SHAKA THE GREAT

Born in 1966, Walton Golightly is a freelance writer from Durban, KwaZulu-Natal – on the doorstep of what used to be the Zulu Kingdom. He's a film buff with a passion for spaghetti Westerns, several action movies and the films of Sam Peckinpah and Jean-Luc Godard. He shares his life with a few thousand books and two dogs. Occasionally the dogs let him sleep on the bed.

Also by Walton Golightly

AmaZulu

SHAKA THE GREAT

Being The Further Adventures Of The Induna &
The Boy Among The People Of The Sky
In The Time Of Shaka KaSenzangakhona, King Of Kings,
In Which Are Encountered Many Strange & Wondrous Things,
Such As Zombies, A Vanishing Man & Sly Sangomas,
Not To Mention White Men & Sundry Other Savages

Walton Golightly

Quercus

First published in Great Britain in 2011 by

Quercus
21 Bloomsbury Square
London
WC1A 2NS

A CIP catalogue reference for this book is available
from the British Library

ISBN 978 0 85738 329 7

10 9 8 7 6 5 4 3 2 1

Typeset by Ellipsis Digital Limited, Glasgow

Printed and bound in Great Britain by Clays Ltd, St Ives plc

For Norm Gillespie
Who had to leave early

Reader, there are, in truth . . . two kinds of history, as different from each other as chalk and cheese. There is *town* history and there is *country* history.

Town history . . . relies on facts and figures. It is knowing . . . Beginning in the shadow of the law courts, at the end of the day your town history tends to the universities – it becomes academic . . . Offering proofs, it never strains credulity. But sometimes it can't see the Forest of Arden for the trees . . .

Your country history is a different matter. Country history is faithful and open-ended. It is a tale told by various idiots on the village green, all busy contradicting themselves in the name of a common truth. It exaggerates and enflames what it talks about. It delights in lies and gossip. It is unwise. Wild and mystical and passionate, it is ruled by the heart. Beginning by the glow of the hearth, at the end of the night your country history tends to pass into balladry and legend – it becomes poetic. Country history is fanciful and maggoty. Easy to mock, it always strains belief. But sometimes it catches the ghostly coat-tails of what is otherwise ungraspable . . .

From *The Late Mr Shakespeare* by Robert Nye

Happy was our laughter there where death became absurd and life still more so.

Wilfred Owen

Contents

Main Characters

The Zulus

Shaka KaSenzangakhona	*King of the Zulus. Born in the 1790s. Seized the throne in 1816*
Mbopa	*Shaka's prime minister*
Mdlaka	*Commander-in-chief of the Zulu army*
Dingane Mhlangana Mpande	*Three of Shaka's half-brothers*
Mgobozi	*Shaka's most trusted general*
Kholisa	*A sangoma*
Ntokozo	*A renowned Uselwa Man*
Vuyile Gudlo	*Two of his sons*
Jembuluka	*The brother of Ntokozo's chief wife*
Masipula	*A brewer renowned for the quality of his beer*
Nyembezi	*A wealthy trader, also known as the Bead Man*
Pampata	*Shaka's favourite concubine*
Nandi	*Shaka's mother*
Mnkabayi	*Sister of Senzangakhona KaJama and hence one of Shaka's aunts*
Melekeleli	*Ntokozo's chief wife; mother of Vuyile*
Dwanile	*Another of Ntokozo's wives; mother of Gudlo*
Zikihle	*Masipula's daughter*

The Izilwane

Ngoza   *Ruler of the Thembus*
Kobo   *His chief advisor*
Pakatwayo   *King of the Qwabes*

Henry Fynn
Francis Farewell   } *English traders*
James King

Jakot Msimbithi   *Their Xhosa interpreter; called*
                         Hlambamanzi, the Swimmer,
                         by Shaka

Prelude

It is Untlolanja, the Time of the Fucking Dog: the month of the December–January moon when dogs are believed to be more interested in fornication than food, fleas and fighting. It's also the month that marks the culmination of the First Fruits. Traditionally, the final Umkhosi rituals are conducted by the various village chiefs around the kingdom as well as by the King, their ceremonies mirroring his, but Shaka has decreed that from this year on only the King himself may conduct the rites that conclude the First Fruits.

And so they have come, the People Of The Sky. Leaving their swollen, alluring crops under the watchful eyes of caretakers threatened with a myriad of dire consequences should any harm befall the fields and groves, all but those in the furthest, most inaccessible reaches of the kingdom have journeyed to KwaBulawayo, Shaka's capital, the Place of He Who Kills.

And the amabutho, the Zulu regiments, they have come as well. The Amawombe, with their dun-coloured cowhide shields. The Umgumanqa, whose white shields are speckled with red hairs like spatters of blood. The Isiklebhe, who have grey shields the colour of the morning mist and pride themselves on their stealth. The Iziyendane, made up of long-haired Hlubis, men of Lala and Swazi stock, carrying rust-coloured shields. And there are others, including, of course, the Ufasimba, the 'Blue Haze', with their black shields; one of the first ibutho to have been taught Shaka's new tactics, they remain his favourite regiment. Each comprising men of the same age group, the amabutho have come in all their finery, eager to outdo the other regiments with their war songs and dances, the discipline displayed in their parade-ground manoeuvres, the skill with which they wield shield and spear. It's the largest mustering of

1

the Zulu army in the whole history of the nation, and a show of force partly intended as an ever-present reminder to the White Men of the chastisement Shaka can call down upon them should his guests forget their place, and the signal honour he has bestowed on them.

For that's something else: it's 1826. The throne of England creaks under the weight of King George IV, while Lord Charles Somerset, second son of the Duke of Beaufort, is pissing off the Whitehall mandarins in his capacity as governor of the Cape (and will in fact be removed from that post later in the year). To the north of Zulu territory, at the start of a reign that will outlast Shaka's by decades, King Moshoeshoe is in the process of establishing the Basotho nation. And this year also marks the first time foreigners have been allowed to attend the climax of the First Fruits.

Foreigners? Some have other names for these izilwane, these barbarians who claim to serve a king called Jorgi who lives far across the waters. But Shaka wants them here, present despite the disapproval of even his closest advisors, for there is more to the Umkhosi – more to the First Fruits – than a mere harvest festival.

And the King has been doctored by his medicine men, his inyangas, and smeared with an especially potent muthi. And his warriors have gathered in the pre-dawn darkness and they have called on him to join them with a chant: 'Woza ke! Woza lapha! Woza ke! Woza lapha!' And the King has emerged from his hut and moved down an aisle lined by his concubines. And he has spat at the rising sun and entered the massive cattle kraal in the centre of KwaBulawayo, where his regiments await him. And now he sits on a throne made from rolled-up mats, and there listens to his praise singers.

And they tell his story, this son of Senzangakhona, the Zulu prince who believed he was tricked into marriage by Shaka's mother. Ukuhlobonga, claimed he, the Pleasure of the Road: a dalliance between clenched thighs, and if both of you lost control and penetration occurred, well, a fine of a few cattle would appease the girl's father and she'd still be regarded as a virgin. Besides, if what's-her-name, Nandi, was pregnant, how could he

2

be certain he was the father? Cha! How could they be certain she really was pregnant?

That was the line taken by Mduli, who was Senzangakhona's uncle and to all intents and purposes, the King's prime minister. Nandi wasn't pregnant, he claimed; merely infected with an Ushaka, an intestinal beetle that made the stomach swell. Fine, replied Nandi, and when her son was born she named him Shaka. Now here is your Beetle, said her family, come and fetch him! And his mother too, for they were only too happy to be rid of the wilful girl. Senzangakhona had by then ascended the throne and was now told by his uncle that he no longer had any choice in the matter. So, reluctantly, he took Nandi as his wife.

Years of abuse and cruelty followed, and things didn't get better when Nandi and Shaka were sent to live with his mother's people, the Langeni. As if the scandal of the 'banishment' wasn't bad enough, Shaka's insistence on his being the heir to the Zulu throne saw him mocked and bullied by the other boys, while their parents shunned Nandi. She had brought this all on herself, yet still she acted as if she were a queen.

Finally it became too much and they left the Langeni to live like refugees, seeking succour where they could until at last they found themselves among the Mthetwas. Inducted into the army, along with others of his age-set, Shaka soon attracted the attention of the Mthetwa king, Dingiswayo, the Wanderer. Forced to flee his home when his brothers accused him of plotting to overthrow their father, Dingiswayo knew how it was to live as an outcast, and thus saw in Shaka a kindred spirit. After Shaka had proved his courage in battle time and time again – especially against the Mthetwas' old foe, the Ndwandwes, who were ruled by Zwide at that time – Dingiswayo persuaded an ailing Senzangakhona to acknowledge his long-lost eldest son as his true heir. And when the old man reneged on his promise on his deathbed, the Wanderer sent Shaka, with the Izicwe legion, to claim the throne. Then, guided by Nandi and his beloved Pampata, this 'Beetle', this bastard son, set about putting to death all of those who had scorned his mother. Next, having reorganised the army, he taught his soldiers the Way of the Bull. He equipped them with the iklwa, a short stabbing spear one didn't foolishly throw away, and made them discard their sandals and toughen their feet by marching across thorns. Then he turned his attention to the nation's enemies . . .

And they sing his praises today, these izimbongi, and tell of his many great deeds. *He is Bull Elephant! He is Sitting Thunder! He is Lightning Fire! Hai-yi hai-yi! I like him when he wrapped the Inkatha around the hill and throttled Zwide's sons. I like him when he went up the hill to throttle Ntombazi of the skulls. Bayede, Nkosi, bayede! Blood of Zulu. Father of the Sky. Barefoot Thorn Man! I like him because we sleep in peace within his clenched fist. Hai-yi hai-yi! I like him because our cattle are free to roam our hills, never to be touched by another's hand. I like him because our water is sweet. I like him because our beer is sweeter. Hai-yi hai-yi! Bayede, Nkosi, bayede!*

★

Now here, on a morning in the Fucking Dog month, following precepts and prescriptions and the rites and rituals laid down by those who were here before Malandela, the father of Zulu – Zulu, the Sky, who begot Gumede KaZulu, who begot Phunga kaGumede, who begot Mageba, who begot Ndaba, who begot Jama, Shaka's grandfather – he has been doctored by his inyangas . . .

Imithi Emnyama, or Black Medicine. Muthi of the dead moon, isifile, and ngolu mnyama namhla, the dark day thereafter, when human beings are especially vulnerable to evil and it's best to sit in the shade and do nothing. Like repels like, and this Imithi Emnyama, this Night Muthi, is conjured from the fragments of that hole in the sky, that *absence* that has been crowded upon, cracked, then shattered by the slow-motion return of the moon. And these shards fall to the earth, to be trapped by inyanga chants, those words woven like nets to catch the blackness, and its power, in the spaces between the sounds. They are incantations that season and add potency to ingredients collected in secret from far and wide.

There is water gathered from the sea and the great rivers that traverse the kingdom; there is the King's own shit and piss; grass from paths used by the King's subjects, thatch from their huts and dirt from their doorways. There is soil taken from enemy territory, as well as samples of all the fruit and vegetables favoured by his nation. There is blood from a black goat, the fat of a leopard, and strips of flesh sliced from various snakes. There are the ground-down teeth and claws of a lion, as well as its heart.

Body, Soul substances, vital essence, unity, power and protection – he will need them all if he is to revive the occult obverse of the festival, reaching out and grasping where others have simply gone through the motions. Therefore let the King become at one with the people, let him be protected from the blackness by the blackness itself, let him draw strength and sustenance from the plants and animals of his kingdom.

Let him not inhale too deeply . . .

★

But who is this mighty ruler, this potentate? Who is this king, who casts a long shadow across the centuries?

Who is this Bull Elephant who has won more than merely territory for his people, whose monuments are pride, honour, courage, myth – alive and enduring where sullen stone crumbles and vain marble shatters?

Who is this monarch who never needed ships of wood, whose praises, carried across the singing veld, were enough to bring the world to his kraal?

★

Hai-yi hai-yi! He is Bull Elephant! He is Sitting Thunder! He is Defiler and Defier! Hai-yi hai-yi! But he is more, too . . .

He is the One They All Forgot, the boy who provided a bedtime story for his half-brothers Sigujana, Dingane, Mhlangana and the younger princes. And not even that; he is the vague memory of a

5

bedtime story – a cautionary tale about what happens to bad boys – of whispered conversations and mocking laughter. How some had to rack their memories, rummage deep within their consciences, when this Shaka returned to claim the crown! As for the older adults, Nandi was the one they remembered best. She was that jackal bitch who tricked Senzangakhona into marrying her, but whatever plans she might have had had come to naught. Although nuptials eventually took place, there was no lobola, no bride price. Nandi had been treated more as a servant than a wife, and soon she and her two offspring – Shaka and his sister – were sent away. Thus Nandi was remembered in the way droughts and plagues were, while Shaka was by and large forgotten. Few had any inkling that the brave warrior who was making a name for himself in Dingiswayo's army (and who could barely even speak Zulu) was also of the royal house of Zulu.

★

Hai-yi hai-yi! Bull Elephant! King of Kings! Sky that Thunders in the Open, Where there is Neither Mimosa nor Thorn Tree. Willow Tree that Overhangs Deep Pools. Hai-yi hai-yi! I like him when he chased Zwide from where the sun rises to where the sun sets! Bull Elephant! Spear Red to the Haft! Hai-yi hai-yi! But he is more, too . . .

He is King Inguos Chaka – the traders' Shaka – and when Francis Farewell went looking for investors after his first trip to the fringes of the Zulu kingdom, this King Inguos Chaka appeared as a benign patron, affable, well behaved. And although they weren't keen to annex yet another beach, the colonial administrators at the Cape were happy enough. And when trader James King returned from England and rather belatedly set about trying to raise money for his own venture, he too reported that this Inguos Chaka was obliging, pleasant, 'stern in public, good-humoured in private'. Chaka's attitude changed, though, when King failed to find any investors. He became a 'cruel monster' and, hell's bells, did they think King was trying to raise funds for a *speculation* – no, they'd misunderstood him! Francis Farewell and the rest of his party were now little better than castaways living in terror of the savage despot. So they needed rescuing; and that's what King wanted the money for – to *rescue* them. Somehow he managed to raise the ready cash, rushed off to save Farewell and promptly sank his ship in the process – meaning it was he himself who now needed rescuing by the 'castaways'. Later, Farewell would intimate that if a 'king' was proving troublesome and treacherous, it wasn't Shaka. Besides, if Shaka was such a terror, why was James King happy to take Farewell's wife along with him when he sailed off to Port Natal? And the *South African Commercial Advertiser* was speaking for the British authorities when it suggested those 'frightful stories' one heard about Shaka from time to time were 'mere fabrications'.

★

Hai-yi hai-yi! I like him when he pulled the Buffalo from its place. I like him when he tore down the thatch. When he swallowed their treachery and then spat out vengeance! Trampler of Burnt Grass! Sky that Thunders in the Open! Hai-yi hai-yi! But he is more, too . . .

He is the 'duplicitous Zoolacratical tyrant' of Nathaniel Isaacs, that halfwit who spent a brief time at Shaka's court, while still a teen, and repaid the King's hospitality by slandering him after his death. As did Farewell and Fynn, it has to be said. To their shame, when later accused of having served in Shaka's army, they sought to vilify their deceased patron by claiming they'd been threatened with death if they didn't accompany the 'Zoola impis'.

★

Hai-yi hai-yi! He is Father of the Sky, son of Mother Africa, this strange southern land with its heat and mist, its frostbitten crags and singing veld, its blossoming deserts and painted caves where elongated wildebeest lope through the darkness. And those other, even more secret places, older than time: man-ape remains; the thumb that twitched, curled and held; the occipital lobe that tilted upward toward the stars. Ancestors of the ancestors. Pleistocene Woman who, fleeing a predator one day, ran into the waves and, to protect the baby clutched to her chest, walked upright . . . And he is more!

He is Rider Haggard's Chaka, which is to say the lover of Nada the Lily, and Umslopogaas' Father, who foresaw his own greatness and who rose out of a time of chaos and cannibalism to bring order and bloodthirsty benevolence. He is E. A. Ritter's Shaka Zulu, a warrior-king in the Arthurian mould, with the iklwa as his Excalibur; visions of Avalon amid the birth pangs of apartheid. He is an aquarium and an airport, a simile and a model for capitalist middle management, a justification and also a metaphor. For certain whitey academics, political toadies who think cynicism and spite acceptable substitutes for scholarship, he is a nobody: just the Paltry Potentate Pushed Down the Coast by the Portuguese.

★

Hai-yi hai-yi! But he is more, too, this man of the moon who understood the power of the sun of the men from across the waters. Come close, my Brothers and Sisters, and I will tell you!

Come close.

Izindaba zami lezi . . .

These are my stories, of long ago and far away.

Uma ngiqambe amanga . . .

If I have lied, I have lied the truth.

If this is not the way things were, it's the way they should have been.

PART ONE
Potsherds & Ostraca

To these white people, Shaka gave girls from his harem, who became their wives. They bore them many children, now comprising several clans, and those clans are still known by the surnames of their fathers. They are distinguishable by being white, but they are black in all other respects.

From *The Black People and Whence They Came* by Magema Fuze
(translated by H. C. Lugg)

Strange to relate there was no Scotsman in the party.

From *The Diary of Henry Francis Fynn* (eds. James Stewart and D. McK. Malcolm)

They came from the sea.

In the beginning it was colonisation by shipwreck, although even that's stretching a point. The Great Scramble would only begin much, much later, and these bedraggled Long Noses were more intent on survival than acquiring territory for their tribes across the waters. You could almost say that the missionary position in those days was to be on your knees gibbering for mercy. And they were helped to their feet and led to the village, where giggling children followed behind them and young maidens peeked at them from behind their fingers. Fed and rested, they were sent on their way, often with the benefit of a guide.

These aliens were too afraid to be fearsome and, if you include the Phoenicians — the Ma-iti of the Nguni chronicles — and the Arabs who reached the Mkuze River on the south-east coast of Africa towards the end of the thirteenth century, they had been washing up forever. Their comings and goings were a part of the folklore shared by the Zulus, Mthetwas, Xhosas and other Nguni nations who had settled on the coast of what would later become South Africa.

Then in 1415, at about the time the Chinese emperor was taking delivery of a giraffe from Malindi, Portuguese forces captured Ceuta on the North African coast. The port had been used as a base by Barbary pirates, when they had raided the Portuguese coast, destroying villages, taking the inhabitants captive and selling them in African slave markets. The Infante Henrique, Duke of Viseu and third son of King João I, took part in that expedition. He was twenty-one at the time, and the experience changed his world view. He got to thinking, considering the angles, as the alidade of his inner astrolabe swung rapidly between exploration, conquest and wealth. He certainly wasn't the first to see how reconnaissance could be disguised as noble and courageous exploration, while paving the way to conquest that

11

would bring in the riches. But the Ceuta campaign enabled him to add an entire new vane to his astrolabe called Africa. Everyone knew about the Mediterranean coast and Egypt, of course, but he was now looking the other way, and saw another coast that could be followed downward and, possibly, even around.

One of the key discoveries of the Age of Discovery being more of a Homeric Doh! *Moment, the prince got to work and, as Henry the Navigator, he initiated the European wave of exploration that would ultimately bring the White Man to Shaka's court.*

About the first thing he did was ensure Portugal equipped herself with the right kind of ship for the job. This turned out to be the 35-metre-long three-masted caravel. With Arab-style lateen sails and a shallow draught, it was ideal for hugging the coast, exploring shallow waters, navigating reefs and sailing up rivers. By the time of Henry's death in 1460, Portugal's influence stretched as far as the Cape Verde Islands, six hundred kilometres west of Senegal.

In 1482, Diogo Cão reached the coast of Angola, where he erected a padrão, one of the two-metre-high stone crosses he'd brought along in order to mark the expedition's most important landfalls.

In the wake of the mariners came the traders, settling wherever a victualling station was needed on the coast. They brought in copper ware, cloth, tools, wine, horses and, later, arms and ammunition. In exchange, they received gold, pepper, ivory and slaves.

But India was still the prize. With Venice controlling the older land and sea routes across the Persian Gulf, the only way Portugal was going to get there was by sailing south, then turning left and left again, as it were, all the while using Africa as a balustrade. Geographers of the time reckoned this could be done without impaling one's ship on an iceberg, therefore João II duly sent Bartolomeu Dias along to give it a shot.

Things went reasonably well until he reached the Namibian coast, and saw lush greenery give way to a moonscape desert as dry as old bones, yet caressed by waters as icy as a pope's heart.

Dias didn't know it at the time, but he'd now entered the realm of Adamastor, tyrant of the seas, ruler of the wind, with his clay-clogged, steel-wool hair, his scowling hollow eyes and his yellow fangs. And Adamastor bided his time, letting a sense of unease grow among the members of the expedition, as they eyed that inhospitable coast and mulled over what they faced should they find themselves shipwrecked. For if they didn't first freeze to death in the waters of the Benguela current, they'd burn up on those sands.

Then, after Dias had gingerly planted a padrão on the promontory of Luderitz Bay, Adamastor finally struck. Herding the mariner and his caravels out into a storm, he tossed them southward into the middle of nowhere.

Thirteen days passed before Dias could set about finding Africa again. First he turned east, groping for the north–south coastline that had been their companion these many months. Then, growing ever more frantic, he sailed due north – and finally made land at Mossel Bay, on a coast that now stretched directly from east to west. He continued on to the Great Fish River, to make sure this wasn't just another bump in the continent, then he turned back.

And it was only now, on their voyage home, that he rounded Cape Agulhas, Africa's southernmost tip, and discovered the Cape of Good Hope. (He, with no little feeling, called it Cabo das Tormentas – the Cape of Storms – but the king later reckoned Cabo da Boa Esperança would inspire more confidence among investors.)

That was in 1488, and Dias had shown it could be done, but almost ten years would elapse before a Portuguese expedition finally reached India by this same route.

That one was led by Vasco da Gama, and in December 1497 he sailed into the uncharted waters that lay beyond the Great Fish River. As Christmas was near, he christened the lush green coast he was passing 'Natal', to commemorate the Nativity.

A few days later, a headland running parallel to the coast caught his eye. He named it Ponta de Pescaria and sailed on, blithely missing the bay hiding behind this imposing bluff. It was only in 1554 that Manoel de Mesquita Perestrello, coming back from India, found Rio Natal for Portugal. Even so, the sheltered harbour was soon forgotten.

In 1652 the Dutch chose Table Bay, at the Cape of Good Hope, as the site of a settlement tasked with supplying provisions for the ships of the Dutch East India Company. As the years passed a mud fort evolved into a star-shaped stone castle, Company employees became settlers, vineyards were planted, and slaves imported. By 1793 the colony had a population of fourteen thousand burghers, of whom only four thousand lived in or near Cape Town. Hunters, traders and nomadic cattlemen called Trekboers had meanwhile pushed the borders of the settlement eight hundred kilometres eastward.

In 1806 the British occupied the Cape. As the century entered its late teens, they began to hear talk of great upheavals further along the coast, but they had other more immediate matters to deal with. Like pacifying the Xhosas, who stubbornly insisted on hampering the colony's expansion beyond the Great Fish River, on the basis that they had got there first.

As a result, the nearest European settlement to the Zulus remained Delagoa Bay, where Lourenço Marques had established a trading post back in the 1540s.

But these Portugiza were different from the other savages who washed up on the beaches from time to time. Familiarity had long ago bred contempt; and they had been there, dying of fever, for so many generations that they were seen more as a mongrel offshoot of the Maputo tribe they customarily dealt with than as representatives of a mighty foreign nation.

Ascending to the Zulu throne in 1816, Shaka was more interested in the other tribes who came from across the water. Or rather — and this is where he differed from most of the other rulers in the region — he knew there was more to learn here than appearances might suggest.

That was thanks to his great mentor, Dingiswayo. For while in exile, fleeing his father's wrath, the Mthetwa prince had befriended a White Man who may have been the last survivor of an expedition despatched from the Cape in 1807 and tasked with seeking an overland route to Portuguese East Africa. Dingiswayo agreed to guide the man to the coast but, after a few months, the barbarian contracted a fever and died. Dingiswayo inherited the man's horse and his gun, then decided it was time to go and claim his own birthright. Although the gun was useless, lacking powder and shot, and the horse would soon die (this long being insalubrious territory for these naked zebra), they were nonetheless impressive talismans that played no small part in helping the Wanderer regain the throne.

And Dingiswayo never forgot all the things the White Man had told him, as they sat around the fire of an evening. Coming from the Cape, the White Man could speak Xhosa, a Nguni language Dingiswayo himself understood, and though the young prince could grasp most of the concepts he raised – trade, empires, wars of conquest – it was their sheer scale that awed him.

And got him thinking.

So it was Dingiswayo, not Shaka, who first set about uniting the tribes and clans along the south-east coast of Africa, organising something approaching a standing army and fighting wars not only to gain territory and cattle, but to secure trade routes with the Portuguese. The Zulu king merely completed what his mentor had started.

And Shaka wanted to know more, wanted to hear for himself. What else could these creatures from the sea tell him? Problem was, whatever trembling specimens his warriors found amid the seaweed could do little more than weep and grovel.

Possibly, in the end, they weren't that different from all the others. Possibly, their claimed provenance aside, they were simply wild beasts like all the rest. For that's how the Zulus saw things: they themselves were Abantu, human beings, while everyone else was izilwane, wild beasts, savages. But even as Shaka was taming the other beasts around him – those indigenous to the region – these newly found barbarians were poking at the map and wondering about the possibilities of this coast.

By the 1820s the British Admiralty was desperately seeking employment for the naval officers left idle and on half pay after the Napoleonic Wars. One of the projects embarked upon was a long delayed and much needed scientific survey of the coastline extending from the Cape of Good Hope up to Cape Guardafui north of Portuguese East Africa. Captain William Owen was the one put in charge of the expedition, which included the Leven and the Barracouta.

The HMS Barracouta left the Cape first, around the middle of 1822. Also tasked with making contact with the tribes beyond Algoa Bay, the furthermost outpost of British civilisation on that coast, the ship's officers discovered something interesting.

The natives they encountered were a pathetic lot – cunning, treacherous and prone to 'drunkenness and gluttony'. However, the Barracouta's officers soon learnt that they were not the 'aboriginal inhabitants' of the coastal strip, but were refugees who had fled 'the merciless and destructive conquests of a tyrannical monster named Chaka'. These reports, which caused a stir back at the Cape, mark one of the first official mentions of the Zulu king whose name would one day be known around the globe.

The despatches were later confirmed by the officers of the HMS Leven. While the ship was at Delagoa Bay, it was learnt the Portuguese were trading with a 'warlike' tribe to the south. They called this tribe 'Vatwas', but it was likely these were the 'Zoolas' the British had already been hearing about.

And why would the Portuguese risk dealing with such a bloodthirsty bunch? That's what a few merchants, and at least one out-of-work Navy man, got to thinking after listening to the stories Owen's expedition brought back to Cape Town. They knew the Portuguese were doing very well out of the gold and ivory coming into Delagoa otherwise why maintain a settlement in such a hellhole? But that the traders should be willing to do business with a 'tyrannical monster', presumably as likely to slaughter them in their sleep as hand over any goods, meant there had to be more gold and more ivory than hitherto suspected.

Consequently, while Shaka was consolidating his power after defeating Zwide, and wondering what to do about the irksome Thembus hunkered down on his western border, other izilwane, the very ones he wanted to learn more about, were making plans to come and find him. And thus ensure any future arrivals and departures were more organised, and less the result of storms and shattered hulls.

1
Enter Mariners, Wet

July 1823

The sea is choppy, the sky glowering; the foam stings and the waves do their best to unseat the boat, as if it were a particularly detested jockey.

Impatience, teeth-grinding, deck-pacing, mouths-to-feed, investors-to-appease´impatience, has seen Lieutenant Francis Farewell, founder of the Farewell Trading Company – and sole bloody leader of this bloody expedition, the whole thing having been his idea in the first place, despite what a certain party might claim at a later date – attempt a landing in such inclement conditions.

The beach they're aiming for keeps disappearing, tilting and slipping behind waves the colour of stone, until the boat rises again like the remnants of breakfast in a burning throat, while the water roars in its rage and the spindrift peppers one's face like specks of gunpowder. Jakot, their interpreter, along with a matelot who's never been the same since a tumble from a yard a few years ago, has broken one of the barrels they've brought with them, and are using the shakes in a clumsy and futile endeavour to bail water. And the other men pull at the oars; for they don't need to be told that survival lies in keeping this surfboat under control.

They're just coming out of another trough, when Farewell rises to check his bearings. *How far to go? How far?* He knows they won't be able to get back off the beach so long as this weather keeps up, but getting there at all will at least mean an end to this constant battering.

He rises and, just as the oarsmen claw their way to the crest, a gust of wind knocks the boat sideways so that it almost capsizes as it drops down into the next trough. The crew fight to bring the bow around, and it's only when they hit the next crest that they realise Farewell's gone. As are Jakot and the sailor who was helping him bail.

But there's nothing to be done about that right now. The surf-boat's perched above another near vertical descent, and they have their own lives to think of.

Down they go, then up again, in a haze of grey and white.

Down, then up . . . and the beach seems to leap at them, closer than anyone would've dared hope.

Carried into shallower water by the breakers, they now have to contend with cross-currents. During any landing, waves breaking against a broad behind can cause a boat to turn sideways to the swell, and capsize. Surfboats have pointed sterns to prevent this from happening, but these greybeards are too cantankerous. Just when it seems as if they're going to make it through the churning water, the boat broaches . . .

. . . and at the same instant the sea snatches the water away, like an optimistic conjurer tugging at a tablecloth laden with plates and cutlery . . .

. . . and the surfboat drops down and rolls forward, spewing men and their fearful cries.

★

It's July 1823 – the time of Uncwaba, the New Grass Moon, for the Zulus – and Lieutenant Francis Farewell has come seeking to establish a trading station on the south-east coast.

Having listened to the reports brought back by Captain William Owen and his officers, he has come to the conclusion that Shaka isn't as bad as the Portuguese have claimed. Yes, there are the other negative accounts gleaned from the refugees encountered by the *Barracouta*, but there you were dealing with the animosity of a defeated foe – a different situation entirely. It's in Portuguese interests to exaggerate the atrocities of the Zoola chief, lest someone else get precisely the same idea as Farewell. Which is to avoid Delagoa altogether, and set about doing business with the Zulu monarch directly.

After persuading various merchants at Cape Town to finance the venture, Farewell chartered the *Salisbury*, skippered by James King. On 27 June 1823, they reached Algoa Bay, recently renamed Port

Elizabeth. That same day, the HMS *Leven* dropped anchor alongside the *Salisbury*.

Captain Owen was making his second pass along the coast, and Farewell eagerly turned to him for advice.

Two things in particular bothered him, and Owen was happy to help. The first was finding a suitable place to make land before reaching Delagoa, and Owen suggested the estuary named Santa Lucia by Manoel de Mesquita Perestrello back in the 1550s.

Farewell's second cause for concern was the matter of interpreters. They'd been able to hire some in Cape Town, but he wasn't sure they'd be up to the task and he cited the example of his beloved Horatio. While serving in the West Indies, Admiral Nelson had found it frustrating having to rely on indifferent interpreters when questioning the crew of French prizes he'd taken. Consequently, after the Peace of 1793, which he realised wouldn't last, he had spent several months in France in order to brush up on his French, so as to be able to monitor what was actually said to an interpreter and assess how well it was being translated for him. Farewell believed their own predicament would be even more fraught. Far from Redcoats and grapeshot, they'd be at Shaka's mercy, and needed someone who would not only translate his employers' questions and requests faithfully, but who could be relied upon to pick up nuances, signs of uncertainty and prevarication that pointed to a possible betrayal.

Owen said he understood, and offered Farewell one of his own interpreters. The fellow had accompanied the captain on his previous voyage and shown himself well able to communicate with the natives they met along the way.

'He's one of these Causahs and reckons the languages aren't all that different,' explained Owen. 'The pick of the litter,' he added. 'In fact, some of the men say he's royalty. I don't know about that, but he handles well, by and large. Won't need much cobbing!'

That the captain might have been laying it on a bit thick only occurred to Farewell a few days after they left Port Elizabeth. For one thing, Owen might have revealed to him that he'd hired Jakot out of the prison on Robben Island but, instead, Farewell had to hear this little piece of intelligence from King, who had in fact once transported Jakot from Algoa to Cape Town, from whence he had been returned to the island.

That was another thing: until employed by the Admiralty as an interpreter, Jakot had been very much a repeat offender, his crimes ranging from murder to stock theft, and to inciting rebellion against British rule. This information came from the three other interpreters, hired at Cape Town, who were angry because Jakot had been lording it over them from the day he first set foot on board.

When Farewell asked him why he was bullying the others, and generally acting as if he was their chief, Jakot said the accusation was preposterous. He'd intimated nothing of the sort, and wouldn't dream of doing so, for they were half-castes, while he was pure Xhosa. Come to think of it, *he* was the one who should feel insulted, for even a dog would think long and hard if it was forced to choose between becoming their chief and, say, contracting rabies.

The upshot of this was that, after the other interpreters were pulled off Jakot, *they* were the ones who found themselves crammed into the cubbyhole that served as the brig, leaving the Xhosa with a little more space in what had till then been their communal sleeping area. Not that the others were under arrest: it was merely considered it would be better for everyone's health if they were locked up at night, when there were fewer people around to keep an eye on them and prevent them from getting themselves into serious trouble.

This was far from being the end of Jakot's trials, though. The half-castes − and the expedition's Hottentot servants − were mere irritations, and easily intimidated. Being treated as chattel, handed from one owner to another, was what stuck in his craw.

That he was being paid for his services was of little consequence. And largely hypothetical, anyway, since he hadn't yet seen a penny in these many months of rolling from port to starboard and back again.

It was also true that, however impressed by the bona fides

20

provided by Owen, Farewell was only willing to take on Jakot if Jakot agreed to accompany the party. But in reality Jakot didn't have a choice, and could only say yes.

He was no longer Owen's favourite, for the captain had become enamoured of a new court jester he'd picked up at Cape Town: a man called English Bill. And Jakot suspected that Owen was planning to leave him at Port Elizabeth, which he didn't want to happen, as there were frontiersmen there who still had some scores to settle with him, notwithstanding the pardon he had received on joining the Royal Navy's expedition.

This aside, the prospect of returning to Delagoa was about as appealing as leprosy to the Xhosa, who counted himself lucky to have survived one voyage there already, travelling with these imbeciles who seemed to actively seek out the most disease-ridden inlets in their never-ending quest for ivory and gold. That he'd been reassured Delagoa was most certainly not the true destination of the Farewell Trading Company mattered not a jot. Despite their fancy brass instruments, these hirsute creatures remained trapped in the palm of the weather, and therefore, as far as Jakot could see, they seemed to spend a lot of time being blown off course. So who knew where they might eventually end up?

*

Well, he knows now: thrashing about in a tempestuous sea.

As the boat turned, he'd been rising to throw out a scoop of water, but had instead been flung in Farewell's direction. The two men collided and somehow Jakot managed to grab the collar of the lieutenant's jacket. Farewell was tumbling overboard, but all was not lost. Jakot remembers reaching out to the nearest oarsman. If the big man had seized his hand, they could have both been pulled back on board. Instead – and now, riding the swells, Jakot remembers this clearly – the man had simply smiled.

In Jakot's mind the man's smile stretches time. With everyone else seemingly frozen in place – including Farewell, halfway out of

21

the surfboat, his eyes wide, his mouth wider as it forms a shocked cry – Jakot sees his own fingers close around the collar of Farewell's coat . . .

. . . and it's as if everything you touch starts moving, too, and Farewell's falling again, dropping fast, thrown into the maw of the emerald trough, and taking you with him . . .

. . . and somehow your fingers are trapped between Farewell's neck and the sodden collar of his coat, and you can't let go, so you reach out for the nearest oarsman, and your desperate fingers must have brushed his shoulder, because now *he* can move, but all he does is smile – a knowing smile; the smile of someone who knows what you have in mind, knows he can help but also knows he's going to do exactly nothing, just smile . . .

. . . and in the end it was the other sailor who came to Jakot's aid, the matelot who'd injured his head in a fall and who moved to his own time in his own world and didn't need a Xhosa prince to reanimate him, but it was to no avail . . .

★

The other crewmen have managed to drag the surfboat up the beach, away from the waves. Now collapsed on the wet sand in various states of fatigue, they can only watch and gape as Jakot staggers ashore, dragging Farewell behind him.

Edwards, the coxswain, is the first to react. He calls on the man nearest him for help, and they rush into the water. Together they get the lieutenant up onto his feet. Jakot stands still a moment, his chest heaving. Slipping one of Farewell's arms over his shoulder, the coxswain asks about . . . But Jakot shakes his head. The coxswain sighs. That's two they've lost today, the second sailor drowning as he got trapped under the boat.

Seeing that Farewell has survived his ducking gives the others a jolt of energy. They converge on the lieutenant, those passing close to Jakot gently clapping the Xhosa on the shoulder and telling him *Well done.* But no one notices how he has eyes for only one man.

First Mate Alex Thomson was thrown clear as the boat went over, only to find the backwash dragging him out towards the breakers. Gasping and gagging, he rolled on to his back in time to see he was about to be reunited with the surfboat, which an incoming wave was kindly carrying towards him. With the boat looming as large as a cannonball the instant before it takes off the fusilier's head, Thomson rolled on to his stomach again and dug in against the current . . . and found himself rising. With one more glance over his shoulder – churning foam the colour of dirty soapsuds, curved planks with edges that suddenly seemed as sharp as the blade of a guillotine – he high-stepped it on a course that took him diagonally away from the surfboat, just as it gouged a gunwale into the sand and ceased to be a threat.

It was only after coughing up several mouthfuls of the salty stuff, and hearing the coxswain urge the other men to secure the boat, that he remembered his rank and levered himself up to take charge.

Now he hoists himself once again, a little more sharply this time, and Jakot's bearing down on him like a ship of the line with all masts square-rigged and staysails fluttering between. Because he doesn't believe in fighting fair, Thomson makes to throw the first punch, the fact that none of his fellow Salisburys seem aware that their first mate is about to be attacked by a black servant adding strength to the blow.

And that punch needs all the help it can get, for both men are so tired that the altercation seems to happen in slow motion.

Just as Thomson raises his fist, Jakot gives the first mate a push. It's a mighty heave as far as the Xhosa is concerned, enough to knock over a mountain, but in truth it's a clumsy child's shove, and Thomson merely takes a step back.

The two men stare at each other, Thomson stunned because Jakot has dared to lay a hand on him, and Jakot thinking, *Well, that could have gone better.* Then Thomson remembers his fist, the one up here by his right ear. But it's as if the air has turned into molasses, or they're still in the water – and both he and Jakot find themselves watching the passage of the first mate's knuckles as if they're merely interested bystanders.

Thomson recovers first, leaping back inside his battered body and reaching down deep into all that loathing and resentment, spite and sadism he's accumulated over the years, to give the punch the extra momentum it needs. Instead of bumping against Jakot's chest, the fist changes trajectory like one of Mr Congreve's rockets, rises with a lurch and Jakot feels the first mate's knuckles bounce off the bridge of his nose. Then it's as if he's back on the launch, for the horizon drops away and he's staring up at the sky.

He should retaliate. He should leap up and defend his honour – and the honour of his people, of course. But these are distant voices of reproach, easily lost in the crash of the surf. Better to rest for a bit.

Then movement to his left causes him to turn his head to see the sack of pus himself, lying on his stomach next to him. Clearly that punch had overbalanced the weary, waterlogged first mate, and he'd dropped alongside the interpreter while Jakot was busy staring at the sky.

Jakot spends a few moments watching as Thomson endeavours to hoist himself on to all four paws, before realising he's thereby missing a chance to strike. Taking a deep breath, he manages to send his right fist over his body in an arc that ends at Thomson's left ear. It's not the strongest punch Jakot's ever thrown, but it's enough to elicit a grunt from Thomson. Even more gratifying is the thump a second later, as the White Man's gut hits the sand.

★

Farewell dismisses the men after they have received their orders. Some will seek firewood, others will follow the strand in both directions, trying to retrieve what they can of their rations. Still more are to seek fresh water, but none is to wander too far (an injunction no one's likely to disobey).

He moves away from the overturned surfboat that will serve as their shelter tonight. The line of the horizon is interrupted by waves and there's no sign now of the *Salisbury*. King rightly won't risk a second boat. Instead he'll wait for clearer conditions before rescuing them – and who knows how long that will be, Farewell wonders, gazing up at the leaden sky heavy with clouds. And behind him lies an even greater weight: terra incognita. Who knows how many eyes are watching them even now?

Damn Owen!

The thing is, on that first expedition, it was the *Barracouta* did most of the work. Owen had taken the *Leven* straight to Delagoa Bay, where he set about trying to fill his own coffers under the guise of exploring the surrounding countryside. But what little ivory and gold he could coax from the Maputos came at a terrible cost, as he would lose half his crew and two-thirds of his officers to malaria and dysentery. Finally forced to put to sea again, in November 1822, Owen set a course southward, needing to return to Simon's Bay. He resumed his survey of the coast, but it was lackadaisical at best, the voyage becoming more a series of burials at sea than a scientific expedition. And when he suggested Farewell attempt a landing at Santa Lucia, it had merely been because the place had seemed promising in passing.

At this time Farewell is unaware of the extent of Owen's dereliction of duty. All he knows is that the affable and co-operative captain who was willing to share his charts (as well as Farewell's private stock of port) has almost scuppered the whole bloody expedition.

Farewell scans the jagged waves, the see-sawing horizon, then shivers and turns up the collar of his wet coat against the gusting wind that transforms every grain of sand into a thorn, as he tries not to think of what lies beyond the battered bush fringing the beach.

He can still see the captain's casual wave as they sat in the *Salisbury's* wardroom: one finger pressed against the chart, then the nothing-to-it gesture as Owen leant back. 'Santa Lucia, old chap.' A burp of Farewell's port. 'That's the spot I'd try for, were I you, and don't I envy you!'

Clearly Owen hadn't even come within a nautical mile of this place, or else he would have realised that, even under the best of conditions, a landing would be difficult.

'Sir?'

Wrenched from his thoughts, Farewell turns to the coxswain, a wiry capable fellow he trusts more than King's first mate, who accompanies the fellow, his face as dark as the clouds above.

'Begging your pardon, Lieutenant, but we have a problem,' says the coxswain.

'Shut up,' growls Thomson, pushing the little man aside. 'I can speak for myself.'

'Stand easy, Mr Thomson.'

Thomson stiffens, his mouth working as he strives to remind himself that Farewell is the leader of this expedition.

After giving the first mate a chance to regain his composure, Farewell asks him what seems to be the matter.

There's no lack of choice in that department at the moment, but something in particular appears to have incensed him.

Thomson half turns; points: 'It's him!'

Farewell's gaze follows the direction indicated by Thomson's trembling finger.

'Jakot?' he asks. 'Blighter saved my life – must remember to thank him.'

'Be that . . .' Thomson gulps. 'Be that as it may, sir, but that . . . that *blighter* has just attacked me!'

Farewell glances once more over to where a sodden Jakot sits, his chin resting on his knees, his eyes fixed on the breakers.

'Attacked you, Mr Thomson?' Before Thomson can reply, Farewell turns to the coxswain: 'Did anyone see this incident, Mr Edwards?'

'Can't say as they did, Lieutenant, seeing as how we were all following your orders and foraging and what not.'

'Quite. And that reminds me: has the water party returned?'

'On their way back now, sir. They sent young Evans ahead to report they found us fresh water and fruit of some kind. Evans has gone back to collect some for us.'

'Good.'

'Begging your pardon, sir,' says the man who should be overseeing these operations, 'but the black bastard *attacked* me!'

'Right, of course. So you say. Mr Edwards?'

'Sir?'

'Be so kind as to fetch that black bastard, as Mr Thomson here chooses to refer to him, although surely in no position to comment on the chap's antecedents.'

'Sir!'

'A heathen bastard he is,' mutters Thomson, as Edwards moves off. 'A lazy, thieving one, too. Get him back on the *Salisbury* and I'll wield the cat myself.' Looking up at Farewell and finding evidence of distaste for his tirade, he adds a belated, 'Sir.'

Another 'Sir!' announces Edwards' return, along with Jakot.

'Well, Jakot,' says Farewell, 'is it true? Did you strike Mr Thomson here?'

As he was being steered towards Farewell by the coxswain, Jakot noticed that those men whose chores are already completed had begun to pay closer attention to the exchange between Farewell and Thomson, drifting a little nearer, but not so near that Farewell will notice their inquisitiveness and order Edwards to find more tasks for them.

The interpreter realises he's underestimated the first mate's cunning. By reporting the matter right now, he draws the attention of the others to the most worrying aspect of their predicament. They'll be rescued soon enough, but for the moment they're stranded on a beach where there are God knows how many black bastards lurking in the bushes over there. And see how this situation has even affected the behaviour of their own black bastard!

Back on ship, Thomson would have found himself in trouble when Jakot explained what had happened on the surfboat, and why he had then attacked – or, given the feebleness of both their efforts, tried to attack – Thomson on the beach. Few would have doubted that the unpopular Thomson was capable of such a callous action – which had also cost the life of one of their own, don't forget that.

But here, under these conditions, he knows the White Men will stick together. A hunting party of Xhosas would do the same, were they to find themselves stranded or lost and the guide they had recruited from a local tribe started showing signs of 'acting up', as the White Men term it. There is therefore no point in trying to explain himself.

Instead, Jakot Msimbithi squares his shoulders and turns to face Thomson.

Addressing the first mate in Xhosa, he invites Thomson to go and fuck himself, and informs the others that he is going to find Shaka. Then he sets off to do just that, his angry footsteps, that windy afternoon, the first in a journey that will eventually see him become one of the most influential figures in South Africa's history. Although that's perhaps a story for another time . . .

2
The Land of the Sweet Grass

Interlude

. . . because you saw through him, didn't you?

What he had to say, his little insights, these weren't without their value, but they required a certain amount of dusting off, to get rid of the malice, the spite and the exaggerations that were a symptom of the desire to ingratiate. (You already had his measure, you knew how many cattle there were in his herd; it was your brother who fell under his thrall; and see what happened!)

Shaka – his forehead, nose and cheeks painted black, his hair and lower face the rust red of dried blood, with lines of ash across his chest – gazes at the footprints that resemble a chain of shadows pressed into the sand.

Perhaps Jakot's greatest service was done to him before he even reached KwaBulawayo. For these footprints leading *away*, were also leading *to*. Bringing Jakot to him, yes, but also bringing him to *them*.

Shaka raises his head to regard the bedraggled white barbarians scattered around the wooden tortoiseshell of the overturned boat. Not these ones, those who followed; but he has the feeling *they* wouldn't have come were it not for this chain of feet.

Then it happens again.

'Where are you going?' It's an alien language, but comprehensible thanks to its very tone. 'Come back!'

And Jakot brushes past Shaka . . .

Who suddenly finds himself back in the hut of his seclusion. Orange thatch, and wet heat, the fire blazing in its centre intended to hasten and amplify the effects of the muthi his medicine men have fed him: the potions and libations that will turn this nightly exile inside out and set his umkhokha free.

And he is standing?

Hadn't started the night standing.

And there's the brush of Jakot's shoulder, the sand, the spoor.

Only now, when Shaka looks down, he sees . . .

★

. . . the Thukela River to the south, the Pongola to the north. No matter how far and wide the name Zulu might be whispered, no matter how deep inland his hegemony might extend, the water ways called the Frightening Suddenness and the River of Narrow Pools will remain the coronary arteries defining the heartland of the nation.

This is where history was leading the People Of The Sky in a trek that started long, long before the birth of Malandela, the father of Zulu, when a chief called Nguni led his people out of Egypt. It's a continental drift measured in centuries, as sons moved away, moved east or west, or kept on coming south, and families became clans that settled where they were, or kept on moving, or stayed a while and then moved on, with drought or warfare snapping at their heels, ever colonising and conquering, or being conquered. Intermarriages occurred between the interlopers and those they encountered and a tribe became a nation. Then the fraying as the grandsons' grandsons, finding the land crowded, moved on again, southward, always southward, until they found themselves on the shores of the Indian Ocean. Found themselves here, in fact, amid the bushel of rivers to be found between the Thukela and the Pongola: the Mhlatuze, or

'Relentless Force'; the Mkhuze, or 'Violent River'; the ragged, jittery Lopsided Y created by the Fig River, the Black Mfolozi, and its tributary the White Mfolozi, so named because of the lightness of the stones along its banks.

Later he'll only remember his sudden comprehension; remember understanding something that should have been wholly incomprehensible. It's like the dream that's vivid when you open your eyes, then is gone as you blink, or turn your head, leaving only the memory of your having been somewhere as real as here and now . . . or of sudden understanding dissipated and lost. But that's on the other side, where the flames cause the red and black to glisten, and dawn brings with it an aching head.

For now, the Father of the Sky squats and peers down at deep, wide valleys: places where a man, a family, a clan can spread out and prosper. Because this is good land for cattle. He nods, for Mgobozi, his old friend Mgobozi, has now joined him. 'Good land,' he whispers.

And it is so. Those who try to raise izinkomo on the rainy coastal belt have to make do with sourveld grass, which is only good for grazing during a short period in the spring – and see how puny those beasts are! Their bellies are hollow, their milk thin and they move like old-timers.

Here, in these valleys, however, you'll find the sweetveld grass that provides nutritious grazing almost all the year round. And the herds grow, Old Friend, producing bulls as strong as the rivers that carved these canyons, and cows whose milk is as sweet as the grass they graze on.

*

And they settled here. And they built their huts, bending the saplings to create a framework, then covering it with thatch. Floors are laid out of a mixture of ant-heap and clay, then covered with cow dung and rubbed hard and smooth until the surface shines. In the centre is the isiko, or fireplace, and to the right side of the hut is the men's side, the isilili samadoda, to the left the isilili sesifazana, the side for the females. And in the rear, where it's cool and dark, there's the umsamo, the place of the ancestors, who divide their time between here and the cattle kraal. And sleeping mats, clothing, gourds and skins containing water, medicine and beer are hung along the wall.

And they built their villages: circular like their huts, like the full moon. The huts arranged on a slope for better drainage and protected by an utango, or outer wall, comprising poles lashed together or a hedge of viciously spiked thorns, with the isango, the entrance to the umuzi at the lower end, and the dwellings of the village's head, his mother and wives situated at the upper end. In the centre of the settlement, surrounded by a second fence: the isibaya, the sacred cattlefold. And at the top of the isibaya, the ibandla tree, where the headman greets guests or where the villagers gather to discuss matters of import and resolve disputes, with every man allowed to have his say.

And the men tended their cattle, the herdboys leaving early in the morning, while mothers and daughters began their chores, fetching water, neatening the hut, working in the fields.

And they celebrated the First Fruits . . .

★

The hoes are taken up. The planting begins. Maize, introduced to the region by the Portugiza, predominates, while sorghum, the favoured cereal before ummbila, is grown mainly for use in the making of beer. Then there's the ipuzi, a large, light-yellow pumpkin, the imfe, an indigenous form of wild sugar cane, various gourds and melons and different varieties of sweet potato.

A period of intense labour as the men clear the fields, hacking away the bushes that have encroached during the fallow time. Then come the mothers and daughters, sisters and daughters-in-law: breaking up the soil, broadcasting the seed by hand, planting it in rows or thrusting it into the loam with their fingers, depending on the crop.

This becomes their time, for the women are feeding the nation, their efforts in the name of Nomkhubula, the Princess of the Sky. And the planting is accompanied by numerous ceremonies held to entreat the Princess to keep away drought and protect the plants from pests.

After the sowing, it's time for the Phukula, when every maiden must go out and beg for beer from her sweetheart's kraal. If she hasn't yet an isoka, it's her chance to make the first move if the man she has her eye on has yet to notice her charms. She'll arrive at his homestead and be welcomed in the usual hospitable manner, for such is the way of the Amazulu, but on this day she will not return the greetings. Instead, she'll signal the reason for her visit with a phukula, or disdainful pout.

When enough beer has been collected, a feast is held, involving only women. Wearing special dresses of woven grass decorated with flowers, they sing and dance and praise Nomkhubula. The following day they'll pick up their hoes and go and plant one more field of mealies. This one is specifically for the Princess of the Sky. Its crop is never harvested, and pots of beer will be regularly left out for the princess to enjoy whenever she visits.

And so Umfumfu, the planting season, gives way to the month of the October–November moon, the fecund month of Uzibandela, the Pathfinding Moon, when everything grows abundantly and the new grass hides the trails and tracks.

And, although it'll only reach its climax in January, the First Fruits ceremony has already begun.

Ukutatamageja, the Taking Up of the Hoes, in October has marked its commencement. The second phase is Ukunyathela Unyaka, the Stepping into the New Year, which starts when the Pathfinding Moon gives way to the November–December moon. Known as Umasingana, the Peering-About Moon, this is when the women start searching the fields and gardens for the emergence of the new crops – the first fruits. This is also when select groups of men are sent out to collect soil and steal bulls from neighbouring tribes. An elite within this elite are those despatched to the coast to fetch the uselwa, and often the men will camp out for several days while waiting for the calabash they've found to ripen before picking it. The King chooses the best ones brought before him, and it is, of course, a great honour for the warrior whose offering is chosen.

★

We did these things, listened to the sangomas, appeased the ancestors, but still we lived in fear . . .

3
Mnkabayi

Umandulo, Moon of the New Fields, August 1825
'It is so, it is so. He would have the First Fruits celebrated at Bulawayo, and only at Bulawayo, and the savages from King Jorgi will be there! I would that it were not so, Mama. Aiee! I would that it were not, but it is so.'

To hide her reaction, Mnkabayi turns away from the sangoma and moves out from under the shade of the tree to stand gazing down upon her cattle.

How hideous things have become. This land. These people. Him!

She folds her arms, a big buxom woman who has yet to start showing her age. That's a testament to her large appetite, her immense will, her vast energy, say some. Others whisper *witchcraft*, and she lets them live to spread such rumours, because they breed fear, which is always a useful weapon. Besides, as a member of the royal family she cannot be openly accused; she is beyond the reach of those who purport to sniff out abathakathi.

Ironically, these same whisperings also make her a much sought-after patron among some of those who wouldn't have hesitated to condemn her had her status been more lowly. If she is untouchable, perhaps she will protect them, make them untouchable as well. Hence the oh-so-eager fool who has now taken it upon himself to ruin her afternoon – this limping Kholisa who sees himself as Nobela's heir. And there are others, too. Even more since Shaka ended Nobela's reign of terror.

Mnkabayi allows herself a grin, for even the maddest dog will do the right thing every now and again. Nobela was one of those who'd wanted her dead before she could even suckle her mother's breast. How Mnkabayi loathed that crone! How she loathes them all.

It had to be thus, they said, if Jama was to save himself from the curse of twins. His life was in danger, for supernatural powers were working to crush him. His only recourse now was to kill one of the babies. He had no choice, said his councillors. Because he was king, the ramifications of having twins might affect the whole tribe, they added.

But, in an act of courageous obstinacy, Jama insisted that Mnkabayi – who had left her mother's womb first – and her sister Mmama would both be allowed to live. And anyone who sought to harm them would have to face his wrath.

Mmama had died while still an infant and, although her immediate family treated her just like any other child, Mnkabayi would never forgive the sangomas. But those who seek her protection do have their uses because, for one thing, their followers tell them things.

Mnkabayi's gaze returns to her cattle. How peaceful it all seems. A soft sun, a mild breeze, sweet grass. But, then, the greatest lies are like that, for how else would they be believed?

Having shooed the sangoma away, Ndlela joins her.

Mnkabayi is about fifteen summers older than him, and they were lovers once, when he was still a herdboy and she played the experienced guide who taught him the warm secrets of a woman's body. Seducing herdboys remains one of her favourite pastimes, but there was something about Ndlela, the glimmer of promise, that saw her take an interest in other aspects of his education as well as his advancement, long after she'd found new cubs to pleasure her. Now the age difference doesn't seem so great, and the induna is her most trusted advisor.

'He is mad,' murmurs Ndlela, referring to Shaka.

'Or wise. He is the inkosi, the King, so why shouldn't the Umkhosi, the First Fruits, be about him?'

'But the people—'

'Will do what, Ndlela? Have they risen up yet? No! And why should they? They grow fat, their cattle grow fat, bayede Shaka!' *Hail! Shaka!*

'There are many widows, Ma. There are many families who are bereft, many fathers who have no heirs, and mothers without sons. Listen carefully late at night and you will hear their cries! There are many who have tasted the sweet words, swallowed the promises and spat them out. They've found them wanting, not even fit to feed a vulture.'

'But there he has us, too, don't you see?' says Mnkabayi. 'There are widows, it is true, but not as many as there might have been.' For has Shaka not had the isicoco ripped off the heads of those who are entitled to wear it? And has he not said marriage makes a man weak, and therefore forbidden his warriors to marry?

'Another calumny,' hisses Ndlela.

The isicoco, or headring, is made by plaiting a fibre around the skull, then smearing it with black gum to harden it, and it is one of the most significant adornments in Zulu society. Only once it is assumed is a male recognised as an indoda, a man, with all the rights and responsibilities of an adult. Before that, no matter what his age, he's regarded as a youth – an insizwa, or hornless ox.

When Shaka came to power, he drafted the men who wore the isicoco and were already married into the Amawombe regiment. Those who wore the headring but had not yet married were forced to remove it, and they became the Ujubingqwana – the Shorn Heads. Not surprisingly, this was the cause of much resentment, as the new king had in effect stripped these men of their adult status.

'Yes,' says Mnkabayi, 'he took that away, but he gave them something else in return. He is no fool.'

Let service in the army be the true test of manhood, Shaka had said. And, before anger and resentment were able to gain purchase, becoming a threat to his throne, he sent his regiments off to war, where striving not to die soon took precedence over a mere headring. The fact that Shaka handed his men victory after victory also helped, for they began to see his definition of manhood offered some very real rewards.

'This is so,' murmurs Ndlela, 'yet I am like a man standing by a fire. I can put my hands out and feel the warmth, and thereby know the fire is there without even looking.'

'You are right, Ndlela, there *is* resentment, despite Shaka's successes. And this is where this current peace aids us. It gives them time to sit and think, time to brood about the horrors that followed Nandi's death.'

'Hai! Our Father turned on his own children, but what have they done, Ma?' asks Ndlela. 'Nothing!'

Mnkabayi nods.

'He turns men into youths, and they are angry. But they are also not angry, because he makes them men again,' says Ndlela. 'His ban on marriage – yes, there's another source of anger! But it's also a weapon, not so? A potent weapon. For see how happy they are when he finally lets one of his regiments marry! The jubilation is louder than the complaints that went before. He makes a mockery of the sangomas, and that makes our people nervous, but they are also pleased to see the sangomas bested.'

The induna shakes his head. 'There is this,' he says, twisting his left palm upwards; 'there is reward. But there is always that,' he adds, curling the fingers of his right hand into a fist. 'Are we walking into the wind, we who can see further? Is it not better to count our cattle and hope the coming storm doesn't rob us of everything?'

Mnkabayi smiles. 'But there is a lesson hidden within what you say. It lies there like a snake, and it's one Shaka hasn't noticed!'

'Aiee, tell me, Ma! Tell me what it is!'

'Very well, everything you say is true. They glower, then they grin. They mutter, then they sing! That is the lesson, Ndlela: they are fickle! My nephew has won them over, he has pampered and pacified them, made commoners into lords, savages into Zulus, but he can never hold them. He has built his kraal and set up his throne on a morass. It holds for now, but who knows for how much longer?

36

He calls them his children, but who knows how long before he realises just how petulant children can be!'

The daughter of Jama, sister of Senzangakhona, lays a hand on her trusted advisor's shoulder. 'We cannot sit back and do nothing, for then our people will be obliterated. And if we are to save our people, we must look amongst those who have lost more than they have gained.'

Ndlela sighs, pats his isicoco. Because he is in Mnkabayi's service no one would think of forcing him to remove the headring. Her patronage also means he's one of a select few whose status has enabled him to assume it without being married, for it is unthinkable that one such as he should ever be seen as a youth.

And it's men like this Mnkabayi is now referring to, clan headmen stripped of power and forced to take the title 'unumzane', gentleman, in place of the more traditional 'inkosi', chief, which is now reserved only for Shaka. This includes former favourites of Senzangakhona and his father, and other members of the Zulu nobility who have also seen their privileges severely curbed. Such as Senzangakhona's sons . . .

Ndlela shuts his eyes as though in pain. They've been through this before. Many times. No matter what path they take, they always end up at the gate of the royal kraal, wondering which of these pampered bulls inside it have what it takes to challenge Shaka. Dingane, Mhlangana, Bakuza, Mpande, Magwaza, Nzibe, Kolekile, Gowujana, Sigwebana, Gqugqu, Mfihlo, Nxojana – who among them has the courage to move against Shaka?

Some of them are still too young, of course. Mpande, for example, is Dingane's udibi, and others haven't even reached puberty. But those who are old enough . . . these are not the kind of bulls a man would want to build a herd with.

And is it not said that Mduli – the cantankerous uncle who sent Nandi's relatives packing, saying she merely had a stomach-ache when they told him she was pregnant by Senzangakhona, and who was among the first Shaka had put to death when he took the throne – is it not said that he asked to die like a warrior, with an assegai thrust, and went to join the ancestors praising Shaka's greatness? Is it not related how he had looked into Shaka's eyes and there seen everything that Senzangakhona and his sons lacked?

Today, however, Mnkabayi surprises Ndlela. Today she chuckles and says he is right to look doubtful.

'However . . .' continues this daughter of Jama and sister of Senzangakhona, who has the status of a queen and to whom Shaka has entrusted the care of his great northernmost war kraal. 'However, I have been watching and thinking, and I have changed my mind, for I believe there might indeed be one who is up to the task.'

★

And to think . . .

Left alone again to admire her cattle, Mnkabayi allows herself another grin.

How peaceful it all seems. A soft sun, a mild breeze, sweet grass. But, then, the greatest lies are like that . . .

The kingdom has grown and Shaka has given the Sky People almost complete control over trade in the region.

It hasn't always been so. Acknowledge that fact, at least.

But Mnkabayi's happy to. She will not dissemble and lie. More importantly, she will not seek to delude herself. Not like those greybeards who look back upon a time of drought and death and try to tell us those were good days, better than now – no, she won't do that.

I wanted him. I wanted him to come . . .

Her uncle Mduli wasn't the only one who spotted his potential. Somehow the spirit of Zulu shone through in Shaka despite her brother's disdain and his rejection of this boy who only wanted to be loved, who couldn't be held responsible for the conniving of his mother – yes, and somehow despite that harridan's influence, the bile she fed him at her breast, the anger she poured into his ear when he was older, the resentment she clothed him in.

Yes, the Bloodline in him kept breeding power, like the lightning strike in the night that sets the flames chewing at the split tree before spreading to the dry grass . . . Like the drumbeat that can never be stilled because it's the beat itself that feeds the drummers, keeps them going after their hands have completely worn away and they are left to pound the cowskin with bloodied stumps . . . Or the trickle conceived deep in the earth, the birth emerging through stone, the stream becoming a river, defying rapids and cataracts, eating away rocks and splitting the ground. And somehow this one has made it to the sea without burning out in a drought or becoming another's tributary . . .

I wanted him. I wanted him to come . . .

Her noble upbringing had seen Mnkabayi treat Nandi far better than her brother's other wives had done. Doubtless this had saved her from an impaling when Shaka became king. But it had been good manners, not foresight, that guided her actions then, in a willingness to grit her teeth and endure Nandi's tantrums. Besides, who could have known! Aiee, even the sangomas' bones had been strangely reticent. Certainly none of them she's aware of had foretold the coming of a great warrior king.

Neither had her support of Shaka once he assumed power – which had gone far in helping assuage the concerns of the people – been driven merely by self-preservation. Far from it! It was her allegiance to the Bloodline that had seen her stand up and declare: here is no usurper, merely the eldest son come to take what is rightfully his.

But now that same allegiance has her wondering how Shaka can be stopped.

And to think I wanted him to come!

★

And then – with almost all their foes vanquished, the pot boiled over, the hut collapsed, the gourd of the calabash shattered. But it wasn't the gourd used during the First Fruits – death had been Shaka's Uselwa Man, and destruction the harvest.

Shaka took to slaughtering whole villages that he felt weren't showing sufficient sadness after the passing of his mother. He forbade fornication, and had holes torn in sides of huts so that his slayers could come round at night and make sure the new law was being obeyed. Another decree conceded that cows had to be milked, but no one was then allowed to drink the milk; instead, it must be thrown on to the ground.

Everyone's still trying hard to forget the madness that erupted after Nandi's death, but Mnkabayi's not sure that Shaka himself has recovered. To her the King seems like a screaming man who has suddenly fallen silent. A cessation, yes, but also perhaps the beginning of a new kind of madness.

Doesn't Kholisa's report confirm this? What other explanation can there be for Shaka allowing these the izilwane from the sea to attend the First Fruits? Such a dangerous move!

A new kind of madness – but not the sort that heralds yet another loss of control.

Mnkabayi believes things aren't that simple. She suspects Shaka's madness has changed from unfettered rage into cold cunning.

And they must act soon to end his reign.

Or who knows where he will take them next!

4
Mgobozi

Interlude

Shaking his head, Shaka lowers himself on to a large flat-topped stone. Sitting on a log at right angles to the King, the old general patiently waits for surprise and shock, incomprehension and anger to work their way across his friend's visage – like swirling cold fronts and cyclones, low pressure systems and battered butterflies.

'Who would . . . ? This is . . . I don't know what to say.' Shaking his head. 'Mnkabayi?'

Mgobozi shrugs.

'She . . .' Shaka frowns, shadows darkening his eyes. 'I saved her.' He seems to be addressing the flames at his feet: orange fronds and white wood. 'I could have . . .' His hands lift from his knees, drop back down again. 'I could have ensured she joined Mduli on the Great Journey. He at least had . . .'

'Balls?'

Shaka turns his head, as if only now becoming aware of Mgobozi's presence. His old friend.

They stood shoulder to shoulder in the ranks of Dingiswayo's Izicwe legion: the mad Mthetwa who constantly refused promotion and the much younger Zulu who had some crazy notion about going into battle barefoot – less chance of slipping that way – and carrying a broken spear. For he claimed that a weapon you wielded like a Roman broadsword was a better proposition than one you threw away – in fact, threw to the very people who were trying to kill you.

'I thought she . . . Well, wasn't she one of the few women who showed my mother any kindness?'

Mgobozi nods . . .

. . . while Shaka frowns, momentarily distracted by the thought that something is not quite right here. It is like a civet lying high in the branches of a tree, this notion; for you know it's there – the barking of the dogs tells you that – but you strain to spot its form amid the greenery.

'And it's not as if she has any good reason to mourn the passing of the old ways,' says the general.

Something is there: now you see it, now you don't. The creature is all tail, easy to mistake for part of a branch. *Something to do with his mother?*

But Mgobozi is speaking.

'What was that?' Shaka asks him.

'I said she had little reason to miss the old ways – or her brother.'

'My father.'

'Your father, yes. And then there's her great love for sangomas.'

'This is so.' A grin. 'The three of us had that in common. Then again,' he adds, 'maybe the sangomas were right . . . About twins being a curse, I mean. She was allowed to live, and now see what she's up to! I saved her, gave her more than she dared dream of, and yet still she turns against me! Is that not a sign of one who is both cursed and a curse?'

'Aiee, old friend, no. I'd take my chances with twins, even albino twins . . . better, at least, that than those hyenas who claim to speak for the ancestors.'

'So why, then? Why this betrayal? Why *her* among all of them?'

'You would have me speak plainly?'

'I expect nothing less, Mgobozi.'

'Do not think I know more! Please, do not think that.'

Shaka frowns. 'I don't understand.'

'You will. But since you have asked me about Mnkabayi, I can simply tell you what I think. I do not know anything more!'

'You are like a man calling to me in a gale, old friend. I cannot make out what you are trying to say to me.'

Mgobozi holds up a calming hand. 'Do not let the wind blow us further apart, then. You ask me why I think Mnkabayi moves against you, and I say it is due to this business of the First Fruits.'

'But, old friend, this is something we have often discussed.' Shaka pauses briefly as another twinge of unease shimmers through his mind, as lightly as the brush of Jakot's shoulder on the beach. 'It makes sense,' continues the King, forcing himself to focus on the matter to hand. 'Let the First Fruits be celebrated by the King, and solely by the King at his royal kraal!'

What better way of drawing the nation together! What better way of emphasising the king's power! Has he not protected his children? Has he not brought them glory? Has he not brought them wealth, measured in cattle (which is to say *catel*, also both 'chattel' and 'capital')? Well, now, let him be the one to feed them!

'That's not what I refer to,' says Mgobozi. 'Your aunt is after all of the blood, so she would understand your reasoning, even applaud it.' Up to a point, Shaka's power is Mnkabayi's power – and has he not elevated her even above his brothers?

'Then what is it about the First Fruits that causes her to contemplate betrayal?'

Mgobozi spreads his arms. 'This, old friend.'

'This?'

'Yes, old friend, it is *this* that makes her afraid.'

Mnkabayi afraid? That's hard to imagine.

Precisely, says Mgobozi; and that she should decide to move against the King is a sign of just how strong that fear must be.

'Hai! Feared, yes, but afraid – no! Even Nobela, that old lizard, never dared to cross her!'

'And again I say to you: read the spoor, Majesty! You are right, but listen to what you are saying! And ask yourself this: what about Shaka?'

'What about Shaka?' asks Shaka.

'Even Shaka!'

'Even Shaka?'

'Even Shaka, Majesty. Even Shaka does not frighten her!'

The Zulu King grins. 'This is so.'

'She knows you intend to revive certain aspects of the First Fruits that have lain dormant over the seasons. As indeed you have for, see, here we are! And she knows you intend to include those savages washed up at your feet by the Great Waters. Aiee, old friend, do you wonder that she intends to move against you?'

Shaka scratches his chin, spreads his fingers and holds his hands above the flames. The izilwane have been coming and going for generations, but what's different about this bunch is that they have sought him out and built a kraal so that they might trade with the People Of The Sky. This doesn't seem to have bothered his children, though. Which isn't surprising because for one thing, the savages are small in number, and that alone makes it difficult to be afraid of them. For another, their presence means the Zulus no longer have to rely on the Portugiza in distant Delagoa, as the men from King Jorgi are closer and pay more for ivory and gold. Add to this the fact that they've settled in healthier environs, and don't rely on middlemen the way the Portugiza do with the Maputos. And they have little to fear from their Zulu hosts – although, if they don't seem to realise that themselves, so much the better.

Shaka slides his palms over his knees and arches his back, stares up at the thatch. It's his own advisors who have urged circumspection when dealing with the savages. Some have pointed to the Maputos and the way a few sickly Portugiza have turned them into vassals. The Maputos might not acknowledge that, and at times it might seem as if they are the masters, but they are fooling themselves.

The greybeards who point this out are right. But the same thing will never happen to the Zulus — of that Shaka is certain.

However, others of Shaka's izilomo, his inner circle, those a little wiser, a little more perceptive, have spoken of having misgivings harder to substantiate or even articulate. A vague sense of unease, apprehension, disquiet. Even Mbopa, his prime minister, has admitted to feeling somewhat concerned.

'Even Mbopa . . .' whispers Shaka.

Mbopa.

He's staring into the night and so doesn't see Mgobozi's stricken expression, doesn't hear his old friend whisper, 'No, Shaka!'

'You remember how he said they were coming? How he believed their arrival to be inevitable? And how, when you said, "Let them come, and we'll kill them on the beach", he urged caution, spoke of a need for cunning?'

Mgobozi's look of relief becomes a smile as Shaka glances towards him. 'I remember,' says the general.

Shaka frowns. *But he changed.*

Mbopa changed. And more than just his mind.

A sudden searing pain. An explosion of fire spreading like a baobab tree. The King recoils, toppling backwards, his arms raised to protect his face, his eyes.

Then, just as he's about to scrabble away, hurl himself into the safety of the darkness, he realises he's still sitting on the rock, while the flames remain docilely within their stone circle.

Shaka swallows, not daring to face Mgobozi.

But if the general has noticed anything, he's too loyal a friend to let on. 'You were saying, Majesty?' he asks mildly.

You were saying . . .

Shaka sighs, glances upward, towards stars twinkling in a midnight blue veld: the armies of the ancestors on the move.

He frowns, thinking he shouldn't be able to see any stars.

'Even Mbopa,' he says, returning to the orange flames and the face of his old friend. 'Even Mbopa, who said to expect their coming, has grown uneasy of late.'

Because they are of his izilomo, Shaka knows the fears of his inner circle can't be dismissed as silly remnants of old superstitions, or a natural suspicion of strangers, exacerbated by their experience with the double-dealing Portugiza – and by the arrogance evinced by these particular savages who would remain Jorgi's men despite Shaka's blandishments.

At the same time, though, this feeling of apprehension is a form of witchcraft – and one he has to be particularly wary of. Look how even those who would later become his most trusted generals cringed and quaked when he spoke of throwing away the ill-fitting sandals Zulu soldiers had always worn and of teaching them how to use the iklwa! Remember the barely contained rage that ran through what was then more a clan than a tribe, when he had the older recruits remove the isicoco and march across thorns!

How tempting had their warnings and complaints been! Concubines calling him to the comfort of warm thighs! How subtle the poison infecting him with doubt: those long, sweaty, sleepless nights when even the mighty Shaka – slayer of all who insulted his mother – would find himself asking the darkness *What if they are right?*

So many things could have gone wrong before his new regiments even caught their first glimpse of the enemy – and where would he be now if he hadn't been able to suck out that poison? Where would he be if he hadn't been able to bite down on the doubt and continue chasing his mutinous men across the thorns, and devising exercises to prove to them the wisdom of fighting with a weapon you didn't throw away, and convincing them of the great strength the Way of the Bull could bring to out-numbered regiments?

So, let him be strong here, too.

Yes!

He will show them . . .

His shoulders sag. But that's not really the issue, is it?

Mnkabayi poses a threat far greater than any of his brothers, or the rulers he has bested on the battlefield.

'I must confess I still do not follow you, old friend. You speak of the First Fruits, then you speak of the savages at Thekweni.' Shaka can't see the connection.

'Aiee, old friend!' says Mgobozi. 'This is me you're talking to! You know it's not that simple! You know what inviting the Long Noses to the First Fruits implies. You know how provocative that is. Yes, yes, many won't consider that, but there are those, like your aunt, who will wonder what you're up to. Those who will know you're up to something simply because you've invited the Long Noses to the First Fruits. They will never fully divine your motives, it is true, but the little they do grasp will be enough to have them reaching for their spears.'

Even Nandi! Even his mother had trusted her!

His mother . . .

'And Mnkabayi will understand this goes beyond power.' Yes, beyond even ensuring the perpetuation of the House of Zulu. 'She is not like your brothers, after all! Power is valuable to her, yes, but perhaps she also realises there are more important things at stake here. Maybe she moves against you, old friend, not to usurp but to save.'

Shaka glances at the general. His head is spinning. Mgobozi's words scurry through his mind like burning ants. Nausea sits coiled in his throat and there's a stinging in his eyes.

Hot, suddenly. So hot.

A wary glance at the flames. But they are behaving themselves.

His mother . . .

Mgobozi . . .

Mgobozi's here, but not Nandi. Why not? What he wouldn't give to see her!

46

Shaka regards his old friend.

'You are dead,' he murmurs. He runs his left hand down the side of his face, then leans forward and examines the black and red smears on his fingers. Imithi Emnyama, Black Medicine – muthi of the dead moon, isifile, and the dark day thereafter.

'You are dead,' he says again, staring at Mgobozi. 'And I will remember nothing of this, will I?' Except perhaps as a presentiment: the same kind of vague unease his advisors feel when he speaks of the White Men.

And she will move against me.

And you have told me why, old friend.

Or at least you have told me as much as you know, hence your warning earlier. What you then meant was: Just because I am dead, do not think I know anything more! Please, do not think that!

Somehow, though, Shaka will have to retain *some* inkling of this encounter. Yet, even as he's telling himself this, something else intrudes. Nandi, his mother – why not her? Why isn't she here?

Not important!

Mgobozi, it's what he said.

Mnkabayi will move against me.

She will . . .

He looks around, finds he is back inside the hut of his seclusion.

Who will move against him?

He snorts. Who indeed!

His shadow curves over him against the walls, as he paces back and forth.

It is the time of the First Fruits. His mighty army surrounds him! He will awe the White Men. They will not realise it, but this will be the beginning of their enslavement. The great army, and a mighty nation awaiting his word . . . these things will distract the barbarians, for they are like children in that respect. They will gape and stare, their greed rendering their precious guns next to useless, making a mockery of their boasts of conquering legions and stone cities. And they will nod and grin, and think they are fooling him!

They will walk in his shadow with their hands clasped behind their backs, and then, when they speak, their gestures will become more elaborate than a praise singer's, and they will think him tamed, never realising that he knows they believe their King Jorgi is stronger. Never realising he thinks they might be right!

But this campaign will not be decided on the battlefield.

What they don't know is that Shaka is something their King Jorgi is not – for if he is King of Kings, he is also Umthakathi Omkhulu, Sorcerer of Sorcerers, and it is with the First Fruits the beguiling will begin.

★

Once he dreamt of stones on a plain. And a journey, then an arrival . . .

Seen from afar the rocks resemble crocodiles sunning themselves, half hidden in the long grass. There is something reptilian about those rocks, those walls, those crude bricks like scales. Move closer and the crocodiles vanish; the rocks rearrange themselves, become something else. Circular walls creating enclosures; walls curving and ending; walls worn down by time and the elements to become rocky paths through the grass. A curse awaiting the awareness of words in order to give it life. A childhood taunt, lying in the long grass of memory, seemingly discarded, but never forgotten. An evil that beckons, but is willing to bide its time, knowing that time will come.

And he wondered about this dream of his. Did it have something to do with his Ubulawu, the talisman every Zulu king must seek out? He thought so at the time, and even sent out a band of trusted warriors to find the stones.

But the more he watched the White Men, the more he wondered . . .

Stones on a plain. And a journey, then an arrival. Perhaps those stones were theirs, and Jakot's footprints in the sand the final stage of the odyssey. (Although that's only a way of seeing that's occurred to him while he's been segregated in here, covered by this vile muthi. Which clearly does serve some purpose!)

Initially he'd agreed with Mbopa that skilful manoeuvring would see the men from King Jorgi help him secure complete hegemony over all he sees, and extend the boundaries of his kingdom even further, since those ruled by greed are so easy to fool. As time passed, though, he began to wonder if they might not be able to offer him more.

Indeed, it was this realisation that finally helped him climb out of the depression he had fallen into since the death of his mother . . .

There is much Shaka can understand about the ways of these savages – they are not so different – but of late he's become intrigued by the things he can't comprehend or imagine.

This is why he thinks they can offer him more than they realise. Although perhaps, in the end, it'll be less about their offering and more about his taking, for this is something these aliens are not even aware they possess . . .

And the taking, the beguiling, begins now at the First Fruits.

Clench your fists, and remember what they said that day you clenched your fists beneath the cliffs that turned Ngoza's capital into a citadel, and say it again: *Everything is ready.* The lion is crouching in the long grass ready to pounce.

He has seen further than his advisors, he has understood more. Now a victory greater than any he has yet won lies within his grasp . . .

Shaka stops pacing. So why, then, this strange feeling, this sense of foreboding, like the sudden stifling heat that precedes a summer thunderstorm?

5
Fynn

May 1824

It lies there in quiet splendour, dozing in the sun, sheltered from the worst of the storms that make sailing along this littoral so hazardous by a bluff of high ground that the Zulus call Isibubulungu, the Big

Long Sweet Potato, while a second peninsula protects the lagoon's eastern reaches. Between the two is a sandbar which is covered by less than a metre of water at low tide. Cross it and you'll be greeted by a tranquil twenty-square kilometres of bay shaped like a pear – or a testicle. Trees alive with chattering monkeys arch out over the water, but the jungle soon gives way to mangrove – full of perfidious hippo eyes and professorial egrets – and then mangrove becomes bush, grassland speckled with wattles, lala-palms and curly podberry trees, while terns and gulls patrol the breaking waves.

Over the centuries, clans and tribes have settled here, then drifted away. Castaways have found succour; even a penitent pirate seeking to atone for his sins, if legend is to be believed. From time to time, mariners have managed to bounce their ships across the sandbar. They have fetched fresh water from the streams that flow into the bay and hunted for food or bartered for provisions with the friendly natives. Then they have sailed away to distant parts, leaving the lagoon to become lost once more.

In 1685, survivors of three wrecked ships built a two-masted vessel, fourteen metres long, which they sailed to the Cape, which was then in Dutch hands. Governor Simon van der Stel bought the vessel, named her the *Centaur*, and despatched her back up the coast to look for other shipwrecked mariners.

He was also interested in the men's descriptions of this mysterious harbour, and four years later, he sent Captain Pieter Timmerman, on the galiot *Noord*, to buy the bay for Holland and the Dutch East India Company. Iron pots and pans, skillets and spoons, bolts of material and several sacks of sugar and salt were handed over to the local chief, and a deed of sale drawn up. A document which was duly lost when Timmerman proceeded to wreck the *Noord*, near Algoa.

In 1705 another Dutch ship crossed the irksome sandbar, seeking confirmation that the Dutch East India Company owned the place. The chief Timmerman had originally dealt with had died, however, and his son sent the White Men packing.

As for the Zulus, they paid little attention to the bay they them-

50

selves called Ethekweni. Initially it was far from their territory, but even when Shaka's conquests saw the kingdom grow to encompass the lagoon, it was ignored. The King was more interested in what lay further south, the territory where the Pondoes and Xhosas had settled.

And Farewell and the *Salisbury* missed noticing it on their first voyage. Outward bound, they had been aiming for Santa Lucia and, while returning to Port Elizabeth after Farewell and the others had been rescued, they assumed the entrance was just another river mouth, blocked by a sandbar.

All the same, Farewell still believed it was possible to find a safe anchorage and establish a settlement hereabouts. King was enthusiastic, too, reckoning there had to be gold higher up the rivers.

After taking on supplies, the *Salisbury* left Port Elizabeth on 11 September 1823, accompanied by a small sloop named the *Julia*.

Returning to Natal, the ships hugged the coast once more. The weather was better this time, but there were always those blessed sandbars. It was as if nature was mocking them, saying *Look, see the wide river, deep enough for a ship with the right draught*, then blocking it off with a barrier of silt and sand.

But not all were totally impassable, as Farewell and King found out one day when the weather changed and a squall started nudging them even closer to the shore. Loath to run aground or tear his keel on an uncharted reef, King decided to seek shelter in a nearby river. The tide was coming in, current and wind were in their favour, and the sandbar was just a smudge in the choppy water. It was worth the risk, and certainly the smaller *Julia* would have no problem crossing the bar.

Past the point of no return, chained to the current and whipped forward by the wind – then a first bump as the bottom leaps up to hit the prow . . . the creaking growl . . . silent prayers . . . and they're over.

They're over, and driven onward by the wind, tacking to starboard, they suddenly realise they're in a lagoon.

A bay!

★

51

It's even more attractive once the storm subsides and they're able to take stock of their surroundings.

Easily accessible to ships with the right draught, 'it abounds with hippopotamus and fish of various sorts,' James King later writes in a letter to Earl Bathurst, Secretary of State for Colonies, seeking to broach the idea of establishing a British settlement at this bay. 'The plains are very extensive, and the pasture for their cattle rich. Near the anchorage is excellent timber for shipbuilding.'

Claiming to have ventured (an unlikely) sixty kilometres inland, he comments that the terrain 'is blest with a salubrious air'.

Natives encountered were at first hostile. 'But when we became better acquainted, they were extremely well disposed and expressed a particular desire for us to remain among them.'

All the same, some reinforcements would be welcome. Although his main aim is to trade with Shaka, whose capital he estimates lies about 250 kilometres to the north-east, King also ventures to suggest this might be a good spot to relocate some of the British settlers sent to the Cape Colony in 1820.

These worthies had been promised a better life, away from the squalor of the Industrial Revolution, only to be placed on the frontier, facing hordes of pissed-off Xhosas, and they haven't stopped complaining since. What's more, precious few have any farming experience and 'settling' for most has entailed recreating the slum dwellings they left back home in an agrarian setting.

'I should not, my Lord, have ventured to offer an opinion of the capability of the soil of this country,' writes the former midshipman, 'but having several very clever men who appeared perfectly acquainted with agricultural pursuits, and who were unanimous in declaring that, if Government were acquainted with its advantages, they would not hesitate to remove the unfortunate settlers thither.'

King's report will be accompanied by an artistic little chart. Along the bluff of land that shields the bay from the ocean is inscribed: *Good timber for ship building*. At the head of the bay is: *Good forests and large trees*. The northern sector King has designated *Hippopotamus grazing ground.* Along the beach that runs north-east, away from the bay, there's *Bush* and, inland, *Extensive grazing flats.*

The report will make no mention at all of Lieutenant Francis Farewell or the Farewell Trading Company.

★

The *Salisbury* and the *Julia* reach Cape Town on 3 December 1823.

As far as Farewell and King are concerned, the expedition has been a huge success.

Fact: the Portuguese are doing very well at Delagoa Bay – why else would they maintain a presence in such a fever-ridden hellhole?

Fact: their main supplier is Shaka. Has to be, since he's the local Napoleon.

Fact: make nice with him and establish a base at Port Natal, preferably with the Crown's backing, and you'll divert all that gold and ivory your way.

Fact: neither Farewell nor King have as yet managed to make contact with this all-powerful potentate, who keeps the Portuguese at Delagoa Bay rubbing their hands in glee (when they're not writhing on their beds racked by malaria, dengue and sundry other horrors, that is).

Fact: neither Farewell nor King are overly concerned they haven't as yet managed to make contact with this all-powerful potentate. Neither are they worried because they can't produce incontrovertible proof that Shaka even exists, or is anything like the figure mentioned in the stories they've heard.

These are details to be dealt with at the appropriate time.

Of more immediate concern is the fact that the two men are now rivals, each vying to be the first to establish a trading station at Port Natal.

Farewell is especially aggrieved. The speculation was his idea, but now King's acting as if he's Clive of bloody India – which is a laugh. Sailing Mommy's ships back and forth is one thing, but establishing and running a settlement is something else entirely. And Farewell possesses precisely that kind of experience.

He was with Captain William Hoste on the *Amphion* when they were attacked by French and Venetian ships off the island of Vis on 13 March 1811. The *Amphion* was accompanied by three other frigates, giving Hoste 124 guns and about 900 men. Commanded by Bernard Dubourdieu, the enemy squadron comprised seven frigates and four smaller warships – or 276 guns and nearly 2,000 men.

With the *Amphion* flying the signal 'Remember Nelson', the British proceeded to thrash the enemy.

Being one of Hoste's favourites, Farewell was placed in charge of the small complement of men the captain sent ashore to occupy Vis, while the captain himself shepherded his battered frigates to a better equipped port for repairs. For a few months subsequently, until Hoste could arrange for a garrison to be sent there, Lieutenant Francis Farewell was the supreme commander of ninety square kilometres of some strategic importance in the Adriatic. (And although the local cricket club is named after Sir William, it was in fact Farewell who introduced that game to the Croatian island.)

So who better to establish a trading post at Port Natal, and start persuading the Zoolas they'll be better off enriching King George?

Not that Farewell's all that surprised by King's perfidy. It's a betrayal very much in keeping with the reefs and shoals he's had to navigate these past few years, where if you're not actually becalmed, you're turning turtle in a tempest.

There he was, his career all shipshape, then Boney's imprisoned on St Helena and he's cast adrift, and 'retired' on half pay. He wasn't alone, since many other Royal Navy officers were in the same predicament, but that wasn't the end of the old vicissitudes.

Drifting south, Farewell had purchased the *Princess Charlotte* and begun to engage in what Fynn terms 'mercantile speculations'. These involved carrying various cargoes from Calcutta to Rio de Janeiro, filling the holds again and sailing to the Cape, and then setting out for Brazil. Farewell had been returning to Rio with a full cargo when the *Charlotte* sank, leaving the lieutenant all but destitute.

Somehow he managed to get back to the Cape . . . and ended

up marrying Elizabeth Schmidt, the stepdaughter of the owner of the boarding house where he lodged. A short while later, Owen's surveying expedition had given him the idea of forming the Farewell Trading Company.

James King has done very well, thanks to Farewell, but now, doubtless spurred on by his mother, who's part owner of several ships engaged in trade with the West Indies, he's developed ideas above his station.

Which is typical.

Although King – who was born in Halifax, Nova Scotia – had also served in the Royal Navy, signing on as a ship's boy at the age of eleven, he had resigned as a midshipman ten years later, which means he isn't in fact entitled to the rank of 'lieutenant'. Yet he has the gift of the gab, can turn on the charm, and few of his acquaintances or employers know of this pretence. As a consequence, *Lieutenant* James King is well liked in Cape Town. His advice is often sought and, as his report to Bathurst shows, he does his damnedest to appear quite the expert in several areas.

He will even on occasion claim kinship with the Captain James King who served under James Cook on the latter's last voyage around the world. That other James King was employed to take sextant readings for Cook's surveys, but after Cook's death he helped lead the ships on the remainder of their course, and then completed Cook's account of the voyage. Like his namesake, the False Lieutenant King fancies himself as more of a scientist and explorer than a mere speculator.

Sheer poppycock, of course. Before Farewell chartered the *Salisbury*, King's main source of income had been transporting troops between Cape Town and Port Elizabeth. Even Mommy didn't trust him with any better ships and longer runs!

Then, even as Farewell is considering scouring the streets of Cape Town to find King and throttle him, the latter makes an incredible blunder.

He suddenly sets sail for London, and Farewell can't believe his luck. King clearly thinks he'll be able to raise more money back home – and perhaps he's right – but now Farewell has both time and proximity on his side. He can have an expedition together, and at Port Natal, before his rival is anywhere near reaching England.

★

On 1 May 1824, he submits a memorandum to the Governor of the Cape, Lord Charles Somerset, explaining how he has discovered Port Natal and outlining his plans for establishing a settlement. Contact will be made with 'the Interior'. With a vessel constantly lying in port, his men will collect gold and ivory from 'the natives' who 'have already requested that we would come and traffic with them'. The resulting 'constant intercourse', adds Farewell, will eventually lead to 'a commerce of importance to the Colony and advantageous to ourselves'.

The trading party will be made up of at least twenty-five men, including servants and crew.

Lest his proposal seem merely a crass attempt to make his own fortune, Farewell ends the memorandum by stressing the hazards involved and how, if successful, the exercise is 'likely to lead to important advantages to the Colony in furnishing articles of Export, as well as new Sources of Trade', not to mention 'tending to the Civilisation of many populace nations hitherto unknown to Europeans'.

Somerset is quick to give his permission, but this is to be a *private* venture, he insists. There will be no annexing of anything for the Crown. Furthermore, all dealings with the local inhabitants are to be conducted in 'a conciliatory manner and upon fair terms of Barter'.

Regarding this, and Somerset's refusal to 'sanction the acquisition of any territorial possessions', as so much fine-print blah–blah–blah, Farewell sets about seeking investors.

He consults his wife's stepfather, Johann Petersen, who in turn approaches other money men in the Colony's Dutch community, who are duly won over by Farewell's tales of cattle kraals constructed entirely of elephant tusks.

'I cannot allow myself to make a statement against the veracity of this gentleman without expressing the opinion that he was either

56

told or given to understand this by some native who intended merely to imply that the elephant tusks were placed *around* the cattle kraal,' Fynn will later write, charitably giving Farewell the benefit of the doubt on this score.

★

Henry Fynn is, of course, another who Farewell persuades to join his party. It's a smart move, not least because Fynn, who arrived at Cape Town in 1818 at the age of fifteen, has some prior knowledge of the region they're heading for.

After knocking about the Colony for a few years, he was hired by the merchants Messrs H. Nourse & Co. and appointed super-cargo on the sloop *Julia*, which was sailing to Delagoa Bay with the brig *Mary*, to trade for ivory. While there Fynn got to hear about Shaka and promptly set out to find him. He managed to reach a Zulu village and learnt (to his own satisfaction, at least) that Shaka was no myth. Now he's eager to repeat the exercise with better preparations, and hopefully more success this time.

His presence in the expedition, then, means Farewell will have an ally, someone else who actually 'knows' Shaka, should mutinous mutterings start up. Not having any money of his own to invest, Fynn will manage the 'trading transactions' and also lead the advance party that will prepare dwellings for the main contingent and mean-while try to make contact with Shaka.

Fynn might, by his own admission, be a little too reserved for his own good, but he can be counted upon in a tight spot. On his trip to Delagoa he looked after the interests of Nourse & Co. admirably, relieving the *Julia*'s drunken captain of his command and putting the first mate in charge instead. Later, he showed himself more than able to deal with the intimidatory tactics employed by the Portuguese authorities to deter foreigners from trading with the local inhabitants.

He's also nobody's fool, therefore certainly isn't taken in by Farewell's wild claims and lavish promises. But neither do they worry him as much as they might have, because the same concern that drives Farewell to ever greater exaggerations also bothers Fynn. This concern is the fact that, try as he might, Farewell can't seem to persuade many Englishmen to join them, while Petersen is having far greater success recruiting his fellow Dutchmen or men of other nationalities.

Even more ominously, a short while before they're due to set sail, Fynn learns Petersen has bribed the junior clerks at the Colonial Office to find for him records relating to the Dutch East India Company's alleged 'purchase' of Port Natal back when the same Company was in possession of the Cape.

What is supposed to be an English initiative is now turning out to be anything but.

★

Why does Fynn go then? It's tempting to suggest a part of him realises that he will remain unformed and unreal, incomplete and indelibly incognito, until Shaka discovers him. That, such is the Zulu King's greatness, Shaka is the one who can give Fynn life through bestowing on him a measure of immortality. After all, those who remember will also be remembered – for a while, at least.

But that's surely the kind of magical thinking best left to plumbers who've fallen off stepladders. It's more likely Fynn goes, despite his misgivings, simply because he said he would, and he is a man of his word – and because 'travelling and new scenes' really are more important to him than 'any pecuniary advantage', as he later records.

Whatever the case, the sloop *Julia* slips over the sandbar and anchors in the northern sector of the bay early on the morning of 10 May 1824, the time of Untlaba – the Aloe Flowering Moon.

At about three o'clock that afternoon, Fynn orders a boat lowered. After provisions and bedding are loaded, he and five others set off for the shore. The rest of the party comprises Michael, a Hottentot servant, Frederick, a Xhosa interpreter, an Englishman called Henry Ogle, a Prussian called Udo and a Frenchman who may or may not have been named Apollonaire. These last three are 'mechanics', handymen who'll be constructing the buildings that will house the expedition and store the deluge of ivory Farewell has promised his investors.

They land on the beach in front of the swathe of soggy terrain that King's chart described as 'Hippopotamus grazing ground' and which will be later named Khangela. After the boat is unloaded and sent back to the *Julia*, the men split into two groups. The three mechanics head one way, while Fynn, Frederick and Michael head the other. Although the Hottentot and the Xhosa are annoyingly nervous, needing constant reassurance and urging every few paces, Fynn by now prefers their company to that of his fellow whites.

He's hoping to meet some locals, but all they come across are hippo tracks. Lots of them.

The mechanics also say they've seen hippo tracks but no natives. Knowing they probably dawdled so as to keep the bay always in sight, Fynn considers retracing their footsteps and moving further afield – but it's getting late. After some gnawing of the bottom lip and a bit of pacing, he's able to fold away his enthusiasm and help the others select a place to spend the night.

They choose a hollow beneath rising ground, reasoning that this will help protect them from the wind. They spread out their bedding, build a fire and prepare supper. It's been a long day, especially for Fynn, who was up and on deck when the *Julia* was coaxed over the sandbar, and beach sand is an ideal mattress for stiff muscles; the men soon fall asleep around the fire.

They're so tired, in fact, that the hollow has already become a fast-flowing stream by the time the storm wakes them.

Somehow they manage to rescue a few burning logs and grab the firewood they collected earlier. And somehow they're able to get another fire going, after scrambling to higher ground.

Thunder, lightning, and rain falling in gusts scattered by the wind, which is possibly why their fire survives, although in truth it's more a collection of glowing embers. And there they sit, shivering beneath their wet blankets, as the rain pecks at them continually, two Englishmen, a Frenchman and a Prussian, not to mention a Hottentot and a Xhosa (but no Scotsman): five nationalities in search of a punchline. Or six characters a Pobble, Jumblie and runcible spoon away from being an Edward Lear limerick.

Thunder, lightning and that irascible wind blowing now from the east, now from the west, slicing right through their blankets to set their teeth chattering. Dark splotches, constantly forming and reforming on the logs.

Thunder and lightning. Malevolent thunder. Whipcrack lightning.

And then the wolves come . . .

A snarling that encircles the men.

And the putative joke and the perhaps limerick mutate into a riddle. As in: when is a wolf not a wolf?

They're surrounded. Now they leave their igloos of blankets to toss every bit of wood they can find on to the fire. They shout and wave their hands, and regret the fact they left the firearms back on the *Julia*.

Brown blurs in the darkness, the wolves are coming closer . . .

Moving in for the kill . . .

The circle tightening like a noose.

But when is a wolf not a wolf?

When you're on a beach on the south-east coast of Africa, being attacked by hyenas.

But perhaps, right here and now, knowing the difference between *Canis lupus* and *Crocuta crocuta* isn't that important (although Fynn will forever insist that they really were attacked by wolves). Especially since both have the carnivore's trademark carnassial teeth which can shear flesh and crush bones, with the hyena a little more powerful than the wolf in this department – although, again, that's a distinction best not mentioned right now.

And these marauders definitely have their napkins tucked into their collars and are looking forward to a late supper.

And, wet, bedraggled and bearded after their weeks at sea, the men are also appropriately dressed for the part, resembling nothing so much as a buffet of Neanderthals about to discover there could

60

just be something to this extinction nonsense everyone's being prattling on about.

'We had no better mode of defence than by standing back to back with firebrands in our hands,' Fynn will later write. When two or three of the creatures decide good manners are one thing, but someone's got to be first at the smorgasbord and come forward, they're met with a frantic waving of spluttering logs.

With the hyenas probing their defences for any weaknesses and the men turning to meet sudden forays, the six have gradually moved away from their bedding . . . and now a hyena goes trotting by, carrying a pair of leather trousers belonging to Ogle. With a bellow, the mechanic flings himself forward . . .

. . . and just manages to grab one of the trouser legs.

A tug of war ensues, with Ogle ignoring the other fangs out there. He's got a sixty rix-dollar-note in one of the pockets – there's no way the beast's going to have that! Pulling hard, he changes his grip and folds his fingers around the band of the pants. That gives him the advantage. With much muffled growling the hyena tosses its head from side to side . . .

. . . and finds itself left with part of the trouser leg. Leaving Ogle to scurry back to his friends, the creature turns and disappears into the night. It has to feel cheated, and not only because it got away with a mere portion of its prey. After all, this tastes like skin, but where's the warm, squishy yummy stuff that's supposed to be inside?

Knowing a diversion when he sees one, Udo the Prussian seizes this opportunity to gather up his own clothes. He's on his hands and knees, when his left leg goes stiff and he's yanked backwards. Dropping on to his right side, he turns his head and shrieks. A hyena has him by his foot.

Fynn: 'He screamed out most vociferously: "My toag! my toag!" meaning his toe. This caused a roar of laughter, as we were now less fearful, finding we were not likely to be rushed upon en masse.'

A firebrand thrown at the animal secures Udo's release. But it's more than likely that it's that lunatic laughter filling the African night,

61

blossoming beneath a sky at last clear and dripping with stars, that finally sees the hyenas beat a hasty retreat – on the sound assumption it's best not to eat anyone crazier than oneself after midnight.

And a Frenchman, a Prussian, a Hottentot, a Xhosa and two Englishmen (but no Scotsman) are left waiting for dawn, as cold as the crabs that crawl on yonder hills . . .

6
The Swimmer

Interlude

And so it was as Jakot had predicted, but not quite as he'd expected.

Was he serious about finding Shaka when he had stormed off into the bushes? Who knows, but Shaka certainly found him – or at least one of his patrols did. Fervently hoping that this Zulu king the White Men aboard ship couldn't stop talking about would recognise his worth, Jakot contrived to ignore the levelled spears and suspicious glances, and tried his best not to act as a captive but as a powerful prince come to offer a colleague advice. And the fact that he would be able to tell Shaka all about the devious ways of these arrogant White Men surely would serve him better than any accident of birth. Let his expertise be his lineage here. As for the Long-Nosed heathens themselves, they'd come to regret the way they'd treated him.

There was just one problem, though. As a child, Jakot had found himself part of the booty following a cross-border raid. He therefore grew up on a white farm, where he learnt Dutch and a smattering of English. When he escaped and returned to his people, they used him as an interpreter in their dealings with the settlers. He was also a useful guide on rustling expeditions. Captured on one of these, he and a companion only avoided being shot when Jakot revealed he could speak Dutch. Then another period of bondage ensued, until Jakot was able to escape once more. He took to roaming the Colony, hiring himself out as a guide and interpreter, when he wasn't stealing cattle.

In other words – and this was the problem – Jakot had spent most of his life among the White Men at the Cape. He loathed and despised them, but had developed a taste for their coffee and jam, for butter and bread baked in the European way, and for rum. Like it or not, he'd been irrevocably tainted, and it had been with a European mindset that he'd gone to look for Shaka. Like his former employers, he expected to come upon Shaka's kraal, astound the King with his superior knowledge, and thus have him awed and eager for his help.

That this might not be the way things were going to pan out became evident once Jakot caught his first glimpse of KwaBulawayo. The sheer enormity of the Zulu capital startled him. Circles within circles showed careful planning – you could even say the city had a neatness that Cape Town with its muddy, shit-splattered streets lacked – and look at all the people, the cattle! But there was now no turning back. Not that Jakot had any choice.

About a week after leaving his employers, then, he found himself on his knees in front of Shaka.

The White Men were coming, whether Shaka liked it or not, and the Zulu King would be needing a loyal interpreter. One who'd not only unwrap their words, but reveal the hidden meanings that lurked behind them. Jakot had to keep telling himself that, as a mantra to ward off the fear.

'Stand,' ordered Shaka, 'so that I might look upon you.'

Jakot obeyed. Although he kept his head bowed, he sensed the King's appraisal – like a stick that sent ants of fear scurrying up his spine.

'Well?' said Shaka, after a while. 'Where are your masters?'

Jakot raised his head. 'No man is my master!'

A grin flickered across the King's lips. His had been a reasonable question, since Jakot was dressed much like the servants White Men employed. He was wearing a cast-off waistcoat, sandals and *klapbroek*, trousers made from cowskin, with a front flap that hid the belt and folded downwards when unbuttoned.

Mbopa, meanwhile, bristled beside the King at witnessing such disrespect, till Shaka told him to calm himself.

'I see,' he addressed Jakot once more, 'in driving their oxen, you also herd the owners.'

As a way of atoning for the brusqueness of his previous response, Jakot inclined his head. 'This is so, Majesty, but in this instance there are no oxen.'

'Do you say you are *not* in the employ of the White Men? But you wear their swaddling,' said Shaka, indicating the Xhosa's britches.

Deciding not to risk correcting the King again, Jakot said he had meant only that he had come over the great waters – in a conveyance that moved across those waters much like a cloud.

'You came by ship, you mean.'

'Er . . . yes, Majesty.'

Shaka sighed. His time had been wasted. Another shipwreck. He used to look forward to quizzing these unfortunates on their strange ways, but had rarely learnt much of interest. They had usually been too scared, and he believed that would be so even were they able to communicate with him in the same language. These days he doesn't even bother to have the shipwreck survivors brought to him. The coastal kraals simply feed them, tend to their injuries and send them on their way, with guides if necessary.

'How many?' asked Shaka.

'I'm not sure I understand, Majesty.'

'How many survived the wreck?'

'There was no wreck, Majesty. These men have come to seek you out!'

'Me?'

'Yes,' said Jakot eagerly, happy to have at last elicited some interest from the King. 'They come to seek you out, Majesty, in order to trade with you!'

And their first transaction would inevitably involve asking the Zulu King for land on which to establish a settlement . . .

'And all this you know, because they are not your masters, and you are privy to their plans?'

'I am there amongst them. They speak. I listen. At times it is as if I am invisible, Majesty.'

'Why do I sense your . . . companions might wish that it was indeed so. But they have come, you say, seeking my favour?'

'Yes, Majesty.'

Shaka glanced around. 'Well?'

'Majesty?'

'Where are they?'

'Ah! I have, uhm . . . pre-empted them somewhat.'

Jakot went on to explain about the botched landing. He didn't, however, go into why he had decided to travel to Bulawayo on his own, but Shaka was grinning by the time he concluded his narrative.

'I see I was wrong to inquire about your masters. I should have asked about your pursuers, for you are clearly a fugitive.'

'Not quite, Majesty. More of an ally.'

Derisive chuckles spread through the ranks of the men gathered behind the King.

'An ally?' said Shaka, after the noise had died down. 'Aiee, who knows what we two might accomplish together!'

'Majesty, you jest at my expense, and I do not mean to criticise you in that, for truly it is the kind of jest I might have made were our roles reversed. However, there is a grain of truth in what you say. Your words do indeed point to a path that might prove profitable for both of us.'

Mbopa could no longer contain himself. 'You *dare* to place the King of the Zulus on the same path as yourself! Your words, earthworm, point to your entrails and you may yet *profit* from the opportunity to view them more closely.'

'Hai, but this one entertains me, Mbopa. I'll stay my anger a while longer.'

'Majesty,' protested Jakot, 'I meant no disrespect.'

'Nonetheless, the hut is now burning. Come now, let us see how you will douse the flames.'

'Majesty, I . . . What I meant was . . . Well, I mean . . .'

65

'Aiee! Now the granny inside the hut is on fire, too! Listen to her shrieks! Yours will become louder if you cannot stop this blaze.'

'I know their ways, Majesty! Yes, yes, it is so, for I have lived among them. I know their ways, their customs – how they think! I can be of assistance to you in your dealings with them.'

'Should I choose to have dealings with them.'

'Yes, well there you go, Majesty. The choice is yours, but you need to know these men will be persistent.' Although Jakot had often overheard his employers complaining about the lack of official support for their project, he knew they were also determined to proceed, no matter what. There were, after all, fortunes to be made. 'And they will reward you!' he added, showing yet again how much a part he was of that society he claimed to scorn.

'Trinkets!'

'Perhaps initially, Majesty, but you should be able to frighten more substantial offerings out of them.'

Shaka led the roar of laughter that erupted among the Zulus, and Jakot allowed himself a wan smile.

As it turned out, Shaka would become enamoured with some of those very trinkets the White Men brought him, when they finally came to pay their respects. He was especially fond of English soap, which he came to prefer over the red paste usually used to 'wash' the King, and he also insisted his barber shave him with a European razor.

'I can help you, Majesty,' urged Jakot.

'*Help!*' growled Mbopa.

'Serve! Serve you, Majesty! I can serve you! Be of assistance!'

★

Jakot had travelled far and wide, and Shaka found him entertaining, naming him Hlambamanzi, 'the Swimmer', after hearing of his escape in the waves. He invited Jakot to stay and advise the Zulu court on how to deal with the White Men when they eventually stopped trying to drown themselves and made their way to his capital.

Shaka knew an arrogant conman when he saw one, but reckoned Jakot's knowledge might just come in handy, if only in helping the King decide what *not* to do.

As for Jakot, the realisation that these Zulus weren't about to be easily duped was somewhat unsettling. It was a sign that he might not turn out to be as indispensable as he had hoped. He constantly did his best to keep Shaka entertained, but when the Zulus went to war against the Thembus he seized the opportunity to 'exile' himself to a kraal closer to the ocean. After Fynn and then Farewell arrived, he began dividing his time between the White Men and the Zulus, favouring the former until he became all but a permanent member of the settlement at Port Natal.

7
Dingane

Untlolanja, the Fucking Dog Moon, January 1826
It suddenly strikes him that things are unnaturally quiet.

He's moving among the temporary huts raised to accommodate the massive influx of people that came to attend the First Fruits. The amadladla in this section are empty, waiting to be torn down, but not every visiting family or clan has yet returned home. Various favourites or those seeking favour, contingents from the existing regiments, heads of the war kraals and their retinues, and sundry others (including Fynn and his interpreter) have remained behind at the King's invitation, to celebrate the end of the celebrations tonight.

And by now the darkness should have become a tangled thicket of lamentations, and night should be day as flames of rage leap up into the sky.

Even laughter! He wouldn't have been surprised to hear echoes of laughter: joyful, gleeful, relieved laughter.

Instead . . .

It seems somehow obscene, this silence.

He clenches his fists, catching and squeezing the urge to keep moving, and forces himself to *listen*.

A brief roaring in his ears, then . . . nothing. Even the air is still. He scratches his nose to reassure himself that his senses haven't deserted him.

He'd heard the shouts and was coming to investigate, when he was suddenly bowled over by a man running fast; a wiry man, now that he comes to think of it, his desperation giving him a strength that belied his size. Dingane had just got his breath back when the Induna's udibi appeared. Since it was clear to the prince that the boy was chasing the man who had knocked him over, he merely pointed in the direction the latter had fled. It was only when he made it to the bonfires, and the milling crowd, that he was told what had happened. Realising it was the killer he had encountered, he immediately set off after him – and the udibi.

That's what he'll claim, at least. And all of it will be true – except the part about going after the killer.

That's assuming he can go back, of course. Is that an option? And he needs to be sure about this, because if it is an option and he doesn't return within a certain period of time, that won't look good, no matter how eloquently he can explain away his actions.

And isn't this what they want? The conspirators – isn't this part of their plan, possibly even the part they reckoned they could be most sure of?

Do it, kill Shaka – and Dingane will run.

So? Isn't that all the more reason he should turn back right now?

No, he decides as he begins to move again. He still can't be certain. And there's no room for mistakes – not on this night, anyway.

So?

So, he thinks, as he passes the last of the temporary huts, *Dingane runs.*

★

The irony isn't lost on him. With the exception of Shaka, who was dragged from village to village by Nandi when he was a child, Dingane's probably done more running – more getting away from –

than any of his other brothers. Yet everyone's always going on about how he lives up to his name and *needs* to be surrounded by life's luxuries. It's a trait he's displayed since birth, they'll explain: for when he showed himself loath to be weaned, to forgo the convenience of his mother's breasts, his father decreed he would be named 'the Needy One'.

But let them think he's soft and weak, only interested in the privileges of his rank, and the opportunities it affords him to indulge his hedonism. Not only has his reputation shielded him from Shaka's wrath on numerous occasions, but Dingane believes it also saved his life, all those summers ago, when his brother seized the throne.

He halts. Grazing livestock and the tramping of thousands of feet have left the ground bare for several hundred metres beyond the huts, and he's reached the other side, where the veld begins again and the grass tickles his knees. He turns to look back the way he's come. He can see the glow from the bonfires where the feast had been taking place, and there's even some movement, but Bulawayo seems strangely normal.

Has he been bewitched? Has he become an impundulu, a zombie, drawn to where his new master awaits?

No, this is too real. He's too conscious of himself as himself. Besides – he glances again at the orange glow around the distant huts – the heat, the blaze of shock that washed over him when he heard what had happened . . . no sangoma could conjure up that.

The thing is, he who is so practised in running, so adept at flee-ing, has set off spectacularly ill prepared. He isn't even armed; he has no waterskins, or sleeping mat, or cloak for warmth.

And that's not all he's forgotten. There's Mpande, his udibi. Where is he? Never there when his master needs him!

They share the same mother, and 'the Root' grew to idolise his older brother, ready to cover for Dingane when the latter couldn't be bothered to do his chores. Not that he ever received any thanks from the Needy One. Dingane simply thought the younger boy was a fool for taking the blame. It took a while for him to appreciate his gullible and eager-to-please sibling had his uses, but there are moments when the old harsh attitude returns. And this is one of them. Dingane's conveniently forgotten how earlier tonight he told Mpande to get lost.

If only Mpande were here! He'd be able to send him back for supplies.

Still . . . not having a weapon is a problem, but as for the other things, he'll be able to manage. Better to be cold than dead.

Or is he deluding himself? Go back, flee – perhaps it doesn't matter. Because what of those living beyond the thornbush walls? How quickly does a loyal vassal put aside his cringing ways and reach for his spear? How long will old foes wait before coming to exact their vengeance, hoping to take back what the Beetle has snatched away from them?

Go back, or keep on running?

Scratching his head, the confusion worse than a swarm of mosquitoes, he glances down. It's dark, but he needs only his sense of smell to realise he's just stood in some shit.

Human shit.

He realises that because he knows the difference between human, dog and cow shit. In fact, the last has never bothered him, for he loves his cattle and is particularly fond of the smells of the isibaya (another trait he shares with his brother Shaka).

So he knows the difference, and this is human shit.

He hops over to a thick clump of grass, and starts rubbing his foot across the stalks. Hops to another and repeats the process. Casts about for a large stone, so he can scrape his foot against one of its edges. But he can't see one, and now the shit is between his toes. Like mud. Only it's not mud; it's shit. Human shit.

Even if his reaction is a decided overreaction, given what's happened back there in Bulawayo, it wouldn't come as a surprise to those who know him well. Dingane is obsessed with his personal hygiene, so will spend hours bathing in streams, or smoothing his skin with animal fat. His friends remark that he can go out court-ing at any time, because he's always looking his best (although that's an exaggeration, as courting necessitates even longer periods spent preening himself).

He also refuses to relieve himself in front of anyone, and hates it when others don't show him the same consideration – especially if shit is involved. When he was younger, it was one of the few occasions when this strapping young prince could be counted upon to resort to violence.

Shit.

Should he be surprised, though? Why *wouldn't* he step in shit? That's where they want him, after all, the jackals!

And since this *is* the time of the Dog Fucking moon, let him be fucked, as well!

Only, he won't make it easy for them.

So?

So Dingane runs.

★

And he still can't leave it alone. As inappropriate and ill-advised as it might be, right here and now, he can't resist another sip from the pot of resentment he regards as part of his inheritance.

Born sometime in the late 1790s, the son of Senzangakhona's sixth wife Mpikase, Dingane grew up in the royal kraal at EsiKlebeni. The marks of Zulu nobility – the broad shoulders, strong thighs and heavy buttocks – were already evident by the time he was twelve. Two years later, he was as tall as most of the men serving his father. His size and strength meant he could afford to act a little more independently than his siblings; no one was going to challenge him if he became ill-tempered or if he neglected his chores. And as a child he had run from others because he preferred his own company, and he had run from his chores, because they bored him in a way they didn't bore the others – those mindless, mundane tasks seem to sap him and drain him, so that avoiding them became a form of self-defence. As a teenager he regularly ran from angry fathers, but then, when he was in his early twenties, the habitual runner was caught – with a girl from his father's seraglio, which was an offence punishable by death. Fortunately for Dingane, Senzangakhona himself was ill at the time, so it was Mduli he had to face. Muttering something about a son following in his father's footsteps, the elder had merely sent Dingane off to live with the Qwabes.

It was a banishment that, initially at least, also involved a fair amount of running. Mduli had huffily reassured Dingane he wouldn't tell Senzangakhona what had happened, but Dingane, with his low opinion of other people, couldn't be sure Mduli wouldn't break his promise, and therefore felt the need to put as much distance between himself and EsiKlebeni as possible.

Mpande accompanied him, and thus Dingane learnt the benefit of having a baggage carrier some time before Shaka insisted that senior herdboys accompany his troops as their udibis, carrying water and extra weapons and foraging for food.

That would come later, though. First there was more running to do.

Dingane hadn't been living at the Qwabe royal kraal for more than six months when he received word that his father had died, and Sigujana had been installed as king. Ndlela had brought him the news, and had a few other things to tell him. A week after Ndlela departed, the prince embarked on his journey home. As instructed, he maintained a leisurely pace, much to Mpande's relief and the bliss of several maidens at intervening villages, where the two brothers would often stay for several days.

Consequently, he and Mpande were still a few sleeps away from the capital when they learnt that Sigujana was dead and Shaka had claimed the throne.

★

He's put several ridges between him and the madness swirling back there when he finally stops to rest. Mist lies across the veld and his sweat is cold on his shoulders. What *is* happening back there? Not for the first time this night, his lips flicker into a wry grin: he could be dead already and just not know it. The order issued, all that remains is the . . .

. . . he drops to his haunches . . .

. . . execution.

Something is moving nearby. A careful pressing of grass and sand that stop the moment he went into a crouch.

Dingane considers issuing a challenge, then decides against it. Without any form of weapon, he's as vulnerable as a baby.

With a quiet sigh, he rises to his feet. He may not be armed, and feels like a bull about to be slaughtered, but he will not die on his knees.

Spreading his hands, his raises his arms to shoulder height and turns around slowly on the path.

If there is someone out there, let them see that the Needy One is ready.

Let them see I do not care.

He turns slowly, then waits, his back towards Bulawayo.

He breathes in. Slowly scanning the grey mist that surrounds him like a fallen cloud.

When he moves off again, it's simply because he's getting cold and not because he's decided he was imagining things.

*

He can understand why, in the early days, his warnings were ignored, seen merely as expressions of jealousy. There were times, when the kingdom was growing and the herds increasing, that he told himself he had misinterpreted the signs. But then came Nandi's death . . .

It was as if she had been a sangoma even more powerful than Nobela, able to beguile the whole nation, and her death had released them from the spell. Suddenly they could see Shaka for what he was. Even the King's inner circle no longer had any words to explain, justify . . . or hide.

And it was as if Shaka wanted to see everyone else join his mother on the Great Journey. They weren't sacrifices, all those put to death for failing to display sufficient grief; nor was it about reminding the ancestors of her greatness. It was as if all those who still lived were an insult, an affront. *How dare they breathe when she cannot! How dare they eat and drink and fuck while she lies curled up in a hole! If she couldn't live, then neither could they!*

And it was Shaka . . . in the end it was Shaka who did what all of his enemies had tried and failed to do so many times. He massed his legions and invaded the kingdom. Only these invaders were the dark legions of an army of terror. The spies, tale-tellers and gossips, the spiteful and the malicious, the disgruntled and the jealous, suddenly all found favour and a sympathetic ear from a king whose distaste for their kind was well known. They were the horns: sneaking around, creeping up, nudging – guiding the prey back towards the powerful chest. The King's slayers, their ranks suddenly swollen – they were the chest, smashing and destroying.

The Way of the Bull, indeed! This was a blood-red, demon-possessed monster come to grind the Zulu people into the dirt.

And it was all Shaka's doing!

Look at what he did to Mbopa! Just when you thought his actions couldn't get more depraved, or more spiteful, aiee! The royal brothers had trembled, and slept with their spears, thinking Shaka might use this as an opportunity to thin their ranks. But see where Shaka's madness had led him: to the kraal of one of his most loyal servants! Instead of coming for those he had to know he could never trust, he pointed his Slayers in Mbopa's direction!

And then it was over. (And in the process Shaka proved to Dingane that one thing about him hadn't changed – his ability to surprise the Needy One.)

It was as if Shaka had merely been ill with a fever – because that's how sudden his recovery was. Granted, the fever lasted a long time and hurt others more than it hurt the man thrashing about on his sleeping mat, but that doesn't make the analogy any less apt. Especially when you consider how there eventually came that crucial phase, that sweaty night when things got worse, and you knew something had to happen. Death was at last reaching out and the illness would be over by dawn, with the patient left either eating dirt or finally rid of the fever.

74

Things had got worse, with ever more insane laws. There was that nonsense with the Umkhokha, which has already entered the realms of myth. There was what happened with Mbopa . . . But then there came the dawn. Shaka sat up and tottered out of his hut, and it was soon clear that something – the rage, the fever, call it what you will – had left him.

There were still relapses, however, when the King disappeared into his hut for days on end and no one dared disturb him, or dark times when his every utterance condemned some unfortunate to death. But these became less and less frequent, and the insane laws were repealed. And the nation rejoiced.

But Dingane can't help but feel Mnkabayi is right.

He hopes he's wrong, but it seems to him that the terrible fever was merely the birth pains of something infinitely worse.

★

And you're still acting as if there's something you can do to change things. But the leopard is already in the kraal, it no longer matters whether you're right or wrong.

He stops, with his hands on his hips, breathing heavily. His brooding thoughts have carried him far, helping him ignore his aching muscles.

He needs to make for higher ground, to get out of this mist.

Instinct tells him to head over to his right . . . and, a few metres from the path, he's soon moving up a slope.

He increases his pace, taking long steps with his thigh muscles bulging.

Get to high ground and rest, work out where he is when dawn comes . . .

Rocks everywhere.

He just manages to avoid twisting his left ankle. Hunched forward, he begins to pick his way between the stones. The big boulders give you something to rest against; it's the small, loose rocks hidden in the grass that you've got to watch out for.

The incline steepens. Must be getting close to the summit.

He looks up. Straightens.

He's even closer to the summit than he realised – and there's someone standing there.

Dingane's about to speak, urge the other man to get it over with, when the greyness thins, parts . . . and he laughs instead.

This is too good! Oh, there has been a truly cunning mind at work here!

For see who has emerged from the elephant-grey mist to stand there peering down at him!

See who they have sent to kill him!

It is his old friend, the Induna.

PART TWO
The Sprouting Moon

The word *umKhosi* is derived from the noun *inkosi*, meaning chief or king, and the ceremony itself, aptly described by one commentator as 'The King's Mass', was a prolonged celebration of the concept of *ubukhosi* – the spiritual power and presence of the king. Its main purpose was to secure the blessing of the ancestral spirits on the new harvest – and by implication on the wealth and power of the kingdom in the coming year . . . The *umKhosi* was the only time, outside major military expeditions, that the army was regularly brought together in its entirety, and the rituals demonstrate like nothing else the overlap between the army's military and civilian roles, and its function as the mobilised manpower of the nation gathered to pay homage to the king and all he represented.

From *The Anatomy of the Zulu Army*
by Ian Knight

'You missed the mermaid, my dear colleague; but perhaps, if we sit quietly here, we may see another.'

'I did not,' said McAdam, 'I saw the brute out of the quarter-galley scuttle; and it was only a manatee.'

Stephen mused for a while, and then he said, 'A dugong, surely. The dentition of the dugong is quite distinct from that of the manatee: the manatee, as I recall, has no incisors. Furthermore, the whole breadth of Africa separates their respective realms.'

'Manatee or dugong, 'tis all one,' said McAdam. 'As far as my studies are concerned, the brute is of consequence only in that it is the perfect illustration of the strength, the irresistible strength, of suggestion . . .'

From *The Mauritius Command*
by Patrick O'Brian

The two factions glare at each other over the fire Jakot keeps feeding. The flames create the illusion of a barrier, however, which is better than nothing. Just don't think of the dwindling stock of wood alongside you, although the warriors on the opposite side have their own supply and throw in a log every now and again. It's as if they're using the fire to keep Jakot, Fynn and the others pinned down. Yes — while another group sneaks up behind them! Jakot twists his head. As luck would have it (about the only bit of luck they've had, and only a smidgen at that) they're on the edge of a cliff. But he didn't get a chance to judge how scalable the precipice might be, while it was still light. Thanks to Fynn, he had other things on his mind.

Meddling meddlesome Englishman!

There they were, finally returning to Port Natal where Jakot feels safest, when the cries of a wailing girl attracted Fynn's attention.

The sounds had led them to this spot, where there'd been a young man on the ground. He was just a few seasons older than the girl crouching next to him. His face contorted with pain, he was pressing his hand over a wound in his thigh, while the girl begged and pleaded with the big man standing over them. This individual was clutching an iklwa and was accompanied by a sangoma Jakot recognised as Kholisa. Both of them were facing down a group of eight men all armed with spears.

And there was Fynn striding forward, demanding that Jakot discover the cause of the stand-off.

Before the Swimmer could master his fear, though, Kholisa had hobbled over. 'He wants to know what is going on,' he said, motioning towards Fynn. The Englishman had already removed his knapsack and was ministering to the youngster's wound.

'This is so,' said Jakot. 'And I apologise for this rude interruption. It

was not of my doing and' — an ingratiating smile — 'I am glad at least that
you are here.'

'Aiee, but I do not know how long Jembuluka and I can hold their
anger in check.'

Jakot eyed the larger group warily. 'They want to harm this one who
you are trying to protect?'

Kholisa nodded.

What do they say? *asked Fynn, turning his head.*

We are still . . . they are angry at your intrusion, Master. I am
still trying to—

What intrusion? They were about to butcher this young fellow.

It, uh, appears as if he is guilty of some sort of wrongdoing.

Well, find out, man, find out . . .

*The young man, whose name was Vala, was accused of murder, explained
the sangoma.*

Murder, your Excellency, *hissed Jakot.* This is not good.

Indeed it isn't, *said Fynn, examining the bandage he had applied to
Vala's thigh.* But it should heal if he doesn't put too much weight
on it for a while. *To the maiden clutching Vala's arm:* Don't worry,
m'dear, be right as rain before you know it.

Turning to Jakot: Kindly tell this to the lad, too.

What?!

*Ignoring Jakot's tone, Fynn patiently explained that he wanted the Xhosa
to warn the young man to favour that leg a while.*

But, but, your Excellency, *spluttered the interpreter, tilting his head
once, twice, thrice, but not wanting to actually point at the glowering men
and their spears.*

All in good time, old fellow. And one more thing . . .

Yes, Excellency.

Don't call me that!

Now, as Jakot prods the flames, Fynn says: When do you think they'll
be back?

*The young maiden, who was clearly besotted with Vala, had told them
one of Shaka's indunas was in the area. As soon as it was dark, and she'd
fetched them food and beer, she went to go and find him. Before that, Kholisa*

had slipped away in the opposite direction, explaining the kraal of the prince he served was close by.

Jakot shrugs. He doubts either of them will be back before dawn.

Just as I thought. Do you think our hosts will try anything drastic?

Vala, who's managed to fall asleep between them, groans. Resisting the temptation to ram his elbow into the boy's gut, Jakot shrugs again. Vala stands accused of murdering the kraal head, and therefore the dead man's brothers and sons want to see justice administered here and now. A scuffle had ensued earlier, with Vala being wounded in the thigh before Jembuluka and Kholisa had been able to force the others back.

Jembuluka, who's the dead man's brother-in-law, had urged caution. This was not Shaka's way, he had reminded the others. Ntokozo, he said, was a much respected Uselwa Man, and Shaka was bound to take an interest in the matter. Vala had to be brought before him while still capable of standing on his hind legs.

Restless as they might seem, the others are holding themselves in check, for now.

All the same, Jakot won't be sleeping tonight, and he quietly damns Fynn for constantly wanting to look and see and find out — and interfere!

The Umkhokha

Long spring grass blurs the rough edges and disguises the fact that the gentle slope is more moor than veld, an eroded badland of dongas and low ridges, drumlins and catsteps. Grumpy, irascible ground, where hidden holes and burrows lie in wait to trip up those who stray from the path. Bisecting this terrain is a narrow trough with steep sides, a crack in the grassland hiding a shallow, fast-flowing stream. At the crossing, the banks fall away and the stream spreads itself out as it races over a slab of slippery rock, before dropping three metres into a pool. Below the pool, the furrow becomes a ravine, then the stream continues on its way through a tunnel of trees. The pool is thus secluded, and it's difficult to see how one might get down there from the crossing.

Standing on the edge of the cascade, the water swirling about his ankles, the Induna notes how the pool has worn away the rock on its left flank, turning the precipice into an overhang. The rim furthest away from the waterfall is made up of huge boulders pressed together like buttocks. Forced into a detour, the stream leaves the pool in what is, to all intents and purposes, the upper left-hand corner. Trees and bushes cluster on the bank here, dense and tightly packed like dancers at a feast. Standing on the path on the other side of the crossing, one can look down on the tops of the trees.

The Induna raises his eyes and traces the course of the stream, this green rope leading to the sea, which is merely a blue band on the horizon, a shade darker than the sky.

One could find where the ravine peters out and then make one's way back to the pool by walking upstream.

He has decided on a quicker way, however. His shield, waterskin and extra spears hidden already, he peers over the waterfall once more, resting his weight on his right foot. The pool is clear and deep in the centre.

He jumps.

A soaring second of suspension, then he hits the water with his knees bent and his arms spread. Straightening his legs, he powers himself upwards and sideways.

The water reaches his chest and he has to throw his arms apart and lean forward, using the water to help him regain his balance as he loses his footing on the slippery stones. Then he changes his mind, allows himself to fall and, using his hands, his chin trailing two long catfish whiskers in the water, he walks himself to the flattened rock. Shaped like a ramp, it slopes up and away from the pool.

There's the spear he tossed down . . .

Raising himself on to his haunches, he reaches for the iklwa and examines the rust-coloured stain that covers the centre of the rock.

Glancing over his shoulder, the Induna checks the angle. This is where Sebenzi's body was last seen, and it would have been in plain view of anyone standing on top of the waterfall.

The men who found the bodies said they saw Sebenzi lying across the sharp edge of the rock, his backside and thighs rising out of the water. Clearly, after leaping or falling into the pool, he'd managed to drag himself that far before succumbing to his wounds. The men called his name and threw stones, but he remained unmoving. They then turned their attention to the herdboy lying in the grass alongside the path, just before it entered the crossing. He at least was showing some signs of life, and they decided not to waste time climbing down to Sebenzi. Better to carry the herdboy back to the village and see if the inyanga could do anything for him.

As it turned out, the boy was dead by the time they arrived at the umuzi.

'And then you returned to the crossing with more men?' the Induna had asked them.

The warriors shook their heads in unison. 'It was dark by the time we reached the village,' said the shorter of the two.

'And Zulus are afraid to travel at night!'

Again the shaking heads, denying the Induna's sarcasm. 'That is not why, Shadow of Shaka,' said the short one.

'No, Nduna,' said the other, 'and we are not cowards, but we are also unafraid of admitting we'd rather stay in our huts when a man's umkhokha roams the night.'

One by one, the search parties had returned to the village to learn that the missing two had been found, and it was only at dawn the following day that a group of armed men returned to the pool . . .

Moving out of the water, the Induna squats on the rock. This happened some days ago, but it hasn't rained, and in the narrow strip of mud between the pool and the trees he can see numerous paw prints. He can also see where broken branches and flattened plants create a circular opening in the bush. It's as the men surmised: during the night, hyenas has pulled the body away.

The Induna slides into the water again, rolling on to his back. It's a hot day and the water is cool, and for a moment he allows his thoughts to guide him back to his own kraal – and his wife Kani. How he misses her! How he misses home! And the two are inextricably linked. He chose the site of his kraal with a soldier's eye for seclusion and safety, but it was Kani who added the finishing touches. She has made their home, nestling away from the world in the heart of a ravine, a place of true tranquillity. Even with Mgobozi's widows and children living with them, little has changed. In fact, the refuge Kani has created has worked its magic on them, too; with the children, especially, emerging from their sadness over the passing of their father. Now, instead of shattering that tranquillity, their laughter makes it all the sweeter.

Kani, he whispers, tasting her name, her loins. *Kani* . . .

However, he is Isithunzi SikaShaka, the Shadow of Shaka, the King's emissary who is allowed to wear the blue crane feather and who speaks and acts with the Bull Elephant's authority, and there is yet work to be done.

But not here. It's not even worth following those paw prints. After the hyenas had finished with the corpse, scavengers will have moved in to feast on the remains. Even if stripped bare, the bigger bones would have been plucked from the ground by vultures, then dropped on rocks from on high so the birds could get at the marrow.

And the Induna sees Sebenzi's angry face again, for he himself was very like a vulture, trying to get at the marrow of this matter. Called to the umuzi's ibandla tree, he hadn't even been able to observe the niceties that normally preceded the main business at such meetings. While the village headman looked on helplessly, Sebenzi confronted the Induna, who had been summoned there because more than a month had passed in which the headman and his own indunas had been unable to identify the murderer of Sebenzi's father.

Whereas the unumzane had begun his investigation by asking who might have murdered the father, the Induna preferred to wonder *why* he had been killed. Approaching the problem from this direction, it was clear to him that Sebenzi himself was the likely culprit. Who but the heir stood to benefit most from the father's death?

'You say I killed my own father?' Sebenzi had snarled at the meeting that day. 'Hai! Then let Shaka have his cattle, if you think that! I don't care. I would far rather see my father's murderers brought to justice!'

When the Induna asked him who he thought was responsible for his father's death, Sebenzi had muttered something about a dispute between his father and his uncle.

But that dispute, the headman hastened to add, had been over grazing land and had eventually been resolved.

'Is this true?' asked the Induna.

Sebenzi nodded sullenly.

'Then watch your tongue,' warned the headman.

'Yes,' murmured the Induna. 'Baseless accusations in this matter are likely to lead to more bloodshed. Shaka will not like that.'

'Master, this is perplexing, is it not?'

Lying on his back in the water, staring at a cloudless blue sky, the Induna smiles. This is not the first time he's heard his udibi's voice. Now old enough to join a regiment, the boy has already left his service, but his presence remains constant and the Induna has not yet found himself a replacement. He prefers to carry his own waterskin and sleeping mat and food sack these days – not least because travelling alone enables him to converse with the udibi in peace.

And the boy would be right: this *is* perplexing . . .

'It is because you thought Sebenzi had murdered his father, is it not, Master?'

Yes, that thought *had* crossed his mind.

'He was as a bird squawking, but doing so in a direction that takes you away from the nest.'

The Induna grins. This is so – but now Sebenzi too has succumbed.

As has his father's fourth – and some would say favourite – wife. She was found on the path that led to the stream where the village collected its water, her head bashed in with a stone.

And, once more, messengers were sent to seek Shaka's help.

And the Induna paid his second visit to the village in as many moons. Only to be told, upon arriving, that two more people had been killed – Sebenzi and a herdboy.

'Your father has been murdered,' the Induna had told Sebenzi, at the end of his previous visit. 'There is no doubt about that. You cannot now give me the names of any enemies without your sense of loss leading you to slander. Well and good, patience is therefore required.' The unumzane and his advisors would serve as Shaka's eyes and ears. With a little patience, the killer would reveal himself.

Sebenzi seemed satisfied. He assured the Induna that he'd do nothing rash. But what of his father's umkhokha? An umkhokha needs to be appeased, especially in the case of violent death. Failure to do so will put the deceased's closest relatives at risk, because it is upon them falls the onus for laying the umkhokha to rest.

That was a matter for the village sangoma, said the Induna.

'The rituals won't help if my father's murderer walks free,' said Sebenzi. He was right, but the Induna suggested the very fact that the murderer was being sought should be enough to hold the umkhokha in check.

But this one has proven to be an impatient umkhokha!

He will visit Sizwe on the morrow, decides the Induna. Perhaps the uncle had grown tired of hearing his nephew malign him and moved to silence him. Which doesn't necessarily mean Sizwe is responsible for the death of Sebenzi's father as well.

Sizwe kills Sebenzi and the herdboy – who just happens to be in the wrong place at the wrong time – but what about the wife? How does her murder fit into the scheme of things?

Or is it the umkhokha angry, lashing out and killing everyone it feels has wronged it?

A man's umkhokha is not his spirit. It's a force conjured up by violent death – a commingling of violence and death – and one of the things that set men apart from the animals. A cow or buck has no umkhokha. It is because of the umkhokha that a warrior who has killed in battle is considered unclean. In the case of murder or suicide, if the umkhokha is not treated properly – through muthi and cleansing rituals – it will cause other family members to die violently, too.

In this instance, though, the village sangoma has confessed himself at a loss. He's performed the appropriate rituals, but the umkhokha still rampages unchecked. The sangoma is extremely unsettled, for this reflects badly on his capabilities.

The Induna can empathise. His inability to find the one responsible for these murders doesn't say much about his own abilities either!

★

The headman shakes his head in disbelief. 'This . . . This is the same as how we found his father.'

The Induna issues orders for the men standing around to start pulling away the thatch. It is early morning, and the herdboys have just taken the cattle to pasture – but even if the sun was at its zenith it would still be gloomy inside the hut, and the Induna needs to see what he can.

While his orders are being obeyed, he questions the wife who discovered the body. She was surprised to find her husband awake, for he was just sitting there, on a stump he used for a stool. It was only when she touched Sizwe, and found his skin cool beneath her fingertips, that she realised he was dead.

That was earlier this morning. What about visitors during the night?

As far as the wife knows, there were none.

The Induna gazes around. It's a small settlement, comprising some seven huts built around a cattlefold, and about a ten-minute walk from the main umuzi. No fence encloses the dwellings, therefore anyone could move fairly easily among the huts after dark.

He turns to one of the dead man's sons. 'Ngabe izinja zakhonkotha?' *Did the dogs bark?*

'No, Nduna.'

'Was your father expecting any visitors?' Perhaps that's something he would have mentioned to his sons, but not his wives.

'He was expecting you to call on him, Shadow of Shaka.'

As well he might.

'There was something he wanted to tell you.'

'Did he say what?'

'No, Nduna.'

'Can you think what it might have been?'

'No, Master.'

'And your brothers, what say they?'

There are five sons, and each shakes his head when the Induna's gaze falls on him.

'The cattle . . .' It's the wife who speaks.

'What about the cattle?'

'He was concerned about the cattle.'

'In what way?'

She shrugs. 'He seemed annoyed when I took him his supper. Vexed.'

The Induna points his spear at the eldest son. 'Know you anything about this?'

'No, Nduna.'

'Well, he *was* in a bad temper,' confirms one of the other sons.

'With one of you?'

88

'No . . .'

'He was a man who could not untie a knot,' interrupts the wife.

'We *were* to go and count the cattle today,' adds the eldest son.

'Whose? His?'

'No, his brother's.'

'Why?'

'We do not question our father's motives, Nduna.'

'Very well then, go and fulfil this, his last request. Go count the cattle . . .'

After the sons have left and he's had the wife sent away, the Induna turns his attention to the body.

Enough thatch has been removed to enable a close examination. Sebenzi's uncle is still balanced on the tree stump. His back leans against the wall and he is held in place by the iklwa that has been thrust through the wall and then through his body, so that the blade emerges just below his ribcage.

And this is how Sebenzi's father was found?

The headman nods. Sebenzi's father had also been stabbed through the wall of the hut.

'By someone standing outside the hut?'

The headman's nod is accompanied by a frown this time. He clearly regards that as an odd question. Of course by someone standing outside the hut! He watches as the Induna steps over the remains of the wall and moves to investigate where the shaft sticks out. This part of the thatch-work has been left intact, and it curves over the body like the back rest of some ornate throne.

The Induna drops to his haunches, examining the strands of dried grass protruding around the assegai shaft.

'I think not,' he murmurs.

'Nduna?' asks the headman.

'No,' says the Induna, standing.

The unumzane looks from him to the shaft, and back at him again.

'Do you not see it?' asks the Induna.

The headman leans forward, squinting, unsure of what he's supposed to see.

'If we are to believe what we see here,' says the Induna, as the headman peers at the broken strands of grass, peeling outwards and away from the spear shaft, 'then we must say that two men were involved.'

The unumzane straightens. 'How so, Nduna?'

The Induna responds with a question of his own. 'Who is the strongest man here?'

A burly bearded warrior steps forward. He is one of the deceased's sons-in-law. 'Fetch your spear,' says the Induna. After the man has left, the Induna examines the interior of the hut and selects a large pot. He tells one of the other men to place another stump by some portion of the wall that remains intact, and then rests the pot on that stump.

When the big man returns with his spear, the Induna tells him to thrust the blade through the thatch, aiming directly for the pot.

Two things happen. First, the man realises he cannot force the blade through with a single thrust, because the thatch is too thick. Trying again, he starts by embedding the tip in the thatch, then pushing with all his might, but even then the blade sticks and he has to change his grip to push it all the way through. Which is when the second thing happens: the pot topples over and shatters.

'Can't you see?' says the Induna. With even the strongest man here pushing the blade, the force is not enough to break the pot. The blade merely knocked it over.

This is why at least two men had to be involved. If resting against the wall, Sizwe would have felt someone trying to push something through the thatch behind him long before the blade could be driven home. And even if he was semi-comatose or drunk, chances are the emerging blade would have sent him toppling over, leaving at best only a shallow cut. There had to be someone holding him in place while the accomplice pushed the spear through the wall.

But . . . the Induna moves back inside the hut, and pulls the shaft inwards through the thatch . . . *there need not have been two killers at all.*

You have seen? he asks the udibi, in a silent question.

'*Yes, Master.*'

What have you seen?

You have seen that the dried grass around the shaft of the spear that killed Sizwe curls outwards, whereas in the Induna's demonstration just now, when the spear was thrust into and through the thatch, it curved inwards. Also, on Sizwe's side, there are tiny fragments of dried grass lying on the dirt at the foot of the wall *outside* the hut; and if the spear had been pushed inwards, those fragments would have been lying only inside the hut.

You have seen there need not have been two killers, after all.

The spear that killed the uncle was first pushed through the thatch from the *inside* of the hut. This was to make an opening. It was then reversed and the shaft thrust in through the wall again. The uncle was then forced backwards, and thus made to impale himself!

'But he was not a weak man,' protests the headman, 'and no one heard shouts, or any sounds of a struggle.'

'That's because he was probably dead already, or near death. The shock would've been great, for after all he was being attacked by a ghost!'

What the sons have to tell the Induna, when they return, only serves to confirm his suspicions. It's midday and the herders have brought back the cattle. The Induna has them brought to his presence. He asks them one question and, in answer, they offer him three options. He chooses the second because of its close proximity to the place where Sebenzi and the herdboy were murdered.

When the headman hears of the Induna's plans, he says he'll lend the warrior a band of armed men. The Induna declines the offer; instead, if the headman wants to help, he can send a group of men to the other places the herdboys mentioned. He doubts they'll find anything, but it's a way of being certain and of letting the unumzane believe he's played a part in the apprehension of the murderer.

★

Without the herdboys' directions he would never have found the kloof. It's some kilometres from the village, and past the crossing. Seen from the path, there's no break in the bushes that line the slope. It's only up close that one spots a faint trail disappearing into the tangle; and even that one would miss if one wasn't looking, because there's no outward sign that the trail will actually take one *through* the hillside.

The ravine hidden by the bushes is a narrow passage along which it would just be possible to lead cattle. And then one is standing at the apex of the hidden kloof, which runs eastward, parallel to the distant ocean.

And some thirty head of cattle are grazing here.

And a man is moving among them.

The Induna whistles.

The man's head comes up. He regards the Induna over the back of a brown and white cow.

'It's a hot day,' calls the Induna, 'and I am in no mood to chase you.' His voice seems magnified by the surrounding cliffs. 'But know this: even if you run, you *will* be caught.'

The man's hands come away from his sides in a gesture of resignation.

The Induna moves down the shallow declivity. The man will be brought before Shaka, who'll want to hear his incredible tale before handing him over to his impalers. But the Induna has some questions of his own first.

'I know why the uncle had to die,' he says, stopping a few metres away from the man. 'He would have realised the cattle were missing sooner or later, for they became his upon the death of the heir. But why the wife?'

The man shrugs. 'She was the youngest, and I thought she had shown a willingness . . .'

'But she refused to come away with you.'

'Yes.'

'And in revealing your feelings to her, you revealed yourself as her husband's murderer.'

'Yes.'

'Hai, could you not wait? These cattle would have been yours some day, and perhaps by then the herd would have grown.'

'My father was threatening to give the herd away, one beast at a time, to his wives,' says Sebenzi.

'As he was entitled to.'

'Yes, but it wasn't generosity — it was to taunt and spite me!'

'So you killed him.'

'Yes, and I do not regret it!'

'But you knew you would be suspected and so, in order to enjoy your inheritance, you arranged to be killed — after you had hidden the cattle here with the help of the herdboy, who would know of secret places like this where one might hide cattle, and who then also had to be silenced.'

'I lay a long time in that pond waiting for those fools to find me.'

'To find you before the hyenas did. Or rather before they sniffed the offal you had with you.'

Sebenzi nods.

'Aiee, it must have pained you to slaughter a cow! But the animal's meat was to be the herdboy's reward for helping you, not so?'

'Yes.'

'Still, it did not go to waste. You used the offal, then lived off the rest.'

Another nod.

'But why did you stay here so long? After all, it is but a short journey to the land of the Pondoes.'

'I was waiting to see what you would do.'

'That was foolish.'

'I realise that now.'

He lies on his back beneath the night sky. Stunned, can't move, can't feel anything. Right now he is simply an aching head. It's as if the dregs of everything he once was have pooled in his skull, stained blood-red by anger.

Woke up angry, woke up fuming.

Woke up ready to be irritated, annoyed, provoked. To kick the day before it kicked him. A seething, roiling rage, because the time is near and that opens the gate to doubt and fear — a puny herd of two, cow and bull, he should be used to it by now, these feelings; he should be able to control them, but the doubt and the fear have intensified as the seasons have passed and the demands on him have grown.

His gourds are always among those chosen by the King, and the more successful he has become, the more 'wealthy', the more they cling to him like ticks, these creatures who think, because they are of the same blood, they are entitled to 'share' in some of his success.

Yet none have realised the strain he is under. At the last Umasingana, it had taken him four sleeps — four! — before he had discovered the first gourd he thought worthy of the King (and it had taken him another five days to find three more).

Was the knack leaving him?

Every season the same grim question. Every season the doubt and fear growing more intense . . .

Perhaps the boy will bring him luck. A surly one, and distrustful. It would be easy to assume — as has that lout Jembuluka — that he is not grateful for having been taken in. But it's not as simple as that, reckons Ntokozo, staring up at the sky. Vala does show definite signs of resentment, but what Jembuluka doesn't understand, what he's too stupid to see, is that the resentment is justified. It's something to be accepted, not an excuse for

94

*harsher treatment, or more severe punishment, as if the boy doesn't bear
enough scars already.*

*Wouldn't resentment become your shadow, too, were you to see your
king's power destroyed and your people forced to flee their homeland?*

*And, with Ntokozo signalling his understanding of that resentment by
not constantly chastising the boy, a bond has begun to form between them.*

*He still disciplines Vala when his chores are not done properly, but he
doesn't include, along with the punishment, a remonstration and a reminder
of how fortunate the youth should count himself.*

This too he feels is strengthening the tie between them.

*And he values the boy's silence when they take to the road. Such a
change from the wheedling and the backstabbing his sons indulge in, when
one of them acts as his udibi.*

*And taking the boy along with him when the word comes from
Bulawayo – that might help. If only because of his enthusiasm. It's one
of the few times he can recall seeing Vala's face light up – when he
mentioned the possibility of his coming with him to find the gourds for
the King.*

*It's also the only time he can remember the boy asking for something.
He'd be happy to accompany his master, he'd said, and he was sure they'd
find many gourds for the King – but would he then be permitted to accompany Ntokozo to KwaBulawayo to present them to the King?*

Boy, *he had thought before saying he would think about Vala's request,*
if we find such an abundance of gourds as you say we will, I'll not
only take you to Bulawayo, I'll introduce you to Shaka as our clan's
next Uselwa Man!

*But his sons and their mothers would . . . aiee, he doesn't like to think
what their reaction will be. Although neither of his eldest have shown an
interest in his craft, he reckons they'll suddenly be wailing their bereavement
at having been denied the opportunity to follow in their father's footsteps.*

But the knack . . . ?

He's desperate.

And afraid.

*Desperate to regain the knack that made finding the 'right' gourds so
easy in the past. Afraid it's slipping away forever . . .*

And it's not just his family. Too many of the other Uselwa Men are jealous of his reputation, so he won't – and can't – give them the satisfaction of seeing him fail.

Woke up angry, woke up fuming.

Woke up ready to be irritated, annoyed, provoked. To kick the day before it kicked him. And to kick his sons while he was at it!

He usually succeeds in dividing the misery equally between his boys, so that all quail before him, but it stands to reason that the two eldest will inevitably attract a little more ire than the others. Currently it's the oldest son, Vuyile, his wrath stalks.

Lazy, lazy boy! Who takes too much for granted!

Although that's partly his mother's fault. She's fed him grandiose ideas, and now Vuyile acts as if he already wears the leopard skin of the clan head.

Not that the next in line's much better, he decides, recalling the look of triumph on Gudlo's face when he said he was considering making him heir. Don't think I didn't spot that, Boy!

When he's finished with Vuyile, he'll cut Gudlo down to size.

And when he's finished with Gudlo, he'll circle the mountain to fall on Vuyile once more.

And Vuyile's mother.

And Jembuluka, her brother, who is truly well named.

And the others!

Ticks, the lot of them, sucking him dry.

And why can't he move?

Must have twisted as he fell, for he's on his back staring at the stars. At the fragment of moon.

On his back, beneath the sky, still too angry to die. How easy he'd made it for them in the end.

A grin.

Didn't think they had it in them.

They are ungrateful, whining cowards, as bitter as bad beer, as insistent in their demands as mosquitoes, as spiteful as some old women. They are never satisfied, always wanting more. He knows how a cow must feel in times of drought, with all those dry mouths tugging at it . . . But he didn't think any of them had the courage to go this far, to even contemplate going this far . . .

Then again, it doesn't take much courage to poison a man.

And he's sure now that's what has happened: he's been poisoned.

But why?

He and he alone is the source of their wealth, so why kill him?

Who among them is that foolish?

Death Of An Uselwa Man

The Induna has breakfasted and is busy gathering together his belong-
ings, when he's summoned by the village headman. Grass mats have
been spread under the tree outside of the unumzane's hut and two
of his wives are tending to a trembling young girl, trying to feed
her milk and porridge. As soon as she sees the Induna, she tries to
clamber to her feet, and has to be restrained by the women.

The girl's name is Zusi and she has come seeking the Shadow
of Shaka, explains the headman. And, truly, she has a terrible tale to
tell. Ntokozo KaLumula, one of the King's most respected Uselwa
Men, has been murdered!

'But he's innocent,' shrieks the girl, milk now splattered down
her chin and across her bare breasts. 'He is not the one who killed
my father!'

'Her beloved,' explains the headman, in response to the Induna's
quizzical look. 'It seems as if he's been blamed for the murder.'

'And he did nothing, Shadow of Shaka,' says Zusi, trying to pull
away from the wives. 'You have to save him! You have to!'

'She walked here through the night?' asks the Induna.

The headman nods.

The Induna was to have escorted Sebenzi to KwaBulawayo, with
an armed guard supplied by the unumzane, but the latter says he'll
put his eldest son in charge of the party in the Induna's stead. The
boy is ready for the responsibility, and will anyway be with older
warriors who'll keep an eye on both him and the prisoner.

He will also tell one of his other sons to accompany the Induna
back to the Uselwa Man's kraal. 'For this one is tired,' he says, meaning the girl, 'and you may require a guide.'

They leave within the hour. At first the girl keeps pace alongside the warrior, telling him over and over again how Vala could never have committed such a deed. Soon, though, exhaustion causes her to falter, and the Induna lifts her on to his back.

He's glad for a respite from her imprecations, for this is a serious matter, indeed. The King's decision to hold the First Fruits only at KwaBulawayo has caused resentment in some quarters and, given the important role Uselwa Men play in the ceremony, Ntokozo's murder will be seized upon as a sign that Shaka's arrogance has angered the ancestors.

Making matters worse, the King is already uneasy. It is mid-August 1825, the month of The First Fields. Spring is due, but Shaka has yet to hear from Mbilini KaZiwedum, head of the clan responsible for informing the Kingdom when the time is right for the sowing of the seeds. As the days have passed, the King has grown ever more impatient; for the longer the soil remains sullen, the more likely this will be seen as yet another augury of the ancestors' displeasure. And now this . . .

The King will not be happy.

'Nduna,' whispers the girl, startling the Induna out of his reverie. He thought she had finally managed to fall asleep.

'What is it, child?'

'I am afraid.'

It is just past midday. A breeze bringing with it the scent of the sea teases the grass, which is beginning to turn green. Some oribi graze in the distance, providing a speckling of black tails. Treelines – broom-cluster figs, their stems splayed to carry a dense canopy of grey-green leaves; the pigeonwood with its smooth grey bark and its untidy branches and unkempt leaves; the similar-looking, but taller, white pear, its leaves marked by a yellow central vein – show the passage of streams down to the ocean, although many will simply be narrow folds filled with grass and carry water only in times of heavy rainfall.

Sneaking a glance over her shoulder, to make sure the unumzane's son is several paces behind them and out of hearing, Zusi moves her lips closer to the Induna's ear. 'I am afraid, Nduna, because I am to blame.'

'For what?'

Her father had been particularly ill-tempered of late, cruel even . . .

The Induna stops, turns and lets Zusi slide off his back. Fourteen summers old, she is no child, and heavy, and the Induna is glad of the opportunity to rest.

'And you feel this was your fault?' he asks.

A shrug.

Had Ntokozo found out about her and Vala?

No, no one knew. Except . . .

'Except?'

'A sangoma, Nduna.' When she was sure Vala was willing to be her isoka, her beloved, and accept her as his isigxebe, his sweetheart, Zusi went to ask a sangoma in a nearby village for a maguqu potion, something to make her father feel even more benevolent towards Vala, and thus open the way for them to reveal their love.

But that's when her father started acting strangely, says Zusi: after she started feeding him the sangoma's muthi mixed in with his porridge.

She went back to the sangoma, who said some of those fed that kind of muthi reacted in this way, and it was testament to how great a struggle it was going to be to get Ntokozo to accept Vala as his daughter's suitor, no matter how kindly disposed he was to him. The sangoma then gave her a stronger batch of muthi, which she was to continue adding to her father's porridge; and a second potion that she was to put in his evening meal on the next night the moon was isilucezu, or in its first quarter. That had been two nights ago. She had obeyed the sangoma – and that was the very night her father died!

'Know this,' says the Induna. 'You have come to me seeking my help and I will help you, for I serve Shaka, who is our Father and who will answer his children when they call out to him. I will help you, but I cannot promise I'll be able to save Vala.'

Holding up a hand to silence her protestations: 'I promise you I will look and see, but if Vala is the one who killed your father, then he will suffer the consequences – and he certainly wouldn't deserve your loyalty.'

Does she understand?

A hesitation as, lips quivering, she fights back the urge to launch into yet another defence of her beloved. Then a nod.

'Now, know this as well. You are not to blame yourself for your father's death, so banish such thoughts instantly.'

A nod and a smile this time, a brave smile.

'Who was the sangoma you visited?' asks the Induna.

'It was Kholisa,' says Zusi.

The Induna grins. 'Now there is a name I know!'

And they resume their journey, Zusi choosing to walk again because they are close to the homestead.

★

Mhlangana arrives just before midday with an escort of ten men looking suitably regal and important amid a profusion of amashoba and headband feathers, the prince liking to see his guard of honour almost as lavishly dressed as he himself is.

He orders everyone to the homestead's ibandla tree, where he commences to address them. They must cease this madness, he says. This is a matter that must be brought before the King, and Jembuluka is to be commended for realising that.

Listen to the cows lowing! They must be milked. Pointing to the mats Ntokozo used to sit on, he insists they must be burnt.

He calls Melekeleli, Jembuluka's sister and the dead man's main wife, or ingadi. Everyone is angry and shocked, he says, with eyes only for the accused. But, as ingadi, she has a duty to ensure that the day-to-day running of the homestead resumes, and that the anger of the sons is kept in check. And Dwanile, Ntokozo's second wife, she is to help Melekeleli.

As for the men, they are to listen to the wives. Mhlangana singles out Vuyile, the murdered man's eldest son, pointing at him with his isinkemba, a broad-bladed spear with a short haft carried for such purposes. 'Come!' he says. 'Do you believe your justice is stronger than the King's? This may well be the murderer,' he adds pointing to Vala, who stands with Fynn and Jakot, 'but what if he serves others? Would you not, as the son of your father, want to see these other miscreants rooted out?' They must leave justice to the King and instead see to the rituals needed to assuage the umkhokha. They must see to their chores!

'You are like old women,' says Mhlangana. 'And here is another one,' he adds, levelling his isinkemba at Kholisa. 'See how he hobbles!'

The sangoma bows. He had gone to fetch Mhlangana, but couldn't keep up with the pace the prince and his men set this morning.

He bows, and smiles to himself. Let them mock him! (Even Jembuluka, his ally of yesterday, is laughing.) He bears his infirmity with honour, because he was a soldier once and sustained the wound at Gqokli Hill. And also because it's a sign of how powerful the Calling was in him – for this is what the ancestors do to you if you try to ignore them: they visit mishap after mishap upon you, until you relent and seek out a senior sangoma to train you.

*

'Cha! He stamps, he throws out his arms, and he raises his voice – but, once the feathers have dropped to the ground and the dust has settled, what has he accomplished? He is merely trying to hide his own laziness! Not that I'd expect anything less from this one. Although perhaps such laziness here has an ulterior motive! Yes, this is a serious matter, and if he could see me thwarted without lifting a finger, what bliss for him!'

Shaka is standing up on the hill, yet able to hear every word, see every gesture in the scene playing out below him. His face is divided by the black and ochre of Imithi Emnyama, Black Medicine: muthi of the dead moon, isifile, and ngolu mnyama namhla, the dark day thereafter, when human beings are especially vulnerable to evil.

Mhlangana had to have known the import of this event, but any anger now will be wasted. After all, these are events that have happened already – and the Induna was there to ensure the matter was handled properly.

No, the frustration he feels – and which is one thought away from turning into rage – has a more immediate cause. It has to do with the fact that he now finds himself here on this hill . . .

★

Ignored by Mhlangana, Fynn and Jakot stand to one side, with Vala between them, watching the proceedings.

At this stage of his sojourn at Port Natal, Fynn, due to a constant lack of supplies from Cape Town, has adopted what might be termed a 'Robinson Crusoe look'. His trousers are a pair of female bloomers that dangle loosely around his knees, because he's found that they dry more quickly and cut down on the chafing. Over this, covering his groin, is a Zulu kilt comprising the isinene and ibeshu. He also wears a sailor's peacoat, with the sleeves detached; these he keeps with him, and he can re-affix them with leather thongs at night when the temperature drops – or when the sun is especially hot. Although his skin has been gradually turning brown, the terrible sunburn he experienced on first arriving here has taught him to be more careful when venturing outside. His hands and shins are still discoloured for, as he discovered, those rays will seek out the smallest patch of exposed white skin. Even the tops of his feet were seared lobster-red when his boots finally gave out, and he was then forced to resort to wearing sandals made for him by one of the refugees who have sought the White Man's protection at Port Natal. For the same reason, his disintegrating straw hat has been augmented with a piece of buckskin. Worn under the hat, it covers his ears – another early target for the African sun – and the back of his neck.

Along with his knapsack, which includes a complement of medicines, Fynn carries his Brown Bess. But his powder got wet while crossing a river the morning before they arrived here (well, in his journal it will become a river; the truth is it was a stream, a slippery rock, and about fifteen centimetres of water that saw the powder rendered useless).

The weapon's intended for hunting – and to protect them from marauding wild animals. When it comes to the locals, Fynn is happy to rely on Shaka's decree that none of the White Men is to be harmed. Or, rather, he has no doubt this decree will be obeyed, since the discipline evinced by the Zoolas was one of the first things he noticed in his dealings with them.

For his part, Jakot wears sandals, the remnants of a pair of nankeen trousers, and a collarless shirt with the sleeves rolled up. He has introduced certain members of the expedition to the joys of the marijuana smoked by the Zulus and other tribes in this region. As the sole supplier, and the only one who knows how to prepare the plants, he is repaid in certain luxuries, such as the shirt and trousers. Items denied to Fynn and some of the others, who have to make do as best they can, these seem to appear magically out of thin air as soon as Jakot produces his special rhino horn.

In addition, the interpreter carries a pouch, blankets and a Zulu isijula, or long hunting spear.

Given the tension of last night, he's happy to be ignored for a while, and has already whispered to Fynn that it's perhaps better if they both remain silent and let Mhlangana take charge.

He watches as the prince turns to Jembuluka once more. 'Hai! But I know you. I thought you looked familiar and now I remember – you are the Skin Man!'

Beaming, the big man bows. 'You do me a great honour, Brother of our Father!'

The prince slaps his right shoulder with his left hand: these items were prepared by him. Jembuluka nods and respectfully suggests he has recognised the garment. It comprises two pelts sewn together, with space for the prince's head to slip through, and reaching down to just above his chest. The pelts, with their black and white stripes, were taken from the inyengelezi, or African weasel, and are testament to Jembuluka's skill as a Skin Man. The creature itself is hard to catch, and small, meaning there's little margin for error and wastage when skinning it. It also secretes a disgusting odour, just like a skunk, and a lot of ingenuity (not to mention a closely guarded family recipe) is needed to get rid of that smell.

'Highness!' calls one of the prince's men.

Mhlangana looks in the direction the warrior is pointing, and sees the Induna making his way down the side of the hill.

★

Him!

The Induna was one of those present when Shaka questioned Jakot on the day he was first dragged into KwaBulawayo. He and the other one, the old general who died – Mgobozi, that's the one! – and a few others . . . Well, put it this way, Jakot believes it was partly due to their counsel that Shaka treated him not as he had expected to be treated. (And when the most powerful King in the region, whose capital is called The Place Of He Who Kills, mark you, isn't sure what to do with you – that's not a good feeling. Jakot will be forever grateful to his ancestors that he was out of harm's way, with the Englishmen, when Nandi died and Shaka went mad.)

Fynn is almost as unsettled as Jakot is to see the Induna. When Shaka had heard that one of the savages from the sea was on his way inland, seeking to make contact with him, he set about ensuring Fynn would be taken 'the long way round', with numerous delays at kraals en route, so he might gain an idea of just how large the Kingdom was. To help accomplish this, the Induna, with ten other men – including big Njikiza, The Watcher Of The Ford, who prefers a massive club with a head bigger than a medieval morning-star over the puny iklwas the others carry – were assigned to keep an eye on the Englishman.

Fynn wasn't fooled, though. Even if they were there to cater to his every need, they were also his jailers. Later, in his journal, he would say of the induna in charge of this 'bodyguard' that there was 'something so frightfully forbidding in this man's countenance that, in addition to the conviction that one of his duties was to spy and report on my every action, I felt he looked as much like a murderer as it was possible to infer from his countenance'.

Not that it's evident in the published 'diary' that emerged years after most of the original journal was lost, but Fynn has since had occasion to revise his initial opinion of the Induna, but he can't

105

stifle that initial jolt of fear whenever their paths now cross and he's confronted by that 'frightfully forbidding' countenance once more.

★

Leaving the girl with the headman's son, the Induna approaches the prince. 'Brother of our Father, I greet you and I am yours to command.'

'Aiee, Nduna, I am glad it is you!' Since the Induna is particularly adept when it comes to these matters, Mhlangana is happy for the warrior to take over.

He will leave eight of his men in the Induna's charge, lest this mob become unruly again. And, because he understands Shaka will want to hear of the death of an Uselwa Man as soon as possible, he will not be expecting the Induna to report his findings to him in person. A messenger that the Shadow of Shaka trusts will suffice. Instead, the Induna is to go straight to KwaBulawayo, taking as many of his men with him as he sees fit.

The Induna inclines his head, thanks the prince for the faith he has evinced in his abilities and for the loan of the men and says he will gladly do as the prince desires.

Him!

But Kholisa is forced to stop skulking among Mhlangana's entourage and straighten up when the prince calls him forward, saying: 'My personal sangoma happened to be here at the time and he found the body, so he might be of some assistance.'

Noting Kholisa's expression – a valiant attempt at stony formality – Mhlangana grins. But of course! He's forgotten that they have met before. Indeed, agrees the Induna, and under slightly similar circumstances. Although this present matter seems to involve finding a body rather than losing one. All the same, does Kholisa feel a Smelling Out might be necessary? 'Although,' adds the Induna, making a show of looking past the sangoma, and scanning the empty cattle-fold behind the wives, 'I do not see your impi about.'

Kholisa's hands come up. Please! The Induna must understand he learnt his lesson that day. Besides, the King has not given his permission.

106

Yes, yes, the King, interjects Mhlangana; they must consider the King. And his wishes. 'Talk of a Smelling Out is surely premature — is that not so, Nduna?'

The Induna nods.

'Nonetheless,' says Mhlangana, pointing his isinkemba at the sangoma, 'Kholisa will remain behind to assist the Induna in any way he can.'

★

Why this place?

He has only stepped back a few paces tonight, but why has the muthi sent him here? What is he supposed to see?

Is he meant to see that those who said this was a bad omen were right?

And thus forget the fact that the Induna's presence could be interpreted as the ancestors favouring Shaka, helping him right this wrong which had been caused by a human agency and had nothing whatsoever to do with the First Fruits.

And he had other things on his mind at the time, indeed other things to worry about. If he stills his heartbeat and listens, he can hear himself berating that stubborn old-timer at the Nkandla Forest, while Pampata tries to soothe him. The season is here, the time is right, so why won't Mbilini give the word? And Pampata telling him to be patient. This he cannot hurry. He cannot be seen to usurp Mbilini over this, not with what he has planned: a whispered conversation in the background, quietly supplanting the sound of crickets and rustling grass.

It was easy, then, not to brood upon this death, to let his inner circle see that while he allowed it was a tragedy — and the killer or killers had to be found, so that his Slayers could deal with them — he didn't think it was a bad omen.

Turning, turning again, in the hut of his seclusion, turning in the sweaty heat so that he is back where he started, is he now meant to realise the Uselwa Man's death was indeed a bad omen? A harbinger of failure?

Because see here, see how he struggles, night after night, reaching for his objective only to be sent somewhere else . . .

No! It will work! It must! He will know their secrets!

He forces himself to return to the hillside, and watches as Mhlangana and the remainder of his men take their leave.

Mhlangana?

Has the Imithi Emnyama brought him here to show him Mhlangana – to show him, in effect, an omen of a different sort?

'Mhlangana,' he whispers, 'my brother . . .'

'Hai, but you more than anyone else should know how troublesome brothers can be to a king! Especially the ones you're likely to forget about!'

'Ngwadi!' The King turns. 'Why am I not surprised?'

'Because I am dead?'

There is that, too, allows Shaka, but he was thinking more of the matter of Sigujana.

'Another brother,' smiles Ngwadi.

'I was not responsible for what happened. Blame the jackal who was my father.'

'Yes, fathers can be as bad as brothers.'

'Forgetful, malicious, or both.'

'And getting worse as they grow older,' says Ngwadi, who is Shaka's half-brother – which is to say Nandi's son, but not Senzangakhona's, and the product of a later liaison. The result of Nandi using her wiles with a grumpy chief so that she and Shaka might be sheltered just a while longer.

'Heirs, too,' says Shaka. 'And this is why I have not bothered with wives and sons.'

Ngwadi nods. The King's views on marriage are well known.

'A man strives his whole life, so that his sons can bicker and fall out over his hard work, trample his memory in their haste to divide his property. And his loving wives are little better!'

'You have just your sisters,' says Ngwadi, for this is how Shaka's concubines are referred to. They are his 'sisters'.

The King grins.

'But what happens to all of your hard work, Brother? A man has heirs, despite the trouble they might cause him one day, because he would see his hard work continued, and his wealth grow. What of your achievements, Brother? Who will—'

'I have something in mind, never you fear.' Although he has spurned the thought of marriage and sons – why raise your own murderer? – it did bother Shaka that his conquests might become merely old ashes blown away by an irritable wind. Look what remained of Dingiswayo's empire. And of Zwide's.

Then the White Men came . . .

★

After the prince leaves, the Induna asks Kholisa to lead him to where they'd found the body.

The path that Ntokozo took on the night he was killed slips through a side entrance to the compound, ducks under some bushes, and opens out on the crest of a shallow slope with a view of the sea.

It was here that Kholisa and Jembuluka had come upon the Uselwa Man's body. Melekeleli had sent them out to look for her husband. 'He was irritable that night, and Jembu said we would find him here seeking solitude,' explains Kholisa.

'What had annoyed him?' asks the Induna.

'Aiee! That one, he didn't need anyone around to feel troubled and put upon! He would chastise a path for being too steep, that one!' But, adds the sangoma, Ntokozo had also been feeling unwell.

But it wasn't an illness that saw the Uselwa Man eating dirt, observes the Induna.

No, it wasn't, says Kholisa. Ntokozo was found lying face down and, as he knelt to examine him, he noted a wetness about the man's head which he suspected was blood. This was confirmed after they had carried the Uselwa Man back to his compound. It was also clear he had been hit over the head, probably with an iwisa – a stout stick with a knob at the end. 'As you know, Nduna, I was a soldier before I accepted the Calling, and I have seen such wounds before,' says Kholisa.

Jembuluka confirms the sangoma's version of events. He was the one to set up the hue and cry after they had carried Ntokozo back to the compound, and Kholisa showed him how the Uselwa Man had been bludgeoned. Although the fragment of moon offered them some light to see by, he knew there was a good chance of missing any spoor left behind by the killer – but something had to be done while the women wailed.

He divided the menfolk up and sent some to follow the paths that radiated out from the homestead. The younger sons, meanwhile, he set to searching the huts.

'Why did you do this?' asks the Induna.

Jembuluka shrugs. There was always the chance the killer had gone to ground somewhere within the homestead, while fully expecting the menfolk to go charging about the open veld.

'What made you suspect Vala?' asks the Induna.

Nothing, says Jembuluka – until Gudlo, Ntokozo's second oldest son, found the iwisa in the boy's hut.

Twice he'd asked Gudlo if he'd personally checked all the huts in the sector assigned to him and to a few of his younger brothers, and twice Gudlo reassured him that he had. 'What about Vala's hut?' Jembuluka had demanded, the second time he confronted the boy. 'Yes, of course,' was the response, which showed what a liar the boy was. 'Well, check it again,' Jembuluka had snapped. Not that he tells the Induna any of this – and he doubts anyone else will remember him singling out the little savage. It was then close to dawn, and everyone was tired and still in shock.

'Where was Vala?' asks the Induna.

Helping with the search, says Jembuluka. They thought he'd fled, but he'd been with the group checking the vegetable gardens.

After dismissing the big man, the Induna asks Kholisa to show him Vala's hut.

It is a sad thing about the general, says Kholisa, as they make their way across the hard-packed dirt. But, then, doubtless that's how he would have wanted to go – in the thick of things, commanding his troops, leading by example.

110

'I always respected him, despite the nature of our last encounter,' says Kholisa, with a rueful grin. 'Aiee, he tormented me, but doubtless I deserved it!'

Certainly, as the Induna can now see, he has learnt his lesson. Mgobozi's words weren't wasted. No longer does Kholisa seek to don the mantle once worn by The Lion or Nobela, and then gather together his own retinue of sycophants.

'I saw I was on the wrong path before it was too late, and I have Mgobozi to thank for that. And perhaps I am mistaken, perhaps I am speaking out of turn, but I believe that beneath *his* bluster there was ... Well, I think I confused him. I think there was even, perhaps, a little surprise, a drop of respect.' Another pause, then: 'Because, after all, I had been in the ranks, and I think that fact must have confused him, because he couldn't call me a coward, or a shirker; because I was there at Gqokli Hill!'

Then, slapping his right thigh: 'That's where I got this affliction. But I was there, and I killed my share of Ndwandwes! And I think knowing that must have confused the general somewhat. Which is not to say he let me off lightly that day! Aiee!'

'Is this it?'

Distracted from his monologue, Kholisa nods.

It's a dilapidated old storage hut, and the Induna doubts there's room for Vala to stretch out fully in it. It would be hard to hide one's breath in this cramped straw hole, never mind an iwisa.

'This boy ...' says the Induna, pausing and dusting off his hands. 'He is an isilwane, not Zulu?'

'That is so,' says Kholisa.

'And you?'

'Me?' says Kholisa, startled. 'I am not—'

'I meant how came you to be here?'

'Ah!' The sangoma gnaws his lower lip for a heartbeat, then says: 'Would I be right in assuming Zusi, the girl, has told you that she came to me seeking help?'

The Induna nods, his eyes fixed on the hut before him.

Noticing this, Kholisa hastens to add that if he'd had any idea of how the boy was treated, he would have told Zusi – gently but firmly – that she was wasting her affections. Some captives become accepted into a clan after a period of servitude, but that would never happen here.

The sangoma's hands come up to indicate the hut. 'But I didn't know, and she never told me,' he says.

'But how came you to be here?'

'Well, if she told you she had come to me for help, she would also have told you that the muthi I gave her to give to her father, so that he might grow more amenable to a savage courting his daughter, only made him more bad-tempered. She came back to me, but Ntokozo got even worse, and I had to see for myself what was going on.'

Indicating the ragged hut once more: 'And I soon saw why my muthi wasn't working – was having the opposite effect, in fact. This love match could never be. And clearly the ancestors were trying to warn us that the savage could never be trusted.'

Did Ntokozo know why he was there?

'Of course, not, Nduna! And I was made to feel most unwelcome.' Jembuluka and Melekeleli were a little more hospitable, though.

'Did *they* know why you had come?'

Kholisa shakes his head. 'They too thought something was seriously wrong with Ntokozo, and believed my coming was testament to divinatory powers I have never claimed to possess.' He let them think that, because it was definitely not the time to reveal to the Uselwa Man the relationship that had sprung up between his daughter and the isilwane Vala . . .

The sangoma shrugs. As things turned out, it was just as well he had been there. There was, after all, the matter of the burial. He had overseen that, performed the ritual the circumstances required. Does the Induna wish to see . . . ?

The warrior shakes his head. Instead they return to the ibandla tree, where the Induna strides over to Vala, grips his chin between the fingers of his left hand and twists the youth's head this way and that, all the while watching Vala's eyes.

When he's done, he orders two of Mhlangana's men to take Vala to his hut so that he might collect his sleeping mat. They are then to return here. It is late in the afternoon, so they will be forced to spend the night in this accursed place. Mbuyazi – Fynn – on the other hand, can go about his business.

'You say your master has been out seeking cattle for his umuzi,' says the Induna, addressing Jakot.

'He is not my master, but this is so,' says the interpreter.

Very well: the Induna knows of a village where the White Man can find cattle. This is the son of that village's unumzane, he says, indicating the youngster who served as his udibi on the way here. He will guide them. If they leave now and hurry, they should reach the umuzi by nightfall.

Having dismissed Fynn and Jakot, the Induna turns to watch Vala and his escort moving along the path.

He has looked into the boy's eyes, and Vala is clearly not a simpleton. Why therefore would he kill someone, then hide the weapon he used in a hut so small and bare?

★

'I have something in mind,' says Shaka again.

'Although dead, I, of course, cannot tell you what will be the outcome of any plan you might have.'

Shaka lays a hand on Ngwadi's shoulder. 'I know this.'

'And reawakening this other aspect of the First Fruits . . .' Ngwadi shrugs. 'Well, who knows what the consequences might be.'

'The same thing could be said before any of the campaigns I've embarked upon,' murmurs Shaka, his eyes on Fynn now. So close. Out there, right now. Not down there, but beyond the walls of the hut of his seclusion. And yet I am here. This Night Muthi can be unpredictable, but he will subvert it to his will!

'This is true,' says Ngwadi, and chuckles. 'Even with Dingiswayo's help, your campaign to take the Zulu throne was, shall we say, fraught . . .'

In the brief moment it takes for Shaka to consider his brother's words . . . it's night and the drums are beating, and they are somewhere else.

He knows this place. It's vaguely familiar.

Turning to Ngwadi, he sees, in the special light created by the Imithi Emnyama whose mask he wears, that his brother is smiling.

Ngwadi's hands come away from his sides, his gaze pointing Shaka's to the firelight in the clearing in the centre of the huts a few metres away, where the sounds of raucous, drunken laughter can be heard even over the drums.

'See where we are?'

'I was only here to witness its destruction,' murmurs Shaka.

Then, conscious of Ngwadi moving away, receding, he raises his voice: 'One more thing, Brother.'

Ngwadi doesn't so much pause as seem to hover. 'What is it?' he asks, his voice already distant.

'I didn't kill you, did I?'

A chuckle. 'No, it was the trembling sickness that got me.'

'Yes, I remember now. But you were happy . . . I mean, I rewarded you amply for your services this night?'

'Of course! Now go – see!'

Nodding to himself, Shaka turns and makes his way to the firelight.

He stands on the fringes, watching the strutting, swaggering, beer-swilling young men.

Now which one is your king? he wonders.

*

In his diary, Fynn says the 'frightfully, forbidding' induna's name is 'Msika'.

He is wrong.

114

'Why did you let the prince come? Is he the one?'

'He came because he had to. Because to do otherwise would have aroused suspicion.'

'But even one more means one more to betray us!'

'Keep your voice down! He'll hear us!'

'Cha! He sleeps up there, with the others.'

'And you know he is there? You know he isn't wandering around somewhere? Do not worry about others – let us be sure we do not betray ourselves!'

'Well and good, but we are talking about someone who, when the wind changes direction, might decide he fears Shaka more.'

'And I say that will not happen. Besides, he had to come here to ensure order was restored – you know that.'

'The Induna—'

'Hai, we weren't to know he would be nearby.'

'Do you think he suspects something?'

'I do not know. It's hard to tell. And, even if he does, who is to blame?'

'Seek you to chastise me now?'

'Well, you told me you would throw the stick away.'

'It is better this way.'

'Think you that?'

'Yes.'

'I do not see that. I see only that you have added ingredients to the beer that might give the Induna pause for thought.'

'It is better this way.'

'So you say.'

'How is he?'

'Who? Our friend?'

'Who else, Brother?'

'I had to feed him some more muthi.'

'Some more?'

'Yes.'

'But you said he can't have too much . . .'

'I know when too much is too much, Brother. Besides we must wait until the Induna departs. And tomorrow night will be too late. It'll have to be during the coming day.'

'I will help you.'

'You know that cannot be. Do not keep pestering me.'

'Yet you pester me, because you did not answer my question.'

'Which question?'

'Is the prince the one we serve?'

'Cha! He merely obeys this other calling we have all received.'

The Moth & The Soil

The Earth turns, freeing the sun, and the khehla feels a warm caress on the side of his face. Rays slant through the bush, turning dew into diamonds. There is a blur of orange above charcoal mountains. It's still cool in the mornings, but . . . The old-timer pauses, tilts his head. Fingers splayed, palm outward, he wipes the air. The older you get the more you seem to feel the cold, yet . . . If your sleeping mat and your coverlets and even your skin feel thinner than they were, and seem to grow thinner with each passing year – well, doesn't that mean you're also likely to notice a change sooner than others do? And while the air is indeed cool this morning, it lacks the bone-scouring chill it had only yesterday.

He inhales deeply . . .

Yes, yes, it even smells differently this morning. When winter reigns the air is as sharp as Zulu steel, but now it's heavier – the old man grins – and *riper* . . .

Then he sees it, fluttering low: a white moth.

His heart beating faster, he casts around, about to call for his stick. But here's his son, handing him his trusty iwisa, and opening his right hand.

Resting on his palm is another of the white moths.

The old man peers at it. It's not just any moth – see those double wings, that plump body – it's the moth that emerges from the tamboti seed.

The khehla feels a surge of paternal pride. His boy, who will one day inherit this sacred task, has done well to spot and capture this little messenger.

Behind the boy hovers a handful of his younger brothers. Beyond them, keeping a more respectful distance, notes the old man, the

117

villagers have also begun to gather. Which is as it should be. He is merely the headman, and the whole clan shares the burden and the honour of this commission.

Conscious of those eager, expectant faces, Mbilini KaZiwedum, unumzane of the EmaCubeni clan, solemnly lays his free hand on his son's right shoulder and the two set off at a stately pace. A command from the son ensures that his brothers – and therefore the other villagers – will keep their distance as the two of them move between the domed huts, around the cattlefold, and out through the main gate.

Like most Zulu villages, the umuzi has been built on a slope, for better drainage. To the east extends a plain of grassland. The soft pressure of fingers curling around his collarbone, and Mbilini's son stops so the old man might gaze upon this vista. The grass has sloughed off its winter-brown colouring, and the marula and acacia trees have begun to don their leaves, like amasoka, courting men slowly and carefully – and with almost feminine finesse – adorning themselves in their finery.

Mbilini nods and they move on, taking a path that peels off from the main track, and leads west.

A tangle of greenery, wider, vaster and denser than the plain that lies to the east; a tempestuous sea to the plain's tranquil lake. The slope steepens rapidly, and soon it's as if they're beneath the surface, or are about to be swallowed by an arboreal tidal wave.

The mighty Nkandla, the forest where Shaka's impis ambushed the Ndwandwe invaders, and one of the nation's special places. A fastness at the core of it, offering strength and sanctuary. Muthi ingredients are especially powerful when gathered from here and this was where Shaka sent Nandi, Pampata and the other women and children, when Zwide dispatched his son Nomahlanjana and his army to die at Gqokli Hill (for that was by no means a certainty at the time, and if his plan failed Shaka was willing to fight a holding action and sacrifice himself to give his people a chance to escape north). But it's more than that. There's awe, a sense of wonder. Children are taught to respect the forest, for, as ominous as it might seem, the forest will reward such respect by offering one shelter and sharing its secrets.

Could it be it's precisely because the towering yellowwoods and cabbage-trees invariably block out the sky that the Sky People are so fascinated by this and other forests in their kingdom? Whatever the case, it's to this particular forest, the mighty Nkandla, that the People Of The Sky turn when the tamboti moth emerges, the grass changes, the leaves return to the trees, and various other signs are observed. And Mbilini KaZiwedum is their representative in this matter, as was his father and his father's father, and all of the other headmen of the EmaCubeni clan for as long as anyone can remember.

There are fields here on the edge of the forest, well tended and kept free of the veld, but currently lying fallow. Mbilini moves past his son and makes his way across the centre allotment. This is his ground, and by far the largest in the patchwork. Crops are also grown elsewhere, but every family in the clan has a plot here. Although the sun has yet to crest the hill, and the grass is still silver with dew, the shift in temperature that Mbilini spotted earlier is noticeable. In fact, there are even pockets of warmth amid the wintry chill.

With help from his son and the stick, being lowered by the former while pushing down on the latter, Mbilini manages to drop on to his knees. Leaning forward, he plunges his left hand into the ground. It goes in at almost the same angle as a spade might, and his fingers are pressed together to catch hold of clods of damp soil. He crushes the first clods in his fist, then, thrusting his hand deeper, he scoops up another handful.

Noticing that his son is watching him, he nods. Squatting a few paces in front of his father, but facing the old man, the son copies Mbilini's actions.

The soil is a deep, dark brown. This handful isn't as damp as the first one, but the earth is still sticky, with the consistency of maize meal porridge, albeit the drier kind that is eaten with one's fingers.

Mbilini glances at his son. 'Can you feel it?'

He nods.

But Mbilini's not about to let his son off so easily. 'What can you feel?'

119

It's damp, but not too damp. Not like dusty itshetshe soil, which is useless for farming: nor is it like swamp-like iboye soil, which will see the crops rot.

Mbilini's impatient nod says that's obvious.

It clings, but is also loose, adds his son.

'Yes?' urges the khehla.

'The belly will swell.'

Good, he's got it. This soil is ugade, tight enough to hold, loose enough to allow for expansion. The belly of this earth will indeed swell to accommodate a growing plant. There's more, of course: the texture tells Mbilini there's sustenance in the loam, felt as tiny fragments – roots, twigs, ant-size pieces of leaf – that are not of the soil but have been taken in by it. But such subtleties can wait, for his son is doing well so far.

Raising his palm to his mouth, the old man touches the soil with the tip of his tongue. Just as there are those who can take a sip of beer and tell you what's gone wrong in the brewing, what process has been rushed, what ingredient was overused, so Mbilini can taste whether the soil is ready or whether they must still wait a while. He's not the only one who can do this, of course. Any farmer who doesn't want to see his family starve needs to learn the taste of soil, but none can do it as well as the headman of the EmaCubeni clan.

And the taste isn't quite right, but Mbilini wasn't expecting any different. There's a lack that the change in temperature will rectify in due course. By the time the messengers have spread the word, the soil will be ready.

When his son has helped him to stand, Mbilini shows him how deeply his stick has sunk into the earth. That the iwisa went in so far, and no further, is another good sign.

Knowing from experience never to take his father's verdict for granted, the youth waits.

Mbilini regards his son's quizzical expression for a moment, then he nods slowly.

'Sekunjalo!' he says. *It is time.*

He rises unthinkingly, lifted by the motion of the men on either side of him. The Bull – which is his Bull – is coming awake, called forth by the swallow-tail axes of the generals, and by the bellowing of the indunas. They are his generals, his indunas. But he is here, in the ranks, the Night Muthi mask as invisible as his identity is to those around him . . .

His comrades, he thinks with a grin, and wonders, if he were to turn and look back, whether he would see himself on the summit of the nearest high ground . . .

But there's no time and it's only a passing thought, for it's good to be here, spear and shield in hand, weapons so much simpler than the arsenal a king must master, and he doesn't want to find himself back in the hut. Not yet, anyway.

And they are on the move, he and his comrades. And he is remembering those days of himself and Mgobozi and the others marching shoulder to shoulder, of sitting on their shields and waiting, while sharing snuff and familiar stories. Then the orders . . .

Of course, that was when Dingiswayo stood on the hill, and the Way of the Bull was still an idea he would sketch in the sand and try to explain to Mgobozi.

The Way of the Bull: the horns to outflank and encircle, with discipline and well-trained officers enabling each to operate out of sight of the main body, for extended periods if need be; the chest to slam into the enemy; the loins held in reserve, comprising the men sitting facing Shaka, keeping their backs to the action and waiting for his signal. Total war.

And now, on this battlefield he can't identify . . . how many have there been? And is that why he is here? To be reminded of the path that has no end, so that he can be reassured he is doing the right thing? No time, though. This is no time for such thoughts. For here, in the midst of the First

Fruits, he is on a forgotten battlefield, himself part of the Bull, which is his Bull . . .

And the Bull has risen and is on the move!

They are running now. First the slow lion-lope, with your isihlangu under your arm. Save it, madoda, save it; marshal the hunger that powers your muscles. Then the cheetah-sprint . . .

Comrades together, and bound by the drills. The stamping of the thorns, the long marches, the running. Sweat-slick backs and heaving chests, burning eyes and howling muscles. Bound by hardships shared: the hunger, the cold, the fear.

We drank the King's milk together . . . we came from far and wide, but we were closer than brothers, for we shared the season, were of a similar age . . . And, when it was time, our fathers brought us to the royal kraal and we drank the King's milk, and set about learning the meaning of pain. Of suffering.

But a cleansing pain, madoda! A suffering that hardened your muscles and set you free. To run all day without missing a breath. To rise up the next day and run again. To wield your shield as if it were no heavier than a cloak, and your arm an iklwa. Ngadla! I have eaten!

Running faster and faster.

Running to and running away from. There will be shouts and groans, whimpers and pleas. There will be writhing bodies. There will be the desperate eyes of young men holding in their intestines with one hand, while reaching out for their mothers with the other. They know this, for theirs are the battle-weary eyes that look beyond the fires of the feast to court the darkness. But they also know that running to it is the only way to run from the horror.

When their wounds have healed and they are called to battle again, they can seek solace in the ranks, and once the axe is pointed, they can rise up and flee the horror. Flee it in the way that makes all soldiers brave: by running towards it. By raising your shield, thrusting your spear, meeting the horror head-on and vanquishing it. It will return inside in your head, late at night, when the beer runs out, or again on another battlefield, when you sit on your shield and watch its harbingers gather before you, listen to their taunts . . . But here and now, on this dusty day at

122

least, you've beaten it once more. And if the blood on your shins and chest, your knuckles and shield, is only the blood of its rebirth, you can still rejoice because you are alive.

There and then, here and now, that's the only thing that matters: you are still alive.

Running faster and faster.

Then the clash of shields.

The Bit About The Zombie

The kloof guides a stream towards the sea. The stream is shallow, narrow enough for a man to leap over with little exertion, but the water is fast-flowing, as though desperate to reach the waves before it can be poached by the sun. Kholisa follows that rainfall sound until he comes to where the water has pooled behind a small dune of silt. Beyond lie the waves, their crashing and rolling now seeming to taunt the trapped water. It has spread out sideways, seeking a way around the sand barrier; then has receded, beaten back by the same sun that paints streaks of silver across its surface.

The sun is at its zenith, and the herdboys have brought the cattle home. It is now or never – it might even be too late. But Kholisa doesn't want to countenance such a possibility, for he has made reassurances, and the consequences of failure don't bear thinking about.

He pauses a moment to let the ache in his leg subside and to examine the slopes for any sign that he's been followed. He doesn't think so, and he carefully took a circuitous route before entering the ravine.

Finally he turns his attention back to the stream. The sand where the water has sought a way around the silt seems dry, but the moment one steps on to it, one's foot sinks through to a layer of dampness, making this an ideal spot for . . .

This.

Across one end of the mound of silt there's a strip of buckskin. It is held in place by rocks on either side of the mound – the rocks are kept from sinking too deep into the sand by the skin. The buckskin is about the size of a Zulu war shield, and turns the mound into a T-shape. The rocks notwithstanding, the skin lies loosely enough over the creature's face to allow for a passage of air underneath it.

Kholisa bends forward and presses his fingers against the rounded sides of the first rock. Straightening up, and holding the rock in front of his groin, he takes two steps away from the mound, and lets the rock drop into the damp sand with a *plop!* It sinks slowly.

Seconds . . . minutes . . . hours later, he finds himself staring at the buckskin, focusing on its patterns. There's a brown a shade darker than the sand he's standing in, a grubby white a shade lighter, and streaks of black. Who knows what he will find when he removes the covering.

Do it!

Leaning forward Kholisa grips the nearest edge of the hide and pulls it aside. And straightens.

Except for a certain grey cast to his skin, Ntokozo could be asleep.

Which, in a sense, he is.

Bending again, Kholisa touches the Uselwa Man's forehead with the back of his hand.

Still warm – meaning there's still a chance he can be revived.

Working fast, he collects some bone-white twigs and branches among the wind-bent trees that fringe the beach, then piles them behind a buttress of dunes and gets a fire going. Next, he removes a small pot from his muthi bag. Before he left the homestead, he placed some of the ingredients he'd need in this pot. Taking out a pestle made from a cow bone, and using the pot as the mortar, he begins to grind up the mixture.

Finding some way of administering the muthi to Ntokozo had been a weakness in their plan, until the girl Zusi had come to Kholisa . . .

She came to him before he even cast the bones to seek guidance about any alternatives – a procedure he'd been putting off, as reading the bones isn't one of his specialities. And was this not a sign that the ancestors favour this undertaking, even though it involves sorcery?

After all, they are planning to bring down a sorcerer! An umthakathi capable of great ubuthakathi, great evil, a manipulator of the manifest

125

moon-less darkness that infests humans. And, by guiding Zusi to him, the ancestors showed their approval. That's a thought to cling to, as Kholisa examines the contents of the pot and decides that it will do. For this too is an act of ubuthakathi, and he runs the risk of finding his abilities as a sangoma diminished as a consequence. Especially if he's wrong about the ancestors. But he's not, he assures himself, as he reaches into his muthi bag and removes a sticky substance wrapped in green leaves. He's not wrong.

The pot is a small ukhamba known as the umancitshane, the miser's pot, since it is bad manners to serve a guest food or drink in such a vessel. After unwrapping the leaves and dropping the foul, malodorous mixture he has prepared beforehand into the pot, he immediately adds some sea water from his waterskin. Placing the umancitshane on the edge of the fire, he picks up a stick and manoeuvres a few embers into place around the pot itself. Now it's a matter of stirring and adding sea water to get the consistency right, while the mixture is slowly brought to the boil.

When Ntokozo had started acting even more erratically than normal, Zusi returned to Kholisa. Feigning concern and mystification, he was able to give her the second batch of medicine the process required, promising her he would come and see her father for himself. He gave her a reassuring grin, and, when the time was right, he paid the clan a visit.

A lazy bubble eases to the glutinous surface of the mixture. Using a piece of cowhide, Kholisa pulls the pot away from the fire, but not so far it will be allowed to cool down too much. After dropping a few more sticks on to the embers, he makes his way over to the mound.

He grabs Ntokozo's legs and drags the Uselwa Man towards the fire.

Can he do this?

Never done it before, never even seen the ritual performed before, but yes . . . Yes, he can do it! He can change Ntokozo into an impundulu who will do anything they desire – or rather, anything *he* desires!

Something he's so far neglected to tell the others: whoever creates the impundulu becomes its master.

He edges the pot closer to the embers. Adding a bit more sea water, he starts stirring again, using the bone that had served as his pestle to break up any clotting that has occurred while he was moving the Uselwa Man.

A glance at the body glistening in the sun – hai, but Ntokozo had impressed him in the end. Kholisa had given Melekeleli a last dose of the muthi and told her to administer it to the man's food secretly. Tired of her husband's moods, Melekeleli had been happy to oblige. That final dose would have seen the Uselwa Man's symptoms greatly intensified. His skin would have been on fire, and his head would have felt as if it was being pounded against a boulder. Ntokozo would have felt dizzy, disoriented, angry for no reason, yet also close to tears. And if he had looked down, he would have seen that his feet had become like swollen waterskins about to burst. But, by and large, he had managed to disguise whatever he might have been feeling, as he blundered out of the hut, announcing that he was going for a walk. And any doubts the sangoma had retained that Ntokozo might not make it to the spot where they were to waylay him were then put to rest.

Can he do this? Yes, he can!

And when the body was found, Kholisa was on the spot to take charge, mutter dark hints, and allow only the two most senior wives – Melekeleli and Dwanile – to view the body. And even they had to keep their distance, for there was clearly evil afoot, and the women had to guard against themselves becoming infected. And also who knew what vengeance this poor man's umkhokha would wreak? Until this matter was resolved, the body had to be buried in a secret location. When the evil that had prompted this affliction had been laid to rest, thereby satisfying the dead man's umkhokha, Ntokozo would receive a proper burial. Until then his body was deemed dangerous, obviously the focus of some malicious sorcerer's ubuthakathi.

That's what Kholisa had told the wives. And in a way it was true.

127

Can he do this? (Having never done it himself before, never even seen it done.)

Yes, he can!

*

Although creating an impundulu is an act of evil that most sangomas won't dare contemplate, for fear of losing their powers, there are some deemed strong enough to have the secret passed on to them.

His aunt hadn't been one of those, but she had served in Nobela's entourage for a while and had wanted to unravel this and all the other secrets known to the privileged few, and thus had become a supernaturally alert and skilled eavesdropper. She had fooled even Nobela – the old hag being too obsessed with Shaka to notice the mamba in her own hut – and who knew what else she had overheard, before being sent to look after her nephew (who clearly, too, had the Calling and had already learnt the consequences of ignoring it)?

It was her ministrations that first of all ensured Kholisa's wound didn't cripple him entirely, then she had taken him on as a student. This was a fairly common occurrence, as the Calling was passed down through the generations of the same family. The thing was, Kholisa soon realised his aunt didn't really like him all that much. She was only doing her duty in training him, afraid that to do otherwise would anger the ancestors. The truth was, they were too alike: vain, ambitious, ruthless and suspecting everyone they met, even family members, of secretly harbouring the same malice.

In the end, though, she had been forced to share this one secret with him. On her deathbed her guard had at last slipped, and she had asked him to cut off her head after she had embarked on the Great Journey. She was at his mercy then, and had to tell him why. If she didn't, he had informed her, her last request would not be carried out. In addition, he would make sure everyone he came into contact with knew that she had been buried in one piece. The assumption being that the news would eventually get back to

128

someone capable of doing to her corpse whatever she so much wished to avoid through having her head cut off.

For all this, he had been stunned when he finally coaxed and bullied the secret out of her. Everyone had heard of, and feared, the impundulu; but that someone he knew and detested should know how to create one – aiee!

Can he do this?

Time to find out.

★

From his muthi bag, Kholisa removes the spike he's had made for him by one of the Zulu ironsmiths in Mhlangana's district. Leaning forward slightly, trying not to think, trying to keep his mind averted from the fear of failure, he inserts the spike's point into Ntokozo's left nostril.

Gently but firmly, using the palm of his right hand, he pushes the spike a little way into the nasal cavity. His head now tilted slightly, listening as much as feeling, he removes his palm as soon as the point encounters resistance.

Straightening up, he clenches his fists, splays his fingers, then leans forward again.

Using his thumb this time, allowing the spike to guide him, as his aunt had put it, with the thumb there for gentle pressure, he pushes the point through the fragile resistance of the eggshell-thin ethmoid bone.

Wait for the red snot, his aunt had told him.

And there it comes, oozing out of the left nostril: blood diluted with spinal fluid.

Wait for the red snot, then – his right fist swallows the end of the spike – a short, sharp, stabbing motion. A mere twitch of the fist. Then a circular motion to widen the passage he's opened up.

He removes the spike and places it on Ntokozo's chest, then picks up the reed that served as its sheath. The pot is close enough for him to dip the reed into, merely by leaning to his left. Holding the reed in his left hand, he raises it to his lips – and sucks. As soon as he feels the warmth reach his little finger, he raises his head and immediately clamps his thumb over the top end of the reed. He doesn't know how or why this should lock liquid inside a hollowed-out reed, but just knows that it does.

Carefully, twisting his wrist around while still keeping his thumb in place, he slips the reed into Ntokozo's right nostril and pushes. Pushes it up as far as he dares, then a little further. Then he raises the reed slightly, removes his thumb, places his lips around the opening – and blows hard.

At the third time Kholisá repeats the process, Ntokozo's legs jerk and stiffen. Taken by surprise, Kholisa almost flings himself off the body. Never done this before, never seen it done . . .

. . . and his aunt had pulled his right hand closer, her own hand becoming a talon as it bit each of his fingertips in turn, starting with the little finger and ending at the index finger. It was an indication of how many times he was to repeat this part of the ritual.

Which means he's still got to do it once more.

After hesitating a heartbeat, to see if there's any more movement, Kholisa dips the reed in the pot – then inserts it into Ntokozo's nostril, and blows hard.

His splayed knees pressed against Ntokozo's sides, he's ready for further movement, but the impundulu remains still.

Tossing the reed on to the remains of the fire, Kholisa picks up the spike he placed earlier on Ntokozo's chest. Laying his left hand over Ntokozo's brow, he tilts the Uselwa Man's head so he can get access to the right ear.

This time he uses his thumb and forefinger to guide the metal ever deeper into Ntokozo's skull. As with the nose, he waits until he sees the blood-red liquid, then pushes the spike a little deeper.

Then he straightens up, leaving the spike in place in case he has to push it in a bit further, and waits.

★

And waits, oblivious to the breeze rustling through the trees, the timeless crash of the waves, the sun beating down on his shoulders and neck.

★

And waits.

★

And lets his guard down. He looks up, looks around, suddenly concerned and momentarily distracted by the sense that someone's watching him. Then he's gasping for breath.

The impundulu has its hands around his throat and is trying to throttle him.

Kholisa jerks back in shock . . . and is free.

He rolls off the impundulu and scuffles backwards. He stops only when he sees how the zombie's arms remain raised above its body, and realises how easy it was to escape its grasp.

It was as if the zombie had simply pressed its hands against his throat, its stiff fingers incapable of holding on or squeezing.

Kholisa rubs his neck. The shock was the worst thing, after being taken unawares like that.

Then, fascinated, the sangoma watches as the creature's torso rises up. He watches as it lowers its arms to steady itself, watches as it presses its right palm on to the coals.

There's a smell of burning flesh, but the impundulu seems unconcerned. Moving its body from side to side, it eventually topples over to the left, then bends its legs and begins the process of standing up.

Kholisa clambers to his feet. He needs to treat that burned hand. These creatures are immune to pain, but that also means it would have left its hand resting there until it was burnt off. By tending to the creature's injuries, one can extend its lifespan.

Kholisa casts about for the spear he brought with him. Just as he spots it, the creature takes a step towards him, its arms outstretched.

This shouldn't be happening.

Ignoring the spear, Kholisa backs away, realisation dawning on him . . .

The bitch!

The sangoma shakes his head in disbelief.

The bitch!

The curse ensnares him, and he misjudges the speed at which the zombie moves. Or perhaps, like some men, these creatures merely require time to wake up, whereupon they become stronger and more determined.

Whatever the case, the impundulu is on him before he realises it. As he turns to avoid the creature, his crippled leg gives way, so it's the zombie's fingers around his throat, gripping him tighter than a python this time, that keep him upright.

Gagging, his eyes wide with fear, Kholisa tries to pull those hands away. His fingers dig into the impundulu's arm and tear off strips of flesh, but its grip only becomes tighter.

Then, black spots swimming before his eyes, his tongue like wet sand clogging his throat, Kholisa notices the metal spike still protruding out of the creature's right ear.

There's no other way . . .

He slaps his palm against the head of the spike, ramming the point deep into the zombie's brain. Its fingers straighten, releasing Kholisa; and the impundulu falls backwards, as stiff as an assegai haft.

★

The bitch!

Sprawled now on the hot sand, massaging his neck. *The bitch!* She tricked him. Not realising how happy he was to see the last of her, and how much pleasure cutting her head off would bring him, his aunt obviously thought he might try and turn her into an impundulu, too. Accordingly, she'd given him instructions on how to make one that turned against its master.

A shadow falling over him.

Cringing in pain, Kholisa turns his head. 'You!' he exclaims, shading his eyes. 'You were watching all the time! You know that is

132

forbidden!' He extends his free hand in the direction of the body. 'And see what you have wrought!'

When in doubt, blame someone else.

'Fool!' hisses Kholisa. 'Our master will not be pleased with us.'

A chuckle as the shadow moves across Kholisa's face. 'Maybe, maybe not.'

You see its spoor first. In converging paths and tracks that become a hard-trodden road, a veritable king's highway heading towards a grey smudge in the sky. And there are more and more people coming and going: striding, ambling, hobbling. Lines of youngsters weighed down by stacks of skins, bundles of assegai hafts, sacks of iklwa blades, led by fathers and uncles. Or else lines coming away, the adults strutting proudly, the sons and nephews herding cattle alongside the road, as a clan's reward for supplying quality goods. Young maidens, marshalled by their mothers, carry pots or sleeping mats, beadwork, decorative headdresses and coverings, collections of feathers for young men to wear when courting, cloaks made from cow or buffalo skin. Parties of older women, expert brewers, are accompanied by assorted sons and nephews carrying their latest consignment of beer.

Striding with a little more purpose, there are those come to seek justice. Their faces grim, they glare at the horizon as though their eyes can pull their destination – and their moment of reckoning – closer, while deviating from this impossible task only to study those coming from, as if their faces will reveal the prevailing mood over there. An exercise in futility, the old hands could tell them, for the mood over there can change just like that! This is not to imply capriciousness, you understand, but with all these ingrates scurrying in every day – well, is it any wonder the Bull Elephant should grow annoyed from time to time? And if the matter involves another party, you might also want to make sure the two of you don't end up sharing the same space of road at the same time – in case an attempt is made to settle the case out of court, as it were. Better to keep going, dodging these others who're moving so slowly they're all but loitering.

Regiments on the march and the King's messengers can take special paths reserved for them the closer they get. And, although entitled to do so, the man doesn't exercise this option because of the need for secrecy. Alongside *him, acting as his udibis, are two of his younger brothers. It's not a misguided sense of self-importance that's seen him furnish himself with two baggage carriers. He's on an important errand — in fact, right now he's perhaps the most important man in the kingdom beside the King — but he can't attract attention by travelling in a large party. However, his message needs to get through and he himself needs to be the one to deliver it, and he can't do that with fewer than two companions — for two can carry an injured companion with relative speed, if need be.*

They've travelled as fast as possible, slowing down when they encounter other wayfarers, and indulging in the niceties expected when travellers meet on the road, sharing snuff, exchanging news, then moving on again, waiting until they're safely out of sight before increasing their pace so as to make up the lost time.

Now, however, so close to their destination, they allow themselves to be swept along by the rest of the human current, the man occasionally reaching up to finger the round hardness in the muthi pouch rendered nondescript and all but hidden amidst the other adornments around his neck.

An important man with an important message, but he allows his brothers a little time to stop and gape and stare, and turn to the many other travellers doing the same thing, so as to share their awe and feel it multiply, when they finally crest the ridge and see it laid out before them, always bigger than you expected it to be, or remembered . . .

KwaBulawayo!

Cities Of The Zulu Moon

There are three kinds of Zulu settlement. Firstly there is the home-stead established by a man when he marries, and leaves his father's fireplace. Comprising a few huts and a fenced-in cattlefold, it might expand to house three or four families, invariably related.

Next there's the village, or umuzi, a larger settlement of numer-ous families. Each village (and the surrounding homesteads) are in the charge of a headman. Traditionally, he's been called inkosi, or chief; but, since coming to power, Shaka has decreed that this title should be reserved for the King. These days, a village headman is addressed as unumzane, a word that means 'gentleman' and implies nobility, if not necessarily one of noble birth. This is in keeping with Shaka's policy of consolidating his position within the kingdom by replacing amakhosi ohlanga – hereditary chiefs – with his own appointees, who are invariably officers who have proved themselves in battle.

The third, and largest, form of Zulu settlement is the military kraal, or ikhanda. These are where the amabutho are stationed when they're called up for a tour of duty, and where youngsters come to be trained prior to being formed into new regiments. The amakhanda all belong to Shaka, and he divides his time between them. These are the Zulu cities, and awe-inspiring expressions of the King's power, but only those war kraals on the borders of the kingdom are kept permanently garrisoned. The other amakhanda are like the moon, waning and waxing, and only truly come alive when the King himself is in residence.

Shaka will hold court there, deal with matters of state and any problems that might have arisen in the surrounding district. He'll also inspect those portions of his cattle and his harem that are kept there. Then he moves on, and the settlement wanes until it becomes a ghost town of largely empty huts, which is now home mainly to women, children, old men, a caretaker regiment and some youthful conscripts who, as part of their training, see to the vegetable gardens and ensure the huts are kept clean and habitable, building new ones as it becomes necessary.

Of course, the King's always going to have his favourite ikhanda, or Komkhulu, Great Place, where he spends most of his time, thus making it to all intents and purposes the Kingdom's capital. In Shaka's case this is KwaBulawayo, the Place Of He Who Kills. The first Bulawayo had been situated near the White Mfolozi but, after defeating Zwide in 1819, Shaka had it moved south to the region between the Mhlathuze and Thukela rivers.

Built on a slight slope, for better drainage, it's laid out in typical fashion, although of course on a much larger scale. That is to say, perfectly round as the full moon, it consists of a series of concentric circles.

First, there's a stout outer fence of poles lashed together; about four kilometres in circumference, this palisade is patrolled constantly day and night. Stretching along the curve of the left and right hemispheres, from the main gate to the royal enclosure, stand the huts of the regiments. Each regiment has its own specific section, which none but new conscripts tasked with ensuring the huts remain habitable may enter whenever the ibutho is elsewhere. So intense is the rivalry between regiments that each sector is separated from the next by the huts of the civilians who serve the King by cultivating the fields, tending to his cattle and brewing beer.

There are also the homes and workplaces of those artisans who make shields and assemble spears. Regiments receive their shields always from Bulawayo, when they're given their names by Shaka, and must come here to beg for replacements when such are needed. And, although weapons are manufactured throughout the kingdom, an iklwa from Shaka's Komkhulu is highly prized, and often handed out by the King himself as a reward for bravery.

Fenced off and well guarded, the isigodlo, or royal enclosure, fills the upper arc of the city, furthest from the main gate. When Nandi was alive, the largest house located here – and in the isigodlo of every other war kraal – was hers. Since her death, every indlunkhulu has been pulled down.

Shaka's hut is much smaller, and occupies its own compound below the former indlunkhulu.

In the isigodlo are also to be found the huts of the King's councillors and servants, a cooking and eating area as well as storage huts for the King's provisions. Traditionally, this is where the monarch's wives reside, in a section known as the 'black isigodlo', where any trespassing means instant death. Shaka, however, will never marry and, in each of the amakhanda spread across the kingdom, the black isigodlo instead houses members of his harem, who were watched over by Nandi, when she was alive, and are now overseen by Pampata.

Hidden deep within the black isigodlo is the Enkatheni: the hut that houses the sacred Inkatha, watched over by an old woman chosen for her age and wisdom. Constantly added to, enhanced and rejuvenated, this comprises muthi made from substances such as the King's vomit and shit, soil from paths he uses regularly, and other ingredients culled from wild animals so as to co-opt their magical powers, and then smeared over a coil of grass rope which is in turn covered by python skins. Shaka has further strengthened the Inkatha by adding fragments from the izinkatha of vanquished tribes, and flesh from the bodies of chiefs that his impis have slain. Some say the coil has grown so large, and is so wide, that the King can barely straddle it.

In the centre of the ikhanda, as in the centre of all Zulu settlements, is the sacred isibaya, or cattlefold. It is here the cattle are brought at night, and there is a collection of smaller pens for calves, cows about to give birth, and those which belong to the ancestors.

It is also here that the regiments parade, and the supplicants gather.

At the top of the isibaya, near the isigodlo's main entrance, is, of course, the ibandla tree, from which Shaka holds court.

★

This morning, the big central cattlefold is crammed with litigants. Many have travelled far, knowing it's here at KwaBulawayo that the King spends most of his time and because they are unwilling or unable to wait for him to visit a war kraal closer to their home. They sit in the midmorning sun, rapt, like a lake surrounded by reeds which are the soldiers who line the fence that surrounds the cattlefold. But, even so, these waters are ruffled, and there's a constant susurration, as what's been said beneath the ibandla tree is relayed through the crowd.

All these people, rows and rows of them; the middle-aged and the aged, young men accompanying their fathers and keeping an eye out for comely maidens, with their younger brothers acting as udibis and unable to stop gawping. And the smooth talkers who sidle up and down the rows, offering to represent you, speak for you, for they know how such things are done and they can get them done quickly, if the price is right! And the soldiers, Shaka's lions, tall and impassive with their shields and spears, held in awe by the udibis. And the praise singers who regale the crowd with tales of courage and victory, hardship overcome and suffering vanquished, while leaping and cavorting, bellowing their tributes to the sky . . .

And, of course, the Father of the Sky.

There he is! This alone is worth the long journey, especially for the youngsters who can't wait for their call-up and have no truck with adult bickering over grazing land, unpaid lobola, or slights both real and imaginary. For them to see the King, even if only from a distance, that's enough.

And there he is, with plump Mbopa, his prime minister, to his right, and Mdlaka, commander-in-chief of the Zulu army, to his left, standing where Mgobozi once stood. Aiee, a Mthetwa he might have been, but the nation is poorer for the loss of that cantankerous old general.

But there he is himself, Shaka KaSenzangakhona, the Bull Elephant and King of Kings, Sitting Thunder, Defiler and Defier. The sun has yet to drape the shadow of the ibandla tree over Shaka's shoulders, so one of his servants hovers nearby with a shield, should the King require some shade.

And see who has come before him now! In his late twenties, the Induna is only a few years younger than Shaka, but taller, with broader shoulders and a waist that has yet to swell from the many rewards the King has already bestowed on him. For, as one of Shaka's most valued officers, he has little time to enjoy those rewards. Like most of the other men present, he wears a tasselled kilt and goes barefoot. Cow-tail amashoba are affixed above his elbows and below his knees. His only other adornment is his war necklace, comprising beads and stones interspersed with lion's teeth. The teeth are an indication of his rank, and the other items are relics from the battlefields where he has fought.

★

'Eshé, Nduna!'

'Eshé, Nkosi!'

'You are well?'

'I am well, Majesty.'

'This I am glad to hear,' says Shaka, 'for you have been very busy of late!'

The Induna inclines his head. Because of Vala's wound, it has taken them four days to reach Bulawayo, and Shaka has already dispensed with Sebenzi. In addition, as a matter of course, the Induna had sent one of Mhlangana's men on ahead to inform the King of Ntokozo's death, and last night, immediately upon arriving at the capital, the Induna was summoned to the King's presence. He was relieved to see that Shaka had already digested the fact of Ntokozo's murder and its implications, and therefore listened to his more detailed report calmly. Such was not the case when the King first heard of the Uselwa Man's demise, Mbopa later informed the Induna. Shaka had been in a high dudgeon, seeming at one point to hold Ntokozo responsible for his own slaying. The King's anger is understandable, though. The death of an Uselwa Man, coming so soon after his announcement about the First Fruits, is something he can do without.

'That Ntokozo has been murdered will not matter to those looking for signs indicating the King has lost the support of the ancestors,'
explained Mbopa. In addition, the King is now faced with the
possibility that someone might be actively trying to sabotage
the First Fruits. It's precisely because of these considerations that the
King had wanted to hear from his trusted emissary before the public
hearing today.

'Let the accused come forward,' says Shaka.

'Bring him,' says Mbopa, signalling to the two soldiers standing
a few paces behind the Induna. They are Mhlangana's men and are
holding Vala by the elbows. As they take up position alongside the
Induna, Shaka raises his hand. Because of his wound, the prisoner
may remain standing instead of prostrating himself on his stomach
before the Zulu King.

'Do not think I concede this because I favour you,' says Shaka.
'Do not see portents of clemency in my words!'

A quick glance at Mbopa, and the prime minister takes over,
curtly explaining that the King merely wants to be spared the tedious
wait involved in seeing Vala lowered to the ground and then raised.

'Although, Majesty, from what the Nduna has told me, this wound,'
Mbopa indicates the grubby remnants of the bandage Fynn had
wrapped around the boy's thigh, 'is but a paltry scratch.'

'But let us hear from the Nduna himself, Mbopa!'

'Of course, Majesty!'

'Nduna, what say you? Does this man deserve the privilege of
being in my presence today?'

'Majesty, I do not believe so!'

'Believe, Nduna?' interjects Mbopa. 'This is a serious crime, for
the murder of an Uselwa Man cannot be taken lightly.'

'This is so,' says Shaka. The exchange of words is meant for their
audience, and intended to be relayed across the isibaya and beyond.

After a brief, almost imperceptible pause to allow the process to
begin, and knowing, without needing to see, that fingers are tapping
shoulders and heads are turning, the King addresses the Induna. 'And
it was that?' he inquires. 'It was murder?'

141

'It was murder, Father.'

'Which is to say a human being was responsible?'

'This is so, Majesty.'

'No abathakathi? No sorcery?'

'No, Majesty.'

'Really? For that is what I hear, Nduna.'

He turns to his prime minister. 'Is it not amazing, Mbopa, how fleet-footed such tales can be?'

'Amazing, Majesty.'

Shaka turns to his commander-in-chief. 'How quickly they spread, eh, Mdlaka?'

'Faster than the fastest Dhlamini,' confirms the general, referring to the Zulu clan from which the King enlists his messengers, since Dhlamini men are noted for their speed and endurance.

'Yes, you are right, although I am reminded of blood-soaked sand, for the way in which these falsehoods seep and spread. They rapidly darken visages and thoughts, and then blot out the truth.'

'Hai, but your children are wise, Father,' says Mbopa. 'They know to trust your word!'

'And I have learnt to trust the Induna's word in these matters,' says Shaka.

Which is why he is happy with the word 'believe', he tells Mbopa. This *is* a serious matter, yes, a matter of *murder* and, yes, one of his Uselwa Men is the victim, but roll these things up and you have a compelling reason for caution and circumspection.

'It is because I regard this as a serious matter that I expect nothing less than certainty before I mete out a punishment that matches the distress this loss has caused me,' says the King.

But, says Mdlaka, what of the iwisa found in Vala's hut? Was not Ntokozi killed with just such a weapon? And wasn't the heavy, rounded head of this particular iwisa sticky with blood?

All good questions, allows Shaka, but what does the Induna have to say?

He was shown the iwisa, confirms the Induna, and the head did seem to be stained with blood. But the weapon did not belong to

Vala. He might be given a spear if they went hunting, but it would be taken away from him afterwards, for he wasn't allowed to keep anything resembling a weapon in his possession.

'But this does not exonerate him, Nduna,' says the general, almost indignantly. 'He could have stolen it, once he had decided to kill his benefactor.'

'You are right, General! But I say this, what *does* count in his favour is the fact that he is not so stupid as to hide that weapon in his own hut, after committing the murder.' Briefly, the Induna describes how small and dilapidated the hut was; how it was a storage hut, and Vala wouldn't have been able to stand upright or stretch out fully when he lay down.

'Is this so?' asks Shaka, addressing the prisoner. 'Are you cleverer than that?'

Vala remains mute, his head bowed.

'Perhaps he meant to dispose of it later, but didn't get the chance,' suggests Mdlaka.

But he could have thrown it into the bushes near to where he killed Ntokozo, counters the Induna. Why risk returning to his hut with a bloodied weapon?

'This hut?' says Shaka, ignoring the exchange between the Induna and the general. He turns to Mdlaka: 'You called Ntokozo the boy's benefactor, but consider a hut like that, where one can't even stretch out after the hard day's work doubtless expected of this fellow, and that says to me there was a very good reason to kill!' And then there are the scars that cover the boy's back. Perhaps in his rage, in his desire for vengeance and freedom, the boy wasn't thinking straight. With his master dead at his feet, perhaps his first instinct had been to flee, and he'd forgotten he still held the iwisa in his hand until he was back cowering in his hut . . .

'And what of the girl? Perhaps he was merely removing an obstacle to their being together,' says Mbopa.

Zusi had resorted to muthi, points out the Induna.

'Perhaps she grew impatient. Or else he did!'

On their journey to the homestead Zusi had told him she would

143

have nothing to do with anyone who'd killed her father, says the Induna.

'Aiee, listen carefully to what you are saying, Nduna,' says Mbopa. 'That comment of hers suggests to me the matter might have been discussed.'

'Possibly, but she only mentioned it as a sign of how sure she was of Vala's innocence.'

'Hai, but just because she says he didn't do it doesn't mean . . .'

'You are right, General.'

'It takes more than one sapling to build a hut,' observes Shaka. 'I also agree with you, General, but perhaps this is something else to lay alongside the fact that we are expected to believe this one might be so stupid as to kill his master and then hide the murder weapon in his own hut!'

And the iwisa is the only thing that points directly to Vala's guilt, adds the Induna.

'His sullenness aside, you really don't think this one killed my Uselwa Man, do you, Nduna?'

'He passed my test, Majesty.'

'Ah yes,' grins Shaka, 'tell us again of this test that had even your own bodyguards scratching their heads in dismay.'

*

On the third evening of their journey, they had found a suitable place to camp and made a fire to cook their porridge. The Induna had already briefed the soldiers travelling with them, and after the meal he ordered Vala to bring his sleeping mat and accompany him. He led the prisoner over a ridge and down to a plain of long grass. Here, under an acacia tree, one of Mhlangana's men had prepared the makings of a fire, and left a collection of firewood. Using flints taken from a pouch he wore on his waist, the Induna got the fire going, then stood up.

'This is where you will spend the night, and I will fetch you tomorrow,' he told Vala, who in a rare display of emotion showed

144

himself to be as incredulous as Mhlangana's men had been when the Induna had first outlined this plan.

Unlike them, though, he had not sought to drench the Induna under a cascade of questions. Instead, he simply stood in silence and watched the Induna walk away.

Now, while Shaka looks on, it's Mdlaka and Mbopa who want to know why the Induna had opened the kraal gate and, to all intents and purposes, invited his captive to escape.

It was a test, reiterates the Induna patiently. And Vala was bright enough to realise that fact, just as he was bright enough to understand earlier that flight would be an admission of guilt that would see him hunted down and summarily executed. But he was welcome to try it, and he was being offered a fair chance – let there be no doubt about that. His wound had been troubling him less and less, and he would have been able to put a fair amount of distance between himself and his pursuers, before the Induna came looking for him at sun-up.

Shaka glances first at Mbopa, then at Mdlaka. Does that answer their questions? Both men nod. The merest possibility of getting away would surely have appealed to a guilty man who faced a terrible punishment at the hands of the King's Slayers. 'Isn't that so, Nduna?' asks Shaka.

'It is so,' agrees the Induna.

★

Well, then, says Shaka, what are they going to do with the accused?

'Majesty . . .' ventures Mbopa.

'Speak,' says Shaka.

Given the absence of other suspects, they cannot know for certain that this one *didn't* actually kill Ntokozo. Yet at the same time they have all learnt to trust the Induna's judgement . . .

'Yes, yes,' says Shaka, his impatience sounding real, for all that this is another prearranged exchange, 'but I am still not hearing any suggestions.'

'I say keep him here, Majesty.' Are not new regiments being formed during this First Fruits? Vala looks the right age to join one of the groups of conscripts, therefore put him with them. What does Mdlaka think?

'It would certainly mean we can keep an eye on him, Majesty.'

'Very well, then,' says Shaka, 'you have persuaded me!'

Addressing the accused: 'You!'

'The King speaks!' says Mbopa.

Slowly Vala raises his head. Even though the youngster must have heard their discussion, Shaka tells him what he has decided.

Vala dips his head and surprises them all by saying: 'I thank your Majesty!'

'Aiee! It speaks!' says Mdlaka.

'So it does,' says Shaka. 'We might yet make a Zulu out of you, boy!'

But Vala must remember this, says Shaka: if he applies himself, he will be fairly treated and will have the opportunity to rise through the ranks; but if he tries to flee, he will be hunted down and killed on the spot.

Now let Mdlaka summon one of his own indunas to take the boy to where the conscripts are quartered. Mhlangana's men can also consider themselves dismissed, but they may stay the night and enjoy the capital's hospitality before returning to the prince. As for the Induna . . . Shaka grins. He is to remain here, for the King he serves so loyally has a surprise for him.

In fact, it's nothing of the sort for the Induna and his former udibi, although both will, of course, humour the King. As happenstance would have it, the Induna encountered his former udibi late yesterday afternoon, just a ridge away from the city. The latter had been sent towards the kingdom's eastern border, to bring back three traders who had been robbed and also the man they accused of being involved in the robbery – although he hadn't actually stolen anything from them, or even knew the bandit who had. It was complicated, the boy told the Induna, after they had exchanged effusive greetings. And was this the one responsible for killing Sebenzi and his father? he asked, as Mhlangana's warriors made Vala join the four men who had been travelling with the udibi.

No, chuckled the Induna, that matter was finished with. This . . . this was something else entirely.

'Ah,' said the boy. Returning his attention to Vala, he had the impression the prisoner had been staring at him and had averted his eyes, turned away, only when he realised the udibi was about to look his way. And the boy caught a glimpse of a scar – a flattened ridge, the skin around it pink – just before one of the traders blocked his line of vision.

The men with the boy wanted to know why they were suddenly surrounded by armed guards.

'Think of them as guides who will lead you to the Great Place,' suggested the Induna, his firm gaze enough to reduce their protestations to a series of harrumphs. They were to go on ahead, added the Induna, for he and his young friend had important matters to discuss.

'If that is the . . .' he began, turning back to the boy. 'What is wrong?'

The boy frowned, shook his head. 'It is nothing, Master.'

'Are you sure? I have seen that look many times before. Something is bothering you.'

'It is nothing, Master.'

'Aiee,' said the Induna, as they too began to make their way towards the capital, 'I do not blame you for being somewhat out of step. For, as I was going to say, if that is the way your companions behaved all the way here, I am surprised they are still alive!'

'I am surprised I am still alive! A more garrulous, quarrelsome bunch would be hard to find.'

The Fools

'Look who we have here, Nduna!' He turned to the young warrior: 'Eshé, Little One – although, truly, you are not so little any more.' By the standards of Zulu society, the Induna's former udibi is still regarded as a boy – an insizwa, or hornless ox – because he hasn't taken the isicoco, but he's almost seventeen summers old and a man in every other respect.

'What do you think, Nduna?'

'This is so, Majesty.'

'Aiee,' says the King, 'and is it true they call him Mthunzi, the Shadow, as he is the Shadow of the Shadow?'

'This is so, Majesty,' says the boy.

Hai, but the way he is growing, the shadow's shadow will soon be bigger than the shadow itself, says the King, earning a chuckle that ripples outwards as the jest is repeated.

'But tell me, Mthunzi, does your head not ache? Do your fingers not bleed? For Mbopa here tells me this is a tough knot you bring before me.'

'Truly, that is for you to decide, Majesty, but I think you will find your fingers especially supple this morning!'

'Aiee,' Shaka is addressing the Induna, 'I taste a strange brew here. He speaks and I hear your voice, but also something of a certain general we all mourn.'

The Induna smiles. 'I do not know about my voice, but you are right about the general's, Majesty.'

'You are too modest, Nduna. You have taught this one well.' Shaka extends his right arm. 'But let these old women approach, for I can see they can barely restrain themselves.'

'You may enter the presence of our Father,' calls out Mbopa.

Four men jog forward, and each one tries to outdo the others in being the first to throw himself on to his belly at Shaka's feet.

Shaka sighs, flaps away the dust, then raises his hand to restrain Mbopa who is moving in to kick the nearest head.

'Let those who come seeking my judgement in this matter stand up.'

Slowly, gingerly, knowing they've come close to getting themselves impaled before they've even said a word, the three men to Shaka's right clamber to their feet. They strive to appear contrite – for having dared to allow their dust to touch the King – yet indignant – for this is after all their moment. They have been wronged and are here to see that justice is done.

Mthunzi speaks each one's name but Shaka's already forgotten it before the man in question has finished bobbing his head. It's easier to think of them as Big Buttocks, Broken Nose and Long Legs.

'You have come seeking my judgement, as is your right?'

Each proffers a bowed head. 'Yes, Majesty.'

'What has gone before matters not. What matters is what is decided here and now. This you know, for it is the way of our people. I merely remind you, for I see the outrage in your eyes,' continues Shaka. 'What matters is what is decided here and now, and what is decided here and now is the end of the matter. Do you understand?'

'Yes, Majesty,' says Big Buttocks.

'Yes, Majesty,' says Broken Nose.

'Yes, Majesty,' says Long Legs.

'Good. Mthunzi – the accused!'

The boy nudges the man lying closest to him, with his foot. 'You heard the Bull Elephant. Arise!'

The man obeys, and stands with his head bowed.

'This is he, Majesty. The accused.'

'Very well,' says Shaka, 'tell me what has led to this dispute.'

'Majesty,' says the boy, pointing to the plaintiffs, 'these three were taking hides and ivory to trade with the Maputos, when they met another party led by a man called Vulani. He was with his brother, and they were going the same way.'

150

'These three were together?' asks Mdlaka. 'They did not know Vulani?'

'That is correct, General. These three are friends and, along with their sons, were travelling together, when they met Vulani and his brother, who were strangers to them. However, Vulani said that he had heard Beja the bandit was abroad, so it was suggested they travel together.'

'Aiee – Beja again!' says Shaka. 'How many times must I kill him?'

Mention of the bandit's name causes the men to fall silent for a moment, as the Induna, his udibi, Shaka and Mdlaka, Mbopa and the other councillors all start remembering . . .

Then, seeking to guide their thoughts away from the smell of burning thatch, avert their eyes from the tangled bodies and the babies, especially the babies, Mdlaka speaks up: 'Who suggested they travel together?'

'Mdlaka,' interrupts Mbopa, 'but I do not see the relevance of—'

'No,' says Shaka, 'that is a good question.'

'Indeed it is, Majesty,' says Mthunzi, 'and one I asked, too.'

Shaka grins. 'Let me see, it was one of these three who made that suggestion. Is that so?' he asks the three men.

Hesitant nods and crestfallen expressions.

'Please continue, Shadow of the Shadow . . .'

'Indeed, Majesty.' A day later the party had come to the accused's homestead, where they were made welcome, fed, and offered a hut for the night. The homestead was two sleeps away from the nearest Maputo kraal and, while they were breaking their fast, Vulani said he'd been thinking . . .

These Maputos and their Portugiza brothers were always look-ing for ways to cheat honest Zulus, so why not get their own back for once?

Here's what they should do, suggested Vulani. They'd leave the bulk of their wares with their host, and travel to the Maputo village with a few hides of lesser quality than the others, and there see what they were offered for them. The Maputos were likely to laugh and tell them what they might have received were their hides better, or if they had brought ivory instead. In this way they'd get a more accurate indication of what hides and ivory were really worth. Then they'd return to the homestead, fetch their wares and take them back to the Maputos, and now be in a better position to barter.

'And they thought this would work,' sneers Mbopa.

'Apparently,' says the boy.

But if they went along with his plan, where would they leave the rest of the hides and the tusks they had brought with them? Vulani thought about this for a moment . . .

'Vulani?' interrupts Shaka.

'Vulani, Majesty.'

'Continue.'

Vulani had considered the matter and said perhaps the merchandise could be left with the accused, their host. Assuming he could be trusted, of course.

'And who asked that question?'

'Vulani, Majesty.'

'Ah!'

'These three had stayed with Kolo before. They therefore knew him and they vouched for him.'

'Little did we know!' mutters Big Buttocks.

'Silence!' orders Mbopa.

So he was honest, continues the boy, ignoring the interruption. That was all very well for them to say, remarked Vulani, but *he* didn't know Kolo. No offence, Brothers, but how did he know they weren't working together to rob him?

'However, he had a solution,' says Shaka.

'Yes, Majesty, they'd make a pact. They'd leave the hides and ivory with their host, and Kolo was only to hand them back when all four came to claim them.'

'Aiee, I can see what's coming next,' says Mbopa.

'Yes.' Shaka nods. 'They left and were gone a day, say?'

'Yes, Majesty,' says Mthunzi.

'Then Vulani came racing back, saying the hides and ivory were needed?'

152

'Yes, Majesty.' Vulani had said a party of Portugiza happened to be right there at the Maputo kraal. They'd never have a better opportunity, for the Portugiza would give them more than the Maputos ever would.

'And this fool,' says Shaka pointing to the accused, 'gave him all of the hides and the ivory. What say you, are you a fool?'

A meek nod. 'I *was* a fool, Father,' says Kolo. 'But he was very insistent and I thought . . . Well, he said they stood to profit, and I thought who was I to stand in their way.'

'But these other three knew nothing! Or, rather, all they knew was that Vulani and his brother had vanished when they woke up that same morning. What say you, Nduna?'

'I say you are right, Majesty,' says the Induna. 'And they were lucky to awake at all, for I'm sure Vulani and his brother would have preferred there to be no witnesses to raise the alarm.'

Yet that is something Beja would have done, says Shaka. He had something of the Trickster about him, that one, and this is surely proof that Vulani was trying to imitate the legendary bandit.

'This is so, Majesty, for see the angry confusion he left behind him!' says Mbopa, indicating the three dour plaintiffs and woebegone accused. 'Beja would have found that prospect almost as enticing as the theft itself.'

'Majesty, if I may?'

'Of course, speak!'

'He also couldn't be sure Kolo would hand over the wares,' says Mthunzi. 'In which case three dead traders would have been an even bigger problem for Vulani.' The boy grins. As there was just him and his brother, while the traders were accompanied by assorted sons, he might also have felt a little outnumbered, he adds.

'This is so,' says Shaka. 'All they needed was for one to come awake and give the alarm, if they had tarried to kill. Aiee, Nduna, you have taught him well. And you are right, too, Mdlaka. But never fear, we'll have men set on this one's trail this very afternoon, and it won't be long before I see him lying at my feet.'

But, adds Shaka, they have not yet addressed this trio's grievance.

He fixes his gaze on Big Buttocks. 'You were robbed, it is so. But surely you do not mean to imply that this man' – he indicates the accused – 'who you know, and whose hospitality you seem to have accepted before, is one of Vulani's accomplices?'

'Speak!' says Mbopa.

'N-no,' says Big Buttocks, the admission clearly bitter in his mouth.

'But . . .' begins Long Legs.

Big Buttocks restrains his friend with a nudge. He swallows, then dredges up the courage to continue. 'No, Majesty. At first, when we realised what had happened, we might have made such an accusation. But we have had time to reconsider . . . and we believe he was as taken in by the bandit as we were!'

'Then you are here simply to waste the King's time,' says Mbopa.

'No,' says Long Legs defiantly, 'that is *not* so!' Jabbing a finger at Kolo, he continues. 'He might not have been an accomplice, but that doesn't change the fact that he broke his word.'

'It is so, Majesty!' says Broken Nose. 'We had made a pact—'

Again Long Legs' finger snakes out. 'And *he* broke his word!'

Shaka holds up his hand, waiting for fear to silence the men, then he addresses the Induna. 'What say you, Nduna?'

'I say, from the look on his face, the one they call my shadow has something to say about this, Majesty.'

'You are right, Nduna.' Now that the warrior mentions it, he can see that the boy looks like one eager to get at the amasi sack. 'Speak, Mthunzi,' says the King.

'Majesty,' says the boy, 'I do not believe the accused had anything to do with the theft. But he *did* give his word, Majesty. A pact *was* made!'

'And, being too cowardly to seek out the real thief, these baboons now demand compensation from an honest man,' says Mdlaka.

'Nonetheless, General, he is right,' says Shaka. 'A pact *was* made. Why *shouldn't* they seek compensation from him? Why shouldn't he pay for his stupidity? For did he not hand over the skins and tusks, after they had expressly agreed this should only happen when all *four* were present?'

'But there you have it, Majesty!' exclaims the boy. 'They agreed the wares would only be handed over when all four were present. And a Zulu keeps his word, Majesty, so let the accused keep *his* word. When the four are reunited – *four*, Majesty, not three – when Vulani comes down from the hills and joins these three and all four go to this man – well, then, let him hand over the hides and ivory they left in his safekeeping, or proffer an explanation as to why he no longer has them! Until then, he is under no obligation to give anyone anything.'

This is the last case of the day, and Shaka adjourns to the flat-roofed shelter alongside his eating hut, where he prefers to be served on a hot day such as this. He asks Mdlaka, Mbopa and the Induna to join him, and for a while he can't stop chuckling over the boy's solution to the problem posed by the outwitted traders. As the meal progresses, however, Shaka finds it harder and harder to smile away his disappointment and frustration. He really thought today would be the day, and he grows quieter, grumpiness clouding his visage.

The Induna notices the change, and sees that Mbopa has spotted it, too. He watches as the prime minister glances away, his jaws rhythmically working at a chunk of isinkwa, a form of bread made from crushed mealies. When Shaka isn't looking, Mbopa nudges Mdlaka, who has sought refuge from the King's change in mood by focusing on his porridge. The Induna watches how the two men exchange glances, Mbopa tilting his head slightly, as if urging the general to say something.

Reluctantly, Mdlaka coughs to clear his throat, hesitates a moment, then remarks on how the regiments are looking forward to the First Fruits and their chance to impress the King.

Mbopa seems to sag. Clearly, this is not the right topic to have chosen.

'Father, does something perturb you?' murmurs the prime minister in a heroic attempt to draw Shaka's glare away from the general.

It works. His eyes now shifting to the man he has wronged so abominably, Shaka responds with his own question: 'What say the people?'

Silence follows. The Induna can clearly hear the rhythmic thock-thock-thock made by a servant banging two hoes together to warn everyone that the King is eating, for no one may spit, cough or sneeze during this period.

Mbopa has leant back almost imperceptibly. As well he might, and as they all might, while gritting their teeth and readying themselves for the squall . . .

It's not Shaka's obvious grumpiness, it's not that his tone is ominously

156

quiet, although these signals are bad enough — it's his use of the phrase 'the people'.

When they are considered his children, they are to be indulged, their failings to be looked upon benignly, every chastisement simply the prelude to being given a second chance. When they are his 'people', they are culpable, scheming, ungrateful, wilful, foolish, lazy, spiteful, greedy cowards — among many other things.

What say the people?

'Well,' says Mbopa at last, because someone has to say something. Prevarication will only exacerbate Shaka's mood.

'I would ask if they are happy, but that would be a waste of breath, for they are never so.'

'Father,' says Mdlaka, 'surely you jest! Your children have never been happier.'

'I have no children,' mutters Shaka.

'Hai, Majesty, you are both right,' says the prime minister.

'Of course, I am right!'

'As always, Majesty, but the general here is also right. You asked what the people are saying, and my answer is that most are saying nothing. For they are happy, Majesty.'

'Happy? Them?'

Choosing to ignore the sneer in Shaka's words, Mbopa nods. 'Indubitably so, Majesty. However . . . you would of course know what those who are saying something are, er . . . saying?'

'Nduna,' says Shaka, 'do you hear this? Do you see what I have to put up with? Aiee!'

Shaka dips a finger into his porridge bowl. Licks it clean. Points the same finger at the Induna. 'You, Nduna! You tell me what the people are saying.'

'Father, I . . .'

'Hai! Don't look to that one,' says Shaka indicating Mbopa. 'I'm asking you what you have heard. After all, don't you travel far and wide for me?'

'This is so, Father.'

'Well, then, what have you heard on your travels?'

The Induna swallows, takes a deep breath. 'They say you have gone home, Father.'

A Propitious Omen

Because of the way it's constructed, the average Zulu hut will only last about four years. By then the rain, wind and insect infestation have taken their toll, and you'd be better off building a new hut rather than trying to keep patching up the old one. Consequently, settlements are regularly rebuilt, and it's not uncommon for the head-man to decide they might as well move the whole village to a new spot while they're at it.

Shaka's decision, then, to relocate KwaBulawayo raised few eyebrows initially; many thought it was high time, as the old place was beginning to look a bit tatty, and getting overcrowded as well.

The grumbling only began when it was learnt how far away he intended to move his Great Place. Many old-timers reckoned they wouldn't be able to make the journey, and it was felt this was a kind of test, with Shaka wanting to get rid of those who couldn't keep up.

Others even saw cowardice in Shaka's actions. His praise singers might go on about how the King and his army destroyed Zwide's capital and sent the Ndwandwe ruler scurrying up country, but the northern border remained unstable and the King clearly wanted to put as much distance, and as many amakhanda as possible, between it and himself.

Perhaps more ominously, however, there are those who said: 'Look, see *where* he has built his new capital!'

They scoffed at his claim that the Great Place needed to be moved simply because the rapid growth of the kingdom meant the old Bulawayo was no longer at its centre – as true as this might be.

No, they said, this was merely a convenient pretext, and he'd have found another one if need be.

No, they said, building the new Bulawayo here all but brought him back to Mthetwa territory . . .

And hadn't experience shown him he'd always been safer here? Much had changed since he caught Dingiswayo's eye, but what did Shaka moving closer to Mthetwa territory say about the stability of his throne?

'Zwide's finished,' says Shaka. 'Is he to be like Beja? How often will he be used to instil fear? How many times must I defeat him? Hai, how can I defeat what no longer remains? And what of the Thembus and the Qwabes? Cha!'

He takes a sip of beer. 'Yes,' he says, 'as for our borders, when have they not been threatened?'

'This is so, Father,' concurs Mbopa.

'But we have brave men and able commanders like yourself, Mdlaka, to keep us safe,' continues Shaka.

'And you can always count on our loyalty, Father.'

'That I know, Mdlaka. That I know. As for this nonsense about the old-timers . . .'

'Well, it's not surprising that some are saying that, Majesty, given your immense fondness for the elderly.'

Shaka's laugh is a bark of appreciation. 'Oh, yes, Mbopa, you have me there. How I loathe them!'

'You mean *love*, Majesty?'

'Yes, thank you. A slip of the tongue. This happens when I must dwell on how much I *love* their bowed legs, their ceaseless coughing, their doddery, decrepit *loveableness*.' Shaka slaps his chest. 'And it pains me to think that I myself will never enter that enviable state. How I lie awake at night, grinding my teeth and lamenting the fact!'

'Majesty, please,' says Mdlaka, 'I speak for all of us when I say it disturbs us to even begin to contemplate—'

'My demise? Why not? At least I'll get to see what these ancestors really want.'

'That's just it, Father,' says Mdlaka. '*You*, an ancestor? Aiee! Will we ever get any rest, with you and Mgobozi watching over us?'

When all four have finished laughing, Shaka turns to the prime minister. 'This talk of me coming home . . . What do you make of it, Mbopa?'

'Well, Majesty . . .'

'For, how many times must I say it, I am not a fucking Mthetwa! No offence, Mgobozi, wherever you may be.'

'And he would say none taken, Father,' says Mbopa, 'for he always said he was really a Zulu.'

'As am I, too! Can't they get it into their thick skulls that it wasn't my fault I wasn't allowed to be raised among my own people?'

'Nonetheless, Majesty, perhaps this is a falsehood we have to endure for now,' says Mbopa.

For the move has also brought Shaka closer to the coast and to Faku's Pondoes. It is something no one has picked up upon, least of all Faku, and that's an oversight the chief might yet die regretting.

'Nonetheless, Mbopa,' says Shaka, mimicking his prime minister, 'we have to ask ourselves how this will affect our other plans for the First Fruits.'

Your plans, thinks the prime minister to himself; plans the King hints at but has never discussed fully with anyone, as far as Mbopa knows – not even with Pampata. And Mbopa is becoming more and more uneasy with the passing of each day. He doesn't object to Shaka claiming the right to be the only one to celebrate the First Fruits – quite the contrary, he supports such an innovation. It's Shaka's decision to revive that other occult aspect of the ceremony that worries him. It's become an obsession with the King, and seems too much like a return to those superstitions they spurned when Shaka took the throne.

But Shaka has asked him a question. 'Majesty, it is as I said just now. Not everyone thinks like this. We are talking merely of an ant in a bowl of porridge. Pick it out, and flick it away.'

'But it's those who are powerful enough to do something about it who are saying such things, is it not?'

'Is it, Majesty?'

'I am asking *you*, Mbopa.'

'And I am truly at a loss here, Majesty. If you already know who these people are, let us move against them.'

'Pick them out, flick them away,' adds Mdlaka.

'As we did with Nobela and her kind? But these are not sangomas, and the benefits of having them eat dirt might not be as immediately apparent to the people. It's bad enough that many still think of me as a usurper . . . no, don't deny it, Mbopa! It's just that they're willing to overlook that fact so long as their bellies are full.'

Shaka takes another sip of beer, swallows it. 'And now there's this business with the Uselwa Man,' he mutters, 'which is bound to be misinterpreted.'

Addressing the Induna: 'Although you acquitted yourself well there.'

'Thank you, Majesty, but the murderer remains at large.'

Which is why he's going to ask the Induna to keep an eye on the clan, and he will assign the boy and Njikiza to help him. Let Mthunzi resume, for now, his role as the Induna's udibi. 'After all, I have noticed you have not yet found a replacement,' observes the King.

When the Induna starts to remonstrate, he holds up a hand. 'I know! I would not be in a hurry to replace that one, were I you.'

'Aiee,' says Mdlaka, 'I know the boy is too old to be an udibi, but this one' – indicating the Induna – 'almost looks undressed without him by his side.'

'Lacks his shadow, you might say,' adds Mbopa.

'Very good, Mbopa,' says Shaka. 'Well put.' Addressing the Induna again: 'There you go; you may have your shadow back, even if Mdlaka's right about him being too old. But he was always more than an udibi to you, I think.'

'This is so, Majesty, and I thank you.'

'I hear you, Nduna, but thank me by finding the killer now, and seeing if there is a plot to unravel.'

'It will be done, rest assured, Majesty.'

'It must be, Nduna.' He wags a finger at Mdlaka and Mbopa. 'I do not say you are among them – in fact, I know you are not –

but I also know there are those, some of whom I regard as trusted advisors, who, even if they agree the First Fruits should be celebrated by the Bull Elephant and only the Bull Elephant, have begun muttering that it would be better if I waited another season. But did the Ndwandwes, or any of our other enemies, wait for one more season?'

It is a rhetorical question, of course, but Shaka lets his gaze rest on each of his companions in turn, as though expecting one of them to proffer an answer.

'No,' he continues, 'they did not wait. They came when they came, and we acted accordingly. See this merely as yet another campaign – and one we *must* undertake if our other campaigns are to be successful. As the kingdom grows, so our grip must tighten. *Tighten!* For if, in growing, the kingdom is allowed to become flabby we will lose all that we have gained.'

★

They are still pondering these words when Shaka's head cook scuttles into their shelter to whisper something into the King's ear. For the Induna it's as if the world around them has suddenly returned . . . he can again hear the knocking of the hoes and, beyond that, the muted rumble of a city of thousands, which cannot be still even though certain observances are necessary while the King eats.

And the head cook is one of the few who would dare disturb the King . . .

And Shaka is leaping to his feet, the others scrambling up immediately, so as not to be left sitting in his presence.

'He's here. Mbopa, he's here! Mdlaka, what say you? He's come at last!' Glee and boyish enthusiasm. To the cook: 'Send him to me. Hurry!' Rubbing his hands, he goes striding into the sun, unable to wait: 'No, no, on your feet!' he calls, as Mbilini KaZiwedum's eldest son drops to his knees. 'Nduna!' The warrior darts forward and helps the messenger up.

'You have something for me,' beams the King, as the Induna guides the young man towards him.

'Majesty.' The eldest son has already opened the muthi bag, and now his trembling hand moves over Shaka's palm.

'Thank you,' says Shaka. 'Tell your father I say thank you!'

Leaving the cook to usher Mbilini's son out of his presence, he turns back to Mdlaka: 'See?' Then to Mbopa: 'I know you do not set much store by such things, but see.' To the Induna: 'Do you see? I have been expecting him for several sleeps, and he arrives just as we talk of this thing. Is that not a propitious omen?'

The Induna nods.

In Shaka's palm rests the rounded seedpod from a tamboti tree.

The jumping-bean moth lays its eggs in these pods, which seem to come to life as the caterpillars inside them grow and begin to move. And when the moth emerges, it's as if it has been birthed by the tree itself.

This metamorphosis occurs in early September, the month of Umfumfu, or the Sprouting Moon. The pods and the white moths are one of the auguries that the Sky People look out for, along with the coming of the rains and the return of the Pleiades, which are known to them as Isilimela. But it's up to the headman of the EmaCubeni to monitor the progress of the season on the fringes of the Nkandla Forest, and to say when exactly the planting and sowing may commence.

And this empty pod is Mbilini's affirmation that it's time to Tatamageja, Take Up The Hoes.

163

Up and running, the Bull – which is his *Bull – has risen and is on the move, and he's right here in the ranks.* We drank the King's milk together, we came from far and wide, but we were closer than brothers, for we shared the season, were of an age . . .

Running, now, first the slow lion-lope, your isihlangu under your arm; then the cheetah-sprint. Then the clash of shields.

Forget what the praise singers say, this is what a battle is: a monster writhing and howling in a storm of dust, blood, sweat and confusion. Comes a moment and you're no longer afraid. For what is there to be afraid of? You're part of the beast, part of the swarm, driven along on numb legs; everything has become instinct. The loud punched-in-the-stomach sound of shields clashing; stepping back to take the impact or pushing on, trusting those behind you to clear the way with their spears as your momentum grinds down in a haze of blood. And your iklwa now has a life of its own. There's only whatever's in front of you; that's all that matters. But somehow you still hear the orders. Or else someone pulls on you, gets you turned around, and it's back up the hill. And every time you have to climb higher, because the lines are becoming denuded. Shaka's lions are tearing the Ndwandwes apart, but many of them are dying in the process.

Gqokli Hill.

Suddenly he's at Gqokli Hill – a soldier in the ranks, trudging back up the slope.

And all you want to do is reach the udibis with their waterskins. Even the baying Ndwandwes behind you don't matter. Besides, they're trapped behind the bodies of their comrades. Aiee! So many bodies! Stepping over them . . . stepping on them, because there's nowhere else to stand. And every now and then one of you stops, drops to his knees by a fallen comrade who won't be making it back up the hill. And you ask: 'Are you ready to

164

make the Journey?' The answer is always yes, and if there's no answer that's taken as a yes, too, and the coup de grâce *is delivered.*

And then you're pushing through the ranks that were held back, re-forming behind them so that you might rest while they bear the brunt of the next attack.

And then the Ndwandwes are coming again, and the indunas are screaming at you to get on your feet, on your feet, because the front lines aren't holding. And you, tired as you all are, are needed to strengthen the Inkatha Shaka has woven around Gqokli Hill.

Dust choking you. Stench of sweat and fear, and shit. Bloody haze, anger made manifest. Screams and shrieks, pleas for mercy drowning in throats filling with blood. This is a feeding frenzy, and you are the carcase.

Twist, then hook the other man's shield, sweep it aside and stab . . . plunge on forward. Twist, hook . . . and that wasn't even a man whose stomach found your blade. He was a screaming mouth. He was an assegai. He was frightened desperation. He was you. A reflection of you in turbulent waters, shattering and re-forming, as you confront the reflection behind him.

And again the bastard on the summit sends you down.

I am that bastard . . .

And, with that thought, the sounds of battle fade away. The killing continues, but there's a parting and he's running down a path between the screaming men . . .

And there's the udibi, the Induna's udibi, appearing in front of him, but looking as he was at the time of Gqokli Hill. Just a child Shaka had set to watch for a smoke signal from a distant hill, so that his attention might be diverted from the slaughter on the slopes . . .

What's he doing down here? Shaka tries to stop but it's too late, and he goes crashing into – and somehow passes through – the udibi.

And all is still. And he is now outside KwaBulawayo, and there's the Induna. And, without knowing how he knows, he realises he's seeing something with the udibi's eyes. Something important.

The Induna. And men from Mhlangana's kraal. A second group: four men in all. Those four fools tricked by the bandit. And Mhlangana's soldiers are herding a fifth man into their midst. Can't see his face; just his profile

*as he looks away, then the scars on his back, one of them standing out like
a big pink worm . . .*

*In his hut, Shaka wills the scene to repeat itself. What is he missing?
What did the udibi, now older, see?*

Mhlangana . . . does it have something to do with Shaka's brother?

Forget the other group. Look at the men he lent to the Induna.

Is there something about one of them?

Or is it the fact they are Mhlangana's men . . . ?

Is this to do with Mhlangana?

But why the return to Gqokli Hill?

*That day, Mhlangana had been with Dingane, who was guiding the
women and children and old-timers to the safety of the Nkandla Forest.
And so both brothers were safely out of the way, where his mother and
Mnkabayi, and a hand-picked contingent of Fasimbas, could see to it that
they didn't get up to any mischief . . .*

*Shaka turns his attention back to the five men now being led towards
KwaBulawayo by his brother's men, and finds himself back in his hut . . .*

And The Induna

And the Induna reaches down, grabs his hand and pulls him up.

The sky is a cavern, and fog hangs from the ceiling like thick, heavy cobwebs.

Dusty, clinging layers spun by the night.

He was almost at the summit, had leant against the rock shelf to regain his breath, to clear his head.

Always running . . .

A shifting – a displacement – above him.

He looked up.

The greyness, these dusty, clinging layers, had thinned, parted . . .

And there, stepping out of the mist to stand peering down at him, was the Induna.

This Shadow of Shaka who, he knows, has come to kill him.

Oh, the irony! He chuckles mirthlessly, like the scratching of a rat in the fog.

And the Induna bends forward, extends his hand and pulls Dingane up.

'So it was you,' says the prince. 'Out there, just now.'

Yes, says the Induna: burdened as he was, he had to run to overtake the prince, couldn't wait for a less risky moment, as they were close to their destination.

'How did you know where I was going, since I didn't know myself?' asks Dingane.

Although it's shrouded in fog, the prince will recognise this place if he just steps this way, says the Induna.

The Needy One follows his friend for a few paces, then finds himself nodding as he spots the fault line that has become a cleft in the rock face.

'Do you remember now?' asks the Induna. 'This is where we would come to escape your father's wrath.'

'And more,' murmurs Dingane. It was where two lonely boys came to share their doubts and fears, the dread and frustration that seem to dog one's days when one feels one is old enough to be treated as something other than a child, yet still fears bullies, ghost stories and girls, and all those inarticulate terrors that lurk on the edges of one's life at that age. That age when one realises there's a world beyond the world one knows. One that can be just as strange and incomprehensible to the adults who seek to confine and constrain one, and you realise that the protection they offer – and you sometimes seek out, just like a child – is largely illusory.

Among the People Of The Sky, a human being's inner feelings and emotions are known as umxwele, the same term being used to describe the inner parts of the throat. This place was their umxwele, their throat.

Then again, decides Dingane, even in the darkness the elongated oval resembles the opening to a vagina.

But he hasn't been here for so long!

'I still can't see how you could have known,' murmurs the prince.

'Your question is both of the Earth and of the Sky,' says the Induna.

'What?'

'Nothing. It is nothing. I knew the direction you had taken, and I remembered this place . . .' Remembered, too, that the prince faced more or less the same dilemma; for they were two men heading out into the night, both unsure of where to go. Heading for the one place he knew Dingane was familiar with, as a refuge that would at least suffice until dawn, was surely better than blundering through the darkness. If he was wrong, and if this hadn't been Dingane's destination all along, or if the vaguely familiar topography didn't reawaken old memories to make this his destination, it was as good a place as any to wait until daybreak, when he could start the daunting task of seeking out the prince's spoor.

168

'All the same,' says Dingane, 'I feel as if I have been bewitched and all of this is planned. Hai, perhaps it is really as I suspected before . . . ?'

'What is that?'

That he is dead, and someone has turned him into an impundulu.

'You are alive,' says the Induna, 'and you haven't been bewitched.'

'Which could merely mean you too are bewitched,' points out the prince.

'Then they have failed!'

'How so?'

'Do the bewitched know they are bewitched?' Isn't that the whole point of putting a hex on someone, so that they may suffer, or do your bidding without realising it?

'Hai, perhaps you are right.' There's a pause while Dingane appears to mull this over. Then, just as the Induna is about to explain to him how — although they can't risk a fire — he has seen to it they will be warm enough, the prince says: 'Another question, old friend. Why are we talking about such things?'

'Why?'

'Yes, why!' The prince's hand comes up, pointing in the direction of KwaBulawayo. 'Are there not more important matters to discuss?'

'Such as?'

Such as? Dingane tries a stare of disbelief, but it soon disintegrates into laughter and head-shaking.

'Such as, have you brought us some beer?' he says eventually.

Sadly, no, says the Induna, there was no time. But, if the prince recalls, there is a spring in this secret place of theirs that offers water they once declared the sweetest they'd ever tasted.

'And yet we each then would have swapped the other for a gourd of beer,' notes Dingane. Or later, as they got older and came here less, a girl!

'This is so,' chuckles the Induna.

'But before we taste once more the sweetest water in the kingdom, I would ask you another question, old friend.'

The Induna nods and waits.

'You have served my brother loyally all these years, but who do you serve tonight?'

PART THREE
How The Induna Came To Serve Shaka

There is some difference of opinion about the manner in which Shaka seized power . . .

From *The Zulu Kings* by Brian Roberts

Whereupon, much to the surprise of his brothers and all the inhabitants of esiKlebeni, Dingane declared his approval of Shaka's usurpation of the throne and solemnly promised to honour, to defend and to serve the new chief of the Zulu.

From *Rule Of Fear* by Peter Becker

Take a look at a map of modern-day South Africa, and you'll see the country is divided into nine provinces. On the east coast, you'll find KwaZulu-Natal. Brushed by the warm Indian Ocean, the subtropical coastal lowland reaches maximum temperatures of 28°C during the height of summer, between January and March, with an extremely high humidity factor especially in and around Durban, the city that gradually grew out of the trading station established on the shores of Port Natal. Temperatures can be higher further inland, for the Thukela Valley often reaches 30°C, but they will drop considerably after nightfall.

KwaZulu-Natal's coastline stretches from Port Edward in the south to Kosi Bay in the north, where the province shares a border with Mozambique. It is here, too, that sandy beaches give way to a vast low-lying plain of mangroves, swamp forests and salt marshes. The Zulus call this region Umhlaba'yalingana, Flat Land.

This is malaria territory, best avoided, although many of the plants required for medicines are to be found in the northern reaches, where the plain meets the precipitous slopes of the Lebombo Mountains, and shrubs and tree cycads cling to the rock faces. It is here that many sangomas and inyangas come to receive their training.

The coastal belt gives way to more hospitable land further south, where rolling hills and fertile grasslands, watered by moist warm air moving inland off the Indian Ocean, invite settlement and promise prosperity away from the tsetse fly and trembling sickness.

Travelling deeper into the province is to travel higher, until one encounters the mighty basalt and sandstone barrier of the Drakensberg or Ukhahlamba mountain range. Beyond this lies the home of the Sothos. The mighty Thukela, the region's largest river, also has its source here.

Even further south, spilling over into what's now the Eastern Cape, is Pondoland, with its often impenetrable thickets of shrubs, low trees and vines, becoming forests and montane grasslands in the higher altitudes.

Between the Ukhahlamba and the granite Lebombo lies a swathe of bushveld: dense thickets along watercourses, and trees in the savannah. They include the buffalo-thorn jujube, whose branches are used to carry a person's spirit home if they have died in a far-off place; the marula whose berries are eaten by all, from wild animals to livestock to humans; the aloe whose nectar children love, and whose dried leaves are ground for snuff; the ever untidy red bushwillow with its heavily scented flowers . . .

The borders of the province mark the great area of land that came under Zulu control during Shaka's rise to power: more than ninety thousand square kilometres gained and never truly lost.

Now take a pencil and make a mark on the map, preferably somewhere in the area between the White Mfolozi and the source of the Mhlathuze River – but it doesn't really matter where.

That pencil mark, on any 1:350 000 map, represents the size of the territory Shaka inherited when he first became King of the Zulus in 1816.

1
A Rude Awakening

'One more thing,' she said, as Ndlela was leaving. 'I think a little fear will be in order. I think a little fear will go a long way to helping him see the wisdom of the course of action we propose for him. What say you?'

Mnkabayi's induna nodded.

'Not that I think he will take much convincing, for he is a smart one. But do not let the nature of our relationship deter you from ordering your men to emphasise the seriousness of the matter.'

'I will also see to it, Ma, that they do not go too far. The special relationship the two of you enjoy aside, that would defeat our aims.'

'Good.' Mnkabayi smiled. 'Go issue your orders.'

As things turned out, it was a refinement to their plan that caused some difficulty for those sent to fetch the young warrior at first light, the next day.

On their own initiative they decided the 'scaring' would start from the moment they woke him up. That, they felt, would set the tone for the rest of the proceedings.

Instead of calling the warrior out of his indlu, his hut, they crept inside with the intention of having him tied up and docile before he was fully awake.

But, even as they moved into position, the warrior was stirring. Sheshayo, the leader of the group, darted forward and clamped his left hand over the young man's mouth. Unfortunately, he was too quick for his companions. Hila had managed to grab an ankle and Radebe was leaning forward to take hold of the warrior's hands, when the man came alive.

He kicked Hila across the hut, caught Radebe a glancing blow on the cheekbone, and brought his other hand up under Sheshayo to punch him in the balls. If he had been able to connect with Radebe properly, things might have gone even worse for the intruders. As it was, Radebe was merely deflected. He regained

175

his balance and, while Sheshayo toppled sideways with a howl, he threw himself on to the warrior, who tried to use Radebe's momentum against him by rolling with him in a move that should have sent Radebe flying. But they were too close to the wall of the hut. Radebe hit the thatch and dropped back on to the warrior.

It was as they wrestled face to face, each trying to grip and pin down the other's hands, that he recognised his assailant.

Suddenly the warrior stopped struggling. 'Have you gone mad?' he asked Radebe.

His lip bleeding, Radebe shook his head.

For a few moments the hut was filled with the sound of three men panting and one keening like a hungry eaglet, his hands covering his genitals.

'Ndlela,' said Radebe at last.

'Ndlela?'

'He has' – gulping in mouthfuls of air – 'summoned you. And . . . sent . . . us.'

'To fetch me?'

'Yes.'

'And this was how you chose to carry out his orders?'

In answer to his friend's question, Radebe glanced at Sheshayo, still curled up a few paces away. It was Sheshayo who had been briefed by Ndlela and, in turn, all he told Hila and Radebe was that they were to take the fellow by surprise.

The warrior nodded his understanding. Sheshayo was known for his eagerness to impress his superiors.

'Let me get up!' he demanded. They could wait for him outside while he got dressed.

Ndlela? That usually meant orders from Mnkabayi. Or even an audience with Senzangakhona's sister.

When he emerged from the hut, he was wearing the isinene and ibeshu that make up the Zulu kilt. The isinene, or front apron, comprises skins cut into circular patches and strung together on sinews to form tassels. These are weighted to prevent the isinene from opening in case of sudden movement. The ibeshu is made of soft calfskin. Sandals completed his attire. If this was the way Ndlela chose to summon him, he would not bother with the feathers and armbands a Zulu male might wear on more formal occasions.

Part of him was aware he might regret such petulance, but he couldn't see what he had done that might have angered Ndlela (or Mnkabayi) and precipitated such a rude awakening.

The induna, however, could scarcely keep from laughing when the four of them trooped into his presence around mid-morning. As he'd later tell Mnkabayi, it was if the warrior was escorting the other three. 'Fear there was, Ma,' he'd explain, 'but it clearly ran in the wrong direction.' And Mnkabayi would ask him: 'Are you surprised?' He'd look at her for a moment, the beginnings of a smile playing around his lips, then shake his head and release the smile fully, saying: 'No, Ma, not in the least.'

There and then, though, he conjured up a stern expression. The warrior was to be given some water, then he could sit in the shade, with Radebe to watch over him, until Mnkabayi was ready to receive him.

After Ndlela had moved off, the warrior asked Radebe if he knew why he had been summoned.

His friend shook his head.

And it was only as they approached his hut, explained Radebe, that Sheshayo told his companions how he wanted them to wake up the warrior. 'There wasn't time to warn you,' he added.

'But you did stamp hard as you entered,' grinned the warrior.

Radebe shrugged. It was the best he could do.

Nodding, the warrior rested his back against the tree trunk, eyeing the huts around them. He could hear the shouts of children at play somewhere nearby.

The king, he asked at last . . . did Radebe think this had anything to do with the king?

'That is unlikely.' Still revelling in the novelty of his elevation in status, Sigujana was at EsiKlebeni, feasting and meeting the maidens brought to him for consideration by the noblemen, it being a signal honour to have a daughter taken into the king's harem.

Whenever a new king assumed the throne, there was a certain amount of jostling as his cronies replaced the favourites of the previous monarch, but the warrior couldn't see how any of this would affect him.

Except . . .

Yes, well, there was that.

2
A Commission

'Welcome,' said Mnkabayi spreading her arms wide.

They were standing in an enclosed section to the side of her hut. Privacy was provided by a fence made of poles lashed together, and shade by the umbrella canopy of a paperbark acacia. This was where Mnkabayi received important guests, a fact not lost on the warrior as he bowed his head.

'I am your servant, Ma. As ever.'

'You look healthy.' She turned to Ndlela. 'Doesn't he? Healthy and strong. Other young men . . . well, they tend to lie around, need to be goaded into doing the smallest chore for their indunas, or even their mothers. Not you,' she added, her eyes meeting the warrior's. For a moment, like a leopard loping between the trees, there was a glimpse of the flirtatious young girl she used to be.

'And don't think I haven't noticed the good influence you have on my nephew.' Mnkabayi grinned. 'Well, in most areas. But when it comes to young maidens, no one can restrain him. Still, we will be seeing him soon enough. I know, for I sent the messengers myself.' At a time like this the princes needed to come together, to show their support for the heir. Differences must be put aside.

The warrior nodded, not sure where this was leading.

Mnkabayi must have sensed his puzzlement. Or else she realised that she had reached the point of no return. It was like the many branches of this tree spreading shade over them: they might be slender, but most would bear your weight – within reason and up to a certain point, of course. Indeed, you'd be able to climb along them further than you'd think. It's only when you tried to retreat that they were likely to snap. Mnkabayi glanced at Ndlela, as if seeking his consent. The induna shrugged – the gesture of one who's more than merely a loyal servant, indicating that he'd stand by her no matter what she decided.

Mnkabayi laid a hand on the warrior's shoulder and guided him over to the pile of mats arranged beneath the tree. Allowing him to hold her arm, she lowered herself on to the mats and indicated that the warrior should sit too. Over here, on this stone, though, where she can see him without twisting her neck, and also close enough so she can speak softly.

Ndlela, the warrior noted, remained standing, occasionally moving away to peer over the wall to make sure no eavesdroppers lurked nearby.

What was going on? What did they want from him?

Dingane had often teased him that Mnkabayi had her eye on him – and everyone knew what that meant! Initially it bothered the warrior, since he most certainly did not want to become one of Mnkabayi's herdboys, her special protégés. But how did you turn down the advances of one who was a veritable queen? It was hardly any less comforting once it became clear seduction was the furthest thing from her mind – what then *did* she want from him? By the time Dingane was sent off to the Qwabes, the young warrior had given up trying to work out why Mnkabayi had decided to take an interest in him. Such ruminations only brought on a headache and whenever she summoned him and asked him to do something for her, he simply obeyed without question.

Now, though, there was a sense of urgency and of some great trust about to be conferred on him, which reignited his unease. The old questions kept flaking off his mind, like the bark from this tree. What did she want from him? And why him? Peel the straw-coloured strips off to reveal a darker yellow bark. Why him in particular?

And there are thorns hidden in this tree: long and sharp.

'Your friend, my nephew, will be pleased to be back, I think.'

The warrior responded with the slow nod of a man who suspects a trader is guiding him to a bargain that will turn out to be such only for the trader, yet finds himself unable to pull himself free from those honeyed words and sweet phrases.

Mnkabayi chuckled like a benign aunt looking benevolently upon the foibles of youth. 'But perhaps not so pleased as when he was sent away.'

A strange thing to say, and an odd way of putting it. Why wouldn't Dingane be happier that his 'punishment' has ended prematurely?

'I'm not sure I understand, Ma,' said the warrior. 'Has the prince got into, well . . .'

'Has he been unable to keep his pizzle where it belongs, do you mean?' Does the warrior have to ask? Chances are, there are several additional reasons why Dingane would be happy to leave his hosts so soon. 'But, no,' said the queen, 'that is not what I refer to.'

Then why? Dingane hadn't been able to believe his luck after his interview with Mduli. The ancestors had smiled on him, he told his friend, before whooping with triumph and relief. Making his way to the elder's house, he'd barely seemed able to walk, now he was leaping for joy. The warrior had also been stunned. Expecting the worst, he'd already gathered together supplies so that he and Dingane could flee Mduli's wrath, should the need arise.

Death was the fate that awaited any who had a dalliance with a concubine from the king's harem – with the woman in question joining her lover at the Place Of Execution. Although it was unlikely that Mduli would have countenanced such treatment for a prince, the cantankerous old bullfrog was more than capable of coming up with some punishment almost as bad. Yet, in the end, he had simply decreed that Dingane go and live with the Qwabes for an unspecified length of time.

'Will I be correct in saying my nephew was overjoyed at Mduli's leniency?' asked Mnkabayi.

'Yes, Ma.'

'Did my nephew ever stop to wonder why my uncle was so lenient?'

'No, Ma.'

Ndlela had ceased his prowling and come to stand before them, listening. After a glance at her induna, Mnkabayi asked the young warrior if he was certain of that.

A nod.

'And did my nephew ever wonder how Mduli found out that the young bull had been inside the old bull's kraal?'

'Not really, Ma. He merely assumed one of the other females had reported them.'

A look at Ndlela. 'He doesn't know!'

The induna nodded.

'Is that good or bad?' murmured the queen. Then, recollecting the young warrior's presence, she placed a hand on his knee. 'You are doubtless confused, so let me make things clear.'

And he must remember she is telling him these things because he is one of Dingane's closest friends.

The thing was, she said, Dingane's dalliance with the girl from his father's harem had been reported to Mduli by Sigujana.

'I suspect he was also infatuated with her. Finding himself spurned in favour of his brother, he decided that, if he couldn't have her, he was going to see to it that Dingane was punished for the very crime he also had contemplated.'

And let the girl suffer, too.

Only he had misjudged the elder's reaction.

'Mduli could not overlook the seriousness of Dingane's crime. He would never have allowed him to escape punishment totally, but he considered Sigujana's betrayal of his brother as an equally serious transgression. This was not the way the heir should act.'

Hence Mduli's leniency, which was also intended as an admonition to Sigujana.

'But there, perhaps, Mduli overestimated Sigujana's sagacity. I do not think he really understood,' said Mnkabayi. 'In fact I know he did not understand, and merely felt thwarted.'

This is why Mduli has now fallen from grace, his counsel being ignored by the new king.

'And this is why your friend needs protecting,' said Mnkabayi, squeezing the Induna's leg.

Straightening again, she continued. 'That Dingane doesn't even know it was Sigujana who betrayed him . . .' The queen shrugged. 'I do not know whether that makes things simpler or more difficult. What say you?' she asked Ndlela.

'I think,' he said, 'the question we should be asking ourselves is how much the king knows.'

'This is so,' murmured Mnkabayi. 'What say you?' she asked the young warrior.

Flattered that his opinion was being sought, he nodded his agreement. 'It is what the king thinks his brother knows that we need to find out.'

'For that will guide his hand,' added Mnkabayi.

Obviously, if Sigujana believed Dingane knew that he'd betrayed him, he'd view his brother's return with apprehension. Guilt or fear of reprisal might lead him to fabricate a reason to get the Needy One out of the way. Permanently.

'And we are surrounded,' said Mnkabayi. 'In fact encircled! We must watch even our allies.' The Zulu nation could not afford a civil war.

The young warrior will do this for his friend, then. Mnkabayi will use her influence to see that he joins the new king's inner circle. 'Sigujana is too callow to think he needs advisors. It's playmates and bodyguards he is on the lookout for and you will fulfil both functions, like the other sycophants he has already gathered around him.'

'A question, Ma!' interrupted Ndlela.

'Speak!'

Won't Sigujana suspect the young warrior's motives, since he knows him to be friendly with his brother?

Boozing and fornicating take up her nephew's time these days, says the queen, and if he gives the matter some thought, he'll probably be flattered and regard the warrior's defection as testament to his own charms. 'And more's the pity.'

'Ma?'

'Think, young one. If he suspected your motives, that would make your task easier. Let him think you are there on Dingane's behalf and, while he asks you questions, seeking to find how much his brother knows, you will learn how much *he* knows.'

'For sometimes the questions people ask us are as important as the lies we prepare for them,' added Ndlela.

'A valuable lesson, young one. But are you willing to help Dingane in this way?' asked Mnkabayi.

'Yes, Ma.' There was no question of him refusing.

Good, said the queen. There was just one more thing: as a safeguard against Sigujana trying to punish him for being Dingane's friend by treating him as a servant, he will enter the new king's service with the rank of induna. Even Sigujana is not so foolish as to undermine the system of favouritism and patronage such ranks signify. He can afford to scorn Mduli, because the elder has never been popular; but that's as far as he will go when it comes to challenging the status quo.

At the same time, the young man must know this is not simply a matter of contingency. Instead, he is to see the rank as a further sign of the trust being placed in him.

He bowed his head. 'I thank you, Ma, and I am your servant, as ever.'

'More than that,' murmured Mnkabayi. 'You are more than that. I think I see in you the makings of a warrior whose brave deeds will be told around campfires long after we are all gone.'

3
The Forgotten King

History barely remembers Sigujana kaSenzangakhona. He becomes a king and then a murder victim, very often all in the same brief paragraph, with Shaka the carriage return that heralds a new beginning.

Even the circumstances of Sigujana's death are obscure. Since an heir who killed a king ceased to be an heir – and could not then claim the throne – it's highly unlikely that Shaka himself steered the blade, tightened the garrotte or held the royal head under water, as some sources claim. Others maintain that, as soon as he heard Senzangakhona had reneged on his promise to Dingiswayo and chosen Sigujana as his heir, Shaka sent his half-brother Ngwadi, who was Nandi's son, but not Senzangakhona's, to assassinate Sigujana. It's also alleged that Ngwadi's brief was merely to 'negotiate' with Sigujana, and that the latter's obstinacy led to a quarrel while they were swimming, whereupon Ngwadi held Sigujana's head under water until the king signalled that he had come to see the validity of the emissary's arguments by dying.

However, it's surely more likely that Shaka would have entrusted the actual task of getting his brother out of the way to someone he knew he could trust unequivocally – a close friend, in other words, for the fog of war and privations shared can forge a loyalty stronger and more enduring than mere blood and the burden of kinship.

As for Sigujana himself, and the kind of man he was – perhaps what's more important is his timing.

When Sigujana came to the throne, the tribe's way of life was already changing. It may have been a quiet erosion not immediately apparent, but change was there all the same. The tree stood, but its strength was illusory, for the termites were hard at work, and had been so for some time.

The land was becoming crowded. Hemmed in, surrounded, unable to expand their territory, the Zulus had reached the point where they could only allow themselves to be assimilated. The People Of The Sky were well on their way to becoming a mere clan – a part of and no long apart from. Not that outright conquest loomed, for things weren't that simple.

Some of their immediate neighbours, like the Buthelezis, would have relished the prospect, but they were fleas caught in the same situation. Attempting a sustained campaign against their old foe would have left them too weak to consolidate any gains they might have made. (Consequently, when conflict did occur, it was kept at the level of an occasional exchange of insults and spears, with both sides claiming victory at the end of play.)

A larger power like the Ndwandwes, meanwhile, merely saw the Zulus as a means to an end, and as bodies they had to trample over to get at Dingiswayo's Mthetwas.

In other words, even though many of the other Nguni tribes in the region were always going to be bigger, stronger and wealthier, and therefore would always treat the Zulus as vassals to be exploited, no one was actively seeking their extinction. Instead, in a trend that was no longer even noticeable as such, more and more young men and women were marrying into those neighbouring tribes. In turn, that discrete grouping of people who regarded themselves purely as Zulus was shrinking.

Land inherited by daughters became the property of the tribe they had married into, while a son who had moved away to stay with his wife's people rarely returned to take possession of any land left to him by his father. You soon realised how much more comfortable life could be if you didn't live in a buffer zone between two of the biggest tribes in the region, whose kings had both sworn to destroy each other. Consequently, you spoke to your mother – and your father's other wives – and traded the family land for cattle. As was customary, the women would in turn divide their own portions of the land among their daughters, who were more and more likely to marry into another tribe . . .

Would this assimilation have reached its apotheosis during Sigujana's lifetime, had he been allowed to live and rule some fifty summers, say? Perhaps not, but chances are there were those alive, when he took the throne, who would one day have looked up and looked around and realised that even if they had been Zulus once, they were now something else.

Of course, Shaka's coming changed everything. Or perhaps it merely delayed the inevitable. Writing in August 1887, Theophilus Shepstone called the Zulu nation a collection of 'more or less autonomous' and 'more or less discontented' tribes, 'a rope of sand whose only cohesive property was furnished by the presence of the

Zulu ruling family'. Then again, despite the depredations of the armies of Empire and Apartheid and the idiocies of the Cult of Mediocrity that crept in with the new millennium, the People Of The Sky are still with us, ruled by a bloodline unbroken since the days of Malandela, father of Zulu. (For which they have Mpande to thank, but that's a story for – and of – another time.)

And yet again Sigujana has slipped out of the narrative, disappeared from the discourse.

And, again, tonight.

★

At least, the Induna can't spot him. The new king is lost amid the dancing bodies in the darkness that the fires can't seem to push away, and amidst the dust awoken by stamping feet before. They're outside, but the closeness of everyone – and everything, because even the drums seem to be pressing in – is stultifying. And their abandon – these strong young men, all swagger and muscle and disdain, and their adoring maidens – adds to the crush, like clods of earth falling on you in an open grave in a bad dream (and you're alive and you want to tell them that, but you can't speak, you can't move, and now your mouth is full of wet sand and your arms are already covered). The booze and grass don't help, either. Hard to pick someone out of a seething mass, when your world is see-sawing. Fresh air and a place to puke, that's what he needs.

His departure involves some sidling, and a certain amount of circumspection. The king has a habit of making a fuss if he spots one of his playmates endeavouring to leave the party before his royal highness himself has passed out. The ingrate is then dragged before the monarch and, depending on Sigujana's mood, his willingness to allow himself to be egged on by the snide suggestions of those who happen to be at his side, his punishment can range from being forced to drink beer until he throws up, to being sent to pull down Mduli's hut or else terrorise some other old-timer who has annoyed Sigujana.

Given the reason he's at court, the Induna also feels he has to be extra careful about drawing attention to himself.

Ironically, though, Sigujana has shown every sign of being flattered by the Induna's defection to his camp, and he hasn't sought to victimise the warrior. Quite the contrary; he's castigated those who've attempted to cast aspersions on the Induna's loyalty. Even the king's brother, Mhlangana, has come in for a public tongue-lashing after sending a few sneers the Induna's way.

This is not to say that the Induna has been admitted into the king's inner circle – his izilomo, where Mhlangana acts the major domo – but he is getting close. The gate might remain shut, but he's allowed to look over the fence because Sigujana values his counsel on at least one subject. He is forever quizzing the Induna about Dingane's intentions, as if the Induna is in constant contact with Dingane, or is blessed with a unique insight into that prince's psyche.

★

This is also why the Induna is one of those that Sigujana orders to accompany him when the emissaries arrive the next morning, after the party.

Hungover, panicking at this sudden and unexpected intrusion of the outside world into his realm of drink and debauchery, Sigujana for some reason believes they've been sent by Dingane himself. That makes the Induna just the man he wants at his side, and it also helps that the Induna happens to be one of the few still upright and seemingly sober at this hour.

After drinking a lake of water the previous night, the Induna had made his way back to his hut to sleep. Rising early, he washed, broke his fast, and is standing amid the slumbering bodies draped around the remains of last night's fires, when Sigujana finally drags himself out of his hut. Blearily, the king listens to the messenger, then spots the Induna. 'You!' he calls, momentarily forgetting the warrior's name. 'Nduna! See what this fool wants. And ask him why my brother feels the need to add pomposity to his impertinence, by sending others to speak in his name.'

'As you wish, Majesty,' says the Induna, moving forward while the king allows himself to be led away by one of his servants.

187

4
The Stranger

He was standing amid the snoring, groaning bodies trying to remember the dream he'd had last night. However, the opening of the pot is too narrow and he just can't get his hand in. The memory of the dream was still fluttering behind his eyes as he woke up, but it vanished while he was readying himself for the day. It was only on returning here, to the scene of last night's dismal merriment, that he remembered.

An axe embedded in his head, dust in his throat . . .

The surge of resentment at having to sneak away.

Fresh air, then.

And hesitation.

Rummaging for the will, if not the courage. The drunk's dilemma: knowing it will be better this way, but feeling his body rebel nonetheless.

The decision.

Moving further into the darkness.

On his hands and knees, and then the finger thrust into his mouth.

The gagging.

Then the flood.

A dog barking in the bushes, but trying not to make a sound. Not quite succeeding, though, it being a process hard to control once initiated.

Still, despite the vile taste in his mouth and the burning in his throat, he'd felt better when he straightened up.

But there was tiredness, too. He had known his evening was over.

Find some water, then find his hut.

That the first task meant moving closer to the flames, and the drums and the sweaty limbs and the shouts and screams, didn't worry him as much as sneaking away had. He had successfully disentangled himself, now he could circle the fringes unnoticed.

He'd found some water, was sucking the skin dry, when a voice next to him spoke: 'Now, which one is your king?'

Running the back of his hand across his mouth, the Induna turned to face a man several summers older than himself.

Noting the stranger was unarmed, the Induna asked him who he was referring to.

Now, the morning after, he wonders if the man had been speaking to himself because, as soon as the warrior spoke, the stranger had glanced at him as though seeing him for the first time.

And, having seen him, was seemingly determined to commit his features to memory, for he'd stood a long while gazing into the Induna's face.

Hard to see his eyes in the darkness, or judge what he meant by this long hard glare, but it was enough to unsettle the Induna.

And it was the memory of that same unease that struck him when he returned to the gathering place this morning. The call that awoke the echoes.

That stare? He can't be sure, but thinking about it now, it's as if the stranger had been taken by surprise, was staring because he couldn't believe his own eyes. Yes, it was as if he, and not the Induna, had seen something out of the ordinary!

'Your king,' he said at last, his eyes now on the strutting, staggering warriors only a few metres away. 'Which one is he?'

Even there and then, caught in this dream that might not have been a dream, the Induna was struck by that odd choice of words. *Your king.*

Stepping over the slumbering bodies, trying to find the exact spot where they had then been standing: who was this man? *Your king* implied he wasn't one of them, wasn't a Zulu, in which case he should not have been there. Yet the Induna had done nothing. He hadn't raised the alarm or tried to detain the stranger. *Why?*

Because things became hazy after that . . . The next thing he knew, it was today.

What happened to the man? Where did he go? The Induna

would surely have known by now if he had intended to make mischief.

Or had it all been just a dream?

Just as the messenger hurries into sight, seeking the king, the Induna remembers something else. Here was one who seemed to be an outsider, who spoke of *your king*, yet, on his face, the black and red muthi sangomas applied to a Zulu chief at the time of the First Fruits. Yes, Imithi Emnyama – and worn out of season, too.

5
Stranger Strangers

But the arrival of these other strangers – a little more strange since there's no doubt they aren't Zulus, and thus far more ominous than some chimera in the night – meant the Induna had other things to think about.

'My brother . . .' began Sigujana, not elaborating, not even mentioning that he was referring to Dingane. Consequently, when the Induna questioned the messenger and learnt that the emissaries were from Shaka, he was more than a little surprised.

All Zulus had by now heard of Shaka's rise to prominence in the service of their powerful ally. Few doubted his bravery – or, rather, they were willing to tolerate the blather of the Mthetwa praise singers – it was his claim to be Senzangakhona's eldest son which they treated with disdain.

Some said the poor benighted brat spawned by Nandi had died during the great famine known as Madlathule, Eat And Be Quiet, and this Shaka was an impostor used by Dingiswayo in an effort to gain greater control over the Sky People. And just how stupid did he think they were, for this Shaka could scarcely speak their language! Others believed Shaka to be Nandi's son, but not Senzangakhona's; and that, impregnated by another, she had shamed the Zulu king into marrying her – but eventually got what she deserved.

Yet here was Sigujana blithely speaking of 'my brother'. Curious.

While the king lethargically went about piecing his consciousness together, and some of his servants set about waking up all the other men, the Induna sent the messenger off to tell Mnkabayi what had transpired. Unfortunately, the queen was at a homestead a few kilometres away from the capital, so it would be some time before she got there.

And Sigujana was ready to meet the emissaries much sooner than the Induna had anticipated. Although the warrior wasn't to know it, this was an indication of how nervous Dingane made Sigujana. He would not be able to enjoy his new status fully until he knew what Dingane was planning to do. It was an anxiety that showed itself as Sigujana pushed aside his servants and shouted for the favourites he'd chosen as his guard of honour to get a move on.

The Induna decided that, in the same situation, he'd also want to get this meeting over and done with so he might learn what this mysterious brother had in mind. Had Sigujana ever even met Shaka? The Induna didn't think so – and he knew Dingane hadn't. He and Dingane had campaigned with the Mthetwas and, although there were times when they saw action, the Zulu contingents were mainly used to cover the main force's flanks or look after the cattle, while the battle itself raged a few valleys away. They rarely even camped alongside Dingiswayo's legions. So both he and Dingane had heard the stories, but they had never seen Shaka in the flesh.

*

'Shesha, shesha!' bellowed Mhlangana. And here was another brother, thinner than Sigujana, taller than Dingane. What did *he* think?

Is this some secret the royal family has kept from the tribe?

'Shesha, shesha!' urges Mhlangana again. *Hurry, hurry!*

After the chosen ten had formed up, Sigujana's inspection of his bodyguard was brief. His gaze moved along the line, which had already become an arc, as those on the fringes moved forward and inward so there could be no doubting their enthusiasm. Then he nodded.

A ruler with a little more experience might have noted how the men themselves were as ragged as the formation they'd assumed.

Knowing there was little he could do about the bleary, bloodshot eyes, the sagging shoulders and the other signs of last night's drinking session, he could have still sent them away to spruce themselves up. For kilts were awry, and only some of the men had managed to pull on amashoba, while others preferred to spend the extra time required for that in throwing up. Some were wearing headdresses, others not, and, while all were carrying spears, their shields didn't match. In their haste, a few of the men had even picked up the smaller ihawu they used while dancing.

Sigujana, however, was more interested in ferocity, and clearly believed this component was all present and correct. And he wasn't wrong; for being awoken while their hangovers were flowing full-bore had indeed induced a sullen aggression in his men.

Would the king like to say a few words? wondered Mhlangana.

After a slight hesitation, Sigujana nodded. Why not? Get them even more riled!

'My brother has at last emerged from the thicket,' he announced. 'But, coward that he is, he's still wary of wandering too far. Instead, he sends two emissaries who now have the effrontery to inter-rupt our rest. But that is not an impudence I will hold like a blade to their throats, for it is time we cleared this field of such weeds.'

So let his men swagger forth and show his brother – and these creatures of his – the way things stand.

'But please, my brave warriors, restrain yourselves! We would not want them dying of fright before they can report back to my brother. Is that understood?'

As expected, Mhlangana answered for the men. 'As you wish, Majesty – until you wish otherwise, of course.'

Sigujana joined in the laughter.

'Yes, well,' he added after taking a mouthful of water from a gourd proffered by a servant, 'a hiding may yet be in order.' But there's every chance his brother will see reason, isn't there? This last question was aimed at the Induna, and was largely rhetorical, since Dingane was known to be circumspect where his own safety was concerned. This nonsense was simply that, nonsense – and it was the prince's way of throwing a tantrum. And, before the Induna had even stopped wondering why Sigujana should be asking him to comment on what Shaka might or might not do, Sigujana and Mhlangana were already discussing how they would deal with the emissaries.

Putting aside his confusion, the Induna moved to where he could see down the main path leading away from the group of huts. It was still too early, and his messenger was probably only now drawing in sight of the homestead where Mnkabayi was tending to a sick relative. But that didn't stop him from wishing she'd hurry up and get here.

Seeing the brothers returning, he slipped back among the ranks.

Sigujana and Mhlangana had decided that two men would be sent ahead. Staying away from the path, they'd keep their eyes peeled for any unpleasant surprises – not that Sigujana believed Dingane would stoop to such treachery, but one couldn't be too careful. For the same reason, the remaining men would encircle the king for his protection, as they marched to the rendezvous. When they reached the emissaries, they would step forward and form an intimidating arc in front of the strangers. Sigujana would be in the centre; while Mhlangana would place himself to his left and the Induna to his right.

★

Believing the emissaries to come from Dingane, Sigujana hopes the Induna's presence in such a prominent position will show Dingane's men how he's perfectly willing to forgive and forget when it comes to defectors from his brother's kraal, and their past lapses in judgement – and taste. If that doesn't work, they can at least be counted upon to tell Dingane what they saw, and this will serve to remind his brother that his herd of allies might not be as big as he believes.

Knowing the men to be from Shaka, meanwhile, the Induna simply assumes he's been chosen to stand next to Sigujana because he's clearly the least affected by last night's depredations, and hence the most alert, and therefore the one the king can count on to spirit him away should things turn nasty.

6
A Brother (Of Sorts)

Birdsong and a sense of busyness just beyond the periphery of one's vision. The *zzz-WIK* of the black-bellied korhaan, its neck stretched skyward, the call coming like a cork pulled from a bottle. The sunbird with its red chest, and its black head splattered with yellow pollen. The red-billed wood hoopoe, called inhlekabafazi by the Zulus because it cackles like an old woman. Blue swallows on the wing, their long thin tail feathers like twin contrails. And in the thatch grass, amid the hidden stones and bumps and in and around the bushes and plants, the wily, wilily willy-nilly of ants and cicadas, robber flies, butterflies and sundry scorpions, spiders and millipedes. And the stamp of sandals, the moving shadows, the strange smells and foreign noises cause only a temporary silence, a brief cessation before the whole business of crawling, creeping, scurrying, stalking and dying resumes.

*

Two ridges away to the south, the two men were waiting for them by a grove of trees about midway between the king's retreat and the capital. A few minutes earlier, the scouts Sigujana and Mhlangana had sent out had rejoined the main group, reporting that the men appeared to be alone. The Induna hadn't liked that 'appeared to be' – they should have made sure – but it didn't seem to bother Sigujana, who ordered the party forward.

As the king's entourage drew closer to the trees, the two strangers moved away from the shade. Neither was armed and, like the Zulus, both wore sandals and kilts, although theirs were longer – a fact Sigujana pointed out *sotto voce*, to the accompaniment of much sniggering, for among the People Of The Sky it was only old-timers who wore kilts that length. In addition, the man who moved a few paces ahead of his companion wore a kind of poncho made of overlapping rows of feathers, in layers of red and green, white and black. This prompted Mhlangana to mutter something about an ostrich, but envy sealed Sigujana's lips. He was wearing amashoba around his arms and legs, and had a leopard skin cloak draped across his shoulders as a sign of his status, like the collection of blue crane feathers curving out of his headband, but these adornments seemed diminished by the other man's attire.

Which – the Induna realised somewhat belatedly as the Zulus took up their position, in front of the two men – identified him as a high-ranking official in Dingiswayo's service. Clearly, Sigujana was expected to understand that not only had these men come in Shaka's name, they also had the support of the Mthetwa king.

'Yes, yes,' said the Zulu king, waving aside the feathered man's courtly overtures. 'What do you want?'

Stifled sniggers in the Zulu line from those who, like Sigujana, mistook rudeness for forcefulness.

A head taller than Sigujana, but with sloping shoulders and a big belly that the feathers couldn't hide, the emissary tilted himself forward in a brief looming motion that he clearly intended as a bow. 'Majesty, I am Ngwadi . . .'

'Who?'

'Ngwadi, Majesty, son of Nandi. And this is—'

'Nandi?'

'Yes, Majesty. And this is—'

'Nandi?' murmured Sigujana again, turning to the Induna. 'Where have I heard this name before?'

Before the warrior had a chance to reply, Sigujana had wheeled on Ngwadi once more. 'But where is Dingane? And why have you come here dressed in this Mthetwa plumage?'

Dingane? thought the Induna.

'Dingane?' said a bewildered Ngwadi.

His companion – older, bow-legged, his chest bare except for the scars of one who has seen many battles, and his only adornment the fly-whisk in his left hand – stepped forward and muttered a few words in Ngwadi's ear.

'And who is *this* person?' demanded Sigujana, as Ngwadi murmured 'Ah' in response to his companion's prompting.

'I'm sorry, Majesty—'

'Pay attention to me, not to him, louse.'

'Yes,' interjected Mhlangana, 'this is the Zulu king, therefore do not squander his day!'

'Answer me! Where is my brother?'

'We are here on your brother's behalf, Majesty.'

'Indeed we are,' added Ngwadi's companion, slapping the fly-whisk against his right shoulder.

'Who is *he*?'

'He is Mgobozi, my escort, and one whose counsel your brother values.'

The older man's response to this introduction was a wide grin and a languid flick of his wrist, which caused the zebra hair on his fly-whisk to caress his neck.

'See?' Sigujana told the Induna. 'You have already been supplanted. Didn't take him long, did it? But this is nonsense! One of the Blood should not skulk and cower, while others come in his stead. Where is he?'

Peering past the two men, he called out, 'Dingane! Show yourself, you layabout.'

'Dingane?' asked Ngwadi, while the one called Mgobozi raised his right elbow slightly and sent his left hand across his stomach, so that the whisk could stroke his lower back.

'Yes, fool, and this behaviour is very like my brother. So you tell him, wherever he is hiding . . . you tell him—'

'Majesty, please forgive me for interrupting,' said Ngwadi, as Mgobozi brushed the fly-whisk across his left knee, 'but we are not here on Dingane's behalf. We come here in the name of your brother Shaka.'

7
Old Friends (I)

'He really didn't know?' says Dingane, standing on a cold hillside some ten years later. Elephant-grey mist, lying low in the valleys and ravines. A sky crowned by the disintegrating moon that marks the waning month, Untlolanja giving way to Undasa, the Time of Abundance.

'No, he didn't.'

'Not at all? Didn't have a clue?' He already knows the story, but it never fails to incur the same expressions of disbelief.

'He was like a newly born calf, in the matter.'

'Teetering, about to fall over, and knowing nothing.'

'Not quite, for he thought he knew.'

'Not a calf, then. More a stupid child who sees the fire, but still thinks he can pluck the sweet potato from among the embers. Stupid, stupid child, what was he thinking? Did he really believe Shaka was only a story told to tame naughty children? If he even gave him any thought at all,' he murmurs, as he pulls one of the wildebeest cloaks the Induna has brought with him tighter around his shoulders.

Nodding: 'Which, mock him as we might, is a mistake we all made.'

Glancing at the Induna, Dingane continues: 'I speak of us, his brothers, for we led the pack when it came to mocking Sigujana. But, in the end, we were just as stupid, because we too forgot about Shaka.'

'But did you? We were often together in those days, marching off to war with the Mthetwas, when someone, not realising who you were—'

'Because my father wanted me to suffer.'

'Not quite, old friend.'

'Wanting me to act as his spy? That is a better motive?'

'Well . . .'

'I am reminded of us marching up the hill to meet Ngoza and

his Thembus. Will you now tell me the same thing as you did then: that this is a sign of how I was valued? Trusted?'

'No, I was going to say . . .' The Induna's words tail off.

'What? Don't let me interrupt you.'

The Induna grins. 'I was going to say this was a sign of how much your father valued you.'

'Aiee! All this praise! All this respect! Funny how it always involves me risking my life. But that's my family for you. They have such endearing ways of letting you know how much you mean to them.'

But he has to realise how important it was for Senzangakhona to have someone he could trust – one of his sons, in fact – moving incognito among his most powerful ally's army.

'Think you it was my father? Hai!' Dingane laughs. 'I detect Mduli's hand.'

'If so, he rewarded you handsomely in the end.'

'Yes, his leniency in the matter of my keeping one of my father's concubines happy was some kind of reward.' And who might know what would have happened to Dingane had he not been exiled when Shaka came to claim the crown. Not that Mduli could have foreseen any of that.

But, in the end, the blow was merely delayed, the prince tells himself. Because . . . well, here they sit.

And we were often together in those days, marching off to war with the Mthetwas, when someone, not realising who you were, would speak of the brave Zulu who had become Dingiswayo's favourite. And you reported all you heard to Mduli, because that was one of the things you were ordered to do – find out more about Shaka. The Induna's surprised he hasn't realised it before.

Senzangakhona was already ailing by the time Shaka rose to prominence. Mduli, who knew the whole story, knew the truth, would have wanted to find out what he could even as he worked hard to ensure that the rumours and tales didn't reach the king's ears. That would not have been too difficult, given the state of Senzangakhona's health, and the way he had, like his father before him, left the running of the tribe's day-to-day affairs to

Mduli (and Mnkabayi, of course). And, even after that night Dingiswayo took it upon himself to see father and first-born reunited, it's clear the old king didn't really understand what was going on.

Since Mduli would have had to tell Dingane why he needed to find out more about Shaka, that meant Dingane knew the truth about Shaka long before the other princes.

The Induna straightens up as the full import hits him.

He knew.

Which means . . .

'Mfowethu,' says Dingane. *Brother.* Is he well, not well?

Which means Mnkabayi knew that he knew, too.

Which means that special task she had given the Induna so long ago had another aspect to it.

They were afraid.

He has spoken those last words aloud, without realising it, and Dingane asks, 'Who? Who was afraid?'

They were afraid that if Sigujana's paranoia caused him to move against Dingane, and he failed, then Dingane might choose to ally himself with Shaka, who had the promise Dingiswayo had extracted from Senzangakhona to support any claim he might make regarding the Zulu throne.

But in the end, of course, Shaka fooled them all!

'Mfowethu, old friend, who is afraid?'

'No one. I was just . . .'

'Cha! No one! You always choose your words so wisely. Do you speak of Mnkabayi? And Ndlela, of course? But why should you be surprised?'

Sometimes it seems to him as if they are doomed to live as the moon, and keep going through the same phases, says Dingane. Doesn't seem to bother the moon but, aiee, it can be vexing if you're a mere human being.

'Do we never learn? Even Mnkabayi, wise and cunning as she is, she meddled, then.' Dingane grins. 'With the best intentions, of course. And she has meddled again now. With the best intentions, of course. And what has changed? Nothing! For, see here, Dingane must still run.'

Not that the Induna need worry about him trying to escape now. That would be beneath him, for he is still a prince. Just as he considers it beneath him to come right out with it and ask the Induna about Shaka's health, or why the Induna has been sent to apprehend him.

This is not to say that he can't resort to devious means to find out more about tonight's events, though. As now, when he chuckles and says: 'And now as then, then as now, you could even say we have a king about to vacate the throne.' He wants to add *not so?* but bites back the words, knowing the question he's asking has to remain hidden if he's to have any chance of finding out if Shaka survived the attack.

But, incredibly, the Induna isn't listening to him.

Something Dingane said a few moments earlier has caught his attention.

She meddled then and she has meddled now.

Mnkabayi?

And then as now, now as then, is he being just as naive?

She meddled then – he already knew that – but until now he had assumed he knew what she was up to. Because hadn't she even taken him into her confidence? Hai, but it seems he was only privy to part of her 'meddling'. All he was seeing was his reflection on the surface of the lake. There were deeper layers he couldn't see, not least because of his own reflection, and the way she had used his vanity to secure his loyalty and cooperation.

Cha! Isithutha! Fool! Just think about it. You were a youngster, a loyal friend of her nephew, it is true, but she didn't have to enlist your service in the way she did. All she needed to do was tell you what she wanted from you, and then send you on your way. Instead, she first set out to beguile you, to ensure you wouldn't think to ask any awkward questions. Not then – but later perhaps, if things went wrong.

And now? She is 'meddling' again, and once more he has obeyed her without question.

Go after Dingane. Find your friend, for his own good! What else lay behind that command couched as a request?

Phases of the moon, endless repetition, has he learnt nothing?

Thinking about it, he realises how she's been a permanent fixture at the capital during the past few months. He'd assumed it was due to her concern about the First Fruits, which was exacerbated by the murders, but now he wonders if something else has been going on. 'Meddling' he missed because he was trying to put a stop to the murders, and therefore only too willing to accept her counsel. And Ndlela's help – never forget Ndlela's help. Seeing him that day, blood splattered across his chest, hearing his words again: 'It is over! It has ended!' How had he come to be there?

Could it all be connected? Rubbing his hands over his eyes, hearing the wind stride past them. Hai! If that's the case, he might have the beads, but he can't read the pattern.

Again Dingane asks if he is well, not well.

'Ngisaphila!' says the Induna. *I am well.*

Unlike I who may be dead already, and am just waiting for the blow to fall. The prince's silent musings, which he won't share with his old friend, who may also be his executioner.

Better to talk of other things, for now.

'What was he thinking?' he says again, seeking the comfort of an oft-told tale. 'Why did Sigujana assume that I would be the one who would challenge our father's decision to make him heir?'

The Induna smiles in the darkness. 'Perhaps, for all his faults, he saw in you something the others hadn't. Certainly, of all the princes, it was you he feared.'

'Cha! You flatter me – which, given our current circumstances, really isn't necessary.'

★

And there they sit, two old friends sheltering from the cold, waiting for the dawn, laughing and joking and making small talk and, as at least one of them might put it, generally killing time until the killing time.

8
Sigujana's Retreat

Aiee! And Ngwadi had said: 'Majesty, please forgive me for interrupting, but we are not here on Dingane's behalf. We have come
in the name of your brother Shaka.'

And Sigujana had said: 'Who?'

And Ngwadi had said: 'Shaka, son of Senzangakhona.'

And the arc of Zulus had retreated imperceptibly.

And Ngwadi had said: 'The son of your father. The eldest son.'

And heads turned, eyes straining for a glimpse of Sigujana's reaction. And the Induna tightened his grip on his spear and willed the
warriors to face the front, to stop acting like nervous maidens, and
to keep their eyes on the izilwane.

And Ngwadi had said: 'Your brother – and mine, too, for Shaka
and I share the same mother, Majesty.'

'You and . . .'

'Shaka, yes. It is so, Majesty.' And his brother, that is to say Shaka,
was perplexed.

'Per . . .'

'. . . plexed, indeed. And sorely so, Majesty. And, dare I say it, a
little hurt, Majesty.'

'H-hurt?' Had there now been a brightening in Sigujana's tone?
Did he think Shaka was injured, and he was being summoned to
the Beetle's deathbed? Surely not! (Then again, this *was* Sigujana.)

'But mainly surprised, Majesty.'

'S-surprised?'

The Induna wished he could have intervened, put a stop to this
mocking of his king. Such effrontery, he thought, as he began to
pace up and down the section of perimeter fence he was assigned
to guard. Here were two men outnumbered, and deep in another
tribe's territory, yet unafraid of taunting the tribe's king to the king's
own face!

202

. . . But it wasn't his place to comment. That was not an excuse or a shirking. He was there merely to help his sovereign get away unscathed, if things went wrong, and to have involved himself in their exchange meant lowering his guard, and being less vigilant.

'Surprised?' said Sigujana again, like a bewildered old-timer who'd forgotten the way home and now thought one of his disrespectful daughters-in-law had stolen his hut.

'Surprised,' echoed Ngwadi.

Shaka was indeed surprised.

Surprised, Majesty, that his own people should prove to be so untrustworthy.

Surprised, Majesty, that a Zulu king would break his word.

Surprised it has come to this, having to send emissaries to beg an audience with the new king.

Surprised he has to be the one to put this imbroglio right.

Surprised that this new king should even dare to call himself king.

Majesty. The honorific seemed an afterthought, a sneer.

★

Such effrontery, and then the emissaries had returned with the Zulus to Sigujana's retreat. Where they, too, were assigned a hut.

The Induna glances over to where they now sit in the shade of a tree on the far side of the gathering place. Look at them! Seemingly the only thing of importance to them right now is the food and drink the servants have brought them.

Ngwadi and the other one . . . what's his name? Ngwadi still wearing his feathers, so that he must sit upright on the log, keeping his back straight if he's not to crush them. His companion. The older man, Mgobozi. (*That's* his name!) He is sitting cross-legged beside Ngwadi, now passing his feathered friend a morsel, now filling his own mouth, now reaching for a pot of beer, all the while playing with that fly-whisk.

Which he was only too happy to show off to the Induna, when he showed them to the guest hut.

Does he mean it as a subtle insult to his hosts?

Hai, but where are the flies here?

And doesn't he know how shit brings with it its own flies!

★

And then a short while later, Mduli and the senior counsellors had arrived with a contingent of older, more experienced warriors who wear the isicoco. They were there to reinforce Sigujana's royal bodyguard, explained Mduli. While some of the counsellors posted sentries, Mduli had joined Sigujana in the royal hut.

They're still there and have since been joined by Mnkabayi and Ndlela, who brought a second impi along with them.

'Be on your guard,' Ndlela had whispered to the Induna. Mgobozi and Ngwadi had friends watching them.

The Induna had started: did Ndlela think . . . ?

A grin. 'I do not think, I know. There are more out there.' Ndlela tilted his head in the direction of the fence surrounding the king's retreat. 'Don't look,' he added, squeezing the Induna's elbow, 'for some are doubtless watching us even as we speak.'

Lowering his hand, he chuckled. 'Watching us as we chase our tails! Aiee, this will warm their hearts, and raise their spirits.'

The Induna's gaze roams across the gathering place, over the huts, the palisade beyond. The King's retreat is deserted now that everyone has been given something to do – even the servants lighting cooking fires and collecting weapons are carrying out their duties unobtrusively – but it still seems ragged and unkempt. Many of the huts need new thatch. One that caught fire during a drinking session a few nights ago has yet to be pulled down, as has a storage hut that collapsed due to neglect. The hard-packed dirt of the gathering place needs sweeping, and the remains of last night's bonfires have still to be cleared away – as do the potsherds and torn waterskins scattered about.

This filthy place, Ndlela had called it, disgust infusing his words. The Induna risks what he hopes seems a casual glance over the perimeter fence towards the bushes beyond. How the watchers must have chortled to see the Zulu king and his court behaving in such a dissolute manner.

Tired, thirsty, his shield feeling as heavy as a boulder, he turns his attention back to the royal hut. What are they saying? What are they telling Sigujana? And what will they now decide?

9
That Night

The Zulu king took a deep breath so as to be doubly sure his voice wouldn't tremble, and said, 'Uhm.'

He pressed his palms over his knees, to make sure his hands wouldn't tremble, and said, 'Yes.'

He slipped his lower lip under his upper lip, and wished they'd all go away. All these faces peering at him: some seeming to hover in the light of the torches held by Mhlangana and the counsellors who arrived with Mduli; others thrust forward, eager not to miss a moment of his discomfort. He wished he could banish them by shutting his eyes. And it was hot in this hut, and he also wished he could tear aside the thatch like a wild wind and breathe again.

Instead, he said, 'The way I see it . . .'

And interrupted himself to scream at Mgobozi to stop playing with that fly-whisk; to stop going like *this* and *this* all the time, like a flea-bitten baboon. Would he have the gall to act in such a manner in Dingiswayo's presence?

'But I don't think you'd have the courage to disrespect your own king so, therefore do me the same courtesy. I am, after all, one of your king's most valued allies.'

'This is so, indeed it is so,' said Ngwadi eagerly, as Sigujana accepted a pot of beer from a servant. 'And please accept my . . . please accept *our* most abject apologies. Mgobozi is more used to the field of battle than a king's court.'

Sigujana drank deep and returned the pot to the servant.

'He is uncouth but he has his uses,' continued Ngwadi, still referring to Mgobozi.

'And you? What uses do you have, bird man? Other than giving a king like myself a headache.'

Mduli coughed meaningfully. He was seated to Sigujana's left, with the other counsellors arrayed behind him. Ndlela was sitting next to him, and just to Mgobozi's right. Being a woman, Mnkabayi wasn't present, but a hole had been made in the thatch so that she could listen to the proceedings.

'What is it?' snapped Sigujana, then silenced Mduli with a raised hand before the counsellor could reply. 'Yes, yes, I know we are here to discuss a matter of the utmost importance, but this behaviour,' he says, indicating the whisk in Mgobozi's hand, 'makes me wonder how much these two are willing to discuss.'

Seated to Sigujana's right, Mhlangana grunted his agreement.

'This behaviour,' continued the King, as a nudge from Ngwadi caused Mgobozi to carefully lay the whisk aside, 'tells me they have come here not to discuss but to instruct – to tell us the way things will be.'

'Majesty,' said Ngwadi, 'I assure you—'

'Silence! You have brought this madness here, this sickness, I have suffered since I laid eyes on you, suffered and been made to suffer by the warbling of these greybeards here' – indicating Mduli and the other counsellors who had held sway when Senzangakhona was king – 'and now . . . now it is time for *me* to tell *you* how things will be.'

Murmurs of 'This is so, this is so' from Mhlangana and the men standing behind Sigujana.

'You and Dingiswayo and this savage who claims he is my brother, and my father's first-born . . . who knows, maybe you even have allies in my kraal. You may have plotted and planned, and it may well be that your willingness to negotiate with me is a sham. So be it. I salute you! But here is something that is not a lie, for be careful of assuming you will ever leave my kraal on your hind feet!'

'But, Majesty—'

'Hai, do not misunderstand me. It is not my intention to be belligerent. This is just something I wanted to bring to your attention.'

'And we thank you for doing so, Majesty.'

'Thing nothing of it, feathered one,' said Sigujana, while glancing at Mduli. He wasn't surprised to see the elder fuming. Aiee, it was a wonder you couldn't hear him grinding the few teeth he had left, and you could be sure he'd pressed his hands between the aprons that made up his kilt so he could clench his fists without anyone noticing. And those eyes . . . hai, those eyes would impale you where you sat, if they could. He hadn't followed Mduli's counsel, and now the old man could do nothing to stop him.

(Now that he thinks about it, he can't remember what Mduli – and the others – had advised. Although they kept on at him, he was in a state of shock, and when he nodded and started trying to look as if he saw the wisdom in their words, it was only to get them to shut up. Still, no matter, after a shaky start he now feels he has things in hand.)

Another sip of beer, just to show how little Mduli's chagrin has affected him. Then a sage nod. 'Yes, well, I merely mentioned that because it was something I felt you should know. Do not think I disagree with you.'

'Majesty, I'm not sure I understand,' said Ngwadi.

'Do not think I disagree with you,' continued the king as if the emissary hadn't spoken, 'and this is what I was trying to tell you, before your pet baboon here interrupted me.'

Sigujana nodded.

Ngwadi waited.

Mduli frowned, wanting to throw something at the imbecile, and never mind the consequences.

Even Mhlangana began to grow a little edgy as the silence stretched out. He tried to catch his king's eye without appearing to.

Mgobozi smirked and suddenly appeared very interested in the embers in front of him. He reached for the whisk and pulled it a little further from the ring of stones that formed the fireplace.

'Your Majesty?' said Ngwadi, breaking the silence at last.

'Yes?'

'You were saying?'

'What? Ah, yes, I was saying this. It seems to me you come here as if this matter has already been decided. And you are right, there *is* nothing to discuss.'

A sick man, said Sigujana, an ailing man no longer able to live up to his name, no longer capable, in other words, of 'acting wisely', is approached by an ally he has served well all these years. This ally, young, strong and healthy, feeds the dying king beer and food, and then demands that he name as his heir a lout of the younger man's choosing!

'You frown, you twist your faces, you and your baboon. *Your* feathers rattle in outrage, *his* arse stings. But is this not what happened?'

There was Senzangakhona, ill, and close to embarking upon the Great Journey, but willing to make this other journey. Dingiswayo had summoned him to a victory celebration and he did not want to insult his ally. Because, after all, the Mthetwa ruler had intimated that the feast was to honour Senzangakhona's contribution to the success of the most recent campaign against Zwide.

'And then what did your king do? Hai, I will not speak of treachery, I will not speak of betrayal, I will not speak of lies, for I would not insult your king this night. That is a treat I intend to set aside until we two can meet face to face. But you cannot deny this is what happened.'

'Aiee, Majesty, two men may say the same thing, and yet by the tone of their voices might be said to contradict each other,' said Ngwadi.

'This is so. Nonetheless, you cannot deny this is what happened, for then you might as well gather up your sleeping mats and be on your way.' Sigujana chuckled. 'Even I do not deny this is what happened.'

'Well, then, Majesty . . .'

'Well, then, brother of my brother, what I *do* say is that it does not matter. For who's to say who my father had already decided would be his heir before dragging himself to Dingiswayo's feast of lies and bombast. He knew he was dying . . . did he not, Mduli?'

He continued, without waiting for the greybeard's nod. 'So that must have been something he had considered. And, who knows, he might have promised one of his wives that Mhlangana or Dingane or even me was to be his heir. He might have even discussed the matter with Mduli, although he's not saying anything. Then what happens? The great, the mighty, the let-us-be-thankful-he-lets-our-men-die-in-his-cause Dingiswayo ambushes the Zulu king and—'

'He did no such thing!' interrupted Mgobozi.

'He might just as well, baboon,' grinned Sigujana, holding up a hand warning Mhlangana and his men to remain calm. 'He might just as well have kicked my father in the teeth, poisoned his beer, thrown him to the hyenas . . . My father who had only ever been loyal to him! But, because insulting my guests is the furthest thing from my mind, let us say Dingiswayo grovelled and wept and pounded his chest and begged my father to acknowledge Shaka as his successor – as that was the only way he was going to rid himself of the loathsome lad and his conniving mother.'

Sigujana scratched his chin. Had he been afraid of his hands shaking, a few moments ago? Had he sat there waiting for them to come, while wanting only to throw himself on his sleeping mat and bawl like a jilted maiden? Oh, yes, it no longer shames him to admit it: their arrival and Mduli's badgering had turned him into a child again; the same fearful, cringing, cowardly child he had once been. He was no longer ashamed, or frightened, though.

They have come to his aid: Zulu and Gumede, Phunga and Mageba, Ndaba and Jama! They are here tonight in this sweltering hut, where his are the only eyes not burning with sweat. Where the leopard cloak that is his badge of office has become his second skin, and he need only leap forward for the claws to click out of his fingers. Where his words fall among the enemy like a shower of assegais.

Which is why the leopard's claws will remain sheathed, for his words are all he needs tonight.

'And let us say, friends . . . let us say it was charity, not befuddlement, that led my father to acquiesce to Dingiswayo's heartfelt plea – the same impulse that will lead a man to fuck an ugly maiden on occasion, when the beer has flowed and he is of a mind to give her a memory she can cherish in her dotage.'

Fine, whatever, says Senzangakhona, wanting only to put a stop to this unseemly beseeching. Shaka shall be my successor.

But what if he had already promised the throne to another son? What would Dingiswayo have done if Shaka had then been made king of the Zulus, and this other son had come forward saying *Wait a moment*, and bringing witnesses with him?

'What would Dingiswayo have done being renowned as a just and fair king?' asked Sigujana. Because, if they were going to be honest, this was all about what Dingiswayo wanted, and his beloved mentor would have to accede to his wishes. 'Which would have been what, do you think – had it been me or Dingane sitting where you are?'

'But you knew of this promise, did you not?' said Ngwadi, addressing Mduli.

A reluctant nod.

'And had Senzangakhona KaJama promised his throne to anyone else?'

'Hai!' interjected Sigujana. 'We are not Maputos! The Zulu throne is not something to be bartered back and forth! Do not forget where you are!'

Ngwadi bowed his head. 'My apologies, Majesty.'

'And do you forget the way kings are? They are always promising the throne to this son, then to that brat, as soon as one of them annoys them.' Sigujana grinned. Hai, perhaps he's contradicting himself now. Perhaps the Zulus are very like the Maputos when it comes to passing the throne around – or at least the promise of the succession. But, if so, they are not alone, and it is not for izilwane to draw attention to this shortcoming.

Even Dingiswayo had experience of the fickleness of fathers, when it came to who would rule in their stead. For he himself was the heir until his brothers saw to it that their father disowned him.

'And the older they get, the more likely they are to change their minds,' added Sigujana. 'This is why the life of a prince is not as happy and carefree as some seem to think.'

Time for more beer now, but what's this? His guests aren't drinking – not thirsty, eh? Well, that's to be expected, since he's done most of the talking. Not that you have to be thirsty to appreciate Zulu beer.

'But Dingiswayo and his pet doubtless are awaiting our decision with much anticipation. So let's not have to light new torches tonight. These will suffice, because it's really very simple. You say my father promised Dingiswayo that he would acknowledge Shaka as his heir. I say, so what? My father changed his mind shortly thereafter, just as he did on numerous occasions before.'

A glance at Ngwadi. A glance at Mgobozi, but held a little longer. 'My father changed his mind, as was his wont – and also his right. He changed his mind, so I am king, and that's all there is to it. If this is gruel to your Mthetwa gullets, so be it!'

10
Afterwards

Mnkabayi steps away from the hole in the thatch, her eyebrows raised.

'What's wrong, Ma?' asks the servant with her. Senzangakhona's sister shakes her head, feeling too stunned to speak.

Inside, Mhlangana and his men rise to their feet like sleepwalkers. No one will ever accuse them of being perspicacious but, for now, they're just as affected by Sigujana's aplomb. There are no jibes, and none seek to bolster the king's words with invective of their own devising. He has but to raise his hand – the languid gesture of a sated man – for them to begin to herd the visiting savages out of the hut. And they do so in silence, without even a threatening glare or any accidentally-on-purpose jostling.

Tarrying after Ngwadi and Mgobozi have left, with their escort, even Mduli finds himself speechless. And, groping for some criticism or something to condemn or disparage, the cantankerous councillor realises there's nothing for him to say. He'd suggested Sigujana put aside the prospect of Shaka and remember that these emissaries were also from Dingiswayo. He'd pointed out how a man's mentor was also his captor. Shaka might have earned the right to be treated as one of Dingiswayo's favourites, through his acts of bravery, but once accepted as thus he was also trapped. Having caught the king's eye he could only retain his status by becoming the king's creature, thus putting his mentor's needs first. 'Remember this,' Mduli had urged, 'and then treat these savages as if they are merely envoys sent from Dingiswayo.' That is to say: listen, hear them out, be cautious and courteous, then send them on their way with the promise that you will consider the claims they have laid before you.

That was, Mduli believed, the only course of action likely to show the young king in a good light. Acting as his chamberlain, Mduli would have presided over the proceedings, and thus Sigujana would have had little chance to display his immaturity – or fear. (Yes, he had noticed how scared the boy was, and it had been hard for Mduli not to rebuke him, warn him that he was in danger of shaming the House of Zulu. But that would have only made matters worse.) All the king had to do was keep quiet, and nod when appropriate. And, with Ngwadi and Mgobozi sent back to Dingiswayo, Mduli and the other elders would have been given a little more time to consider their options before approaching Dingiswayo himself. There had to be a way of persuading him that the People Of The Sky would be even more valuable allies under Sigujana. After all, protégés have a habit of turning their backs on their mentors once they get what they want, because isn't that precisely when they realise how like servitude this patronage can be?

Mduli had even allowed Sigujana to think it would be that simple: meeting Dingiswayo face to face and reminding him how easily a favourite might rebel once he had a taste of power. Therefore rule in their favour here, and the bonds between the two tribes would be strengthened. It might have worked, but Sigujana had chosen to follow his own path. And Mduli knows he should be angry with the callow fool, but he can't be, because the path Sigujana chose shows him to be anything but a callow fool. He has stood up to Dingiswayo tonight. Suddenly, without any warning, he has acted like a true Zulu king. Mduli's plan might have worked, but it also involved the swallowing of pride, the tacit acknowledgement that it was acceptable for Dingiswayo to meddle in the Sky People's affairs. Mduli had realised that, of course, but what else could he do with a drunkard on the Zulu throne?

Tonight, though, Sigujana had raised his chin. Tonight the Blood had spoken. And see how stunned Ngwadi and Mgobozi were. Their plan had collapsed on them like a poorly made hut, so their only recourse had been to slink away into the night. Mduli suspects they would have liked to leave the king's presence with the air of reasonable men whose attempts to please and appease had been rebuffed, and now the other party must suffer the consequences, but such superciliousness had been beyond them. And Mduli has only to glance at Ndlela to see he's thinking much the same thing, in fact is as impressed and surprised as the greybeard himself. There will be consequences, have no doubt about that: messy, dire, dangerous consequences. For as a child, Shaka was known for his tantrums whenever he didn't get his way. More importantly, there's Dingiswayo's response to consider. (However, who's to say Mduli's original plan might not still work? Choose someone with the right skills – Ndlela springs to mind – and delay the departure of Ngwadi and Mgobozi, so that the induna and his escort reach the Mthetwa capital first, where Ndlela will explain to Dingiswayo the advantages of leaving Sigujana on the Zulu throne.)

But when Mduli, Ndlela and Mnkabayi come together a few minutes later to discuss what has transpired and make plans for the immediate future, they are like three tired travellers who have been heading into a gale the whole day. They can merely shake their heads in wonder and, after some desultory conversation, the only thing they have decided is that Ndlela should warn the guard command-ers to ensure their men are especially vigilant; to watch all the approaches to the homestead and make sure the Mthetwa emissaries don't slip away.

Then they repair to their sleeping mats where, of course, their tiredness will be dispelled by thoughts too restless to be disciplined by the shutting of eyes.

Only Shaka is of a mind to make a noise, to whoop with joy and punch Sigujana's shoulder and tell his brother he didn't know he had it in him. Tell him how proud he is of him. How it doesn't matter how short his reign was – he can take his place among the other Zulu kings with squared shoulders and a straight back.

Sigujana's finest hour . . . what a pity it's also one of his last.

11
Kings Out Of Time

But he doesn't want to be here!

Still, a revelation of sorts.

Time moves differently for a king wearing the Imithi Emnyama. There's an overlapping, a slow-motion speeding up, sluggish minutes as wide as the mighty Thukela, and hours banished with a blink. And when he steps from the shadows on the opposite side of the hut, it's as if he sets off a displacement that bow-waves across to the others, forcing them out of the indlu. A blur of movement that catches itself and stops, whenever he looks that way, pays attention. There's Mhlangana with his blank face – there's an emptiness inside that one that's disturbing – but the fact that he's lost his sneer shows that Sigujana has surprised even him. And there's Mduli suddenly looking his age, while Ndlela manages to appear a little more composed, but only just.

And, of course, there's Ngwadi. And Mgobozi.

Shaka grins. When they reported to him what happened here, they downplayed this encounter. Doubtless they reassured themselves

214

that other events had rendered this meeting a mere side show, and scarcely worth mentioning, but the truth was that they had both been bested by a Zulu king.

Shaka turns back to Sigujana. Fires flare and subside, as time leaps forward . . . and Sigujana lies on his sleeping mat.

I never knew, Mfowethu.

Shaka moves closer, would reach out and calm his sleeping brother if he could. For Sigujana sleeps in an anthill tonight, his breathing shallow, his arms and legs twitching and jerking, his head rolling from side to side.

I never knew, and so I have betrayed you these many seasons, these many moons.

Ants scurry to and fro beneath Sigujana's eyelids, becoming whimpers as they finally escape out of his lips.

I have betrayed you by adding my voice to the many calumnies uttered against you, speaking of you with disdain when in truth you proved yourself worthy of my ministrations, and the energy we expended, when many said a child leaping out from behind a bush could have scared you into submission.

Yes, the Night Medicine has brought him here, to show him something he surely needs to see . . .

. . . but why now?

He has brought them to him. He has separated them. He has even visited their kraal, beating a path for the muthi, should it require him to go there. But even with them right here . . .

. . . not *here*, of course, but beyond the walls of his hut of seclusion at KwaBulawayo . . .

. . . even with them in his capital he cannot seem to reach them!

Are these White Men protected by some kind of spell?

But they don't think that way – Fynn has told him so!

And if Fynn is lying and there *is* some kind of spell he would feel it as a barrier, or if the izilwane sangoma was more skilled, he would feel a subtle but insistent pushing away that many a Night Muthi man less experienced than himself wouldn't even notice.

What is going on?

215

Why can't he get to them?

However, he also knows frustration is a slope that will see him crashing back into his own hut, so best then to keep moving.

One last glance at his brother. What happened will happen soon and he'd better not be here, because that will be as bad as having been here (and he wasn't, of course, since that would have cast further doubts on the legitimacy of his claim, for one heir cannot be seen to be directly involved in the death of another). Then he backs away, passing through the thatch as though it's a waterfall.

Turning, he catches sight of the Induna.

Another grin. *You saw me.*

Someone was sent to relieve him, shortly after the meeting in the royal hut broke up, but the Induna hasn't yet returned to his quarters. Instead he leans against a nearby storage hut, close to his king, and dozing. His shield lies face-down next to him; his spear is resting across his lap.

You saw me — which was surprising because, as far as I know, you're not dead — but obviously you'll forget the incident, because you have never mentioned it to me.

The Induna's head jerks up, and Shaka quickly steps behind a hut.

Blearily the Induna looks around, and Shaka shuts his eyes and presses his knuckles into his eye sockets, and pulls his fists down his cheeks, stretching the skin taut, smearing red into black as he realises he's back in the hut of his seclusion.

And there's a scream . . .

A scream and a thrashing about, as the king the King left behind reaches the end of his own time.

Launching himself to his feet, clutching his spear but leaving his shield behind, the Induna is first into the hut.

Sigujana rises up, as though to greet the Induna, then drops back on to his sleeping mat, his fingers clawing the air.

Movement, and voices outside, but the Induna daren't turn around, and he refuses to be distracted. Instead he watches Sigujana closely

216

as if the two of them are involved in a duel, each waiting for the other to let down his guard.

He watches as Sigujana raises his head.

Watches as the king howls like a wounded dog.

Watches as the king howls, then points in the direction of his own feet.

The Induna moves forward, his eyes scanning the hardpacked dirt beyond the king's sleeping mat.

A shiver of movement, a sliver of darkness.

And Sigujana howls again as a spasm tosses him on to his back.

And now Ndlela is in the hut, too, pushing through the sentries who hover around the entrance but are too scared to cross the threshold.

He sees the Induna kick a pot out of the way, but knows enough not to say anything. Instead he turns his attention to the king. Sigujana writhes in agony, his skin wet mud, his lips foam, his limbs no longer his to control. Ndlela glances back at the Induna; sees him reach for a rolled-up sleeping mat leaning against the thatch, and pull it aside.

And, as he pulls it aside with his right hand, the Induna brings his spear into play. But, when he raises his left shoulder and extends his arm in a downward thrust, the warrior realises he's got it wrong.

Stupid, stupid, to be wielding his assegai in such an awkward fashion – underarm and then, as his elbow locks, relying on his wrist to angle the blade even further downwards. And he pulls back just in time to save himself time: precious seconds he would have wasted trying to recover his balance or to pull his blade free from the floor; precious seconds during which he would have lost sight of his quarry.

That's something you don't want to do, because this one has a habit of turning and attacking. It will rear up and launch itself a metre high.

Think! Put aside your fear! You're aiming at a crack in the night, at a slender stream of piss, at a slithering nothingness. Think!

Ndlela turns and ducks out of the hut, calls the other senior indunas to join him. They are to make sure the men return to their posts, for an attack might be imminent. One of the officers from Ndlela's own regiment pushes his way through to him. As soon as Ndlela had heard the screams, he sent this man to make sure Ngwadi and Mgobozi were in their hut and to double the contingent guarding them. Now the same officer reports that the emissaries are where they're meant to be, and Ndlela's instructions have been followed.

'Good!' says Ndlela. 'Now get back there and tell those two that I proffer my apologies, but they are to remain in their hut until further notice. Tell them I said it's for their own safety.'

'It will be done, Master.' The man gazes past the Induna. He swallows, takes a breath. 'Master, the king . . . ?'

'Go! Be gone!'

The Induna wrenches another pot out of the way and pounces. A downward movement; his knees hit the ground first, then his right palm, fingers splayed. Wielded like a knife in his left fist, his spear is raised, then strikes true.

And strikes again, as the snake squirms and twists, like Sigujana on his mat. It twists and turns, its head flaring and flattening, for this one is like a cobra in that regard.

The Induna brings his blade down yet again. And again. And one more time.

Then, keeping his hand as high up the haft as possible, he gingerly raises the spear and steps into the light, so that Ndlela can see how he's caught the cause of the king's suffering.

The snake's dorsal scales are the colour of an assegai blade, and its belly is a pale grey. It's the reptile's mouth – as tenebrous as the moonless night and the dark day thereafter that the Zulus dread – which gives the creature its name: black mamba.

12
Old Friends (II)

He remembers confusion, panic, fear. And a rushing to and fro. The sense of things happening simultaneously, time compressed, cause and effect mixed together like milk and porridge, but a poisonous porridge. People fleeing the flames, yet engulfed at the same time. But he also remembers how wiser minds remained calm, ensured that the homestead was encircled by spears; men facing the darkness beyond but also holding back the terror behind them.

Ndlela had him wait, with the snake draped over the blade of his spear, while two of the elders hacked away a portion of thatch at the rear of the hut. The Induna then passed the snake through the hole, twisted the assegai, and let the creature drop on to the small ihawu shield held ready by Ndlela. For there was a chance the mamba was an umhlangwe – a familiar employed by a wizard, an umthakathi. If so, it would have returned to continue its attack, if carried out through the hut's doorway, even though its body was split into two where the Induna's blade had sliced it.

Ndlela carried the shield round to the front of the hut and carefully placed it on the ground. Then he ordered four of his best warriors to equip themselves with torches and spears, and to guard the shield lest the umthakathi tried to retrieve the snake and use it in a ritual that would see the whole tribe cursed. Ndlela also hoped to let a Zulu sangoma examine the reptile the following morning. The shaman would look for signs that the mamba had been doctored, smeared with insila – dirt stolen from the king – and other substances, and so confirm that it was an umhlangwe.

The Induna smiles in the darkness as the wind stalks the slopes beneath their hideaway, making the grass rustle like rain. That was the one thing of which there was no doubt: it had not been an accident. The snake had been sent by a wizard – or somehow introduced by the Mthetwa emissaries. It was even possible that one of them was the wizard.

And, while Ndlela was seeing to the dead snake, Mduli had been dealing with Sigujana. The king had started vomiting. Every time he took a breath it was as if he had been stabbed, and he seemed shrunken by the pain and the flailing – although every now and then an especially harsh spasm would cause him to stretch out and twist and claw the air.

Where was the king's inyanga?

After Mduli's voice became a bellow, it was Mhlangana who admitted the inyanga was dead. A few weeks previously, Sigujana had wanted to see that if one drank until one vomited, the amount one vomited would be the same as the amount of beer one had drunk. He had chosen the inyanga – who had annoyed him for a reason Mhlangana could no longer remember – to do the drinking and the puking. Unfortunately, the inyanga had passed out between the drinking and the puking; immediately losing interest, the king and his cronies found something else to occupy themselves. When they later remembered the inyanga, he was dead, lying on his back with his mouth full of vomit.

There was little an inyanga could have done, anyway. Moving fast, striking multiple times before its prey can react, a black mamba can bring down a buck. Just one bite contains enough poison to kill fifteen men, and Mduli and two of the other elders could only try to make Sigujana's passing a little less painless.

The Induna, meanwhile, had been sent by Ndlela to keep Mnkabayi informed of developments. She had remained in her hut, with guards posted outside. Unlike tonight, she'd been quiet and ruminative. She listened to the Induna's report and nodded, and then it had been as if he wasn't there. Although, when he had at last asked permission to leave, she had told him to stay a little longer. 'Ndlela knows where you are, and he will send for you if he needs you,' she said, before looking inward again, like a wayfarer contemplating the embers of a campfire – although this was a fire only she could see.

Unlike tonight . . . when she had known what to do. When she had taken charge – the Induna glances at Dingane, who seems to have dozed off beneath his wildebeest cloak – when she had told the Induna not to follow his udibi, who had seen the assassin, but to go and find Dingane instead.

'Make sure your waterskin is full and take an extra cloak,' she'd added. At the time, wanting to be with the boy who was no longer a boy, the Induna had been annoyed, thinking that such a womanly thing for her to say. But Mnkabayi had clearly suspected that finding Dingane would take the Induna some way from the capital.

What is going on back there?

Does Shaka now writhe like Sigujana did? The Induna stifles a shudder, still remembering how the pain had pulled Sigujana's skin tight around his skull. As if death's decay was already beginning.

But Shaka has Fynn . . . Fynn and his special muthi: izilwane muthi but effective, for all that. Remember the old woman? Assigned to watch over Fynn when the White Man had first been summoned to KwaBulawayo, as part bodyguard, part jailer, the Induna had witnessed how Fynn had opened a large wooden box that one of his half-breeds carried, and then healed a sick old woman at a village where they'd stopped to rest.

Shaka had scratched his head on hearing that. He allowed that he was impressed, but he couldn't understand why the White Man should waste his muthi on one who was so close to making the Great Journey anyway.

Of course, he saw things differently once Nandi fell ill – and Fynn was the one he sent for. Shaka wouldn't let any of the Zulu inyangas touch his mother . . . But that is not a time the Induna wishes to dwell on. Nandi's death was very like a mamba bite, one that left the nation howling like Sigujana did, Shaka's pain being the venom pumping through its veins.

Aiee, and no matter how much you and your family suffered, you were always coming across those who had lost even more. Like Mbopa.

The Induna turns his head to gaze out at the sky, as if turning away is enough to rid oneself of such thoughts.

But Mbopa – where is he? *What is* he *doing tonight?*

He remembers how, at the height of Shaka's depredations, the prime minister had suggested that the Induna return to his home kraal. Driven insane by Nandi's death, Shaka was of a mind to condemn everyone around him, even his most loyal servants. He was seeing plots and disobedience everywhere, explained Mbopa, and even when he recovered, those he had accused would be forever untrustworthy in his eyes. It was better, then, that the Induna absent himself. 'You who have served our Father so valiantly, I would not see you being so tainted,' said Mbopa. 'For the time will come when our Father will need trustworthy men – men whose loyalty is beyond reproach – and I would rather you become one of those he turns to.'

Is Mnkabayi doing the same thing now? Is she simply trying to protect him?

Cha! He should be on the trail of the assassin, and ready to restrain the other hunters, for the man must be questioned before he is executed.

Is *that* why he's been sent away? So the assassin can be killed before he's made to talk? Another thought he wants to avoid, because that means Mnkabayi is . . .

Dingane stirs and yawns, catches sight of the Induna watching him and laughs. 'I was asleep,' he says.

'This is so,' says the Induna.

'Some things never change.'

'This is so.'

'When we marched together to fight Dingiswayo's wars for him, you would always shake your head and say you couldn't understand how I could manage to sleep even if we were sitting on our shields, facing Zwide's jackals.'

'Especially then.'

'And what would I then tell you?'

'What else was there for you to do, and it wasn't as if you were going to be left behind.'

'No,' grins Dingane, 'more's the pity.'

'I thought your sleeping was a very princely thing to do, for it helped the men stay calm.'

'Yet it irritated you.'

222

The Induna chuckles. 'That was my envy baring its teeth, for I wished I could fall asleep as easily.'

'And under such circumstances?'

The Induna nods, in his mind seeing Mnkabayi again, hearing her tell him to go and find Dingane, then get him out of the way. It would be good to shut his eyes and escape these thoughts, if only for a little while.

'Well, as you said, it's a princely thing, you might say a knack vouchsafed to us princely things,' says Dingane.

The wildebeest cloak rises and falls as he shrugs. 'And here we sit,' he says, 'and it is as if we are in the ranks again.'

'Drawn up,' murmurs the Induna.

'Yes, and waiting.'

Waiting for the enemy, knowing dawn will be his herald, the sign the swallow-tailed axes have been waiting for, when they will rise up into the air, straining to break free from the generals who hold them, and pulling the Zulu Bull to its feet . . .

Knowing there is nothing to do, and nothing that can be done, until then.

'And, because it is as if we are sitting here awaiting the call to arms, and some things never change, I sleep,' says Dingane.

13
The Umhlangwe

Ndlela led the Induna to the rear of an empty hut, where Mnkabayi was sitting on a tree stump. It was early the following morning and she had positioned herself there, with two of her servants, so she could overhear what was being discussed by the elders and officers only a few paces away.

She didn't have to strain her ears either, for the men were agitated and unsettled. Before Ndlela and the Induna arrived, they had been discussing whether a Smelling Out was called for, and which sangoma might carry it out – and the thunderclouds began darkening

223

Mnkabayi's visage, for at this time, in 1815 or thereabouts, the nation's most influential sangomas were The Lion and Nobela. And, because they were the most influential, with Nobela preferring to let the Lion garner the reputation while she herself gathered power, Mnkabayi loathed them the more.

Now the men were mired in irrelevancies, such as adumbrating Sigujana's profligate ways, as if these had led to this.

'Go and tell them to keep their voices down,' she told Ndlela. 'Tell them they make our guests grin and our own men look off towards the hills.'

Turning her attention to the Induna, she asked him if he felt rested. Feeling his cheeks grow warm, the Induna stammered an apology. He had waited for her to dismiss him last night, but she hadn't, and he hadn't meant to fall asleep inside her hut . . .

'Nonsense,' said Mnkabayi. 'It was a mere morsel of rest, I know, but better than nothing. We all need to be as alert as possible today.'

The Induna bowed his head.

'Now,' said Mnkabayi, 'Ndlela says you have something to say to me – and a request to make.'

The Induna nodded. Perhaps she was right about sleep being a muthi that revives, refreshes and sharpens, because something had bloomed in his mind while his eyes were shut. The snake had been real: that's what he had realised on waking up.

It was no phantom that had slithered out of the spirit world. It was no shade called upon to kill for an umthakathi. It had been used as a weapon, and was thus as real as a spear or iwisa. And, if it was real, it had to have been deliberately introduced into Sigujana's hut in some way.

The Induna swallowed, then proceeded to ask Mnkabayi's permission to examine the royal hut.

There were numerous reasons why she might refuse to grant this request. For one, although Sigujana's body had been removed, his possessions still remained. These would be sorted through by his servants, under the watchful eye of an elder such as Mduli. A few items would be buried with the king, but most would be destroyed, crushed, obliterated, burnt, and their remains hidden lest they be used by sorcerers to attack the entire tribe. Therefore it would not do for someone to be left in the hut unattended, before this sorting has occurred.

Then there was the matter of the dead man's umkhokha, which would be seeking vengeance.

And this one, this young man before her, the one who she must strive to keep at arm's length, no matter how much it pains her – she would hate to see him placed in such jeopardy. Yes, yes, he is a warrior, a soldier, and she aches until she hears of his safe return, the pain intensifying then because she can't seek him out, or see for herself that he has escaped major injury. On the battlefield he has his prowess to aid him, but when it comes to an enraged umkhokha, a spear and shield are useless.

But this one, this young man before her, pondered a moment, his brow furrowed, then – hesitantly and with due deference – asked if he might speak. Mnkabayi nodded, her eyes never leaving the Induna's face, even when his shyness caused him to look away.

He's going to be searching for the spoor of Sigujana's killer, he insisted, so might not the king's umkhokha be restrained, held in abeyance, because he is after all seeking to appease it?

Mnkabayi conceded that he had a point. And they listened a moment to one of the greybeards gathered in front of the hut wanting to know when they were going to discuss the king's funeral arrangements, because there's the matter of protocol, of assigning guest huts to the village heads and clan chiefs who will come to pay their respects (although the king will have been buried long before then) – and have messengers yet been sent to the tribes currently on friendly terms with the Zulus?

Mnkabayi frowned at this. She knew she shouldn't be surprised, but she still couldn't believe what she was hearing.

'Very well,' she said, turning to the Induna. At least here was someone with a definite plan of action. 'You may examine the royal hut, but stay on your guard.'

225

14
The Royal Hut

The royal hut's entrance – the ikotamo, or door-arch – was slightly larger than normal because this was a king's dwelling (and would be considered as such until after the funeral, whereupon the indlu will be collapsed – not pulled down but made to fall inward). In other words, there was an opening right there that a tubby baby rhino could fit through, never mind a snake. But a Zulu hut also had a door of sorts. Inside the indlu, a stout upright post is planted on either side of the ikotamo. A square wickerwork screen is slid between the thatch and the poles to cover the doorway at night. The gaps between the intertwined leaves allow some light through, so the isivalo can also be used on windy days without having the interior too gloomy. When the entire family is away from home, the wicker door is put in position and held fast by a wooden bar thrust crosswise through a series of loops, one in the centre of the isivalo and one on either side of the door arch, as a sign that the family is away, and might be for some time.

Here too there were cracks and gaps that a snake could easily use. But the king's hut was permanently guarded, with the sentries even more vigilant last night. A snake would have been one of the dangers they knew to watch out for.

Straightening up, turning away from the hut's entrance, the Induna looked over to where the councillors stood, a throng of senior indunas, also isifunda, who act as judges in outlying districts, and izilomo, men of influence at court . . .

'. . . what is to be done? What are the precedents? Are there any precedents?' The question is aimed at Mduli, who in turn defers to the oldest councillor present. Talking in a slur that a great-grandson has to 'translate', he says he can remember no other situation quite like this one.

'But what are we talking about exactly?' asks a senior induna in Mduli's service.

'What does he mean?' responds a greybeard. The elder is an isifunda *who from time to time manages to pluck up the courage to dispute Mduli's decisions, and his present tone suggests that the induna's question was a waste of breath. How can anyone not know the trouble they're in?*

At a nod from Mduli, his man explains himself. 'We speak about precedents, but precedents for what?'

'For what?' asks the isifunda, with disdainful disbelief. He spreads his hands. 'For this!'

'What Nqoboka means,' interjects Mduli, 'is we need to know what this is! We need to know the nature of the beast we are dealing with!'

'Beast,' sneers Mhlangana. 'He is a Beetle.'

Instead of the laughter he was expecting, a glare from Mduli is the only response he gets. And now one of the councillors is saying this is why they should be waiting for the sangomas. They need to be guided by the bones here; the bones will help them see beyond . . .

The Induna circled the hut. It was newly built, with the thatch still tight. In three places he found what appeared to be holes. Two were at ground level, the third a hand's width above the hard-packed dirt. However, when he inserted his spear haft, it did not penetrate all the way through in two of those holes. With the remaining opening, one of those at ground level, he was able to push his spear haft deeper until, with a modicum of exertion, he could force it through to the other side.

He's seen a dog kick dirt over its mess, and often, as a herdboy in the veld, he has watched as a titihoye, or plover, tricked a predator by feigning a broken wing and running away from the nest where her young were hidden, screaming 'Tit-tit-titihoye, titihoye, abantwana bami bathathwa nguwe' (*Tit-titihoye, titihoye, dare you deprive me of my children!*). Could a mamba be as devious? Of course! But a dog uses its hind legs to cover its mess, so how exactly would a snake be able to hide its point of entry, even if it was a wizard's familiar fortified with muthi and then sent forth to kill on behalf of the umthakathi?

'. . . the bones, the bones, always with the bones, Qumo. And you, Bala,' adds Mduli, fixing on the judge who most often challenges his rulings, 'you who provide refuge to our most beloved and esteemed Nobela, before you

227

scurry back muttering about my disrespect, let me emphasise that I am all for throwing the bones, for this is our way, and their guidance is valuable. But look you to the sky now, Brothers. See how high the sun is.' For whatever reason, the sangomas who specialise in these things have yet to make their appearance.

'Our guests are still there, in their hut,' continues Mduli. 'We cannot detain them much longer without making matters worse by being seen as ill-mannered hosts. And there is Shaka. And there is Dingiswayo. Decisions have to be made now!'

'The battle has commenced,' adds Ndlela, who's been sent around the hut by Mnkabayi with the purpose of joining this cacophony of hisses that passes for the Zulu senate today, and of endeavouring to point them in the right direction . . .

The Induna straightened up and stretched. Who could know how many other similar holes there were in this hut?

Besides, how much will be gained by finding out where exactly the snake got in?

But there was surely one thing he could be certain of . . .

'. . . Ndlela is right,' says Mduli after some of the older councillors have looked around anxiously, as if expecting to see Mthetwa shields and spears come sweeping down the low hills that surround the homestead. 'Strategy governs those who move forward to meet the enemy, and certain objectives have to be seized, but often an induna will find his progress slowed, or be faced by obstacles or circumstances that his generals did not foresee.' And then he must act on his own initiative. To blunder forward blindly or withdraw and wait for guidance from his superiors – both of these paths will lead to destruction. And, in turn, the outcome of the battle might be threatened.

'This is where we now find ourselves, Brothers,' says Mduli. 'We have only our own skills and our own wisdom to rely on.'

There was one thing he could be certain of: the mamba had to have been introduced into the hut last night. And that was precisely when the security measures around the hut had been increased. Someone trying to make a hole in the thatch would have been spotted, as this was no easy task and required time.

The Induna knew this because there had been such a hole and

228

it had taken several minutes of hammering to make, with one man pushing the end of an iwisa into the thatch, and another hitting the stick's rounded head to drive it further in. This was where Mnkabayi had positioned herself in order to listen to the meeting.

But the mamba had to have been introduced sometime last night, for the simple reason that Sigujana would have died earlier had the snake been brought in earlier.

Across the way, Bala is inviting Mduli to share his wisdom with his fellow councillors, because he himself feels very unwise. He hears this talk – aiee, all this talk – and yet no one, not even wise Mduli, will condescend to answer a few simple questions.

'Such as?' asks Mduli, scratching his chin.

'What precisely is going on here?' No, wait, adds Bala, holding up a hand. He will be even more specific: who will tell him what has happened here?

From her place behind the hut, Mnkabayi grins. Every now and then the detested Bala gets the better of his rival, and she wishes she could see Mduli's face.

'What has happened here . . .' says Mduli, repeating Bala's words to allow himself time to think.

But the isifunda won't give him the chance. 'Yes,' he says. 'Men have come from Dingiswayo, claiming that Senzangakhona KaJama promised the throne to Shaka. The king Senzangakhona chose on his deathbed then meets with these men. Then he dies.' Are these things connected? And does it matter?

'Does it matter?' asks Mduli incredulously.

'Well, does it? These men from Dingiswayo, they are merely messengers, and here we are now without an heir. Does the death of our king, Sigujana KaSenzangakhona, render Shaka's claims irrelevant? Sigujana left no heir, and in these cases does not the crown go to the next eldest son of the old king? Who is that?' The final question is rhetorical, sneering.

The opening specially hacked in the rear of the hut meant that the interior of the dwelling was well lit, depending on the position of the sun. The Induna returned to the entrance of the indlu, to retrace his steps of the night before.

Mduli shrugs. 'Matters of succession – these are important, yes, but they will resolve themselves.' Is there not a river to cross before they reach that

place? A raging river, swollen by floodwaters? Bala tries a dismissive grunt,
but a quick glance at the faces around him shows him too many of his
fellow elders understand what Mduli's getting at. Surely the first issue to
be addressed is how far Dingiswayo is willing to go when it comes to inter-
fering in Zulu affairs. His championing of Shaka is one thing, but that he
should resort to − or at least condone − an assassination, when the People
Of The Sky have never ever given him reason to doubt their loyalty . . .
well, what does that say about the future of the Zulu–Mthetwa alliance?

He had kicked in the isivalo last night, and now sees someone
has gathered up the pieces and laid them neatly to the left of the
door. He moves further into the hut, avoiding the space where
Sigujana had lain and screamed and suffered.

He turns, noting the position of the mats, arranged in a U-shape
before the pile of skins that served as Sigujana's throne − and which
he then spread out whenever he went to sleep.

Judging by the way these things are usually done, those seeking
an audience would have been seated directly opposite the king, on
the other side of the fireplace.

And, yes . . . the Induna moves forward . . . there's the fly-whisk
Mgobozi had carried. He had even showed it to the Induna, yesterday afternoon. Weighing it in his hand, the Induna had been struck
by the intricacy of the carving on the handle, its thickness, too, and
the skilful way the plaited zebra and quagga hairs had been worked
into the top of the handle. The Induna frowns. Remembers thinking how surprisingly heavy the whisk had been . . .

'What's this?' Aware of a sudden darkening of the hut's interior,
even as those words are spoken, the Induna turns towards the hole
as Mhlangana inquires, 'What are you doing here?'

The Induna explains how he has been given permission to examine the royal hut.

'Why? What for?'

How to answer those questions? Fortunately, the Induna is saved
from making the effort, by a new commotion outside.

Ngwadi and Mgobozi have been brought forward, to be questioned about last night.

15
Tapetum Lucidum

A familiar feeling. One she has worn so often, it has taken her shape.

(. . . just like, dare she say it, the skins that Nobela wears become and have become her . . .)

Familiar as the grave, where bones have found their notches, their niches, these impedimenta left by the spirit when it embarked on the Great Journey . . .

(. . . left behind . . . discarded . . . ignored . . . familiar feelings of a different kind, which she must strive to leave behind . . . discard . . . ignore . . .)

Familiar.

Listen to them talk, listen to them bicker. They have lost their way.

These men, they have lost their way.

And she can say nothing.

(Let him come . . .)

She must hide here – a pretence, of course, for they all know she is listening in but their pride and their vanity must be indulged – and she can only eavesdrop. She cannot rise up and stride into their midst and tell them what must be done!

(Let him come. If even half of what she's heard about his courage is true, and the nobility they say shines in his eyes, he will be the one who will speak the words she cannot.)

Listen to them!

For once Mduli has got it wrong, showing his age not by cloudy thinking but by letting his stubbornness overrule his better judgement. Why goad the other councillors into seeing this as an act of war on Dingiswayo's part? But better that than admit he is sowing what he reaped all those years ago. His mistake hadn't been in saying that Nandi had a stomach-ache when she claimed to be pregnant; that was simply a stratagem to be expected from one tasked with protecting the reputation of the royal family. His error had been in allowing Senzangakhona to treat Nandi so despicably, once they were married. Because Mduli was his uncle and a respected elder, Senzangakhona would have felt obligated to obey him if Mduli had suggested the young king treat Nandi as he would any wife he had courted and paid lobola for. Instead, the elder had turned a blind eye when Senzangakhona's resentment at having been forced into a marriage saw him raise his hand against both the mother and her son. It was a wife's duty to obey her husband – so she could expect the occasional beating – but it was also possible to go too far. When this happened, it was up to the family elders to protect the wife, either by having a word with the husband or, if this failed to curb his abuse, to send for the woman's father (and uncles and brothers). Nandi's family wanted nothing to do with her – or Shaka – but Mduli could have intervened, in their place, and warned Senzangakhona to restrain himself. Instead he did nothing and when Nandi, realising there was no help coming from that quarter, sought to protect herself and her son, he was one of the first to suggest that the wilful bitch be sent to live with her own people.

Just listen to them!

How dare Dingiswayo interfere in our affairs! Who is he to say who will be king of the Zulus? And now Mduli's the wilful one. In another time, another place, she'd be able to view the man's behaviour with a certain amount of compassion, realising the fear behind his exhortations.

Shaka is coming home – and not as a mere soldier but as a king with the power of life and death over all.

(And let him! Let him come!)

But Mduli's adamant that Ngwadi and Mgobozi had something to do with Sigujana's death, and that they were acting under Dingiswayo's orders, not Shaka's.

'How?' asks Ngwadi, for they were confined to the guest hut, surrounded by sentries.

'We came here in peace and under the protection of one of *your* protectors, Zulu, never forget that,' adds Mgobozi.

It has to be so! There can be only one way out of this predicament — and what does it matter if Shaka planned it?

And it's Shaka's hand she sees here; Mduli is wrong to blame Dingiswayo. Shaka has merely been assured of his mentor's support, everything else has been left up to him.

Mnkabayi turns to one of her servant girls, telling her she must go and fetch the Induna.

And the men continue to bicker, some trying to question the Mthetwas, others arguing among themselves.

So familiar, these feelings of frustration and impatience. And this constant need for subterfuge, always having to take the long way round. But what can she do? Despite her rank, she is a woman. And because she is an ambitious woman . . .

She smiles. That alone makes her different, as being one of a pair of twins made her different, suspect, one to be watched. Maybe Nobela and the other sangomas, who would suck her gall, eat her spleen and gnaw on her heart to gain her powers, are right when they whisper *Witch!*

After all, doesn't she have her familiars?

These feelings, these *familiar* feelings of frustration, impatience, resentment, do they not also protect her as some familiars do? It is true there are bitter moments when they are painful reminders of her predicament, the way she is trapped, enslaved by her body, her cunt a curse, the scar that will never heal. But most of the time they do their job, protecting her by biting at her in the same way that stiff, not-quite-healed muscles and tendons warn one against overexertion.

Hai! See how well this female umthakathi has learnt her craft! Such is her power, the strength of her will, she can use her anger, her frustration, to pull her up, and give her the chance to re-evaluate and regain control of her impis. (Whereas one of these baboons, these men, would allow themselves to be goaded into a duel or confrontation that is likely to see whatever pathetic plans they might have thwarted forever.)

A wizard also has familiars — snakes, owls, wolves, baboons — who help him achieve his ends. And it's not surprising that the umhlangwe favoured by female abathakathi is the impaka, or wild cat. It can do many things for its mistress, such as make livestock ill or collect hair from a sleeping person who the witch wishes to curse. But the part of the story Mnkabayi has always liked is how a witch can use an impaka to spread malice, ruin the reputations of women she has taken a dislike to, make husbands think they are being cuckolded, cause old friends to become bitter enemies.

The way her mother had told it, all a female umthakathi had to do was go to a wedding celebration or beer party, and then set the impaka free when no one was looking. She'd have it hidden under her skirt, and she'd simply rejoin the festivities while the cat scampered about, spreading malice wherever she had sent it.

But her impaka . . . Mnkabayi grins, lowering her face so her attendants don't see this softening of her stern expression. She speaks the words to herself: *My mpaka is always under my skirt . . .*

For that which confines her can also be a powerful weapon.

Men speak of feminine wiles . . . Cha!

When unleashed, its claws unsheathed, full-moon pupils aglow, her impaka rules the night.

★

And yet . . .

And yet there is this one.

She rises as the Induna bows, takes his elbow and leads him away from the assembly, where they are still speculating on how Ngwadi or Mgobozi managed to escape from their hut, elude their guards, elude all the sentries patrolling the kraal, slip past those surrounding the king's hut . . .

'Ma, may I speak?'

Distracted, rehearsing her words, Mnkabayi nods.

'Ma, I think . . . No, I know how . . .'

'. . . how it was done?'

'Yes, Ma.'

'You speak of the snake?'

'Yes, Ma.'

'Good, good, but I say no.'

'Ma?'

Looking around to make sure they are alone, Mnkabayi moves in front of the Induna. 'I say no because, truly, this affair was started before you were even born. So you cannot be expected to know how it was done – or why. Although you will shortly witness the consequences.'

'Ma, I do not understand.'

She is looking down, gnawing her lower lip, ignoring his question. 'But not suffer,' she murmurs. 'You will not suffer, not if the betrayed, the wronged, honours his word to not wrong or betray in turn.'

Her eyes are on the Induna's. 'There will be blood, there will be suffering . . .' Then, as if recognising him for the first time, she draws back a step.

And yet there is this one . . .

Pulling together her thoughts, her resolve, she informs the Induna that he must go and find Dingane.

'But, Ma—' He wants to tell her what he has found, but she waves away his words.

He must go and fetch Dingane. Where once to tarry on the road was in the prince's best interests, he must now be encouraged to make haste.

'It is up to you to see he gets here as quickly as possible,' says Mnkabayi, pressing a finger into the Induna's chest. 'And, even if he is a prince, he will listen to you because he knows you speak with my words.'

The queen smoothes her breast covering. 'But you might have to remind him of this. This thing has come to pass, and when he gets here he is to do as we have discussed.'

Does the Induna understand? When he nods, Mnkabayi asks him to repeat it.

'Good,' she says. 'This is very important. And just as you have been a good friend to my nephew, by curbing some of his wilder instincts, so I expect you to see that he does what is expected of him here, and what he has agreed to do. This is why I'm sending you.'

She regards him a moment. 'I know you feel your place is here – but doing what? Shouting loudly? Waving your spear?'

'But, Ma, I have . . .' Earnest, eager features, desperate to tell her. This one! Harden your heart.

'Go!'

Harden your heart, because this is another way of ensuring his safety.

'This is how you can best serve your people on this dark day! Gather the supplies you'll need, and go. Leave by the gate Ndlela will show you. Go fetch Dingane, and bring him back.' They will have returned to the capital by then, and he is to bring the prince there.

Does he understand?

Crestfallen, confused countenance, but a nod. 'Yes, Ma.'

'Then go!'

★

When unleashed, claws unsheathed, full-moon pupils aglow, her impaka rules the night, and yet . . .

And yet, she thinks, as she watches the Induna move away, there is this one.

This one!

Harden your heart!

For while others must fear you and your impaka, this is one *you* have to fear, the more so because he is unaware of the power he has over you.

16
Old Friends (III)

He was a young man – a warrior and an induna too, but one who some considered too young to hold such a rank – and he had heard the old tales of the heroes who now marched across the sky on stormy nights. He wanted to prove himself in battle and gather together daring deeds, like the cow tails of the amashoba that made a man seem to grow in stature. He should have been livid, enraged, instead he had been too taken aback by Mnkabayi's dismissal. And that's what it amounted to, he told himself, as he gathered together his sleeping mat and extra spears. He was being dismissed, sent off on an errand which could just as easily have been entrusted to another of Mnkabayi's 'favourites'. There was supposed to be a Mthetwa legion out there, getting ready to surround them, and he was being sent away. Was he going to fetch reinforcements? Or appeal for aid to Pakatwayo, chief of the Qwabes? No, he was going to fetch a disgraced prince who, having been cautioned to take his time in returning to EsiKlebeni so as to give Sigujana an opportunity to feel more secure on the throne, had taken this as an opportunity to fornicate his way from there to here. And who . . .

'And so it is,' says Dingane ten years later. 'I boast of my ability to sleep whenever and wherever, and here I sit with my eyes as wide open as an owl's!'

'A bird of ill omen, some say.'

Dingane's shrug says *Look where we are!* 'I think we are past worrying about omens,' he remarks. 'But where were your own thoughts, old friend?'

'I was remembering the last time I was sent to fetch you, and how angry I was.'

'Understandable,' says Dingane, gazing at the sky. There's a lightening now, just the slightest blush of blue that makes the stars seem brighter. 'You expected to die defending Zulu honour. You were like a child denied amasi.'

The Induna chuckles. 'This is true.'

Back then, the nation found itself threatened in a way it had never been before. Heirs had bickered and fought, but never had one who was, to all intents and purposes, an outsider, ever come to claim the throne. Shaka was no invader, no usurper, for he was of the Blood (although there are still those who would dispute that), but he might as well have been an isilwane, for he'd spent most of his life away from the Zulus and could barely even speak their language.

And his coming was presaged by a promise, and an assassination. Similarities?

We have slaughtered those who dared to march against us, we have broken tyrants and dynasties – but once more we face a threat we have never encountered before.

And, because so little is known of the White Men, they have to be seen as a threat, even though they are greatly outnumbered and have mostly obeyed Shaka's edicts.

And they are here . . . and an assassin has moved through the ranks around the King. What was the promise? Who made it? Who accepted? Similarities?

Mnkabayi's involvement – her meddling, as Dingane said earlier – then as now.

Another similarity: he was misled then, so could it be he's been misled now?

There's also a difference, though. Then, when he was sent to fetch Dingane, there was no king. But now he serves Shaka.

★

Plans, plots, conspiracies . . . the lookout, the low, urgent voices. Promises and compromises.

An umfazi, a wife, will cover her breasts with a garment made from buckskin and decorated with beadwork bearing a message only her husband can understand. Dingiswayo affecting a 'reunion' between a father and a loathed elder son was just one arrangement of beads in an intricate pattern. One that was interwoven with other 'meanings' and 'messages' the Mthetwa ruler probably wasn't even aware of.

It's like the silence that slowly smothers all the sounds around you, so it takes you a few paces before you realise that something is wrong. Although, in this instance, those paces have been measured in years, in the phases of the moon, the seasons . . .

Something is wrong . . .

★

How like Sambane, the aardvark, his mind seems tonight, with claws and snout burrowing here, burrowing there . . . And how like ants and termites that Sambane loves are these thoughts he chases in the darkness.

Plots and conspiracies . . . and that silence. Another kind of enigma to decipher: the silence of the stalker, or the ambush waiting up ahead?

Or something else.

Always another possibility.

One of the things he's learnt by serving as Shaka's Shadow, sent around the kingdom to settle disputes, seek out those responsible for breaking Shaka's law: there's always another possibility and it's invariably something you haven't even considered.

As when he met up with Dingane and Mpande, fully expecting to receive complaints and cursing when he delivered Mnkabayi's message to Dingane, the Induna had been surprised at the sense of urgency Dingane had shown. The prince had even helped his younger brother gather together their baggage.

17
The Homecoming

The three reached Senzangakhona's old capital in the late afternoon. Shaka had arrived three days before, they were told, on the day after Mnkabayi had sent the Induna to fetch Dingane. It was proof – not that any was needed – that he had been somewhere close by, awaiting the outcome of the 'negotiations' with Sigujana. He came with the Izicwe legion – the Mthetwa regiment he had joined when his age-set was eligible for call-up – which was proof, if any was needed, that he engaged Dingiswayo's backing. However, in his first address to his people, Shaka had made it clear the Mthetwa ruler had intended the legion only as an escort to protect Shaka and his retinue against marauding Ndwandwes . . .

For he was also the bearer of troubling news: Dingiswayo's spies had told the Wanderer that Zwide was eyeing Zulu territory. And, having heard of this discord over the accession . . .

Exaggerated tales, of course, added Shaka for, in truth, what was there to dispute?

But Zwide swallowed such tales the way he liked to say he swallowed kings, maintained Shaka. Believing civil war was in the offing, he was preparing to test the state of Zulu preparedness with raids made to seem like mere acts of banditry. So said Dingiswayo's spies, reported Shaka. If the Zulu response lacked aggression, or in any way showed signs of a divided, indecisive leadership, there was every possibility that these forays would become an all-out invasion . . .

Which would be inconvenient for Dingiswayo, at this point, because the bulk of his army was dealing with the Thembus.

Indeed, added Shaka, he and Dingiswayo shared the opinion that these two occurrences were not unrelated: the Thembus ignoring the Zulus in order to probe the Mthetwas' northern border, while Zwide proceeded through Zulu territory to attack Dingiswayo's eastern flank.

Aiee, and all of this made possible by a misunderstanding here among the People Of The Sky!

At any rate, then, these men – these five hundred Izicwes – were a guard of honour and potential reinforcements, and their presence was in no way intended to seem threatening, or an insult to the prowess of the Zulu warriors – who Shaka knew were ever willing to give their lives for their king. The officers of the Zulu impis were to remain in their posts, he said. For he needed their help, the nation needed their help, and they all needed the courage of the men they commanded.

(At this point, Ndlela later told Dingane and the Induna, cheers reverberated across EsiKlebeni's cattlefold.)

These brave warriors would be divided into two units, said Shaka. One would guard the perimeter of the capital, night and day, forming a wall of men against any Ndwandwe units who might let their enthusiasm and desire to spill Zulu blood get the better of Zwide's caution . . .

And let them not forget the Thembus! Some of them, fearing
Dingiswayo's legions and believing the Zulus to be easy pickings,
might come this way.

Aiee, said Shaka, momentarily forgetting the faces and shields
and spears arrayed before him, he fully intended to see Zwide eat
his own entrails, but the Thembus could be even more vicious, therefore he would see them destroyed too . . .

(Ndlela who, as one of the tribe's most senior indunas, had been
standing close to Shaka and thus was one of the few to hear these
last words, this aside, had told Mnkabayi and, later, Dingane and the
Induna what Shaka had said. What he didn't tell any of them, not
even his beloved queen, was the tone Shaka's voice had slipped into,
and the strange reaction it had evoked in him. This tall, broad-shouldered young man, who bore the scars of one who had fought in the
van of countless attacks, whose legs were those of one who could
march all day over the roughest terrain, and whose hands and arms
bore the calluses of spear hafts and shield straps, had let his voice fall
into the musings of a rich man, wondering whether to move this
herd or that herd to better pasture first. In other words, these weren't
boasts intended to inspire his men. Had they been, he would surely
have raised his voice, bellowed his intentions aloud. Just as the wealthy
man had his cattle, he now had the power. So these were things he
was going to do, and it was simply a matter of when and where. And,
at that moment, Ndlela had the sense of sand spilling down his spine,
and a singing in his veins. Not a sound but a colour, though. *White.*
White, the colour of the sky. For everything in the sky is white –
white like the inside of Umunka, the Thunder Tree, planted by the
Great Spirit himself. And so like a human, for does this tree not bleed
red sap when its thorns are broken off? White, the colour of lightning and the heavenly herds. White, like the shadows of the shades,
the amathongo. Could it really be? Did this singing, this blaze of light,
mean that Shaka had the blessing of the ancestors? Was he, in fact,
imbued with the power of ezimhlope, the white ones, who stand
against the forces of evil? Despite himself, and his preconceptions,
Ndlela had begun to feel himself drawn toward this man!)

241

Pulling himself away from thoughts of the future, Shaka went on to explain that the other contingent of brave Zulu warriors would be broken up into smaller units, and set to patrolling the surrounding countryside. They would be accompanied by officers from the Izicwe legion, so that these men might gain knowledge of the lie of the land. In addition, Izicwe soldiers would be sent to the far-flung villages, to warn the menfolk there to be on guard against Zwide's raiders, and not to venture too far from their umuzis.

And so it could be seen that their powerful ally had not deserted them, even though his own land was being threatened, said Shaka.

Bayede, Dingiswayo! Bayede!

And spears went up as the men echoed Shaka's praises.

Bayede, Dingiswayo! Bayede!

★

That was how things stood when the Induna brought Dingane back to EsiKlebeni. Senzangakhona's older sons had all been sequestered in the huts at the lower end of the capital, those located on either side of the entrance that led towards the great cattlefold in the centre of the settlement.

The princes weren't prisoners, explained Ndlela, amid snorts of derision from Senzangakhona's sons. Shaka, he continued, turning to Dingane, had simply made it known he was aware that it would be a gross breach in etiquette for him to meet his other brothers before he had met Dingane.

'Etiquette?' growled Mhlangana. 'Is there an etiquette for usurpers now?'

'You appreciate the wisdom,' murmured Ndlela, ignoring Mhlangana.

Dingane nodded. It was a smart bit of diplomacy, showing the prince some respect since, after Shaka, he was now the eldest of Senzangakhona's sons.

It annoyed Mhlangana no end, however. He and Dingane had different mothers and, to his everlasting chagrin, he was but a few days younger than the Needy One . . .

Now *there* was a lesson about pride and vanity. For all they knew,

Dingane was going to his death the next day, yet Mhlangana felt slighted! He could scarcely conceal his jealousy, and looked ready to go out and kick his mother to death for allowing him to remain just that little longer in her womb.

★

Hai, but a brother's resentment was as nothing compared to the discomfort the Induna felt the next day.

Dingane had chosen his friend to act as his attendant when he went to meet Shaka. The Induna regarded the chance to serve — and stand by — the prince in this way as an honour. The discomfort only started when it was time to help Dingane get ready for the meeting itself.

With the crowds beginning to gather in the great cattlefold, Dingane stunned his friend by saying that he would don only the isinene and ibeshu that comprised the Zulu kilt. He would not wear any of the regalia or adornments he was entitled to, as a prince. The feathers, the leopard skin, the necklaces and bracelets were all laid out and ready, but Dingane merely turned his back on the aghast expressions of his friend and his servants.

He remained adamant in the face of their pleas and, with Ngwadi hovering impatiently outside, there was no time to send for Ndlela or someone else who might talk some sense into the Needy One.

The Induna accepted the fact that he and Dingane could very well be walking to their deaths that morning. It wasn't the fear that Dingane's bizarre decision might annoy Shaka that unsettled him, for whether they were to live or die had already been decided. The Induna simply thought a prince should be properly dressed even — and especially — if he was about to face his death.

An induna, too, for that matter.

But Dingane had made up his mind, and reluctantly the Induna signalled for one of the terrified servants to help him undo his amashoba.

'No, no,' said Dingane hastily. The Induna was to remain dressed as he was.

★

It was a long, long walk from the huts at the entrance to EsiKlebeni up the slight incline of the cattlefold towards the ibandla tree standing just outside the gate that led to the king's compound. On either side stood the men, women and children of the Zulu nation – or at least those who resided at the capital. And since most of the young males were guarding the perimeter fence, or patrolling the surrounding hills, the men gathered were grandfathers or the middle-aged who had performed their stint of carrying spear and shield for their king. They stood in silence behind a rank of Mthetwa soldiers. Even the capital's sangomas remained quiet, although theirs was a seething, chagrined silence. Instead of being allowed to stand up at the top of the cattlefold, near the king's retinue, they had been consigned to the opposite end, so were among the first onlookers that Dingane and the Induna passed.

A long walk under an azure sky and a stern sun, one that tested the endurance of soldier and civilian alike.

A walk of shame for the Induna, wearing the regalia of his rank while the prince wore so little.

The people were edgy enough, and now this! What was Dingane thinking? Any sympathy they might have felt for the prince's (presumed) fate would hardly be ameliorated by what seemed to be churlish, childish behaviour – and, worse, an act of defiance that might have dire consequences for all.

The Induna found himself recalling what one old-timer had told him the night before. He had been sent to find himself some food, while Ndlela and Dingane conferred, and had joined the greybeard at a nearby cooking fire. After finishing his meal, he offered the man some snuff and asked him how things had been since Shaka's arrival.

'Aiee, so you were on the road?' said the old-timer.

Perplexed at what seemed an evasion of his question, the Induna nodded.

'You were a wayfarer?'

Again the Induna nodded.

'And when wayfarers meet on the road, we greet each other and share a fire and food. Is that not our way?'

'It is,' said the Induna.

'But there is a need to be wary,' added the greybeard.

'This is so.'

Questions were exchanged, and the answers mulled over. You could expect to be asked to recount your clan history as far back as you could remember, and quizzed on where you were coming from and going to, and the places you had been. It was an understandable precaution, a way of ensuring that strangers were who they claimed to be.

'So, on the road, we are welcoming and we are also wary,' said the greybeard, 'and this is how we feel now. Or, rather, this is how I feel – and, see, I have travelled far and wide, have met many wayfarers, shared many campfires, and I have lived to see my sons grow lazy and my daughters-in-law cheeky. But I know many others feel the same way.'

'Wary but welcoming,' murmured the Induna.

The old man nodded and shifted closer. 'You remember how things were when Sigujana ruled?'

'But he was king for such a short time.'

'And see how many weeds sprang up in that time. An infestation!'

The greybeard lowered his voice. 'But this one, this Shaka . . .' A co-conspirator's pause; asking for encouragement to continue, a nod from the Induna provided that spur. 'This Shaka, some say he isn't even Zulu. Isn't even of the Blood.' A quick look around. 'I do not believe such stories, of course.'

'Of course! They are silly stories unlikely to fool even a child.'

'There you have it.'

'But you were saying . . . ?'

The greybeard gripped the Induna's elbow. 'We are wayfarers, welcoming but wary, but already this stranger, this fellow wayfarer, has shared with us something most precious in these trying times – order!'

Already Shaka was restoring an order trampled upon during Sigujana's brief reign – and not a moment too soon! For see where Sigujana's decadence had led them. Wasn't Zwide even now eyeing Zulu cattle and Zulu women?

What would that old-timer be thinking now, wondered the Induna, as they drew closer and closer to Shaka.

And Mnkabayi . . . the night before she had entertained Nandi and now, while the Induna and Dingane walked across a cattlefold as wide as the world to meet Shaka, she was with Pampata and the King's mother. Safely ensconced, in other words, in Shaka's most inner circle. What would she think of the Needy One's display?

A walk in silence, the occasional rustling of the Induna's amashoba producing a stab wound of shame. Why hadn't his friend at least allowed him to tear off his adornments?

It was as if the prince was his prisoner, and he was now delivering him up to Shaka.

18
Brothers

Shaka watches them approach. To his left stands Mgobozi; to his right is a plump, bald man. This individual, Shaka had learnt upon his arrival at EsiKlebeni, was awaiting his execution orders from the king. That there should have been just this one 'miscreant' in custody has told Shaka a lot about Sigujana's approach to law and order. And this man, Shaka was told, was only hunted down because it was claimed that he was a cannibal. Struck by the prisoner's cheerful demeanour, Shaka asked him if the charge was true. The man shrugged his shoulders and allowed that he was a good cook, and that his skill in making anything edible, especially during times of great drought, might have given rise to such rumours. 'Rumours?' had inquired Shaka. 'That I enjoy eating human flesh, Master, but this is not so. Not so at all, for I have a preference for beef.' That Shaka could see, and he grinned, prodding the prisoner's paunch with the rounded head of the iwisa he carried. 'And cooking?' he had asked. 'Cooking?' frowned the portly prisoner.

'Yes, cooking,' said Shaka. He might not enjoy eating it, but what about *cooking* human flesh? 'Ah, but, Sire, that is another charge entirely! I am only accused of eating human flesh.' At this Shaka had burst out laughing and ordered the man to be released. Now Mbopa stands alongside Shaka, to act as an interpreter if needed, Shaka's grasp of Zulu being inadequate to pick up on nuances and ambiguities.

Dingane stops two paces before Shaka. The Induna moves a step forward, tightens his grip on his assegai, so he can be ready to defend his friend.

'Eshé, Mfowethu,' says Dingane.

The Induna sees how Shaka's eyes narrow. 'You greet me as your brother?'

Dingane nods. 'This is so, son of my father.'

'Hai, but there are many who would say you have been misguided and misled – bewitched even.'

'I say they are fools. For who cannot recognise his own brother? Who cannot feel the pull of blood shared?'

'This is so, but there are many who would say you speak these words thinking only to save yourself!'

'I say they are blind.' Dingane spreads his arms. 'For see? Here I am! I have not run and hidden. I was told to come – and here I am.'

'*Told* to come? Who dares order a Zulu prince around?'

You do, thinks the Induna, but Dingane's answer is a little more diplomatic. 'Another Zulu prince,' he says. 'And an older brother.'

'Hai, and again you call me brother!'

'Yes,' says Dingane, 'and this is why I approach you dressed in this manner. This is the way we would have known each other, were our father not so ill-disposed toward you and your mother. This is the way we would have roamed these hills together, as boys.'

Shaka grins and, to the Induna's dismay, not to mention the horror of the King's attendants, he rips off his headpiece.

'And we will yet roam these hills together,' says Shaka, pulling off the slightly longer kilt favoured by Mthetwa men, 'but as men now. And our excursions will take us even further afield, beyond these hills and the next, and let our path be over dead men, and our sustenance their blood.'

Dingane leans back slightly, as if Shaka's words are fingers, their palms pushing intently against the other prince's chest.

He coughs. Yes, well, he himself is more partial to amasi, he says. A form of fermented milk, amasi is regarded as a delicacy among the Zulus and a family treat. It's considered a great honour to be invited to share a family's amasi.

Shaka claps Dingane on the shoulder. 'Why am I not surprised to hear that?' he grins, for amasi is also believed to make men strong, healthy and more desirable to the fairer sex. And the prince himself has a reputation as an isoka, a ladies' man, more charming – and successful – than Sigujana ever was.

'Now, such stories as I have heard about you, I am gleeful . . .'

It's the wrong word. In the Mthetwa dialect it can mean 'pleased', but not in Zulu usage. There's a discreet cough from the portly man to Shaka's right, which manages to convey extreme fear and a brave adherence to the instructions that are partly responsible for that fear. Slowly, his face turned to stone by the interruption, Shaka inclines his head to the right. The portly man rises on tiptoe and whispers into Shaka's ear. Fracture lines extend across Shaka's brow, then he nods. And, sweating profusely, Mbopa lets the soles of his feet take his weight again, and digs his toes into the dirt to retain his balance.

'I am *glad* these stories are true,' says Shaka, as if the interruption hasn't even taken place.

Dingane tilts his head, raises his shoulders, explaining that even here, as loath as he is to malign his reputation in this respect, there are exaggerations . . .

'And allegations,' grins Shaka.

'Aiee, too many!'

'You take after our father in this respect, I think.'

'No!' Dingane shakes his head. 'Never! I would never shun a wife of mine!'

Shaka stares at his brother long and hard, a bull elephant wondering whether he's going to have to lower those big old tusks after all. Dingane is, of course, referring to Nandi and the way his father − their father − treated her, and Shaka's wondering whether this isn't a display of sycophancy too far. One that borders on mockery? On reflection, though, he reckons Dingane is not that stupid; which is to say not so stupid as to think Shaka is so stupid as to swallow such a statement without a certain amount of rumination.

'That is good to hear,' he says at last. 'And you know why I say that.'

Dingane nods.

'And I know, too, how our father made his other sons suffer.'

That is true − aiee, is that true! Never mind himself, as much as he despises Mhlangana, Dingane knows his father's constant beatings must have done something to create the dead-eyed, vindictive jackal his brother has become; and also to turn Mpande into a buffoon. But the prince sees Shaka's observation for what it really is: another test.

And he lowers his head, and says, 'These are the words of a brother, and I thank you, but no hardship can compare with what you and your mother went through.'

That is true but, as the People Of The Sky and their neighbours (including Nandi's home clan) will soon find out, Shaka is going to do his damnedest to try and give a whole lot of lying, spiteful jackals a taste of what he and Nandi endured.

But Dingane's answer has pleased him.

'You call me Brother, Mfowethu − but will you call me King?'

'It is as this one,' says Dingane, indicating Mgobozi, 'and your brother here say,' pointing to Ngwadi who is standing behind Mbopa, 'that our father recognised you as his first-born and named you heir?'

Shaka nods. 'Dingiswayo was there too. We can—'

'No, Brother.' Dingane holds up a hand. 'Because you are my brother, your word is good enough for me.'

249

Ngwadi pushes his way between Shaka and Mbopa. 'Do you acknowledge Shaka's claim?' he asks, displaying that pedantry that will soon see him usurped as one of Shaka's chief advisors.

'My brother has already said so,' says Shaka.

'But we must be sure.'

'Enough!'

A discreet cough and Shaka's glare is then transferred to the portly man. 'There is, anyway, something as important to be acknowledged,' says Mbopa, displaying the acumen – and courage – that will see him become the one to displace Ngwadi.

'What is that?' The bull elephant seems ready to lower his tusks again.

But Mbopa is like a yawning hippo safe in the deep water. He knows that he's about to, if not impress Shaka, then at least plant the thought that he's worth keeping around, the cannibal business notwithstanding.

'It is to do with the manner of the, er, previous incumbent's passing,' he says and *gleefully* notes the *Ah, yes!* flicker across Shaka's features. Clearly this idiot Ngwadi has advised him that it's enough to get Dingane to admit the validity of Shaka's claims, but that's a hut without the thatch.

Ngwadi says he doesn't see what that has to do with anything. And he is told to shut up and step back, as Shaka finally lowers his tusks.

'Yes,' he says, turning back to Dingane, 'that was tragic.'

'And sudden,' says Dingane. This diplomacy is like the summer heat that burns the plains, a man has to escape it every now and then by diving into the nearest river.

'Some would say merciless,' adds Shaka.

A cough. A whisper.

'I mean merciful,' Shaka corrects himself. 'Some would say the suddenness of it was also merciful. It meant he didn't suffer.'

Not for long, adds the Induna to himself, eyeing Mgobozi.

A glance and a nod from Shaka indicate that Mbopa can continue. (It's a good omen as regards his own future, reckons the plump man; but he's not so naive or vain as not to realise it's also a sign that Shaka needs to recover his composure after that slip of the tongue.)

'Do you acknowledge that your brother did not have a hand in your king's sad demise?' Mbopa asks Dingane.

In the way that you occasionally have a hand floating in your cooking pot? Then no. But did he plan this sad demise? Do you think I'm a fool? Of course, he did! Such is the response that flows through Dingane's mind, but it's time to return to the hot, dusty plains of diplomacy.

He turns to Shaka. 'Did you, my Brother, have a hand in Sigujana's death?'

Shaka's response is a solemn shake of the head. 'No, I did not.'

'Then, because you are my brother, your word is good enough for me.'

And the People Of The Sky have a new king.

19
Old Friends (IV)

And he was confused, and he sought out the one person who might have explained it all. And it was as if Mnkabayi understood his confusion, felt his pain, for although there was feasting and celebrations, and she was expected to act as a lady in waiting for Nandi, she made herself easy to find, was willing, even eager, to see him and speak to him.

He had to serve Shaka, because Shaka was his king, she said. He was to forget the nasty stories he'd heard over the years. Shaka was of the House of Zulu and he was Senzangakhona's first-born.

He can still remember how close to tears he had been. He had proof that Sigujana had been murdered. Didn't that mean anything?

'Do you mean to say you have proof Shaka murdered Sigujana?' asked Mnkabayi calmly.

'No, Ma.'

'Then you know our way,' said Mnkabayi.

Brave and young and foolhardy, he had to try again. 'But, Ma, if a man plans a murder, isn't he as guilty as those who strike the actual blows?'

'You know our way,' repeated Mnkabayi. And he was intelligent enough to understand why the law was so – for it allowed kings to sleep a little easier in knowing that an heir who struck the actual blow could not become king.

'I hear you, Ma,' he said.

But what about yesterday? What about Dingane striding across the cattlefold to meet Shaka? How many had assumed he and the Induna would be eating dust before sunset?

Brave and young and foolhardy, he had dared to inform her, and he was mentioning this not because he was angry at being called upon to risk his life alongside his old friend. No, he wanted to know what that said about all this nonsense about heirs and kings not killing each other. Yes, even if Shaka was then able to convince the people he was not killing an heir but a usurper.

'It said what you say it said,' said Mnkabayi, a smile playing across her lips.

'What?' asked the Induna incredulously. 'That it's all nonsense?'

'Just so. But *our* nonsense.'

'Or think of fences,' she said. 'They guide and protect, but they're also often moved and rebuilt. We need them, but we also need to break them down from time to time.'

Although he didn't know it, his next question made Mnkabayi glow with pride: 'Then, Ma, I humbly ask you why we had to break down *this* fence?'

'Because *he* is the one we need. And he is of the Blood, never forget that! He is no usurper. But never forget this either: he is the one we need and you are among those who *he* needs. Young men like you – brave, strong, willing to learn new ways, so full of potential – he needs your loyalty if we are to achieve the greatness that is our due.'

★

252

He had listened to her and he had obeyed, but he still sought out Mgobozi.

It was two days before he was finally able to find the Mthetwa general alone.

He smiled in the face of the older man's irritable reaction, 'Yes, what is it?'

Smiled and held out the fly-whisk.

'I believe this belongs to you.'

Mgobozi stared at him, for what felt like a long while, with a penetrating, appraising stare. Then he turned his attention to the object still lying across the Induna's open palm.

'I believe it does,' he said, but made no attempt to reach for the whisk.

The Induna raised and lowered his palm. 'It seems to lack a little heft now, but I may be mistaken.'

'Maybe.'

'But, other than that, I do believe it has suffered no real damage while out of your possession.'

So saying, the Induna slipped his finger into the opening at the bottom of the hollow handle, which was once blocked by beeswax or some other substance that would melt if the whisk was left close to a fire for long enough. And extended the whisk.

Mgobozi smiled, bowed his head, and took the whisk from the young warrior.

'I think such fripperies are not for me,' he said, examining it.

'Perhaps.'

'I think I need now to turn my attention to Zulu beer, but I will need a guide.'

He received a tight, humourless grin. 'Perhaps another time.'

'Aiee, are all Zulus so equivocal?'

'What of our King?'

'He is anything but, Nduna. Which is doubtless another reason why he is King, and we are left free to drink beer.'

'Still I must decline.'

'This time?'

'This time,' agreed the Induna.

'There will be another.'

'I'm sure there will.'

★

It's Mnkabayi's words that stick in his craw, though. Think of fences, she had said; they guide and protect, but they're also often moved and rebuilt.

And where had *she* been the night before he and Dingane were to meet Shaka? She had been entertaining Nandi. And when he and Dingane had walked to meet Shaka, Mnkabayi was to be seen in company with Nandi and Pampata.

And what about tonight?

Plans, plots, conspiracies. The lookout. The low, urgent voices. Promises and compromises.

Where was Mnkabayi tonight?

Who had she entertained last night? Or whenever it was . . . ?

And he'd reached down through the elephant-grey mist and pulled Dingane up – obeying her orders! – and a short while later the prince had said, 'You have served my brother loyally all these years, but who do you serve tonight?'

It's Mnkabayi who needs to be asked that question.

And what of Dingane? He had come to EsiKlebeni already knowing an arrangement had been made: a form of lobola, with his approval of Shaka being the price for his life. He couldn't be sure that his long-lost brother would honour his side of the bargain, though, so his trepidation had been real . . . But in the end it had all gone according to plan.

But whose plan?

And how much does Dingane know about this matter?

And it's dawn, and they are making their way down the slope. The Induna is walking in front of Dingane, his eyes fixed on the path.

'Nduna,' hisses the prince.

254

He looks up and sees men arrayed in a line across the opposite ridge. From their shields he recognises them as the Iziyendane. That's the regiment made up of Hlubis, men of Xhosa stock who can be counted upon to slaughter Zulus as willingly as they slaughter the King's enemies, if the right person gives them the command.

PART FOUR
Alarums & Excursions

The reorganisation of society on military lines was accompanied by a new ethos . . . A pride almost amounting to arrogance and an indifference to human life were accompanied by a sense of discipline, order and cleanliness which at once attracted the attention of European travellers. At the same time political loyalty was enhanced to a high degree, and came to be regarded as an absolute value.

From *The Zulu Aftermath* by J. D. Omer-Cooper

Shaka must die.

Shaka will die.

Let that be the drumbeat that sustains him.

Let that be the drumbeat that guides him through pain and suffering.

Shaka must die.

Shaka will die.

He is known by many names, and will be known by many more – but that's all to the good. It's the way it is when one has no past, no tomorrow. Besides, to know his real name would be to instantly divine the nature of his quest.

And he can't have that – at least not until the day of reckoning, when it no longer matters and everyone will quake and cringe at the destruction wrought by his fury . . .

Let the pain and suffering also be his punishment for being too young when his family fell; too young to stand by his brothers, his father; too young to do anything but whimper.

Let the pain and suffering, the snarls and sneers, the setbacks sustain him, as well. Because the worse it gets, the greater his trials, the closer he is to fulfilling his vow.

Let the pain feed him, because he is unstoppable. He knows this the same way he knows the sun will rise tomorrow and set tonight. It's in the sky; it covers the rocks like moss, slices through the valleys like a young river, slips through the long grass like a snake.

And if, like a snake, he'll sometimes have to move sideways in order to move forward, so be it.

Every move brings him closer to the Zulu King.

And he will be – and is already – all but invisible.

Shaka must die.

Shaka will die.

The ancestors guide him, but he doesn't need their help. There is the pain, the drumbeat, anger in his heart, his throat, anger powering his muscles, giving him the strength to endure.

That's all he has to do, endure, and he will find his prey. His prey will deliver itself up to him.

And he knows the pain will then fall away, leaving him free to deliver the killing blow.

And if he falls too, so be it.

He will die a happy man if his assegai blade is drenched with the Beetle's blood, and the monster lies writhing at his feet . . .

The Wayfarers

There are three of them, and their captive. But he doesn't count, not being one of them and therefore not human. That doesn't save him from taunts and torments intended to enliven a dull journey, though. Today, Thin Son's weapon of choice is a slender green branch, and he walks behind the isilwane, whipping the thing's left shoulder in a downward motion. The idea is to see how many times he can hit the same strip of pink and red, lay the switch exactly within the same cut. Short Son, meanwhile, being the first-born, gets to bully both the thing and his younger sibling. He moves ahead of the group, hides himself a few paces from the path, and waits until they pass. His father, the captive and his younger brother, in that order – the last's antics ensuring that he and the isilwane have fallen several paces behind their father. Then Short Son pounces. He yanks his brother aside and sweeps a foot across the thing's heels. He's got so proficient that he can have both down in one pulling-and-tripping motion. Thin Son, who is very dim, is caught out every time. He will, in fact, watch his brother move ahead and disappear around a bend, and then still yelp in surprise when he feels those hands close around his elbows several paces later.

Their father, meanwhile, chortles every time this happens, his laughter an invitation to further repetition. Seeing the thing fall is especially funny, as it has both its paws tied behind its back. That his sons might be damaging the goods is clearly neither here nor there.

What *is* a reason for curtailing this frivolity, however, is the approach of night. The trees and bushes are yawning shadows, and it's time to find a stream and a nice, safe, sheltered place to camp. Without slowing his pace, the father turns his head, tells his younger

261

son to stop dawdling. It's an instruction the boy conveys to the captive walking between them with another mamba-like strike of the green branch, its end frayed now and sticky with blood and sap.

Several paces later, the three round a bend to see Short Son standing rigid next to a pool of water.

Frowning, the father tells Thin Son and the captive to wait there. Raising his spear to shoulder height, the blade bobbing slightly, he approaches his first-born. His eyes aren't what they used to be, so the seventeen-year-old is a plump blur – and it's only when he comes up alongside his son that he sees what has caught the boy's attention.

For a moment, instinct tightens his grip on the haft of his spear. But, even with his poor eyesight, he soon realises there's no threat here and lowers the assegai. The man sitting on a smooth shelf of rock alongside the pool is elderly. A cobweb of grey mats his chest and follows his jawline.

The two adults exchange ritual greetings, and the greybeard, whose name is Xola, indicates the pool. 'I have water, and food. Would you share my fire?'

Food? The father scratches his head and wonders where this food is. He can see a sleeping mat, an iwisa and a leather sack, but these seem to be the greybeard's only possessions, and the sack is too small to hold enough food for four.

As though divining the other's thoughts, Xola explains that he and a grandson were taking a bull to the next village. A section of the path ran along the side of a kloof, and the nervous animal had stumbled, lost its footing and gone careering down the slope. Xola chuckles ruefully, saying he doesn't know why he didn't let go of the leather rope they had tied to the animal's horns so they could guide it more easily along this stretch of path. It wasn't as though he could have single-handedly stopped the bull from taking a short-cut into the ravine. When he did think to let go, choosing to save his life rather than this sizeable chunk of his wealth, it was already too late. He was entangled, and the rope now had him as surely as the slope had the bull. When they reached the bottom, sliding through dirt and grass and a collection of stones sharper than a mother-in-law's tongue, he had a twisted ankle and the bull had a broken leg.

The bellowing beast was killed to put it out of its misery, then Xola had his grandson bring him back here, where he knew there was fresh water. After collecting firewood for the old man, the grandson continued on to the umuzi to fetch help. Knowing the boy will only get back tomorrow, the old-timer has resigned himself to spending the night alone and hungry. But now the father can send his eldest son to butcher the animal, for most of the bigger scavengers won't have moved in yet, and the boy should be able to at least rescue some fine cuts of meat.

'It pains me to lose a bull, but let us make the most of this tragedy,' says Xola. 'Let us eat like kings!' Better that than leaving the carcase to the hyenas and vultures.

The father readily agrees. After the greybeard has told him where to find the bull, Short Son ambles off down the path. He doesn't need his father to remind him to put aside some extra pieces of meat for tomorrow night and, if possible, skin the animal. (Let them make the most of the old-timer's tragedy as well!)

A whistle from the father brings Thin Son and the isilwane to the pool.

'This is my other son,' he says, introducing the former. Xola nods a greeting, intrigued by the way the irises of the boy's eyes are like feuding uncles and seem to be trying to reside on opposite sides of his head, as far apart as possible.

'Er, erm …' continues the father. Faced with the stranger's generosity, he has to make his own contribution to the evening's festivities. Biting down his resentment, he says he will supply the drink: a gourd of beer and also one of Sweet Innocence, a hard-kicking liquor made from honey.

'A potent combination,' says Xola, 'and I salute your generosity.'

The father hopes it's worth it. He hopes Short Son can find them enough meat for tonight, and for tomorrow when they'll be free of this old fool, and be able to save the animal's skin. (Will he remember the horns and hooves? He'd better, if he wants to sit down again before the next full moon.)

'And who is this?' asks Xola, referring to the captive standing next to Thin Son, and thereby proving to the father that he is a fool and a tactless one at that. Aged and outnumbered, he ignores common decency and good manners to ask such a question and even indicate that he has noticed the thing! Is he senile as well as stupid?

'He is nothing,' says the father, trying hard not to sound annoyed.

'By his features, I would say he is a Ndwandwe.'

'You are right,' allows the father grudgingly.

'We caught it sneaking towards its old feeding grounds,' adds Thin Son.

'This is so,' says the father, mentally promising Thin Son a hiding he'll never forget.

And now they are taking him to the Portugiza at Delagoa Bay?

Another impolite question!

'This is so,' says the father.

He is young and seems healthy, so they can expect a good price.

The father nods and, seeking to divert Xola's attention, tells Thin Son to unroll their sleeping mats and start the fire.

'I would help you look for firewood, but . . .' Xola makes a vague gesture towards his ankle.

'Hai, no, this one can do that as well,' says the father.

After chivvying the boy along, he ties their Ndwandwe captive to a nearby tree and rejoins the greybeard. The two men proceed to exchange news, speak of their clans, the places they have visited. The questions they ask each other are unashamedly probing, for this is the way of the road: establishing that those you're about to spend the night with are actually who they say they are.

And the father is naturally suspicious, like a jackal buzzard always on the lookout for prey or predator, congratulating himself on his slyness but almost always ending up with mere carrion. The stranger's generosity has only amplified his distrust. Even when it comes to his own kin, generosity is anathema to him, and he's always uncomfortable when he encounters that quality in others, seeing in it only subterfuge, an attempt to lull or out-manoeuvre. What's more, Xola's been a little too curious about their captive. The father doesn't want word of his intended transaction getting back to one of the district heads; Shaka has decreed that selling slaves to the Long Noses is punishable by death.

For his part, the greybeard can afford to be a little more relaxed, since he has nothing to steal. All the same, he ensures his stout iwisa remains a quick snatch away.

And because he enjoyed seeing the father's obvious unease when he mentioned the family's prisoner, he alludes to him again once he feels they've asked each other enough questions to be satisfied that each is who he claims to be. (Although it's clear to him that, as far as the father's concerned, any sign of satisfaction will be a sham, simply a chance to let his distrust regain its breath, stretch its legs a little, before re-entering the fray.)

'I am surprised to see a Ndwandwe,' says Xola. 'I thought our Father had dispensed with them, once and for all. Although . . .'

He pauses as though in thought, his eyes on the fire Thin Son has built, but in truth he's savouring the father's expectant gaze. One of anxiety mixed with annoyance.

'. . . I have heard the stories,' he continues. 'Could it be true?'

'What have you heard?' asks the father.

'But we have heard them, too,' interjects Thin Son. He's on his knees, stroking the burning wood with a green stick, spreading it out in the circle of stones so that coals might form faster.

'You have?' asks the greybeard.

Seizing this chance to show off his knowledge, Thin Son goes on to say they have also heard the rumours that Zwide has died, and that his heirs are planning to return his body to their old homeland. And perhaps then attempt to retake that homeland by force.

'Aiee, they never learn!' chuckles the greybeard.

'They are animals,' says Thin Son, leaning away from the fire to snort out a chunk of snot from his right nostril. 'You cannot teach them anything,' he adds, straightening up. 'Like this one.' He indicates the isilwane. 'See its shoulder! I've tried to teach it, but it won't learn. All it does is bleed. It will do nothing to help itself.'

The venomous glare the father turns on Thin Son goes beyond angry censure to encompass wrath, rancour, animus and demonic disapprobation, and it is enough to make even a basilisk blink. Terrified and unsure what he's done to provoke such a response, Thin Son's limited mental faculties are saved from overexertion by Short Son's return.

He's found the bull and is able to display some prime cuts of meat and favour his father with a slight nod to indicate there's more where that came from, all safely hidden from scavengers for the family's consumption tomorrow.

The boys thread dried sticks through the beef and cook it over the coals. The meat is then placed on a flattened stone, from which the men proceed to help themselves while the youngsters cook their own portions. At the greybeard's suggestion a few scraps are tossed the captive's way.

'See? No gratitude,' growls the father. 'You are wasting your food.'

Xola watches the young Ndwandwe a moment. He seems the same age as the man's younger son, say sixteen summers old. And when the youth's eyes meet his, Xola allows himself a brief smile to show the Ndwandwe that he appreciates the self-restraint it takes him to sit there and not fall upon the meat immediately.

'All the same,' he says, returning his attention to the father, 'I would've thought you'd want to deliver your cargo in the best possible condition.'

'We give him what he needs, not that which he can't appreciate.' Realising he's close to being rude, the father sits up straight and tells Short Son to pass him the gourds.

'Now we will drink,' he says.

With due reverence, the greybeard takes a mouthful from the first gourd. Smacks his lips with pleasure. Good Zulu beer.

He accepts the second gourd, clasps the rounded bottom in both hands and raises it slightly, offering it to the father. The latter inclines his head, indicates that Xola should drink first. This one contains the lethal Sweet Innocence, and Xola's gulp and swallow is a lot more controlled than the coughing fit that follows it might lead one to think.

The boys' laughter is stilled by a raised hand and a cobra hiss from their father, but Xola himself chuckles, when he regains his breath, to show he doesn't mind being the source of their amusement.

'Aiee,' he says, 'we need not fear the cold tonight!'

'What of Beja?' asks Short Son. 'Is he not worse than the cold?'

'And more cunning than a python,' adds Thin Son, his brother's interjection giving him the courage to speak out again.

'This is so,' says Xola, stroking his grey beard. 'This is so.'

'Our Father sent one of his best regiments after him,' says Short Son, 'and even they couldn't catch him.'

'Couldn't catch him!' adds Thin Son.

'What do you expect?' says the father. 'The King has been kept busy destroying our many enemies.' He indicates their captive. 'Zwide's crocodiles, for one.'

'This is so,' agrees the greybeard, noticing the scraps of meat thrown to the young Ndwandwe have now vanished. He raises the gourd to his mouth to hide his smile.

'And the Thembus are proving a nuisance, now that Zwide is gone,' he adds, after swallowing a mouthful of beer.

The father nods as Xola passes him the gourd. It's dangerous to seem critical of Shaka, especially among strangers, and Xola's response is a reassurance that he won't hold the father responsible for any nonsense his boys might utter.

'Aiee! You are right there,' says the father.

'So you have heard these other stories, too?'

'That Ngoza of the Thembus grows restive? Yes.'

'Hai, but we are strong!'

'And stronger now that the Qwabes have joined us.'

'Has that come to pass?'

The father shrugs. 'So I've heard.'

Both men fall silent, contemplating the coals, and the prospect of another war. But the youngsters don't know any better, and soon, at his brother's prompting, Short Son breaks the silence to ask the greybeard if it's true this is Beja's land.

'To hear them speak, young one, everywhere is Beja's land!'

Yes, but they have heard that Beja was born somewhere in these hills and, no matter how far he roams, he always returns here. Is that so? The greybeard is also from around here, so he must know. Perhaps he even knows Beja!

Xola laughs, and the father tells Short Son that is not the kind of rumour their host will welcome, and he'd better be still.

'Your father is right,' adds Xola. 'But I have never met Beja. And I will say this, too, I am not even sure he exists.'

Aghast looks from the youngsters. In fact Thin Son is so stunned by this prospect that Xola is sure he sees the boy's left iris disappear completely and reappear momentarily alongside his right iris. Then again, perhaps that's the beer and the Sweet Innocence kicking in.

'It is so,' he grins. 'If all the stories are to be believed, many is the time Beja was in two – even *three* – places at once!'

'Well, he *is* a wily one,' says Thin Son, which earns him a punch from his less gullible brother.

'But he is real,' adds the latter.

'Perhaps. And there is respect in your voices, I think, so you admire him?'

'Well,' says Short Son, 'he *is* Beja.'

'What will he do, do you think . . . what will he do should he overhear your words tonight? Will he say: Hai, let me find some less admiring wayfarers to rob?'

Short Son grins. 'That is not Beja's way.'

'No,' adds Thin Son, 'he is Beja. He fears nothing!'

'But there are many of us here, so what have *we* to fear?' says the greybeard. 'Unless,' he adds, tapping the father's knee, '*you* are Beja . . .'

A moment of stunned silence, fringed by the sounds of stridulating crickets and the guttural *wur-wurrr* of the bullfrogs.

Then the father chuckles. 'That *would* be interesting,' he says.

'Because that is his way,' says Xola, suddenly solemn.

'How so?' asks Thin Son.

'Let beer refresh my memory!' says Xola.

The gourd is passed around, with the brothers now allowed to partake.

'It is so,' says Xola, slapping his stomach with both hands. 'I have heard it told how Beja, and his friend Mi, will approach travellers in the night. Strangers, they say, we come in peace.'

'This is a familiar story,' grins the father.

'Indeed.'

'And do the strangers share a fire?'

'Indeed,' says Xola. 'And there they sit, and eat and drink. And soon talk will come round to Beja, as it always does in these parts. Because you are right, young one, this is Beja's country. These are his hills and valleys, his streams and ravines.'

And the leader of the strangers will regale his hosts with tales of Beja the Bandit. And they'll drink and laugh, laugh and drink, bellow and burp, and they'll say, 'Tell us more. Tell us more!'

Xola leans towards the rapt faces of the two boys. Tell us more, they plead, tell us more. For whose heart doesn't beat quicker to hear of Beja's exploits?

And the leader of the strangers will say: *Cha! There is but one more thing to say!* 'What is it?' ask the wayfarers. And he'll leap up and roar: *I AM BEJA!* And before they know it, the travellers have tasted the assegais of Beja and his friend Mi.

Xola takes another swig of beer, and burps. 'This is Beja's way.'

'Then our ruse is ended,' says the father.

The men stare at each other for a second, then burst out laughing. It is a braying fit to scare away the jackals and silence the bullfrogs.

The father is the first to recover. He upends the gourd. 'The beer is finished, so we are left with Sweet Innocence.'

'That is not altogether good news,' says Xola.

'Perhaps a drink of it will help you to better face the prospect.'

'A good idea! But now I must piss. Will you help me?' Because the greybeard has asked him, the father can't delegate the task to one of his sons without appearing rude. Besides, he realises as he stands up, he could also do with a piss.

'Let the regiments come,' says Short Son, as the two men move away into the darkness. 'They will come, they will go, and Beja will remain.'

'Your sons, they are good boys,' murmurs Xola, leaning on the father's arm and using his iwisa as a walking stick.

The father looks back towards the fire and shrugs. Praise is a foreign concept to him.

'A moment, please!' The greybeard's iwisa is stuck between two roots. 'Yes,' he continues, after freeing it, 'good boys. You must be proud.'

Again the father shrugs. 'I don't know about that,' he ventures.

'Aiee, do not let their veneration for Beja concern you. They speak with the brashness of youth.'

As Xola steps away, the father turns aside, reaching for his own kilt.

'Yes, the brashness of youth. How well I remember it,' says the greybeard, pissing into the darkness.

Turning towards his companion once he's done: 'Do not worry, for they will soon see Beja for what he is: a bloodthirsty scourge. Oh, yes,' a sigh, 'this I know better than most.'

'How so?' mutters the father, still concentrating on getting his own flow going.

'Because I am Beja.'

A sudden searing, tearing pain. The father looks down.

The old-timer's iwisa hadn't really got stuck between the roots back there. It was simply the means he used to remove the tip and unsheathe the slender blade.

Which is now sticking in the father's gut.

Beja, who is not as old as a bit of judiciously applied ash has made him appear, raises his foot and pushes the other man off the blade – pushes him backwards into the long grass.

By the time he reaches the pool, Mi has emerged out of the night to dispense with the two brothers. Now, his iklwa blade raised and glistening red in the firelight, he's eyeing the captive.

'Wait!' calls Beja.

Later, surrounded by the African night, their fire an orange glow within its circle of rocks, the boy asks him how he knew.

The Induna grins. He lays a branch across the embers, to give himself a little more time to gather his thoughts. For these are like the snail shells the boy carries in a small hollowed-out horn stuffed with dry grass: it takes a while to find the right ones, and then they are delicate, and have to be handled with care. And the tongue can be so clumsy at times.

'Your question is straightforward,' says the Induna, at last, 'but the answer . . . aiee, the answer isn't so simple. It can never be simple!'

'How so, Master?'

'In a way, your question is both of the Earth and of the Sky. How did I know? I can answer by speaking of the things I thought were wrong, of how I wondered what if this, rather than that, or why not that other thing. I can speak of stories that begin to make less sense the more you listen to them, although for others the repetition only seems to strengthen their belief.'

The Induna points at the boy. 'This you know, for we have often stood alone, you and I, listening for another story amid the murmuring; looking for the message hidden in the beadwork, where some patterns are meant only to distract. This you know, and this is the part of your question that's of the Earth. I can point to fragments and footprints, things that make no sense and things that make too much sense, or trivial things missed by others, or lies and contradictions. There can be debate, disagreement.'

The Induna sighs. Scratches his chin. He gazes upward at the stars, before returning his attention to the boy. 'And then there is the Sky. And here your question is really about how I knew what I knew. How I knew to follow this spoor instead of that one, to talk to that gogo instead of this maiden . . . Do you understand?'

A crooked grin. 'I'm not sure I do, Master.'

'A pot lies shattered at your feet, and you have to put it back together again before the sun dips behind the mountains. All the pieces are there, but you still have a tough task ahead of you. You still have to try first this shard, then that one. This is the Earth question.'

The Induna reaches for the waterskin and takes a mouthful of water.

'Now let us say many pots lie broken at your feet, but you have to put together only one of them before the sun sets. However, only one of the shattered vessels still has all of its pieces in the pile, and the rest have a fragment or two missing. To build that particular pot again, you have to start working on all the pots . . . but, because the sun is sinking ever lower, the moment will come when you have to make a guess and choose one pot to continue with, while ignoring the others.'

The Induna scratches his chin. 'That is the Sky question,' he says. If you do happen to choose the right pot, you'll be hard pressed to come up with an answer as to how you came to choose that specific one. If you make a habit of always choosing the right pot, then some will call you wise and say you are blessed by the ancestors.

The Induna chuckles, takes another mouthful of water. He hands the sack to the boy. 'And I can see you are saying to yourself: all I asked was how he knew! Yet now he speaks of Earth and Sky and broken pots.'

He holds up a hand to pre-empt the udibi's protests. 'Well and good, I will answer your question, and think of the Sky another time. Although' – a wry grin – 'as you know pots feature prominently in this tale . . .'

The Pots

The Induna found her sitting among some of Shaka's newest 'sisters', as the King's concubines are called, overseeing their beadwork. Shaking her head at the efforts of one of the girls, and telling her to start again, she led the Induna away to the shade of some nearby trees. After seeing to it that he was served beer, Nandi allowed herself to be lowered on to a pile of skins under a paperbark acacia. Resting her back against the tree trunk, she accepted a hollowed-out rhino horn from one of her serving girls.

'It is a time of peace,' she said, after taking in a few lungfuls of marijuana — or dagga as it's known in these parts. 'One which, like a maiden's sudden acquiescence, we must make the most of, Nduna. For where once our enemies treated us with disdain, now they envy us — and fear us, too.' Smoke snaked out from the corners of the Queen Mother's lips. 'And, as you know, that can act as a goad as surely as greed. But I have not summoned you to talk of the future, for we have enough bother in this time of peace.'

A smile. 'You are one I can trust, Nduna, and this is why I summoned you. I do not believe he did this deed, but I cannot be certain. If anyone can uncover the truth lurking here, it is you. And if that truth is unpleasant — if everything is exactly as it appears to be — well, then, I know you will not seek to mislead me. And this is why your loyalty can be relied upon. It is not a sham, a boast, or the hut that falls down before the first stern wind.'

Another lungful of dagga. 'So,' she said, exhaling, 'let us talk about Nyembezi the Bead Man . . .'

It was less than six months since Shaka had defeated the Ndwandwes, under their brilliant general, Soshangane. First, the King had his people remove themselves from the path of the invaders, taking with them every item of food they could find. It was harvest time and Soshangane had been hoping to live off the land. Instead, Shaka led him deeper and deeper into a country denuded of sustenance, while Zulu marauders made off with the few head of cattle the Ndwandwe general had brought with him. When Shaka finally attacked, his regiments faced a starving enemy. Then, his force easily defeated, Soshangane was allowed to go free, while the Zulu impis went rampaging through Ndwandwe territory. Zwide eluded them, fleeing north with his sons, but Shaka was able to see Ntombazi punished. Zwide's mother collected the skulls of the chiefs her son had bested, and, when he caught up with her, Shaka ensured her death was painful and prolonged.

Always one unafraid of a risk, the Bead Man had been dealing with the Maputos and Portugiza for a while, gradually accumulating wealth and a reputation for the quality of his wares. Now, with the trade routes firmly under Zulu control, his impis have become like ants, chuckled Nandi.

'I do not believe there's a time when a group of his bearers, usually led by one of his brothers or sons, isn't either going to or returning from the Portugiza settlement.' More often than not the parties pass each other on the road, one herding cattle or carrying ivory to Delagoa Bay, the other bringing back stocks of beads and cloth.

In other words, they were talking about a clever, hard-working, wealthy man known for his honesty. Nandi inhaled. Savoured the smoke filling her lungs. Exhaled. 'Which is to say he seeks to cheat only the Maputos and their Portugiza masters,' she added.

She handed the horn to one of her servants, and waved the girl away.

'He is a good man,' she said when they were alone again. Yet now, at a homestead in the middle of nowhere, this good man had chosen to kill a fellow Zulu. To protect his goods on the road, yes, but to kill a man in cold blood? That was not the Bead Man's way.

'Or maybe I am wrong,' said Nandi, with a shrug. 'And if I am wrong, so be it, but it will be Nyembezi who suffers.'

He is in custody? He has not fled?

'Mzilikazi watches over him,' said Nandi, referring to one of Shaka's favourites.

But they were getting ahead of themselves, she added.

The Induna nodded, inquiring: who was the man Nyembezi was supposed to have killed?

His name was Masipula, said Nandi, and he was known throughout the district as a bitter and twisted recluse. A thief in the night had stolen his happiness away from him, and henceforth no one else was going to experience the smallest iota of joy, if he could help it. His sons couldn't wait to leave home and he treated his daughter like a slave. Although she was regarded as a great beauty, Masipula had discouraged all suitors and now she was deemed too old for marriage, even though her looks had somehow managed to withstand her years of drudgery.

'Or so I have been told,' said Nandi.

'The thief in the night, though . . .' said the Induna. 'That is where their paths first crossed, is it not?'

'As ever, you amaze me, Nduna! But even you will be surprised by what I have to tell you next . . .'

★

After leaving the King's mother, he didn't immediately call for the boy or send one of Nandi's servants to fetch him. He had much to mull over and, instead, readied their baggage himself and collected the provisions they'd need, before going to look for his young charge, so that the udibi might have a little more time with Pampata.

The two were by the river, sitting under a tree several metres away from the crossing where the women of the village went to fetch water. Pampata sat with her knees bent and her feet tucked under her thighs, while the boy hovered before her on his heels. In between them, he'd smoothed out a swathe of sand.

Even from a distance, it was easy to see what the boy was up to, and the Induna held back. He knew how much the boy had wanted to show Pampata this trick . . .

★

The udibi has placed three striped, pointy shells on the sand before Shaka's Beloved. Each little bigger than a man's bellybutton, they are land-snail shells. It had taken the boy a while to find some that were undamaged and almost identical. In the meantime, the Induna would often come upon him sitting on his heels glowering at three stones placed in a row. The boy's expression was intense as he moved the stones, suggesting this wasn't so much play as practice. As a result, the Induna said nothing, or ignored the boy's embarrassed scramble whenever the need to be on the move forced him to interrupt the udibi's communion with those stones.

He'd soon realised what the boy was up to, and the pride he felt was almost paternal. This was Mgobozi's trick, one whose secret the old general stubbornly refused to share with anyone. And here was the boy patiently trying to work out how it was done, on his own. He didn't quite succeed, but his efforts were duly rewarded by the dismay displayed by Njikiza and the others when he finally performed a variation on the trick for them.

'What is this?' asks Pampata now. 'Would you bewitch me?'

Balanced on his toes and gripping his knees, the boy shakes his head.

'Would you trick me, then?'

A nod and a grin.

'Hai!' says Pampata, pushing out her lower lip in a feigned pout. 'You would do that to me?'

Another nod, a wider grin.

This time Pampata's 'Hai!' is a growl of mock challenge. 'Very well, we will see! For you are not the only one who knows some trickery.'

The boy shrugs.

'What must I do?'

The boy holds up a tiny stone and topples sideways.

'Aiee! A drunk frog! That *is* a clever trick,' says Pampata, as the boy sheepishly rights himself.

Deciding it will be better if he rests on his knees, he shows her the stone again. Leaning forward, he lifts the first shell, places the stone in the centre of the impression left by the edges of the shell, and then replaces the shell. Next he swaps the other two shells around. After retrieving the stone, he places it under the shell to his left and swaps the positions of the remaining two.

'And now?' asks Pampata, as he drops the stone into her palm.

With his open hand, the udibi indicates each shell in succession.

'Hai! Now I understand. Inside one of these you have hidden your voice.'

The Induna grins. For some reason known only to the boy himself, he deems a solemn silence and accompanying mummery crucial to the successful performance of this trick.

Patiently the boy points to the stone in Pampata's palm, and then to each of the shells in turn. She knows he wants her to place the stone under one of the shells, then shift the position of the remaining two. She'd already worked that out after the boy was only a few grimaces into his mime-act, but didn't want to spoil his performance. And she, too, is secretly impressed by this variation on Mgobozi's trick.

As she makes to place the stone under one of the shells, the boy holds out his right hand to stop her, then places his left hand over his eyes.

'No,' says Pampata. 'How do I know you will not peek? Turn around.'

As the boy scoots around on his toes, Pampata picks up the shell to her right. Then, unaware the Induna is watching, she hesitates and glances at the boy's back. With the sudden vigour of one reaching a decision, she scoops up all of the shells in her right hand. Transferring them to her left hand, she uses her right palm to smooth out the sand. After carefully lining them up again, she places the stone under the shell to her left. And then straightens and thinks about it – and reaches forward again. Retrieving the stone, she places it under the shell to her right.

'I am ready!'

The boy turns and makes a show of scratching his chin. He passes his hand over each of the shells in turn. Then, gently, using the tip of his forefinger, he pulls the centre shell towards him . . .

'Aiee, Little One,' says Pampata, clapping her hands, 'this is clever. You have shown me where the stone isn't!'

A smile playing across his lips, the Induna retraces his steps quietly, waits for a few moments, then summons the boy.

★

The homestead that was their destination was a day's journey away. By leaving in the early afternoon, the Induna intended to break their journey into two segments, with a sleep in between. This would enable them to arrive at the kraal before midday.

They moved quickly, following well-trodden paths, wispy fan lovegrass giving way to hardier thatchgrass with its flattened stems, buck nibbling the seed pods of flat-topped acacias, and among rocky outcrops, and along watercourses, quilted sagebush.

As night approached, they made their camp. After a supper of porridge and amasi, the Induna told the udibi about the Bead Man and the accusation of murder. He also told him the second part of the tale Nandi had recounted . . .

★

Two suitors, one maiden, and a father who cared only about the lobola. As the bride price is an indication of how her family values their daughter, a wise father would be governed by his daughter's wishes, where two suitors are involved. Not surprisingly, though, there are those who abuse the custom, seeing it merely as a business transaction, with profit as the aim. And although Nomleti, the maiden, loved Nyembezi, Masipula's father was wealthier, so it was Masipula who married her.

The result was an unhappy marriage and many believed that Nomleti's death, while giving birth to her second son, was brought on by her treatment at Masipula's hands.

'He knew, Nduna . . . he knew he wasn't the one she loved and he set about making her suffer,' Nandi had said. 'They say he kept her out in the field, hoeing until she could scarcely stand, and then

279

he took his time sending for the midwife. As far as he was concerned, he couldn't make her suffer enough.'

At least Nomleti was free of Masipula's tyranny, once and for all, but the same couldn't be said of their children. As the eldest, Zikihle did her best to shield her two brothers from their father's wrath, and suffered for it. Like a disease, Masipula's hatred for his wife had metastasised into a hatred of all women, including his daughter.

Then he began to poison her brothers' minds, the boys she herself had raised. He'd beat them when he was drunk and had become bored with picking on Zikihle, yet he was happy to enlist them as allies in his mistreatment of her. At first they joined in eagerly, because at least it meant they weren't the ones in trouble, but all too soon abusing their sister became second nature to them.

Upon hearing of Zikihle's plight, Nandi had intervened. She could do nothing about Masipula's treatment of his daughter, but she could arrange for the brothers to be called up as udibis, thereby removing them from the influence of their father.

'A bitter, brutal man,' murmured the Induna, watching the embers for the billowing of colour that follows the ever-shifting movement of the life within the fire.

'Who had a grudge against Nyembezi,' said the boy. 'Yet *he* was the one who died.'

That was just it. 'This is another reason why I have sent for you, Nduna,' Nandi had said. 'If they had told me Masipula had murdered Nyembezi, I would have said "Hai, what are you waiting for. Let the King's impalers have him!" For, say what you like about the man, he had every reason to feel wronged, with the desire for revenge growing ever stronger in the passing of the years.'

'Especially when he heard how his rival, the Bead Man, prospered!'

'There is that too, Nduna. But see what has happened.'

*

Whenever a human being dies in their hut, a special exit for the body is constructed at the back of the dwelling. Under normal circumstances, a person is considered rude if they leave the hut back-

280

wards, but this does not apply to those who carry the corpse. The ingadi, or right-hand wife, will walk on the left side of the body, while the ikhohlwa, or left-hand wife, will walk to the right. As a sign of mourning, they'll wear their skirts inside out. Immediately after a chief's funeral, cows in the kraal will be milked from the left side of the animal, instead of the right side as is usual.

In other words, things are inverted.

And that seemed to be what happened here. Everything was the other way around.

★

A contemplative silence. Then the boy opened his pouch and checked to see if his shells were still intact.

'She cheated,' said the Induna, his gaze fixed on the embers at his feet. Pampata was supposed to put the stone under one of the shells, and then move only the other two before smoothing the sand. Instead she had shifted all three.

The boy nodded. 'This is so.'

That earned him a look and raised eyebrows from the Induna. 'You knew?'

'Yes, Master.'

'Kobo!'

'Sire?'

'Am I wrong? Do my eyes deceive me? Or are we experiencing a surfeit of Zulu sangomas?'

'Hai, Sire! Ngoza, the Great Buffalo and ruler of the Thembus, master of all he surveys, scourge of his enemies and the dreadful one even the shades fear, can never be wrong. They are indeed flocking here, these Zulu sangomas, like animals fleeing a drought.'

'The drought in this instance having taken the form of a big fat Beetle . . .'

'This is so.'

'But why must they come here?'

'Erm.'

'Kobo?'

'I have, er, made it known in your, uhm, name, Highness, that they will be welcome here.'

'Why? Am I not taunted enough by our own sorcerers?'

'They loathe the Beetle, who is constantly striving to restrict their influence, Majesty, and I thought they might be able to provide us with valuable information about the state of affairs over there.'

'And have they done this to your satisfaction?'

'Er, no, Highness. I must confess the harvest has been paltry, to say the least.'

'Idiot! I could have told you that. Were one planning to usurp a king, one would prefer to remain as close to him as possible. Failing that, one must work on his subjects, show them the error of their ways, and seek allies among his inner circle. Take whats-her-name . . .'

'Nobela, Sire?'

'Yes, Nobela, whose reputation caused even some of my own medicine men to bang their knees together. Did she flee? Of course not! Not even when it became apparent that to stay was to die. It's only the cowards who darken our doorway.'

'I will see the message is spread. None will make it this far in future.'

'Yes, tell them to go and pester Pakatwayo and his Qwabes, or else Faku.'

'Since the Beetle has been courting Pakatwayo, I doubt they will feel safe among the Qwabes. As for Faku, he appears to hate everyone, and why travel so far when they can eat dust at home?'

'Which shows a distinct lack of mettle on their part. Not only do they value their innards over putting a stop to the Beetle's tyranny, they prefer to seek out what they clearly think is the easier path even when they flee.'

'But they compliment you, too, Majestic Awfulness!'

'I need their words of praise like a bull needs udders.'

'This is so, Sire, this is so, but I meant they compliment you by coming here. Is it not a sign they believe that you, the Mighty Magnificent Buffalo, are the one – the only one – who has the strength and the wisdom to succeed where all others failed, and crush the Beetle?'

'No, Kobo, the only sign I see here is how eloquent you can be when trying to justify your errors of judgement. Which isn't surprising, since those are legion.'

'I am humbled by your Cognoscence's shrewdness!'

'As well you might, Kobo.'

'And, more, see how my hands tremble at the thought of what might have been, Sire!'

'When do they not tremble? But why particularly this time?'

'What if the Beetle sends an assassin disguised as a disgraced sangoma, as he did with Zwide on the eve of Gqokli Hill?'

'Do you seek to insult me, now?'

'Majesty! Fount of Wisdom! That is furthest from my thoughts.'

'To think that I would fall for such a puerile trick. This smacks of treachery. Treachery, Kobo – betrayal!'

'Please, your Dreadfulness, I did not mean to—'

'You are slobbering now, Kobo.'

'May my bountiful apologies cause your fields to blossom with mercy, Sire.'

'I might be master of all I see, but apparently not of all I hear.'

'Sire?'

'I have absolutely no idea what that means.'

'What what means, O Frightful One?'

'Forget it! Let us return to the matter of these Zulu sangomas . . .'

'Rest assured, Majestic Terror, I will see to it that your wishes are carried out.'

'What wishes?'

'I will see those Zulu sangomas removed before they foul our land any further.'

'Tell me this, Kobo; are you enjoying your journey along the path of stupidity, this morning? For it seems to me you have packed your sleeping mat and are set on ranging far and wide.'

'Majesty? Bellowing Buffalo? Profuse apologies, but I do not—'

'Understand? Clearly! Let me put it this way, Kobo, and heed my words carefully. You will continue to allow the Zulu sangomas to come to us, seeking protection, and you will leave them unmolested until you are able to discover whether they have anything of value to tell us. I do not see this ever happening, but let us not miss any opportunity to get behind Shaka's shield. Do you understand?'

'Such wisdom, Majesty!'

'Yes, and then, when you are certain they have nothing of value to tell us, you will kill them. As you will kill those who are here already, for you have already ascertained how that land is fallow.'

'That is so, sire.'

'However, this talk of how Zwide was tricked has got me thinking.'

'Ah!'

'So spare a few of them.'

'A few?'

'A modest herd. Have them sent northward. Let them discover the veracity of these whispers we've been hearing. Personally, I do not believe it, for it will take more than old age to rid us of Zwide.'

'And so it did, Sire. It took Shaka.'

'And so, Kobo, we leave the path of stupidity for the perilous passes of pissing off a pissed-off monarch.'

'I only meant, your Ruthlessness, that Shaka's defeat of the Ndwandwes was total. There was no need to hunt down Zwide afterwards. He had lost everything, Sire, he was as good as dead. You could even say this way was better, a fate worse than death, because imagine the agonies he must have suffered, as a mighty warlord reduced to leading a band of vagabonds.'

'I'm still not smiling, Kobo, or saying "Oh!" '

'Y-yes, I can see that. I mean . . . what I meant was . . .'

'What you meant, Kobo, was that Zwide became a spent force after Shaka had finished with him. This I know, Kobo. I am, after all, king, and there's a reason for that. It's because I know things.'

'This is so, Sire. But, if I might humbly point out, you also have many other fine qualities.'

'Kobo—'

'Oh, right. Profuse . . . No, abject . . . No . . . uhm.'

'Are you finished?'

'Uhm, yes, Majesty. Thank you for asking, Majesty.'

'So it is agreed?'

'A-agreed, Sire?'

'That we will send a few Zulu sangomas to see if Zwide really has joined the ancestors. That is all we will ask of them, and when they return we will listen to them very carefully, Kobo, because the thing we really want to know is if the second part of the rumour is true. Are the surviving sons planning a campaign against the Beetle?'

'Ah.'

'Your awe is noted, Kobo. Now . . . what are you waiting for? Choose your sangomas, then kill the rest. Dumo and his henchmen will be only too happy to help you get rid of this infestation.'

'It will be done, Sire.'

'One more thing, Kobo . . .'

'Sire?'

'Do try to wait until the first group has left, before you start killing the remaining sangomas. It will only confuse those you have chosen, if they have

285

to step over the bodies of their brothers and sisters of the Calling on their journey northward. They might even come to doubt any reassurances you might have given them.'

The Bead Man

'Master, forgive me. . . but which pot are we putting together now?'

The Induna grins, hearing an echo of Mgobozi in the udibi's words. Cheeky words but not insolent; the same way the old general will sneak through the King's grumpiness to draw Shaka's attention to an important consideration . . . or to ask an apposite question.

'We speak of matters of the Earth now, Boy.'

The udibi frowns. 'Because . . . because, even before we began our journey, it was clear there was something wrong.'

A nod of approval from the Induna. 'There you have it, Little One.' The story Nandi had told them, the same tale that had sent them on their journey two days ago, had provided a jarring ending. As Nandi had pointed out, the wrong man had been killed.

'Earth questions?' muses the boy.

'Yes, things we can touch and hold, examine and discuss.' It was quite possible things were as they seemed, and the Bead Man had killed Masipula; in which case it was merely a matter of finding out what the rest of the story was. But there was enough strangeness to warrant Nandi asking the Induna to investigate the matter.

'You have asked me how I knew,' continues the Induna. 'It can be as simple as that, as simple as realising there is something wrong, right at the outset.'

Is he stating the obvious? Perhaps, in this instance, yes; but there are other times when one has to look long and hard before one spots an anomaly. Of course, this is often when the distinction between the Earth and Sky blurs. Then one needs to rely on one's instincts, those Sky thoughts that tug at one and whisper that, while everything seems placid, one must look deeper.

But the strange inversion was only the start – the first few words in the alternative narrative the Induna was seeking out.

★

Nyembezi was about fifty summers old, and almost as tall as the Induna, with the strong thighs that told of a man used to travelling long distances.

'Why did you come here?' asked the Induna, speaking as the Shadow of Shaka, with the blue crane feather in his headband.

Much to the warrior's surprise, the older man essayed a grin. 'Clearly you have heard the tale: a battle won but the war lost.'

'He won the battle but lost the war, for it was you that Nomleti loved.'

'This is so.'

'But your victory – if it can even be called that – was sour.'

'This is true, also. I loved her, she loved me, but he was the one her father chose.'

'And Masipula made her suffer.'

'Yes, indeed. I left the district shortly after the lobola negotiations concluded, but my family kept me apprised of how he treated her.'

'In a way he suffered, too.'

'Hai! I cannot think of him without . . .' The Bead Man paused, grinning again.

'You were about to say . . . ?'

'I was about to say I cannot think of him without loathing, even though he has now set like the sun. But I see your meaning.'

'She loved you, not him, and he had to live with that.'

'Yes, but don't you see, Nduna? I told Nomleti . . . The last time I saw her, I told her, pleaded with her, to forget about me and concentrate on being a dutiful wife. And I know she would have tried! But could *he* see that? Could Masipula appreciate that? No! She had to be ground down, and when he was finished with her, it was her daughter's turn.'

'This may be so,' said the Induna, 'but you have not answered

288

my question: why, after all these seasons, did you go and see Masipula?'

A family matter had brought him back to the district, explained Nyembezi. It was the death of an uncle, his mother's brother. He had to oversee the parcelling out of the estate. The uncle and his family were the last surviving relatives in the area. As the Bead Man's wealth had grown, he had arranged first for his parents and siblings to come and live with him at his kraal, then the uncles, aunts, cousins and nephews who wanted to join what now amounted to the 'family business'. Few demurred – even this uncle. Although he had remained here, he supplied cattle for Nyembezi's many trading expeditions.

'However, this is the first time I have been back here since leaving,' Nyembezi told the Induna.

A day after his arrival, Masipula's daughter brought him a message that her father wanted to see him.

'And that is why I went to see him, Nduna – because he invited me. Let us put aside the past, he said as he greeted me at the entrance to his kraal. After all, he laughed, neither of us were getting any younger! And we had been friends once.'

What did Nyembezi make of such an effusive welcome?

'I wasn't sure, Nduna, and I wasn't ready to lower my guard so soon. But I will tell you this: when he laughed, and said we weren't getting any younger, the sound was like stone sliding across stone. Here is someone unused to laughing, I thought to myself.'

All the same, Nyembezi had put aside his misgivings and allowed himself to be guided to the meeting place in front of the main hut, where there were two tree stumps positioned at opposite ends of a grass mat. Two serving pots had been placed in front of the host's seat and, once Nyembezi had been installed on the other stump, Masipula went to fetch some beer.

'Masipula went for it? Not his daughter?'

'No, he was very proud of his beer, as you must know, and when showing it off, he did the pouring . . .'

The Induna nodded. Masipula's beer was the source of no small part of his income – men came from all around to barter beads, fruit and vegetables for his brew. And, whether preparing the malt or serving up the finished product, he'd allow no one else to help him.

'It seemed to be the one set of tasks she was spared,' added Nyembezi, 'although . . .'

'Although?'

'I couldn't help but notice that Zikihle seemed agitated.'

'Agitated?'

'It was such a small thing, Nduna, but she was fretful about the pots. For it seemed one of them had a chip in it.'

Zikihle had at last found the courage to pick up the drinking pot, and it was in her hand as Masipula turned away from the Bead Man. For an instant his mask of bonhomie had then slipped, and Nyembezi was treated to a glimpse of the terror Zikihle had to endure. In fact, Masipula's outburst had been so abusive that Nyembezi momentarily thought he'd misheard Zikihle's stammered explanation, and there was more than just a cracked pot involved.

★

The tyrant who was tolerated only because of his prowess when it came to brewing beer.

Even here there was a reversal of sorts.

Beer is made from sorghum, with the malt prepared by sewing grain into a sack and allowing it to ukucwilsa, or soak, in a stream. Grain placed in the water in the morning is removed at sunset. If placed in the water at sunset, it must remain in the stream until the following sunset.

Afterwards, the grain is put in a large earthen pot called an imbiza, and covered up. After two days in summer (three in winter), the sorghum will have begun to sprout shoots. It is then spread out on a mat, to dry in the sun.

Three days later, it's ready for brewing. The malt is mixed with dry sorghum and water in an imbiza, then removed and crushed on a grinding stone. This creates intlama, a dough-like substance, which is put back into the pot, then covered with water and brought to the boil . . .

And, among the People Of The Sky, it's women who oversee the constant pouring, boiling and ladling that brewing involves. And they also have to abstain from sexual intercourse for the duration of the process, or else the beer will taste like a thirsty man's piss.

But Masipula did all of this himself, including fetching and pouring beer for his visitors – another task usually left to women.

And, that day, Zikihle noticed something was wrong. But when the dutiful daughter made to put things right, her father shouted at her . . .

★

'Hai, it's easy to see how she could have been confused,' says the Induna.

Sitting with his feet together and his chin resting on his knees, the udibi thinks a moment, then nods. 'He was shouting at her for trying to do the right thing.'

'Yes, here was a man who liked things just so, a man who'd beat her and harangue her until she got things just so, suddenly saying that things didn't have to be just so.'

'But there was a guest, Master.'

'Hai, Masipula's nastiness was well-known, remember. Those who came to fetch beer often witnessed him chastising his daughter. *Their* presence didn't stop him.'

'But Nyembezi was different, was he not?'

'Yes, you are right there. For he was a true enemy!' And Nyembezi loathed him with equal vigour.

But that brings the Induna back to the point the Bead Man had made that same day at Nyembezi's kraal, while watched over by Mzilikazi and his men. 'If I'd had murder in mind when I came here,' he'd told the Induna, 'would I have killed Masipula in such an obvious fashion?'

Looking into the night, the Induna conjures up the scene . . .

Masipula returns, carrying two gourds.

He pours the beer into each of the serving pots.

To remove any scum or other impurities, he skims the surface

291

of each with a spoon-like isiketo, made from strips of palm leaf plaited together.

There is a reverence in his actions as, holding the heavy ukhamba with both hands, he passes the pot to Nyembezi. Then he picks up his own ukhamba and lowers himself on to his tree stump.

He takes a deep gulp of the pinkish liquid.

He smacks his lips in pleasure . . .

In what starts as pleasure, but soon becomes alarm.

He stands up.

He gasps.

He clutches at his throat.

He gags.

Turns. Falls against the wall of the hut, his nails digging into the thatch.

Sags and falls.

★

'There was still beer in the two gourds, when you arrived?' the Induna had asked Mzilikazi.

'Yes. Nyembezi saw to it that they were not emptied.'

'And one of those gourds contained poison?'

'Yes. One was half empty – and the poison was in that one. We dipped dried lumps of porridge in it and left them out for the birds. Three ate, and three died.'

★

He smacks his lips . . .

His eyes bulge.

Putting the pot down, he stands up, confused, bewildered . . .

He clutches at his throat, making a *ka-ka-ka* noise . . .

Stands up . . . Clutches his throat . . . On his face . . .

★

'Fear, Nduna. Horror.'

'Horror?'

292

'That is not too strong a word. And then he was like a man who's been stabbed, and is now writhing in his own blood – only there was no blood. But I knew immediately this was no illness.'

'And you thought it was the beer?'

'What else could it have been?' asked Nyembezi. 'For we hadn't yet eaten. If there was indeed poison, it had to be in the beer. Besides, I was right, was I not, Nduna?'

★

'And he was,' says the udibi.

He was, agrees the Induna.

And would a murderer have ensured the suspect beer was kept safe until the matter could be more fully investigated?

That was something else to consider and place alongside the Bead Man's observation. For, if he had wanted Masipula dead, he wouldn't have killed him in a way that made himself the chief suspect.

'He need never have gone near the kraal at all, and could have got someone else to kill Masipula.'

The Induna nods.

'And these are Earth matters?' asks the boy.

'Yes, things I heard that began to point to the Bead Man's innocence.'

'But then things changed,' observes the boy.

'Indeed they did,' agrees the Induna.

★

Nyembezi's calm insistence on his own innocence evaporated after the Induna said he was going to speak to Zikihle next.

'Why?'

'She was there as well. She saw.'

'Yes, she saw her father die a terrible death. And don't say that must have gladdened her heart! For she is not like that. He was still her . . . For all his cruelty, she still looked upon him as her father.'

'But there *is* that cruelty . . .'

'Do you think . . . ?'

'I do not think anything yet, which is why I must speak to her.'

'No!'

'Do not let your distress blind you. See who you are speaking to now.'

'I am sorry, Nduna – Shadow of Shaka – but if you persist in speaking to her, then I will save you the trouble!'

'How so?'

'By confessing. I killed him! I poisoned him and watched him die like the jackal he was. I saw his writhing and his pain, and I laughed. As I will laugh when the King's Slayers come for me.'

'Well, then, this matter is concluded!'

His head bowed, Nyembezi nodded.

'Good. Then my speaking to Zikihle shouldn't cause you – or her – any distress.'

'Nduna, no! You can't!'

'If this is the condemned man's last request, then I cannot grant it.'

'But . . .'

★

Women brew the beer. Then the daughters serve it to guests, after the eldest daughter has taken the first drink from the ukhamba to show them the beer hasn't been poisoned. But not there. Not at that homestead where the dutiful daughter was kept busy by fetching and carrying, cooking and cleaning. Hai, the place was so neat it was hard to believe it was all the work of one person!

But this dutiful daughter wasn't ever allowed to touch the beer.

★

There were those, Nandi and Pampata among them, who said the years of drudgery had made remarkably little impact on Zikihle's beauty. The Induna thought they were being kind, however. Her face was round and her lips comely (he supposed), but a lifetime of being chastised for the smallest infraction of an insane man's

rules had given her eyes a nervous, flickering quality. If he hadn't
known her story, the Induna would have said here was someone
with *dishonest* eyes. And that was still a fair assessment when you
took her background into account, for doesn't constant and sustained
abuse force dishonesty upon the victim? Doesn't a tyrant, who
would control every aspect of their lives, force his subjects to
become dissemblers?

It probably didn't do her much good – truth, lies, it was all the
same to a father who'd decided in advance to find fault and take
umbrage – but it was a tendency worth noting.

And her hands and knees were the knees and hands of an old
woman; and her shoulders sagged in the way of one who has not
only given up hope but who can't remember when last she wished
for something other than an end to her misery.

Hai, but there *was* a sudden flaring in her – like a torch being
carried through a forest at night; now you see it, now you don't –
when Mzilikazi began leading Nyembezi away.

Her eyes lost their nervousness, she stopped fidgeting with her
skirt, and seemed to straighten up. 'Where is he going? Where are
you taking him?'

Seeing the boy's chest rise as he made ready to reprimand Zikihle,
to remind her she was talking to the Shadow of Shaka, the Induna
lay a calming hand on the udibi's shoulder.

'Please, where are you taking him?'

'There is no longer any need to worry yourself over this affair,
for he has admitted he is the one who poisoned your father.'

'*No*, that is not true. He is lying!'

'Then he is a strange one, for a lie like that can lead only to
the impalers!'

'No, he is lying to protect me!'

★

'He would do that? He would lie to protect you?'

'Yes!'

'As you would lie to protect him?'

'Yes. No!'

'Well, which one is it, Little Sister?'

'I killed him! Nyembezi had nothing to do with it. I killed my father.'

'No, no! It was I! I killed him!' shouted Nyembezi, trying to pull away from Mzilikazi. 'I killed him, you fools.'

Gripping Zikihle's elbows, the Induna told her to look at him directly.

The authority in his voice, as much as the sudden pain, made her obey. 'You will do this for me,' he continued. 'You will stand here with my udibi, and you will be still. Do you understand?'

Zikihle nodded, and the Induna turned his attention back to Nyembezi. As he approached the Bead Man, the Induna extended his left arm and took the iklwa one of Mzilikazi's men proffered. Pressing the point of the blade against Nyembezi's chest he said: 'And you . . . you will remain still.'

'But she—'

'You will calm down and tell me what you have neglected to tell me!'

'She didn't . . . She couldn't. I'm . . . I am the one who . . .'

'That is not what I am asking. Tell me what you have neglected to tell me.'

He arrived. There were greetings, and small talk, then Masipula went to fetch the beer. Is that what happened?

'Y-yes.'

'Yes, Nduna!' bellowed Mzilikazi.

'Ye-yes, Nduna.'

'No! Something happened before that,' said the Induna. 'Before Masipula went to fetch the beer.'

'I don't know what you mean.'

'Think! You told me once, now tell me again.'

'Nduna, I don't . . . oh!'

'Yes?'

The pot . . . Zikihle had seen one of the pots was chipped, and she wanted to change it. Masipula had shouted at her. 'It was

296

like he was two people fighting each other,' said Nyembezi. 'I could actually see him forcing down his anger. Then he smiled, tried to act as if nothing had happened, and went off to fetch his precious beer.'

'And then?'

'He returned, and . . .'

'And? You've remembered something else. What is it?'

'It's nothing important, Nduna. It's just that I remember then thinking how his whole face changed when he came out of the storage hut with the beer. He almost looked happy. Proud, even. But I do not understand what this has to do with anything, Nduna.'

'How long was he gone?'

'Nduna . . . ?'

'You heard me. How long was he gone, when he went off to fetch the beer?'

'I don't know!'

'Think! How long was he gone? Long enough for you to say a few words to Zikihle?'

'No.'

'Why? Was he back before you could even blink?'

'No, but I didn't get the chance to say anything to Zikihle.'

'Why? No, I know why. Because she was too busy, am I right?'

★

She was too busy being pulled apart. For here, pulling her in this direction, was a confused, fear-filled desire to please that, for reasons she couldn't begin to understand, felt like she was disobeying; while, on the other side, there was the inexorable pull of habit, the familiar this-and-not-that drummed into her by her father, where to obey was to win, if not praise, then at least a modicum of respite. Hesitant steps. Apprehensive glances towards the hut where her father kept his beer. Patting her skirt. Rubbing her neck. Another glance. Then, while Nyembezi looked on, mystified, she darted forward and picked up the cracked pot . . .

She replaced it and, when her father returned with the beer, she was on her way back to the cooking hut, for she had to finish preparing their meal.

It had been Masipula's death throes that brought her back out.

★

Masipula returns with the beer.

And his beer and the renown it's brought him, these are the only things that give him pleasure. All else had been tainted when the woman he loved couldn't bring herself to love him . . .

And he pours the beer, thrilled by the thought of how apt this is.

And they drink.

And Masipula smacks his lips in pleasure . . .

In what starts as pleasure, but soon becomes alarm.

A look of shock as he realises the bowls have got mixed up somehow – *how did that happen?* – and he himself has swallowed the poisoned beer intended for Nyembezi . . .

★

'Get out your shells,' says the Induna, rising. 'It was your game I thought of when I was told of two calabashes and two drinking pots. So much to remember! Better to mark one, not so?'

Stepping past their campfire, he sits down beside the boy. Picks up one of the shells. Shades of brown like the patterns in a semi-precious stone. 'To everyone else these look alike – but not to you. Fill a kraal with screaming babies, and they will all look alike to us but not to their mothers. And it is the same with you and these shells.'

The udibi nods.

'I have seen you studying these shells,' says the Induna examining the one he's selected, holding it up and towards the fire as though checking to see if it's translucent.

After finding three shells that were similar in appearance, the boy had chosen one of them and studied it intently. Studied it until he knew it as well as he knew his own teeth. He can instantly tell which

298

of the three it is whenever the shells are arranged in a line – just as the Induna's doing now. The 'special' shell, however, isn't the one the warrior picked up; rather it's the one to the boy's left.

The Induna reaches forward and straightens up again, his finger-tip covered in ash from the fringes of the fire. 'You do not need to do this, but I do,' he says, touching the ash to the shell in the centre. 'Let this one be *my* shell.'

Once he's identified where his shell is, in the line, the udibi asks someone to place a stone under any one of the shells while he is looking away. To complicate matters, the person can switch the two shells that do not house the stone.

'So,' continues the Induna, 'I look away and you place the stone, and move the other two shells. I open my eyes when you tell me to, and I look for my special shell, which is this one,' he indicates the centre shell, 'and see it's still there, exactly where it was when I closed my eyes. That means *that's* where the stone must be!'

The position of the 'special' shell reveals the position of the stone. If the shell was in the centre but is now on the right, say, that means the stone must be under the shell on the left.

'That you thought of this . . .' The Induna shakes his head. 'That is remarkable.' He has only a word of caution to add. The boy must be beware of performing this trick too often on the same occasion and before the same group of people, since the risk of someone spotting what he's doing is increased. 'Because,' he says, 'they cease being awed and start looking more carefully.'

And he was reminded of the udibi's trick when told the story of the beer. Masipula could ensure he knew which beer was which by putting the poison in the calabash that was half-full, but when it came to the drinking pots he needed a more discreet way of being absolutely certain that Nyembezi got the one with poison. So he used a chipped pot. That would be his own, the 'safe' one. When he couldn't feel any chip on the rim of the first pot he handled, that was where he poured the poisoned beer. Then he reached for the second pot and, in his glee, he didn't bother to double-check to make sure this was the one with the chip. Instead he poured and drank, hoping to get Nyembezi to follow suit with the same alacrity.

But his dutiful daughter had replaced the chipped pot.

'That's the only way it could have happened,' says the Induna. Nyembezi was nonchalant when the Induna started questioning him, positive he'd be the chief suspect and felt certain nothing could be proven, because he knew he wasn't the murderer. It therefore had to be Zikihle, and he was trying to protect her.

'When you said you wanted to question her, he got desperate...?'

'That's right,' says the Induna, resuming his seat on the other side of the fire.

'Because he thought her guilt might lead her to confess. Or give herself away.'

'Yes.'

'But then she also confessed, because she assumed the Bead Man had killed her father.'

The Induna nods, for Zikihle had been in the same quandary as Nyembezi. She knew *she* hadn't killed her father, which left only Nyembezi. It didn't matter what his motives might have been, because he'd rescued her and she resolved to protect him. What's more, knowing Nandi had taken an interest in this affair, she may even have reasoned that she could count on a degree of leniency.

'Two of them confess, then,' says the Induna, 'each sincerely believing the other to be responsible, but both are wrong!'

'The Sky question.'

'Precisely! Ask me how I knew both were wrong, and I cannot tell you. But I knew there had to be someone else. And the only other person there was Masipula.'

★

Thumb smudge of orange against a black background.

A man and a boy.

The man is stretched out, resting on his left elbow, his feet pointed towards the embers.

The boy sits opposite him, resting his chin on his right knee and toying with three snail shells.

African night.

The man lies back, his hands behind his head. Now he can look past the canopy of the tree and see Impambano, Orion's Belt – and Indwendweni, the string of stars to the right of that constellation.

'Nduna!'

The Induna's head comes up with a start. He has dozed off, doesn't know how long for. The boy is fast asleep beneath a cowskin cloak, on the other side of the fire.

It's Shaka who has spoken. He sits on a rock to the Induna's left, and waves a calming hand when the warrior makes to rise.

'It is late,' he says, 'so let us dispense with some formalities. Besides, they become of little importance when you consider this meeting shouldn't be possible.'

Noting how the Induna glances at the boy a second time, the King adds that he need not worry, for they will not awaken the udibi.

As Shaka speaks, the Induna realises he is wearing the muthi of the First Fruits – Imithi Emnyama, muthi of the dead moon, isifile, and ngolu mnyama namhla, the dark day thereafter when human beings are especially vulnerable to evil.

'And, no, you are not dreaming,' says Shaka, as the Induna wonders why his King should be here sitting next to him, wearing Night Muthi out of season.

'At least I don't think so.' Shaka frowns. 'You may be dreaming, but I know I'm not.' A glint of ivory appears between the black and ochre hemi-spheres of his face, as he smiles. 'Although I do not know why I am here.' A shrug. 'Then again, maybe I do. Maybe I was guided here to hear you speak of knowledge that is of the Earth, and knowledge that is of the Sky. Or is it knowing?'

The Induna hopes the flicker of a shrug he proffers will manage to convey to the King that – whether it's knowledge or knowing – he is happy with either description.

302

'And then there's what you said about the little one's trick . . . hai, do you know that old goat Mgobozi would never even tell me the secret of his trick?'

Another flicker of a shrug, this one intended to indicate that the King can decide for himself whether the Induna does or doesn't know that.

'But what you said about repetition, and how those who once watched spellbound cease being awed and start looking – that was well put. I know that feeling.'

Shaka regards the Induna a moment, then smiles. And the warrior has to fight not to flinch as the King reaches out to squeeze his shoulder.

'I know that feeling, as I know you are disconcerted. But do not worry! For I too am confused.'

At last the Induna finds his voice. 'Confused, Majesty?'

Shaka chuckles. 'You? Confused, Majesty? You? Indeed I am, Nduna, because you are not dead.'

'Ma . . . majesty?'

'Dead, Nduna.'

'But I am not . . .'

'Precisely – which is why I am confused. I have been roaming the night and on occasion I have met and spoken with old friends . . .'

. . . but not her, never her . . .

'. . . and all have this in common. They have made the Great Journey.'

As she has, yet she eludes him as surely as the White Men!

'Except for you, Nduna.'

The Induna's arm comes up. 'You mean' – he indicates the space between them – 'we have . . . You and I, we have . . . before . . .'

'Yes, but do not ask me where or when. There is a mist, so I see only glimpses when I return from my wanderings.' As in knowing he spoke to Mgobozi, and knowing that the general told him, or let him see, something important, but being unable to remember what it was.

That reminds him . . . Mgobozi is still alive tonight. That is, he was still alive when Nandi sent the Induna to help the Bead Man. He must be careful, therefore, of inadvertently revealing to the Induna who he has spoken to. It will not do the warrior any good to know their fate, especially when it comes to Mgobozi.

And Nandi, his mother, she is still alive tonight . . .

But, before he can dwell on that thought, Shaka finds himself gazing at the sleeping udibi and finds his memory tingling. There is something the boy knows . . . or will know.

Is that why he's here?

'Majesty?'

Shaka does know this for sure, though. The harder he tries, and the more agitated he becomes, the quicker he is likely to return to Bulawayo. And so he allows the Induna to distract him.

'Yes,' he says, 'we should not be talking like this.'

'Because I am not dead?'

'That is so.'

'Then perhaps it is because I am not real, Father.'

'I hadn't thought of that.'

'I merely state the obvious, Father. Something beneath your notice.'

'Hai, Nduna, I said let us dispense with some formalities. Indeed, let us dispense with silly questions, as well. Instead, let us talk. Let me tell you how a king allowed himself to be guided by the Sky — which is to say a sense of knowing he could not explain to his advisors . . .'

★

African night, African sky: Impambano, Orion's Belt, and Indwendweni, the string of stars to the right of that constellation. African sounds: grunts and growls out there, lion roar, jackal howl, and the crunching of bones.

A King & His Mother

'Mother, if you have come to pester me about my Bulawu again . . .'

'Boy, you know how important it is that you should find your talisman, but that is not why I have come to see you.'

'Everything in its time.'

'Aiee, and it is time your hut was cleaned. Look at this dust! Are your servants blind?'

'I'll attend to it, Mother, although . . .'

'Yes, yes, *you* might not mind. You might be happy to let those lazy jackals get away with the bare minimum, but you must remember that your people look to you to set an example.'

'My children . . .' says Shaka with a rueful grin.

'Hai, you're talking to me now, boy. Save such nonsense for your court. Your children! Aiee, if you knew the pain of childbirth and parenthood . . . well, you wouldn't look so pleased with yourself.'

'But someone once said they look to me to set an example. Is that not how children look to their father?'

'And where would we be if you judged yourself according to your father's shadow?'

'Mother, you wound me!'

'Enough of this flippancy, then. You are their father, and they are your children, well and good – but beware of treating them as children!'

'As always, your wisdom enlightens me. I thank you.'

Nandi raises her hand, and Shaka leans forward with the unconscious indulgence of a son expecting a loving pat on the cheek. Instead he finds his ear tweaked.

'Mother!' he exclaims, stepping sideways, instantly regretting the girlish shriek that carried that word. But he was taken by surprise, after all.

'Sarcasm is something else you can save for the ibandla tree.'

'I did not mean . . . That was sore!'

'Enough! I have an important matter to discuss.'

'It's always important,' mutters the Bull Elephant.

'What was that?'

'Nothing.'

'Remember what I said about sarcasm?'

'I would say I am all ears, Mother, but I am not sure I'd be telling the truth,' says Shaka, gingerly rubbing the left side of his head.

'Ngoza.'

The King's hand comes away from his head. 'What of him?'

'The Buffalo is sick. He must be destroyed.'

'What ails him?' asks Shaka, fully aware that Nandi is speaking metaphorically.

'Do not cheek me, boy.'

'But you make it so easy, Mother.'

Nandi raises her hand in a mother's *I'm-warning-you* gesture.

'My apologies, Mother.'

'Cha, only apologise when you mean it.'

'Very well, Mother, but my playfulness is prompted by finding ourselves on the same path this afternoon.'

'Really? Think you that?'

'Well . . .'

'Think you that — as you swallow Pakatwayo's lies?'

'His lies?'

'His lies. Do you really think you can trust the Qwabes, simply because Qwabe and Zulu were brothers? Look how trustworthy *your* brothers are!'

Shaka has to work hard to hide his grin. If his overtures to Pakatwayo's Qwabes have fooled even his mother . . .

'What makes you say that?' he asks.

'Hai! Are you blind?' Everyone talks about Dingane, but in

Nandi's opinion it's Mhlangana who needs watching.

'I meant, Mother, what reason do you have to cast aspersions on Pakatwayo's honour?'

'The Bead Man.'

'*Who?*'

'You know him, Thutha!' *Fool!*

Yes, he does, agrees Shaka. He merely said '*Who?*' because Nandi seemed to expect some kind of response.

Not deigning to reprimand her son once more, Nandi says Nyembezi has reported to her that Ngoza's ambassadors are courting Pakatwayo as energetically as Shaka has – and with more success, it seems.

'You can trust this Bead Man?'

'Of course! He is a Zulu.'

'Cha! And all my children are loyal!'

Nandi grins. 'He also owes me his life.'

'Yes, I remember the affair.'

'Anyway, he would have reported what he heard, regardless, for he is a loyal Zulu.'

'The Qwabes and Ngoza's jackals . . .'

'Yes, even as our cousins have reassured you of their loyalty, they have been plotting with the Thembus.'

'And there is no chance of intervening?'

'You'd be wasting your time.'

Shaka nods. Even if, at the last moment, he could convince the Qwabes to join him, he'd never be able to trust them.

'You must also see how there can be no quarter given,' adds Nandi.

'Even if they are our cousins,' murmurs Shaka.

'Forget that. They have! Their king crawls before Ngoza, and have any of our cousins come to warn us? They are happy to follow him? Well, then, let them follow him to the grave.'

'Aiee! I thank you, Mother. That Pakatwayo might be untrustworthy and be working to betray me. I had not thought of that.'

'Beware, Bull Elephant, you have two ears and my fingers are strong.'

Shaka holds up a hand in submission. 'My apologies, Mother, but I am only jesting.'

'This is no time for flippancy, Boy.'

'I am aware of that. Just as you need to be aware of something else I have in mind.'

'What is that?'

He will continue to court Pakatwayo, and the Qwabe ruler will know nothing of his suspicions.

'Suspicions? I bring you more than suspicions, Boy.'

'Please, Mother, let me finish.'

'Then finish, Boy.'

'That is what I said I wanted to do.'

'Now *you* interrupt *me*! I was about to say: finish but choose your words more carefully!'

'I will, Mother.'

'Then finish, Boy!'

'As I have said, I will continue to flatter Pakatwayo, but I will also be sending emissaries to Ngoza to speak of a possible alliance between Thembu and Zulu.'

'Why?'

Nandi's shocked incredulity is a joy to behold.

Shaka grins, taps his forehead, clutches his crotch. 'Because two ears aren't the only things I have.'

Hai, but you would know of Mnkabayi and Ndlela . . .

At this time Mnkabayi is content to spend most of her time in the nation's northernmost war kraal. Next to KwaBulawayo, it is the Sky People's most important ikhanda. And, of course, that is a testament to her status, and the trust Shaka has placed in her. And his cause is still her cause, and the qualms that surface from time to time are easy to put aside.

It's more often than not Ndlela who brings these potential problems to her. He's probably even more knowledgeable about the intricacies of Zulu lore than Mduli was. And matters such as the isicoco, and Shaka refusing to let his warriors marry, bother him.

Ndlela's conservatism is a trait Mnkabayi finds amusing at times (even endearing, although that's not an adjective that readily springs to mind when thinking of a veteran soldier who has a scar stretching from his hairline, just in front of his right ear, down to his jawbone, where the tip of the blade caught but was bumped free, as well as several smaller scars, like fossilised mopani worms, embedded across his body and thighs). His knowledge is also useful, especially in predicting how people will respond to royal decrees that might be considered controversial.

But his conservatism can be annoying, too. Why must the traditions be so scrupulously honoured? Because the ancestors deem it fitting, he'll say, and it's a way of keeping them happy. But how can he be certain this tradition or that ritual is exactly the same as it was in his great-grandfather's day? Even she can see how some of the rites have changed since she was a little girl! It's a debate they've often had, with Ndlela always resorting to some vague declaration that the ancestors will guide one, if one is willing to honour them by upholding the traditions . . .

What does worry her is Jakot's revelations about certain savages wanting to seek out Shaka. She's just as sceptical of his pronouncements as her nephew is, but like him – and Mbopa and Mgobozi – she feels there's no reason to doubt this aspect of his tale. Plans will have to be made. As yet unaware of the depths of Shaka's obsession with the White Men, she agrees with Mbopa that some kind of accord needs to be reached with those barbarians. If all they want is gold and ivory, well and good! But let them see what the izilwane offer in return.

Nandi is the only one of the King's inner circle who doesn't seem interested in the Swimmer's claims. She's more concerned with encouraging her son to complete his wars of conquest by subjugating the remaining tribes in the region – and perhaps moving further afield. Like Ndlela, she is also bothered by Shaka's refusal to seek out his Ubulawu, the talisman every Zulu king must find. The king will know it when he lays eyes on it and, once he's found his Ubulawu, he'll become stronger, more powerful. This is very like Nandi – she's always been short-sighted and lacking in imagination, in Mnkabayi's estimation – and it's another cause for concern. Instead of being pestered about such nonsense, Shaka would be better advised to consolidate his position and first deal with the White Men.

Yet now Nandi also seems to want him to taunt the Thembus into taking the field.

The only consolation is that the last time Mnkabayi saw the Queen Mother, she was shocked by how frail Nandi had become; and Shaka's mother is younger than her! Perhaps the Great Journey is not far off, in which case Mnkabayi has plans to take Nandi's place in Shaka's inner circle. To this end she has long been cultivating Pampata's friendship and trust.

The Vanishing Man

The sangomas who arrived yesterday afternoon have ordered the villagers to gather in the cattlefold in the centre of the umuzi. They have supplanted the village chief, and now they are calling his people to their death. And they will be obeyed. For no matter how much you might curse them behind their backs, you can't stop from shrinking before their gaze, because you have been raised to fear them. The respect and reverence everyone talks of are simply alternative words for dread and terror. Nostrils flare, a finger is curled or pointed, and that's that – you are guilty. And so sons will be pulled from mothers, wives from husbands, fathers from shrieking children. Guilty because they say so; because they dwell where *then* and *now* overlap to create something else: a glimpse into the future. And they rule this land, having been called to rule by the ancestors. And when they stride forth . . . watch out! Young or old, a mother or a grandmother, a baby or an invalid, it matters not to them, for they know wizards and witches assume many forms, though no umthakathi's disguise can fool them. And they are never wrong, no never; their nostrils cannot be deceived, for they are guided by the ancestors. And the village unumzane can do nothing but stand aside. No one protests, for to speak out against the sangomas is to draw suspicion upon oneself. To challenge them is a sign of guilt akin to being found holding a bloodied spear over a dead body. Until Shaka came to power, even kings had to tread carefully. And some of the old ways have returned today, because there is, after all, the matter of the vanishing man.

He has gone away, stolen by wizards, and in his place have appeared these creatures.

They are led by a sangoma called Kholisa. Shaka long ago punished the Lion for his treachery, and later forced a showdown with Nobela that saw her sent to pester the ancestors personally. With a personality as fit for inspiring loyalty as his right foot is for walking, Kholisa will never be as powerful or respected as those two, but for now the matter of the Vanishing Man has enabled him to gather together this band of six sangomas and their retinues, which triples their number. And he is aided by the fact that many of the villagers are genuinely unsettled, and believe a Smelling Out is needed.

Wearing their animal skins and pelts, and with their faces painted or hidden by masks, the sangomas will move among the villagers, chanting and wailing, hissing and keening. Some of their apprentices will assist them here, while others beat the drums.

Meanwhile, in a conscious attempt to imitate Nobela, Kholisa will stand aloof with the two men he has designated as his bodyguards. Like Nobela, he would like to make it clear that such exertions are not for him. Like Nobela, he will focus on those who have been chosen by the others and dragged forward, while seeking the ringleaders in this band of abathakathi – these wizards who have brought misfortune upon the village.

And the drums are beating, and the izangoma are working themselves up into a frenzy. Here a short, wiry male wears the head of a hyena; there, naked except for a loincloth, a woman has painted her body, hair, breasts and limbs ochre, and is shaking a rattle made out of a calabash and the teeth of a leopard. A man smeared with ash from burnt assegai hafts is moving backwards, guided by two apprentices; his body bends and twists while his legs jerk and twitch. Another sangoma, wearing the horns of wildebeest and a necklace fashioned from the vertebrae of a python, screams at the sky. Nearby, her body rigid and her neck at an angle, a woman is held upright by two helpers; she'll begin to twitch once she comes anywhere near to an umthakathi.

And the drums are beating, like a pounding headache, and the terror is as palpable as the dust. Babies wail and are forcibly silenced, but better that – better a mother's hand pressed over a tiny mouth – than attracting the attention of a sniffing, snuffling, snorting sangoma.

Old-timers faint in the heat, and are left where they fall. Men clench their fists in helpless frustration, knowing there's nothing they can do to protect their loved ones. The unumzane's eyes burn with shame because he is powerless against the onslaught of these who have the Calling. And haunting all is the fact of the Vanishing Man; the feeling this might indeed be warranted, even deserved.

And a man . . .

No, wait, there are two men: a short, slightly bow-legged man about fifty seasons old and, behind him, his younger companion who is tall, broad-shouldered.

These two have broken through the front ranks, and both are wearing amashoba, and each carries a shield and an iklwa . . . which can't be right.

Five paces forward and they stop.

And wait.

And the izangoma cavort and squawk, and the drums keep up their monotonous, sweaty beat, and the two men stand firm where they are, and wait. And whispers sneak through the villagers, and their eyes are drawn to the two men.

Then Kholisa spots them. This is his moment! This is a chance to show all he is even more powerful than that bitch Nobela, who laughed at him and had him chased away when he came seeking to be taken on as one of her apprentices. He is well aware of the importance of showing authority, defiance, yet for all this he cannot stop his heart from beating faster when he sees the two men, realising they are armed. Before he knows it, his mouth is dry and he no longer feels aloof, just . . . exposed. He tightens his grip on his staff, tries a soft growl, anything to rekindle that sense of entitlement, of a prerogative that extends beyond the caprices of a king.

And gradually the others become aware of these interlopers, who have dared to leave the crowd. And they grow quiet, some falling before they fall silent.

And finally the message, the sense that something's not right, that something has gone wrong or is about to go wrong, reaches the drummers, and they leave off beating the cowhide to gape at the two men, the short old one and the tall young one. The men who shouldn't be here — and who certainly shouldn't be carrying spears.

Once silence has settled over the kraal, the two men amble towards Kholisa, the sweating, panting sangomas and their apprentices parting before them.

'I hope we are not too late,' says Mgobozi. 'We came as fast as we could.'

★

'And now this!' Shaka had said. 'I have the Thembus and the Qwabes to tend to, and now this. These root-gnashers have a knack for choosing the most inopportune times.'

'Mayhap it's their only knack, Majesty. And perhaps for them the inopportune is opportune,' said Mgobozi.

'You state the obvious, old friend.'

'I merely wish to remind you . . .'

'. . . without seeming to remind me, for that would be . . .'

'. . . dangerous, Majesty?'

'I was going to say impolitic, but never mind. You were saying? No, wait, you were *reminding* me . . . ?'

'That perhaps they do indeed choose well their moment of striking, Majesty.'

'Instead of having it chosen by the ancestors?'

'That is what they would say. A most disingenuous response!'

'So what would you have me do? Impale the lot of them? Cha, but look who I'm asking!'

'Indeed, I believe your Majesty is well acquainted with my views on the subject.'

'This is so. But will impaling do the job? There are always more of them springing up.'

'But are they not weaker each time, Majesty? For, if our informants are to be believed, this one . . . this Kholisa is no Nobela.'

'True, although that only brings us to another question. Who is behind him? Nobela needed no prompting, and would be guided or ruled by no one. This one is timid by comparison. Yet suddenly he comes out of hiding, hobbles forth, his own praise singer.'

'Cha, Majesty, maybe it is what it is! This preposterous tale of a man vanishing in front of a friend, it's just the thing to goad a pompous fool into overreaching himself. So let us investigate, Majesty!'

'By us you mean you, with some Fasimbas and the Nduna, I take it?'

'Yes, Majesty. I know you granted him furlough, Majesty, but he has not gone back to his homestead. He's at Nkululeko KaDingwa's kraal, which, as you know, lies in the direction we must take if we are to make the acquaintance of this sangoma who has grown tired of life.'

'Very well, let this not become an ember that flares up. We have Ngoza of the Thembus already growling in the distance, and we cannot have a fire in our own kraal.'

'I understand, Majesty.'

'That's also why, Mgobozi, I order you to find the truth behind the lies that encircle this preposterous tale, as you call it, like a thorn fence. Thwart the sangomas that way. No impalings, hear? There will be more lies and rumours before Ngoza is mine, and the people will be unsettled enough. We cannot have them thinking the ancestors are angry, and punishing me for allowing one of my generals to indulge in one of his favourite pastimes.'

'And one that gives me so much pleasure, too, Majesty, but I hear you. I understand! I will . . .'

'Restrain is the word you're looking for. You will restrain yourself.'

'If you say so, Majesty.'

'I do, old friend. Now go! Proffer my apologies to the Nduna, although he will understand the need for prompt and decisive action, and let us see this matter dealt with!'

★

A vanishing man? That certainly smacked of sorcery! Within days of the first search parties being sent out, the lies and the rumours were racing across the kingdom. Witness the way the Induna, Mgobozi and their Fasimbas have made good time, but have still been beaten

315

to the village by Kholisa and a conspiracy of his cohorts . . .

And it's not lost on the Induna or the general how hard Kholisa is trying to emulate Nobela. In a low voice that will never be as ominous as Nobela's, he addresses Mgobozi, who is wearing the blue feather that identifies him as the Shadow of Shaka. 'There is sorcery here,' he says. 'Sorcery!'

'So *that's* what it is, Nduna,' says Mgobozi, turning to his companion, 'and here I was thinking it was the stench of another hyena's arsehole.'

There's a shifting behind them. For how can the general speak to a sangoma like that? At the same time, though, word has begun to filter in, from those on the fringes of the crowd, that other armed men have made their appearance. These two are not alone.

'But, speaking of sorcery,' continues the general, 'you're not about to conduct a Smelling Out, are you? Not without the King's permission!'

Another ripple. This is an interesting revelation, for many don't know the King's permission is needed.

And, of course, it isn't. Not as far the sangomas are concerned.

'The ancestors do not need—'

'No, but *you* do!' interrupts Mgobozi.

'There is evil here! It must be smelt out!'

'Perhaps. But that is why *we* are here.'

'And again you insult the ancestors!'

Mgobozi raises his spear. 'Look up,' he tells Kholisa. 'What do you see? The sky! And Shaka is the Father of the Sky, and so long as we are beneath the sky we are in his realm. Let the ancestors tend to their own affairs. Besides, how does the King rule if not with the ancestors' blessing?'

'But if he should insult them . . .'

'Speak you now of Shaka?'

'No,' says Kholisa hastily, 'of any king.'

'Hai! Shaka is not *any* king. And the Great Journey awaits those who think otherwise.'

★

316

Later, after he has told the villagers to go about their business, and ordered his Fasimbas to keep the sangomas confined in the same cattle kraal where they were going to herd those they had identified as witches and wizards, Mgobozi summons the headman and his elders. 'Know this,' he says softly, 'the Bull Elephant does not blame you for allowing this to take place – this invasion, this infestation of lice – for he knows you had no choice.'

'This is so, Shadow of Shaka,' says the headman. 'This is so.'

'But you are a Zulu, are you not? And so are your people! And I am here to see that you act like Zulus. There will be no more such cringing before drivelling men and incontinent old ladies, understood?'

'Yes, Shadow of Shaka. But . . .'

'I know. This vanishing, it is strange. Or maybe not. We will see.'

★

What happened was that Magema was walking along late one afternoon, when he met his friend Sitheku approaching from the opposite direction. After exchanging greetings, they hunkered down in the shade of some bushes, for the setting sun was still strong, and each had a pinch of Magema's snuff. They chatted a while, then said their goodbyes. About a hundred metres on from these bushes, the path rose to join a wider track. When he reached this spot, Magema turned and hailed his friend. Upon hearing him, Sitheku also turned. Raising his arm, he shouted something Magema couldn't make out – and shouted it again when Magema made a show of tugging at his right ear. Then both young men made dismissive, forget-about-it gestures and turned away almost simultaneously.

Then something, he didn't know what, made Magema look back again . . .

. . . and Sitheku was gone.

Gone?

Gone.

Magema had already told the story many times, before Mgobozi and the Induna arrived – and would tell it several times more under

317

the Induna's disconcerting gaze – and this was almost always the response of his listeners. *Gone?* Soon the question didn't even have to be spoken aloud. It was there in Magema's unconscious hesitation – itself a result of having been repeatedly interrupted at this point. It was in the tensing of his listeners: the swallowing and the leaning forward of one about to speak, followed by a second stiffening as one decides it's better to keep quiet. Like the slow shattering of the moon, it was disbelief, it was incredulity, it was denial, the shrinking slivers finally giving way to fear. The fear that was like isifile, the dead moon, and the dark day thereafter.

Gone?

Gone.

In the direction Sitheku had been heading, the path entered a grove of tamboti trees, a parade of spear-straight trunks now thrown askew as the setting sun laid shadows across their massed ranks. Was Magema sure that his friend could not have quickened his pace, started running even, so that, when Magema looked back, Sitheku was already in among the trees, becoming lost amid the zebra stripes of light and dark?

That was a fair question at a time before the search parties had been despatched. But Magema could only shrug, tilt his head to the side, twist his lips. He'd be relieved if that was what had really happened; it was just that Sitheku had been too far away from the tambotis. Magema didn't think it was possible for anyone to run that fast. Neither, for that matter, did he think his friend could have reached the bushes that lay between them in the brief time it took for him to look away and then look back.

And there was that feeling, he said – which he'd like to forget, but couldn't – that strange feeling, the tug, that had compelled him to look back, even before he realised what he was doing. It had kept him standing there, gaping, while that strange feeling had become a sense of certainty that, although he hadn't actually seen it happen, his friend had vanished off a path running through the middle of the open veld.

★

'So, this Beetle . . . aiee, this Beetle sends me a message. Me! *And he says let us unite. Let us join forces and rule this land together!'*

Ngoza, the Mighty Buffalo and paramount chief of the Thembu nation, waits for the laughter of his lieutenants to die down.

'Yes, this is what he says. He invites me to join him. I have many things to say to that, and here is the first of them . . .' With a pah! he spits on to the ground.

They are at the Place of Wisdom, a flat expanse of rock just below the summit of an escarpment. It's the larger of two steps, and able to accommodate Ngoza and his twenty advisors, as well as their servants. To the left, in a niche in the sheltering wall, there's a fireplace where food can be cooked. On the opposite side, there's the trickle of a stream that has its source atop the escarpment. It descends on to the second ledge, and then falls a few hundred metres, becoming a thread of silver that will eventually reach the sea, growing stronger all the way.

A variety of bones – skulls, femurs, ribcages – litters the second ledge. It's here that special executions are held and the bodies then left to the elements, so that the Thembu shades, in the guise of vultures, might feast on these offerings. Every so often the nation's chief shaman and his helpers will grind the bones down, using special stones, and feed the powder to the river, to appease the spirits of the land.

The top step is reached from the escarpment by following the cleft carved by the stream. The second, narrower, ledge is less than two metres below the first. Prisoners are forced to leap down there to reach it, while their guards use a ladder.

Ngoza raises a hand to silence the sneers and sniggers of his men. 'And then,' he says moving to the edge, 'just to prove to me how sincere he is, the Beetle sends an impi sniffing around my feet!'

He shakes his head and stands for a moment, staring down at the four Zulu emissaries. Their wrists and ankles tied, the men lie at the feet of their captors, one of whom is a monolith bigger than even Njikiza, with hands each as large as a full moon, and thighs that will make any chief's best bull look scrawny.

'Look!' says Ngoza, and his lieutenants crowd forward. 'See the Beetle's lions! See the anger in their eyes. See them struggle. See them suffer as their bonds bite back.'

Turning away and moving back to the wooden throne that is carried down to the Place of Wisdom every time there's a meeting, Ngoza waits for his men to gather around him.

'Mark what I say,' he says, keeping his voice low. 'Set those men free and they will try to devour us even though we have them at our mercy, and though we are many and they are but four. We must not underestimate the Beetle – or his lions.'

The River's Secret

A Qhumbuza takes place at the time of uma inyanga ihlangene, when, much like the blooming of the moon, a child on the cusp of puberty becomes a full member of the family, and thus is expected to play a larger part in the life of the family.

A few days before the ceremony, children of the requisite intanga, or age-set, are summoned to the district head's kraal. They're accompanied by their parents, who bring beer, mealies and livestock for the feast that will follow the ear-piercing.

Until then, however, the children are kept in seclusion to ensure they don't come into contact with anyone who might be unclean, such as menstruating or pregnant women, and those who've been to a burial recently or couples who've just had sexual intercourse. Anyone else may visit the children to offer advice, and the Induna's udibi remembers well how the abafana, the boys in his age-set, were told to be courageous; to love cattle, for one cannot be a man without cattle; and to always sit qoshama, with the knees drawn up – not bazalala, or flat, like women – so you can be ready to rise in an instant.

The piercing itself is performed at the entrance to the cattle kraal. The children are lined up according to the rank of their parents. When the abafana are finished, it's the turn of the amantombazana, the girls. The instrument used is a strip of iron sharpened at one end. After the piercing, the top of a corn stalk is placed in the newly made hole. As the ear heals, larger and larger pieces are inserted. An infection is regarded as scandalous.

The piercings over, the children return to the huts set aside for them, where their seclusion continues for another three days. They're still believed to be vulnerable to the unclean, but this period of seclusion also enables those in charge of such things to ensure the wounds are kept clean until properly healed.

An induna yesigodi, or district head, whose umuzi was situated near a tributary of the White Umfolozi, Nkululeko KaDingwa had been at Bulawayo when Shaka granted the Induna a furlough and had invited his old comrade-in-arms to be among the honoured guests at the Qhumbuza due to be held at his village.

Since this Qhumbuza involved some sixty boys and forty girls, the piercings would be spread out over three mornings. The boy had looked forward to attending the ceremony, as a spectator and as an honoured guest's udibi. After all, if the Qhumbuza marked a definite stage in a child's development, and signalled a change in how he or she was treated, being able to watch others undergo the piercing surely meant one had oneself moved even closer to adulthood. But, shortly after midday on the second day, Radebe quietly approached the Induna. The general sent his compliments and . . .

Needless to say, the boy was bitterly disappointed when he heard he wasn't going to accompany his master, but he knew it was no good arguing.

He helped the Induna pack, saw him off at daybreak, and since then he's been in a prolonged mope.

'Hssst! Hey!'

Sitting in the shade of the tree, the udibi ignores these utterances made with such melodramatic intensity. His head bowed, he's listening to the screech of the cicadas and watching the ants patrol the dirt. Nothing feels worth doing any more, and even the prospect of the impending feast has palled.

'Hssst! Hey!'

The Induna had patiently explained that the need for secrecy meant they both couldn't leave this ceremony before it was over. Otherwise it would be all too obvious that something was afoot. What's more, all the ensuing talk and speculation could ruin the Qhumbuza, for it would cease to be the focus of attention. They couldn't do that to their host! Nkululeko would know the real reason for the Induna's departure, of course, but the story would meanwhile be put about he had sick cattle to tend to. If anyone doubted the truth of this explanation, there was continued presence of the udibi. If it had been something serious, he would have gone with the Induna, but no, he had remained behind to represent his master. 'Hai,' chuckled the Induna, 'they already call you Shadow of the Shadow, so now become the Shadow of the Shadow!'

The boy should have savoured this compliment, a sign of the great trust the Induna had in him, but it still feels to him as if he's being punished.

'Hssst!'

The clouds are high today, almost touching the roof of the sky. Winds up there pull them into slender ropes, frayed and unravelling, but down here the wind is merely a breeze, like a calf struggling to walk. When it stands, teetering on its long, ungainly legs, the grass rustles; when it topples over, the grass is silent. And the heat steps forward to remind you that it's still around, and it will take more than such a little whisper to chase it away.

'Hey!'

The voice comes from behind the tree. If the speaker wants to hide himself, it seems a redundant precaution, as the trunk is narrow and the boy just needs to turn around to see who's trying to attract his attention. Not that he needs to do that, for he knows who it is.

'What do you want, Philani?'

Philani has been following the udibi around ever since the older boy arrived, and stepped up his pestering after the Induna's departure two days ago. His parents are dead and he lives with a married sister, understands loneliness in the instinctive way of the solitary child, and perhaps sees in the udibi a kindred spirit. Or just a temporary older brother.

'I have something to show you,' he says.

★

Magema stood staring into space, oblivious to the approach of the village elder. Hafa, quickening his pace, was about to chastise Magema for his lack of manners, but his annoyance became concern as he

323

drew closer to the youth. It was as if Magema was fast asleep on his feet with his eyes open, he tells the Induna. And he didn't respond when the elder's grey-tipped fingers closed around his arm. A gentle squeeze . . . then something a little firmer, Hafa's callused fingertips pressing deeper, leaving leopard spots when he let go.

That seemed to revive the youngster. To his credit, as both the elder and the village's unumzane agree, Magema proceeded to tell the truth. He could have shrugged and said there was nothing wrong, and proceeded on his dazed way after apologising for his rudeness. Instead, risking ridicule, not to mention Hafa's wrath, he told the elder what had just happened.

How Sitheku had been there – *right there!*

How both of them had turned away, at almost the same time . . .

How he'd looked back again . . .

Hafa immediately instructed Magema to lead him to the exact spot on the path where Sitheku had been standing. But, looking around, he couldn't see anything out of the ordinary. The grass was undisturbed, the softer edges on each side of the path a quilt of faint footprints. There were no convenient rocks or bushes that Sitheku could have hidden behind – and Magema was adamant that Sitheku could not have darted back into the buffalo-thorns where they had taken snuff.

Sitheku was playing a joke on Magema, decided Hafa. 'What else could I think?' he tells the Induna. It would not have been out of character, for Sitheku had a reputation for being something of an isilawuli, a prankster.

'You did not consider that *both* of them intended you to be the prey?' asks the Induna.

'No, never,' says Hafa. For they knew all too well what trouble they would have found themselves in; and even if Sitheku had been tempted, he would not have been able to involve Magema.

'Yet they were friends . . .'

'But, Nduna, we have all seen this before: the one pushes, the other pulls, and together they are stronger.' When it came to play-ing a trick on a village elder, it was doubtful Sitheku would have been able to persuade Magema to join him, while in fact the latter would have endeavoured to restrain his friend.

'I told Magema that doubtless he would find Sitheku at his father's hut, waiting there to laugh himself silly at his distress.'

With that, the two parted. Magema returned to the main trail, while Hafa, who'd been intending to take the other path anyway, headed for the trees with a little more purpose in his stride, half hoping he'd catch up with Sitheku.

Magema got back to the village after dark and only went in search of his friend the following morning. That was when he learnt that Sitheku hadn't returned home, after taking a bull to Bubula's homestead. His father wasn't all that concerned – Sitheku could certainly look after himself – but he was decidedly less sanguine after Magema related his strange tale.

They immediately went to seek an audience with the unumzane of the village. He in turn summoned Hafa, who confirmed what Magema had said, and agreed this was taking a practical joke too far even by Sitheku's standards.

The headman then sent Hafa, Magema, Sitheku's father and two other men to the spot where Magema had last seen his friend.

★

'How far till we reach this secret?'

The udibi's annoyance is unnoticed by Philani as he turns round. 'Not far,' he says.

Not far? How far is *not far* to a child? And this one seems a most inside-out child, and upside down. Wearing his isinene around his forehead, in a manner of speaking. For most children, the shortest distance can seem far, an interminable trek, but they've been following the river for a long way already. In fact, they're following – in the opposite direction, of course – the path the udibi and the Induna took to get to the umuzi. Does Philani want them to go all the way to Bulawayo?

'How much farther?' asks the udibi again, well aware he's the one who sounds like a child.

'We are near,' says Philani, stopping. 'But we must hurry,' he adds.

'Why?'

'I do not like this place.'

'What place?' And if he doesn't like it, why has he brought his new friend here?

'This place . . . the river.'

'The river?'

'Yes.'

'*This* river?'

'*Yes.* I am scared it will take me. It won't take me, will it?'

Ah! Now the udibi understands: Philani's thinking of the Cat Man's story . . .

The little boy nods vigorously.

'That was just a story.'

'But that is what I want to show you.'

'What?' The udibi frowns. 'What do you want to show me?'

'We must go further on.'

'But I thought you were afraid.'

'Hai, I am. But I think it has also eaten, so we should be safe.'

'Eaten?'

'Yes. Come now, please.'

'Hai! Hai, what's this? You are far from home, my little brothers!'

Philani all but leaps into the udibi's arms. It's Lungelo, the Cat Man's nephew. The udibi gently but firmly eases Philani aside, bristling at being called 'little brother'.

'And you, too,' he says, 'you are also far from home, *Little Brother.*'

'Aiee! It's my lot to be far from home. At least, this is what my uncle says. It is our lot, he says.'

That superior tone grates, especially since the same can be said of the udibi. Hai, he has probably travelled further and seen more than Lungelo, all the while serving the King. 'And now?' he asks. 'Are you practising?'

'I don't understand . . .'

'Roaming,' says the udibi. 'Are you practising your roaming?'

A mirthless grin. 'No, I thought there might be some pools where

I can catch fish, but I could find none, and the river flows too fast.'

'This is so.'

'And you?'

Out of the corner of his eye, the udibi sees Philani straighten up, ready to speak and he brings his hand down on the younger boy's shoulder to silence him. They have come in search of imphepho, he says in a flash of inspiration, referring to the yellow flower used as a form of incense in the sacrifice of beef that follows the piercing ceremony.

Well, then, says Lungelo with a snigger, he will now leave them to look for their flowers.

They watch him until he's disappeared from sight. Then Philani says: 'You lied.'

Yes, and the udibi's not quite sure why. Possibly it had something to do with Lungelo's superior tone, the way he already acts like a man, although he has yet to join his regiment. And probably never will, for such is the shiftless existence of those like the Cat Man and his kind. 'Peddlers', others in another time and place might call them. And their children are as unruly and shiftless as the lifestyle they've chosen. Surviving on services rendered, on the occasional usefulness. But shiftless and shifty. Watch your cattle when they're near, and your pots, even. Guard your secrets, no matter what they might be, as anything and everything it seems can be fashioned by these people into something that is needed or wanted by others.

And Philani says, 'You lied.'

And the boy shrugs. 'So?' he asks. 'Did you not say this thing you want to show me is a secret?' Staring sternly at the little one. 'Or did my ears deceive me?'

Philani shakes his head, grinning. He would have told all, for Lungelo scares him, but the udibi has saved him. Clearly his faith in the wisdom of his new friend hasn't been misplaced.

★

After they had searched the immediate area, including the stand of tambotis, Hafa went to the headman and requested some more men.

327

For the rest of that day, and the next, search parties roamed the region. Sitheku's brothers were questioned almost as many times as Magema was made to retell his story. Had Sitheku let anything slip that might suggest he was planning to run away or, for whatever reason, was going to pretend to run away?

They knew nothing; neither did Magema, or Sitheku's other friends. The youth had no reason to run away. He hadn't been accused of theft and, although he considered his charms too much for even the hardest feminine heart to withstand, he hadn't got any of the maidens in the village with child, or incurred a father's wrath while exercising some of those charms.

'Of this you can be sure?' asks the Induna.

Both Hafa and the unumzane nod.

'General, Nduna, will you be able to help us?' asks the headman.

It's Mgobozi who wears the blue crane feather, and is the Shadow of Shaka here, and it is he who answers this question that is also a plea. 'We will,' he says. 'Have no fear of that! And if we cannot make the vanishing man reappear we can at least make those who have appeared since his passing, very like dung appearing after a herd of cattle . . . we can make them vanish!'

★

The river has narrowed to the width of three hunting spears, but it remains deep and fast-flowing. Incema and eelgrass grow along its soggy banks, making access to the water difficult. Philani leads the udibi to a small inlet where the current curves in a slight detour, like a brief aside that soon rejoins the main cacophony. Further in, however, the depth decreases, so that for the most part the inlet is comprised of stagnant pools little more than puddles surrounded by dark brown mud peppered with hundreds of tiny holes, and fringed with a mat of glasswort samphire, a segmented perennial that resembles flattened millipedes.

And Philani stands there, shaking his head in disbelief.

'Is this the place?' asks the udibi.

'Yes, but . . .'

328

'But?'

'But it was there!' says Philani.

'What was?' asks the boy.

'The body.'

The udibi stiffens. He can't have heard right? 'The *what*?'

'Body,' hisses Philani.

'A body? Of a human?'

'Yes. One such as you.'

'Me?' asks the udibi, wondering what sets himself apart.

But Philani simply means that the body belonged to a youth close to the udibi's age. 'One in your ntanga,' he explains.

'And it's . . . ?'

'There!'

The udibi frowns. Philani seems to be pointing at a spot near where the inlet becomes a bed of eelgrass. Or is he pointing at the reeds? Or to a spot within the eelgrass? Or . . . ?

'He was there yesterday. In the shallow water.' An anxious look. 'You must believe me. I wanted you to see, because of the Cat Man's story. About the little sister who was fed to the river. And then here, yesterday, I found . . .'

A body, swept into the inlet. The boy's eyes scan the mud, its cracked, flaking, brown scabs a shade darker than his own skin. He scans the sluggish, sickly water.

'I wanted to show you, but now it's gone.'

'I believe you,' says the udibi, more to calm Philani than anything else.

'The Cat Man's story – it's true!'

The river has taken him, taken this boy, and what if its hunger has not been sated? Who will be next?

'The King broods, Mother.'

'I know.'

'What I had hoped would be a lesson to our enemies, leading to a lasting peace, has turned out to be but a respite.'

'Such is the way of this land, Daughter.'

'I know.' Pampata sighs. 'And I know it was foolish to even wish they might see the folly of trying to challenge us, after Zwide was vanquished.'

'Folly is right,' says Nandi, 'but you weren't foolish. They might be our enemies, and some might even see them as beasts fit only for slaughter, but you and I see mothers and wives, and it's not foolish to want to see them spared the pain of losing their loved ones. No, it is their leaders who are foolish!'

'And our women, Mother? Do they not also stand to lose sons and lovers? Their tears will join the river, and all tears are alike, are they not?'

Nandi sighs, for Pampata is right. Rhetoric is all very well, and has its place under the ibandla tree or on the eve of the battle, but one must face facts as well — and sooner rather than later.

'My son is concerned because the emissaries he sent to Ngoza have not yet returned?'

Pampata nods. 'They should have got back by now.'

Face facts: Shaka's position remains far from secure. Ironically, his success against the Ndwandwes has made his position even more perilous. Viewed in the context of the ongoing jostling for power within the region, Shaka's defeat of Zwide was akin to an ambush: coming out of nowhere and startling everyone.

Now no one will underestimate the Zulus to that degree again. Shaka is still viewed as an upstart, and few doubt that his impis can be crushed,

330

but now his enemies have a clearer idea of his tactics, a greater respect for the discipline that drives his army. There will be no more such ambushes. Not if they can help it.

Now they are working at setting their own traps. Witness the way the Qwabes have smiled at Shaka, while busy weaving an alliance with Ngoza, ruler of the Thembus.

But, right now, Shaka's mind is pointed westward. He still seems to think he can bring Ngoza into his kraal, or at least see what the Thembu chief is willing to offer in exchange for his intestines being allowed to remain inside their stomach cavity.

And although Nandi can't understand her son's reasoning here, she's not surprised that Shaka is in one of his moods. The fact that the emissaries are overdue is not a good sign, for you can be sure they haven't been detained while swilling beer in Ngoza's capital in celebration of a new alliance.

What The Induna Saw

Situated about two kilometres from the village, the homestead comprises five huts arranged in a V-shape, with the dwelling of the head of the family at the apex. The other huts belong to his four wives and his daughters. Storage huts and the homes of his unmarried sons lie to the rear of the compound. The homestead is encircled by a fence made of poles lashed together, and the cattle kraal is situated in the front, itself encircled by a hedge of thornbushes.

On the day he disappeared, Sitheku had come here bringing with him the bull his father had promised Bubula. He had also used the opportunity to visit with Bubula's eldest daughter, Nomona. It wasn't that he had any designs on her, rather it's just the way he was. He fancied himself as the isoka, or sweetheart, every maiden longed for; and if they spurned his advances, they were simply playing hard to get. Not for him uqume, ipopomo or the other potions that lovesick youths sometimes had recourse to. His words were all he needed. Watched over by Nomona's mother, Sitheku had chatted and flirted with the girl until she had been obliged to return to her chores.

'And when he left, he went that way?' asks the Induna, pointing his iklwa towards the main trail.

'He went the same way he came,' agrees Bubula. 'I saw that for myself, for I came to ask him to thank his father once more, on my behalf.'

It's the day after they had arrived and interrupted the Smelling Out. It's also about the same time in the afternoon that Sitheku disappeared, and the Induna's now retracing the youth's steps.

After leaving Bubula's kraal, Sitheku was spotted by a woman and her two children. She had noticed nothing strange about him.

Then there were the three herdboys letting their cattle drink as Sitheku passed through the ford. They are sure it was him, and the Induna's inclined to believe them.

The Induna lowers himself on to his heels. Resting his right hand on a convenient rock, he leans forward and scoops up some water from the stream with his left hand. He swallows, stands up.

Perhaps it was not where he was coming from, but where he was going to that's important, he tells himself.

'Or perhaps it was something along the way, Master.'

The Induna wheels round. Those words were spoken with his udibi's voice, and for a moment he had forgotten that the boy isn't with him . . . This boy who is no longer a boy, and who won't be with him for much longer.

To shrug off such thoughts, the Induna tastes those words again. *Something along the way.*

A chance meeting . . . ? Someone Sitheku didn't expect to see . . . ? It's certainly something to consider.

But here is Magema, accompanied by two Fasimbas.

He's standing at the point where the path leaves the main trail. It runs down the shallow slope, then through the knee-high grass of a strip of flat land – a natural meadow of sorts – before entering the grove of tamboti trees on the opposite side. Its ultimate destination is the village. The main trail also leads to the village, but this path is used as a short cut by those who live on the southern edge of the settlement.

As the Induna and Mgobozi found, after walking this stretch several times this morning, there's an optical illusion here. The clump of bushes, where the two friends sheltered to share some snuff, lies in the centre of the meadow and the path passes through these same bushes. But the bushes are located in a deep, elongated donga. Standing where the path leaves the main trail, you can't see that there's a fold in the land. For the path itself adds to the illusion. The place where it drops into the donga and the spot where it emerges on the other side are directly in line – at least from the vantage point of anyone standing at the spot where the path joins the main track. That means the donga itself is invisible, and therefore the path seems to travel in a straight line through the bushes.

So, if you're watching from here, anyone walking along the path will suddenly drop out of sight. Look away at the right time, and it'll be as if they've just vanished.

'I have walked here every day of my life and never noticed that,' says Magema, after the Induna has had one of the Fasimbas run along the path to demonstrate how a 'vanishing' could take place.

'But, Nduna,' he adds, 'are you saying someone might have been hiding in those bushes, and attacked Sitheku after we went our separate ways?'

'What say *you*? Could that have happened?'

'Hai, we were sitting right there, so I'm sure we would have spotted anyone else hiding in the bushes.'

The Induna nods.

'Could it be that the sangomas are right, Nduna? Is witchcraft at work here?'

Both men find themselves gazing in the direction of the village, where the crippled sangoma waits, fuming, under Mgobozi's watchful eye. He's no Nobela — imagine her earthworm lips pursed and sucking, trees bent horizontal, leaves, branches torn off, sand and stones, and legs and arms flailing, fingers trying to dig into rock, all being pulled back into the hurricane whistle of her call — but old fears die hard. He's no Nobela, but he stands for the same things she did; claiming to have received a Calling, and therefore a rank and an authority from beyond the realm of mortals. Those like Mgobozi might laugh, and speak of a 'rank authority', but many more will be haunted by a niggling thought, the late night what-if, for who's to say Shaka isn't wrong. What if the sangomas really are the ones who speak for the ancestors, the ones who endure while kings come and go? What if they genuinely see — and know — more?

As though seeking to dismiss such thoughts, the Induna sends Magema, and the two Fasimbas accompanying him, to go and wait by the tangle of red bushwillows, just where the two friends had shared snuff.

★

Hafa has been asked to wait a little way down the path, out of earshot. Now, at the Induna's signal, he rejoins the warrior.

Yes, he says, the trail is straight, and therefore he could see Magema long before the youth spotted him.

He saw Magema come up the bank. Saw him wave, then heard him shout. Saw the ear-tugging. Saw that dismissive wave. Saw him turn back.

And then he was right next to Magema, and Magema was staring at him, his eyes wide, his mouth open . . .

After he had calmed the youngster, they went to where Magema had said Sitheku had been standing. As the Induna knows, their search proved fruitless.

After thanking Hafa, and saying he can return to the village, the Induna stands a while, staring down the main track, then gazing down the path Sitheku had been proceeding on.

Looking down the main track, where Hafa can be seen walking away from him, then switching his attention to the path, where Magema and the soldiers stand just beyond the bushes in the donga.

And again a glance down the main track; a glance down the path.

'Wait!'

When Hafa turns, the Induna holds up a hand, signalling him to remain where he is. Then he jogs down the slope and slowly makes his way back up the path. It joins the main track at an angle that for a moment has one facing down the trail in Hafa's direction.

Perhaps it was not where he was coming from, but where he was going to that's important: the Induna's words, spoken as if his udibi were present. The boy's response: *Or perhaps it was something along the way, Master* . . .

The Induna turns to gaze down the path one more time.

Something along the way . . .

The Induna jogs over to Hafa, asks him a question, asks him if he's certain, then cuts through the long grass, heading towards Magema and the soldiers.

★

The shadows have met and merged and night has started to spread by the time the Induna arrives back at the village. A series of bonfires create a rough circle a few metres from the main gate. Mgobozi and some of his men are waiting here with Kholisa and the other sangomas.

'Eshé, Nduna.'

'Eshé, General.'

'You are well?'

'I am well, General.'

'Would that I could say the same for myself.'

'General?'

'Yes, I have had to endure the stench of a hyena's arsehole, while you have at least been able to enjoy the fresh air.'

'Aiee, General, but such are the penalties of rank!'

'Penalties? Hai! This was torture, Nduna. In *this* Smelling Out I was the one who failed, for I could not take it much longer. You arrived not a moment too soon. Now assure me my nausea has not been for nothing.'

'General, your suffering has not been in vain!'

Mgobozi raises an eyebrow. His lips twitch with the beginnings of a smile, which he manages to smother by adopting a grave mien.

'You have identified the miscreant?'

'Yes, General.'

'And Kholisa, most esteemed of our estimable sangomas, has been vindicated? There is a sorcerer at large?'

'As much as I know it will pain you, General, I have to say there has been no sorcery here.'

Mgobozi slaps his chest, over his heart. 'Nduna! I will try to restrain my disappointment.'

'While your sarcasm rampages unchecked, like a disobedient child sorely in need of his mother's knee!'

Mgobozi frowns. 'Do you smell that, Nduna? Has the hyena farted?' He turns towards Kholisa. 'Or perhaps *you* had something to say?'

'You heard me. I will not stand here any longer listening to this nonsense.'

'I will happily see to it that you have a spear to lean on!'

'Cha! Silly words while danger looms over us.'

'Hai, but we are trying to resolve this matter.'

'No, you would look the other way and insult the ancestors. But I forgot! What do you care about the ancestors, for you are not a Zulu, are you?' Mgobozi is a Mthetwa, an isilwane!

'*Now* who is indulging in silly words? Besides if I am a beast, I am a beast who eats up sangomas ... although, truly, you have nothing to fear from me, for what beast could stomach you? But never mind,' says Mgobozi abruptly turning away from Kholisa. 'You said you had something to report, Nduna.'

As always, when it comes to putting the sangomas in their place, there can be no equivocation, no doubt, for it's Shaka's children who are the judge and jury here. Meaning those who peer over the walls of the village, straining for a glimpse of the showdown, and those all around the kingdom who will hear of its outcome quicker than one would think possible (aiee, now *there's* sorcery for you, the speed with which news travels, with bad news and falsehoods always outpacing good news and the truth).

'Speak, Nduna. And the esteemed sangomas, I'm sure, will condescend to keep the terrors of the night at bay while you let your wisdom enlighten us.'

'General, this matter can be speedily resolved.' The Induna points to his left. 'Bind that man!'

Before he can do anything, two soldiers grab his arms and Magema's held fast.

'What do you think?' Mgobozi asks Kholisa. 'Shaka's warriors have no need for your drums and masks, for there's the guilty one. And we have not had to stand about in the sun, watching you and your pets shriek.'

'Who am I to argue with you, wise General? If you and your induna say this is the guilty one, I will not argue. It's just . . .'

'What? Out with it! Or if it's stuck, might I suggest a finger down your throat? Your own finger of course, as my fingers prefer my own arse.'

337

'It's just . . .' Kholisa shrugs. 'Well, who is behind this one? Where is the evil that has guided him? Perhaps our noses might still be of some use to you. And the King, of course.'

'Nduna?'

'That is easily answered as well, General.'

'Tell us, then.'

'As you wish, General. It's jealousy. A few words carelessly uttered, a sudden rage. These were the things behind Magema's actions. And a certain amount of luck, as well. But' – the Induna's eyes dart to Kholisa then back to Mgobozi – 'not the kind of luck a witch's muthi might bring one. More the luck of the falling man who feels his fingers curl around a branch.'

'Not that this branch held him for long.'

'No, General.'

'Thanks to you, Nduna.'

'Cha, General, I only saw what there was to see.'

'And what was that? I am curious, for I and these others saw the same things, but we didn't see what you saw.'

★

Sitheku took his father's bull to Bubula. He lingered a while, chatting to Nomona. On the way home he met Magema, and the two settled down and shared some snuff.

The Induna turns to Magema. 'What did the two of you talk about?'

'Nduna, please! I am not the one who—'

'I am ready for you to prove me wrong. Do it by answering my question!'

'I don't . . . We spoke of many things . . .'

'Like what?'

Wide, pleading eyes. 'I can't remember, Nduna.'

The Induna taps his iklwa blade against his knee. 'Can't remember?' he asks. 'This thing takes place, this frightening thing that even has the sangomas sniffing for sorcerers, and you yourself told me how often you have thought about it, knowing that anything – any

338

little thing – might lead to an answer. Yet now you tell me you have forgotten what you spoke about.'

What they spoke about is the one question no one has thought to ask Magema. And it's clear he did not expect to be asked such a question, because he has not had time to gather together a herd of lies. 'And he needs to lie,' adds the Induna, 'because if he told us the truth, he'd condemn himself!'

'What then did they speak about, Nduna?' asks Mgobozi.

The Induna says he'll answer that with another question that Magema never expected to be asked.

He addresses the captive once more: 'Where were you going, when you met Sitheku? I'll tell you where – you were going to visit Nomona.'

And that's where Sitheku was coming from. And did he suddenly then remember that Magema was infatuated with the girl? Did he think here was a chance for a little fun at his friend's expense, Magema's obvious discomfort being the breath that fans the ember?

'No, he said more!' interrupts Magema. 'He said he was of a mind to visit her again. He said this, knowing of my feelings for her, knowing I would be her soka and she my gxebe . . .'

'And you lost your temper,' says Mgobozi.

'Yes, but there is more. He would've done just that, don't you see? Yes, maybe he was joking, there and then, but he'd planted the thought in his own mind. And I knew he'd come to see it as a matter of pride – as something he had to do lest he be accused of idle boasting. I'd seen him do it many times before, but this time it was with Nomona, who he knew I loved!'

Mgobozi turns to the Induna: but why this bizarre subterfuge? This outlandish tale of a vanishing man? Couldn't Magema see that would only have drawn more attention to his crime?

'Hai,' grins the Induna, 'we have Hafa to thank for that. And a little luck.'

Magema killed Sitheku in anger, hid his body in the thicket, then fled. As he reached the main trail, however, he saw Hafa coming from the village. He knew the body would be discovered sooner or later and, since Hafa had already spotted him, he'd be marked as one of the last to have seen Sitheku alive. What's more, the body was in the thicket, and Magema knew that Hafa would be taking the path passing through those very bushes. How was he to know the elder wouldn't find the body there and then?

'So he said the first thing that came into his mind,' says Mgobozi. 'That Sitheku had vanished before his eyes.'

The Induna nods. Without thinking, Magema called out to Sitheku, and the subterfuge grew from there, with Magema becoming ever more entangled in lies.

When his panic subsided, Magema might have congratulated himself on his quick thinking. Calling out to Sitheku, as Hafa approached, surely made his story even more believable. But when the Induna questioned the elder, Hafa made no mention of having heard Sitheku responding to Magema's calls.

The Induna had almost missed the significance of that, he admits. It was only this afternoon, on the main track, that he realised Hafa should have heard Sitheku's calls, since he was certainly close enough. And so the Induna had jogged over to him, to check. But, no, the elder reassured him, he'd only heard Magema.

And Hafa hadn't thought anything of it, because . . . well, there was the vanishing! And Magema had happily led Hafa through the thicket, so they could search for his friend.

'After that he waited until dark, possibly using the time to dig a deep hole,' says the Induna, looking to Magema for confirmation.

The youngster nods.

'Then he went and fetched the body.'

'And that was when the vanishing man truly vanished,' observes Mgobozi.

'This is so, General. And Magema had little to fear when there was talk of sorcery and a Smelling Out, for he would be one of the victims!'

★

340

'And there we have it,' says Mgobozi, after Magema has told them where he buried his friend's body.

'And there we have it, General.'

'Now it is late,' says the general, addressing Kholisa, 'and wickedness rides out at night – which means you won't be alone. But you will leave now. No!' He holds up a hand, to silence the sangoma's protests. 'I speak as the King, and I say you *will* leave now. Hai, should you wish to rest at the bottom of a crevice or a cliff, I do not mind, so long as you shriek softly. But you and your troop of monkeys – you will go now!'

Leaving his Fasimbas to herd the sangomas out into the darkness, Mgobozi heads to where Magema lies. With a glance at the Induna, he drops on to his haunches. 'Boy,' he says gently, 'look at me.'

Magema raises his tear-streaked face to the general.

'Look at me,' says Mgobozi again. 'Attend to me,' he adds, lowering his voice even further. 'You have heard me when I say I speak as the King, have you not?'

After a moment, Magema nods.

'Well, I think the King will be of a mind to be merciful in your case for, more than others, he knows how hurtful idle banter can be – the lazy words that soon become cruel taunts. He knows. He cannot let you go unpunished, but he can ensure your end will be swift and painless. Do you understand?'

Magema nods again. 'Yes, and I thank you, General . . .'

And he gasps and his eyes widen and freeze as, coming up behind him, the Induna rams his iklwa blade into the back of his neck, killing him instantly.

I will now tell you how Fudu the tortoise and his brother Dufu tricked Giraffe (says the Cat Man). *At this time, the giraffe was only a little bigger than a zebra. He was a lazy creature who preferred to bend down and eat the grass close to the ground, rather than stretch his neck to eat the leaves in the upper branches. This angered Fudu, as these creatures were stealing the only food that tortoises could reach. So, one day, he challenged Giraffe, saying: 'You are very tall and I am only small, but this I can do: I can leap over you.' When Giraffe had finished sniggering, Fudu continued: 'You have heard me right,' he said. 'I can leap over you. Even with my house on my back, I can leap over you.'*

Giraffe was welcome to laugh, he added – but why leave it at that? Wouldn't it be even funnier to see Fudu try, and fail? Oh, yes, indubitably, concurred Giraffe. 'Hai,' said Fudu as if it had only just occurred to him, 'if I am to entertain you, it is only fair I should get something if I succeed!'

What about . . . hmm, what about this. If Fudu succeeded in jumping over Giraffe, then Giraffe had to promise to eat only the high leaves in future. If Fudu failed, however, he would stop complaining and Giraffe could eat whatever he liked.

Giraffe agreed to these terms, and Fudu said: 'Watch closely!'

Positioning himself to the left of Giraffe, the tortoise rose up on his hind legs, so that a stone seemed to become a boulder, and he raised his front legs and, with a 'Hup!', he leapt into the air. And Giraffe couldn't help himself. Instinctively, he swung his head to the other side – where he saw Fudu on all fours, with his legs slightly bent to cushion his landing.

Giraffe swung his head to where Fudu had been, and saw only flattened grass. Returning his attention to where the tortoise was now, he saw Fudu was favouring him with a wide grin. The tortoise had won his bet, and no more would Giraffe and his brothers and sisters eat the lower leaves.

342

'Don't be lazy and eat only the leaves in front of you,' advised Fudu, 'or else you'll just have to stretch higher and higher.'

Which is exactly what happened, and how the giraffe gained its long ungainly neck.

And, of course, Fudu hadn't really leapt over Giraffe. While he spoke to him, his brother Dufu hid in the long grass on the other side of the path. When Fudu pretended to leap, and Giraffe looked away, swinging his head in a slow arc, and giving the brothers ample time, Fudu hid himself and Dufu stepped out of the grass on the opposite side of Giraffe, to stand with his legs slightly bent.

★

And then the Cat Man tells a story about the Trickster, and one about the magic bowl and magic spoon, but these are merely preludes to get his audience warmed up. He knows full well who they want to hear about.

Of Puddles & Lakes

'Now Shaka is our Father,' declares the Cat Man. Tall, slender, bearded, and quite a few seasons older than the Induna, he's not only popular with the children; the udibi has noticed how his audience seems to comprise more and more adults every night. That's not surprising, though, since the Cat Man's livelihood depends partly on his ability to convince and persuade, and all know that his stories are his way of ingratiating himself. No one enjoys them any the less, for all that, and there are always those who will stay and listen whenever he decides the time is right to do some business . . .

Aside from guns, the Portugiza exploring the coast of southern Africa introduced the Zulus to tobacco, maize . . . and cats. The People Of The Sky found the tobacco much too weak compared to the marijuana they already grew and smoked. The beautiful yellow grain, the Europeans explained to them, would grow in places where sorghum would not, and the crop soon became the tribe's staple diet. And the cats, the Portugiza assured their sometime hosts, would be useful in catching the mice and rats that ate the grain.

These felines were smaller than the civet and the genet the Zulus already knew, but they were, of course, domesticated, and soon there was a brisk trade in the creatures, as the Zulus introduced these 'pest exterminators' to other tribes.

This was a long time ago, but the three amakati the Cat Man has with him are still regarded as valuable commodities. He can certainly afford to bide his time, and travel from village to village, until someone is able to meet his price.

'Shaka is our Father,' repeats the Cat Man. 'He watches over us and protects us. He is the Bull Elephant who keeps our enemies at bay. But sadly . . .' The storyteller's brows and lips curve downward in a mask of mournfulness. 'Sadly there are those who look at the way he would hold us safe in his fist, and they see tyranny.'

The mask becomes enlarged eyes, arched brows as the Cat Man leans back and extends his right arm, with fingers splayed, to fend off disapprobation. 'No, oh no, do not look at me like that! I merely speak the thoughts of others, those malcontents among us who sneer at the King's kindness.'

He leans forward, eyes narrowed. 'And there is one who mocks Shaka the loudest. Is he a king commanding a massive army? No, you know who he is, and he is no king, or general, or wizard even!'

The Cat Man chuckles. 'You know who he is,' he says. 'Of course, you do, for who doesn't! Who hasn't heard of Beja! Beja the bandit?'

Nervous laughter from the younger children, an overflow of anticipation becoming a shifting about and getting comfortable. Then the tensing, the concentration. Even the adults drop the pretence that they are here listening to children's stories because they have nothing better to do, and they attend more closely.

'No king with an army to command,' says the Cat Man stroking his beard. 'There is just Beja!'

'Hai! Do not forget his loyal friend, Mi,' interrupts Owethu.

'This is true,' says the Cat Man, taking the gourd of beer from his travelling companion. 'There is Beja and there is Mi . . .'

'Two men!'

'Two men! And yet Shaka sends an impi after them. How many men? Fifty? A hundred? All those shields, all those spears, all those feet pounding the dust – just to catch two!'

This the udibi knows to be true, for Shaka sent Nqoboka and the Amawombe regiment to try and find Beja.

'So many men!' says the Cat Man.

'So many!' adds Owethu.

'Too many!'

'This is so.'

The Cat Man peers out at his audience. 'You frown, Little Ones. You are confused.'

'Like Shaka's soldiers,' says Owethu.

Another flutter of unease among the adults: a feeling that such comments are unnecessary, needlessly provocative.

And perhaps the Cat Man realises this, too, for he glares at Owethu briefly . . . then continues with his tale.

'But think about it, Little Ones,' he says. 'One man, two men, three men, five even, can easily hide in these hills. But fifty? Cha! Beja watched them come, and Beja watched them leave.'

And he goes on to tell how Beja tricks travellers. Regales them with tales of his own exploits, before revealing his identity.

The udibi turns away and finds Philani has quietly moved up to stand beside him. He's been sticking even closer to the udibi since their expedition upstream. Clearly the way the older boy handled Lungelo impressed him. Now he has no doubt the udibi can protect him from the hungry river.

Aiee! If only the Induna were here!

★

'You are well, General?'

'My old legs are not so old that I cannot keep up with you two.'

'This is true, for you exercise them enough in fleeing your wives,' chuckles Radebe.

'To no avail for, however fast he might run, a dog cannot flee his fleas.'

'But he may forget them in a fight!'

'Ah, there you have it, Nduna.'

The Fasimbas who were with them earlier have been sent directly to Bulawayo to inform Shaka that the matter of the Vanishing Man has been resolved. Mgobozi has decided to accompany the Induna back to Nkululeko's kraal – with a little luck they'll be in time to join the feasting that marks the conclusion of the Ear Piercing ceremonies. Radebe accompanies them because he is the old general's unofficial minder (Mgobozi refuses to take on an udibi), with instructions from Shaka himself to never leave Mgobozi's side.

346

They cooked their supper – a dassie caught by Radebe, and not the fare you might choose had you a choice, but it'll do – in the late evening, when the smoke from a fire is less likely to be seen, then they moved on half a kilometre or so to this spot scouted out by the Induna, where they'll spend the night. To make up some time, they've chosen a course that takes them along the fringes of Qwabe territory; hence the need for a certain amount of caution.

But they've decided to risk a little marijuana – a few medicinal puffs to soothe aching muscles.

'There you have it, Nduna,' says Mgobozi again, with a contented sigh. 'Some men, like our Father, have minds like lakes, wide and deep. That is to say capable of deep thoughts, and an understanding as wide as the sky. But, like the Great Waters, these lakes are prone to storms, to a rise and fall, a turmoil, are they not?'

Both the Induna and Radebe nod solemnly.

'And so men like our Father – not that there are any men quite like our Father – feel tormented from time to time.'

'This is so,' says the Induna.

'For having to constantly tend to the needs of his children, I cannot imagine, cannot even *begin* to imagine, what that must be like,' adds Radebe. 'Even herdboys, sentries, sangomas, they can sleep, but our King must remain ever vigilant.'

Mgobozi nods. 'If Shaka is the Bull Elephant who tramples our enemies, if he is the Father of the Sky who watches over his children, he is also the lake that gives us sustenance. With a wisdom wide and deep. And this is good, this is good, but, as for me, my mind is like a puddle!'

The Induna has just sucked in a lungful of smoke from the hollowed rhino horn they've been passing back and forth and now he leaps to his feet in a coughing fit, while Radebe topples backwards with a hand clamped over his mouth to stifle his guffaws. For to bellow with laughter in the darkness would be to try the indulgence of the ancestors, who they hope will watch over them and ensure the sweet scent of dagga won't give away their hiding place.

'It is so,' says Mgobozi, watching the Induna trying to cough, exhale, laugh and not spew, all at the same time. 'The mind of a good soldier should be like a puddle.'

'A puddle, General?' asks Radebe, pushing himself up on one elbow and wiping his eyes with his other hand.

'A puddle, Radebe. There is no need for depth, or width. Show him the enemy, and that is all he needs. That and the cattle his king rewards him with.'

Reaching up, Mgobozi takes the horn from the Induna. Inhales. Holds the smoke in his lungs. Exhales.

'Yes, a good soldier cannot think too much. He can be afraid . . .' Mgobozi nods. 'Indeed, he *must* be afraid. Fear can be a valuable ally, for fear can mean speed, fear can be the instinctive, unthinking thrust of your blade – and Ngadla! You have eaten without realising you were hungry. And fear, of course, also clears the mind, leaving the soldier in the ranks free to follow the orders that will save his life. And then, when it is over, the man who is the puddle, which is to say the good soldier, knows but one emotion: he is happy to be alive.'

Inhale. Hold the smoke. Exhale. 'Of course,' he continues, the word extending into a hiss, 'the soldier who has killed in battle must then be cleansed. But is this not simply another kind of command he needs only to obey without thinking? For, my Brothers, I tell you, this is when the troubles begin.'

Mgobozi passes the rhino horn back to Radebe.

'When a soldier begins to think too much, to question the orders of the axe during battle . . .' he says, referring to the swallow-tail axe that senior officers carry to direct troop movements, 'when he looks past the warm glow of the cleansing ritual, and sees the ghosts in the darkness beyond, when he begins to think too much and be tormented, there is trouble. He might as well leave his iklwa at home, for all the good it'll do him in battle.'

'And so,' says the Induna, having recovered his voice after several mouthfuls of water, 'the good soldier must be a puddle.'

'Indeed . . . but we have strayed from the path here. You already mentioned those terrors who claim they are my wives – that is why I am happy to be a good soldier.'

'Who must, of necessity, be a puddle,' interjects the Induna.

'Yes, and there lies true contentment for me, in the ebb and flow, crash and clatter of battle. For there, where *forward, forward, ever forward* is the only way to go . . . why, a warrior has no time for worry.'

★

'What are you thinking of, my love?'

Shaka grunts in the darkness. 'I was thinking, let that old goat make haste. Let him be as quick as he is garrulous. I need his counsel.'

'Mayhap they are even now on their way back.'

'Yes, but if that's the case . . .' Well, the moon is still full and Shaka knows his old friend too well. The return journey for him will involve a detour. 'That one can smell tomorrow's feast today, and so he will offer to keep the Nduna company. I do not begrudge him that, but I only hope he will be quick about it.'

'The Thembus are preparing their spears?'

A wry chuckle. 'Oh, yes, and, in a manner of speaking, you could say they are the spears I myself have given them.'

'They have learnt from your achievements?'

Shaka nods.

'But have you not said that it is who wields the weapon that matters?'

'That is so, but what concerns me more is the Qwabes. They are weaker than the Thembus, but if they join up with Ngoza both will become immeasurably stronger.'

Because then geography will come into play. If those two tribes can coordinate their efforts, Shaka will end up fighting on two fronts. He and his generals have considered – and rejected – a variation on the strategy he used against the Ndwandwes when they came looking for war a second time. To attack the Thembus now, say, and leave a rearguard to draw the Qwabes away from the main force, and lure them further from their homeland until Shaka can dispense with the Thembus, that would be suicidal. His army is still too weak to be split up in this way, especially when you consider the rearguard would need to be almost as big as the main force, because it would have to engage the Qwabes and win, if the latter choose to break off their pursuit and seek to link up with the Thembus instead.

There is this fact too. Soshangane burnt numerous Zulu settlements as he stalked through the kingdom, and the people and the land itself haven't fully recovered from these depredations. Shaka doesn't know if they can face another 'retreat'.

And, as Mbopa has warned him, he mustn't forget that his enemies will be expecting just such trickery.

'You have taught them too well,' murmurs Pampata.

'This is so.'

'But their feet remain tender, I think. They might imitate us, but they'll never be us! They'll only ever be hobbling somewhere behind us.'

'Nonetheless, they can still prove irksome.'

In sending emissaries to the Thembus, Shaka is simply hoping to play on Ngoza's vanity. Let him savour the thought of the mighty Bull Elephant grovelling, and desperate to win his friendship! Let him enjoy the thought of Shaka's fear for a while . . .

Pampata runs her fingers over Shaka's chest. 'So it is a matter of being patient, beloved.'

And of handing over the initiative to Ngoza – something that makes Shaka want to roar with frustration!

Although Pampata's right when she speaks of the need for patience, he's worried he might have been too successful in convincing Ngoza that the Zulu army is more vulnerable than it really is. And he's haunted by the sense that these feverish preparations, this back-and-forth between the Qwabes and the Thembus, are merely the deluded to-and-fro of ants oblivious to the descending foot.

Who's fooling who . . . ?

What if Ngoza strikes first? Although not as badly off as Shaka has led the Thembu ruler to believe, the Zulu army *is* in a weakened state. Morale and discipline might be good, and shields and spears plentiful, but the amabutho are undermanned. They'd be hard pressed to deal with a Thembu invasion, especially if its accompanied by a Qwabe incursion from the south.

Patience? Yes, he needs to be patient. But what if Ngoza is more reckless than he's bargained for?

This is why he needs Mgobozi, for the counsel of his old friend will help ease the pain of waiting. More than that, Mgobozi's wisdom will help him formulate a strategy to deal with a war on two fronts, should that dreaded likelihood arise.

'I hope they have not met with any mishap.'

'Mishap? Mgobozi? Hai, no! He is the mishap that befalls others, never fear.'

Shaka chuckles. 'This is true.'

'So is this,' whispers Pampata, her hand enfolding his hardness.

'Let it speak,' says Shaka, rolling on to his back.

'Your wish is my sweet delight, Beloved.'

★

As it turns out, at this very moment, both Mgobozi and the Induna happen to be holding a prick as well – although in this case each has his hand around his own prick.

'You are right. We have untied this distance very rapidly,' says the general as they both piss. Below them stretches the veld: shades of turquoise and purple under the same moonlight that attends the Qhumbuza being held a few kilometres to the north. 'And just as well, for it makes my teeth ache to know that we must leave any Qwabes we encounter unmolested.'

'Even though we are supposed to be still at peace with them?'

'Cha! Peace for them is merely a way of biding their time before they can next strike.'

'This is so, General. And, who knows, your iklwa might yet get to feast.'

'Yes . . . aiee! I almost stepped into your puddle.'

'My apologies, General.'

Mgobozi lays a hand on the Induna's shoulder. He murmurs that he meant what he said, just now, about puddles and lakes. But the

Induna . . . there are those, like the Induna, who are something else altogether.

'Hai, General!'

'It is so.' For as long as great deeds are praised, Shaka's name will be remembered. This is so. 'But,' continues Mgobozi, 'it is your muscles and sinews, and the muscles and sinews of those like you, who will bind this land together, give it its strength and ensure there are future generations to discuss great deeds and praise Shaka's name.'

'Hai, but that also could be said of any and all Zulus!'

'Perhaps,' chuckles the general.

'And what of Mgobozi?'

'Oh, he will be remembered, too. Long will they speak of the torments he suffered at the hands of his wives.'

Philani could be making the whole thing up. That's the thought the udibi finds lingering with him, when he opens his eyes that morning.

What would the Induna do?

The boy smiles to himself. The Induna would urge him to think it through, to tell himself this story and see how it sounds.

A river that eats children . . .

Perhaps, there, Philani's imagination is in danger of leading them astray. Because of its very obvious source — one of the Cat Man's stories — one might be tempted to dismiss everything Philani says. But, as tempting as that might be, the udibi feels that if the Induna were here, he'd say that such a dismissal would be dangerous.

What if the child really did come across a body?

If he did, that raises an ominous possibility.

It's easy to imagine a corpse being washed down a river and becoming snagged in an inlet . . . and then becoming unsnagged again. But the river runs past the village, through a shallow ford in constant use. A body is sure to have been found, noticed, and no one's reported finding one. Neither has anyone reported coming upon a body further upstream.

To the udibi that implies that, after Philani saw the body, someone came looking for it and removed it. And why do that, and so surreptitiously, too, unless you had something to hide — like the fact you were responsible for the body becoming a body?

There are at least two villages further upstream that the boy knows of, for he and the Induna passed through them on their way here. Does one of these settlements harbour a killer?

★

What is he to do with this story, these thoughts and suspicions? He can speak to Nkululeko, who'll take him seriously simply because he is the Induna's udibi. That's the obvious and the right course of action. But why take to him mere suspicions? Why not ensure he can hand Nkululeko certainties? Won't that make the Induna even more proud of him?

Spear Of The Spirits

Into the kraal comes the bull singled out for sacrifice, accompanied by five other beasts. The animals were chosen a few days ago from the herd of the induna yesigodi who is hosting the Qhumbuza – not that he himself had much say in the matter. It was the ancestors who guided his feet and his eyes, as he and his brothers moved amidst the cattle. Hock, withers, neck and horns taking shape amid the brown and white, the black and grey, solidifying, seemingly called into existence by his gaze. A sense of knowing. *That one, there* . . .

And, when it was removed from the herd, there were those other cattle who tried to follow it, thereby identifying themselves as its izinceku. These are the men who tend to the king's pots and eating utensils, as well as his food, and it's a fitting nickname for, in this context, the izinceku cattle are the ones who look after the sacrificial beast. And this afternoon they follow it again into the cattlefold in the centre of the village, accompanied by the host's brothers and closest friends, who take the place of the herdboys today, just as they did when the bull was selected, guiding the animals towards the middle of the byre.

The whistling and clapping of the men sets off another movement, a silent surge. The cattlefold is empty . . . then it's not. Seeming to have appeared from nowhere, the villagers move forward, like a giant's cupped hands coming together to enclose the animals and herders.

Then those hands part, one fingertip at a time, at the top end of the cattlefold, where the ibandla tree is, to allow Nkululeko to enter the ring.

He's a short, stout man, with a pot belly and heavy buttocks, but he manages to look regal as he strides forward. He is wearing amashoba, and the isinene and ibeshu that form the Zulu kilt. Draped around his shoulders is a quagga skin. This is the isiphuku, the cloak kept specially for such occasions by the oldest woman in the family – in this instance the last surviving wife of Nkululeko's great-grandfather. The cloak was already ancient when she was a young makoti, a new bride, never thinking she'd one day become the isiphuku's guardian.

But it's not as old as the spear that Nkululeko carries. Every family has an Umkhontho Wamadlozi, a Spear of the Spirits. It's used to slaughter animals and the blade is never cleaned; for to remove the nsila, or gore, is one of the worst forms of desecration known to the People Of The Sky. But no other Zulu family has an Umkhontho quite like this one. Indeed, Nkululeko's clan is famous throughout the kingdom because of it, and the village, too, for being the home of the Spear. With a haft made from a wood unknown to the region, and a long slender blade more finely formed, stronger and easier to sharpen, than any Zulu equivalent, it's said to be a Ma-iti assegai, a relic from the days of the Phoenicians. Whether that's so – and it doesn't seem likely for the spear is old but not that old – is neither here nor there. Nkululeko's Umkhontho Wamadlozi is deemed extremely valuable because of its age, because of what it is – a thing of fine craftsmanship from another world – and because it's the potential source of much magic.

Raising his arms, with the blade of the Umkhontho Wamadlozi pointing skyward, Nkululeko begins naming the amathongo, the ancestors of his family and his clan . . .

. . . and the udibi's thinking of a thirsty land, a hungry river and another sacrifice. And a young herdboy who, on overhearing his father say the spirit of the river was angry, set out to appease it so that all might once more go to sleep with their bellies full. 'Mighty River,' he said, 'I bring you my father's best cow. It is yours if you let us quench our thirst once more!' But the next day the cow was still there, and the level of the river was even lower.

The ancestors' names crowd the cattlefold. Their praises fill the air like the finery they once wore in attending occasions such as this. And then Nkululeko is done. He stands gleaming with sweat, his eyes shut, his head thrown back. He stands motionless save for the rise and fall of his chest. It's as if the years of indolence have fallen away and he is young again and strong, able to march all day, carouse all night.

. . . and the boy offered his father's best bull to the river. But the following day the bull was still there, and the level of the waters had dropped even lower. The boy wept and punched the ground and beseeched the sky. What could he do? What sacrifice could he offer the river that would see their crops grow again?

Now he must giya. Calling on his newly regained youth, Nkululeko rises up out of his sweat, as he leaps and lunges in, fighting an imaginary foe, while the spectators urge him on to greater exertions. Some even point out to him where opponents might lurk. *Here! There! Behind you!* And the tempo increases, for the more energetic the giya, the better, and there's always a chance the host will pass out. Although that's not something to be ashamed of – quite the contrary, it's a sign the warrior has literally fought himself to a stand-still – masculine pride prefers this does not happen. Instead, the idea is to attain a frenzy that leaves one tottering afterwards, but not face down in the dust.

And the amathongo are in a good mood this afternoon, and the strength of youth flows through Nkululeko's arteries, powering his muscles to lift his body and legs in leaps and kicks that a man half his age (and weight) would be proud of . . .

. . . what, oh, what could he offer the river? What could he offer as a sacrifice to end these burning days, these hungry nights?

Thrust and parry. Leap and kick. Twist and lunge.

Let all evil, let all the agents of bad luck and misfortune, be banished from this place . . .

. . . his little sister, Nompofo! He would offer her! 'What say you, Mighty River, Giver of Life, will you accept my little sister?' asked the boy. 'Will her life see our lives returned to us?' And, as soon as the words left his lips, water swirled around his ankles. That was it! That was the sacrifice that would appease the river!

357

And Nkululeko's on his knees. Sweat stings his eyes, but he daren't wipe them. His muscles and his chest and throat are raw. His body wants him to lean forward till he's on his hands and knees, the better to catch his breath, but he fights that urge. That would be undignified. But the need to open his mouth as wide as a python's and suck in as much air as possible can't be resisted. And his lips feel as rough as dried mud. And he realises that, as his muscles cool, he'll have an even harder time getting to his feet . . .

It's a consideration that overrides all his other aches and pains. Freeing his arm from his shield, but keeping a firm grip on his spear, he manages to somehow get himself aloft. His knees already aching, in a harbinger of what is to come once he has a chance to relax, he tries not to hobble as he circles the cattle.

When he feels able to do so without coughing, he starts speaking.

His tone is even, and it's as if he's talking to his friends. This is the bika; he's reminding the ancestors he's fulfilled his obligations, and telling them he's ready to sacrifice the bull. His voice is calm so as not to disturb the animal and, even as he's speaking, he stabs the bull in its side.

It happens that fast, that smoothly. There's no pause and flourish, no cruel hesitation. Nkulukelo stops in mid-sentence, his soothing words giving way to a grunt of exertion as he drives home the blade of the Umkhontho Wamadlozi.

And the shout goes out: 'Cry, bull of the amadlozi! Cry!'

Even as the bull drops, the butchers move forward, accompanied by young girls carrying an assortment of bowls. Skilled in their art, these men will skin the animal in such a way that not one drop of blood or splatter of gore remains unaccounted for. Mixed with the right ingredients, such substances can be used to create powerful muthis capable of bringing forth all manner of hardships for a village, for it is said that 'aguqule amadlozi ukuba abulale' – the spirits will listen to anyone in possession of blood or offal from a sacrifice.

★

He offers his younger sister to the river, but that isn't the end of the story. As the Cat Man had told it (and he's not the first from which the udibi has heard the tale), the herdboy fetches his sister and brings her down to the river. When she eventually falls asleep, the boy steals away. But, just as the spirit of the river rises up to pluck the little girl from the bank, Nompofo comes awake and, screaming, she runs as far and as fast as her plump little legs can carry her.

So far and so fast does she run, she enters a distant kingdom ruled by King Ndlovu, the elephant. She doesn't realise this at first, though. She's more interested in the ripe mealies growing in the fields, for by this time she's very hungry.

After building herself a shelter in a thicket, she collects some mealies and cooks them over a fire. Then she goes to sleep again.

Early the next morning, she's woken up by voices. It's a group of dassies, who are the king's izinceku and who have come to collect food for his breakfast. While Nompofo watches from her thicket, they reach the place where she'd helped herself to part of their crop.

Consternation follows! The hyraxes scurry this way and that, their noses twitching in agitation, their tiny incisor tusks bared in impotent anger.

There's a thief nearby! His smell is still strong. He must be caught and punished for stealing from King Ndlovu.

Remaining hidden and using embers from her campfire, Nompofo sets the field ablaze, and the dassies flee in terror.

'Mighty lord,' they tell the elephant, 'there's a thief in your fields, and he's set them on fire!'

Angrily, the king calls Mpungushe, the jackal. 'You who sing to the moon,' he says, 'go and find this thief and kill him.'

But, as Mpungushe approaches the thicket where Nompofo is still hiding, the little girl shakes the branches, causing the leaves to rattle. Making her voice as deep as possible, she calls out, saying: 'I am not afraid of you, scrawny rat, for I am Nompofo! What you think are branches are my horns and I will tear you apart. I could eat ten of you, and still hear my stomach growling. Make yourself ready, then, for I am coming for you.'

With a yelp, Mpungushe tucks his tail between his hind legs and races back to the king's kraal. 'My lord,' he cries, 'a monster is loose in your land!' And he describes a creature with trees for horns, who could crush even an elephant!

While King Ndlovu's working himself up into a high dudgeon, Fudu the tortoise sidles forward. *Crush?* Did someone say crush? Well, who can crush *him*? He will go and confront this enemy. And, so saying, he moves off down the path in a bow-legged swagger.

By this time, little Nompofo has used up all her courage and she's very frightened. When she sees Fudu, she rushes out of the thicket and begs him to help her. Happy to oblige, he carries her on his shell to the border of the kingdom and shows her the path that will take her home.

Chuckling, he returns to the king's kraal, singing about how the mighty tree giant fled at first sight of Bold Fudu.

He's duly rewarded by King Ndlovu, while the jackal's cowardice sees his kind cursed. And, to this day, he never has the courage to hunt for himself, but follows others like the lion, the leopard and the cheetah, and his songs to the moon are tinged with mournful regret.

★

The meat must all be eaten the same day, but, before it's doled out, the ancestors are given their share. They get two portions. The first is the isiko. This includes the impukane, a cut of meat taken from the outside end of the shoulder blade, and considered a great delicacy, the umhlwehlwe, which is the adipose tissue covering the viscera, and also pieces of the abdomen. Then, because this is a Qhumbuza, a piece of the inanzi, or stomach, is added to the isiko. After the cuts of meat are thrown on live coals collected in a broken pot, imphepho flowers are added as a form of incense. Then the burnt offering is placed on the umsamo inside the host's hut.

The second helping is the umbeko, the meat set aside for the ancestors to 'lick'. These slices are placed on the umsamo in the hut belonging to the induna's mother. A pot of beer and some snuff are added to the offering, for the additional enjoyment of the ancestors.

After smaller cuts of meat have been handed out to various families in the village for medicinal purposes, the feasting begins.

The boy joins the other younger members of Nkululeko's family in collecting the skin and bones, while the fires are being lit. This is no menial chore, since it's of great importance, and a sign that one is regarded as responsible and on the path to adulthood. For, as with the blood and gore, not even a sliver of bone or the tiniest scrap of skin can be left unaccounted for.

The story of Nompofo and Fudu has been an itch in his mind the whole day, and the udibi has to force himself to keep focused on the task at hand, channelling his concentration. His eyes scan the ground at his feet with an intensity that all but cracks the hard-packed mixture of dirt and dung – don't want to miss a single piece of slaughtered bull – as the noises around him recede, his tastebuds barely aware of the enticing smell of beef being grilled.

The larger bones will be tightly wrapped in skins, and then burnt on a bonfire built out of sight of the village. The smaller fragments go into a pot which will also be tossed on the fire. It's a ritual watched over by Nkululeko in person, because whatever remains, once the fire has burnt down, has to be buried in a spot known only to the induna yesigodi.

'They are, as you know, a stupid bunch,' says the Cat Man, later that night. 'Incorrigible snot-eaters who regularly forget where they placed their backsides, and their women are indescribably ugly.' However, this clan, by some incredible good fortune, had managed to amass a fine herd of cattle. When Beja and Mi heard of this, they went along to witness this frightening spectacle for themselves.

Sure enough, from their hiding place in the hills, they saw that the stories were true. This, they decided, was an affront.

When night fell, Beja entered the umuzi. The villagers were suspicious at first, but he soon had them under his spell. It wasn't long before a feast was under way, for this is the saving grace of these savages, that they enjoy singing and dancing, drinking and eating.

Beja knew this, of course, and, as the evening wore on and the beer flowed like a suitor's promises, he silenced the drums and said, 'I will teach you a new song.'

And he then said: 'Listen!'

And he began to sing in his fine, deep voice: 'Wo-vula ngase zantsi! Hou hou hou! Wo-vula ngase zantsi!' Wo – open at the bottom! Hou hou hou! Wo – open at the bottom!

Louder and louder he sang. Louder and louder did the maidens clap.

Then, after a while, Beja called out that it was time to change the song again.

This is what he now sang, in his fine, deep voice. 'Vula kwe samatole! Hayo hayo hayo! Vula kwe samatole!' Open the pen! Hayo hayo hayo! Open the pen!

Louder and louder he sang. Louder and louder did the maidens clap.

Then, after a while, Beja called upon the company to see if they could better his song, and the young men strutted and stomped while trying to outdo the friendly stranger's verses.

And Beja melted into the darkness, to where Mi waited with the clan's cattle. Their plan had worked. Through his song, Beja had instructed his companion when it was safe to approach the cattlefold, and when it was safe to open the gates and herd the cattle out. The villagers continued to feast and drink, and it was only the next day that they discovered what had happened.

'By this time, Beja and Mi and the cattle were long gone,' says the Cat Man. 'And long afterwards could they hide out in the hills, growing fat on the stolen beef.'

★

And the boy can't loosen this fragment of meat stuck between his teeth, this aspect that's worrying him about the Cat Man's stories. There's something in one of those stories, but he just − can't − get − at it.

But is it in the tale or has it something to do with the teller?

Hai, the Cat Man might annoy people with his jibes at Shaka, but there's nothing sinister about him. If anything, it's his companion, Owethu, and the nephew who travels with them who need watching. Morose, sullen, suspicious, they're like dark clouds accompanying the Cat Man. Such is his way with words, however, he soon makes one forget those two dour presences.

★

And if it's not the Cat Man or his companions who are the cause of the udibi's unease, it has to be something in one of the stories. But what? What is this finger that keeps tapping his shoulder? What is that distant, distorted, but desperate, voice trying to say?

Grey Matter

A sycophantic chorus of *No, Sire!* and *Wise words, Bold Buffalo!*

'It is so. We must not underestimate the Beetle, or his lions.'

All know what the outcome of this meeting will be, but a certain amount of ceremony is needed, for his subjects to feel Ngoza and his ministers have the blessings of the shades. And many, many eyes will be fixed on this eyrie high in the sky. For there, in the valley below them, laid out over the gentle hump of a hill, and seen now in the moonlight as a collection of dark domes, is the Thembu capital, the Place of the Buffalo.

'Oh, how I would like to see this Beetle suffer,' says Ngoza.

'We'll do what we can, Sire,' says Zibhle, his commander-in-chief, who is a lean, scarred man only a few years younger than Ngoza's fifty-seven summers.

'For we would see him suffer at your feet, Sire,' adds one of the younger lieutenants, eager to attract his chief's attention.

'Yes, yes, suffer,' says Ngoza, with a languid wave of his hand. 'That prospect is beguiling.'

'Which is why we must tread with caution,' says Zibhle with a glare in the young lieutenant's direction. For puppies need to know their place.

'Too true,' says the chief. 'The important thing is for him not to escape. Convey my wishes to the men. Tell them I will be content with Shaka's head. And the man who brings it to me will profit greatly, as will his comrades and his commander.' Ngoza stands up. 'But suffering . . . there can still be suffering.'

He strides to the edge of the ledge, the group of officers fanning out on either side of him. 'Dumo!' he calls out. 'Are you ready?'

'I am ready, Highness,' answers the big man, his voice like thunder rolling across the veld.

'Well, gentlemen, what's first?'

The men know to save the best for last – even the young lieutenant who spoke earlier. For when Ngoza leans forward to peer along the line and fix him with a stare, saying, 'You, who were so eager to see suffering, tell me your pleasure,' the lieutenant grins and says, 'I would see his head twisted, Sire.'

Ngoza nods and gives the order to Dumo.

Two of the guards lift one of the Zulu warriors on to his knees, and crouch beside him, each holding an arm.

'See,' says Ngoza. 'See how he stares straight ahead.'

'But not for long, Sire,' says one of the older officers standing next to him.

Dumo moves up behind the Zulu. Pressing a hand firmly against each of the soldier's ears, he turns the man's head gently to the right. When the Zulu's chin is poised above his shoulder, Dumo steps briefly to the left, past the Thembu soldier crouching there.

Once more he twists the Zulu's head to the right. This time there's a loud crack, and the man is left staring backwards.

'Well, what say you, my friends?' asks Ngoza, as the guards drag the limp body to one side.

'Too quick,' says one of the lieutenants.

'He didn't even cry out,' says another.

'Sire, Honoured Buffalo,' says Zibhle, 'we must not forget old Enza!'

He's referring to the tribe's head shaman, and Ngoza nods. 'Yes, yes, of course. Dumo!'

'Sire!'

'Gather what Enza needs.'

Another bow from the big man, which brings to mind an avalanche, or at least the beginnings of one mysteriously curtailed by the ineffable whims of the gods. 'Sire!'

The second Zulu is hauled to his knees and held fast.

This time Dumo reaches over the warrior's head, slips two python fingers into the man's nostrils, and tears off his nose with a single backward jerk.

This time Ngoza and his officers are rewarded by a shriek.

With the Zulu panting, and trying to turn his head away from the giant's big fingers, Dumo calmly grabs an ear – and twists that off, too, taking with it a flap of skin that reveals the Zulu's molars.

The sudden pain drives the Zulu upward and backwards. Dumo steps aside, but the two guards foolishly try to hold on to the man, and so are carried alongside him over the cliff, with a plummeting scream.

'Do you see?' says Ngoza calmly. 'We must not underestimate these Zulus.'

'Wise words, Mighty Malefactor,' adds Zibhle, 'and therefore let our men know the price of failure.'

'Indeed. Did you see that?' calls Ngoza, addressing the remaining guards standing down below. 'You will tell your comrades that they underestimate these Zulus at their peril.'

The men swallow their shock, and bob their heads in acknowledgement.

'And now,' says Ngoza, rubbing his hands together, 'our big friend's speciality. Dumo!'

All move closer to the edge in greedy anticipation.

*

Two men yank the Zulu's arms away from his body. With his ankles tied together, there's no easy way he can get to his feet. His pupils are like pebbles rolling about his eye sockets, as he tries to track Dumo's movements. The big man is toying with him, making as if he's about to step right, and then moving left, all the while laughing at the way the Zulu twists his head. As Dumo's helpers chortle, the Zulu tries to regain his composure. But he's seen a friend's face turned around so that he's staring at the ancestors; he's seen another comrade's face torn apart, bit by bit – better to die on a battlefield than this. If only he, too, could throw himself over the cliff, but right now it's as far away as the moon.

Then the men on either side of him are raising his arms behind him, forcing him to bow his head. Do they mean to tear his arms from his shoulders?

Suddenly, amid writhing, screaming tendons, and as vivid as the snap of a dry twig in a world of silence, he feels a point – a point he just knows is the tip of a spear-blade – pressing down and then *into* the top of his skull. The pain retreats long enough for him to note that the movement has two parts to it: first you feel the tip of the blade touch your scalp, then there's the pushing-into that dents, but doesn't break the skin.

Why is he noticing this? Think of your family. Of your proud father. Of your mother, always concerned, always pleading with you to be careful, but proud in her own way. Think of . . .

Why's he noticing this? Because it's a positioning, an aiming, a getting just right—

—and before the Zulu can respond, Dumo has brought the stone down on the flattened end of the blade.

Brains are a delicacy among Ngoza and his inner circle. You fast, you eat the brains, you become a god, or at least until you defecate. But that gives you time enough to decide the fate of nations with a god's wisdom.

★

As Ngoza and his myrmidons watch Dumo practise his speciality, the Zulu's screams becoming the sweetest sounds they have ever heard, Thembu messengers make their way through the night. There are three of them, each approaching their destination from a different direction. Ngoza's taking no chances: the message has to get through, and the message in this instance is simply the arrival of the messenger himself. The generals know what to do next.

Too soon, too soon . . . But you precipitated this, so no sense in whining now. You knew it was too soon, your regiments still below strength, the new call-ups still busy with their training.

He's pacing up and down the enclosure that's his own special space. Sent the guards packing. Stop. Raise your face to the stars; squeeze your balls. What to do?

Too soon, too soon – it becomes the beat that accompanies his feet. Silly to ask what to do. You precipitated this. He remembers Nandi's response, when he told her he was going to send a deputation to meet with Ngoza. 'Are you certain this is what you want to do?' she asked.

He'd frowned, sensing a warning behind her words. 'Yes,' he'd said, 'but I think you think it's a mistake.'

'No . . .'

'Then what, Mother?'

'I just . . . well, are you sure you're ready for the consequences?'

'Yes, of course. Why wouldn't I be?'

'Are you sure you know what those consequences will be, Boy?'

'Clearly you think I don't. Well, then, tell me what you think those consequences will be.'

'The child sees a mealie he likes, but it's at the bottom of the stack. Hai! No matter! That's the one he wants, and he reaches for it and . . .'

'The other mealies all come tumbling down. I know what is meant by consequences, Mother.'

'But you do not really see my meaning, which is this. The child reaches a point where he can't change his mind. Once the mealies start tumbling, he cannot say: That's enough, I don't want to do this any more! And, once your messengers arrive at Ngoza's kraal those mealies will start falling. Do you understand?'

Shaka had nodded.

'You nod, Boy, but your eyes still say no. Listen, once those mealies start falling, the child cannot change his mind. The only thing to be decided now is the severity of the end.' The child might, for example, be able to gather up and restack the mealies before anyone else is the wiser. Then again, he could be found out and punished, before he even has time to react. When it comes to what Shaka is proposing, however, he has to assume the worst.

'If you send your messengers, you must expect them to fail. You must expect Ngoza to see this as a provocation, and you must then expect him to come for you, for all of us.'

She had a point. He was happy to concede that then, but now he realises he hasn't really spent much time contemplating – and preparing for – the worst.

And now it's too late.

Shaka wheels round, fists clenched.

'As always, you are a lion ready to pounce!'

'Mother!' exclaims Shaka, relaxing. 'You must not startle me like that.'

'I come to see what ails you.'

'Sent no doubt by Pampata and the captain of the watch!'

'Your soldiers feel they cannot be fulfilling their duty, when they see you so restless. They feel you doubt their ability to guard you, and it pains them.'

'Better they do not know the real cause of my restlessness.'

'Perhaps.'

'Hai, Mother, I was just now recalling your words about the mealies.' A wry grin. 'Your warning.'

'I intended no warning, Boy. I sought merely to guide you.'

'And I should have listened.'

'But you have this churning in your gut . . . ?'

'This is so.'

'You are like a man pestered by mosquitoes. There are sparks in your blood that would become a roaring fire.'

'You are truly wise, Mother.'

'No, just a mother. And I know how you feel because you have always been this way. It's impatience that burns inside you. It's impatience that *forced you to try and hurry things along, deal with the Thembus before you were quite ready. And it's impatience that keeps you awake tonight!'*

'Tonight?'

'Yes! For now there is no more uncertainty. The way is clear: you must go to war — and I think you realise that. And now you are impatient for things to begin. But things can only really begin when that old Mthetwa bull returns.'

Shaka grins. 'This is so, Mother.'

The Wily One

The man grips the wicker door, tugs it to one side and enters the hut. Without hesitating, he makes straight for the umsamo, the sacred section, in the far interior of every hut, which is allocated to the ancestors and where Nkululeko keeps the precious spear. But the boy holds it and is standing close to the entrance – to the left, on the isililo sesifazana, or women's side. He crouches, ready to make his move, relying on the fact that the intruder's eyes will take a while to adjust to the gloom of the hut. And expecting that the man knows exactly what he wants, and where it is. Or where it should be.

As the man crosses the centre part of the hut, his back is to the udibi. Time for the boy to get out of there.

The ikotamo, the door-arch, is just one step away. One step and he's out.

There can be no hesitation – he's already worked this out beforehand – and he'll have to go through the door in a somersault because, the moment he's in the doorway, the interior of the hut will darken, thus alerting the man to his presence.

A step . . . keeping his eyes on the man, who's now tossing aside the saplings that mark the borders of the umsamo. Pushing pots over. Where is the spear?

Another step, then the udibi throws himself through the door.

Head over heels, clutching the spear tightly in his right hand, and up on to his feet again.

Running . . . He should be out and running, calling for help . . . But that doesn't happen.

Head over heels, chin tucked into his chest, spear clutched tightly, his feet just missing the upper arc of the doorway, then powering him upwards . . . He rises, and bounces his face off the knuckles of Owethu's fist.

He's thrown backwards, hits the thatch, and sprawls across the mats laid out in front of the hut's entrance.

'See what I've caught!' says Owethu.

Chuckling, the Cat Man emerges from the ikotamo, steps over the udibi and wrenches the spear out of the boy's hand.

'A wily one!'

Blood streaming from his nose, his head full of mud, the boy stares up at the two of them. Today's the day the seclusion ends for the first batch of boys and girls who've had their ears pierced. Everyone else will be down at the cattlefold to greet them, and he'd thought Owethu would be there watching to see if Nkululeko or any of his family seemed about to return to the hut early. Doubtless that task was left to the nephew – who he had thought would be with the Cat Man, and who he had thought he could beat, had it come to a fight.

'*I am watching you, Little Nephew, never forget that. He calls you "nephew" because he's so trusting. But not me, I'm not like that. I expect the worst from human beings, for I expect them to act as anything but. Hai, these savages that they mock – many of them are better than they are. And I'm rarely disappointed, Little Nephew, rarely. Nor do I think you'll be one of those who surprise me. No, I do not see that happening, do you? Because I can see you. I see your wounds have healed, but only on the outside, which is the way things normally go. We all have hidden scars, but yours aren't scars. Your hidden wounds continue to fester. And they poison you.*' Owethu's words, snarled at Lungelo when he met the former at the cattlefold, after slipping through the hole in the fence he had prepared yesterday, and then taking their baggage to the meeting place they'd agreed upon – a clump of rocks on a hillock overlooking the umuzi.

'Were I to tell you . . . Stand up, Boy!'

The udibi obeys, swaying slightly. He lets his eyes meet the Cat Man's, uses the older man's gaze to steady himself.

'Were I to tell you that the induna, your host, *our* host, sent me . . .' A glance at Owethu. 'Sent *us* to fetch this extremely valuable Spear of the Spirits for him, would you believe me?'

The udibi shakes his head.

'Impudent little shit, isn't he?' observes Owethu.

'It is not impudence that makes me say no. I say no because I do not believe it's in Beja's nature to run errands!'

The Cat Man's grin spreads. 'Ho-ho, I see I wasn't mistaken when I said you were a wily one. How did you know?'

'Hai!' interrupts Owethu, who must be Beja's companion, Mi. 'They will be back soon. Let us slit his throat and be gone.'

'No, no, Lungelo will warn us, and I always have time to learn how I might perfect my craft. And if a herdboy can see through us . . .' allowing his gaze to rest once more upon the udibi, 'although I do not think this one is an ordinary herdboy. So speak, then! Tell me what makes you think I'm not a humble cat man.'

'Your hidden wounds continue to fester,' said Mi, 'and they poison you. And they poison those around you. You should be showing gratitude to your uncle, but instead you are sullen. Why he rescued you, I don't know. I told him, I warned him. It was a stupid risk, for those three had nothing of value, but he wouldn't listen. And don't think I haven't heard the two of you talking when you believe me to be asleep. Don't think I believe you. He might, but not me. We already have one Shaka, we do not need another shunned prince seeking vengeance.' Spiteful words! Words made even more hurtful by the fact that Mi knew he couldn't retaliate.

It was jealousy, of course. Mi had his uses. He was a shield. A spear. A pack animal. A threatening snarl. But he would never be Beja's equal. And it hadn't taken Beja long to realise just who it was he had adopted as his nephew. Unable to see beyond his jealousy, Mi refused to believe it, but Beja knew . . .

'Speak,' demands Beja. 'Tell me what makes you think I'm not a humble cat man.'

'You say you are a cat man, yet you avoid your little herd,' says the boy, whose nose feels as if it's been stood on by an elephant.

'You leave your nephew to look after them,' says the boy, tasting blood. 'Yet his arms are covered in fresh scratches. Would one who works with these creatures be so clumsy?'

And, yes, those creatures are free with their claws, but why has the boy only ever seen fresh scratches on Lungelo's forearms?

'We already have one Shaka, so we do not need another shunned prince seeking vengeance,' said Mi. 'But be whoever you want to be, for I don't care. Just know this: we are soldiers on the eve of a great battle! We are outnumbered, but we are brave and cunning. We will triumph. We have to triumph. Failure is death here: a painful, terrible death. This is why I warn you that my eyes are on you. We all have our tasks to perform, and failure for one is failure for all, and failure means death. So be who you are, or who you want to be, but just do not let us down. Because before they get to me, I will get to you. And I will enjoy it for, unlike your uncle, I do not like you, and I certainly do not trust you.'

They were words meant to hurt, but now Lungelo can afford to smile. Even given the current circumstances – this unexpected, exceedingly dangerous contingency – he can smile. Mi, of course, had been referring to the theft of the spear, but he's about to get his battle. Oh, yes!

Which reminds him – as enjoyable as this might be, he has to get out of here alive.

Aiee! Can it be? Will surprise be so complete?

Another smile. That's not something he has to worry about.

He pulls aside the poles they had carefully cut, so that this portion of the fence would seem untouched, and steps boldly through the opening, not caring if he's seen, because he knows he needs to be seen if he's to survive this.

The amakati and the 'disguise' probably came from the last group of wayfarers Beja and Mi robbed and murdered, says the udibi. It was the body of one of these unfortunates that Philani had found. And doubtless Lungelo went out that day to make sure the gang had covered their tracks. What a shock he must have got when he saw one of the bodies had surfaced.

'He said nothing about it to us!' Mi tells Beja angrily. 'I told him to slice open the bellies.'

374

'We can discuss this on the road!'

'Then there was the other story you told . . .' interrupts the boy, hoping to play for more time. If only someone will return to the hut!

'What story?'

'The one about how Beja tricks wayfarers.' This is what had been bothering the boy all the while: that fragment of meat stuck between his teeth. 'When Beja attacks travellers, he leaves no survivors. Who, then, would know how he goes about winning their trust, except for Beja himself?'

'Aiee, wily one, do you not know the purpose of a story is to thrill and entertain?' asks Beja. 'Beja has to trick those he robs somehow. What you say – that is not necessarily proof that I am Beja, merely that I am a good storyteller. I see now, though, that I am also perhaps one who is too fond of irony.'

'I've warned you about all those stories,' mutters Mi.

'So you have.'

'Now let us kill this one, and be off.'

Beja opens his mouth to speak.

But then . . .

A moment of incomprehension. Are they really hearing what they are hearing?

He had returned to the fence and, glancing through the gaps between the poles, he had seen them. Three, four, five men spaced far apart, moving through the grass, heading towards the palisade. They weren't carrying shields, just a spear each. As one drew closer, Lungelo saw his face and upper body were covered in dried mud of a khaki-grey hue that helped him blend in with the grass. Thembu scouts! And they wouldn't come so close to a settlement of this size if they weren't part of a larger group.

Lungelo waited while the Thembu moved along the palisade, pushing at the poles. Waited until he found the loose ones, and then carefully stepped through.

Then Lungelo was on the man, taking him by surprise.

They went down, the spear flying out of the scout's hand, and Beja had taught Lungelo well, for he rolled over, pulling the man with him, and had snapped the Thembu's neck before the warrior could make a sound.

Lungelo did the best he could with the waterskin the Thembu had been carrying, making earth into mud and smearing it over his chest and face, reckoning it could be expected that some of the covering would rub off, as the scouts crept and sweated.

By the time he's done, and has another look between the poles, the grass surrounding the umuzi is empty. But then one of the other scouts entering the village must have signalled, for over to the north men appear: a Thembu legion charging towards the umuzi.

Lungelo pulls aside the loose poles and steps boldly through the opening. Not sure what the agreed signal might be, but reckoning a raised spear will be sufficient, he does just that, and raises the Thembu spear above his head, keeping the haft parallel to the ground.

And the opposite hillside becomes a wave of men.

Shouts and screams. A drumming. A tearing. A tempest moving on a thousand feet.

Screams of pain, of terror, but also, soaring like mad gulls above a blood-red sea, shouts of delirium. Joy.

And here they come, racing between the huts, chasing those who've managed to flee the cattlefold, cutting down everyone in their path — old-timers, women, children, everyone.

Mi tosses the Umkhontho Wamadlozi at Beja, and disappears in the opposite direction. However, as he soon finds out, there is no opposite direction. The Thembus have surrounded the village, and are closing in from all sides. His size and weight carry him forward, knocking aside both Thembu and Zulu. But then he's brought down, ironically, by a dying Zulu thrusting his spear upward as the big man leaps over him. Wounded in the groin, Mi turns around and around — seeing huts, twisted faces, smoke, a woman stabbed through the baby she's clutching to her chest, shields smacking together, a haze of blood, burning thatch . . . Then four Thembus fall upon him, like wild dogs bringing down a wounded zebra.

Lungelo steps aside, waves them on. An officer shouts some orders and a few soldiers stop to help Beja's 'nephew' enlarge the opening. It's only when they've raced on into the village, eager for Zulu blood, that Lungelo

*is able to move away. Initially he follows the fence, but then, when there's
a curve hiding him from the opening, he jogs off into the long grass. The
place where he stored their baggage is only a few metres away. There aren't
many rocks, and the slope is exposed, which is probably why a contingent
of Thembus wasn't positioned there – but there's enough cover for him to
hide in while he considers his options.*

'Come here, Boy!' says Beja, still gripping the spear tightly.

He charges to his left, plunging the blade into the gut of a Thembu
warrior coming round the side of the hut. Snatching the man's spear
as he falls, he withdraws the Umkhontho and uses it to parry the
thrust from the next warrior, then drives the second assegai past the
soldier's shield and into his abdomen. Transferring this spear to his
left hand, he reaches out with his right and grabs the udibi's arm.

'Come!' he hisses, pulling the boy along with him.

They move between the huts and come upon a group of three
Thembus who are kicking a greybeard. Without hesitation, Beja falls
on them, stabbing one of the warriors in the back. As he brings
down another, the third Thembu lunges.

Beja tries to twist away, but his spear is stuck in the second
soldier's ribcage, and he can't quite avoid the third man's blade. It
slices through his side, opening a fissure of blood. Dropping the
Umkhontho, and letting go of the haft of the spear still stuck
between the second Thembu's ribs, Beja staggers backwards and trips
over a body.

Smiling rapaciously, his mouth all teeth, his eyes like those of a
leopard enjoying its kill, the Thembu moves in.

But the udibi has at last roused himself from his daze. Rising up
through the screams and the confusion, through the billowing black
smoke and the flood of movement all around them, he rams the
Umkhontho's blade deep into the man's spine.

His hand covering the gash in his flank, Beja scrabbles across dirt
slick with blood: maroon dirt, sticky blackness oozing between the
bandit's fingers.

Before the udibi can help him up, three shrieking women run
past, chased by two Thembu soldiers. The latter all but skid to a halt

when they spot Beja and the boy. Panting and covered in sweat, they reckon these Zulus will be easily dispatched, affording themselves a chance to rest in the process. But, before they can move, the udibi has launched himself at them. He crashes into the smaller soldier's shield, and thrusts the Umkhontho sideways. He's aiming at the bigger warrior's neck, but the man jerks back his head, so the blade of the spear grates across his collarbone.

The boy might have missed the man's jugular, but the resultant spray of blood causes the man to panic all the same. Believing his wound to be worse than it is, he staggers away, clutching his throat, his shield and spear lying forgotten at his feet.

But the boy still has the companion to deal with. The man's shield twisted sideways, the two are now face to face. As the soldier raises his spear, the boy headbutts him, and curls his arm to punch the Umkontho's blade into the soldier's exposed armpit.

And is knocked sideways.

The other Thembu!

But Beja has already seen to him, and the man has merely fallen against the boy.

The boy recovers his balance, and is at Beja's side just in time to slip an arm around the bandit's shoulders to keep the older man upright.

Breathing heavily, with a fern leaf of blood and spit dangling from his lower lip, the bandit glances around. Wipes his mouth. 'This will do,' he mutters.

Taking a deep breath to steel himself, he steps away from the udibi.

'Here,' he says, dipping his fingers into his wound. The boy closes his eyes as the bandit smears blood over his face. The headman's compound will be the first place the intruders sack, explains Beja. That's why they had to get away from there. Now the boy is to lie down among these bodies, and play dead. It's his only chance. Once night falls, he should be able to make his escape. And he can keep the Umkhontho, for it's of little value now. It's far more important that someone survive and get a warning to Shaka, as soon as possible.

'And you?' asks the udibi.

Beja's chuckle becomes a grimace of pain.

'As for me,' he says, 'I will go and die like a Zulu! Which is to say I will be taking a few of these savages with me before I eat dirt. But, even then, I will not be done, never you fear. The Great Spirit will have to guard his cattle well tonight.'

PART FIVE
How The Induna Went Up A Mountain To Beard A Buffalo

A party of infantrymen appears in front of us. One of them throws his machine-gun at us in desperation. He dies under the tracks together with his comrades.

'If only blood wasn't so sticky,' grumbles Porta. 'Can't get it off. If God'd thought of tanks when He created the world He'd've made blood that wasn't sticky, and could be washed off with plain water before inspection.'

Heide enters into a complicated explanation, involving red and white corpuscles, of just why blood sticks to tanks.

From *Blitzfreeze* by Sven Hassel
(translated by Tim Bowie)

'So, now the king of the Zulus would bend his knee. Aiee! Wasn't that the most frightened soldier you ever saw? The rattling of his teeth announced his imminent arrival before we even saw him.'

'And that one was all, Highness, for all Zulus are bullies at heart. Show them a stern countenance and they flee in terror.'

'But not your men, General?'

'No, nor any Thembu man, Sire.'

'Kobo, you look doubtful?'

'Hai, but it is not because I doubt the courage of our soldiers—'

'— or any Thembu man—'

'Yes, or any Thembu man — thank you, Zibhle.'

'Why do you look so concerned, then? You are my most trusted advisor, speak.'

'It is not our courage I wonder at, Sire, it is theirs.'

'So do I, Kobo. So do I! I wonder that they can call themselves courageous when they are so lacking in courage!'

'Now, now, General. Let Kobo speak. What do you mean, Kobo?'

'Merely that we must be careful not to underestimate these Zulus, your Cognisance.'

'Underestimate them? How is that possible? They are the lowest of the low.'

'General, please . . .'

'I am sorry, Sire.'

'Still, perhaps he's right, Kobo. There was a certain amount of swagger before, then we taught them a thing or two about Thembu terror, and now they grovel at our feet.'

'But look at these messengers, Sire . . .'

'What about them?'

'First, Shaka sends four emissaries—'

'—who dare to speak of an alliance.'

'Quite, your Horror. And you kill them and destroy a Zulu village.'

'To teach that oaf a lesson!'

'Well and good, Beneficence. Then he sends a messenger and . . . well, you kill him.'

'To remind the Beetle that I really don't care about anything he might have to say.'

'Yes, and then he sends a second messenger, Sire, who you also kill . . .'

'To emphasise my previous point.'

'Then he sends a third messenger . . .'

'Who I killed to see how persistent the Beetle would be, and how desperate he was to grovel. Is this leading anywhere?'

'To the fourth messenger, Sire.'

'Well, him I had killed because I had a headache that day and couldn't bear to listen to those vile sounds that emerge whenever a Zulu opens his mouth.'

'The fifth messenger, Sire?'

'Toothache.'

'The sixth?'

'My stomach pained me.'

'Which brings us to the seventh, Honoured Ogre, who you let live, listened to and sent back to Shaka.'

'That's correct, Kobo. I was there, remember?'

'Indeed, Highness.'

'I trust you are coming to the point.'

'Indeed! For now my stomach aches from having to listen to him.'

'Or perhaps from having too much beef this evening, eh, General?'

'There you have me, Sire. I admit I overindulged, but this Zulu beef is so puny.'

'Isn't it? And stringy, too.'

'Aiee, that is true!'

'Mighty Buffalo, if I may . . .'

'Ah, yes, Kobo. Please . . . continue, or should I say conclude.'

384

'My point is, Sire, Shaka kept sending these messengers, even when he knew he must be sending them to their deaths.'

'Why should he care how many Zulus die, so long as he gets what he wants?'

'Yes, Sire, but those men also kept coming. Shaka kept sending them and they kept coming, even though they knew the chances of their returning were slim.'

'No one said Zulus are very bright, Kobo.'

'Be that as it may, General, but they kept coming. They had every chance to desert, and knew that no one would miss them because no one was expecting them to return, yet still . . .'

'They kept coming.'

'Yes, Benevolent Malevolence. And those two things – the will of iron it took to send them, and the courage it took for them to obey – those two things tell me that the Zulus are far from beaten.'

'Hmm, yes. Well, I have always said your counsel as my first minister is invaluable, have I not, Kobo?'

'I am only doing my duty, Sire.'

'Invaluable, Kobo – which is to say it is only valuable in how I choose to make use of it. Indeed, your advice has often proven most valuable when I have seen in it a warning of what not to do. As I do now. Yes, Kobo, I choose to disregard your advice, because it is quite simply the stupidest thing I have ever yet heard spew from your porridge smackers. Aiee! Are you sure you're not standing upside down?'

'How perceptive, Sire. That explains everything.'

'General?'

'Yes, Sire?'

'Shut up!'

'Sire!'

'As for you, Kobo, let me tell you why the Beetle sends them, and why they come. He sends them, Kobo, because he is a bloodthirsty imbecile, and they come willingly because death is better than anything else he can offer them. What say you to that?'

'Your servant, as ever, your Monstrosity.'

'As am I, Belligerent Buffalo.'

'And let me tell you both something else. I do not underestimate the Zulus! Haven't I said that many times? I do not underestimate the Zulus. And do you think that when Shaka says he wants to negotiate, discuss this state of hostility that exists between our nations – do you think I open my legs like a trusting maiden? I am not that stupid!'

'Sire, we never—'

'Shut up and listen! Shaka wants to talk? I say, Good! Come to me! And when he does come to me, no matter what he has planned, he'll be in for the biggest surprise of his life.'

1
These Thembus

'These Thembus are crazy.'

'That's it, is it?' asks Dingane, after they've walked several paces in silence. 'You've looked, you have seen the multitudes, and this is your conclusion?'

Big Njikiza shrugs.

'This is your considered opinion, that these Thembus are crazy?'

'Hai, one does not need the Calling to see this is so. One does not need to throw the bones. Some things are easy to divine.'

'Really?'

'Yes.'

'But here, in this instance . . . hai, Brother, but you will have to say more, because my poor understanding cannot grasp the way *your* understanding works.'

'I don't understand.'

'Now *that* is obvious. *That* is easy to see.'

'Brothers, please,' says the Induna, 'lower your voices. You are disturbing our hosts.'

'My apologies, old friend,' says Dingane. 'We would certainly not want to disturb our hosts.'

'Yes, that might be dangerous to their health.'

'Aiee, there you go again, Njikiza. They are not the crazy ones here. *You* are.'

'That may be, but they are crazier still.'

'Why?' hisses Dingane. 'What makes you say that?'

'Isn't it obvious?'

'Obvious how?'

'They are crazy because they have let us inside their kraal.'

'They are . . . This makes them . . . They have let the four of us into their kraal, and you say *they* are crazy? Are you blind? Look . . . *Look!*'

'Easy, easy,' murmurs the Induna.

'See how many they are!' exclaims Dingane, but lowering his voice. 'They are everywhere.'

'So? We are Zulus.'

'Yes, but we are *four* Zulus, and they are . . . everywhere.'

'You have a point.'

'Ah! At last, understanding dawns.'

'Yes, it *is* unfortunate. We are three too many.'

Dingane's response starts at the back of his throat as a growl, and ends with lips pursed in an explosion of exasperation.

'Why is that worrying?' asks Radebe, who's been following this exchange with interest.

'The praise singers will likely think this day not worth mentioning,' explains Njikiza, the Watcher of the Ford. 'For, truly, to praise our deeds here will be like . . . I don't know, like remarking on the setting of the sun – which really shouldn't surprise anyone.'

★

Aiee! Shaka willing to parley? That amounts to surrendering. Can this be? See how the praise singers hide their faces. Some are even weeping! The Bull Elephant, Father of the Sky, what is he thinking? Aiee! Who can penetrate the wall of silence that surrounds him? Who dares even try? And Mgobozi? Where is he? Some say he has headed south, saying better the savage Xhosas than a spineless Zulu king. He's taken most of the Fasimba impi with him. They, too, are disgusted.

Oh, Father, Father – what is happening?

Mbopa! Can't he do something? Hai, but the King's prime minister stands mute on the other side of a barrier of silence. And Mdlaka, our commander-in-chief, even he is powerless. Even he can only stand beside Mbopa and watch the King from beneath furrowed brows.

Father, Father – why are you doing this? Are we carrion already, and do you merely await the coming of the vultures?

Vultures? They say that what you found that day, wading through Zulu blood, broke your spirit, shattered your blade. They say you claim this is for our own good, this bending of the knee, but how can that be? You would bow to a murderer, yet how can you trust anything he says?

Father, Father – why, why, why?

Nandi! Pampata! Perhaps they can . . . But, no, they are far away already, with the children and the other women, being taken to safety by Nqoboka. Hai! Will anywhere be safe for them, once we have fallen? You must see that! As you must have heard the mutterings, Father: only cowards bend the knee and we, your lions, your loyal soldiers, would fight . . . would rather die fighting, even if it means disobeying you. You – and we – cannot give up this easily! But here we sit, on our shields, and there you are . . . Do you shun us, your loyal children?

★

'He toys with me, like a lion with its prey. But, no, even a lion is not that cruel. What say you, Nduna, old friend?'

The Induna's response is to pull Dingane further away from the sentries. Further into the darkness.

'I say, old friend, that you need to watch what *you* say. Your brother, our Father, does you a great honour!'

'Aiee! I don't even think Fat Mbopa could make me believe that, and he has a way with these things. He could make you believe you're standing in a downpour, a deluge, even as the dust swallows your feet and your stomach is hollow and your mouth as dry as the fields around you. What honour, old friend? He sends me merely because I am expendable.'

'He sends you to convince Ngoza of his sincerity.'

'Indeed! I am to be an offering!'

'Come, come, you know that is not true.'

'Hai, I know you admire my brother – and I do not hold that against you. I cannot hold that against you, for you show respect to the Bloodline. But I am not Zwide, so do not now seek to make me an offering of my brother's shit and tell me I must be grateful for this fine repast.'

'But there you have it, old friend, the Bloodline. The delegation must be led by one of the Bloodline. This is why Mgobozi cannot go, or Mbopa . . .'

'They are too valuable to the King.'

'No, because they are not of the house of Zulu.'

Dingane turns away, gazes up at the hill they must climb tomorrow, a dark mass filling the sky.

'Why doesn't he just kill me and have done with it? Why this slow torture?'

'Hai! He does you a great honour!'

'Are we even talking about the same person? Because honour and my name, those are not cattle we'll ever see in the same kraal, as far as he's concerned.'

'But, old friend, you must see how important you are to the success of this undertaking. This is why I speak of honour.'

The prince shakes his head. 'And yet again you do it. There is thunder, but you tell me it is elephants crossing the sky. Do not try to console me as if I'm a child.'

'I don't mean to, but think of what it means to *them*,' says the Induna jutting his chin in the direction of the sentries outlined by the glow of the campfires. 'The men are nervous and confused enough as it is. Just let them see you ready to do your duty, and they'll be a little mollified. The Bull Elephant must know what he's doing, they'll say, for he sends his brother to speak with the Thembus.'

'More likely they'll say my brother has at last decided to get rid of me!'

'But who says his Majesty wants to get rid of you? That's nonsense!'

'How do you know? Who are you to speak with such certainty?'

'I know, because it's so obvious . . .'

'Obvious?'

'Yes. You snap at his heels like a little dog. You pull faces at his back – and sometimes to his face. Or else you make a point of being morose and sullen in his presence. In short, old friend, you do not bother to hide your animosity. It's clear to everyone, including his Majesty. Don't you see, if he wanted to get rid of you, he would have done so long ago!'

2
The Place Of The Buffalo

The Place of the Buffalo lies on a plateau that rises gently to the north, and it comprises a series of concentric circles. In the outer ring are the huts of vassals, who congregate here seeking safety, in return for working the fields and other menial tasks. This ring is protected by a palisade of poles lashed together; the wall that separates the outer from the inner ring is much higher and sturdier. In fact, it's not a true circle, but an octagon with towers at each of the corners, joined by walkways from which defenders can repel invaders. Next come the huts of those who regard themselves as true Thembus. In the two lower arcs, which meet at the main gate to the south, are the huts of Ngoza's legions and their dependants. Then come the dwellings of the civilians: the greybeards and the married men who've done their time in the army.

In the very centre of the city, and surrounded by a thorn fence, are situated the cattlefold and the chief's compound. But, unlike in a Zulu city, these do not form the main focus of attention. Instead, one's eyes are drawn to the highest point in the settlement where, several metres in from the outer perimeter fence, and protected by its own palisade, there stands a large dome. This is where Ngoza receives visitors. It's surrounded by several huts, some of which are for important guests, while others house servants and bodyguards, or serve as storerooms, but all of them are dwarfed by the large thatched dome. Its apex reaches higher than the watchtowers, while the fact that it's sited at the very top of the slope makes it seem even bigger. A forest of stout poles support the dome, surrounding the meeting place in the centre. At the apex of the dome, an opening almost the diameter of a normal hut provides illumination, but the large structure also has no outer wall. Instead, depending on the weather and the amount of privacy required, skins can be hung to create a temporary screen. Decorated with markings not unlike those found in the caves once inhabited by the Old Ones, each is said to represent a Thembu victory on the field of battle, and it takes many such skins to turn the big roof into a big hut.

This structure can therefore be said to symbolise Thembu power, resting on or arising from military might, and supported by that might. And not only can it be seen from all parts of the city, but visitors are escorted to it down a wide avenue that bisects the capital, and which seems to magnify the size of the dome even further. The avenue starts about a kilometre away from the main gate, at the very edge of the plateau. In this part of its course it is a broad track, with an even wider swathe of land on either side, comprising an expanse of stubble and dark brown earth stolen from the dense bush that grows on the slopes of the plateau. This tangle is still very much in evidence to the east and west, where it's been left to form an almost impenetrable barrier that would make an assault from either side all but impossible, assuming an enemy could send enough men up the steep slopes undetected.

To the south, the plateau drops away in a gradient that's slightly steeper than the anterior slope. This rear portion of the plateau is also much smaller, and comprises grassland, with the bush continuing along the western and eastern fringes until reaching the cliff face that is the table's southern edge. This is where the city draws its water. It comes up from a spring, flows into a large, shallow pool, and drops a level into a smaller pool, before flowing over the cliff in a slender waterfall. A second stream drops down the opposite slope, flowing past the spot where the Thembu ruler and his generals go to commune with the ancestors. It joins the other stream in a deep pool on the floor of the canyon, to become a river that flows through the echoing canyon and turns to follow the eastern wall of the plateau, before widening as it ox-bows across the plain that forms the southern approach to the city.

It's here that the tribe maintains its cultivated land. An array of huts, under some trees on the river bank, houses the regiment whose turn it is to guard the crops and intercept strangers. The barracks are deserted today, of course, as this is where Shaka and his advisors are expected to stay while the Buffalo meets the King's delegation. Shaka, however, has declined the dubious comfort offered by Thembu thatch, and has slept with his soldiers under the stars.

Now he makes his way past the ordered ranks of his amabutho, who were as restless as he was and, despite the presence of picquets, have remained on the alert throughout the night. The few soldiers who managed to doze off are kicked awake, and all watch as the King moves through the cold early morning air, beneath a sky as grey as a pigeon's plumage. He's followed at a discreet distance by Mbopa and Mdlaka and the Induna's udibi, who carries waterskins and the King's shield. They halt a few paces in front of the first line of Zulu warriors and watch as Shaka strides ahead through long grass dripping with dew. When he's gone about a hundred metres, he too stops.

'Go!' Mbopa orders the udibi. 'But not too close, mind.'

With a nod, the boy jogs forward.

'That's far enough, Little One,' says Shaka, without turning.

Taken by surprise, trying to stop and retreat a step at the same time, the udibi drops on to his arse with a spine-jarring thump. Although winded, he's back on his feet almost instantly.

'Are you all right?' asks Shaka, keeping his eyes on the heights before them.

The boy nods, his ears aflame with embarrassment. But a nod won't do, since the King still has his back to him. 'Yes, Majesty,' he wheezes.

'Deep breaths, Boy. You will not choke.'

As his breathing returns to normal, the boy tries to work out what Shaka is examining so intently.

You can clearly see the path that leads up to the summit. It zigzags between the trees and bushes, now emerging to follow an outcrop of rock, now disappearing behind bracken ferns and silver sugarbushes, tree-fuchsias and cabbage-trees.

That's the same path the Induna and the others will be taking. As his eyes get caught in the rhythm of the track, the udibi realises it's as if they'll be swinging, in wide arcs, from this end to that, from that end back to this side, climbing slightly higher each time.

It's a reminder this is not a place an army can easily attack. Any force, no matter its size, will be forced to move along that path in slender columns, like ants, and like as not will be crushed like ants, too, slaughtered before they even reach the top.

But to talk? Is that all Shaka can come up with?

Philani dead, bloated, grey. Missing an arm. That's why he won't − can't − believe Shaka would even contemplate some kind of accord with the Thembus. Because Philani is dead.

And because of the babies.

And everything else.

But especially Philani.

And especially the babies.

3

A Massacre

Herdboys dead in the veld, hunted down by contingents of Thembus, who then drove the cattle away. Burnt huts, burnt bodies; dead livestock, dead humans. And a king standing amid the carnage. A few survivors, the boy among them. Reporting to Shaka, describing what has happened. Broken voices. Hoarse voices. The Fasimbas here with the King; three other regiments abroad, roaming the countryside. But the Thembus have already been tracked back to the Place of the Buffalo, where they doubtless await Shaka's response − or are getting ready to strike again.

A massacre. Charred corpses. Bodies torn apart. Groups here and there, shields and spears and tangled limbs bearing testament to an attempt at a holding action. Signs that women fought fiercely to protect their children; and that those children fought alongside their mothers. Curled fingers, scraps of flesh caught under the nails. Human meat trapped in the clenched teeth of six-, seven- and eight-year-olds; their older brothers clutching iklwas, sticks, broken pots even. And many Thembus fell, but the surprise had been total. There was no stopping the wild animals that fell upon this village, then rampaged through the huts.

A massacre.

And at the entrance to the umuzi, impaled on sharpened stakes, their tiny heads removed and replaced by heads torn from dogs, is a row of babies. Zulu babies. Blood-stained snouts, lolling tongues, bared incisors above chubby stomachs and curved arms and legs. In some instances, if the dog had been big enough, or the baby small enough, the infant's head has been forced between canine jaws opened unnaturally wide.

★

Shaka, who insisted on being the first to enter the village, had immediately ordered his older indunas to begin disposing of the little bodies. But is that to be it? A burial and a forgetting? Broken bodies thrown together, then relighting the fires so that the destruction begun by the Thembus could be finished. A decree that no Zulu settlement be built on that site ever again. Indicating a willingness to negotiate a treaty with the savages who did this.

Or is it, as some say, that Mgobozi hasn't deserted Shaka; and that the King is merely playing for time while the general goes to fetch the Qwabes, so that together they might bring down Ngoza!

But Philani . . . always, amid the howl of tormented spirits demanding their deaths be avenged, his dreams return to Philani. The little boy who befriended him. The udibi knows, in the way he knows the sky is blue, that others died but Philani's the one whose loss he truly feels. Deep inside, his gut twisting like fat in the fire. Like the limbs of those trapped in those burning huts.

Always, he's back there, wading through rotting flesh, looking and hoping, knowing he was silly to even think Philani might have survived.

He'd finally found the child. Had at least made sure his body was taken care of.

Scant comfort, though, because there are the dreams still. None of the battles he's endured has ever left behind such a legacy of thrashing around and sweating. It's a fever even the cleansing ritual couldn't vanquish.

★

The udibi straightens up with a start. Lost in thought, he's been looking without seeing. The sun has shrugged off its pigeon plumage and is easing its way across the veld. And now he can see that enemy soldiers line the path that leads to the Place of the Buffalo. The udibi can make out their shields, and the bristling of spears.

He shoots a look at Shaka, but the Bull Elephant stands immobile, his gaze still fixed on the slope.

★

'Aiee, Zikhle! Do not let your excitement tire you out so soon.'
'Sire . . .'
'He reminds me of one trying to make fire the old way, Kobo.'
'Sire . . .'
'Mayhap he's about to give birth, Highness.'
'Now you are being too cruel, Kobo. Shame on you!'
'My apologies, Sire.'
'This one is way past childbearing age.'
'H-highness . . .'
'What is it, General? Have our guests roused themselves?'
'Y-yes . . .'
'And you rushed here to acquaint me of this fact. Would it not be wiser to husband your strength for the more important tasks? I would not want you to miss out on all the fun.'
'Y-yes, Sire, I u-understand but . . .'
'But?'
'The Beetle, Sire.'
'What about him?'
'He's just standing there.'
'So?'

396

'Perhaps it would be best if you came and saw for yourself, Highness.'

'Sire, if I may . . .'

'You may, Kobo.'

'That would not be a good idea. Everything is ready, and any deviation should be avoided. Hai, maybe this is what the Beetle wants. Although I can't see why the fact that he's, er, standing there, as the general claims, should be the cause for so much concern. Least of all a fast run undertaken by one who should perhaps stick to a more sedate pace.'

'Highness! How dare he imply I might not be speaking the truth, or might be confused . . .'

'Be that as it might, General, I agree with Kobo for once. I don't think we should deviate from our plan.'

Anyway, so the Beetle stands there – so what? If that's how he chooses to spend his last few hours upright, who is Ngoza to interfere.

4
Stalwart Companions

'The setting of the sun! It is more likely us who will set here today.'

'Then so be it. So long as we take some of these crocodiles with us. Yes, you! I see you.'

'Do not taunt them, Njikiza.'

'I am sorry, Nduna.'

'They are unsettled enough.'

'This is true, Nduna,' chuckles the big man.

The Induna's comment wins him a disbelieving glance from Dingane, though. 'Hai! You, too, Nduna? Have you also gone mad?'

'No, we just need to be careful of . . .'

'Frightening them? You were going to say frightening them, weren't you?'

The Induna nods.

'Frightening them! You're as mad as he is.'

★

There they go, to meet with the monster.

See their finery. Feathers and tails. Isn't that a sign of their courage? A way of mocking the monster, even as they obey his imperious summons?

We would send them on their way with our war cries, but the indunas among us tell us to keep quiet. And our cheers are left to wither in our throats, for it is the King's wish that we clench our teeth.

That's what the indunas tell us. That they give us a reason for this order is surely a sign they too are disgruntled. They, too, would raise their voices and tell those savages to come down here and taste Zulu steel.

Yet the King would have us remain as silent as he is.

And there he stands, apart from us.

The sun is climbing ever higher, growing ever hotter, and there he stands, unmoving, watched over only by a single udibi. He carries a shield to protect the King from the sun, and waterskins so he might quench his thirst, yet he also is ignored by the Bull Elephant.

Just as he ignores the four brave men who pass him on their way to meet the monster.

Just as he ignores us, his brave warriors who want to fight.

But there they go . . .

And we must remain silent.

And docile.

It feels as if we are already captives . . . We have lost a battle we didn't know was being fought, and now, abandoned by our King, we await our fate.

★

The four are dressed for the occasion. The Induna, Njikiza and Radebe wear amabeshu made of black calfskin. Dingane's, however, are white and slightly longer, as a sign of the prince's rank. In addition to the weighted strips of skin that form the isinene, the front piece of each man's umutsha bears additional ornamentation in the shape of monkey and genet tails. As a further sign that

398

he's a member of the royal family, Dingane wears a leopard skin over his shoulders. The Induna's rank is signified by his necklace of lion's teeth and stones taken from the battlefields where he has fought.

Along with Njikiza and Radebe, he also wears his regimental ubushokobezi, a headdress worn above the forehead and comprising six dressed cowtails standing erect. Dingane's head, by contrast, is unadorned except for the blue crane feather, for he is the one who will be speaking as the Shadow of Shaka today. None of the men carries a shield, and all are unarmed. Completing their attire are the amashoba worn around the lower legs and upper arms. Made of cowtails, these are meant to 'enlarge' a man, give him additional stature, and the amashoba chosen by the four today are especially generous.

They move along the path up the mountain, behind the Thembu warriors who show the Zulus their backs.

'Do you see, Brothers? Do you hear?' asks Dingane, after they have passed the second batch and are on a stretch of the path that is too narrow to accommodate a line of men. 'Who would have believed a back could be so eloquent.'

'I see nothing pretty about these . . .'

'Eloquent. I said eloquent, Radebe. Loquacious.'

'Lo—?'

'Garrulous,' interjects the Induna. 'Like Mgobozi.'

'Ah,' says Radebe, who is bringing up the rear.

He falls silent as they pass yet another row of Thembu shoulder blades and backsides.

'But,' he says when they are alone again, 'I do not hear them say anything.'

'Exactly. In a word, eloquent.'

'The prince means they insult us, Radebe.'

'How so?'

The Induna steps aside and lets Njikiza and Dingane ease past him, before falling in step behind Radebe.

'They insult us by turning their backs to us, as if we are not to be feared.'

'But that is not all,' calls Dingane from the front.

'No. For by letting us walk behind them, while they face our comrades, they would make us feel like deserters . . .'

'Traitors!' adds the Needy One.

'Yes, traitors who have betrayed our King and gone over to their side.'

'Eloquent, as I say,' remarks Dingane.

'Hai!' grunts Njikiza. 'Have you heard the cows when a leopard is nearby? Fear can be eloquent too. And this is what *I* hear in their silence. This is what their backs tell *me*. They are afraid to even look at us.'

★

Where's Mgobozi? Why aren't Mbopa or Mdlaka saying anything? Fetch Nandi! Fetch Pampata! Perhaps they can talk some sense into the King.

★

A massacre! The boy barely remembered being led away by Beja. Lying motionless among corpses that smelt of shit and urine, and later of putrefaction, had rendered other memories inconsequential. And there was fear, too, with Thembu soldiers passing close by, one or two even entering the hut next to where the boy lay. It was as if they were drinking the suffering all around them, for every time the boy heard them, they sounded drunker and drunker. Then, as the shadows began to lengthen, they withdrew. The boy, who'd begun to drift in and out of consciousness, vaguely recalled a moment of lucidity once he realised they had gone. Something – he didn't know what, but a passing perhaps; feet making the dust dance, then an absence – something had roused him, caused him to raise his head. Caused the thought *they are gone* to form in his mind before he went under again, going deeper now, knowing he was, for the moment, safe or at least safer than he had been before.

Cries and groans, whimpers and pleas offered to the night, and the sounds of the flames chewing the huts, these were his companions. And he later remembered to be thankful for those flames, for they probably kept the natural scavengers at bay.

★

Thirsty, surreptitiously leaning against the King's shield, the udibi's dragged out of his thoughts by Shaka's soft words. 'See, they are almost there.' The King hasn't moved, and still has his back to the boy, and maybe he's imagined those words. But the udibi dutifully raises his head, and sees that Shaka is right. First Dingane, then the Induna, then Njikiza and Radebe, disappear from sight as they move on to the plateau . . .

★

There! Now they are gone, those brave men. Now we await the impalers!

★

Morning reveals a grey haze of smoke and rotting flesh. Cries and groans and whimpers. And a few survivors staggering through the ruins, as lost as ghosts. And what to do about those cries? Get them away, get the living away from here – that was the only answer. Stunned, dazed, barely aware they were alive, the others were easily led. There were also those who had returned to their senses, and helped the boy. Two of these, a young girl not more than fourteen summers old and a greybeard, left later that day for the nearest village.

Someone said he knew of a cave with water nearby. Those cries and groans and whimpers would eventually drive them mad, but there was another reason why they had to get away – there was always the chance the Thembus might return. But there was misery in the cave as well, as the full horror began to sink in. Everyone had lost everyone. All were orphaned. And, to get away from these other cries and groans and whimpers, the boy found himself a vantage point from which he could see if anyone approached the village. He knew he should try to find Philani, as well as . . . all the others he knew, but he couldn't bring himself to walk again among

401

that smouldering horror. At least not until he saw the Induna, the next day.

No one knew what to do, the boy would later tell him. 'Even I, Master,' said the boy, 'I who have been with you in battle – even I didn't know what to do.'

5
The Missing Dead

The summit . . .

. . . and they knew to expect something, but not quite this.

On the cleared ground lying on either side of the track that leads to the gates of the city stand four or five ranks of men, and behind them there are women and children and old-timers.

Clearly no one wants to miss the chance of seeing the Zulus brought to their knees and shamed.

Or else, decides the Induna with a wry smile, no one wants to incur the Buffalo's wrath by not obeying his command to come and see the Zulus brought to their knees.

The moment the Zulus appeared at the top of the path, the Thembu ranks moved forward so that they seemed to grow in number, while the path the Zulus were due to take narrowed.

A wall of shields closing in, trapping them.

And there's no turning back. Each of these men carries a long, heavy assegai, wielded like a pike and, as the Zulus pass on, those in the front rank lower their spears behind them.

It's yet another instance of the 'eloquence' Dingane remarked upon. This is the Thembu salute, the lowering of the spear a warning that one should keep one's distance until one has stated one's intentions, whereupon the spear is raised again. However, the recipient of this salute is normally in front of the warrior. That the spears are being lowered behind the Zulus is therefore a calculated insult that is underscored further by the fact the spears are then kept in a lowered position.

Does Ngoza expect them to know enough of Thembu customs to realise this? Is Dingane expected to fulminate about this at the impending meeting?

He's made a slight miscalculation, though, for the length of the spears means the soldiers can't move close enough to force the Zulus to remain in single file. And, several paces into this grove of shields, Dingane spreads his arms and the others move up alongside him, the Induna to his right, Njikiza and Radebe to his left.

Edging closer to Dingane, keeping his voice low, the Induna says: 'You will say nothing of this, I think.'

The prince has looked back once or twice, and seen the lowered spears and understands what the Induna is getting at. 'That is good advice, old friend.'

'For we are being tested.'

Dingane nods. 'They would see how chastened we are.'

'Chastened!' growls Njikiza. 'Hai! These Thembus are crazy . . .'

★

'Boy, you are thirsty,' says Shaka, without turning.

'No, Majesty, I am fine.'

'You are brave, Little One. And stubborn. Very well, then. I am thirsty . . .'

'Majesty, I am sorry . . .'

'No, do not move. Stay where you are. Or rather, move a little, for I know your legs must be stiff. I am thirsty, and I command you, as a loyal warrior, to drink for me. You will do this for me?'

'Majesty, I . . .'

'You will do this for me and not disobey.'

'Very well, Majesty. I . . . I thank you, Majesty.'

'Hai, you are drinking for me, so *I* thank *you*!'

★

'That's it, is it?' asks Dingane, after they've walked several paces in silence. 'You have looked, you have seen the multitudes, and this is your conclusion?'

403

Njikiza shrugs.

'This is your considered opinion, that these Thembus are crazy?'

★

'Can you feel it?' asks Mdlaka, keeping his voice low. 'The men are growing ever more restive.'

Mbopa nods. It's more noticeable if you don't turn around and look, for then you'll simply see men standing at ease. Keep your back to them and you're gradually aware of . . . not fidgeting, not muttering, but a constant churning, a shifting underfoot as if the ground's about to give way. It's as if you can hear the anguished, agitated thoughts not as words, but as a cricket buzz of unease.

'We try their discipline,' says Shaka's prime minister.

'There is no other way.'

'Just as long as it will hold.'

'It'll hold.'

★

Can you feel it? Yes, here, too, heads have opened and thoughts and emotions have become as palpable as the sand under their feet, or the dust in their throats.

Only, up here, it's hunger, impatience, disdain that ease their way between the shields, to buffet the Zulus.

And, looming in the distance: the great dome of the Thembu meeting place.

But first this, for Kobo, the Buffalo's chamberlain, is standing just over the threshold of the main gate. He is a lean, pompous-seeming man, the kind who uses his height to gaze down upon one, as if that accident of birth alone confers superiority upon him.

There's no bowing of the head, no elaborate greeting, no acknowledgement he is dealing with one of the Blood. Just: 'Welcome, Zulus. The Mighty Masticating Buffalo awaits you.'

To mark the occasion, the avenue has been covered with some kind of fine, silvery-white sand. No footprints sully its surface, which means either servants have followed after Kobo, smoothing his tracks

404

with branches, or he's come to the main entrance via another route.

So they enter the city, which is really a citadel given its position, with Kobo walking a few paces behind them. The Induna doesn't have to turn round to know the chamberlain has a self-satisfied smirk splattered across his face.

There's just one line of Thembu soldiers on either side of the avenue, but these hold back a mass of people so tightly packed they resemble a big, thick rope. These are the vassals and servants, the Induna surmises, for there's a certain glumness about them that contrasts markedly with the crowd outside. These are people used to being herded, doing what they're told, but they'll never do any more than what's expected of them. If forced to cheer, they'll obey, but the result will be an unenthusiastic imitation of the sound a man might make if he's thrown off a cliff.

Looking down, the Induna realises there's something familiar about the way this fine, silvery-white sand coats his toes . . .

★

'So, do not think like that,' the Induna had told Dingane last night. 'See this as a sign of the faith the Bull Elephant has in you. For ultimate success depends on you . . .'

'And you, old friend, and Njikiza and Radebe. Which is why I have no doubt we'll succeed.' Dingane grinned in the darkness, away from the fires and the picquets. 'It's what happens afterwards that concerns me.'

★

Had the Induna ever run so fast? He and Mgobozi and Radebe had arrived the next day, quickening their pace when they saw the birds in the distance, knowing they had to be circling the village, as that was the only human habitation in the vicinity capable of attracting such a hunger of vultures. And the three had set off at a sprint.

A massacre. Ash and smoke, and beaks pulling at rotting flesh. A sense of the world tilting, as the Induna's gaze took in babies piled on top of toddlers; a pregnant woman with her belly ripped open; a greybeard who had had a

405

stone pressed into each eye; and, as a sure sign they were confronted with the
work of Thembus, a preponderance of bodies where the head had been twisted
around so that unseeing eyes stared up at you over shoulder blades.

And then the smoke shifted to reveal a slender boy covered in dried
blood and dust and soot.

He'd used all his reserves to get himself to this moment, and now it
was all draining out of him, and suddenly he could barely put one foot in
front of the other. But nothing – nothing! – was going to stop the boy
now. And the Induna was on his knees, catching his udibi as the boy fell
towards him.

★

'Aiee, look at that,' whispers Njikiza, meaning the big dome looming ever nearer. 'There's a hut that's swallowed every single hut ever
built, and is still growing.'

When he fails to get even a chuckle from his companions, he
glances to his left, at Radebe, then to his right, where Dingane and
the Induna are. All three, he realises, are trying to examine their feet
without being too obvious about it.

The Watcher of the Ford gazes down over his belly, looks up to
maintain his bearings, then looks down again . . . and at last sees
what first the Induna, and then Dingane and Radebe have spotted.

A large number of bodies were found to be missing after the
massacre. Those tasked with burying the dead and pulling down the
rest of the dwellings had assumed these people were burnt inside
the huts. They were wrong, and the four Zulus have just discovered
what happened to the missing dead. They are walking on them.

This is not sand. This is human ash.

6
Détente

Ngoza allows his eyes to rest on each of them in turn. Radebe . . .
the Induna . . . the Needy One.

'Dingane,' says the ruler of the Thembus. 'Dingane KaSenzang-akhona . . .' The Buffalo's tone is soft, ruminative, and his gaze drifts past the prince to rest on a spot outside the hut, a spot only he can see amid the dazzling glare that fills the open section and makes the stout posts seem like slender twigs.

The Induna examines the two men sitting on either side of the chief: Kobo the supercilious chamberlain, and a general called Kingale. Only he's no general, for he's too young, and he has a brooding, almost sullen air about him. He's not even listening to Ngoza. He's watching the Zulus. No, thinks the Induna, not a general but a bodyguard.

Ngoza's head snaps round. 'Tell me,' he says, raising his voice to address Dingane, 'these stories we hear about your king being illegitimate – are they true?' A smile. 'We have heard that your father and his mother weren't married when the Beetle was conceived. And no attempt was ever made to even begin lobola negotiations. What else have we heard, Kobo?'

'Dingiswayo, Sire . . .'

'Ah, yes! We have heard too that Dingiswayo, that eternal, infernal meddler, sought to bully your father into acknowledging Shaka as his progeny.'

'That is, Senzangakhona's progeny, not Dingiswayo's,' adds Kobo.

'Yes, quite. Doesn't say much for Dingiswayo's opinion of your father, does it? But, then, he was sick at the time, wasn't he?'

Kobo: 'Your father.'

Ngoza: 'And did the Beetle help him on his way? Did Dingiswayo send him to your father's kraal, fortified with muthi so he might slaughter both your father and Sigujana, who was the rightful heir?'

The Induna knows such stories will never die. They will always be among the footprints Shaka leaves behind. They will be his bastard children: pale, weak and infirm but venerated by those who fear courage and bravery, because those are the things they themselves lack. Dingane must not allow himself to be goaded, taunted . . .

'How can you know for certain the Beetle really is your brother?' asks Ngoza. 'How could your father know for certain that Shaka was his son? Nandi seduced him – how many others had she done the same thing to?'

'Aiee, Sire, all this talk of mothers and fathers,' chuckles Kobo. 'It's hard to imagine him being born!'

'Perhaps one day Nandi lifted a rock.'

'Or perhaps one day her shit moved,' adds the chamberlain.

'That I can well believe,' interjects Dingane. 'Yes, I can well believe that, since here I sit listening to a talking turd.'

Before either of the Thembus can respond, Dingane addresses Ngoza, his voice oozing politeness: 'And I thank you for your concern. Doubtless you have also heard that Shaka and I don't always see eye to eye. There are even some who say I plot against him. But rest assured, just as I am my father's son, I'm my brother's brother, especially in a matter such as this.'

Ngoza regards Dingane with narrowed eyes. 'Yes,' he says. 'Yes, I can see that now. But tell me this. Since you are so close, would you like to die like your brother?'

'Of course! We both fully intend to die of old age.'

'If you think that, you are both fools.' Ngoza holds up his hand. 'But we are not here to bicker.'

Dingane shrugs.

And the Induna sees how the bodyguard's attention has begun to wander. Even the billowing anger in Ngoza's voice has failed to remind him of the importance of his assignment, and the need to be extra-vigilant.

'No,' says Ngoza, as if to reassure himself. 'Enough of this small talk. Tell us why you are here, Dingane KaSenzangakhona.'

*

Looking left, looking right, making sure the other sentries are out of earshot, Dumo brings his face up close to Njikiza's. 'They don't know it in there, little man, and I'm not supposed to tell you, but none of you will leave this place alive.'

Njikiza meets Dumo's glare. Then yawns.

*

408

'The King wants to know since when has it become Thembu practice to butcher women and children?'

'Hai! Let's be serious,' says Ngoza. 'They weren't women and children. They were Zulus!'

★

'Aiee! My knees tremble, but it'll take more than bad breath to best me.'

'Not much more, though.'

'It speaks. Amazing! Now start working on your last words.'

'Last words?'

'You heard what I said,' hisses Dumo. 'Today you die. Today the ford runs dry, Watcher!'

'I also heard that you weren't supposed to share this far-fetched possibility with me.'

'For you I make an exception.'

'Why? Would you bore me to death?'

'Oh no, I have something far better in mind . . . or should I say in hand.'

'Not that! We'll be here all day if you try to whip me to death with your pizzle.'

★

'Besides,' adds Kobo, 'since when has killing women and children bothered Shaka? We follow his lead in this matter.'

'Listen to your chief, minion,' says Dingane. 'He's right. These were Zulu women and children. That's what makes them different.'

★

The punch doubles Njikiza over, and brings the other two sentries running. There's a silent, tense struggle as they grab Dumo's arms, a man on each side, and force him back a step. Anguished whispers, for they don't dare disturb the meeting behind the partitions. *What is he thinking?* He'll get all of them into trouble! Even if the king

409

calls him his favourite weapon, Dumo mustn't think he can do whatever he likes . . .

Casually, Dumo raises his arms and breaks free of his comrades. But his palms are open, placatory. They mustn't worry. Everything is fine. He and the Zulu are merely having a discussion.

After the two have retreated to their posts, trailing anxious glances behind them, Dumo steps up to Njikiza again. 'You will die today, Zulu, and I tell you this, since you asked, so I can stand here and watch that knowledge fester behind your eyes. Because *that's* what guides my hand to my prick: watching a man who knows he's about to die, and seeing how he prepares himself for the Great Journey.'

★

'Let us not overlook the more important issues here,' says Ngoza. 'Let us not be distracted by the flames, and instead look to the coals. That your king professes perplexity is what perplexes *me*. How else did he expect me to respond to his arrogance?'

'On the battlefield,' says Dingane.

'Hai, then none of you would have been here!'

'This is true,' interjects the Induna.

'Yes, see – even *your* minion can see that,' grins Ngoza.

But Kobo has caught the double meaning of the Induna's words. When their eyes meet, the chamberlain inclines his head ever so slightly, acknowledging the fact the Induna's throw was a good one, and the spear hit the target.

'So it was for your own good, Zulu,' continues Ngoza. 'Even you must see that. Let a few fall so the others can learn how they might prosper.'

'But that is not all,' says Dingane.

'Well . . . a tribute every season would be a fine way of ensuring the lesson won't be repeated.'

'Not that we really need anything you might have,' adds Kobo.

'Hmm, do not discount their women. We might be able to accommodate a few of those.'

410

Kobo makes a show of trying to suppress a shudder. 'As you wish, Sire, but not for me. However . . . it's the principle that matters.'

'Precisely.'

'A way of measuring their allegiance.'

'Quite.'

'Yet . . .'

'What is it, Kobo?'

'Perhaps, in addition to this, we require something a little more meaningful.'

'Require?'

'Yes, I will not say ask, for asking implies there's a choice involved.'

'Whether to say *yes* or whether to say *no*.'

'Yes, Sire.'

'Whereas Shaka has no such luxury.'

'Exactly. You have seen to that, Sire.'

'Hai, no, it was nothing.'

'Birds,' says Dingane addressing no one in particular. 'I am reminded of birds.'

'I can see why,' says the Induna.

Ngoza: 'Birds?'

Dingane: 'Birds.'

Ngoza: 'Is it the heat, do you think, Kobo?'

Kobo: 'I couldn't say, Sire.'

Ngoza: 'For he seems delirious . . .'

'Quite the contrary,' says Dingane. 'I was merely saying this reminds me of birds.'

'What does?' asks Ngoza.

'This . . .' Dingane indicates the space between Ngoza and Kobo, with a lazy hand. 'This exchange, this delicate to and fro – it reminds me of birds. The one chirps, the other answers. The one sings, the other chirps. Or perhaps the exchanges between a soka and his beloved, perhaps *that's* what this puts me in mind of. Sweet words swapped as if no one else existed.'

'Very well, then. A tribute every season and we get to deal with

411

the Portugiza. You want to deal with them, you deal with us. What else, Kobo?'

'That's all for now.'

'Yes, for now. There, Zulu – since you would sneer at sweet words, is that bitter enough for you?'

Dingane scratches his chin, rubs his neck.

'You surely aren't . . .' Kobo turns to his chief. 'He's surely not thinking about it! I mean, there is nothing to think about. Doesn't the fool know that?'

'Clearly not. What say you, Zulu?'

'Hmm, yes,' says Dingane. 'It's not so much what I have to say on the matter, but what our neighbours might have to say about an agreement of this nature.'

'Agreement?' Ngoza raises a finger. 'No, there is no agreement. We say, and you do!'

'Nonetheless, Sire, he raises an interesting point . . .'

'Yes, he does.' Addressing Dingane, he inquires, 'Are you talking about your cousins now?'

The Needy One shrugs.

'Is it their opinion on the matter that concerns you?' Ngoza turns to his chamberlain. 'For we have heard the whisperings, have we not, Kobo?'

'Yes, Sire.'

'Malandela's sons, the brothers Zulu and Qwabe, who both went off to live in different valleys. And some say the bond of blood beguiles a man so that he will see foolishness as loyalty, and the Qwabes have entered into a secret alliance with the Beetle. What say you, Zulu? After all, that would go a long way to explaining your brother's rather strange behaviour.'

'Strange?' asks Dingane.

'We had expected a little more . . . well, gnashing of kingly teeth and pounding of thorns. Instead, he comes here meekly. He cringes, he cowers, he sends you to sit here. Strange behaviour.'

'You say you expected more?' says Dingane.

Ngoza nods.

412

'Do you now contradict yourself? You said the massacre was to punish, yet now you seem to be saying it was to provoke . . .'

Kingale, the bodyguard, is staring into the middle distance. It must have seemed a good idea, choosing one who is too stupid to follow – or be interested in – what's said at this meeting, the theory being that he will not be distracted from his role. In practice, though, with the Zulus sitting where they are sitting and not moving, Kingale appears to have drifted off into a stupor – as one will when one is bored. The Induna can only hope Radebe hasn't drifted off in the same way, although, unlike the bodyguard, he has something to wait for.

'Ha!' A bark of laughter from Ngoza. 'Perhaps you and he really are related. For you, too, are mad if you think you can sit in my house and call me a liar. Besides, if anyone's dissembling here today, it's your king. Coming here meek and quivering, when he has the Qwabes lined up with him! Am I to be surrounded while you entertain me? Is that what your brother intends?'

Ngoza's hand comes up again. 'But why assume *you* would know? You might be of his blood, but you are not trusted by the Beetle. No, let us ask someone who *will* know.'

He straightens.

And calls . . .

'Pakatwayo!'

The ruler of the Qwabes emerges from behind the hanging situated a few metres to the Induna's right. The Zulus watch the portly, grey-haired chief waddle forward. The Induna notices how he avoids their gaze; spots the slight tremble in his hands.

'What say you, my friend?' says Ngoza, and the two go on to exchange the customary greetings. Then the Buffalo shoos away Kingale, and offers the latter's seat to the inkosi of the Qwabes.

★

'Do you hear that?' demands Dumo, stalking back over to where Njikiza stands. 'If you thought your cousins would help you, you were wrong.'

Njikiza shrugs. 'And if you think you can punch me in the stomach again and live, you are wrong!'

Dumo turns to the sentries standing a few metres away. 'Did you hear that, boys? A challenge! You surely do not expect me to ignore such foolishness.'

The other two look at each other. They have their orders, but Dumo is a favourite of Ngoza's. And the Zulu has had the effrontery to challenge the executioner . . . and besides this should be good . . .

'Very well, Dumo, one punch.'

Dumo nods and slams his fist into Njikiza's gut, as he turns back to the big Zulu.

For the second time that day, the Watcher bends forward. Joining his hands together, Dumo steps sideways, raises his arms and brings them down . . .

It's as if Njikiza has been hit on the back of the head with his own club, and he drops to his hands and knees.

'Dumo,' hisses one of the sentries.

'Oops, sorry.'

Turning back to Njikiza, he extends a hand: 'Here, let me help you up.'

★

'So,' says Ngoza, patting Pakatwayo's knee, 'what's this I hear? You have allied yourself with Shaka?'

'Hai! I do not consort with dead men!'

Ngoza turns back to Dingane. 'Did you honestly think they would side with you? Or did you think the mere suggestion would scare me into submission? First you imply I am a liar, then you try to take me for a fool. Have you come here to insult me? Is that it?'

'No,' says Dingane, 'we have come here to kill you.'

7
Accord

Partially hidden by his two comrades in front of him, a few moments ago Radebe had been able to remove the assegai blade secreted in his left amashoba, leaning forward and pulling it from the legging just as Pakatwayo entered. Consequently, he's the first into action. With a cry of 'Njikiza!' he bounds past the Induna, and stabs Kingale in the throat before the bodyguard has even begun to raise his spear. It's a perfect strike, the blade finding the notch between Kingale's collar bones on its downward arc and travelling on through the wet softness of the throat. And even as the bodyguard topples away from him, Radebe's on his left knee, pulling a second iklwa blade from the amashoba wrapped around his right leg.

Over on the other side, Kobo was rather quicker than Kingale. As Radebe pounced on the bodyguard, the chamberlain threw himself forward, trying to make it past Dingane. Ironically, he's too quick. If he'd waited just a few seconds, the prince would have been leaning forward, fumbling for his own blade. As it is, however, Dingane moves even as Kobo moves, his dive bringing down the Thembu at the same time as Kingale hits the ground. The chamberlain manages to call for help just once, before Dingane's on top of him, pressing his face into the floor.

Pakatwayo's the next to jerk himself out of shock. Rising from his seat, he kicks out wildly at Radebe. The Zulu dodges the chief's foot easily enough but, because he's still reaching for his second blade, he overbalances. Pakatwayo swerves, leaps over Kingale's body and heads away from the Zulus, and the partitions, looking to get out of the dome through its open rear section. Blinded by the glare, he careers off a pillar, but fear and adrenalin send him forward again, out into the sunlight, bellowing: 'To arms! To arms!'

★

The blade has been broken off an iklwa, but with enough of the haft left for you to be able to grip it firmly. And each of you carry two of these, one in each of your leggings. And you lean forward, slipping your hand between the cow tails below your left knee. Then you rise and free the blade, in one fluid movement. And there's Ngoza, half on, half off his throne. He looks like someone who's had a pot of boiling water thrown at him: rooted to the spot, horror splashed across his face, in that split second before stunned nerve endings recover and start screaming out in pain. Although, in this case, it's you who'll supply the pain.

And the Induna steps forward, twisting his body slightly, bringing his left hand across his face.

And then your arm is freed, launched, sent swinging away from you in a smooth slashing motion that throws Ngoza's chin backwards. And you follow through, follow the blade, so that you turn your back to him and protect your eyes from the spray of blood.

★

Dumo has his palm pressed against the pillar next to Njikiza. 'What did you expect, Zulu?' he says. 'Telling me not to punch you . . . hmm? What did you—?'

NJIKIZA!

Dumo's head snaps up, and he pushes himself away from the pillar, frowning. Then looks back at Njikiza. A burning wetness. He looks down. Sees the broken haft protruding from his stomach.

'And what did *you* expect, savage? That we would fight as challengers before a battle?' says Njikiza, who had removed the blade from its hiding place when he dropped to the ground, after Dumo had hit him the second time.

HELP! HE—! A desperate cry truncated.

And the sentries are moving towards them. Njikiza slips past Dumo, pulling the blade free as he does so. Grabbing the first sentry's long spear and wrenching it from the man's hands as he lowers it, he rams the bloodied iklwa blade into the soldier's chest as he passes him, then gets the spear pointing the right way.

Somewhere a frightened cow is bellowing 'To arms! To arms!'

And the second sentry has already turned, and is running along the curving corridor formed by the hanging skins. Only he doesn't get far, because there's Radebe coming the other way. The sentry stops, then makes ready to charge, but it's too late. Because, coming up behind him, Njikiza skewers him with his comrade's spear. The warrior drops forward, and is left dangling at a forty-five-degree angle as the assegai blade embeds itself in the dirt.

'All is well?' asks Radebe.

'As always,' says Njikiza, clapping him on the shoulder.

★

'Need help, old friend?' asks the Induna, moving away from the dead Thembu king.

Dingane shakes his head. 'See to the others.'

Pressing his knees against Kobo's shoulders, the prince leans back, reaching for the blade in his right amashoba. At the same time, Dingane feels the chamberlain's ribcage expand, as Kobo tries to find his voice amid shattered teeth and a bleeding tongue. Gripping the broken haft with both hands, Dingane raises the blade above his head and brings it down into the back of Kobo's neck.

★

Outside, Pakatwayo blunders across an empty yard where storage huts have been torn down to allow for the passage of a large body of men. He heads to a section of the perimeter wall that has been cut free and then put back in place, thereby creating a hidden gate allowing that same large body of men access to the city. Should the Zulus attempt to attack from the rear, following the lone slippery, vertiginous path that snakes its way up alongside the waterfall, the men will be there ready and waiting to parry such a foolhardy manoeuvre. Should a Zulu impi somehow manage to hack its way through the dense bush to the east and west of the city, the regiments can also move to counter it. Or, in the unlikely event that the Zulus make significant headway with a frontal assault, the men can be directed through the gate, and straight down the avenue that

417

bisects the city. This was the eventuality Pakatwayo had most wished for, even though he knew his bulls had more chance of growing udders. Because those would have been his men out there. And, although Ngoza kept on about what an important role they would be fulfilling, Pakatwayo was well aware that he and his warriors were expected to know their place, their main reward being relief that they weren't Zulus, while all the honours and most of the spoils went to the Thembus. That they might get a chance to come to Ngoza's rescue, then, was a possibility you wouldn't want to relinquish, no matter how faint . . .

And, well, see . . . you weren't so stupid after all!

That's his finest regiment, waiting out there. Let it come through the city like a flood, carrying the Thembus ahead of it. Let them know they're not leaderless, even though their king is dead, for he, Pakatwayo, will be there urging them to avenge this betrayal.

A sudden vision of how things might be!

And why not? Why shouldn't that be the way things turn out? Clearly Shaka's aim was to sacrifice his brother and the men with him, thinking that, if they killed Ngoza, the Thembus would panic, as the Mthetwas did when Zwide captured and killed Dingiswayo. It might have worked, decides Pakatwayo, in a mood to be charitable despite the circumstances, but Shaka hadn't reckoned on the secret treaty between the Thembus and Qwabes. And to think he'd vacillated when Ngoza's emissaries had approached him! But that was understandable, for it wasn't to be an agreement between equals. Hai, no, Ngoza was graciously consenting to accept the Qwabes as vassals – or else. Still, Pakatwayo had agreed, and look what's happened!

And there's no time to waste. He kicks down the gate and strides on through the dust.

There are his men, his strong Qwabe men, sitting on their shields and waiting patiently in the sun. A quick glance over his shoulder – no one seems to have followed him; so where are those Zulus? – and he waves his men towards him.

'To arms!' he calls.

*

418

More sentries have poured into the hut. Unfortunately for them, they seem to have forgotten the walls are mere animal skins, tied tightly in place, it's true, but easily breached for all that. Instead they come down the corridor created by the hangings, and are thus easily held at bay by Radebe and Njikiza, who have each armed themselves with the long, heavy spears their adversaries carry. In fact, after the first few Thembus had dutifully impaled themselves, the others hung back, and there now follows a kind of fencing, as blades and shafts scrape and bump, parry and thrust, seeking an opening. Leaving Dingane watching the walls in case the guards finally remember these aren't made of thatch and try to outflank the Zulus, the Induna joins the other two, adding his spear to the tangle.

★

'Hurry!'

An officer who's been resting in the shade of the palisade, a few metres past the makeshift gate, pushes himself away from the wall and ambles towards Pakatwayo.

Last night the Qwabe regiments had camped on the banks of the stream, well away from the gorge and the waterfall.

'You,' calls out Pakatwayo, after another quick glance over his shoulder. 'Yes, *you*! Get the men moving!'

The man continues heading towards him.

That's where a raiding force of Fasimbas, led by Mgobozi, had found them an hour before daybreak. A few Qwabes escaped but, chased by Fasimbas, they were steered away from the gorge and the Place of the Buffalo.

'What are you waiting for?' shrieks Pakatwayo.

At first light, Mgobozi had led his Fasimbas up the path alongside the waterfall. The Thembu sentries scarcely paid them any notice before they had their throats slit. Then Mgobozi had positioned his ibutho where Qwabe spies had told them Pakatwayo's forces had been ordered to wait, and where they were ignored by their Thembu hosts, who clearly believed their allies' services wouldn't be called upon.

Without hesitating or deviating from his course, and keeping his eyes on Pakatwayo, the man raises his right arm. And now Pakatwayo sees the axe he's carrying. It's an axe with a blade shaped like a swallow's tail; the kind Zulu generals use to direct men in battle.

Pakatwayo swivels towards the ranks assembled in the long grass, as if to appeal to them – and sees them rise to their feet as one, sees their shields.

Bare feet toughened by marching over thorns; big oval Zulu shields.

Pakatwayo turns back to the man just in time to catch Mgobozi's axe with his forehead.

8
Lions Unleashed

'Are you awake, Little One?'

The udibi, who has indeed been dozing while he leans against the king's isihlangu, straightens up with a start, almost dropping the shield.

'I . . . yes, Majesty. I am here, Majesty.'

'Do you see what I see, Little One?'

The udibi frowns. What can the King see? A twinge of panic. Trembling hands. The feeling of being caught out. Where . . . ? What . . . ?

'Look up, Boy.'

Reports of a disturbance to the rear of the city have led to movement along the path. Suddenly those smug, sneering ranks have become a mob that is pushing and shoving, doing anything to get back on to the plateau.

As the boy wonders what's happening, figures appear on the summit. Distant shouts. Arms gesturing.

Now Shaka turns to the udibi. 'You have stood here with me all this time,' he says, 'so it is only right that you should do it.'

'Do what, Majesty?'

'Unleash our lions.'

'M–me, Majesty?'

'You can do it.'

The boy lifts the shield . . .

'But perhaps you should drink some water first.'

The boy nods: that *would* be a good idea. 'Yes, Majesty. Thank you, Majesty.'

Shaka watches as the udibi rests the shield against himself and reaches for a water-sack, taking a long deep gulp.

Shaka extends his arm, and the boy hands him the waterskin. 'Now,' says the King, 'raise my shield and shout loud enough for the ancestors to hear you!'

The udibi turns.

Takes a deep breath.

Thrusts the shield upwards.

And almost topples backwards.

Shaka steps forward to help, but the Induna's udibi grits his teeth and steadies himself.

Then, before all the breath drains out of him, he bellows as loud as he can: 'Ayi hlome!' *To arms!*

It's all Shaka's lions need. At last they've understood, and they're eager to enter the fray, if only to assuage their shame. To think that they doubted Shaka! That they thought he'd actually deliver them to the Thembus!

They surge forward, and sweep past the King. But he doesn't smile, even when he sees the regiments forming into a column on the run, with no orders necessary.

The shame. The thought that, somehow, he had willed this on them: the massacre, the dead babies.

Was this ultimately of your choosing, Oh, King Who Has Yet To Find His Ubulawu?

Circumstance! His regiments undermanned, his children tired. Discipline and morale: needing to draw the former tighter and enflame the latter, so as to pull the people together, invigorate and enflame!

And circumstance had handed him just such an opportunity.

Circumstance, which had been holding him back, had now opened the way for him – just as the little girl had opened the Ntunjambili Rock, in the story. Somewhere deep inside of him, the word 'Vuleka!' – *Be opened!* – had been uttered . . .

But such a sacrifice! He can only be shamed.

As are his soldiers, too . . . For when it is over, and the Thembu nation lies dying amid the ruins of its own capital, Shaka's warriors refuse their part of the spoils. The memory of their King standing in front of them, facing the enemy in the company of a lone udibi, while they themselves whined and muttered behind his back, doubting his wisdom, his courage, is almost too much to bear. They refuse to be mollified when they're told they could not be informed of the plans earlier lest their swaggering give things away. They had to stand there looking sullen and defeated. And soon it will be recounted how Shaka stood alone that day, clenching and re-clenching his fists so tightly that the bones in his hands were breaking, cracking like thunder, and then re-forming almost instantly, to be shattered yet again. And how the sky grew dark as the King's rage, the thunder within his bones, unleashed the lightning that destroyed his enemies . . .

9
First Contact

And Shaka sends three regiments to the coast, under the command of Mgobozi, to deal with the remaining Qwabe clans. The Induna and the udibi go along with the general. Their iklwas feast and, for close to a month, huts burn and rearguard actions are shattered before they can even be properly mounted. However, let it be said, settlements willing to swear allegiance to Shaka are left alone, their headmen rewarded with cattle taken from their more stubborn neighbours.

The only thing that mars this triumphant campaign is when Mgobozi overreaches himself. For, in a fit of zeal, he leads the

Fasimbas against Faku's Pondoes. Later he will say that he was merely probing their strength and preparedness. If that was the case – and he wasn't hoping to sweep the Pondoes away with very little effort, and a single ibutho – then he found Faku's men ready and waiting. All too prepared, they stood their ground and repelled the invaders. Even more worrying was the fact this force wasn't much larger than the Fasimbas. Fortunately, Faku himself did not reach the battlefield in time, and, suspecting a trick, the Pondo general in charge of the contingent didn't press home his success and turn the Zulu retreat into a rout. The officer escaped punishment only because Faku realised he needed to focus his military resources on preventing his land becoming swamped by the Qwabes and other clans that were fleeing Shaka.

And it's the middle of the day sometime during Untlaba, the Aloe-Flowering Month of the April–May moon, and the regiments are at last returning home. As an antidote to the heat, Mgobozi has led them on to the beach, and they run on the hard sand beside the waterline, where the spray cools them. And the waves sigh and roll forward in a blinding whiteness, as though drawn to the war songs that now echo along the shore.

The Fasimbas, with the general and the Induna, are in the van. Look back, when the shore straightens, and you can see vast brown rectangles, as the orderly undulation of shields and spears and heads becomes lost amidst the breath of the sea. Look ahead and . . .

What's this?

A man.

Wearing a straw hat, a faded blue coat and white trousers rolled up to his knees, he stands there resolute.

Knowing the soldiers can't fail to see this remarkable apparition, Mgobozi bellows the Zulu equivalent of *Eyes front!*

Then, as the column draws nearer to the man, Mgobozi and the Induna peel off, leaving the other officers to hurry the formation along.

'I see it but I do not believe it,' murmurs Mgobozi. 'I see it and I am thinking: *Not again.*'

The Induna nods, aware that the general is referring to their encounter with a Sotho hunting party a few years ago.

'Perhaps this one is different.'

'Aiee, indeed he is that.'

As the second formation approaches, the two warriors move closer to the stranger.

In his usual way Mgobozi has managed to be both right and wrong, decides the Induna. This one *is* a stranger, but he's not strange. They have both encountered his like before. At the same time, though, there *is* something different about him . . .

'Could it be that swimming lizard wasn't lying?' wonders Mgobozi, showing that he's guessed what the Induna is also thinking; or at least is on the same path.

'There is a first time for everything, General.' Even when it comes to Jakot telling the truth.

'This is so.'

'See how straight he stands, General.'

'This is so.'

'And he is not alone.'

'I have noticed that, too.'

Another formation passes them.

'In the bushes somewhere, I suspect.'

The Induna nods. Normally they know that hiding is futile. They understand how they must take a chance and deliver themselves to whoever has stumbled upon them, or else they risk starvation. Yet here . . . ?

'They run, but he stays,' observes the Induna, whose udibi is currently dallying somewhere towards the rear of the column, along with the other herdboys and the captured cattle they are guiding back to Bulawayo.

'Yes,' murmurs Mgobozi, 'he stays. And he watches. Do you see? Aiee, there he looks away, would pretend my eyes chase his away but, as soon as I look away, they'll be back . . .'

'And he doesn't seem hungry. Does he look hungry to you, General?'

'No.'

'But he *is* scared, probably just as scared as those who fled . . .'

'Yet he is trying to hide it,' says Mgobozi.

It's almost as if the stranger understands him, because at that moment he becomes aware his hands have started trembling and he thrusts them into his coat pockets.

Somewhat taken aback, Mgobozi and the Induna exchange a glance.

Can it be that he understands them?

No, impossible!

If that were so, why would they need the likes of the Swimmer?

Another question: is Mgobozi right? Has Jakot been speaking the truth, after all?

Certainly this one doesn't seem like your average shipwreck survivor spewed up by the sea. He's far too self-contained – despite his obvious fear. He lacks the desperation they've seen in others of this strange tribe who regularly try to drown themselves along the coast. He's scruffy and unkempt, without being . . . dirty. That he smells is neither here nor there, for that peculiar stench infests all of their breed.

He . . . The Induna looks at Mgobozi. Mgobozi looks at the Induna. Both look at the savage . . . Frightened whimpering is to be expected, as is some wailing and weeping, but *this* sound has the two Zulus looking at each other in dismay, yet again.

And, no, they haven't heard wrong. Because there . . . he makes the sound again.

And again, even more persistently.

And again.

Speaking. A savage speaking! And making the one sound they'd never expected to hear from an isilwane thrown up by the sea.

Shaka! he is saying. *Shaka! Shaka! Shaka!*

★

Which is how Henry Fynn makes contact with the Zulu nation. Standing rooted to the spot while what, there and then, seems to be the biggest fucking army he's ever seen jogs by, singing blood-curdling songs, and his companions Frederick and Jantjie cower in the bushes (or, who knows, have disappeared into the wide blue yonder, and he can't say that he blames them; the desire to join them is growing stronger every moment), standing there on the white sands, irresolutely resolute, and repeating Shaka's name over and over again, as a talisman he hopes will give these extremely intimidating (not to mention murderous-looking) fellows pause for thought.

PART SIX
Shattering The Calabash

Why have they put on bracelets with so many amethysts,
and rings sparkling with magnificent emeralds?
Why are they carrying elegant canes
beautifully worked in silver and gold?

Because the barbarians are coming today
and things like that dazzle the barbarians.

From 'Waiting For The Barbarians' by C. P. Cavafy
(in *Collected Poems*, translated by Edmund Keeley
and Philip Sherrard)

Eyes, swivelling, stereoscopic. Pinprick apertures between fused lids, encircled by the concentric ripples of tiny wrinkles.

Stained, streaked armour. Spots and splatters. Shades of brown, the darkness of wet mud, the faded khaki of drought-dry winter grass, rusty stripes around the limbs.

Tiny ridged dragon spine becoming a long tail, tightly curled at the end. Chamai-leon. Earth-lion. Air-eater. Fire-fetcher. Unwabu.

Stiff-necked equivocation. The sense of a double chin, a wealthy old-timer's disapproving jowls, but also a tightrope walker's concentration. Jerky, sawing motion atop scrawny limbs; a dapper daintiness that's a hit with the females, while at the same time signifying the slow-motion approach of death for assorted beetles, grasshoppers and flies. Like this one — two or three tongues away.

Got. To. Get.

(Something . . .)

Got to get. Clo. (. . . something . . .) *Ser.* (. . . wrong . . .)

Clo. Ser.

Closer.

A growing unease. Not the fear of losing the prey. Not the dipping diaphragm rise and fall of this slender green branch, gripped so tightly by zygodactyl feet. Something else . . .

(A sense of movement somewhere . . . A disturbance . . .)

Hai, but the People Of The Sky do not like unwabu. It was the chameleon that Unkulunkulu sent to tell the Abantu they could live forever. Lazy loiterer that he was, though, the chameleon stopped along the way to catch grasshoppers with his long tongue, and to admire his wardrobe of colour changes. Thinking the chameleon had delivered his message, and seeing ungratefulness in their silence, Unkulunkulu angrily despatched the lizard to tell the human beings that immortality was theirs no longer. Although leaving some time after the chameleon, the lizard arrived first, schadenfreude *giving him the speed of a cheetah. 'Let you know death, thou sluggards!' he told the Abantu, speaking with gleeful pomposity. 'For so sayeth the Great Spirit!'*

(. . . something . . .)

In this way the human beings became the only creatures to know death, to know they would die, which led them to foolishly regard Life and Death as upper-case opposites, when, truly, like birth, death is but a phase — a motion towards — while Life endures (before, beyond, above language) without end or antonym.

(. . . something odd . . . out of place . . .)

When the chameleon finally arrived, it was too late. People had begun to die and, like all knowledge, the knowledge of death could be suppressed or ignored but never banished.

(. . . some thing . . .)

And so, feeling tricked and betrayed, the People Of The Sky came to loathe the chameleon, and would always seek to kill him whenever they came across him. To this day those considered untrustworthy, or simply slow and dithering, are called 'izinwabo', chameleons. It didn't help that, on hearing what had really happened, Unkulunkulu relented somewhat and instituted marriage as a means for human beings to attain some kind of immortality, if only through their children. Cha! This is often the cause of an even more enthusiastic vengeance being wrought upon the reptile.

(. . . wrong . . .)

The sides of the ravine are sheer here, as though the walls are trying to restrain the spread of the bushes. An upward motion: a leaping, clinging, creeping; but a tangle, too, — a buzzing, hissing, singing tangle.

Hesitant sawing motion, forward-back, forward-back, left front foot raised, the pair of fused toes parted . . .

Raised, hovering, should-I-shouldn't-I, then dropping on the forward slant, toes becoming tongs to grip the branch, as it dips then rises again.

His tongue compressed, spring-loaded within its U-shaped hyoid bone, moments away from being unleashed, the chameleon's equivocation now has less to do with a fear of disturbing his prey and more with a sense of disruption, displacement, something . . .

(. . . not right . . .)

The cells lying in layers beneath unwabu's skin mirror this growing fear, as pigments merge and the chameleon's colour darkens. Something . . .

(. . . imminent . . .)

Something's not right and, somehow, eyes swivelling wildly, the reptile knows he's going to become a part of this fast-approaching something.

Suddenly it's as if the chameleon's darkening skin colour dissipates, escapes into the air around him in a swarm of chromatophores, because, for an instant, he's covered in shadow . . .

Then a plummeting crash, a shattering of branches and leaves. Sound that's also movement: an explosion expelling the reptile from the branch, as though the chameleon has become his own tongue.

★

Wild ratcheting. A spinning away. The flung and the fleeing. A sense of screaming shock, noisy bewilderment, a shuddering. Thunder and lightning from a blue sky. The bruise forming beneath the knuckles. A gulping, gasping, gagging.

Then . . .

The rearranging.

It's as if the ravine gets its breath back, brings its heartbeat under control. There's an easing, a moving on and around, the explosion forgotten, its cause a fixed feature that's been there as long as the rocks themselves.

The chameleon scuttles off to more salubrious environs. The ants continue trooping. The beetles and crickets return to doing whatever crickets and beetles do in ravines on sunny mornings, where the passing of time is just a moving line combing shadow into the leaves and grass.

And, at the centre of all this scurrying: eyes.

Staring, unseeing eyes, cornea and iris, floating on a shattered and flayed face.

431

The Valley Of The Kings

Blue sky. Green grass. Flat-topped acacias, tall and aloof, as digni-
fied as tribal elders. Scruffier marula trees standing slightly askew,
like husbands trying to feign sobriety after drinking the beer that's
made from the same trees' berries. Brown columns, five men abreast
and eighty men long, with indunas jogging up and down their flanks
to ensure the stamping feet keep in line, while others set the pace
up front so that there's always about fifty metres or so between the
formations. Each man carries a small ihawu shield and a stick.
Because the warriors aren't armed, they're watched over by a contingent of the Fasimba ibutho. Some are roaming the surrounding
countryside, while a larger group sit on their shields at the entrance
to the valley.

Umasingana, the month of the Casting About Moon when women
begin to search their fields and gardens for the new crops, has given
way to the month of the December–January moon, and the climax
of the First Fruits is approaching. With Shaka in seclusion, the
processions are watched over by Mbopa, Mdlaka and various other
dignitaries and high-ranking officers. They've spread themselves out
under some trees, just below the crest of the highest slope which is
near the entrance to the valley. With them are a group of udibis,
who keep them supplied with beer, slices of pumpkin, and with
platters of amacimbi, a plump, edible green caterpillar.

The last column has just gone by. Tramping the flattened grass,
it's as if the men are following a giant rope plaited and played out
by the first formation.

In terms of numbers, this is only a small foretaste of what is to
come. Though involving only a few companies from the regiments
quartered closest to this special place, it's nevertheless an important

part of the First Fruits. For this is sacred KwaNkosinkhulu, the Place of the Great Chief, and they have come here, these brown columns, to pay homage to the Bloodline. For it was here in this shady, fertile basin, surrounded by a rampart of hills and fed by a spring on the Tonjaneni Heights, that Zulu and his clan settled and prospered and grew. Here, in this place of plenty between the White Mfolozi and the Mhlatuze rivers, the seeds of greatness were sown as a clan became a nation and the AbakwaZulu – the People of Zulu – became the Amazulu.

Let us recite their names, those who oversaw this slow metamorphosis . . .

Zulu was succeeded by his son Phunga KaZulu, then came Mageba KaPhunga, then Ndaba, Jama, Senzangakhona . . .

And they are all buried here, each king's grave marked by a euphorbia tree.

The columns will visit each grave site in turn, where praise singers wait to regale them with tales of the king who is buried there. Then the men will move on while others take their place, in what amounts to a gigantic circular movement that will eventually bring the warriors back to where they started. A pilgrimage that is also a dance, each step measured by the rhythmic tread of marching feet that follow the lead of the praise singers and indunas. Compression and tension: being drawn into the past and then pulled back again. The whole mirroring the moon, the umuzi, the sacred cattlefold in the centre of every village, the Inkatha and Shaka's ring at Gqokli Hill.

★

Ndlela KaSompisi regards the spectacle with distaste. If he could have done so without attracting undue attention, he would have avoided being here. It's not simply a matter of his growing dislike for the King colouring his attitude towards anything involving the King – for he might be, first and foremost, a soldier but that doesn't mean he's not practised in the art of diplomacy, and adept at hiding his true feelings behind a mask of smug imperturbability. It's those boys . . . the sight of all those boys . . .

The concept of a guild or age-set, comprising youths born within the same period, is common among the Nguni peoples. It was Dingiswayo who started employing these groups on the field of battle as distinct units. Shaka simply took the process further, using the amabutho as the basis for a standing army, while at the same time defusing any potential threat such an army might represent to himself.

Before, the local chiefs would be responsible for sending men to serve the king when the need arose. If they were opposed to a campaign the king intended to mount, or were loath to see their own power base eroded, the chiefs would send fewer men than were actually available, claiming that's all they possessed. Even if a chief condescended to despatch all the men he could manage, they remained loyal primarily to him. They were his men, and more likely to do his bidding than the king's.

By forming his regiments according to age rather than region, Shaka changed all this. Males born within the same four-year period are summoned to Bulawayo from across the kingdom and formed into a new fighting unit, with its own name and unique shield markings. Regional and clan loyalties are thus negated, and loyalty to the regiment itself comes to the fore.

This also enables Shaka to enlist males from conquered nations into his army. Units comprised solely of 'foreigners' are notoriously unreliable, and a threat to internal stability if drawn from vassal tribes, but now, integrated according to their age, the boys are split up and mixed with Zulu youths.

While in training or on active service, the regiments are stationed at war kraals sited in areas of strategic importance or political vulnerability. Thrown together, and each of them far from home but of the same age, the young men soon refer to themselves by their regimental rather than their clan names. But traditional Zulu custom threatened this coherence. For once a man married, he was allowed to leave his regiment and return to his clan lands to establish his own homestead. This, of course, brought him back under the sway of the local chief. Shaka's solution was to withhold all permission for his warriors to marry, while he set about consolidating his own power.

Ndlela fully understands the need for an army that won't melt away, should the enemy prove stronger than expected. But, in his eyes, whatever Shaka may have accomplished there is negated by the very presence of those younger regiments.

They should not be here!

They should not even be thinking of war!

Not allowing his older men to marry is one thing . . . And look, see! Hasn't he heard Mbopa will announce today that some of the regiments will be allowed to take wives? Shaka merely sent the custom the long way round the mountain to buy himself some time, and then he had it fetched and laid before the feet of his warriors as a reward for their service.

But, when it comes to the youngsters, the King has gone too far! For he has abolished the old Zulu coming-of-age ritual. Not simply moved, withheld or changed, but abolished it! Would he do away with the funeral rites and say that bodies must be simply dumped in the veld? No! That would be like telling his people to stop breathing. Look how he's now twisted the First Fruits to suit himself – but he'd never do away with the ceremony altogether. That would be unthinkable! Yet that's exactly what he's done by abolishing the coming-of-age ritual. The unthinkable.

And no one seems to have noticed, or care. Even Mnkabayi. The import is lost on her. Can't she see this is perhaps the greatest evil that Shaka has perpetrated against the tribe?

Seemingly no one can. If pushed, the sycophants clustered around the King simply mouth Shaka's own words. Service in the King's army is now the one true test of manhood, and nothing else matters!

Can't they see how that's meaningless rhetoric? And dangerous, too! Military service cannot simply be substituted for the old coming-of-age ritual! When those youngsters die in battle, they are not quite men, not quite boys, and therefore they cannot join the ancestors. Instead they're lost in a kind of limbo, each one of them alone, eternal travellers with bloody, torn feet, racked by pain and the knowledge

that they will never make it home, yet forced to keep on walking
. . . to keep on trying.

★

And, yes, through Mbopa, Shaka will let it be known that he intends
to allow some more of his regiments to take wives, after the First
Fruits, and the men will thank him, and he will form new amabutho,
calling them into being by giving the age-sets their regimental names
and the shields by which they'll be identified. And these children
will sing his praises, and no one will realise the great harm Shaka
is doing the nation.

He has to be stopped!

Ndlela's eyes seek out the group comprising Shaka's brothers:
Dingane, Mhlangana, Bakuza, Mpande, Magwaza and the others.
Scuffling, fidgeting, seemingly more interested in the food and
drink – or cuffing their younger brothers who serve as their udibis
– than in the men down in the valley. Unseemly, disrespectful
behaviour!

Then Ndlela sees the Induna's former udibi approach his master;
sees the Induna lead the youngster away from the gathering of
dignitaries.

Something's happened.

Ndlela knows that Shaka suspects elements within his own kraal
might be plotting against him, and therefore has tasked the Induna
and his former udibi – the one they call Mthunzi – and a few other
trustworthy men to discover if there is such a plot and, if so, to
bring the conspirators before him.

Aware that Mnkabayi will want to know what the udibi is now
telling the Induna, Ndlela makes his way over to the two men.

The udibi spots him first and says something to his master, who
turns to greet Ndlela.

'What's the matter, Nduna?'

'A death, Master.' Mthunzi has just brought him news that a boy
has been killed.

436

'Murdered?' interrupts Ndlela, the question directed at the udibi.

'It seems so, Master.'

'Aiee!' Ndlela turns to the Induna. 'The King has asked you to be on the lookout for such incidents.'

The Induna nods.

'Then go, see what has transpired!' And, since he has already spotted eyes turning their way, Ndlela will mutter something about there having been an accident, if anyone asks him where the Induna and his shadow have gone off to.

'Who knows', he adds, 'I might not be lying. See how our regiments have to be kept separate.' In any large gathering, tempers are likely to flare. 'How old was this boy?' he asks. Some fifteen summers old, replies the udibi. Well, there you go, remarks Ndlela – at the risk of sounding callous that is not too young to want to enjoy the Pleasures of the Road or get yourself into trouble in some other way.

'Now go,' he says. 'See this matter resolved before any rumours spread too far and wide.'

★

'You didn't tell him,' observes the udibi, as they jog away.

'No, I didn't,' says the Induna.

'Neither did you . . .'

'You are right. I didn't mention that either.'

Grass brushing their knees, the singing fading with every pace they take.

'Might I ask why, Master?'

Ndlela's not one of those Shaka has instructed the Induna to report to, but that's not really the reason he held back.

'I'm not sure,' he tells the udibi. Then a grin. 'Perhaps I hope it will turn out as Ndlela suggested – mere happenstance.'

'But—'

'I know, I know.'

They've been arriving for several days now. From all the war kraals and villages across the land they come: men, women and children, bringing cattle and other provisions. Only the frontier amabutho are manned, as regiments stream in from the north and south, the east and west. Scarred veterans whose necklaces bear the relics of many battlefields, eager young cadets in age-sets that have yet to be named and turned into regiments by Shaka.

And there's a frenzy of building beyond the capital's outer palisade. The regiments are here in full force, and the areas allotted to them within the city aren't big enough. As a result they'll be billeted in temporary camps in different locations around Bulawayo. Then there are all their families to be accommodated. These additional campsites are positioned between the outer ring formed by the regiments and the city itself.

Almost overnight it's as if the capital doubles in size, expanding outwards in concentric circles.

And still they keep coming, bringing with them cattle and dust.

The Face In The Firelight

'Speak up! Make sense!'

'I-I am sorry, Nduna,' stammers Jembuluka, the Skin Man, as they stop outside one of the temporary huts set away from the sector specially assigned to Ntokozo's clan – for, even though he is now dead, his family will continue to benefit from his standing for a while longer. 'It's just that this – seeing what he did – has affected him badly, and his mother fears he may have been bewitched.'

For this reason Jembuluka is happy to allow the boy to be sequestered here, away from the rest of the family, and watched over by Fasimbas.

'What of the inyangas who have been treating him?' asks the Induna.

'Their muthi has made him less agitated and he is sleeping more, but . . .' Jembuluka shrugs. It seems Vuyile still spends most of his waking hours staring into space. 'And I dare not summon a sangoma, Nduna. For obvious reasons.'

The Induna nods, and points. 'That one!'

At the udibi's signal, one of the sentries chases after the man walking away from the hut.

'It is just Gudlo,' says Jembuluka, as the soldier and his captive approach them.

After Vuyile, Gudlo is the next eldest. Dwanile is his mother, while Melekeleli is Vuyile's. He was just visiting his brother, he explains.

'Is he talking?' asks Jembuluka.

'No,' replies Gudlo. 'I think he knew it was me, but I said nothing.'

'His concern is real?' says the Induna, as Gudlo is allowed to go on his way.

Jembuluka thinks for a moment, then nods. Since Melekeleli, the Skin Man's sister and Vuyile's mother, was Ntokozo's ingadi, his right-hand or chief wife, and Gudlo's mother, Dwanile was his ikhohlwa or left-hand wife, and second to Melekeleli, there have been rivalries and disagreements between them, with the other wives being cajoled into joining one side or the other. But there is no sign of this animosity between the brothers, adds Jembuluka.

'They have argued and fought,' he says, 'but no more than other brothers do, and they are a lot closer than some.'

He shakes his head. 'Aiee, poor Vuyile!'

'He is his father's heir, and almost a man,' says the Induna.

'This is so. And he is no coward who seeks to skulk in his mother's hut, but that makes what he must have seen even more shocking.'

'And you do not know the other clan involved in this incident?'

'No, Nduna. As I have told you, they come from the high country.' It was here in Bulawayo that they first met.

The Induna nods, thanks Jembuluka, and says he may go – for he wishes to speak to Vuyile alone.

'And I will wait here,' says the udibi.

'I think that'll be wise,' says the Induna. 'If we are too many, we might crowd him and unsettle him further.'

It's hot inside the temporary hut. At the inyangas' insistence, a fire is kept burning. Periodically they throw on certain kinds of herbs and wood, believing that the muthi and the heat will help Vuyile sweat out the poisons within his mind.

Certainly, the Uselwa Man's son seems thinner than the last time the Induna saw him. As his treatment has also involved purgatives, he has undoubtedly lost weight since the murder. But that was only four days ago, and the Induna suspects that what he's seeing is more a diminution of the youngster's natural arrogance. Vuyile has witnessed something that truly scared him. The real world reached out and grabbed him, and all his masks and shields, poses and postures, couldn't protect him. He will recover, of that the Induna has no doubt, and he will gradually pull together again the growls and guises that help him on his way, but for now the youth is naked in more ways than one.

He sits cross-legged, staring at the flames, and the Induna positions himself at right angles to the youth, and a little further from the fire.

Jembuluka doesn't know it, but the Induna came here and sat in the same spot, on the night he arrived to investigate the murder. And the next morning, and the following evening; as well as this morning. He knew the inyangas allowed the family to visit Vuyile at midday, and so he had stayed away then. Besides, after viewing the body, there was the dead boy's family to talk to, as well as his brothers and friends.

'I have seen your mother,' says the Induna. 'She is concerned about your welfare.'

'Mothers,' whispers Vuyile.

'They do have our best interests at heart,' continues the Induna. 'But they have the strangest ways of showing it – so that sometimes a man must get away.'

'She has a sharp tongue. She . . .'

When it's clear Vuyile isn't going to say more, the Induna declares he is thirsty. After reaching for his waterskin, and taking a few gulps, he passes it over to Vuyile.

'You were saying?' he asks casually, after the youth has almost sucked the skin dry.

'She . . . she nags.'

'And so a son has to make his escape from time to time.'

A nod, the flicker of a grin.

He had got away that afternoon, and soon he was enjoying the sights and sounds, the busy activity around KwaBulawayo. Soon he was flirting with maidens, helping carry baggage for their mothers. Soon he was enjoying something he hadn't had for a long while – a good time.

He had stayed out longer than expected, for no fewer than four families he had helped that day had invited him back for supper, and he had visited them all in turn. When he was about to leave the last party, the father advised him to take that path, over there. It was a short cut that would lead him through land already cleared for the erection of still more temporary huts. These hadn't been built yet, but there were bonfires to show him the way.

It was in one of these clearings that he saw . . .

Vuyile falls silent. 'No,' he whispers, 'I heard, then I saw . . .'

'You heard?' asks the Induna softly.

Slowly, Vuyile's head turns towards the Induna. 'Hyena sounds.' His voice is barely audible above the crackling of the flames, which have yet to die down, and the heat coats the Induna's chest, arms and face in a sheen of sweat.

Hungry, snuffling, slurping hyena sounds.

'Yet you went on, because you couldn't believe your ears,' says the Induna. Mpisi the hyena might be a much misunderstood creature, but one that was unlikely to roam so close to a settlement of this size, especially with all the shouting and movement, the beating of drums and drunken laughter lasting until almost dawn. 'You went on because it had been a good day and a good night, and so you didn't want to believe your ears.'

An almost imperceptible nod.

The Induna reaches across to place a hand on Vuyile's knee. 'I know what this creature did, therefore you do not have to go there again tonight. Instead, I would know this: did he see you?'

'No.'

'Are you sure?'

Vuyile begins to nod, then stops himself. 'Yes.'

'Why can you be sure?'

Because he had approached the clearing, and the sounds, in a crouch. And when he saw – when he took it all in and understood what he was seeing – he had stopped – and sunk backwards on to his bottom . . .

. . . and the figure by the bonfire must have heard something, because that was when he looked up . . .

. . . but Vuyile had dropped out of sight, although he could still

442

see the creature, even though he's sure the creature couldn't see him – and that was when he saw who it was.

'Are you sure?' asks the Induna, because this is a serious allegation to make. Especially at this time.

'I am . . . sure . . .'

'Then why do I hear indecision in your voice?'

★

A good day, a better night – then those sounds.

Biting, slurping, sucking, crunching hyena sounds.

And then he was creeping forward, because there was something about those sounds that just wasn't right. They didn't belong with the distant whoops and shouts. And he crept further forward. And there, in the orange light of the bonfire, a body lying on its back. And doing something to its face, gnawing and biting, tugging and pulling, was a creature the like of which Vuyile had never seen before.

On its hands and knees, with its torso twisted, it resembled a giant lizard, but had no tail. And it was going at the body's face with a hyena's vehemence.

Somehow, Vuyile managed not to shout out. And then he was sitting on his arse, and he could still see through the branches of the bush in front of him, and he must have made some noise, because, as he watched, the creature's head came up. That was when he saw the creature's face, saw who it was. And, as the creature sniffed the night air, Vuyile shut his eyes.

When he looked again, the creature was gone. Without thinking, he turned and ran back the way he'd come, crashing into the campsite he'd just left, with a tale that, garbled as it was, had the men reaching for their spears and calling to their neighbours for help.

★

'He says he saw this sangoma, Kholisa?'

The Induna nods.

443

'Who he knows, so there can be no mistaken identity?'

Another nod.

'But you say he said the sangoma looked different . . .'

'Yes, loose-skinned, not quite human.'

'But it was Kholisa.'

'So he says, Master.'

'And you have no reason to doubt him?'

'No.'

'Aiee, this clan!' says Mbopa. 'You said there was something odd about the whole affair, when you came before our Father after the death of this Uselwa Man. Now this!'

'Some would say it's happenstance, Master.'

'This is so: it could just as easily have been some boy who saw what Vuyile saw. Do you believe that, Nduna?'

'It could indeed have been another boy, Master. And if it had been, we would not know to seek out Kholisa.' That it *was* Vuyile who stumbled on the scene could be a further sign that Ntokozo's Umkhokha is angry and restless, and still seeking vengeance.

'Which means you were right to doubt that the boy Vala was responsible for Ntokozo's murder.' Because, if the Induna had been wrong, the dead man's Umkhokha would have come after *him*, seeking to punish him for thwarting justice.

'Master, if I may . . . ?'

Mbopa makes a be-my-guest gesture.

Perhaps the Umkhokha was the force that brought those two together: Kholisa and Vuyile, who was one of those able to recognise him. And the Umkhokha chose Vuyile because it wants others to know that this madness does, in some way, involve the clan – or at least Ntokozo's murder.

'Kholisa killed him,' muses Mbopa, 'now he has killed again.'

'This is the way things might be, Master.'

'And Ntokozo's body? Did you recall anyone saying it had been . . . abused?'

Jembuluka and the dead man's wives would surely have noticed, but they said nothing of that. However, the sangoma might have done something to the body, after it was left in his care . . .

'Hmm, I ask because the boy who was killed here . . . you know what his wounds signify? Of course you do. The nose and surrounding skin and the lips – powerful muthi. Especially if ingested on the spot.'

'He seeks the boy's youth, and his stamina. Perhaps even his balance.'

'Yes, that's right, for Kholisa walks with a limp.'

'This is so.'

'And now all who know him suddenly realise they haven't seen him since Ntokozo's death.'

'This is so, Master.' After his encounter with Mgobozi a few years ago, Kholisa stopped trying to draw attention to himself. And everyone who might be counted upon to become worried by this recent absence believed they knew where he was. Mhlangana, who arrived at KwaBulawayo a few days ago, was under the impression that the Induna had forced Kholisa to accompany him to the capital, when he had brought Vala before the King. Kholisa's students, who had been in the prince's party, believed their master had been stung by his inability to save Ntokozo's life, and had then gone on a retreat to commune with the ancestors and to collect muthi ingredients from more potent areas. But they had pretended to agree with Mhlangana's theory, out of loyalty to their master. According to the Uselwa Man's family, Kholisa had simply not been there one morning; after agreeing such behaviour was rude, even for a sangoma, they hadn't given him much more thought. Jembuluka was more forthcoming, adds the Induna, for he had encountered the limping sangoma on the morning he left, and Kholisa had told him he was returning home to the war kraal overseen by Mhlangana. Kholisa had seemed unhappy, said Jembuluka.

'And now we are looking for him, I assume?'

'This is so, but as one who is missing.'

The Induna and his men have put it out that the boy was killed by a wild animal, although it's unlikely that particular story will be able to compete with the other more lurid accounts doing the rounds. However, he has been able to ensure that word of Kholisa's involvement will not get out.

'So we hope,' murmurs Mbopa.

The Induna shrugs. The inyangas who are treating Vuyile don't know; and the Induna has threatened Jembuluka into secrecy. He's also had a word with the father of the clan Vuyile had gone to fetch that night, and explained that Vuyile had panicked and was merely calling for Kholisa. He didn't mean to imply the sangoma had been involved in the killing. As for Vuyile, the youth himself has promised he won't say a word to anyone.

'A story like this is like trying to squeeze sand. Some of it always gets out.'

'We will do our best,' says the Induna.

'You will have done that if you find this crippled sangoma. That's all I ask. That's all Shaka asks!'

And to KwaBulawayo she comes . . .

. . . with her retinue, of course. As Senzangakhona's sole surviving sister, and a princess who's treated as a queen by Shaka, she'll be one of the most powerful dignitaries present at the First Fruits.

And by the time she's made sure her quarters are to her liking – and set her servants to fix the things that displease her, and has paid her respects to Shaka and Pampata, and visited her other nephews and caught up with Ndlela who arrived a few days before her, and listened to her ladies in waiting – she knows where to find him.

The one she loves above all else.

The one she was forced to relinquish, and who can never know her.

And, as always, when he's close by, she ensures their paths will cross, the banal pleasantries they exchange having to stand in for all the things she wants to tell him.

And when she can't make their paths cross, she'll watch him from afar . . .

(Working hard to hide her eagerness, but enjoying the giddiness, feeling like a young girl awaiting her suitor – she who has never had any suitors, only clandestine couplings, and off to the impalers for those who betrayed her trust.)

That no one else knows this, except Ndlela, somehow makes the bond between her and him – the one who can never know her – even stronger.

And she can tell herself this, too, as she waits for her nephew. She is doing this for him . . .

The First Calumny

The climb wasn't arduous at all but, at the summit, she allows him to take her arm. She's found it's always good to be thought of as more fragile than one is, especially the older one gets. Although it's scarcely to his credit that he falls for this simple ploy, for looking beyond appearances is an ability that should come naturally to one of the Bloodline. Cha! But she is letting Ndlela's doubts get to her. They taint her beer, making it sour, making herself sour and a little too ready to find fault.

Mnkabayi pats her nephew's hand. 'I am pleased you found the time to accompany me.'

'I will always find time for you, Aunt.'

At least he can hide his boredom and be charming, Mnkabayi tells herself. Although that's nowhere near as important as possessing a talent for being manipulated, moulded and shaped according to her wishes – which trait she believes this one has in abundance.

'I am sure,' she says, 'there are many pleasures more alluring over there than spending time with an aged relative.'

A courtly chuckle. 'All those people! I am glad to escape their noise for a while.'

And also the eyes of your brother's spies, thinks Mnkabayi. She nods in agreement. The Umkhosi seems to get bigger and grander every year. Which is as it should be, thanks to his brother.

'Indeed.'

Who seems to have planted his kingdom in fertile soil, for see how it grows . . .

A cough. 'This is so.'

And, of course, this season some special guests will be present at the climax of the First Fruits . . .

448

They have reached the edge of the hill, and KwaBulawayo is merely a smudge in the distance. At their feet is a circle of stones. It is an isiguqo, a kneeling-place, where one can come and commune with the Great Spirit. Hills where these circles are to be found are never pointed at with a finger; only a clenched fist is used. Judging by the flattened grass, this one has seen a lot of use recently, most likely by those seeking some extra protection for their crops. Perhaps they've been made more nervous than usual this year, because Shaka has invited izilwane to attend the Umkhosi . . . Or is that wishful thinking on her part?

'Tell me,' she says, 'have you had much to do with these savages that your brother finds so diverting?'

'Not really.' A shrug. 'They bore me.'

'There are some who find their presence annoying.'

'Would you be one of those, my Aunt?' he asks, showing her he might be shrewder than even she realises.

Hiding her smile with a hand, Mnkabayi lets him think she's wondering how far she can trust him.

'No,' she says drawing the word out, 'not quite. Which is to say, I haven't formed an opinion of them yet.'

'I'm not sure what to say, Aunt. They come and go. And especially Mbuyazi,' he adds, referring to Fynn.

'Ah, yes, Mbuyazi. My nephew, your brother, says he has quite domesticated him.'

'He seems to enjoy Mbuyazi's company.'

'But I interrupted you. You were saying how they come and go?'

'Yes, and especially Mbuyazi. Possibly this is why they amuse my brother so. They are so eager to please, so afraid. And they smell.'

'Like all the others,' observes Mnkabayi, meaning the various parties of shipwreck survivors who have traipsed along the coast and then sought Shaka's protection over the years.

'Yes,' agrees her nephew.

'Still, as bedraggled and lost as they might seem, these are not like the others, my boy. To think so would be a grave error.'

449

'But' – his free hand comes away from his side, to sweep the air – 'they smell.'

Mnkabayi chuckles, shakes her head, pats her nephew's knuckles once more. 'You say they come and go—' she begins.

'Indeed,' interrupts her nephew.

'But what of their floating kraal?'

'What of it?'

She's been told it disappears for long periods of time.

That is so, agrees her nephew. They go to fetch supplies, and to consult with their King Jorgi.

'That is what makes them different.'

'I still don't understand.'

'They may come and go, as you say, but they remain here among us. It's their floating kraal that goes away.'

They stand for a moment, enjoying the view, the sky and the veld – with KwaBulawayo the join between the two. Her words must sink in. He must understand. The barbarians have asked for, and received, land from Shaka. They are not mere wayfarers forced to remain where they are by circumstances beyond their control. They are not lost, and the sea hasn't eaten their ships and spat them out at Shaka's feet. They have come here to stay, their floating kraal providing a path that still connects them to their tribe.

. . . and who knows how many more might come down that path, as perilous as it seems to be!

They might be here to trade with the King, but they are also the vanguard: their settlement at Thekwini not the end of the path, but a gateway . . .

'Your brother claims he can keep them docile and says they will make valuable allies. But do they think they can trust Shaka?'

'That's a strange way of putting it, Aunt, but who knows how they think? They are not like us.'

'It is important, nonetheless. If they do think they can trust Shaka, then his position is strengthened.'

A pause.

'After all, you can see how too much trust might let them lower their guard.'

'Well, my brother has certainly gone out of his way to win that trust.'

'And I would be confident of his success, were it not for the mamba in the hut.'

'Mamba?' he asks, looking around anxiously.

'By mamba I mean the Swimmer, Nephew. You have heard the story going around, haven't you, about Shaka and Dingiswayo? What if the Swimmer takes it back to his white masters?' All know how the Swimmer regularly falls in and out of favour with both groups, fleeing to Bulawayo when his former employers threaten to flog him, scurrying back to the bay whenever he's annoyed Shaka. A juicy, tasty story like this one would be just the thing to bargain with, should he need the protection of the White Men at Ethekwini once again.

'Those who know and love your brother will see it for what it is – malicious gossip!' But to izilwane ears it will sound ominous, and they will regard it as a warning. 'They too will be wondering whether this king can be trusted to keep his word, and in that story they'll have their answer.'

Mnkabayi pauses a moment. 'You know the story I speak of, naturally.'

A neutral shrug from her nephew, followed by a sniff. 'I do not really concern myself with gossip.'

'Neither do I, but I'm still surprised you haven't heard it. I had heard it before, a while ago, then it vanished. Now it has re-turned – possibly because of all these people coming together.'

That's why she's mentioned it. With the story having resurfaced, and spreading further afield than it might have done under normal circumstances, the Swimmer is more likely to hear it, and pass it on.

'But what story is this?' he asks, barely able to hide his impatience.

★

451

You have heard of how Dingiswayo recognised Shaka's greatness (she says). *You have heard how Dingiswayo spoke to my brother, your father, and persuaded him to acknowledge Shaka as his heir. But then Senzangakhona went back on his word! And Dingiswayo sent Shaka and the Izicwe regiment to seize the Zulu throne. All this you have heard. These are among the baubles the praise singers string together to amuse us.*

And they tell of the dark day Dingiswayo decided to march on Zwide. Of how Dingiswayo neglected to send word to Shaka, telling him where exactly their forces should meet. Of how Dingiswayo blundered into Zwide's arms while out scouting.

Some say that the king of the Mthetwas was bewitched; that his semen was stolen and delivered to Zwide's medicine men.

Some say Shaka saved the nation by refusing to attack when he heard his mentor had been beheaded by Zwide. The Mthetwas were thrown into confusion by the death of their king, and Zwide's forces were able to eat them up; and Shaka withdrew with a few of Dingiswayo's remaining allies, to bide his time.

This is what they say, and this is what you will have heard.

But . . .

Aiee, my tongue burns me for uttering these things, repeating these slanders. Would that the earth open and swallow me! But it must be said. It is our duty, as loyal servants of Shaka, to know these things so that we can root out those who spread such lies!

And there are those who say that Dingiswayo offered succour to Shaka and Nandi. That he saw in Shaka the makings of a great warrior. That Shaka became as a son to him. Yet, despite this, he demurred when Shaka begged him to help seize the Zulu throne, because Senzangakhona was one of his most loyal allies. But Shaka persisted, and getting Senzangakhona to acknowledge Shaka as his first-born and heir was Dingiswayo's attempt at a compromise. He wouldn't help Shaka overthrow Senzangakhona, but let his favourite be assured the throne would be his one day soon. Then, of course, after Senzangakhona betrayed him on his deathbed, Dingiswayo had no choice but to help Shaka claim the crown by force.

And, after the throne was his, Shaka set about building up his army. Soon he was eyeing the empire of the man who'd previously been his mentor.

The Zulu kingdom was growing, but it would always remain stunted by the presence of the Mthetwas. And who would ever want to rule as a vassal!

Then Dingiswayo went to war against the Ndwandwes, ordering all his allies to join him. That was the chance Shaka had been waiting for. Even though he loathed Zwide, he sent emissaries to the Ndwandwe capital, to tell Zwide of Dingiswayo's plans . . .

★

'He betrayed Dingiswayo?'

'Hush!' Mnkabayi puts a finger to her lips. 'That is only what they say.'

'Who?' It's a stupid question that she decides she'll ascribe to shock.

'Those who would malign the King,' she says.

'And they say—'

'—claim—'

'. . . claim that Shaka betrayed Dingiswayo?'

'Yes, through his emissaries, he told Zwide where and when Dingiswayo could be found. Then he took his own time about joining up with the Mthetwa army.'

'He betrayed Dingiswayo. That's—'

'—preposterous!'

Her nephew's head snaps up. 'Oh, yes. Of course, preposterous.'

'Ludicrous.'

'That too.'

'Do you see why I am concerned?'

A vigorous nod.

'This herd of lies cannot be allowed to reach the barbarians!'

A frown. 'But this story we've heard . . .'

'Is just the version given to the praise singers,' she says. 'At least, that's what those who spread the calumny would have us believe. And you must keep your ears open. We must stamp out this story wherever we hear it!'

'Of course, that goes without saying.'

453

Looking around, it was hard to believe these savages were the servants of a mighty ruler. Their kraal was little better than the homesteads of the outcasts and criminals they insisted on protecting.

The settlement that Farewell had rather optimistically named Port Natal consisted of a three-metre-square wattle-and-daub house and some other ramshackle dwellings, surrounded by a fence of thorny branches to keep out hyenas (which the traders still insist on calling 'wolves') and other predators.

To the Induna's eyes, this Port Natal was a sun-blasted, inhospitable place, plagued by mosquitoes from the nearby marshes. Drums and planks, mainstays and ropes littered the site. Over here, someone in the process of stripping the bark off a tree trunk had wandered off, leaving his saws and chisels in the dust. Over there, flies swarmed around a pile of ivory.

Hai! Zulus couldn't live like this. And where were the cattle? In an enclosure when they should be grazing in the veld. See, too, how close the ivory was to the cooking area! Even the ground, the very ground they walked on, was wrong, for these foreigners did not know how to spread dung to prevent the central areas of a kraal from becoming dusty when the wind blew, and muddy when the rain fell.

Truly, this place resembled a temporary settlement suddenly abandoned. Did these barbarians have no discipline?

Yet the spies Shaka had posted, to keep watch over the encampment, reported how every daybreak the White Men gathered around the pole outside the hut to raise their flag. Then at sunset they were back to watch the flag being lowered. They'd even taken to having those who they protected form up in lines, while they performed this bizarre ritual.

Truly, these servants of Jorgi were a strange people!

454

But it's partly because of this development that the Induna has been sent to the *izilwane* kraal, as the second phase of the First Fruits draws to a close. It annoyed Shaka when these savages took it upon themselves to harbour those fleeing his wrath, but he stayed his hand. They were of little consequence, those thieves and other rubbish; however, he could not countenance them being drawn into a ritual that seemed to involve Zulus swearing allegiance to someone other than himself. Whether they liked it or not, these *izinwabo* were still his subjects. They did not belong to this other king across the waters.

The first sign of human life the Induna and Njikiza discerned was a man dozing on a ship's hammock strung in the shade of some trees. It took a few gentle prods of the Induna's *iklwa* before the man finally came awake . . .

Shrieking and rolling off his hammock.

'Aiee,' chuckled Njikiza, 'we have helped this one escape the net.'

'But is he worth it?' asked the Induna.

'Are you, Xhosa?' inquired Njikiza.

Jakot's answer was a sullen glare, as he picked himself up off the ground. He was wearing britches torn off at the knees, and sandals. Bending, he retrieved the straw hat that had shaded his face on the hammock, made a production of dusting it off, then carefully pushed it on to the back of his head.

'Something ails you?' asked the Induna. 'You are very quiet today.'

'It is bad manners to disturb a man during his nap,' muttered the interpreter. 'Especially in such a way!'

'Manners?' chuckled the Induna, turning to Njikiza. 'Did you hear that? This Xhosa dog would teach us about manners.'

'Speak,' Njikiza told Jakot, 'and we'll be as dung beetles collecting your words of wisdom.'

'In which case you have no need of my guidance, for a man who knows his station is truly a wise man.'

'Let my club teach you your station, Xhosa.'

'He is a wily one,' said the Induna, soothingly, 'with an answer for everything. But we have a task to perform.' Addressing Jakot: 'Where are your masters?'

'Aiee,' grinned Jakot, 'I have looked and looked, and have yet to find the man who is master of me.'

Njikiza growled, tightened his grip on his trusty club. The Induna held up a calming hand. 'Talking to you, Xhosa, is like climbing a very steep slope, and' – the Induna's hand came up again – 'before you say it is true that you tower over all, let me tell you such a tedious journey is rarely worthwhile.'

Indicating the wattle-and-daub structure with his spear, the Induna told Jakot to go and fetch one of those Long Noses who were foolish enough to let him cower in their midst.

The Xhosa obeyed and, a few minutes later, Henry Fynn staggered into the sunlight. In his mid-twenties with a beard that seemed an afterthought on his youthful features, like a disguise hastily donned, he wore a pair of light-brown corduroys rolled up around his ankles, and was pulling his braces over his shoulders. To the Induna he seemed emaciated, with only a child's chest, but the White Man appeared cheerful enough. He even grinned when Jakot told him why the Zulus were there.

'Tell him they flee Shaka for good reason, for they are criminals,' added the Induna.

Wondering if he was included in this generalisation, Jakot obeyed.

'Tell him they must be returned to us, so that justice can be done.'

Uhm, right, said Fynn. I think you should point out . . . er, remind him, Jakot, that Shaka has ceded the bay and, er, environs to His Majesty. And, as such, this is Crown territory and it is, uh, the King's laws . . . our King, that is . . . uhm, it's his laws we must obey. These unfortunates he speaks of have not – not yet, anyway – er, broken any of our laws.

'He says no.'

The Induna looked from Jakot to the Englishman, who was glaring at the interpreter.

Now, see here, old chap, said Fynn, when it became clear Jakot wasn't going to say anything more, I have to ask if you have conveyed what I have said in toto, er, and in a proper manner . . .

'He berates you,' chuckled the Induna, 'and so he should, for his words were many and yours were few. But tell him this, too: our King would discuss these matters with him in person. He and the other Long Noses

456

will be attending the First Fruits. Tell him it is a great honour. And tell him that messengers will arrive when it is time for them to come and sit at the King's feet!'

Night Muthi

This Imithi Emnyama is dangerous stuff. It's the stick thrust into the hornet's nest. If it protects, it's also meant to provoke; it's both shield and spear. Part of the way it works is to make the King aggressive, sharpening his mind with anger, so he can face his forebears, and move among those who have passed on. Because the ancestors can be cantankerous and capricious, the King needs to watch himself with them, needs to be as careful with them as he is in avoiding the evil forces that prey on those who move through the fragile bubble-skin that separates our here-and-now from the spirit world.

Aiee! They have scarcely begun, and see how morose the King has become!

He is the purple darkness that weighs down on the mountains when the lightning bird comes. He is the distant rumble that precedes the flash flood, when the Thukela, the Frightening Suddenness, lives up to its name.

He is Sitting Thunder, sitting naked on a tree stump. With his back straight and feet firmly planted flat on the ground, he's barely conscious of the inyangas working around him, smearing the odour over his body with trembling hands.

He is narrowed eyes beneath a lowering brow, but it's not the clamour of the spirit world that has him scowling, or the thought of possibly meeting old adversaries he's helped to make the Great Journey sooner than they might have expected . . .

Palms skating across his skin . . . sticky stench . . . trembling fingers raising his left arm . . . these are discomforts experienced by someone else.

He is angry because last night, for the first time in his wanderings, he saw her.

Hearing the rustle of anxious whispers – intense, insistent, inveigling – he'd turned around in the hut of his seclusion, and found himself in his private compound in the old Bulawayo.

Enraged because of his inability to find *them*, those whose gullets he would see, whose thoughts he would listen to and use as incantations to see further (across the waters), he had wheeled round, ready to spew his rage, and there she was.

Nandi standing with her hands clasped in front of her skirt, her eyes fixed on him.

His frustration forgotten, he had let his tears flow freely.

Here was the balm he needed to still the pounding in his skull, and the tempest raging in his ears. Not even Pampata, his beloved Pampata, had that power, for he would have heard the anxiety and fear behind her soothing words. And they would have become fingers biting into his arms from behind, trying to hold and control him, but only causing him to thrash about even more violently.

Nandi's gaze, by contrast, was a gentle but firm hand against his chest, which said *Easy!*

No judgement, no watching and waiting for a chance to pounce and chastise. It was patient and understanding: a mother's gaze. And, when he spoke, his words were a son's plea: 'What am I to do, Mother?'

A pause in the wiping and polishing, a discreet clearing of a throat to his right. If his Majesty wouldn't mind raising his arm just a little higher . . .

This muthi, it covers him like a second skin, slick and oily the way he imagines a snake's skin feels to the reptile itself, after it's shed its old covering.

'I did it,' he had told her.

And so he had: he had showed the tamboti seed to the people, and sent out the messengers who'd been standing by for several days.

He'd issued the decree.

When the seeds have been sown . . .

When you have had to search for the paths . . .

459

When you have seen your labours rewarded with the emergence of the crops at the time of the Umasingana moon . . .

When these things have come to pass, let the Umkhosi be held at KwaBulawayo, and only at KwaBulawayo.

For is he not the embodiment of the tribe? Is he not the Father of the Sky, the King of Kings, the unifying force? Who better to intercede with the ancestors?

'Are we not one nation now? That is what I told them, Mother. We are the fist, its fingers clenched together, power and strength. We are the fist that defends and strikes back. That is what I told them.'

Standing with his hands on his hips, that day, knowing his words would be relayed around the isibaya: 'But do not delude yourselves, my Children. We cannot lower our guard, enemies surround us. Whereas once they thought they could crush us, without blinking, now they covet our wealth and bide their time.'

Knowing his messengers were well on their way, he reaffirmed his decree: just as there is one Inkosi, one King, let there be one Umkhosi – one First Fruits!

'I issued the decree, Mother, knowing there would be dissent, grumbling, fear even, for there are always those who are terrified of change.'

And there *was* discord. From the usual quarters, of course. No surprise there. That was one of the good things about such potentially unpopular rulings – they gave your informants a chance to pick out the malcontents whose momentary sense of outrage overcame their discretion. And the army remained behind him, as always.

But now this: roaming the night, unable to reach them, unable to bring the next phase of his campaign to fruition, the White Men eluding him . . . always eluding him.

★

He had been with the Induna that day; they had travelled to Ethekwini incognito. Moving into place just before sunrise, he'd witnessed their

460

strange flag-raising ceremony. And when the Induna and Njikiza returned later, they had lingered to watch the flag being lowered at sunset. It was just as Mnkabayi had told him, but was she right in claiming this was a sign that Jorgi's men worshipped the sun? When he pointed out that Fynn had tried to explain to him their beliefs, and how it had seemed to him the izilwane worshipped an entity akin to the Great Spirit, she'd diplomatically suggested perhaps they were ruled by more than one deity. Mnkabayi was, of course, basing her assumptions on reports made to her by Ndlela, so Shaka had resolved to go and see for himself. And after doing so – and seeing the peremptory nature of their ceremonies – he wasn't sure that 'worshipped' was the right word. It was more a simple acknowledgement of the sun's coming, he decided. Greeting its arrival and then, later, saluting its passing. But did such a distinction really counter Mnkabayi's claims? And why should this business about the sun concern her so much?

And he remembers something else. Vaguely. Remembers talking with Mgobozi, remembers the old friend he now misses so much showing him something . . .

Something important. Something to do with Mnkabayi. But what?

He knows that she is annoyed with him – what more is there to know?

*

The stench of this medicine fills his head, invades his nostrils, coats his eyes. Gently, delicately, the inyangas indicate that he can lower his right arm, and raise his left . . .

He obeys with a soft growl.

Unlike his other encounters, the longed-for one with Nandi remains vivid. But not for the reasons he'd like.

He had explained to her how their plans regarding the First Fruits had at last been put into action, and how he missed her.

He had told her how he'd revived that other aspect of the ceremony, the one hitherto overlooked, with generations of chiefs and kings merely going through the motions.

461

He had tried to explain what he wanted to do, how he was trying to marshal the power of the Imithi Emnyama . . . and how he was failing.

And then the son's plea: 'What am I to do, Mother?'

But she'd stood there and said nothing.

Then he was back in the hut of his seclusion, his tears smearing the Night Muthi. And it was a long while before he called Pampata, and before the maidens guarding the hut could begin their singing.

★

She was there, then she was gone, before he even had time to scrutinise her face.

Nandi.

This Imithi Emnyama is dangerous stuff. It has a life of its own.

And he is a lion looking for the slightest provocation, a leopard poised to spring, an elephant ready to gore all around him, as those trembling hands continue to apply the Night Muthi.

★

It's been three days since the boy was murdered and the Induna's men have still been able to find no trace of the sangoma. He must speak to the limping jackal's students again, impress upon them how important it is they find Kholisa. Perhaps one of them knows more than he's letting on.

Hai, perhaps a better plan would be to take them all into custody, so the Induna can tell them exactly why he's looking for their master; let them understand the consequences of lying and ensure that secrecy is maintained, because, involved or not, none will be released until Kholisa is found . . .

★

She had said nothing.

He had asked her, begged her to tell him what to do.

But she had said nothing.

Then she was gone.

Had she been trying to show him her disapproval?

Hai, but she was never one to resort to silence, when her sharp tongue was so skilled at slicing away a man's pomposity and smugness.

How desperately he needs her counsel, her guidance, even her angry chastisements . . . But what he longs for most is her comfort: the arms that enfolded him and allowed him to be a little boy again, for a short while.

The inyangas are finished. As ever they have done their job superbly – which is to say he now smells like a cesspit. But he remains seated and, turning away from Nandi's silence – the confusion, the pain, the bleeding in his throat – he directs his thoughts towards Mnkabayi.

Once his mourning had spent itself, she'd come down to him from the great northern war kraal she oversaw, and has been a regular visitor ever since. Occasionally her attempts to take Nandi's place have been too obvious, and have annoyed him, but she had been one of the few to have shown his mother kindness all those years ago. Never mind Nandi's high regard for her or the way in which she helped smooth his path to power, that alone – her kindness to his mother – would have seen her status greatly enhanced once he took the throne.

Now he wonders if he shouldn't let her take Nandi's place . . . Insofar as anyone can take his beloved mother's place . . .

But Mgobozi! What had that garrulous old goat told him?

Aiee, these are trying times, he thinks, hiding his wry grin from the trembling inyangas who aren't sure he knows they have finished doctoring him.

And again he's got to ask himself why he has to fear Mnkabayi. His power is her power, and her power has grown immeasurably, thanks to him. He can no longer trust Mbopa – and not because Mbopa will betray him, but because he has betrayed Mbopa. Why not speak to Mnkabayi, for her counsel would be valuable if only because she seems to have spies everywhere. What would she make of this latest killing?

They laugh and they boast, these soldiers of Shaka, but they know noth-ing of true courage.

Yes, courage . . . and I spit in your face if you think otherwise.

Because you don't know, can't know, what I have endured.

Can't know what it took to get here.

And, before that, the shame.

The impotent rage!

But even these have been weak muthis, unable to sustain me on my journey.

And then it was up to me.

To endure!

To take another step. And then another.

To endure when I was held back, beaten and punished.

And those few who tried to help him, they were only there to be used, their generosity enabling him to get closer to his destiny. And he spits on them!

His one regret is that he's not certain he'll survive to speak of their weakness.

Cha! He won't have to. Not if he succeeds (and dies). There won't be any need to damn them, for they will cease to be.

When the time comes, he will rise up and make a mockery of all their boasts and conquests.

They will never know how hard it was for him to get here. They will never comprehend the depth of his suffering, the long road he had to travel. He'll make it look so easy. And that will terrify them even more.

I cannot fail.

It's simply a matter of waiting. You'd have thought all their chores would have worn them out, but he himself seems to be the only one on the brink of sleep. And he drifts off, listening to the others talking about the wonders of the day, and the wonders still to come. And he dreams he is drinking the blood of a calf, with warm, sticky blood covering his chest. And even in his dream – glancing up as he swallows a mouthful of that warm, sticky blood – he recognises this as a good omen.

The Lizard

The first thing the Induna does is to ensure some order is restored at the campsite. He is glad to have Ndlela with him. Although he outranks the Induna, Ndlela insists the Induna take charge, and he is happy to oversee the removal of Zusi's body. The girl's mother remains inconsolable, while Melekeleli, Dwanile and the other wives tend to her.

Aiee, this clan seems truly cursed!

'He came back,' says Jembuluka, when he finally raises his head. 'He came back,' he repeats, wiping away the tears. 'Kholisa came back!'

Then, with a hiss, pulling him to his feet, 'You spoke about the need for secrecy, Nduna, and no doubt you and your men did your best. But somehow he found out!'

Somehow Kholisa had heard that he'd been seen and identified by Vuyile. Now he wants vengeance.

'Let us help you,' says Jembuluka. All the clan's able-bodied men are willing to track down the sangoma. 'He is clearly still here and, with that leg of his, he can't get far. Let us help you, Nduna.'

The Induna shakes his head. Jembuluka and the other men will be better used watching over the clan.

Jembuluka seems to sag. He hadn't thought of that. 'Are we still in danger, do you think?' Had Kholisa come looking for Vuyile early this morning, and fallen on Zusi because she was the easier prey? Is he only after Vuyile? Or does he mean to kill all of them?

'It is better that you and the others organise shifts, and guard yourselves,' says the Induna.

Zusi had been returning to the campsite, after collecting fire-wood early this morning, when she was attacked, and her body was

466

still warm when it was discovered. Once more footprints litter the area but, moving further afield, Ndlela has found a trail that seems to indicate the passing of a man with a limp.

'It could be him,' he tells the Induna.

The latter nods. It could be. Then again, it could also be that the tracks Ndlela has found have been there since before the body was discovered, and have merely become smudged by the wind. Whatever the case, they soon peter out, with little indication of where the one who's left them was heading.

Kholisa . . . ?

'Does he really think he's the Lion?' asks the Induna, as they return to the temporary huts where the clan is quartered.

Certainly, in the history of the nation, this First Fruits is likely to be as propitious as Gqokli Hill. And there it had been the Lion's conscience which had forced him to act so hastily, and destroy the Inkatha on the eve of the campaign; here there is a little more planning in evidence.

'I mention this,' says the Induna, 'because Kholisa did not strike me as one capable of being so cunning.'

'Yes, you and Mgobozi shamed him in the matter of the Vanishing Man,' says Ndlela.

'And he certainly seemed chastened, when he and I met again.'

'Hai, perhaps that meant he had learnt his lesson, but in a way neither you nor Mgobozi could have foreseen.'

'Yes, perhaps we merely taught him to become more cunning.'

And perhaps to seek out accomplices who were as wily as he . . . ones who could help him imitate the Vanishing Man. Although, unlike that worthy, he has managed to stay *vanished*. Which might possibly be seen as proof of his accomplices' prowess; as is the fact they have managed to smuggle him into KwaBulawayo and keep him hidden. The first part was, perhaps, not so difficult, bearing in mind the recent great influx of people – and the fact that no one realised Kholisa was missing – but it's the second that speaks of skill, and power.

The Induna orders his men to retrace their steps, but the fact that they have still found nothing is ominous. Someone always sees . . . think of Vuyile, stumbling on Kholisa's depraved slaughter of the youth. For all his plans and precautions, the sangoma must have been spotted by one who could recognise him. Someone always sees . . . and speaks! And what would have seemed commonplace to a passer-by might become more meaningful in the light of subsequent events. Especially with the Induna's men on hand, to prod their memory. But, so far, silence!

'This is why I speak of power,' the Induna tells the boy later, after Ndlela has left. 'If he is being helped, which seems likely, his benefactors are very powerful indeed – if they can ensure such silence.'

'Then the King is right,' says the boy. These events are part of a larger conspiracy to thwart the First Fruits.

'It seems so,' murmurs the Induna.

But, in putting together this particular pot, there is an odd piece, one which may or may not fit. It's to do with the nature of the murders. The teenager's nose and upper lip had been bitten off, and Ndlela has been able to confirm what the Induna and Mbopa suspected. Whoever had done this had been seeking to 'imbibe' the youth's stamina and vitality.

Zusi has had her breasts and all the surrounding skin removed, and Ndlela has pointed out that this means the two murders are related. Related, that is, in a way that goes beyond any mere revenge.

'I have never witnessed them done before, but I do know these are ancient rituals,' said Ndlela. 'First, he sought the stamina of youth. Now, by killing this poor girl and mutilating her in such a fashion, it's a sign that he seeks a following.'

'I do not understand,' said the Induna.

'He took her breasts, Nduna, because he would suckle a new army, and have them obey him as willingly as young children obey their parents.'

The Induna looks around, to make sure he and the boy are alone. 'For let us say,' he says, keeping his voice low, 'there are those who believe in such things . . .' That means *they* are willing to let Kholisa acquire supernatural powers.

468

Hai, do they know what they're doing? Do they *know* Kholisa? It was obvious to the Induna, from their first encounter, that he would never be the threat that Nobela or the Lion were. He lacked their skills because he lacked their stability. Misguided as they were, the Lion and Nobela thought they served the tribe; Kholisa served only himself. To allow him to arm himself with even more potent powers . . . aiee, who would be so foolish?

★

Ndlela has returned to his hut and he sits there now, letting the sounds of KwaBulawayo swirl around him, the thatch providing a barrier that both allows his thoughts to expand and yet contains them.

He is afraid, very afraid.

He has, of course, also had dealings with Kholisa – and, like the Induna, is under no illusions as to the sangoma's abilities. The man might have had his uses as a spy, but other than that . . .

His status, as a senior induna in the service of a woman regarded as one of Shaka's queens, enabled him to quiz Mbopa about the first murder without raising any suspicions. In fact, the prime minister was only too glad to discuss the matter with one so knowledgeable when it came to Zulu lore. Mbopa had an inkling there was even more to this than he suspected, but Ndlela wasn't ready to enlighten him just yet. He was after information, and what he'd heard . . .

In his hut, he lowers his head.

What he'd heard sent him to Vuyile, who was much recovered after speaking to the Induna. Fortunately, he believed the promise of secrecy the latter had extracted from him didn't extend to one of Ndlela's status, so he had told the older man what he had seen.

And this is what Ndlela had wanted to know: not that Vuyile had seen Kholisa, never mind that; but what *exactly* he had seen!

Look beyond the face, he'd urged the boy, and describe to me how he moved, and what he looked like.

And even thinking about it now is enough to make his mouth go dry, his throat contract, his stomach churn.

He knows Vuyile had told the Induna much the same thing, but does the Induna realise the significance of what he's heard? Cha, how can he! These are practices abolished long before he was born.

Vuyile's words: a body on its back in the orange light of a bonfire and, doing something to the body's face, a creature the like of which he had never seen.

Ndlela: 'Why a creature? Why was that your first thought?'

Because of what it was doing to the body's face, that hideous gnawing and biting, tugging and pulling. Because of the way it was positioned, on its hands and knees, its torso twisted . . .

Ndlela: 'You have said it resembled a lizard?'

A nod.

Why a lizard? Was it just because of the way it was crouching?

Not crouching, countered Vuyile. It was lying half on, half off the body, and for a brief instant he'd assumed it had four legs . . . 'It lay, and moved, like a lizard.'

'And its skin?'

'Yes,' said Vuyile, 'that was something else! Its skin seemed to hang loose, the way it does on big lizards.' How did Ndlela know that?

The induna calmed Vuyile down, saying he was simply seeking a clearer understanding as to what the boy had seen.

'It was Kholisa!' said Vuyile.

'That is so,' said Ndlela. And what Vuyile had seen before . . . well, given the horrific nature of the killing, it was easy to see how shock might have initially misled him into thinking he was witnessing the feeding frenzy of some terrible monster.

Vuyile nodded thoughtfully, for Ndlela's words made sense. Then he grinned. 'Because who could have believed a human being capable of such a thing?'

Ndlela had been hoping he was wrong, until Zusi was killed and mutilated.

Another possibility, and one he hadn't mentioned to the Induna . . . Kholisa is doing these things, collecting these things, on behalf of another.

★

'But, Master, what you say about this, this gathering of body parts –
it assumes there are those who believe such things possible!'

'Are we witnessing a return to the old ways, perhaps?'

'But because they believe such things possible . . .'

'. . . doesn't mean they *are* possible. You are right.'

'So perhaps we must listen more carefully, Master. Listen for that
other tale!'

The Induna smiles to have his lessons repeated back to him.

'You are right.'

'No, *you* are right, Master, for this is your way!'

'Such flattery! Beware or else even I shall take to calling you
Mthunzi.' The udibi has already confided to the Induna that it's a
nickname he abhors – and no offence to his master. He is not
offended, the Induna has told him, for he can see how being called
'Shadow of the Shadow' might rankle. But the boy better get used
to it, for he suspects that the name will be with him for a long time
to come.

'Aiee, then I apologise most profusely,' begins the boy. Then he
points past the Induna. 'Master . . . ?'

The Induna turns. It is his wife Kani, accompanied by Njikiza.

She has travelled to KwaBulawayo for the First Fruits, and will
be one of those who attend Pampata as a lady in waiting. Right
now, though, decides the Induna, after listening to her, she might
as well just be the herald of the other tale his udibi has suggested
they investigate.

Aware that Kani is close to Shaka's beloved, as well as being the
Induna's wife, a maiden called Thaki has sought her out. She was
friends with Zusi, and has something to tell the Induna.

471

Cha! But who would trust such a jackal with such an important under-taking!

Ndlela wouldn't. If the limping sangoma was successful, there was a chance he'd use the ingredients he was gathering for his own ends. And, if he was caught, there was no doubt he'd betray those he served.

Yet another possibility: that those he serves have turned Kholisa into an impundulu.

And Vuyile was mistaken about one thing. In his horror, he thought the sangoma was eating the boy's face — but he wasn't. He'd merely been remov-ing the portions needed for the ritual.

And now he has killed a young girl, and torn off her breasts . . .

Those he serves have turned Kholisa into an impundulu, so that he might collect these items for them.

And Ndlela is afraid, because he thinks one of those he serves might be Mnkabayi.

And he's not sure if she's aware of the enormity of what she's done, and of how the forces she has set in motion won't stop merely with the fall of Shaka . . .

472

The Maiden's Story

After speaking to her family, and leaving the udibi to make sure no one tries to listen in on their conversation, Kani and the Induna lead the maiden away to the shade of a nearby tree.

Her family had met up on the road with the party comprising Ntokozo's widows and children, and various other members of the homestead, says Thaki. The youngsters were happy to be coming to Bulawayo for the First Fruits, she adds, and all were looking forward to the celebrations. There was, she admits shyly, a certain amount of flirting.

The Induna nods, hiding his impatience, letting Thaki come to the point in her own time. This was to be expected, for any get-together involving other families and clans was a chance to meet someone new, or to move a courtship forward.

Zusi joined in as best she could. 'But,' says Thaki, 'she made it clear there was one who had won her heart already.' She looks up at the Induna then at Kani. They clearly know of whom she speaks. 'That one . . . Vala.' The Induna notes her hesitation, for the natural inclination is there to refer to Vala as a savage or isilwane, but Thaki's loyalty to her dead friend wins out in the end.

'Vala,' she repeats again. When Mhlangana's men had returned home, they spoke of what had occurred when Vala was brought before Shaka – and word of her beloved's lucky 'escape' had duly reached Zusi's ears. Knowing he was at Bulawayo, she couldn't wait to see him again. She even had some crazy idea of trying to speak to Shaka himself, says Thaki. 'She said that, after all, she had no father, and that Shaka was the Father of all.'

Kani squeezes the Induna's hand: another warning for him to keep his impatience tethered. 'So she still loved Vala,' she says.

Thaki nods. 'But there was one who pestered her.'

'On the road?' asks the Induna.

'Yes, Nduna.'

The Induna can imagine how it must have been . . . A herd of strutting, flirtatious boys, and in their midst one who was different. Betraying himself by a certain intensity; a way of looking at her: the stare that followed her, and cut through the chatter of the others, seeking to pin her down. That all too apparent happiness when he got her alone, out of all proportion to the moment itself, which might have involved sharing some mundane chore. The all too obvious sulkiness whenever they were in a group: looking away when her eyes met his, quietly willing her to come over and ask him what was wrong. Something she wouldn't and couldn't do precisely because she knew it would be misinterpreted, would be considered leading him on . . .

Zusi might have been still too young to know what to do about it, but she would have instinctively realised how he studied her in a different way when she wasn't looking, his eyes narrowed, and hardening when she turned her attention to others.

'She was pestered, Nduna, and it frightened her.'

'Why didn't she speak to her mother?' asks Kani.

'Because she was also ashamed, so I was the only one she told.' And that was only when things had become really bad; when the boy had made his intentions all too clear.

Kani nods, indicating the Induna can ask the obvious question.

However, aware that Thaki is afraid, and close to tears, he chooses a circuitous route.

'You say Zusi was ashamed, but why should she be ashamed?' he asks quietly. He had known her previously as a strong-willed girl unafraid to acknowledge her love for Vala, and prepared to travel through the night to seek his help. (And Kholisa, he reflects grimly. She also possessed the courage to sneak off to Mhlangana's war kraal, to ask the sangoma for a potion that might help her father accept her relationship with a boy the clan considered as worse than a slave.)

But why should she suddenly feel shame?

'Thaki, answer my husband,' whispers Kani. 'He will be able to protect you and your family. And you will also help him see the killer of your friend delivered to the Bull Elephant's impalers. Why was she ashamed?'

'Because this man was one of her clan.'

Now it's the Induna who has to squeeze his wife's hand, so that her angry 'What?' remains trapped behind her shocked expression.

'Did she tell you his name?' he asks.

Her head bowed as though the shame is hers as well, Thaki nods.

'Who was it?' says the Induna. 'Was it Jembuluka?' Snatching at this man's name because the alternative is far worse.

However, Thaki's head comes up and she even manages a scornful laugh. 'Smelly Jembu? Hai, we barely saw him on the road.' Sadness clouding her eyes once more, she says, 'No, it wasn't him.'

'Who, then?' asks the Induna. 'Who was it?'

★

'Mbopa, have you seen Ndlela?'

Mbopa bows before Mnkabayi. 'My apologies, Ma, but I have not!'

'Cha! It is as if he seeks to avoid me!'

'Oh, I think not, Ma, if I may be so bold. Like you, he is highly esteemed by the King, and with the First Fruits upon us he has many additional responsibilities.'

'Very well, then, I shall have to make do with you.'

Another bow. 'I am yours to command, Ma.'

'Do not worry, I will not detain you for long. I would only know if what I hear is true.'

'What have you heard, Ma?'

'That a young girl has been murdered within the precincts of Bulawayo.'

'It was in the temporary settlements erected for the First Fruits.'

'But that is terrible!'

'It is being attended to, Ma.'

'You seem dismissive.'

'These things happen.'

'But during the First Fruits?'

'As I said, Ma, the matter is being attended to.'

'You haven't answered my question.'

'My apologies. I wasn't aware you'd asked one.'

'Very well, if you would behave like a child, let me be more precise. Doesn't the very fact that this crime should have taken place during the First Fruits strike you as significant?'

'Why should it, Ma? It has surely nothing to do with the First Fruits.' There have been other deaths since the gathering began: three old-timers, a woman in labour (along with her baby); two children drowned, the one while trying to help the other. Such things are to be expected, and the inyangas know to be ever vigilant for any signs of disease. 'These things—'

'They happen, yes, so you say. But I tell you this: there was a time when everything that took place during the First Fruits was seen as having something directly to do with the First Fruits.'

'Perhaps that time has passed, Ma.'

'I hope not, Mbopa, for I have also heard that the family of an Uselwa Man is involved. And yet you say this has nothing to do with the First Fruits?'

'That's not quite what I said, Ma. I do not believe this has anything to do with the First Fruits, but the induna investigating the matter has nevertheless been instructed to consider that possibility.'

'As unlikely as it might seem.'

Mbopa inclines his head. 'Indeed, Ma.'

'Understand that I raise this matter because these First Fruits are special.'

'As is every First Fruits, Ma, but your meaning is clear. The presence of the White Men bothers you.'

'As I think it bothers you, too, Mbopa. Have you not often said we must be wary of these creatures?'

'Other barbarians have attended the First Fruits, over the years.'

'Cha! Speak you of the Mthetwas and Khumalos, and others who have allied themselves with our King?'

Mbopa nods.

'Oh, come now! I know some were made uneasy by the presence of those creatures, but I was never one. You know, as well as I do, they have attended the First Fruits as Zulus. These Long Noses from the sea, though, they are another sort altogether.'

'Perhaps.'

'Perhaps, he says!'

'Well, Ma, I must be honest. I cannot see how these deaths have anything to do with the White Men. You are surely not saying they're somehow responsible.'

'I may be old, but I'm not senile. I'm not saying anything of the sort. But perhaps it is the ancestors who are speaking, and seeking to warn us.'

'Then they have chosen a particularly brutal way.'

'Your sudden fastidiousness isn't becoming, Mbopa. But if they have chosen a brutal way, perhaps it's because we haven't listened to their other warnings.'

'Other warnings? Yes, well, I can see how one might be inclined to misconstrue Shaka's many victories on the battlefield as evidence that the ancestors favour him.'

'Make light of these things, if you will, Mbopa, but I think I detect unease behind your glib dismissals. And you have once again avoided my question. Have you yourself not often said we must be wary of these savages?'

'I still believe that, Ma.'

'I hope you do, Mbopa. I hope you do.'

★

'No, Nduna! Please, no!' His head bumps against the thatch as he tries to move his throat away from the tip of the Induna's spear. 'Nduna, please! It wasn't me!' Wide owl-eyes now trying to catch a glimpse of the iklwa, now meeting the Induna's gaze to plead for mercy.

'Please!'

The Induna and Gudlo stand in the afternoon sunlight, the latter pressed up against a hut, while Njikiza, the udibi and Jembuluka look on.

'Did you pester her? Was her *no* merely an invitation to try harder?'

'No! I beg you, Nduna . . . No!'

The Induna lowers his spear and brings his face close to Gudlo's. 'Do not lie. Do not try my patience. Cease your cringing and just tell me!'

'What madness is this, Nduna? They were brother and sister!'

'Tell him,' says the Induna, as Njikiza pulls Jembuluka away.

'Well, why not, Nduna?' says Gudlo, meeting Jembuluka's hiss of outrage with a grin. 'It's not like we shared the same mother.'

'You fool!' shouts Jembuluka. 'She was still your sister.'

'That we shared the same father – that was neither here nor there.'

'What, would you bring even more shame on this family?'

The Induna tells Jembuluka to be quiet. Then he punches Gudlo in the face.

At a nod from the Induna, the udibi helps Gudlo to his feet.

'Let me see that grin again, and you will feel real pain,' warns the Induna.

Gudlo wipes his nose. Examines the blood on his knuckles, looks at the Induna. 'I do not understand this outrage,' he says. And the hint of a sneer is evident, but the Induna chooses to restrain himself.

'Why has nobody said anything about the shame *she* brought upon us when first she started fondling that savage! Hai, the day *that* started, she ceased to be my kin. And besides, I have always regarded her as a tasty morsel.'

After the udibi has helped him up a second time, and he has spat out a globule of blood, Gudlo remains defiant. 'Beat me as much as you like, Nduna, but that doesn't change the fact I was doing her a favour. No one would touch her once they found out about her fondness for animals.'

This time the Induna's fist has Gudlo bending over, has him clutching his stomach and gasping for breath.

'Leave some for me,' says Jembuluka, and he's sure that Zusi's assorted uncles and brothers would like their turn, too.

Still panting, Gudlo straightens up, favours Jembuluka with a glare that becomes another one of his sardonic grins.

But the grin has gone when he addresses the Induna once more. 'As I say, you can beat me as much as you like.'

'You issue an invitation many are willing to accept.'

Another glance at Jembuluka. 'This is so,' coughs Gudlo, leaning aside to spit out a tooth. 'But,' he continues, 'you surely do not believe that I killed my beloved little sister? Hai, we were still only at the courting stage. I had not yet . . .' He holds up a hand. 'Before you hit me again, Nduna, let me say I mention this merely to point out I had no reason to kill Zusi.'

'Unless, of course, she threatened to tell your uncle,' says the Induna, indicating Jembuluka.

'Him? Why should I be afraid of him? Or his sister, for that matter. Neither had I anything to fear from Zusi. Who would believe her, after the shame she had already brought on this family? So I say again, Nduna, beat me, but you will not be breaking Zusi's murderer beneath your fists. No, if it's her murderer you're after, I suggest you speak to her lover instead.' He spits the word out.

'Her lover?'

'I mean Vala. And I say this knowing full well how you suspect Kholisa. Speak instead to that savage, who I believe has been taken into one of the King's regiments.'

Speak to Vala, he repeats, and ask him about the iwisa.

★

The stories told by Gudlo's friends tally. An all-night beer-drinking session had continued into the morning. Gudlo and his friends had not been the only ones present – many others had come and gone. At the time Zusi was last seen, their drinking was still going on.

'What say you?' asks the Induna, as the last of Gudlo's friends is allowed to stagger away.

'I say he contemplated a terrible thing, and bullied this poor girl, but I do not think he killed her,' says the udibi.

But what does the Induna make of Gudlo's mention of Vala? And the iwisa?

'Yes,' says the Induna, 'that was interesting.' Especially since Gudlo was the one who'd found the murder weapon among Vala's meagre possessions . . .

'But we won't know until we can speak to Vala himself,' he adds.

Unfortunately, it's too late now, and it might be a few days before they can get to see him. The First Fruits is reaching its climax, and tomorrow is the Calling of the King.

Ornamental fur ropes for wrapping around the upper body and headdresses such as the isidlodlo, a bunch of feathers worn at the back of the head, and the isiyaya, a circlet of standing feathers, are stored in a large earthenware pot. Hanging against the hut wall is a hollowed-out tree trunk, called an isambo: in this cylinder are kept the more precious head-plumes made from ostrich and black finch feathers. Amashoba and other 'furry tails' are kept rolled up in a large rush mat, called an umbuma. The ends of it are tied close, to prevent the ingress of smoke, and then the rolled-up mat is hung horizontally from the wall. Carried on an udibi's head, the mat also serves as a suitcase to protect the warrior's attire if the wedding or feast he must attend is somewhere far off.

He sits, oblivious amid this finery, having sent his udibi away. And not just because he wants to be alone. Brave soldier, and veteran warrior that he is, he doesn't recognise this feeling – fear? terror? shock? horror? dread? – but it runs through his blood like a fever, and he feels that others need to be kept away, in case his very thoughts might be contagious.

She didn't come to him, simply because she knew he would have done everything in his power to thwart her plans – but if only she had. If only she had!

I would have told you why! No matter how long it took, I would have told you why you could not do this.

Ndlela shuts his eyes as the enormity of this business hits him afresh – as if he hasn't already been sitting here agonising for so long; as if he hasn't been gnawing at it, twisting it, turning it around in his restless mouth.

Hai, but recriminations won't help. Neither will asking why, or how.

There's even a chance that Mnkabayi might not be involved! (Yes, don't forget that! For maybe he is doing her a great injustice.)

Either way, though, she might be in danger.

481

What few realise about the impundulu – even some of those claiming they can create such a creature – is that one has to get both the muthi mixture and the dosage just right. Apply too much during the reawakening part of the ritual, and the subject will die, either before or shortly after being revived. Apply too little and the effects will soon wear off. That may take a while but it can happen. It's not unknown for someone believed dead and buried to come wandering out of the bush a few years later. This is one of the ways an induna like Ndlela has been able to find out more about how the process works.

To date he's questioned two men and one woman. In the case of the latter he had been with his father and Jama had then been king. The two men had both 'surfaced' during the early years of Senzangakhona's reign. Ndlela has always suspected the same wizard was responsible for 'doctoring' all three. None had been quite the same after their ordeal, and they told vague tales of being put to work in the fields; with the woman also claiming she'd been sent out to steal babies. None could remember exactly where they'd been kept, and all three had died shortly after returning home.

Ndlela had then ordered the original graves of the two men to be opened, and so was able to confirm that one aspect of the ritual did indeed involve the substitution of the victim's body by a 'dummy'. (And both families had offered similar descriptions of the mysterious 'sangoma' who just happened to be on hand when the 'death' occurred, ready to mutter about a curse and argue the need for a burial service that involved just him and his apprentice. The relatives could visit the grave only after the appropriate cleansing ceremony had been conducted.)

At the time, he had spoken to Nobela. Trusting him, and acknowledging that it was good for an outsider to know something about the process, if only to recognise the signs and thus know when to summon her, she had said he could ask his questions. However, she would tell him only what she felt it was safe for him to know. (He'd been much younger then, and had replied: in that case, why didn't she simply tell him what she wanted him to know. Nobela had chuckled and said it was the nature of his questions that would allow her to see how much it was safe to tell him.)

Even if the right amount of muthi was applied, the extent of the reawakening could not be controlled, she explained. At first the impundulu would seem as groggy as a drunkard, as clumsy as a child. Then it would become more conscious, more aware, for what use was an impundulu you couldn't train or teach?

She'd poured some water into the sand. 'But even many of those I have sniffed out, who have performed this hideous ritual, don't realise how far this reawakening spreads' – she indicated the puddle at their feet – 'or how deep it seeps.'

And so sometimes the creature will regain some of its old memories, and at other times the impundulu may gradually become aware of its current state. Without knowing why, it will realise that it's trapped in an unnatural limbo. Driven by pain and rage, it'll then turn on those who control it. 'Hai, and perhaps this opens the gate and, at last, allows the ancestors to come to its aid,' she had suggested. 'For somehow it knows not only to seek out the sorcerer who created it – and who himself may be long gone – but the ones who have controlled that sorcerer.'

So this is one way Mnkabayi might be in danger.

However, there is a pattern to these recent killings, a method to this madness, and even if Mnkabayi is not one of those who ordered the creation of an impundulu, she might very well become the zombie's next victim.

And again it's as if the floor tilts, and he has to fight not to let himself slide down into anger and recriminations.

What was she thinking? How could she not have realised what a terrible mistake this would be? Why didn't she tell him what she had in mind? If only, if only, if only . . . Again that assumption of guilt, those foolish pleas as efficacious as a mud spear.

Instead, you can do this, and you know this . . .

Like a crocodile, an impundulu has a lair, and it's been built for it by its masters. It will return there once it's carried out its instructions, bringing with it whatever items it was asked to fetch. Even in its altered state, it still needs to be fed, and if you want to prolong its life, you'd also do well to tend to any wounds it might have since acquired. It might be impervious to pain, but those wounds can still fester and rot. All of this can be *accomplished after feeding it, because the paste it receives will also put it to sleep. And so the creature is kept hidden, and out of the way until you next require its services.*

He knows this, which means he can search out the lair.

Calling The King

Quietly they gather in the darkness, a creeping, seeping, shifting mass that parts whenever they brush up against thatch, parting like jaws, then closing again, moving on. And it's as if the ground has come alive and the huts are being carried away. Dawn arrives quickly in these parts at this time of year, so that when the boy is momentarily distracted by the shoulders and elbows of another udibi inserting himself next to him and looks back, the sky has suddenly lightened and the shapes have become warriors. They have surrounded the king's abode, leaving only an apron of space around the doorway.

'Hey,' hisses the boy, as the other youth, who has pushed in next to him, now uses his bulk to try and ease him sideways.

The other udibi looks down at him, and the boy sees it's Mpande. The boy's reassignment to the Induna is only temporary; yet, despite being older than the one they call Mthunzi, Mpande continues to serve as Dingane's udibi, and there's no talk yet of him joining a regiment.

'Oh, it's you,' says the prince. 'Please accept my apologies, Little One. I did not recognise you without your Nduna.'

The boy is saved from having to respond by a lone voice calling out to the King. The words rise through the silence, and are repeated to become a song. Then, one by one, other voices, one from each of the regiments present, join the first voice. Plaited together, they strengthen the song as it moves, gradually, around the circle.

Then all the soldiers join in a refrain, calling to the King. 'Woza ke, woza lapha!'

Just as it seems the clamour can't get any louder – and see how it has scoured the last stains of night from the sky – the King himself is there, appearing, as if by magic, at the door of his hut.

After a dip in volume to acknowledge his appearance, the song grows louder again.

'Woza ke, woza lapha!'

Louder and more insistent, for the King isn't moving. He's simply standing there with his arms at his sides.

'Woza ke, woza lapha!'

He glistens in the morning light, for he has been daubed with Night Muthi.

'Woza ke, woza lapha!'

The King must come. The King must come now.

But still he doesn't move. Instead he seems to be listening for something within – or beyond – the song.

'Woza ke, woza lapha!'

Mpande bends down. Stale breath in the boy's ear. 'I can smell the stink from here.'

Aghast, Mthunzi tries to move away from the prince. But there's no space, and Mpande waits for the boy to look around and see if anyone else has heard those mocking words; and waits for him to realise that, even if they have heard them, none of the others will dare chastise a prince of the Bloodline. Then he says, 'And I'm not talking about the muthi!'

Gripping the boy's elbow he pulls him closer, turns him round so he can see the King's hut once more. 'Come now, you are going to miss the best part!'

An ululation. Shrill, vibrating, bending the air. The wing-beat of a million swallows. Silver crickets in the moonlight. And the boy sees how the ranks next to the fence of the isigodlo move aside to allow the King's concubines to come forward. And the ululation becomes a song.

'Woza ke, woza lapha!'

And the men join in. *The King must come. The King must come now.*

486

At last, with the women still several metres away, the King begins to move.

Increasing their pace, the concubines split into two lines as they cross the clearing in front of the King's hut. Just as they reach the warriors on the opposite side, the assembled ranks part. The women run down the corridor opened up, so as to line the route Shaka will take.

When the boy's eyes seek out the King again, he sees Shaka has been joined by four inyangas, who follow several paces behind him.

Now the udibis, and various other servants who have commandeered this spot, must run forward if they are to see what happens next. Not that they have to worry about finding a place, for the very youngest among them have already been ordered to keep an area free for them at the cattlefold.

★

The King stops at the royal entrance to the isibaya. The inyangas draw closer. One is holding a potsherd. Shaka turns to him. The inyanga bows his head, raises his hands. Gooey, glistening blackness thicker than molasses. The King slips three fingers into the mixture. It's a more concentrated form of the medicine that covers his body. In the same way the warriors had seemed to envelop the huts in the predawn darkness, so this muthi seems to come alive and reform around his fingers.

Muthi of the dead moon, isifile, and the ngolu mnyama namhla, the dark day thereafter. Body dirt and soul substances mixed with ancient incantations, now coating his fingers.

Shaka opens his lips . . .

Draws the muthi into his mouth . . .

And turns to face the rising sun, a blaze of orange smeared across the horizon, the purple sky changing to blue overhead . . .

. . . and spits.

The ncinda, then the chintsa – licking the Black Muthi off his fingertips, then spitting it at the rising sun.

'Wo vuma Ndaba, hayi zi zi!' It's a chant picked up by a lone

487

voice, then by another, and another: 'Wo vuma Ndaba, hayi zi zi! Wo vuma Ndaba, hayi zi zi! Wo vuma Ndaba, hayi zi zi!'

Then comes the refrain from the warriors gathered in the massive cattlefold. 'Wo vuma, Ndaba, wo ye wo ye. Wayi vuma indaba yemkhonto.'

Now Shaka can enter the isibaya.

Accepting a shield and iklwa from his inceku, or body servant, he strides on past the ibandla tree . . .

★

While he was spitting at the sun, the men who summoned him out went sweeping past the huts that line the inner palisade, so as to enter the cattlefold from the bottom. This is their space, for they are the Black Regiments, the newer amabutho, comprising younger men, and they are identified as such by regimental shields in which black markings predominate. The amabutho at the top, closest to the isigodlo, are the White Regiments, or the older formations, such as the Wombe and Fasimba impis, whose members wear white feathers in their headbands on official occasions. The men squatting, the regiments are formed up in semicircles, radiating like ripples away from Shaka himself. Despite the size of the cattlefold, there's not enough space to accommodate all of the regiments in this great muster, so the four newest amabutho have formed up outside the main gate.

As for the civilians, several hundred of those, who are lucky or influential enough, line the inner palisade and stand on whatever they can to peer over the wall or else they try to catch a glimpse of the proceedings through the gaps between the poles. The rest, the majority, stand or sit among the huts located between the inner and outer walls, looking as rapt as if they were sitting right at the King's feet.

Various dignitaries, meanwhile, have entered the isibaya through a side gate and lined up to Shaka's left, between the servants and udibis and the King himself, well within his line of sight, but far enough away for one to never be sure if he's looking in one's direction.

Shaka's brothers, his aunts and members of his inner circle are in this group . . . but not his mother, for she has gone, left him. Desperately his eyes seek out Pampata. There she is, flanked by Kani and by Mgobozi's wives. In good hands, then, and she is his beloved. But not his mother, not Nandi, who *should* be here . . . even if she never could understand his obsession with the White Men, with *these* White Men – and now his eyes seek out Farewell and Fynn and King. But she should be here, anyway, because this is no ordinary harvest festival. For these are the first fruits of a new way of living, a new way of doing. And see how tasty they are. How succulent! How sweet! And she helped him get here . . .

Hai, never mind these savages from King Jorgi, she'd said; he'd do better to find his Ubulawu. And he wasn't being facetious when he'd told her he regarded his army as his Ubulawu. But, in a way, she too was his Ubulawu, for it was her strength and wisdom that led him here. It was she who gave him the courage that helped him face all the sneers and taunts when he was a child. And how much greater were the indignities heaped on herself! Yet she never let herself be cowed, never let him forget that he was the royal heir. She should be at his side today!

A twinge of anger, even now, as he considers all the ingrates who remain behind while she has set with the sun. And his bellow, as he approaches his regiments, is real.

★

The shout goes out: 'Ima! Ima! Ima!' *Stand! Stand! Stand!*

And all the regiments rise to their feet.

And the praise singers, who've quietly entered the isibaya behind Shaka, also come to life. They move forward, each addressing a different section of the semicircle. 'They hate him!' they bellow. 'They hate him!'

It's a harangue answered by the refrain: 'Ima! Ima! Ima!'

'They hate him! They hate the King!'

Again, 'Ima! Ima! Ima!' There's something onomatopoeic about that word, an effect strengthened by the repetition, the low rumble that rises to a growled exhalation. *Stand! Stand! Stand!* And since they are on their feet already, it's as if they swell in size, seem to climb even higher. 'Ima! Ima! Ima!'

'They hate Phunga! They hate Mageba! They hate Ndaba!'

'Ima! Ima! Ima!' The army will stand. The army will fight. The King will reign.

Now the call changes.

The praise singers have fallen silent and begin strutting up and down, glorying in these reassurances. Suddenly, they wheel round, as one, to face the regiments and punch the sky.

'Bayede! Bayede!'

The royal salute is first picked up by the regiments, then the civilians. It echoes across Bulawayo and the surrounding plains, and reverberates even further afield, adding to the whispers and rumours as it shimmers across the veld. It'll reach the izilwane at the Cape, and some say it will even travel as far as the Great Lakes – rumours fading into myth but still carried along by a sense of unease . . .

And she knows, just knows, that she'll be able to spot him, even from this distance. And there he is!

Pampata sees him, too, and nudges her, and is about to point him out when she realises Kani's already seen him. The two women exchange a smile, before Kani turns to seek him out again.

She knows he has much on his mind, but she can see by the way he stands that he has pushed that all aside, to be here and only here. Like Shaka, he has little time for rites and rituals, but he will participate with all due solemnity today for the sake of his men.

And won't that alone give this ceremony more potency? She has heard him tell his udibi that one of the great secrets of power – of gaining power and using it and seeing it increase – is knowing the difference between acting and enacting. Which is the difference between words and stories, trying to be and being, tears and laughter – although these things only give you a glimpse of that difference. For, ultimately, it can't be explained or described, only experienced.

A smile: that's what she'd learnt that night . . .

The wedding festivities finally over, it was the first night they were truly alone as man and wife. And suddenly everything came rushing back. It was all to no avail, the way she'd sought to cleanse herself . . . The way she'd gone to find the Induna to signal her intention of marrying him (a custom permitted by Zulu society and known as ukubaleka) . . . She'd had Nandi's support and Pampata's help, and Shaka had eagerly gone along with the womenfolk, standing in for Kani's father, but it was all pointless. She was dirty, for Zwide infested her body, and she'd never be rid of him. Her husband would never be able to have all of her, no matter how much she wanted to give of herself. And because she'd gone to baleka the Induna, that was her

491

fault as well. She'd pulled him down along with her. What he must think of her! How he must despise her!

There was a time when her heart soared like a fish eagle whenever she saw him. Here was the man for her and he would be hers, for she knew her charms were not insignificant. And she knew how to work her wiles. And here was one worth the effort. Her knees turned to sand whenever she wondered how his lips would feel as they caressed her skin.

But that girl, that silly young girl, had died when her family was butchered. Only the need to take care of her remaining siblings continued to animate her, but it was a weak flame threatened by the slightest breath of despair. And it was blowing a gale, those first few months. She was trapped in a tempest, where the only thing she could do was keep her head down and keep on pressing forwards. Somehow the flame wasn't extinguished, however – and when she became Zwide's concubine it grew stronger. Here was a way to avenge herself. Patiently, she worked at becoming his favourite and then, when that goal was achieved, she planned how she might make contact with Nandi.

All of this required a certain deadening within her. She had to be like Shaka's soldiers marching back and forth across a parade ground strewn with thorns to toughen their feet. She had to toughen her heart, her very being. It was the only way to keep madness at bay. And there was always that option of seeing how many times she could stab Zwide before his body-guards rushed in and put her out of her misery. But that was too easy, for Zwide had to be made to suffer – and the only one who could ensure that was Shaka.

And when it had come to pass, and she'd seen the Induna again, she had thought perhaps all was not lost. Love never went away completely; like the paths at the time of the Uzibandela moon, it merely vanished from time to time – and it would find you again no matter how far you ran, or sank. She'd thought she was incapable of love, that same girl who'd admired the Zulu officer who regularly visited her father was gone forever but, seeing the Induna again, she realised she could be that young girl again – in his arms.

That first night, though, when they were truly alone . . . she realised she'd been wrong. She was still dirty, and therefore worthy only of her husband's scorn.

492

And the Induna himself had noticed how she was trying to distance herself from him. He could have taken her by force, but he didn't, for he knew that would only increase the hold Zwide had over her. She would struggle, despite herself, because of the memories that fingers biting into her flesh, or the knee pushed between her thighs, would evoke. And that would make the memory of Zwide stronger, like fanning coals into flames.

And that night, the night when they were alone as man and wife for the first time, he told her about a special kind of muthi . . .

White muthi, he called it. Those thoughts he could see moving across her face, and haunting her eyes . . . white muthi would see them vanquished.

He could spend forever seeking to reassure her about how little her past mattered to him, and how, when he did think about it, it was to dwell on her courage, but she wouldn't listen to him, he observed gently. Only the white muthi would help.

There were things no one could tell her, things she would only believe if she experienced them for herself. And the white muthi would let her do that. The white muthi would set her free.

Did she want to try it?

She knew of the white muthi the King used towards the end of the First Fruits, and realised this couldn't be that, but of course she wanted to try it. Well, she was with the right man, the Induna had said, trying to lighten the moment – for he knew the secret of this other kind of white muthi.

She would sleep tonight, and tomorrow she would go down to the river with her sister and she'd bathe, and let the warm sun caress her. And she was to have only a light meal, before retiring as soon as it got dark. In her hut, she was to wait for him. She would be naked, and there would be no torches or fires lit.

'And you will bring me the white muthi?' she asked.

'And I will bring you the white muthi,' said the Induna.

'And I will be healed?'

'You will be released from Zwide's grasp. He will torment you no more. You will be free.'

Kani did as he suggested, and that night, in the dark, he came to her. She heard him enter the hut, was surprised to find herself trembling . . .

trembling like the young virgin she had never really been, having had her maidenhead stolen by one of Zwide's generals before being passed on to Zwide himself (who had the officer executed after Kani became his favourite concubine).

And there was movement.

And then he was on top of her, and her legs were apart, and she was wet, so wet . . .

And it was only later, after she had got her breath back and was moving in rhythm with him, that she thought to ask about the white muthi. Not that she was unhappy about the direction things had taken, but . . . Well, where was it? Where was this white muthi he had told her about?

His reply was a whisper in her ear: 'I carry it inside me.'

Formidable Fellows

Fynn watches Shaka watching his warriors. The emissaries from King Jorgi have been placed between the Zulu dignitaries and the first of the regiments. They have a perfect view of the proceedings, and one might be tempted to feel honoured and flattered that one has been given the best seats in the house, as it were, but Fynn has noted that they're also directly in Shaka's line of sight. He can watch them carefully while appearing to be admiring his own regiments. It's a form of craftiness wholly in keeping with the King's character, decides Fynn. Because it's yet another reminder that one is at all times surrounded by thousands of spear-carrying warriors one is loath to use the term, but there's no getting round the fact that Shaka's hospitality has been very much like a double-edged sword. He gives freely, but with the knowledge that the day will come when he will expect to be repaid.

Fynn has already seen how Shaka has tested their loyalty in little ways, allowing them to return to Port Natal after a visit, then sending for them before they've even got halfway home. Farewell and the others see this as capriciousness, and a form of showing off, but to Fynn it's more like the flexing of muscles. His companions give the matter little thought, their eyes focused on the ivory and the gold (although the latter has so far been sorely lacking). They will bow and scrape, thinking they have the advantage over the Zulu king because they are merely indulging him, but it hasn't occurred to them that he might instead be indulging *them* – while he sizes them up and decides how much use they can be to him.

Take Farewell's casual references to King George. He's happy to let Shaka think they're as close to their king as Shaka's own advisors are to him. He expects Shaka to be impressed, but it hasn't occurred to him Shaka might see through the subterfuge. For one thing they appear a bedraggled, miserable bunch compared to the Zulu King and his inner circle. What sovereign would allow such a motley crew to represent him? More importantly, how will Shaka react if he decides he's been lied to? The thing is, Fynn suspects the Zulu king has realised that already – and remains unperturbed only because it's something he expected. Shaka is willing to be used (up to a point, of course), because he will be using them in turn. Quite how he will use them remains to be seen. There are their guns, of course . . . but Shaka and his men remain unimpressed by these signs of the White Man's superiority.

Fynn has warned Farewell about this. For, as he'd found during his stay in Delagoa, when he had hiked south until he found a Zulu village, the Zulus he met showed no fear and very little interest in such dunnage as he was able to carry with him, while his Brown Bess attracted no comment from them at all. And, if one thought about it, there was no reason why it should have. Farewell had only to listen to his own arguments for establishing a trading station to deal directly with Shaka. That undertaking was in large part feasible because the Zulus (and the other tribes in the region) had been trading with Europeans for generations. So of course they would know about guns!

And, if Shaka knows about guns, what else does he know about European ways? How many of his suspicions have they already helped confirm?

Shouts and chants fill the air. Fynn has heard and seen the like before: the King's troubadours singing his praises to the crowd. They seem to be all around today, though, as some move among the ranks to the rear of the cattlefold, while others entertain the troops assembled outside the main gate. They deliver familiar formulae, almost Homeric, which are greeted with groans and guffaws, laughter and cheers. An oral history of sorts, like a verbal Bayeux Tapestry. And as accurate as the old chronicles? Who knows . . .

Fynn's gaze returns to Shaka, still unmoving in the sunlight. Some of Fynn's companions are using spyglasses, but he prefers not to let

Shaka see he's watching him (after all, two can play at that game) . . .

The foul substance his servants have smeared over him seems to soften his outline in some way, although that could be due to the heat melting the concoction, and causing it to run. God knows what he's going through, yet, there he sits . . .

And what does he want from them?

★

Pampata would also like to know the answer to that question. There being no spoor, her beloved's intentions remain hidden from her. For Shaka refuses to be drawn on the subject of these izilwane from the sea. Does he assume she finds their presence as loathsome as some of the others do? If that's so, he'd be wrong. They have come. They are here. The tales they've already heard about the settlements far down the coast and across the waters are clearly true. It would be foolish, and also dangerous to pretend otherwise. She knows how, at various times, Shaka has been urged to move against these savages, so as to make them vanish. But, rightly, in her opinion, Shaka has ignored such imprecations. Let these ones become dust in the wind, and more will come. Besides, from what she's heard, trade has become easier now that the savages have built a kraal at Thekwini. Shaka might have secured the older trade routes, but isn't it even better to have their own 'Delagoa' within their own territory? For one thing, it would be that little bit harder to cheat a King who has let you settle on his land, in the shadow of his impis . . . But why has he invited them here to the First Fruits? Shaka clearly expects something more from these savages, but what?

★

Mnkabayi wishes she knew as well. Standing three places along the row from Pampata, she too finds her eyes resting on Farewell and Fynn and the other White Men. It's occurred to her that Shaka is using the First Fruits, and his infatuation with the barbarians, as a way of drawing out the conspirators within his own kraal. It's a

497

possibility not to be dismissed too lightly, but this infatuation of his . . . it goes deeper than that. And she has a horrible feeling that the very things that make her wary of the White Men – of *these* White Men – and the very things that make them so abhorrent to her, intrigue him, haunt him, fascinate him, arouse him. Has she left things too late, hesitated for too long, before trying to put a stop to Shaka's madness?

★

Ndlela stands to attention, shoulders squared, his spine stiffened. The old soldier's trick of flexing the muscles in one's feet, surreptitiously curling and splaying one's toes, and every so often slowly rising on one's heels, have long ago become second nature to him. It's also good to pay attention to what's going on – for that's another way of distracting the mind from aching joints, and the blaze of the sun – but today his mind is elsewhere. Despite the spectacle, this largest mustering of the Zulu army ever seen, his mind is elsewhere.

He will be consulting a sangoma soon, but he already has a very good idea of where the zombie's lair might lie.

The Induna and his men have been like swarming locusts in their attempts to find Kholisa – but the younger man still believes he is looking for a straightforward murderer, a human being. Mbopa might be concerned about the pattern that's emerged, the inescapable fact that those killings involve a ritual that has yet to reach its climax, but he sees merely subterfuge and an attempt to mislead, and therefore also believes they are dealing with a mere man. This is why the Induna has confined his search to Bulawayo and to the amadladla, or temporary huts, that now surround Shaka's capital.

By his lights that makes sense, for a man would need a bolt hole close to the scene of his crimes. That accommodation wouldn't be practical for an impundulu and its masters, though, as the creature's lair would have to be secluded. And it's not merely a matter of prying eyes, since there would be the smell to consider too; and the work required to get the creature pacified after each assignment, and then revived it for its next 'outing'.

At the same time, the hiding place can't be too far away. No doubt the Induna will expand his search sooner or later, but Bulawayo remains overcrowded, teeming with visitors. With all the coming and going, there always seems some place his investigating locusts have yet to alight.

Doubtless those who chose the impundulu's roost – and here Ndlela allows himself a quiet smile behind lips stretched as taut as an iklwa haft – thought they were being cunning . . . And just look around, look beyond the huts, see the hills and veld. Where would one begin one's search, especially if one had managed to work out that time was in short supply? And look at all those huts; they would only add to the confusion, increase the enormity of the task one believed one was faced with . . .

They thought they were being cunning, but they didn't realise that a process of elimination – such as the one applied by Ndlela without moving a muscle – would drastically cut down on the list of possible sites.

For the influx of people means the herdboys must roam further afield. The need for more water sends women to rivers and streams not usually visited for such a purpose by the inhabitants of Bulawayo. Then there are the menfolk setting out for a walk, perhaps hoping to bag something for the cooking fire. The immediate environs, beyond the amadladla, are almost as busy as the campsites themselves. That leaves only two areas unlikely to be frequented.

The first is the Place of Execution, but that's too far from the city, and it lacks any caves or other forms of natural cover. The second is a low ridge lying to the west of Bulawayo. It comes close to the temporary settlement in that section; or at least the north end of it does, while the rest of the ridge curves away from the capital. Just a ragged edge of rock, it's shaped like the blade of an axe, with no summit as such, and the lower slopes on both sides are covered by a dense tangle of bushes. Two paths run along the outer slope, one heading through the bushes, but they're rarely used because they simply rejoin the main track skirting the base of the same ridge.

He can't be sure of this, but he suspects the impundulu would need to be fetched from its hiding place, and led as close to its potential victim as its master dares approach.

And if he himself was to create a lair for an impundulu, that's where Ndlela would locate it – on that ridge just to the west of the capital, where the thorny thickets are likely to deter even lovers desperately in search of privacy.

★

They have called the King out and he has spat at the sun, and now, protected by his Night Medicine, he faces his regiments and listens to his praise singers . . .

★

And the praise singers have fanned out, and some are addressing the spectators. And Mpande tries to pinch the Induna's udibi whenever the boy seems particularly caught up in one of these tales of great battles and heroic deeds . . .

★

Standing with the older princes, to the right of Mnkabayi, Dingane once more displays his mastery of the art of napping while seeming to stand upright and attentive. But he can't quite lose himself in pleasant daydreams, because his brother Mhlangana is standing next to him, and he just won't stop muttering under his breath. For some reason, he seems especially bitter and irritable during this First Fruits. When will that hyena's arsehole ever learn? Let big brother strut and congratulate himself, it only means something if you let it.

Mind you, he can afford to be so sanguine, for things between him and Shaka have improved after he helped defeat Ngoza. There were many tense nights after Nandi died, it is true, but, by and large, their relationship remains better . . .

(Now, if you don't mind, he has some breasts to get back to . . . He must remember to find out the girl's name, hmm, yes.)

★

Mbopa? Her eyes seek out the prime minister. What does he really think? Not just about all of this, but of Shaka's shocking betrayal of his loyalty. Starting with his very life, the old cannibal owes Shaka a lot, though he's repaid the King many times over, in the role of diplomat, chamberlain, advisor, strategist. Yet see what Shaka has done. Pampata has told her of the King's anguish, but how does that compare with Mbopa's? 'He didn't know she would be there,' she's told Mnkabayi, on numerous occasions – probably after each time his disgraceful deed came back to haunt Shaka, and he'd turned to his beloved, knowing that his justifications would be met with sooth-ing caresses and tender kisses.

He didn't know. Hai, that's like a man who, unprovoked (and unthinkingly), slaughters another's herd, then apologises when he learns the man's best cow was among the herd, claiming, in effect, that he didn't mean to kill that cow. For how does that ameliorate the fact that he set out to slaughter the herd in the first place?

Mbopa. She wishes she could shake him, shake him like a tree until something drops out. Until she gets some inkling of how he feels, where he stands, whose side he might take . . .

But he's like a sandstorm, his feelings well hidden.

Mnkabayi shifts her attention to her induna. She's missed his counsel. Both she and Ndlela have duties and obligations during this time – and part of Mnkabayi still hopes she can take Nandi's place in Shaka's eyes – but she knows the pair of them will need to find a chance to speak. And soon.

★

He still has to consult his sangoma – a wise, wise old man who is probably even more powerful than the Lion and Nobela put together, but who has escaped Shaka's wrath because he is a hermit who prefers to concentrate on honing his own abilities. But, all the same, that's where Ndlela intends to start his search: on the ridge. And as soon as he can slip away unnoticed. Which may not be for a while, what with tomorrow requiring his constant presence as well.

Also, it won't simply be a matter of finding the hiding place and putting the zombie out of its misery. The place will have to be watched, so he can see who else is involved.

Ndlela wonders if he should take the Induna into his confidence, but decides it's too early. If Mnkabayi's somehow involved, he can't put the Induna in a position where he has to choose between her and Shaka. Mnkabayi would never forgive him. If her old friend and retainer traced the spoor back to herself, she wouldn't think to accuse him of betrayal, or ask for mercy, or even a chance to flee. Instead, Mnkabayi would bare her breast to his blade, and would want Ndlela to be the one to deliver the killing blow. But she would never forgive him, indeed would die cursing him, if he did that to the Induna, and placed him in such an invidious predicament.

Since the Induna is about the only one he would want to take into his confidence, Ndlela will wait and see. And, if Mnkabayi isn't involved, well then . . .

*

The main party of White Men arrived last night, to be greeted by Mbopa, as Shaka was in seclusion with his inyangas. They comprise Farewell and his Dutch business partners, and King and his party – who are to be considered as separate entities, given King's underhand tactics back at the Cape and the moderate success he's had in charming Shaka. He and Nathaniel Isaacs and the others are only tolerated because members from the visiting side tend to stick together when the home team outnumbers them by something like five thousand to one. King's 'reinforcements', such as they are, also mean they have been able to leave a stronger contingent behind to guard the settlement at Port Natal. There, Mrs Farewell has been tasked with keeping an eye on Jakot. Not that the Swimmer has any intention of leaving the bay just now.

Fynn, meanwhile, seems to have reached KwaBulawayo a few days before the others, for in his journal, written closer to the time of the events described in the (published) *Diary*, he tells of encountering 'groups of warriors marching to the King's place, dressed in their best. Out of gorges and river beds, emerging from thickets and mountain passes, they came – formidable fellows singing their war songs.' Their destination was, of course, Shaka's Komkhulu, or Great Place. Fynn mentions a continuous 'roar and hum' of voices in the distance, and then seeing 'temporary huts of green branches' being erected in the veld around Bulawayo. 'Late into the night they'd sit around their campfires telling old stories and singing songs . . .'

Now, on the first day of the climax of the First Fruits, he turns his attention away from Shaka in order to watch as the praise singers retire, hoarse and close to collapse.

After a brief pause, a bull is herded into one the smaller kraals within the cattlefold. 'There, with the eyes of the King and the army on them, a group of unarmed youngsters fought the bull,' writes Fynn in his journal. 'I later learnt the group was comprised solely of unmarried men, as they are believed to be "pure", whereas married men are deemed "impure". It was clearly a great honour to be chosen to fight the bull and these men went to it with gusto.' Several were injured, Fynn tells us, but that had no effect on the 'enthusiasm of the others'. He admits he couldn't see exactly how the bull met its end. When the creature started to show exhaustion – or possibly had gored enough unmarried men – an inyanga entered the kraal, carrying a spear. The remaining warriors then threw themselves on the beast, bringing it down – 'and I couldn't tell whether they broke its neck or whether the *coup de grâce* was delivered by the spearman,' writes Fynn.

★

The carcase is carried before Shaka. The inyangas skin the animal and remove the gall bladder. Then strips of meat are cut off the carcase. These are thrown on a fire made in the old way, by rubbing sticks together. When the meat has blackened, a strip is removed, dipped into a pot containing a watery medicine, and presented to Shaka. He bites into it and sucks out the juices, thereby absorbing the strength and courage of the bull.

The indunas leave the ranks and move forwards to form two lines of three men abreast, so it's as if they become the horns of the regiments. Each officer receives a strip of meat covered in muthi . . .

★

. . . she sees him and, momentarily, everything else is forgotten. And if her eyes admire his broad shoulders, his narrow waist, his muscular thighs, the yearning to hear his voice, to sit and listen to him, to prepare his food and bring it to him, to watch him eat . . . that yearning crushes her chest like the jaws of a hippo.

★

Back with his own section in his regiment, the officer bites off a small piece of meat, sucks out the juices, then throws the strip into the air. The warrior who catches it bites off a small piece, sucks out the juices, and passes the meat to the next man.

And so the process is repeated, as the army thus doctors itself, taking in the power of the bull, for the Umkhosi is also the time when the amabutho are fortified and strengthened.

While this is going on, other inyangas have been busy collecting the horns, bones, skin and offal — in fact everything that remains of the bull. Even the blood is scraped off the ground. These are all placed on a larger pile of wood specially prepared for this purpose, and set on fire. The ash will be placed in a large pot, for use later in the ceremony.

No trace of the bull must be left behind, as even the smallest part of it can be lethal to the King if it falls into the wrong hands.

★

Here is the awe that Farewell hoped to evoke with his guns and tales of Jorgi's mighty empire, thinks Fynn, gazing at the warriors closest to his party and noting how these 'formidable fellows' follow the progress of the strips of meat with a mixture of reverence and eager anticipation. They truly believe, and Fynn feels humbled and chastened in some way. It's as if he and his companions are the exotic creatures here: weak and woebegotten blind men who've blundered into the land of the sighted.

★

By the time the meat has been fully distributed and the ashes of the bull collected, it's growing dark. The regiments return to their temporary camps, while Shaka goes off with Pampata. She will lead him back to the commoner's hut where he has been staying for these many weeks past. It is the eya emsizini, the hut of his seclusion. After spending some time alone there, allowing the Night Muthi to guide him where it will, Shaka will eventually call for Pampata. For the duration of the King's stay, the hut will be guarded by a regiment of young, unmarried women. After Pampata has entered the hut of seclusion, they will sing and try and coax the King out, but he will not emerge, will not allow himself to be tempted and led astray. And Pampata will wash him, in a purification ritual called ukuqunga, then she will straddle him and they will fuck . . .

He moves through the night, a silent song, a black mamba in the darkness, an overwhelming urge.

He is naked, knows that is wrong.

Knows that to be seen – spotted, espied – is to put everything in jeopardy.

(But this hunger, this urge . . .)

Yet is he mistaken? Or does it feel as if he will no longer have a need for such . . . things?

It might be wishful thinking – he might only be looking for an excuse that will justify taking such a risk – but he doesn't think so.

The becoming . . . it's happening.

And soon, very soon, it will be complete.

(But first . . .)

This hunger. The like of which he's never experienced before.

A grin. Hai! If only they knew!

Stupid children, with their stupid games.

Chewing the meat . . .

Sucking the juice . . .

Fools!

If only they knew . . .

This is the way to do it.

This.

Is the way.

And he moves among the makeshift huts, dodging the voices and the laughter.

And the urge pulls him to the nearest cattle pen . . .

And the cattle barely stir as he eases between them . . .

And he has an iklwa blade in his hand . . .

And he's on the calf and has slashed its throat . . .

. . . not a human, no, but better than nothing . . .

And he gulps down the warm sticky blood, and is gone before the herd panics and the watchmen come running . . .

Peregrinations

Quietly, unnoticed by his companions, Fynn leaves the fire. He's reminded of a village fair or market day, although none he's ever seen could match this in scale. And there's laughter and shouting and a constant coming and going, as old friends are sought out. Despite the lateness of the hour many children are still up and about, playing their games or gathered around storytellers. Women carry pots of water and beer, sure-footed even in the darkness.

Finally he's free of the smoke and flickering flames, and soon the people noises merge with the crickets and the frogs. He's seeking high ground, a spot from which he can view the whole spectacle.

And a spectacle it most certainly is. He understands he should feel privileged to be here, but what's even more fascinating to him is the fact that this is a spectacle for the Zulus too. That realisation struck him a few hours ago, when he was trying to update his journal and ignore the antics of those insufferable Dutchmen – although Farewell and King are just as bad, with their constant one-upmanship. He'd been on the verge of writing something suitably grandiose about being one of the first white men to see this magnificent harvest festival, when it occurred to him their hosts were also awed. This particular harvest festival is clearly something unique and different for them, too.

Fynn settles himself on a rock. If Shaka invited them here primarily to show off his power, he's succeeded. That he can still awe his own subjects, though, says more than those regiments massed around his capital – although that's something to take the breath away, too. Fynn grins in the darkness. He still can't believe it. If, that day on the beach and during the dread-filled weeks that followed, someone had told him he'd soon be able to wander among these people without fear, he would have laughed in their face.

Mind you, if he'd known then what he knows now, would he have ventured so far?

What *had* he been thinking that day?

He should have instead heeded the words of Frederick and Jantjie, and of Mahamba, a local man they met near the bay and who, of course, knew more than they what they might be letting themselves in for, if they followed the impis.

Later, referring to that day, he'll write: 'My life evidently was saved on this occasion by that wonderful talisman of this country, the name of Shaka.' What he doesn't mention is how the glamour of that name had an effect on him, too, drawing him on in the wake of the regiments.

It was as if he'd been bewitched.

Well, yes, but the same might be said of Farewell, Petersen, Hoffman and the others. There is something about this land that enthrals and holds, that gets into your eyes and under your skin . . . But it's a spell that touches different men in different ways. Farewell, Petersen, Hoffman and the others . . . their faces are aglow with greed. Like horses who have thrown their riders, they have cast aside reason and move towards what they see as untold wealth, believing they know the way and their destination is in sight.

That day on the beach, Fynn stopped being one of them. He was no longer a trader seeking to make contact with a king, because he'd suddenly realised there was no longer a king.

There was Shaka.

. . . calling him on.

★

Peregrinations. Other regiments overtaking his valiant little party. Then a village. And Mbikwana, an emissary from Shaka, waiting to inform them that the Bull Elephant was relieved to see they'd stopped trying to drown themselves and were at last on their way to visit him. Instructing them to adjourn to his village.

Before they left, Fynn was presented with some cattle. When he asked if three of these animals could be sent to the others at Port Natal, Mbikwana readily agreed, and despatched them under the care of a group of warriors.

Peregrinations and winding paths. The constant need to reassure his interpreter and servant that it was by no means certain they were being guided to their deaths. Then Mbikwana's kraal. An induna and five men tasked to look after the strangers. They were to stay there until Shaka made his further wishes known.

'I remained in this locality 14 days,' Fynn writes in his *Diary*. On each day he was given an ox. 'I distributed the meat to the immense numbers that came to see me,' he notes.

While working as a loblolly boy at Christ's Hospital in London, he'd picked up a smattering of medical knowledge and, after his experiences in fever-ridden Delagoa, he had resolved, on coming to Natal, to bring with him a well-stocked medicine chest. During his stay at Mbikwana's kraal, he'd had occasion to delve into his pack – 'two blankets, a feather pillow, a coffee-kettle, some sea biscuits, rice' – groping for the medicine chest so he could treat a sick woman.

The woman had recovered, much to the astonishment of his hosts who'd believed her close to death.

A short while later, another emissary arrived, bringing from Shaka 'a present of 40 head of cattle, oxen and milch cows, that my people might not starve'. There were also 'seven large elephant tusks'. And the news that Shaka wasn't quite ready yet to welcome this persistent isilwane. Fynn was to wait until the King's army was fully rested, after their recent campaign.

As luck would have it, Jantjie returned, after delivering the livestock and ivory to Port Natal, with the news that Farewell and the rest of the party had now arrived on the *Antelope*. Fynn therefore told Mbikwana he would wait there for word from Shaka.

How impatient he had been, with Shaka so close, but returning to the bay gave him a chance to come to his senses. Jantjie and Michael had been right – what a risk he'd taken! How was he to know that the generosity shown wasn't a way of gulling them into letting their guard down.

But, no, how could that be? Their hosts could have killed them any time they felt like it!

Feeling the need to justify his actions, looking to tamp down the shuddering what-ifs, was surely a sign that the spell was working (because it was also a way of plucking up the courage to retrace his footprints).

Or perhaps not.

This feeling is not something that stands up to close scrutiny. It's akin to a drunkard's reverie, the grandiose plans that fill his mind while the booze fills his gut. It's the silliness that enters your thoughts when you're alone.

Fynn himself struggles to pin it down in his journal, leaving a mess of scored-out lines: next morning's reason editing midnight's epiphanies. A wringing-out that's all but complete by the time he comes to (re)write the *Diary*. Only, he can't quite bring himself to simply follow Isaacs' advice, and do as Isaacs did in his own memoir, and describe the Zulu kings as 'blood-thirsty as you can and endeavour to give an estimate of the number of people they murdered during their reign, and also describe the frivolous crimes people lose their lives for'.

Echoes remain: whispers between the lines that are easily dismissed, yes, but at what cost?

For one there's his own growing disgruntlement with the rest of the group.

Farewell had arrived with thirty men and eleven horses, bringing the complement up to thirty-five, with Farewell, Ogle and Fynn being the only Englishmen.

The Union Flag is raised. The two cannon the traders have brought with them are fired. Port Natal thus becomes British, whether Whitehall likes it or not.

Mbikwana arrives with an escort of about a hundred soldiers, and announces that Shaka will see them now. Leaving the others to finish the building, Farewell, Petersen, Fynn and Frederick, their Xhosa interpreter, set off together with the Zulus.

The going is slower than Fynn would like, as Farewell insists on panning for gold in every stream they cross.

Then there's Farewell's father-in-law, Petersen, who's sixty-three, 'corpulent and subject to ill health, not of the sweetest temper', and who seldom speaks without swearing. After nearly throttling himself in the monkey ropes dangling along the hippo path they're following, he's all for turning back and going home to the Cape.

However, as he's also eager to get an 'ocular demonstration' of those cattle kraals made from elephant tusks, he requires 'very little soothing', writes Fynn.

A little later, however, Petersen causes his horse to roll over in a bog. Since he's on the animal at the time (and therefore ends up underneath it), 'here was a new scene of difficulty' which necessitated a change of clothes and the making of coffee, 'interlarded with strings of Dutch oaths'.

When they stop for the night at a Zulu umuzi (and are presented with two oxen for slaughter), there follows 'several hours' of 'crimination and recrimination between father-in-law and son-in-law', with Petersen suggesting that Farewell has dragged him to this barbarous land with the intention of killing him.

And so they gradually make their way to Bulawayo, with Shaka ensuring they take the scenic route, so they can catch a good glimpse of his mighty war kraals.

The barbarians from across the Great Waters are suitably impressed.

'We were struck with astonishment at the order and discipline maintained in the country through which we travelled,' writes Fynn. 'Cleanliness was a prevailing custom' at the 'regimental kraals', he adds, 'and this not only inside their huts, but outside, for there were considerable spaces where neither dirt nor ashes were to be seen.'

★

Peregrinations, thinks Fynn with a wry smile. They've certainly done their share of riding and walking since then – and himself more than the others.

And then they were there.

Here.

He remembers dancing shields and prancing blades.

He remembers men, screaming men, being put to death before their very eyes.

He remembers feathers and tails, plumes and bristling adornments.

He remembers dust and singing women; and drums and ranks of warriors looming nearer, then retreating, as though daring the strangers to advance a few more paces.

He remembers wide eyes from Frederick and Jantjie, and wouldn't be surprised if they could have said the same thing of him and Farewell. Even the Dutchmen remained quiet.

He remembers still more men dying right at their feet, staining the dirt red.

But where was the king who ordered such callous, casual slaughter simply to impress – or terrify – his guests?

Where was this Shaka?

And suddenly the spears and shields parted, and there he was: a profusion of plumes and skins, monkey, genet and leopard tails, dried mealies and stalks of the wild sugar cane that grew in those parts, pleats and beads and feathers.

He was helped to his feet by his retainers and embarked on a long, baying harangue that Frederick, their interpreter, was unable to translate. And every so often this apparition would pause, and a roar would go up from the crowd.

★

But one man standing to the side, a big tall man, who unlike the others was wearing no adornments, caught Fynn's eye. He hadn't moved forward to help the feathers and skins to rise, yet he was dressed as a servant, or commoner . . .

And suddenly Fynn *knew*.

Leaning towards Farewell, he pointed to the same man and said: 'Farewell, there is Shaka.'

He'd had to speak loudly, to be heard over the bellowing, and the man had heard him, too.

513

And their eyes met. And Shaka smiled. He held up his hand and wagged his finger at Fynn.

★

Returning to their huts, Fynn is almost knocked over by a man running through the darkness. But he thinks nothing of it, and doesn't notice the blood that covers the man's chin and chest.

Certain 'luxury items' have, from time to time, been reverently laid at Shaka's feet. A brass telescope, razors, soaps, silk, braid intended to adorn an admiral's dress uniform. But beads and a form of thick cotton cloth make up the main type of currency used by the Farewell Trading Company (est. 1823).

The cloth comes from the Dongari region, near Bombay in India, while the beads originate from Venice. Given the smugness evinced by certain traders at various stages during the Age of Exploration, it would be all too easy to assume that the Zulus were being ripped off. Ivory, gold and land in exchange for beads and dungarees – come on! Farewell and his partners were nothing more than thieves out to exploit the poor natives!

Accusations of chicanery, extortion and exploitation are not without substance in instances where trade was imposed by gunboats and the like, or where a European monarch decided a certain portion of Africa was his to do with as he liked. But that certainly wasn't the case when Fynn valiantly bellowed Shaka's name, after being confronted by two 'ferocious fellows' of our acquaintance. These traders were in no position to proselytise or force Shaka to do anything the Bull Elephant didn't want to do.

Shaka had the upper hand when it came to trade, and, as it was with the Portuguese at Delagoa, so it was with Jorgi's men. For the People Of The Sky thought they were the ones getting the better part of the deal.

Shaka was happy to 'sell' them the bay the Zulus called Ethekwini. Jorgi's men were few in number, so if some wanted to move away and establish their own kraals, that wasn't a problem. All they needed to do was obtain Shaka's permission.

When it came to gold, the Zulus were a little more ambivalent. They didn't consider it valuable, and found it too soft to have any practical use. But they knew, from the tales that had come down to them through the generations, that there were those, such as the Ma-Iti and the Arabi, who prized this metal considerably, and would therefore seek to enslave human beings and force them to burrow deep under the ground in search of the stuff. For this reason, the places where gold could be found were kept a secret, and traders were fed only a paltry trickle.

Ivory the Zulus had no use for, which is why traders and travellers speak of piles of ivory lying outside native settlements, as if there was a surplus. The Zulus (and other tribes in the region) rarely hunted elephants – a laborious, time-consuming, not to mention dangerous, process when you're armed only with spears and ferocious expressions. When they did kill an elephant, the Zulus used all parts of the creature except for the ivory. And here came these grinning, cringing, albino Long Noses wanting to buy the tusks! Quite what they did with the ivory was anyone's guess – but the consensus was that they ate it.

Things would change but right now, in the 1820s, in the absence of blockades, bombardments and blankets infected with smallpox, one has to ask who was exploiting who.

It's easy to see the uses hardy Dongari Kapar might have been put to, but it's those beads that are really interesting.

Many cultures have deemed beads valuable, and throughout the ages these decorative objects, ranging from a millimetre to several centimetres in diameter, have been fashioned from stone, bone, horn, ivory, pearl, coral, wood and seeds.

Say the word 'bead' these days, however, and most people think of wooden orbs spun on a lathe, or the cheap, garishly coloured plastic kind. But the beads used for trade purposes in Africa and the Americas from the fifteenth century onwards were Italian chevrons created by glassmakers in Venice and Murano.

Making them involves a time-consuming process that starts with the initial core formed from a molten ball of glass called a gather. An air bubble is blown into the centre of the gather, and then the molten ball is dropped into a star-shaped mould with anywhere between five and fifteen points. Once several layers of coloured glass have been applied, the hot substance is drawn out into a long rod. The bubble at the centre of the gather stretches with the rod and forms the threading hole in the bead. The diameter of the

516

resulting beads is determined by the amount of glass in the original gather, and also by how thinly the glass is extended out. The cooled cane is then cut into short segments, which will reveal a star pattern in cross-section.

The beads brought by Farewell are composed of green, white, blue and red layers. If not quite miniature works of art, they are artefacts created by skilled craftsmen, and one could say as much work has gone into their creation as a latter-day run of banknotes of whichever currency one cares to choose.

Shattering The Calabash

The call: 'The King comes!'

And the soldiers in the cattlefold start drumming their spears against their shields.

The regiments have become one army again, as happens before battle, and the men stand shoulder to shoulder behind a wall of overlapping shields. And, in the ranks behind the van, each man drums his spear against his neighbour's shield.

Motion and sound.

Sound that is motion.

The pumping-blood beat of a living creature born out of the merging of the many; the something else that makes the whole more than just the sum of its parts. Steel claws beat against stony cowhide: knock-knock-knocking.

No let-up, no respite; easier to tell your heart to stop beating. Those hungry blades demanding blood: knock-knock-knocking.

The rumble of thunder, slowed down but called closer, so it seems as if it'll never end. And watch out when it does: knock-knock-knocking.

On the battlefield itself, the storm that follows the thunder, the flood of charging feet, the falling-rain hiss of the Zulu war cry, they are even worse: a torrent able to swamp forests and sweep aside mountains, never mind cringing savages whose knees have already begun to bang to together in time to that same knock-knock-knocking.

And today? See what the iklwas call forth . . .

★

Just as the many here have become something else, so we have a man who is more than a man.

518

Called forth by the iklwas, he has legs, he has feet just like a man, and a head; but his body, from shoulders to knees, is thatch.

Three overlapping layers adorned with a profusion of lichen and moss, maize leaves and branches, and cuttings from other crops.

Accompanied by an elderly man carrying a selection of uselwa gourds dangling from cords draped around his neck, he enters the cattlefold – and the drumming stops.

Thatch and leaves and branches.

When he's a few paces away from the wall of shields, the old-timer steps in front of him and helps him remove the thatch coat. Then Mbilini KaZiwedum, for it is he, turns round, and the man who is more than a man affixes the thatch around the greybeard's shoulders, himself becoming something else in the process.

Becoming Shaka.

Greasy, glistening Night Muthi – fragments of the dead moon – covers his limbs. And the left side of his body – arm, torso, leg – is black, while the right side is yellow – a grubby, sandy yellow. And his face and neck are red – the fierce dark orange-red of some sunsets.

A mixture of baboon, genet and hyena pelts form his kilt, while the amashoba beneath his knees are made from the skin of the black bull his men slaughtered yesterday afternoon.

As the thatch was placed around his shoulders, Mbilini ensured the gourds were left hanging on the outside. Now he hands one to Shaka.

The King moves still closer to the shields.

A hush.

He throws the uselwa up into the air, once . . .

Twice . . .

After he catches it for the third time, he flings the calabash at the shields closest to him.

A lunge, with his right leg slipping forward so the bended knee can take his weight, then a slight twisting of the shoulders, before executing a throw – a single, fluid motion – that sees the calabash shatter against the shields.

Begone evil spirits! Begone disease! Pestilence! Misfortune! Go!

And Shaka has his hand extended for another uselwa gourd.

Tossing it into the air and catching it, he moves along the semi-circle of shields with a studied insouciance that's disrupted by a sudden lunge . . .

Begone! Go! Drought! Disease! Pestilence! Away!

And again Shaka throws a calabash, shattering it against cowhide.

Go! Begone! Begone! Begone! Begone!

And the spears flicker again, and the drumming shakes the skies, as the army reminds the ancestors of its presence as guardians not only of the King and his children, the People Of The Sky, but also of their crops and livestock. It is they, not the cringing sangomas, that the forces of darkness will have to deal with, should they be plotting evil.

★

Now they're naked and in the water, arranged in orderly rows with enough space so they can squat and touch the surface with their chins. The King is upriver, out of sight behind a tangle of bushes, at his favourite spot, and he is in the water too. His inyangas are washing him, using ash from the carcase of yesterday's bull, covering him in ash, washing it off, using it to remove the Night Muthi, then covering him again, so that the river turns grey. And this greyness finds the warriors downstream, and they are strengthened by this sacred water that has passed over the King's body . . .

★

Back in the royal compound, the King is dressed again and treated with White Muthi, full-moon medicine. He oversees the burning of the rush garment handed to Mbilini, as well as the sleeping mat he used last night. Then, accompanied by Mbopa and his other advisors, he returns to the isibaya, where the people await him expectantly.

With his words repeated and spread through the crowd by low whispers, he names the new regiments. Then he reaffirms his earlier promises, giving his final permission for the men in two of his regi-

520

ments – and the corresponding female guilds – to marry. The men may now wear the isicoco, and the women the top-knot.

While the cheers wash over Shaka, a line of warriors forms up in front of the first row of spectators. These are men of the Dhlamini clan, renowned for being fleet of foot. Called forward by a signal from Mbopa, each of them carries two small reeds.

Shaka raises his left hand, and waits for the cheers to die down. He watches the ripple of excitement that flows away from him, as those in front spot the men and pass the word back.

Silence.

The moment the nation has been waiting for. The message that need not be relayed, for it will be instantly understood by all.

Each man has two reeds, the one longer than the other. The umtshingo and invenge.

And now, says Shaka, these special messengers are to go forth, playing their reed flutes, so that all might know the nation now has his permission to partake of the First Fruits . . .

★

Arranged in great circles around the cooking fires, the regiments will continue to feast and drink for the rest of the day, and most of the night, while being entertained by the praise singers. In the meantime, the inyangas will be preparing a special medicine called imshikaqo. Tomorrow morning, officers will move among the hungover ranks to find volunteers. These men will dig long shallow trenches in the veld, some distance away from the campsites. By the time these are ready, the men will have been roused and formed up, cringing beneath headaches, their mouths dry, their eyes tortured by the sun. The inyangas and their helpers will move among them, and each man has to drink three mouthfuls of the imshikaqo. Then there's a rush to the trenches for a mass vomiting . . .

The Induna won't take part in these activities, however. Because there is a killer roaming free, and because Shaka fears conspirators might still be working against him, he's in charge of the contingent tasked with guarding Bulawayo tonight.

Sections of the regiments roam the countryside, so there's little chance of a surprise attack. With the rest of the populace also indulging in beer and beef, the Induna's men will be keeping the peace within the confines of the expanded settlement. Some, though, will be looking out for Kholisa, as it's on just such an occasion that he's likely to let his guard down, or his protectors may become sloppy.

The Induna turns to his udibi. 'When you yourself are a greybeard, they will hold you in awe because you were here at this time!'

Gqokli Hill was the end of the beginning. It announced to the world, to the growling, quarrelsome relatives who surrounded them, that the Sky People were no longer going to be vassals. Then, a few seasons later, Zwide had invaded Zulu territory once again, and Shaka had first led the Ndwandwe army deep into Zulu territory, then chased them all the way back to Zwide's kraal. Then, after a few smaller irritations had been done away with, it had become the turn of the Thembus and the treacherous Qwabes. Yet these, and other victories, were only experienced vicariously by the people. As the Induna explains to the udibi, they got the cattle and increased opportunities to trade; they felt the benefits, but not the glory. For it was the army who basked in Shaka's approbation, becoming almost a separate caste, a form of nobility in itself, with soldiers exempt from most of the laws, and protected also from sangomas.

However, in ruling that the First Fruits be held at KwaBulawayo, and only at KwaBulawayo, and there led by the King, Shaka was at last giving the people a chance to experience at first hand some of the glory won by his army. Had the nation ever witnessed such a gathering? Here was an opportunity for those who were less well informed to see just how the nation had grown. And Shaka knew that the vast majority of those who had been made uncomfortable by his ukase about the Umkhosi, and by the invitation he'd extended to the White Men, would lose their qualms the moment they laid eyes on the capital with its expanded perimeters.

That sound, that beautiful alluring din heard from kilometres away, a wind-rustling-leaves noise that gives new energy to tired limbs. That pewter canopy created by thousands of cooking fires in close proximity, seen from afar, a rain cloud about to favour the Great Place with its bounty. It was enough to overawe them before they even reached the city's environs. And then they'd be a part of it all, learning that in these masses there was strength, and unity.

'In years to come, you will see these days and nights grow, overflow, as each one tries to outdo the other in describing the wonders they have seen or heard about. And you will hear' – the Induna grins – 'hai, you might even add your own fables, although I think that will never be your way. And you will listen and you will smile to yourself, for you have seen for yourself. You will have been here at the time they speak of with such reverence. You will understand that their embellishments are an acknowledgement of just how important this moment was. But, because you have seen for yourself, you'll also know that no amount of exaggeration will ever be able to properly describe this occasion.'

They're standing on a rise alongside the main road, and from here they can see over most of Bulawayo and its temporary dwellings. With so many fires, it resembles a giant bed of twinkling coals.

The Induna lays a hand on the boy's shoulder and they stand in silence before this teeming, flickering vision.

The Induna is plagued by the murders, the feeling of having let down his King, but he hasn't had much chance to do anything about it these past few days. Being on the fringes tonight will finally give him an opportunity to ponder the problem at length. Perhaps his participation in the First Fruits will enable him to approach things from a different path.

Yet, right now, standing right here with the boy, he finds himself distracted once again.

Has any Zulu king gathered together so many of his subjects?

Has any Zulu king been able to conjure up such unity?

Has any Zulu king ever believed they could grow and prosper, and move so far from that tired old valley rightfully revered only as a place of beginnings and endings?

★

Back then we had no story, only myths to console us.

Now those days are gone forever. For we have a story, our (own) story, and it begins with Shaka. And let him be called King of Kings, for that is who he is. He has shattered the calabash, and here tonight we are tasting the first fruits of greatness.

I wanted him to come . . .

I saw what my uncle saw . . .

And see how it was! Remember how we were!

Zulus? Who were the Zulus?

We were clawless and clueless.

(But we knew we were meant to have claws. Somehow we knew that.)

We were spineless and gutless.

(And yet somehow we knew this was not the way things were meant to be.)

We were poor relatives expected to be grateful for what we had — because things could always be worse.

(Yet somehow — by a stirring in the blood, a quickening heartbeat, the sense of a lion about to pounce — we knew this was our motherland, and that the sky was our father. We were in the right place. This was our home.)

We were slaves, with history's foot on our back, keeping our faces in the dirt — and if we were allowed up, it was only so we might bow down again.

We were expected to be timid and obedient. Humble and meek. Ever diffident and always servile. Beggarly, sycophantic and abject.

(And always . . . always the vague sense this was wrong. The world was upside down and the sky trodden upon, and this was not the way things were meant to be.)

We were also trapped, children surrounded by bickering adults who could slap us down at any time.

Shut up! Avert your eyes. Be placatory. Grin and bear it.

Yet, even then, there'd be the nudging that became shoving: grazing lands impinged upon, cattle going missing, Zulu farmers accused of stock theft, insults plaited into a tightening tension leading to an inevitable clash . . .

Our old foe, the Buthelezis, delivering yet another thrashing . . .

Or the Ngwanes sauntering down along the map to ask you what you're looking at . . .

Aiee! Back then it was the fleas, and their fleas, who came to taunt us. The likes of Zwide barely even acknowledged our existence.

But we were there all the same, hiding in the valley of the White Umfolozi, trying to survive.

We were surrounded, yes . . .

To the north, the Ndwandwes and the Ngwanes. To the south, the Mthetwas. To the west, a tangle of cantankerous tribes and clans like the Qwabes; between us and the coast: the Mbo, the Thembus and the Khumalos. And among these, too, the Buthelezis, Langeni and others.

We were surrounded, yes, but we could feel it all the same . . . Like a breath held, a waterskin about to burst, a tautness only a few tugs away from snapping . . .

We were insignificant and ignored, yes, but we could still see how things were going. Lions were present among the zebra, and the zebra had two choices: either flee or be eaten up.

A clamouring, then . . . and, when the dust settled, the many had become two. The Ndwandwes to the north, the Mthetwas to the south, with everyone else allied to one or the other – or, like Matiwane KaMasumpa's Ngwanes, now looking for somewhere else to settle.

And for once her brother Senzangakhona, He Who Acts Wisely, lived up to his name. He threw his lot in with the Mthetwas and, because the Zulus formed a buffer zone between the two great enemies, Dingiswayo KaJobe, king of the Mthetwas, allowed Senzangakhona a certain amount of latitude and encouraged him to build up the Zulu army.

Encouraged? That was the rhetoric, but even then, in the hour of their need, the reality was a little different.

We were leant against, and encouraged to strengthen ourselves only in the way a fence is strengthened. We were told how important we were, but we were only valuable as objects: men who, in dying and women who, in being raped and villages that, in being burnt, would serve only to slow Zwide down, and give Dingiswayo time to deploy his forces.

Where would we be without Shaka? How long would it have been before the Zulu nation vanished, in the same way a river – all that potential, that what-could-be – disappears when it becomes only a tributary?

Our fire would have become merely smoke, before vanishing. It would have been as if we had never lived.

★

I wanted him to come, so now let me be the one who sees he is stopped!

★

And as Mnkabayi lies awake, listening to the drums, the shouts and laughter, Ndlela roams the night. He has consulted with the sangoma, and has had him throw the bones. 'And see here,' said the old hermit, pointing to the fragment of tortoise shell that had landed between a bone from a cow and a lion's tooth. 'The one you seek,' he said, indicating the tooth. 'The one you seek to protect,' he repeated, his finger moving to hover over the bone. 'And see here,' he said, indicating the shell. 'The one you seek has been deflected. I do not know why, but the tooth points to the stone.' It's a shiny semi-precious stone, indicating something of value, or something valued, which could be a person or an artefact. 'But, know this, the one you seek to protect will be safe for now.'

And now, mulling these things over, Ndlela moves among the festivities, trusting his instincts, going where his feet carry him, pausing only to avoid crossing the Induna's path. He is a hunter but he is also offering himself as prey. Although, an indication that his suspicions were correct, the cow bone, the 'one he seeks to protect', might not actually be Mnkabayi, but he's not about to take any chances. Perhaps the deviation the sangoma spotted in the bones means the impundulu will seek out an alternative victim, in its quest for wisdom. Or perhaps the deviation is Ndlela himself, as an obstacle the creature will seek to remove so it can get at Mnkabayi.

Whatever might be the case, he is ready for it.

Death In The Morning

They were supposed to stand guard. They were supposed to look after each other. But last night the festivities got the better of them. Should he have seen to it that some Fasimbas were sent to swell their ranks and therefore ensure that his instructions were carried out?

But now is no time for self-recriminations. He had ordered a patrol to pay regular visits on the clan, and it had discovered the body. A kill still fresh (yet not a kill); and enough men to protect the area, keep inquisitive feet off the closest paths, ensure that the family members are kept calm. And how brave the menfolk are suddenly, the cries of their women puffing out those chests; now they are ready to do their duty. Yet they're also tired, and toiling under the effects of last night, and therefore easy to pacify. In fact, this early in the morning, almost the whole of KwaBulawayo, including (and perhaps especially) the temporary dwellings, is suffering from a humungous hangover. Which is why there are only a few people out and about to sully the spoor.

And that's the thing: there is spoor this time. And the Induna knows he and the udibi will have to move fast, if they are to have the trail to themselves. The sun has yet to rise, but the sky is blue, unfurled and awaiting the sun's arrival, presaged by a golden glow in the distance. Soon there *will* be more people out and about.

All the same, there's a need to pause. The Induna orders the men who have arrived with him to see that Dwanile and the wives she deems closest to her are separated from the other women. Then he joins Njikiza at Gudlo's body. The big man was in charge of the patrol that found Dwanile's son, which is why everything has been done precisely as the Induna had outlined when telling the patrols what to do, should they be among the first to stumble upon Kholisa's handiwork.

But it is as Njikiza says. This one is different, not quite a kill. Two assegai thrusts: one delivered below Gudlo's ribcage, the other through his throat. The animal ferocity that has had them speaking of (and expecting) a kill, as if they are dealing with a deranged lion, is lacking.

'Perhaps you disturbed him,' says the Induna.

'Or someone did.'

The Induna looks up, looks around: 'Where's Jembuluka?'

They were not the first ones to find the body, explains Njikiza. That had been Jembuluka and, according to his sister, he has gone off after the spoor.

'He is knowledgeable about such things?'

The Watcher of the Ford shrugs.

'Hai, then we have also his footprints to make our task more difficult!' murmurs the Induna, his eyes fixed on the body.

There is no mutilation.

And the Induna doesn't think that's because Kholisa was disturbed.

Two spear thrusts? The first one to the throat, probably to silence Gudlo . . .

It's something else that's been plaguing the warrior: why hadn't either the boy, or Zusi, screamed? Both were likely to have been heard, and both must have known that. Yet there had been no cries for help. And no obvious attempt made to silence them during the attack – as is clearly the case here.

A courteous clearing of the throat and fingers brushing his elbow. It's the udibi. 'Master? The spoor . . .'

Yes, indeed, the spoor . . .

Let them go and catch this insane sangoma – and then all their questions will be answered.

And, truly, the killer has been unlucky this time. Because this is a temporary camp, the ground around the makeshift huts is soft, welcoming to footprints, and, in striking so early, Kholisa ensured there was a greater chance that those prints would be preserved.

The Induna examines the tracks Njikiza points out to him. 'These have to be his,' says the Watcher, 'for they were clearly made by a limping man.'

When the Induna nods, Njikiza asks him if he wants some Fasimbas to accompany him.

That won't be necessary, replies the warrior. He squeezes the big man's shoulder. 'We two will be enough,' he murmurs.

Njikiza nods as if he understands, and the Induna smiles. All the same, he adds, if the Watcher hasn't heard from them by, say – he looks up at the sky – selilidala, when the sun has matured, and is well up, then he and the other Fasimbas can come looking for them.

'We will make it easy for you to find us,' says the Induna.

'As you wish, Nduna.'

★

Having left their shields with Njikiza, and carrying only an iklwa each, the Induna and the boy set off after the spoor. The residents of the temporary huts they pass continue to be reluctant to face the sun. Only children seem to be up and about, but the Induna and the udibi are moving fast enough to pass them by before their curiosity can be aroused. Paths criss-cross the area, but they're narrow, and with a bit of patient searching at each intersection the Induna's able to find where the killer in his haste stepped off the path and ran alongside it for a few paces. Or else overbalanced – for it's clear even to the boy that there's something wrong with the way he moves.

'See here,' says the Induna, the first time the path forks and they have to split up temporarily. His fingers tracing the shapes so the udibi will know what to look for amid the older tracks, he shows the boy how the right foot is always at an angle, turned inwards, and how most times you see only the toes and the pad behind them. The imprint left by the other foot is deeper, a sign that their quarry's hobbling, favouring his right leg.

Finally they find themselves on a path leading away from the capital. It's a narrow band of hard-packed dirt, but the Induna's still able to discern traces of the spoor. Then he's not so sure . . . Their pace slows to a walk as the warrior casts about, seeking signs that they're still heading in the right direction. He has the boy look for any place at which the killer might have left the path, but the dew has now gone and there's no easy way to see if someone has cut through the long grass.

Reaching a ridge a few minutes later, they come to a fork. One branch runs through a tangle of bush and trees; the other climbs the slope, to skirt the thicket.

The Induna glances backwards and thinks for a moment. They're out of sight of the capital. Perhaps believing that, by this stage, his pursuers will have come to the conclusion he's given them the slip, and return to Bulawayo, their quarry may have become a little more careless.

The udibi will take the path through the bushes, while the Induna will follow the other – the one he suspects a man in a hurry is more likely to take. The boy is to listen for his master's call, which will be the sign to turn back again – and they'll meet here. Two calls mean one of them has found something, and the other is to make his way to him directly.

★

Jogging to overcome the gradient, his eyes on the fringes of soft sand on either side of the path, the Induna still finds himself pestered by the manner of Gudlo's murder. How different his death is to the others. If Njikiza (and Jembuluka before him) hadn't found tracks that indicated the passing of a limping man, he'd be more than willing to entertain the thought that Gudlo's killing had nothing to do with the other two.

But see how closely this clan has been involved in all three murders. Two of their number have been victims, while Vuyile witnessed the first killing. Could it be that they really are cursed?

The Induna pauses. Drops to his haunches, takes a closer look at an indentation in the sand to the right of the path.

Let us say they are cursed. Let us say they have done something to rile

Kholisa, and now he wants vengeance . . . And it could well be that Vuyile was his intended victim that night, the other poor boy who had died merely blundering into the wrong place at the wrong time.

Ndlela stands up, dusting his hands. That footprint is too old. He moves on.

Let us say this, then surely Shaka's concerns fall away. There is brutality and bad blood here, but it's hard to see that becoming a conspiracy to disrupt the First Fruits — or even a more ambitious one to overthrow the King.

Something else now to consider: the First Fruits are all but over. In what way have these murders disrupted the ceremony? There have been the rumours, certainly, but the spectacle itself has been too overwhelming. Was this a case of little Nompofo shaking the tree and fooling Jackal into thinking she was a monster, when she was something else? Was the conspiracy to disrupt the First Fruits merely a ruse, in other words? One that hid not a frightened little girl, in this instance, but something far more dangerous than the tree-monster had made herself out to be. And what might that be? The second option then; the one he's considered in passing, as a mere aside? That the real goal is to overthrow Shaka?

For there are the mutilations, and what they signify.

Doesn't that point to something that is more than a mere ruse, or some way of getting back at a clan that has angered a sangoma? And speaking of which, what had happened to turn Kholisa against the clan? Hadn't he actually tried to help first Zusi, and then Ntokozo?

The Induna pauses for breath. Below him are the bushes that hide the udibi from sight. On the hillside across the way, a herd of cattle grazes; so at least the herdboys are doing their duty. The sky remains cloudless.

He is missing something.

But what?

★

Suddenly the path leaps up at the boy. He's stubbed his big toe and has stumbled. Aiee! Has someone tried to trip him? No — he wheels round – it was just that root. Shaking his head at his lucky escape, due to the acrobatic exertions he was able to employ to ensure his chin and nose didn't smack against the path, he turns again, ready to continue on his way. And that's when the pain hits him.

Even then he takes two, three steps, before he's fully aware there's something wrong with his left foot. And then he blunders on for a few more steps, before he thinks to look down.

He sees blood, slows his pace, but doesn't stop. His big toe ends in blood. It's sore, but not that bad. Still walking, still looking down. Blood . . . but not that bad . . . stupid. Fortunately nobody was around to see what happened. Still walking, looking up to make sure he doesn't stumble off the path, then looking down at blood . . . And what's that flapping at the end of his big toe?

He stops, and the pain that's been ebbing away catches up with him once more, as he realises the nail of his big toe has been wrenched off the quick, and remains attached only by the merest fragment of skin.

He looks away, looks back. The nail is still lying there loose. A sense of dislocation, a jolt, a flutter of panic as when your tongue finds that a piece of tooth is missing. He fights a powerful urge to bend down and touch and pull, to make sure he's seeing what he's seeing. But he fights the urge, because he realises that not only does his big toe not look right, it also feels odd. Moving his foot even slightly causes the nail to lift, and causes him to feel a slight chill as the air slips in.

Carefully he sits down at the side of the path. And it's in twisting to get a better look at his toe that he notices the footprints. There's a set of them right here next to him, though he's scuffed one of the prints. But there's another . . . and another . . .

Raising his head, he sees there's a faint path leading off the main trail. It cuts backward, moving through the bushes spreading up the slope, meaning he could have gone right past it, without seeing it. You'd have to be coming from the opposite direction to have a chance of spotting it, and even then you'd be likely to miss it.

Ducking low, his toe forgotten, the boy enters the bushes. And then the smell! The sickly sweet scent of rotting meat, stirred up by the flies. So many flies! Leaves crackle; slender branches brush against his head. Within a metre, he's able to straighten up in the fragmented shade, like one coming up for air, but the smell has now become of secondary importance. The boy's eyes are on the body and the man sitting next to it . . . and he doesn't see the half-buried root, and stubs the same toe a second time.

*

Ndlela is standing over the udibi, when the Induna arrives in answer to the latter's calls.

'It's over,' Ndlela says.

The boy's spear is nowhere to be seen, but the older man is holding an iklwa, with blood glistening on its blade.

He is changing.

He can feel it.

He feels stronger.

Even his limp has gone.

(Although, of course . . .)

Soon it will be time to shed this skin, this face . . .

Soon he will rise up, a king more powerful than the sun.

And they will suckle at his breasts and do his bidding, as his loins and his hard cock plant the seeds of future generations of followers.

See how he moves among them!

(He's changing; it's starting to work. He's growing stronger with every breath.)

See how he moves among them, able to choose the path that allows him to slip by, behind their backs, their chatter hiding him like long grass.

You'd think with so many people around . . . for this First Fruits . . . but Shaka has made it easier for him. So many strangers. So much movement. So many parties. How easy it is to vanish.

But do not forget the ancestors, for they have helped him, too. Getting in and out is easy, but finding those who suit his purpose — the right ingredients, you might say — has been a little more difficult.

But always, he has found the one he was looking for!

And he will thank them. Has already decided how: Shaka will be theirs.

When he is finished, the King will be a nobody to him. He will not waste his time crushing that beetle. Since Shaka has angered the ancestors so, they can have him.

Aiee, right now he would like to witness the torments Shaka will be made to endure, but he knows that's the residue in the gourd. Once he is finished, the calabash will be shattered, and such things will no longer attract or amuse him.

And the change has begun.

He can feel it.

He moved to protect himself tonight, and it couldn't be helped. But it won't be long now.

Once he has eaten the old lady's brains, the transformation will be complete.

★

He was thinking all these things — as a kind of chant, a war song that carried him along — when he ducked into his special place amid the bushes, the isigodlo from which change would radiate outward into the world. And therefore it was a while before he'd spotted the man squatting in the shadows.

Lair Of The Limping Man

It is done.

Ndlela steps aside and the Induna enters the gap in the bushes, through the natural covering formed by interlocking branches, and moves on through the smell and the flies, the rustle of leaves telling him that Ndlela is following him.

'I was perturbed by these killings,' murmurs Mnkabayi's induna, after the younger warrior has had time to take in the scene. 'Like you, I was haunted and taunted by these deeds that were so clearly more than they seemed. Although' – a wry chuckle, his left hand indicating all of this – 'that was bad enough.'

'Truly, I have never seen the like before!'

'Neither have I, Nduna. Neither have I.'

Two or three skins have been spread out to form a floor in the centre of the clearing. Hidden and protected by layers of branches, the space isn't very large. There is just enough room for a man to store a few supplies, some trophies – and his insanity. He can also stretch out and rest after his labours, or stand up to get changed . . .

'I knew we were in good hands, with you and your men watching over us,' says Ndlela. All the same, he himself hadn't joined in the festivities. He had retired early and spent a restless night, till rising before sun-up. 'I had to do something,' he explains. After some prevarication, he'd armed himself and went out to roam around among the temporary huts. He realised that, in doing so, he ran the risk of making the Induna's task harder. What if he was spotted? Despite his rank, he would have been stopped and taken into custody while the Induna was summoned. An understandable precaution with all this talk of conspiracy, but one that would have needlessly distracted the Induna and his men, perhaps – another wry chuckle –

giving Kholisa the opening he was seeking. A shrug. But he had to do something.

The Induna waves away a fly that seems to prefer his face to the dead man's mask. 'And you witnessed the killing of Gudlo?'

'So that's who he got,' murmurs Ndlela, in the tone of one thinking aloud. The distraction! But why him? (Not that it matters any more.) Realising the Induna's watching him, he hastens on. 'No, but I saw Kholisa.' The sangoma had clearly been fleeing; had clearly killed again. 'But I didn't know who. I merely went after him.'

And a limping man, too. Hai, as old as he is, Ndlela could easily have caught him.

But he wanted to see where he was going.

And, of course, this was no limping man.

'I think you must have seen that for yourself, Nduna.'

As the Induna nods, Ndlela leans over, looking past him. Using the tip of his iklwa blade, he forces the mask higher, sliding Kholisa's lips and nose over Jembuluka's nose. And higher still, to reveal Jembuluka's staring eyes.

And the Skin Man wears 'sleeves' and 'leggings' made from the sangoma's hide, and tied in place by strips of Kholisa's intestines.

And hanging from his neck like a big bib, or like the breast-covering married women wear: a ragged rectangle of skin and Zusi's breasts.

★

It is done now.

Ndlela had thought an impundulu was responsible for the killings. For a start, there was the loose skin Vuyile had mentioned, which was to be expected since such creatures do not eat. They subsist on a form of paste fed them by their master. And if Vuyile had said he had seen Kholisa that night, then the impundulu had to have been the sangoma. And Ndlela had followed Kholisa this morning, thinking he would be led to whoever had turned the limping sangoma into an impundulu. But then the limping sangoma had stopped limping.

'Did you and he . . . ?'

'Speak?' Ndlela nods. 'A little.'

The Induna had seen that for himself; had seen how, when the limping man had got far enough away from Bulawayo to feel safe, he'd stopped limping. And where was Jembuluka? His sister had told Njikiza the Skin Man had gone off after the killer, yet nowhere along the way, from there to here, had the Induna spotted his footprints. He had to have been the killer. How he came to be mistaken for Kholisa, the Induna didn't know at the time (perhaps the two had been working together; or Vuyile and Jembuluka were accomplices, the former helping to cast suspicion on the sangoma.)

'Did he say why?'

'He spoke of a mountain, of being a mountain. He spoke of becoming a king. With the guile and cunning of a sangoma, with the strength of youth, with new followers hungry for his sweetness, also with the wisdom of age . . .'

'Wisdom? He would have killed again?'

'Yes, an elder this time. And, with these qualities, he believed he would be invincible. But I do not understand why he killed . . . who was it?'

'Gudlo.'

'Yes, I do not understand why he killed him last night.'

The Induna says he thinks he knows why – and also why the boy's body wasn't mutilated. Jembuluka was killing to protect himself. Briefly, he reminds Ndlela how he became involved with this clan in the first place, and how it was Gudlo who had found the murder weapon among Vala's possessions.

'I do not think he and Jembuluka were working together,' says the Induna.

'No,' agrees Ndlela. 'This monster was his own master.'

But Jembuluka himself had told the Induna that Gudlo had found the iwisa on the second or third occasion he had searched the tiny, ramshackle storage hut where Vala was made to stay. Like the Skin Man, the Induna had seen it as a sign of the youngster's laziness: Gudlo shirking his duties even in a time of emergency. And he had

539

been right, of course. But now it's clear that Jembuluka also knew the iwisa was there—

'Because he himself had placed it there,' interrupts Ndlela.

'Yes,' says the Induna. 'He therefore knew that Gudlo was lying every time he claimed to have searched Vala's hut.' But, finally, Gudlo had done what he was supposed to do, and he had found the incriminating iwisa. Events then assumed a momentum of their own, and he had other things to occupy his mind. But with these other murders, the way they seemed connected to the clan, he began thinking back to how it was he had come to find the weapon.

'And the one who had literally pushed him in that direction,' adds the Induna.

'Then there was the fact that our Father hadn't punished Vala. And if the King – and you – didn't believe Vala had killed Ntokozo, then maybe he hadn't,' says Ndlela.

But Gudlo had to be totally certain, hence his uncharacteristic concern for Vuyile. 'Doubtless he tried to question him whenever he visited,' says the Induna.

Even if he had been able to get something out of Vuyile, given the latter's state of mind at the time, and was assured that his brother really had seen Kholisa, that would merely have led him to assume that the sangoma was working together with Jembuluka.

'And that might have been so at first, when Ntokozo was murdered,' adds the Induna as an aside. 'The two of them together . . . yes, I can see how that would have made killing Ntokozo a little easier.'

Ndlela nods. He agrees, although not for quite the same reasons as the Induna.

And assuming he knew who was behind the killings, Gudlo had remained quiet. For here was something he could use against Jembuluka. But with the death of Zusi one of his own secrets was made known, and he had been forced to throw a sly hint in the warrior's direction.

'And Jembuluka was there to overhear and to do some thinking of his own,' says the Induna. Unfortunately, he still hasn't had the chance to question Vala . . .

'Hai! What more could he tell you? I think those words were aimed at this one,' says Ndlela, indicating Jembuluka's body.

Let the Skin Man know he knew and perhaps Jembuluka might have been able to see him installed as head of the clan.

'Only . . .' Ndlela shrugs.

'He didn't know everything.'

'But he knew just enough to be silenced.'

'And Kholisa?'

'This one here was mad. Perhaps the sangoma thought he could control him.'

'What did he do with whatever else was left of the sangoma? Did he tell you?'

'He threw him into a ravine, after he had removed whatever he needed.'

Ndlela's iklwa blade comes up to point at a leather pouch hanging from one of the branches. The Induna will find what remains of Kholisa's heart, liver and kidneys in there.

'Morsels to nibble on,' says Ndlela.

'He brought them all the way here?'

'To sustain him until he could get started on the rest of . . . well, whatever he called this insane scheme of his.'

Noting the *Ah yes!* expression on the younger man's face, he prompts: 'Nduna?'

And the Induna tells him how Zusi's friend Thaki had referred to the dead man as 'Smelly Jembu' and how, although the two families travelled together, they rarely saw Jembuluka.

'That's understandable, given his burden,' says Ndlela.

'Did he say anything else?'

'I didn't give him a chance,' says Ndlela, straightening. 'Let us get away from this stench,' he adds.

Back on the path, they move several paces from the opening in the bushes. The udibi still hasn't returned with Njikiza and the Fasimbas the Induna has asked for by name. Over in the direction of KwaBulawayo, the smoke from cooking fires rises into the cloudless sky. People are at last beginning to rouse themselves.

'Do not let my rank prevent you from expressing your anger and frustration, Nduna. He needed to be questioned, although I'm not sure what else he would have had to share, except his madness.'

Talk of a mountain, of becoming a mountain. Talk of gathering together the vitality of youth, the ability to bind his followers to him as surely as those who suckle a mother's teat – and don't forget also the cunning of a sangoma. Possibly he believed he had even imbibed Kholisa's knowledge, and the special powers bestowed upon those of the Calling.

'A madness as overpowering as the stench that surrounded him. But, yes, I know how skilled you are, so you might have got something more out of him. However . . .' Ndlela is still clutching the bloodied iklwa in his right hand. Now he raises his left hand, its fingers splayed so that the Induna can see the tremor in it.

'I did not know how far behind you were, or if you had even found the body and a spoor you could still read. And I had followed him a long way, for someone of my years . . .'

The Induna lays his hand over Ndlela's, gently forcing him to fold his trembling fingers into the safety of his own palm. Squeezes his fist. 'I am not angry, Master,' he whispers, 'for I know you were acting in self-defence. I know your humility forbids you to admit that, if it was wisdom he was after next, he would have had to look far and wide to find one wiser than you.'

Ndlela chuckles. 'Let us just say, as horrified as I was, it didn't take me long to realise that I had, to all intents and purposes, brought him his next victim.'

*

It is done.

But what will he tell them?

Mbopa, he knows, will be satisfied with a rehash of the tale he has told the Induna.

Mnkabayi will be the difficult one, though. She will know there are aspects he has left out, and will assume they are meant for her ears alone.

But even if he wasn't so tired, so drained, and feeling every one of his years, he's not sure he's ready for the confrontation that meeting will lead to.

Even if I was wrong, I'm still right.

Clearly, they had intended to turn Ntokozo into an impundulu – and how Kholisa (of all people) had acquired the knowledge to do such a thing, he'll never know. Then again, Kholisa was clearly not as knowledgeable as he let on. Or something else went wrong . . . and they failed.

He had thought the impundulu was Kholisa – and in hindsight that doesn't make much sense, does it? It meant using another sangoma. And he knows even someone like Nobela would have baulked at that idea, when alive. In fact, he suspects her animosity to Shaka would have been set aside while she dealt with those who had dared to ask such a thing. Even knowing they sought to overthrow Shaka would not have stayed her hand.

Because she knew . . . as does Ndlela.

He may have been wrong about the impundulu's identity, but there had been one, and he is right about this: once the ritual reaches a certain point, there is no stopping or controlling the madness unleashed.

See how Jembuluka had been infected!

And he doesn't want to know that Mnkabayi was behind this.

And he doesn't know how he can make her see it isn't over.

Aiee, and if she *is* behind this, she will see that as a good thing. *All is not lost*, she'd say. *There is cause for hope!*

But she'd be wrong, and he doubts she'll believe him when he tells her she was to be Jembuluka's next victim. She'll say that's merely his love for her speaking, and he doesn't know if he can bring himself to tell her how Jembuluka had confirmed his suspicion. By laughing, as Ndlela raised his spear, and saying: 'You have no need to fear me, old man, although you will soon be lying on the ground, twitching like a lizard's tail. No, it's your mistress I'm after.' Her sister might have died, but Mnkabayi was still one of a pair of twins, which made her brain very appealing indeed.

543

She'd be wrong, therefore, and he doesn't know how he can tell her, or how he can explain it. Explain how whoever set this thing in motion will see it ripple and reverberate – so that the way things are will never be the way they should have been, and that which is still to come will never be what it could have been.

★

'The Zulu harvest festival ends with a truly strange series of events,' writes Fynn in his journal. 'The morning after the feasting and the drinking, trenches are dug and the warriors are made to regurgitate in these hollows. I believe they are fed a purgative of some kind. Thereafter, looking somewhat the worse for wear, they are summoned to the King's presence once more.

'Here, while Shaka and the Zulu royal family watch, the king's chamberlain promulgates new laws – which, apparently, one can count upon to be disseminated throughout the kingdom within a very short space of time. He also issues final instructions to the men and women who have been given permission to enter marriage.

'There then follows a ceremony that's even more remarkable in the light of the casual executions we have witnessed at Shaka's "Great Place". Representatives from all the king's regiments come forward to sit in a semicircle before him. They then proceed to harangue him, often quite volubly. I am told this is their opportunity to speak freely, without any fear of retribution. They question the king's decisions in some matters and demand to know why he has or hasn't done this or that.

'As noted, things get quite heated. If I may be allowed some conjecture, here, I would say the king is able to keep his anger in check by knowing it is not the answers he gives that matter, but his demeanour throughout the interrogation. Should he retain his equanimity, he shall emerge the victor of these strange jousts, no matter how serious the allegations made against him.

'All the same, sanctioned or not, it takes courage to beard a monarch in this way, specifically one who can order one's death by bending his finger.'

Possibly these stained, brown pages were filled up that very night in KwaBulawayo, in the flickering glow of a bonfire. Certainly, Fynn must have felt a weight lifted off his shoulders, precisely the kind of 'lightness' that can give rise to a burst of creativity. Not only was the First Fruits over, so was the constant need to monitor one's every gesture and reaction, and to behave with the utmost propriety while ensuring one's companions did the same. Farewell, King and the others had by now returned to Port Natal, but Fynn had been ordered to remain behind, along with Frederick and Jantjie. And he didn't mind one bit, pretending to be stoical when Farewell commiserated with him before leaving that morning. It was almost as if Shaka could read his mind, and knew how much he appreciated a chance to be rid of the others for a while.

PART SEVEN
A Night In Africa

The sea-reach of the Thames stretched before us like the beginning
of an interminable waterway. In the offing the sea and the sky were
welded together without a joint, and in the luminous space the
tanned sails of the barges drifting up with the tide seemed to stand
still in red clusters of canvas sharply peaked, with gleams of polished
sprits. A haze rested on the low shores that ran out to sea in vanishing flatness. The air was dark above Gravesend, and farther back still
seemed condensed into a mournful gloom, brooding motionless over
the biggest, and the greatest, town on earth.

From *Heart Of Darkness* by Joseph Conrad

Thumb smudge of orange against a black background.

Only, look closer and see copper at the core, becoming an apricot mist as it catches the curve of a branch, the flicker of leaves. Look closer and see how the darkness loses solidity, becoming layered, for the sky tonight is a midnight blue, and even shadows have shadows.

The boy is asleep on the opposite side of the fire. And the Induna's knees and shins seem dusty in the firelight, while his eyes are pockets of black, deepening, swallowing up his face, as he tries not to think too much about that which shouldn't be — the anomaly of Shaka sitting there at right angles to him, wearing Night Muthi out of season. Shouldn't be there, but he is.

African night, with the campfires of the brave warriors who've made the Great Journey twinkling in the vaulted distance. Or maybe those are holes made in the firmament by the passing of the sky herds. Or perhaps it's the milk sprinkled by Nomkhubulwana, Princess of the Sky, so that lost children may at least find some sustenance even if they can't find their way home.

African night, and the veld stretches out, happy to be free of the sun for now. A waterhole truce so that all might part front legs, lower long necks, wade in, and try to find some coolness.

African night, when the soul expands and becomes at one with the darkness. When space joins you at the fire, and says Look!

1
Eating Stones

Once upon a time, long long ago, Mahala, the headman of the Omadla, a clan renowned for eschewing cattle in favour of fish and other kinds of seafood, had introduced him to mussels. Shaka was a young lad at the time, and the headman was one of the few male adults to pay him any attention. He showed the youngster how the brown mussels clustered together in tidal pools, and how to pry them free from the rocks. He claimed that these strange wedge-shaped 'stones' were in fact living creatures, like the crabs they saw scurrying along the waterline. Although the boy adored Mahala, he refused to believe him: how could you eat them without breaking your teeth? (And Nandi was always on at him to watch his teeth, saying a lion who broke his teeth was a dying lion. 'You may have other weapons, my little king, but if your teeth hurt you'll be as weak as a calf.' Never mind beer – sore teeth and a sore stomach, those were the things to be avoided, as they led one into making disastrous decisions, as far as Nandi was concerned.) The headman had chuckled and showed Shaka how you cooked the mussels in seawater, in a pot on the coals of a fire you built in a sheltered spot along the beach. For Mahala, consuming the mussels as soon as pos-sible was an integral part of the process. He said they tasted better that way. Shaka had been willing to take the headman's word on that, though he was still leery of the eating part. However, he'd been suitably amazed when, a few minutes after the water started rumbling, the stones began to split open. He'd been wrong to doubt Mahala, for these . . . things were truly alive!

Mahala had tipped the pot over, spilling the mussels across the sand. After much pinching and blowing, he showed Shaka how one could pull the valves apart to get at the good stuff within. Trying hard not to think of snails, or slugs, or snot, Shaka obediently gulped down the pale yellow globule Mahala handed him. Soon he was prying open and tearing and biting, as if he'd been eating stones all his life. This became Mahala's special treat whenever Shaka was in trouble with Nandi: his way of cheering up the youngster, getting him out of his mother's sight for a while. At the same time, the creatures came to fascinate Shaka. He realised their shells were scattered everywhere. They soon became the inhabitants of the kraals he built with sticks and twigs, a population herding clay cattle and marching off to war. There was the king, there were his subjects, and there were his warriors.

How long has it been . . . ? A long, long time. Many moons, many seasons, many . . . He clenches his left fist, stares at it a moment, struggling to bring it into focus . . . Many battles.

(How many by now? How often has this hand of his curled around the haft of a spear?)

When he came to power, he ensured the Omadla received his full protection without the need for tributes. What's more, declaring Zulu food to be too bland, he'd summoned women from Mahala's kraal to come and teach Zulu abafazi how to cook.

Staring at his fist: Mahala? When had that muddy old fish-man died? He frowns. He can't remember right now. Must ask Pampata. He looks around instinctively, then realises that, of course, she won't be here tonight.

Some beer . . . ?

He has but to raise his hand, and one of his serving boys is already crouching before him. Shuffling forward, Shaka takes the pot in both hands and throws back his head. Beer dribbles on to his chest, but he waves away the boy who would tend to that, and runs a hand across his chin. After gulping down the dregs, he hands the pot to the first boy, who scurries away to get a refill.

Smoke. Heat. Noise.

He's back.

The drums and the dancing have stopped for now, but the dancers – the young warriors from the regiments he named a few days ago – have left their sweat behind them. It clings like a fever, like the Night Muthi he had worn during those days of seclusion . . . and defeat.

551

Shaka squints, and sways. The chatter and laughter, the boasts and the jests, seem louder than the drums ever were.

Mahala . . .

He is on a throne made of rolled-up mats, and can lean back if he wants, but for some reason seems unable to, preferring a spine as stiff as a mast, and a port and starboard that rise and fall with mesmerising gentleness.

There is a space around him. Others can sit next to him, if invited, but for a while now even his favourites have been avoiding his eye. Not that he isn't being watched.

He raises his hand and the boy is there. This time he takes only a sip of the beer, and waves the boy away. He will savour this one.

Mahala.

Shaka frowns.

Somehow he's back with Mahala.

Who is dead.

But it's not him the King is thinking of, but the mussels. How he would once lie for hours watching them in their watery kingdom and marvel at how that shell encased a life. Wind, storms, high seas, treacherous tides – none of these touched the softness inside. Fudu the tortoise also had his own shell, and was wily, but he had to be because he was still vulnerable. He had his weak spots, unlike these stones that lived. They were totally encased, enclosed . . .

And that's the way he himself feels tonight.

That's the way he often feels, but of late the sensation seems more potent, and he finds himself in his own shell more and more frequently.

Everything recedes like a wave, but it stays there, twice removed. And it's like that, exactly. As if he has to reach and reach again to touch anything or anyone. To make contact. And sounds and smells, these too recede.

It feels as if he still wears the Night Muthi, and could stand or move among them, those around him, and never be seen by them. He could tweak their noses, spill their beer, place this one's arm around that one's shoulders, turn this one so he's about to bump

552

into that one, pull down his kilt, douse that one over there in urine, and they still wouldn't be aware of anything. At least not until something grates and grinds and that wave of sound and laughter and movement comes back, and then suddenly people will be wondering why they're falling over, or are naked, or smell of piss.

And things do come crashing back, but not before he becomes aware of himself as himself, and experiences a terror that's like nothing he's ever felt before.

2
A Night In Africa (I)

There are grunts and growls out there, but on a night like this, still, cloudless, the darkness is soothing. Besides, you have the fire at your feet. Abantu is a puny creature, outrun, outclawed and outcast. All other things being equal, Abantu would've been stomped, chomped and chased into extinction long long ago. Except that human beings know the secret of fire.

An opposable thumb, a language that slices and dices reality into edible chunks, and fire. The original, the true, trinity.

The thumb gave us the ability to shape the world, to grip and grab, twist and tie. Our language, verbal as opposed to sensory, gave us an inner life (enclosed, encased?), enabled us also to think big thoughts, to dream of shaping the world in ever more elaborate ways. But fire gave us the time to think these thoughts. No more need we cower in fear. Fire was warmth and safety, offering the leisure to begin to look around.

'The Sky. Yes, the Sky . . . matters of the Earth, matters of the Sky. As you told this one, who will not awaken, you need not concern yourself about that,' says Shaka, gesturing at the Induna's udibi.

'Because . . .'

'This shouldn't be happening.'

'Because . . .'

'You are not dead. Although it might be because—'

'I am not real?'

'Possibly.'

'But I have interrupted you, Majesty.'

'What did I say, Nduna? Let us dispense with such shit for this night at least. For . . . for I would speak of the Sky. This is a good place to start. And, as you know, Nduna, many say the Sky is a cavern covering us, protecting us. But I would ask you this, Nduna. What if there are other caverns?'

'Other Skies, you mean?'

'In a manner of speaking.'

'That is hard to imagine, Father. I have spoken with Mbuyazi, and he has not indicated to me the sky is any different from where he comes.'

'Yet I am not his ruler! For is it not said I am the Father of the Sky?' Shaka grins, waves away his own question. 'Yes, yes, I know. One must be careful of taking the inventions of one's praise singers too seriously.' His mother's warning.

But he must admit, he adds, the thought of Fynn and the Induna having anything approaching a meaningful discussion fills him with mirth. 'For that one is terrified of you. He has told me so himself.'

'Yet, I have never . . .'

'Threatened him? You don't have to, Nduna.'

They sit in silence a while, watching the flames of the fire the Induna has revived.

Shaka has realised there's something wrong with the conversation they've just had. Something . . . out of joint. But, before he can put his finger on it, the Induna coughs, clears his voice.

Aware of Shaka's eyes on him, the Night Muthi the King wears frightening enough to turn away a stampeding rhino, the Induna keeps his gaze fixed on the flames. 'Father, you indicated that we . . . that I could talk freely.'

'This is so.'

'Very well, then, I sense disappointment in you. I sense frustration. You spoke of other skies, and you think I did not understand,

554

and so you diverted the conversation. But, with respect, Father, I say you are wrong. With the coming of these barbarians, I have also been thinking, Father. You speak of the Sky, Father, but for me . . .' The Induna shrugs.

'Go on,' says Shaka softly.

'For me it's as if we have all been living together in the same hut, even our enemies, even the Portugiza, and now suddenly we have discovered that there are other huts . . .' He frowns. 'Not other skies, but other interiors – all around us.'

3
Disgruntled

The big hut has been built especially for this occasion. It will be torn down tomorrow, along with the remainder of the temporary huts that surround the capital. Bulawayo feels deserted, a settlement decimated by plague, now that most of the families and clans have left to go and harvest their crops. Harvesting must begin here, too, of course, but tonight Shaka and the recruits from the new regiments, as well as a few veterans and favourites, will drink and dance and celebrate the end of the celebrations.

And it's hot and steamy under the thatch, the apex of the dome invisible amid smoke and dust. Udibis try wetting the dirt floor, but it's to no avail. The hut is too full, and the new recruits too eager to catch the King's eye with their exertions: warding off enemies called forth and goaded by the drums, defending with their amahawu, lunging with their spears. Just as the amahawu are much smaller than the war shields, so these assegais are shorter than the iklwa and with smaller blades, although some of the young warriors have shunned such 'toys' and proudly wield the ingicawe, a narrow-bladed spear with an ornamental handle.

Then the beat changes, becomes a breeze that shapes and reshapes bodies in graceful contortions, the tread of those honouring hallowed ground, the rhythmic pointing of the spears. Next the umphendu, slow-motion movement with the upper body, then an interval of sorts, the lines making a right face, becoming a single file, handing their spears and shields to the waiting udibis. A full circle and they're facing the King once more. The umgebhulo: sinuous smooth, an entwining of hands and arms climbing to the sky.

Tired, so tired . . . He is a man who thinks he's reached the end of a journey only to discover the path continues. The ceremony of First Fruits has concluded, and here we are! But, before you know it, Mbilini KaZiwedum's son will make his appearance with the tamboti moth again. He has destroyed the Thembus and Qwabes, but now he hears that Zwide's heirs are aching for vengeance. He stamps on one, and another pops up. And the path never ends. Always another bend, another valley beyond this one.

Fresh air.

He needs fresh air.

He's rising, just as the Induna passes by, and the warrior extends his arm so that Shaka might regain his feet with as much dignity as he can muster under the circumstances. For a moment, doubt-less waiting for the world to stop spinning, Shaka eyes the pot he's knocked over, watching the beer darken the sand, then signals for a serving boy to pick it up.

'Where—?' The Induna interrupts himself to wave away a cadet from one of the new regiments. In his zeal to assist the King, the youngster doesn't realise he's come close to getting himself killed, for he's darted forward still holding his dancing assegai. Although regarded as a toy, its blade is real and it's not something one wants to be brandishing when one makes a sudden move in the King's direction.

'Where to, Majesty?' asks the Induna, after the youth has backed away.

'To piss, Nduna. Let us go and piss!'

The hut has an eastern and western doorway, and the Induna leads Shaka to the former. Outside, Shaka stops. 'Mbuyazi! Where is Mbuyazi?' Dropping his voice, so the Induna has to strain to hear him, he murmurs, 'Where is my weakness?'

Noting the Induna's alarmed expression, he indicates they should continue walking. 'Oh, yes,' he adds, 'save your surprise and your erstwhile denials, for I know what some say.'

'Must I have him fetched for you, Majesty?'

'Who?'

'Mbuyazi, Father.'

Shaka lays a hand on the Induna's shoulder, and again it's as if his surroundings withdraw. Only this time, the Induna is with him.

'It's not that I am beguiled by their promises. Their sangomas are no different from ours. Let anyone say otherwise and they can meet my Slayers, for someone that stupid shouldn't be allowed to live!'

It's as if they're alone in the King's council hut; or sharing a campfire together.

Wagging a finger: 'And, another thing, you were wrong, Nduna. As was I. All this talk of other skies and other huts . . . it sounds clever, but it's misleading. For we have always known there is an out-there.'

'Other huts?' The Induna frowns. How does the King know?

'An out-there, Nduna. We have always known! We have always known there were others.'

And why should they be any different? These ones, he means. A snigger. 'Our ones!' Why should they be any different, even Fynn?

'I know the worth of their promises,' says Shaka, slurring his words. 'I know they will seek to use me, as if such a thing were possible. But so what.' Staggering away from the Induna, he throws up his right hand. 'So what!' Drawing closer again, dropping his voice into a drunkard's whisper. 'Because I fully intend to use them, in turn.'

★

And, even as he reaches under his kilt, the mood of sullenness hits him, the sagging, deadening remembering. So far, he's failed there, led astray by the old stories of the true potency of Imithi Emnyama,

557

the Black Medicine, muthi of the dead moon, isifile, and ngolu mnyama namhla, the dark day thereafter.

Aiee, and to think the White Men are eager to lead him astray! He's been betrayed enough by his own ways.

A grunt. Why should he be surprised, given how often he has trampled on the old ways and mocked the superstitions of his children.

'Majesty?'

'It is nothing, Nduna. Let us piss.'

4
A Night In Africa (II)

'Yes, another hut! And when these people emerge, they turn out to be like us in so many ways, but they are also different. And that . . . that, Nduna, is what I wish to discover. Their difference. It's not the similarities that count, but how different they are.'

The analogy has its limits, but tonight it might still contain some value. Or, then again, maybe not. Shaka's hands come away from his knees in a gesture of helplessness, for how impotent words can be.

Does the Induna understand? It is the uncharted terrain of their *difference* he wishes to explore; the secret geography of cause and effect. What it is exactly that makes them different.

And where that road will lead.

For he is tired now, so tired . . .

Shaka grips the Induna's arm. 'It never ends,' he hisses, 'never! Once I dreamt of stones on a plain' – walls and chambers lying there like lizards in the sun – 'and I thought I understood, and I sent you, but maybe I was wrong.' These savages value stone so maybe the path was leading to them.

The King's hand drops away. 'You know what happened then. You know how the stones called me on. And, whether I was right or wrong, it didn't matter. The path didn't end there. It continued past the stones!'

That's why he has to be right about the White Men, why he is eager to concede that his initial interpretation was wrong. Because of that path leading on and on and on . . .

The Induna nods. He, too, has been haunted by a dream of late . . .

'I reached them, *you* reached them – and see the outcome!'

. . . *rain falling as a depthless blur . . . tighten your grip on your iklwa. . .*

'See what has changed? Nothing!' He is nodding to himself, muttering like a drunk old man. 'So I had to be wrong. I had to . . . I had to.'

. . . *and the rain is falling sideways, a swarm of mosquitoes stinging your skin, and there is a man lying in the mud . . .*

Squeezing the Induna's shoulder: 'Do you understand?'

Snatched from his own reverie, the Induna nods, understanding nothing.

'We showed them. We showed these barbarians from the sea, didn't we, Nduna?'

'Yes, we did, Majesty.'

Ensuring the White Men were taken the long way round, so that they might marvel at the size of the kingdom . . . Having the same regiment march past them three, four times a day, so that they might quail at the size of the Zulu army . . . Having groups of men already sentenced to death standing there among the ranks that received the White Men at KwaBulawayo, so that the barbarians would be awed by Shaka's cruelty, the way he could summon slaughter with the merest nod . . . These and other games dreamt up by Shaka and Mgobozi, to keep their guests rattled.

'We showed them, Nduna, we showed them. Now they must show us!'

'I'm not sure I understand, Majesty.'

Shaka waves aside the Induna's words: 'You will see, Nduna. You will see!'

And he will! Suddenly Shaka realises what's been bothering him about this conversation. The Induna has somehow joined him. At the time he went to save the Bead Man, Fynn and the others hadn't yet arrived (and Nandi was still alive). But somehow the Induna has joined him, and is able to talk about things he shouldn't know anything about.

Strange?

But, then again, not so strange when you consider that Shaka shouldn't be able to converse with him in the first place (because he is not dead).

They stare at the fire, its flames like leaves; a plant that grows as it dies, and dies as it grows. The boy sighs, shifts under his isiphuku. Stars overhead, and a moon fragment.

For once, in what Fynn might term his 'nocturnal peregrinations', Shaka feels at ease, feels as if he can relax a little and not fear he'll find himself back in the hut of his seclusion, cursing the vagaries of this Night Muthi.

Perhaps this is why he tries again. 'I want you to understand, Nduna,' he says, shifting his position, and easing a little closer to the warrior. 'Earth knowledge *is* involved here, but these things are mainly of the Sky.'

The same distinction the Induna had discussed with the boy. Earth knowledge: aspects one can see and point to, debate and discuss.

'So many similarities, Nduna. They eat and breathe, they sweat and bleed, they speak a language of sorts and they feel, can laugh and cry, grow tired and irritable, as we do.'

So many similarities, but one signal difference. Sky knowledge: something he knows, without being able to explain how he knows.

'It is this I would learn, Nduna. This is the goal of the campaign I wage, while my advisors stand with slack jaws and my enemies sharpen their blades. This is the secret I would learn, for there is power there, great power. I just know it.'

Shaka chuckles. 'But I know something else, Nduna. I don't think they understand it. I would take something from them they don't even know they have.'

African night – and the veld stretches, sighs, wallows. The night is scarcely much cooler than the day, but for now it's enough simply not to have the sun blaring out of the sky. A screaming that will never stop; a ceaseless, relentless nagging. But the sun has been caught by the mountains, and for now there is a silence of sorts, the relief of sweat at last being allowed to cool against the skin.

5

Evasions

'Majesty?'

It is Mbopa come looking for the King. A quizzical glance at the Induna; a shrug in response. Are they heading for a relapse, and a King who would kill everyone in sight? The Induna's not sure.

'Come, Majesty, let us return to where your new warriors wait to impress you,' says the prime minister, although the drums haven't stopped during the King's absence.

The two have just entered the hut, when the udibi moves out of the darkness. Acting under the Induna's orders, he has been keeping watch over Mnkabayi's compound and has just seen Ndlela enter the queen's hut.

The Induna thanks him. They have already discussed this, and the boy knows the Induna must confront Mnkabayi and Ndlela alone. Nonetheless, he tells the Induna that he and Njikiza will be at the other entrance to the big hut, free of the drunken tangle and therefore ready to assist the Induna should he need their help.

The Induna thanks the udibi once more and moves off into the darkness.

Shaka and Mbopa have praised the Induna, the boy, Njikiza and the other Fasimbas for the role they played in ending Jembuluka's madness. All have been well rewarded, with the Induna insisting that Ndlela be given the credit he was due, and thus the largest portion of the livestock Shaka presented them with.

The irony is that it's precisely Ndlela's involvement that continues to pester him, even though Shaka and Mbopa consider the matter concluded.

Given Ndlela's status, and the many responsibilities he had during the First Fruits, why did he take the time off to become so involved? The Induna can understand him being deeply troubled by what was going on, and wanting to stay apprised of developments – but to become an active participant?

Fine, so he was acting under Mnkabayi's orders. Or he felt his expertise would be useful. Or he was a loyal subject doing his bit to protect the King. Or just a nosy old man who was bored with the matters of protocol and diplomacy associated with the First Fruits.

Fine, but even more serious is the matter of the footprints. As it was with Jembuluka, so it was with Ndlela.

As the Induna has explained to Njikiza and the boy: 'Gudlo is murdered. There is spoor. Jembuluka has gone after the killer. We follow, still believing we are after Kholisa.' But not only did the limping sangoma stop limping after a while, they found no trace of Jembuluka's tracks.

'I remember now,' said Njikiza, 'you were worried he would spoil the killer's spoor.'

This was so, agreed the Induna. He and the boy had been so intent on following what they still thought of as Kholisa's tracks, it was only later the Induna realised they hadn't seen any indication that someone else had been following the sangoma. It was something that would have aroused his suspicions, even if Ndlela hadn't caught the monster in his lair and exposed him as the Skin Man.

'And, as with Jembuluka, so with Ndlela,' mused the boy.

'Yes, we were the only ones to follow that spoor!'

Ndlela had lied. But why?

Now, making his way to Mnkabayi's hut, the Induna can imagine the older man's response.

So easy to use the Induna's own words against him. He and the boy had been so intent on not losing Kholisa's spoor, they could easily have missed Ndlela's. Especially when you considered how he tried to keep off the path whenever possible, so as to preserve the trail for the Induna. Or so he might allege.

Well and good, but what would Ndlela say to this? For that day in the thicket, after Ndlela had left, the Induna had examined the older man's prints and then followed the path leading in the other direction.

That's where he had found Ndlela's spoor. It meant Mnkabayi's induna had approached Jembuluka's lair from the opposite direction.

Which showed an amazing prescience. Unless he already knew where the hiding place was.

If that was so, how much else did Ndlela know?

Angry voices, taut with the effort of keeping themselves low, draw the Induna up short in front of Mnkabayi's hut. He might have his suspicions, but he will not stoop to eavesdropping. Since none of Mnkabayi's servants are around, he announces himself loudly.

Seconds later, Ndlela beckons him into a hut, where the tension is as palpable as toothache. It is precisely because something is so obviously amiss, and his presence is clearly an intrusion, that the Induna finds the courage to forge ahead with his questions.

But Ndlela rouses himself from a very obvious bad temper, to offer the evasions and explanations the Induna was expecting.

The older man has just finished explaining how he circled round the ridge, as soon as he saw which path Jembuluka had taken, when Mnkabayi extends her hand. Thinking that if she believes this will distract him from the ludicrousness of Ndlela's tale, she's mistaken, the Induna helps her up. And finds himself being guided to the hut's entrance.

'You will surely remember another time,' she says, once they are outside, 'when you spoke of a snake and of what you knew, and how I said no.'

There is a question in her eyes and the Induna nods.

'I said no – you did not know, could not be expected to know – because that affair was started before you were born.'

Taking his hands in hers, she fixes her eyes on his. 'I say the same again' — with a half grin — 'although do not think the situation is the same.'

She is squeezing his hands. 'You heard our voices as you approached, don't deny it. You heard Ndlela, my loyal Ndlela, berating me. The wounds we have just inflicted on each other will heal, but for now you are the only one I can count on. These questions you raise, put them aside. Allow me to say *no* again, and just put them aside for now.'

The vehemence of her plea stuns him and he can only nod.

'Now go and enjoy yourself,' she says. 'We will talk tomorrow.'

6
A Night In Africa (III)

'Majesty, this difference whereof you speak, this hidden power, could it not be . . . ? Well, we have heard the Swimmer speak of their strange beliefs, so could that not be the source of this difference?'

'You mean the deity they consume like cannibals? Hai! That does not make them different — we have known others like that.' There's the Thembus, for one. Did they not believe that by eating the brains of their enemies they became godlike?

And the Induna must not misunderstand him. The White Men have many strange ways, just as the Ndwandwes or Mthetwas or Pondoes have their own way of doing things, which a Zulu might equally find distasteful.

'It's a different kind of difference I seek,' says Shaka.

And the two men sit mulling that over, their eyes focused on the fire.

An opposable thumb, language, fire the original true trinity — with fire the power that enabled us to sit around and think.

But fire is also metamorphosis. It is matter changing form. Oxygen and heat, the cocoon; wood becoming char and smoke, the process of change given form; incandescence as the butterfly that springs forth into the African night – growing and shrinking in flapping flight. Nature's deadly weapon, the lightning strike that frees the flames to feed off the veld, predators now the prey. Human Being's temperamental pet, as quick to sink its fangs into hissing flesh as it is to do Abantu's bidding. Respect it, be wary of it, but know this, too. Fire will always be in the thrall of those who know how to make fire. For this was Abantu's first great discovery, not fire but the ability to make fire.

Then again, fire is also time: the shortest distance between now and then, what was and what will be. Its ever-changing, ever-shifting nature is precisely what makes it unchanging. Looking into the blue heart of the orange butterfly, we see what our ancestors saw, and what their ancestors saw, and what those who will come after those who come after us will see.

Hai! Hai! Hai! But fire is blather, too. It is the idle words spoken around the flames wherever humans gather, the shimmering ideas fed by the flames as the chatter tapers off.

Big dreams, big thoughts. Butterflies and metamorphosis. Thumbs and language. A different kind of difference.

Blather.

7

Impundulu

'Did you hear that?'

Mhlangana emerges from behind the array of Buthelezi, Ndwandwe, Thembu and Qwabe shields that Mnkabayi's regiments have presented to her. 'He knows,' says the prince. 'He must be silenced, but I will see to that. Or perhaps you would prefer the honour, Ndlela, considering the accusations he has made?'

The old induna turns away, so the prince cannot see his disgust, and Mnkabayi says, 'No.'

'Very well, then, I will take on the pleasure myself. And I'll be lying if I say I haven't been looking forward to silencing that one for a long, long time.'

'No,' says Mnkabayi, for the second time.

Her tone is so even, matter-of-fact, that it takes the prince a few moments to understand she is actually issuing a command.

'You say *no*. What do you mean *no*?'

'I mean *no*, you will not touch one hair on his head, not that you alone are capable of doing so, for you would need several impis. But that is neither here nor there, for I say no and I mean no.'

'Esteemed Aunt, you may be a source of invaluable wisdom, but do you now seek to interfere in the affairs of men? Worse, do you seek to order a prince around – one, moreover, who is soon to be king?'

Mnkabayi nods.

'This . . . this is outrageous,' splutters Mhlangana. 'Do not think your support and, yes, your connivance entitle you to treat me like some lackey, like this old fool here.' He indicates Ndlela, who still not dare look at the prince. For his loyalty to the Bloodline will not permit him to reveal his anger to one of the Blood. Or to reveal his distaste.

'Connivance, Nephew? I think not.'

'What?'

'This old fool here, as you call him, and soon you will be apologising to him—'

'I will do no such thing!' he interrupts.

'Shut up!'

'How dare you!'

'Oh, I dare. Indeed I do, and more. Now put aside your petulance and heed me well, Nephew. I was saying Ndlela might be angry with me right now for letting this thing occur, but it is over. And your own foolishness has come to naught.'

'My foolishness?'

'Indeed.'

'But, but you . . .'

'I did what? Kholisa was *your* sangoma! Jembuluka came from *your* district! How long will it be, do you think, before your brother, our King, realises this? After all, he has been speaking of a conspiracy. All he needs is for his gaze to be turned in a certain direction . . .'

Ntokozo will be dug up and the substitute 'body' found. The Induna will then be sent to see if traces of Kholisa's corpse can be discovered. Perhaps no one will ever know what went wrong, but the mere existence of the substitute 'body' will be enough to have Shaka's advisors whispering of an impundulu. And, given the facts surrounding the death of the Uselwa Man, who but Kholisa himself could have created such an impundulu?

Your sangoma, Nephew!'

'But this was all your—'

'And if the King is a little slow to see the pattern in the bead-work, or if the Nduna, out of deference to me, is hesitant to share his suspicions with the King . . . well, there are other ways of getting the message through to him.'

Nothing too blatant, of course. Simply a few hints and suppositions.

'That should do it,' she concludes.

'But Kholisa was known to visit your kraal.'

'So what? Many sangomas seek my protection, despite my known enmity towards their kind. Which enmity, I might add, is also well known to the King.'

'You . . . you . . .'

'Be careful of what you say, Nephew, for you stand at a fork in the path. One track leads to the impalers, and the other . . .' Mnkabayi shrugs.

Mhlangana swallows. 'And the other?'

'We will see. You want to be king? Then listen to what I say, and *do* as I say!'

She now has him. She has her own impundulu.

'You mean . . . ?'

'You have failed miserably in your efforts to disrupt the First Fruits and thus discredit the King, but that is no reason why you might not yet take his place.'

'So long as I forget it was you who courted Kholisa, and learnt of his secret knowledge, and—'

'I do not know what you're talking about, Nephew. Do you suppose you might be coming down with a fever?' She makes as if to lay her palm against his forehead, but the prince steps back quickly, saying, 'Don't touch me!'

'I am only concerned about the heir's health. As for the other business, why make things so complicated? If you want to be king . . .'

'I just have to do exactly as you say!'

'Now you have it.'

And Ndlela can scarcely contain the bile that now fills his throat. It's a clever game, a strategy worthy of Shaka – but she still doesn't understand. Still doesn't understand the horror she has unleashed by allowing Kholisa and the others to dabble in such unspeakable practices. She still doesn't understand how the horror will reverberate down the ages, through who knows how many generations. And the ways in which things will never be the same as they might have been.

'Ma! Ma!' The Induna's voice sounds uncharacteristically frantic.

The three inside the hut exchange glances. Then Mnkabayi shoos Mhlangana back into his hiding place and, followed by Ndlela, ducks out of the hut.

The Induna, panting and trembling. 'Ma, come quick!' he says. 'The King has been stabbed!'

8

The Umbhekuzo & The Ingicawe

The boy sees it happen. He is standing with Njikiza at the hut's western entrance. Mbopa has guided Shaka back to his throne, and remained by his side for the past thirty minutes or so. The King's expression is hard to read, and the two haven't exchanged many words. The dance is the umbhekuzo, which has the new recruits drawn up in rows and surging forward to raise their shields, thrust their spears forward and stamp their feet before retreating. Ebb and flow. And Mbopa has moved some paces away from Shaka, to call for more beer, when he and the King become lost behind the surging ranks, the heads and shields.

When they withdraw, after stamping the ground, Shaka has risen . . . then he sags. It takes the udibi a few seconds to understand what he's seeing, and it is Mbopa who is first to react. Turning back to Shaka, as the King slips to the floor, Mbopa darts forward. Then the udibi moves, pulling Njikiza along with him. The dancers are heading back again, so he and the big man thrust themselves into their midst, disrupting the first ranks and breaking their rhythm. Leaving Njikiza to position himself a few paces in front of Shaka, his arms spread out to keep the dancers at bay, the udibi swiftly joins Mbopa.

The prime minister is holding an ingicawe, its narrow blade gleaming with blood. 'Check his wounds!' he shouts to the boy. The boy glances at the King's pain-racked face, his apologetic gaze wasted − no time for such niceties anyway − and gently but firmly peels the King's hands away from his side. Blood oozes from two stab wounds. Carefully, the boy guides the King's hands back to cover the narrow gashes.

And then he becomes aware of the shrieks. Njikiza has called for help and now a wall of Fasimbas keep the dancers away from the King. And sometime while this was happening, as the boy checked the King's wounds and Mbopa stood looking on, still clutching the weapon used in the attack, and which must on no account be allowed to vanish, the drunken recruits have realised what has happened. And now they are screaming like women: *The King! The King! Someone has stabbed the King!* Njikiza is already hoarse from bellowing at them to keep quiet. The boy stands up, calls the big man towards him, notes how officers are moving among the dancers to slap and prod them into order.

'We must get him outside!' says the boy.

Njikiza nods, and drops to his knees. 'Majesty?'

'No,' whispers Shaka.

'What is it? What is he saying? We must get him help!'

Ignoring Mbopa, Njikiza asks: 'What is it, Majesty? What would you have us do?'

'I will not be carried. Just . . .' Shaka winces, 'help me to stand. And do it quickly.'

'I understand, Majesty.' Trying to make sure that his own bulk hides the King's pain-racked face, Njikiza helps Shaka to his feet.

'Mbuyazi,' hisses Shaka, as Njikiza guides him to the hut's eastern entrance.

'Majesty?' asks Njikiza.

'Fetch Mbuyazi.' Shaka coughs. 'Tell him. Muthi.'

He wants Fynn and his medicine chest.

'What's that?' says Mbopa, looking over their shoulders.

'Our Father wants . . .' They're out of the hut, and Njikiza spots the Induna. 'Master,' he calls, realising shock has rendered Mbopa useless, 'the King has been stabbed and asks for Mbuyazi.'

The Induna stands for a moment, taking in the scene: the King clinging to Njikiza, now that they are out of the hut; more Fasimbas arriving to form a protective cordon, as the shouts within the hut that brought him running settle into an anxious babble; the spear still clutched in Mbopa's hand. Then he turns and sets off for Fynn's hut, even as the prime minister begins to remonstrate with Njikiza.

The Watcher has clearly misheard the King. Shaka's inyangas must be summoned instead. Njikiza shrugs, calls for more torches. At least the prime minister has retained the presence of mind to keep hold of the weapon used to stab Shaka. If taken back by the attacker, the blood on the blade could be used in a ritual to finish off what an unsteady hand and a last-minute lapse in courage have failed to get right the first time. In the hands of Shaka's inyangas, however, it can be used to create a muthi that will speed up the King's recovery. He doesn't know why Shaka has called for Mbuyazi, though, and doesn't care that Mbopa is giving instructions to one of the Fasimbas to go and fetch the King's

570

inyangas, for his main concern is making the King comfortable, and keeping him safe until someone can end this nightmare.

★

After waking up Fynn, and Frederick his interpreter, and ensuring that the latter has apprised the White Man of the seriousness of the situation, the Induna makes for Mnkabayi's hut.

★

The udibi stands, panting, in the flickering light provided by the torches around Shaka's throne. If he looks down he'll see the blood-stains. But he won't do that, because it'll be a reminder that this is really happening.

★

Mnkabayi tells the Induna and Ndlela to go on ahead. She will rouse her servants and send them to fetch the other counsellors. And Pampata . . . someone needs to tell her, too. The Induna is about to suggest that Mnkabayi needs protection as there could be more than one assassin abroad but, before he can say anything, Ndlela pulls him out of the hut, insisting they must hurry to attend Shaka.

★

Shaka's lips are moving, and he seems to be trying to say something again. Njikiza glances up at Mbopa, wondering why the prime minister is just standing there, for he should be here crouching by the King's side. This situation is not something Njikiza is comfortable with. In fact, he's terrified.

'Yes, Majesty?' he says leaning forward.

Shaka grins. 'They were more like horns. I thought of them as stones but they were more like horns, flattened horns.'

★

Mhlangana raises his hands as though that will ward off Mnkabayi's anger. This was not of his doing, please. She must believe him! The

571

queen doesn't need much convincing, however, because, for all his swagger, Mhlangana isn't capable of initiating a deed like this. Very well, she says, he is to wait here until she has sent her servants on their errands, before getting himself safely to one of his more trustworthy concubines. Let that be where a messenger finds him. The prince nods eagerly, and Mnkabayi leaves the hut. Roused by all the commotion, her servants are awaiting her instructions – and her reassurances. Is it true the King has been attacked?

★

Even though he'd rather be facing a thousand spears than crouching here, holding Shaka's hand, Njikiza has to fight off a momentary urge to resist, even lash out, when Mbuyazi nervously tries to ease him aside. But this is the one the King himself called for, so hastily Njikiza stands up. He tells the warriors clutching firebrands to move closer.

Fynn has his medicine chest already open, but Frederick . . . he's lost Frederick. Fynn glances around, seeing only knees, and then Shaka's face. The interpreter has held back, too afraid to enter the cordon of Fasimbas along with the Englishman. Fynn's just about to call for him, when the Induna crouches by his side.

Somehow Fynn makes it understood that he'd like someone to fetch him some Sweet Innocence. When the Induna makes to rise, though, the White Man grabs his forearm. He'd rather have the Induna beside him. He points to Mbopa, and the Induna nods. He tells Mbopa what Mbuyazi wants – and to hurry up!

'Thanks,' mutters Fynn. 'Give him summat to do, as he doesn't look like he'll be much use.'

But, while the prime minister looks around as though wondering who's speaking to him, it's Ndlela who calls for the liquor.

'And if rum and other spirits will work, why not your concoction, eh?'

Fynn twists his head so as to examine the wounds in Shaka's side. By now a double circle of flames surrounds the King. The warriors with the firebrands want to be howling at the sky, pounding the dirt, pounding themselves, spewing their shock and horror

572

into the darkness – but their discipline holds. They obey their orders, remain where they are, providing the light Fynn needs. But they can't smother their grief, and all have glistening cheeks as the tears flow unchecked.

Keeping his eyes on Fynn's fingers, hovering around the wounds, the Induna takes a deep breath and wonders if it's possible to, somehow, blow strength into the White Man, the way one blows strength into a fire.

'Yes, why not,' says the trader, speaking just to keep himself calm, and not caring if no one in earshot can understand a damn thing he says.

'Should work. Should help to keep the wound clean,' says Fynn, selecting a short, slender object that seems to be made of silver. The Induna has to fight back the urge to snatch it away from the trader, because it looks sharp and lethal.

'Not this,' continues Fynn, mistaking the Induna's glare for curiosity, and holding up the instrument. 'Spirits are good for cleaning wounds, don't ye know.'

Trust him.

'Another good thing, no clothes. See, that's what gets 'em,' says Fynn, hearing again one of the doctors he worked for as a lad; hearing old Maynard's voice clear as a bell. Either a charlatan or ahead of his time, depending on which of his colleagues you were eavesdropping on. 'It's the fragment of dirty clothing that the ball takes into the wound that causes the problems. And one would presume the same applies to knife wounds.'

Trust him, the Induna tells himself.

'Makes sense, the blade driving the dirty cloth deep into the old organism. Not here, though, fortunately.'

You have to trust him. The King does. Watching Fynn at work, washing the wound in Sweet Innocence. *Not that you have much choice in the matter.*

But then again neither has Shaka.

An anxious glance at the King's face. Even in the orange light of the torches, the Induna can see how pale he's become, and his breathing is shallow. He has to look long and hard before he detects a flutter in his chest.

★

Ndlela's eyes drift away from Fynn's ministrations towards the spear in Mbopa's hand. *Can it really be?* he wonders. *After all this . . . ?*

After all this, the King is brought down by a toy spear − or, rather, the kind of ostentatious ornament a wealthy father would present to his eldest son when the latter is called up.

A whisper in his ear. It seems Mnkabayi would speak with him. After one more glance at the King, Ndlela turns and eases his way out, between the torches.

★

Njikiza's return breaks the udibi's reverie, helps remind him why he's remained here, facing the dancers as if he and they are his adversaries . . .

Because they are, in a sense.

Remembering the surge, then the retreat . . . and Shaka.

Shaka!

The udibi meets Njikiza's gaze with raised eyebrows. Aware that many hungry eyes are on them, the Watcher's shrug is almost imperceptible.

The udibi turns back to face the rows of dancers . . . remembering the advance, the stamp, and the retreat as they leave Shaka sliding to the floor . . .

The assassin has to have been one of the dancers!

★

'Mhlangana?'

'No.'

'Are you sure, Ma?'

'No . . . Yes, as sure as I can be for now.' Moving closer to Ndlela: 'And the King?'

'Still alive.'

574

'But . . . ?'

'Who can say? Mbuyazi tends to him now.'

'*Him?*'

'The King asked for him, apparently.'

'Perhaps it is for the best.'

Ndlela nods distractedly. If not Mhlangana, then who?

★

A depthless blur; wire-thin steel icicles shattering on the hardpacked dirt. Huts lose their shape in the gloom, seem to sag into mounds of waterlogged thatch. And the rain is falling sideways, a swarm of mosquitoes stinging your skin. You tilt your head, wipe your face. You tighten your grip on your iklwa, the wood burning your hand. (Where is your shield?) You move forward, toes pressing into the puddles. A softness underfoot. Your vision is blurred. You wipe your face once more. An instant of clarity, before the swarm surrounds you again.

Where are the sky-herders? Why do they not come to chase away this deluge that threatens the crops? What is wrong?

There is one . . .

Something is wrong . . .

An irritated sweep of your arm. A brushing away that, miraculously, reveals the body in front of the hut.

The body. A big man, lying on his side, his back to you.

There is one, blood of your blood . . .

You move forward, but knowing instinctively it's no use. He is dead, this man, so there's nothing you can do to save him.

And you see yourself drop to your knees.

A statue of mud slowly being eroded away by the rain.

And you watch yourself place your hand on the man's shoulder. A stiffness in the wet. Cool skin.

★

'See here?' says Fynn, pulling the Induna back to the present. 'See?'

He pauses a moment as he notes how intently the warrior – this man with the 'frightfully forbidding' countenance and 'murderous disposition' – is examining the wounds.

'Two of 'em, d'ye see?'

Two wounds, forming an L-shape.

'This chap, here, is the deepest.'

The Induna has noticed that already. The upper gash resembles a fish's mouth when it lies panting on the river bank. However, it's the other one that interests him more. Unlike the first, it's almost hidden by the band of dirt and blood and sweat which coats Shaka's side.

Wetting the tip of his finger, the Induna touches it against Shaka's flank, then examines it.

Watching him, Fynn continues, 'I'd say that was the first wound. It caught his attention, you might say. He managed to turn away, but still too slowly to avoid the second strike. I'd say the weapon was one of those small spears you chaps use when you dance, and that's why I also say he was very, very lucky. Had it been one of those bastards you normally carry, he'd be dead now. As it is, it's going to be touch and go, but I reckon he's going to pull through. Well, he has to, hasn't he, or else I'm not getting out of here. Pulse is weak, but no vital organs were affected, and he's probably not lost much more blood than he would have done during a particularly enthusiastic phlebotomy. I saw you looking at his pallor, by the way, and I wouldn't worry too much about that either. They call it syncope, and it's much more unsettling if the patient has a fair skin. Looks like Hamlet's ghost. Or Hamlet after seeing the ghost. But of course you don't understand a blind word I'm saying, do you? And, for once, I'm relieved about that. Because as soon as my servants heard the words "Shaka" and "dying", stout-hearted yeomen that they are, they vanished before you could say "Metternich", leaving me hoping and praying I'd heard your big henchman wrong and it wasn't me and my medicine chest your King was calling for! As much as I respect and admire him – and you need have no bones on that score – I'd really rather not be the one entrusted with saving his life. But here I am, and God knows what's keeping my bowels in check, because *I* don't. I rather think I know how Boney felt when he heard old Blucher had decided to come to the ball after all – and with nary an RSVP either. The cheek of some people. And the luck of others! So here I am, old boy, all present and correct. And, even though you can't understand a blind thing I'm saying, what say you we let the terrified Englishman clean up the nice king's wounds, and then attempt something of the seamstress's art, followed by a nice bandage and some fervent prayers, eh?'

He realises the King's eyes are open, and watching him . . .

★

He's been lucky, very lucky. He was able to force his way into the front rank during the dance, then retreat several rows back amid the confusion that followed the stabbing. But now his luck runs out . . .

The udibi's gaze finds him – and he looks away too late. And, knowing he's looked away too late, he looks back – and sees how the udibi's gaze has moved on. He is already breathing a sigh of relief and is about to resume working his way towards the western entrance – a barely noticeable shuffle – when he sees it.

Sees the recognition form on the boy's face as his eyes seek out familiar features again.

★

Vala!

Who the udibi had seen when he met up with the Induna on the outskirts of the capital, and who had seemed familiar . . .

The udibi turns to Njikiza. Turns back to see Vala moving out of the hut.

'What is it?' says the Watcher.

Can't cause a panic! The udibi moves close up to Njikiza, says he knows who the assassin is—

'You mean that one who just—'

'Hsst!' says the boy. Yes, that one, but they do not want to cause

577

a stampede. 'I'll follow him, you go tell the Induna, then come after me!'

9
Flight

Blundering through the dark, then stopping. Wait! Why is he running? He had nothing to do with this. Nothing whatsoever!

Biting back the laughter, for that's half the problem, right there. First of all, no one will believe him.

Nothing to do with this? Who do you think we are – these izilwane the Bull Elephant loves teasing and leading astray and frightening and confusing? Cha, nothing to do with this? Better to tell us how Fudu the tortoise jumped over Ndlula the giraffe, for we'll believe that before we believe you had nothing to do with this.

The distant commotion had taken a while to rouse the maiden. Extricating herself from underneath him, she went to see why the sounds of revelry had changed into something else. When she heard what had happened, she rushed back and frantically tried to rouse the prince. That had taken some time, though, and then more time had been wasted in trying to comprehend the . . . well, the enormity of this event.

Finally he was up and dressed, and making his way to the big hut. He was still cursing her, refusing to believe her tear-drenched words, when he'd been knocked over by a figure racing through the night.

Then someone, obviously chasing the first man, had leapt over him. 'You!' he'd shouted at him. 'Stop!'

The second man had obeyed, turning round so that he could now see it was the Induna's udibi. 'What is happening?' asked Dingane.

Recognition was clearly mutual, for the boy hesitated long enough to tell him that his brother the King had been stabbed, and he was going after the assassin.

Suddenly sober, Dingane had leapt to his feet, and started for the big hut again before he stopped and asked himself what he thought he was doing.

Acting as though of their own volition, his feet turned him around, and had him heading roughly in the same direction the boy had taken.

Because who would ever believe him?

Who?

No one, that's who!

Wiping the sweat from his face; suddenly craving a torrent of beer. No one will believe him when he says he had nothing to do with this. And even those who know he is telling the truth will be just as eager to see him eat dirt.

After all, he'd had his chance, hadn't he? They – for he knows the crocodile wasn't acting alone, and he's fairly certain he knows who is behind him – gave him a chance to join them, didn't they? And if he didn't exactly say no, neither did he grovel in gratitude. Which means his loyalty will now be in doubt. Yet again!

And so Dingane runs. Yet again.

★

'Nduna, over here!'

Hiding his frustration, the Induna leads Njikiza over to where Mnkabayi and Ndlela are standing. They've seen the Watcher force his way through the circle of torches, and re-emerge with the Induna, and now, when time is so crucial, they want to know what is going on.

The Induna tells them how the boy had recognised the assassin and set off after him.

'Good,' says Mnkabayi. Njikiza is to follow him, bringing as many Fasimbas as he can, while Ndlela will organise a more orderly hunt.

The Induna is about to follow Njikiza, when Mnkabayi grabs his hand. He is to wait, for she has a special task for him.

'Ma?' asks the Induna, with annoyance in his voice.

Mnkabayi calmly waits until Ndlela and the Njikiza have moved on, then she pulls the Induna further away from the cluster of men surrounding Shaka.

She knows that he would follow his udibi, she says, speaking softly and urgently, hoping to outpace the Induna's growing anger, but she has a more important commission for him.

'Dingane,' she hisses before he can risk showing her outright disrespect by demanding what could be more important than capturing the one who tried to kill the Bull Elephant. 'You must go find your friend.'

'Dingane?' asks the Induna incredulously. Does she think the Needy One . . . ?

'No, no,' she says, waving his question away like a bothersome fly. 'I think nothing of the sort.' But that is precisely why he must go find Dingane. 'It's for his own safety.'

And the Induna had better take a moment to collect some water-skins and cloaks because, if she knows her nephew, he will be somewhere far off when the Induna catches up with him.

'And it has to be you,' she says, 'because I trust you to keep him safe. And you are the one most likely to know where he will have fled to.'

★

Running through the dark. Free! Invincible! Was he a coward at the very end? He doesn't think so. The ancestors have protected him, shown him he needn't die along with the monster. Better to live and see all these creatures completely annihilated.

10
A Night In Africa (IV)

He stops. Turns again to orientate himself. Things are still so quiet! Where is everyone? He's seen torches moving five or six huts away, but no one approaching any closer.

A few deep breaths and he sets off again, but he doesn't get far. A shadow flies at him from the side, and fire enters his gut. Then, even as he's spinning away, the spear strikes again, a glancing blow that scores a furrow across his chest. And he's on his back, and the shadow is on top of him, and the spear is raised again . . .

And then it's lowered.

'You!' hisses the udibi. 'I thought' – sharp stones inside his throat – 'you . . .' – wetness, he's swaddled in wetness – 'were dead!'

The spear laughs. The spear slaps against his cheek, touches his lips.

'You are dying, Zulu! But I'll leave you be, because I want you to tell them who I am. With your dying breath, I want you to tell them who killed their precious king. They know me as Vala, but you know me as Lungelo. And they told you I was his nephew, or some such thing.'

'Beja!' A hiss of pain.

'Yes! So you knew who he was. Now know who I am. Beja was just one of many I used to get here. Now know me! I am Khanzijana, son of Zwide.'

And, seated on the log adjacent to the Induna, Shaka says, 'Yes, that's it!' Squeezing the Induna's knee: 'We will both forget this, but let it be known in case one of us remembers.' Pointing to the sleeping boy, he tells the Induna of visiting Gqokli Hill and seeing the udibi there.

'Something will happen to me. Yes, that's it! He will come for me, and your udibi will know who.'

'You mean someone will try to . . .'

'Kill me? Yes! But why Gqokli Hill? Why was I there?'

'And the boy will know who . . .'

'Yes,' says Shaka, then he half rises. 'He will know who it is, and it will be a Mthetwa. That's why I was taken to Gqokli Hill.'

'But, Majesty, surely . . .'

'We can do something?'

'Yes, Majesty, you've had a premonition, so surely we can move to prevent this thing from coming to pass.'

Shaka chuckles. The Induna still doesn't understand.

'No, because we will forget this. And you are not real, anyway.'

And then the King is gone.

And the udibi is lying on his back, staring at the stars. The only sound he can hear is his own laboured breathing, every gasp a grasp at life, and it's as if he's floating in a pool of blood.

And he's back in the hut. And he watches the ranks close in on Shaka, then withdraw . . .

And he's crouching alongside Mbopa, staring at two wounds.

And the prime minister still has the murder weapon in his hand, had the forethought to pick it up, keep it secure and safe from those who wanted to do the King further harm.

And his eyes roam across the ranks until he spots a familiar face. One he should have recognised that same day he met the Induna outside KwaBulawayo.

And Shaka waits until Fynn's eyes meet his – and at last, with the Night Muthi still strong in him, there is the connection he has been so eagerly seeking . . .

★

It is as if Fynn's wearing a mask, but a mask that's like the mirrors the white men have brought Shaka. (Farewell's offering was in an ornate faux-gold frame, the looking-glass itself shattered in transit, the remaining jagged shards bigger than iklwa blades, but still usable. King, who had arrived later, had presented Shaka with a smaller mirror. About the size of three hand-widths, it had a humbler wooden frame, painted black, but on the glass itself was a second frame, providing a red border. Along the top, in that newspaper's venerable old typeface, ran the legend *The Times*; and across the bottom, just above the red border, in the same font the publication used for its banner headlines, was: *Man Of The Year*.) Yet it's also transparent, this rectangular mask that Fynn wears. Shaka can see himself and Fynn, with his own features, strangely quiescent now, superimposed on Fynn's anxious visage: a man looking through a window and seeing his own reflection and also the face beyond the glass (this amorphous fusion of silica, soda-lime, magnesium oxide and other ingredients that is one of their achievements, yet perhaps not of their invention) and other images – *other images* – flowing upwards.

A moment of queasiness, until Shaka's eyes adjust to these palimpsests . . .

★

Lemon yellow deserts. Violet skies. Fractured barrens. Gorges and kloofs. Monoliths and hoodoos in the distance. A lonely tor standing sentinel over orange sand beneath a pink sky. A frown, then his brows rise in comprehension. *She was right! Curse her, but she was right!* A frantic, hunched-over scurrying, three crooked, ungainly limbs fighting the sand, while the fourth clutches the baby to her chest. Wide eyes, desperate whimpering, as the predator lopes across the dunes in long, easy strides, its tawny muscles bringing those fetid fangs ever closer. Then suddenly she swerves, crashes into the waves and, to keep the baby clinging to her chest, to keep his head out of the water, she walks upright. The gentle waves help her stay erect, and she turns to watch the befuddled beast, suddenly timid as it draws back to escape the breakers smoothing the shore. Lurid swirls across the sky, the passing of time, the loss of hair, footprints in the dust, tiny beads on a thread: this mother, returning to womb-warm waters, and teaching us to straighten our spines, had three daughters. Their names are letters and numbers, like the designations given to some stars, a barbaric tongue beyond Shaka's ken . . . But he knows that these three daughters became the mothers of Humanity. A myriad of threads leading back to one of just these three, nurtured in the bosom of Mother Africa. And some stayed and some walked away, following the cracks in the world that continue to race across Fynn's face, across his own face. Some stayed and some walked away, and she was right, curse her, because he sees it now. With the Night Muthi still singing through his veins and Fynn's fingers forming the umbilicus he has sought these many sweaty nights, he sees deep into the White Man's gullet, where his umxwele reside, his innermost feelings, some of which will be hidden even to Fynn. He sees how far they walked, the trails of their travails still visible in Fynn's throat (just as they would be in the gullets of others of his tribe, for these are the ancestors of his ancestors): faint markings of thirst and despair

583

and the determination to endure, like the cave drawings left behind by the Ancient Ones. Some found the Great Waters and friendly winds and boats that responded to hands expert with sail and oar to speed them further away. Salubrious oases where the more weary chose to settle. Cities rising and falling, deceit and betrayal picking at their foundations. Horsemen on the tundra. War, Pestilence, Famine – and the most potent, most iniquitous of all, Ennui. Oh, how well he has come to know this invincible conqueror of late, who rides with Decadence and Depravity. A heap of broken images (potsherds and ostraca) and somewhere along the way, probably without even realising it, time measured in generations, those who continued on their way entered the whiteness of cooler climes. Shaka has seen such whiteness on distant mountaintops, but here it was everywhere, a blaze that hurt the eyes. And Mnkabayi was right: for those who walked away – lines in the dust beyond the savannah becoming something more enduring, becoming a lineage – the sun eventually ceased to be a foe. Shaka: *But we do not see it as an enemy.* Mnkabayi: *Except in times of drought. But you are right, the sun is not an enemy to us, for do we not allow it a summer house and a winter house? It is the eye of our day. We respect it, but we do not seek it out, because we know we cannot trust it.* Shaka had nodded at this, for their crops are very much slaves to the vagaries of the sun. *It is the moon that guides us,* continued Mnkabayi. Yet those who moved away shunned the moon as they entered forests thicker, denser than fog. In the icy shadows, they became as larvae, maggots. The sun's presence was to be sought out as a palliative to the whiteness. It was to be flattered, appeased. *You know this,* Mnkabayi had hissed. *Look deeply enough, beloved Nephew, and you will see I speak the truth.* (What Fynn had told him, the reversal he should have paid more attention to. How ironic it was, said Fynn, that the People Of The Sky should welcome the full moon, when his own people feared it as a time of madness.) And they turned to the sun, and the sun showed them how to build armour to protect their puny bodies, the stout weapons needed to ward off the monsters who howled in the vastness of the forests. They turned to the sun, those who walked away and have now returned, but the sun exacted a price: it burnt off their Humanity. (*And do we not say albinos are cursed?* she had asked.) *We are the same, yes,* his eyes now on Fynn's sweaty brow and worried countenance, *we have the same mothers, but you are of the sun, while we are of the moon.* This is where the difference lies. This magnificent difference you have been seeking, Shaka, and which now might as well be a bone hurled high, high into the sky – because what does this difference truly mean? See how the sun, which they salute every morning, fills the land. Our moon changes, providing cycles that order our lives. But see what changes with the sun: only the shadows, always shifting. Mnkabayi: *And that means the ones you would idolise, place so much faith in, will always be changeable! You'll never be able to trust them.* Moments of valour, great deeds, then the shifting shadows bringing deceit and betrayal. Because it fills the world, this sun of Man has led them to believe all is knowable and can be known and if there are shadows they will shift, patience being the obverse of faith. They will believe this and fight the night (Mnkabayi speaking of the lowering of the Union Flag at sunset, urging Shaka to go and see for himself: *See how they protect their precious talisman.*) They will always think they can and should see clearly (for the sun fills the world). Her voice becoming his, becoming hers: *They will think this is their birthright. And that is why they fear the mysteries of the night, why they will bring monstrous machines to decimate us and yet still continue to fear us.* She was right, but so was he. In a way that's scarcely any consolation at all – he would smile if he could feel his lips – but there you go. Throw it out. Throw that bone high, watch it spin: these savages are unaware of this divide, unaware of the way the sun has ordered their minds and shaped their lives. Instead, as he knows from listening to Jakot and Fynn, this knowledge has been lost behind a welter of beliefs, so many of them it seems there's been a conscious effort to disguise the sun's influence not only from outsiders, but from others of these tribes living across the Great Water. So he was right about them possessing a knowledge they aren't aware of. But driven to his knees, bleeding under Fynn's fingers, yet as calm as a man enjoying a meal by himself, his day done, he still sees more . . .

An old man on his deathbed reaching out to his younger self through tears of regret. She is right: they are of the sun, we are of the moon, but how different are we really? Bored . . . so bored. Why? The truth a lesser ruler might never have the courage to face: *Because from now on all is repetition.* All. Another battle. All. Another betrayal. Another sangoma (or brother) rising up to challenge him. Repetition! The path to the stone houses on the plain continues past them. The journey continues. It was there all along. I needed no muthi. I needed only to look. *Oh Mother, Mother, beloved Mother, please help me!* Is it so? Can it really be? But it can and it is. All is and will be now and forever more *repetition.* I have reached and grabbed – and held. I have fought and grappled and won. *Now what? What now?* He thought he had an answer, when the White Men came; thought he saw glimpses of a difference behind the similarities. It's like those layers he noticed just now: first the difference – the skin colour, the hair, the language, the way of dressing – which proved illusory as contact was established and the similarities came to the fore – but then, as he got to know them, he saw or thought he saw, hidden like an ancient temple in a screaming jungle, another kind of difference. It was strength, a source of power, he thought that even they didn't know they possessed. (Saw or thought he saw.) He'd thought they were both the gateway and the path, these savages – these aliens. A new realm and a new road for the King to follow. Layers? A mask like a mirror? Overlaid faces? What is this nonsense going going gone, leaving him surrounded by black-ness, the penumbra of isifile, the dead moon, and ngolu mnyama namhla, the dark day thereafter, consciousness now trickling away from him like sand.

*

A familiar face that snags his attention. The immediate movement sideways – he has already been edging in that direction and now, with the udibi's recognition screaming a warning at him, he has but a few paces to cover and then he's outside, with those he pushes past barely aware of his dash to escape.

Another reason for the udibi to curse himself. A face he should have recognised, and then Vala still reacting quicker than him, after he places that familiar sneer. Lungelo at the river that day, when Philani was with him . . .

And there is a burning in his gut as the assassin stands over him, with spear raised.

Khanzijana, son of Zwide.

Who will spare him a killing thrust, so that his agony might be drawn out long enough for him to tell someone who has done this thing to Shaka . . .

The Induna's head comes up. He's had the strangest dream. He glances over at his udibi, half expecting to see the boy writhing in pain. And Shaka was here . . . He looks at the spot the King had been occupying moments before in his dream . . . wearing Imithi Emnyama, and out of season, too.

The Induna stands up and yawns.

A stretching.

A final piss.

Laying a few of the bigger branches on the fire.

Then lying back. The warmth on your face warming your eyes, making their lids droop . . .

No idyll, this African night. No Elysian dream. Don't be fooled: there is nothing idyllic about it. The sun came and stamped on the thorns, stamped and stamped and stamped, a thousand impis driving their moist heat into the ground. Then it went away, and the veld sprawled in its wake, its head buried in the crook of an arm. Happy just to be rid of the blaze, finding relief in a darkness veined with tender breezes. Little gusts that blow up, tickle the leaves, then ripple through the grass, and vanish. But this stillness is merely a phase. Soon the nap will be over, and the veld will be on the move again, stalking and fleeing, creeping and crawling, hiding and dying, as the crickets thread their melodic beads and, somewhere far off, a jackal laughs.

And the udibi's thinking that can't be.

He's thinking: two wounds. One covered in sand, one clean.

(Three, if you count the blood pumping between his fingers.)

But two wounds. One clean because it was administered *after* Shaka fell – and the assassin had fled, taking his assegai with him. (Because a dancer without a spear would have been spotted quicker, even in that mob.)

Two wounds. Two spears. And someone seeing their chance in the confusion, and seizing it.

And the udibi is thinking: *Mbopa?*

Acknowledgements

This is a work of fiction. Which means some things are made up, while others aren't. Shaka, for example, did change the way the First Fruits was celebrated, and there really was an attempt made on his life by a Ndwandwe assassin.

In *Amazulu*, I sought to explore the popular view of Shaka within the parameters of that, ahem, paradigm and see how things might have been. E. A. Ritter's *Shaka Zulu* was, therefore, the logical place to start. Hugely influential in the way Shaka has come to be seen, it cannot be ignored; but it would be of little value to anyone attempting a more scholarly study of the period. Then again, neither are more recent 'revisionist' histories which seek to debunk 'the myth of Shaka' out of hand – not least because they arrogantly ignore the oral accounts diligently collected by the likes of James Stuart and others.

Such nonsense only serves to underscore the 'con' in 'deconstructionist', and a powerful antidote is Carolyn Hamilton's *Terrific Majesty*. It was a key source for this novel, and a book I always turned to with awe and pleasure. Doubtless she will find much amiss with my own 'historical invention', but I would recommend *Terrific Majesty* to anyone wanting to learn more about Shaka's life and times, as well as the ways he has been 'interpreted' and '(re)invented' by subsequent generations – especially readers who find military histories heavy going.

Speaking of which, as with the first novel, I found John Laband's masterly account of the Zulu army, *Rope Of Sand*, indispensable. And then there was Ian Knight's *The Anatomy of the Zulu Army*.

Eileen Jensen Krige's *The Social System of the Zulus* (first published in 1935), A.T. Bryant's *The Zulu People* and C.T. Binns's *The Warrior People* were similarly indispensable when it came to the lifestyle and culture of the Zulu nation at this time.

Also deserving of special mention is Axel-Ivar Berglund's *Zulu Thought-Patterns and Symbolism*.

As regards Fynn, Farewell, King and their attempts to establish a settlement at Port Natal (which would later become the city of Durban), I found so many discrepancies in the oeuvre of 'classic accounts' that I finally threw in the towel and relied on Brian Roberts' account in *The Zulu Kings* and Fynn's own *Diary*. The latter has rightly attracted a fair amount of controversy, but what the hell – this is a work of fiction.

★

As I've said, some things in this novel have been made up, but it should be noted there really is a form of Zulu zombie. Two cases of relatives believed dead (and buried!) returning home with tales of being held captive by a witch were reported even while I was writing this book.

Also there really was a bandit called Beja. He lived a little later, in the latter years of the nineteenth century – and gun-running was one of his crimes in addition to cattle rustling and robbing travellers – but his modus operandi (including the singing of the songs) was as described here. Readers seeking more information are directed to W. T. Brownlee's *Reminiscences of a Transkeian* (Shuter & Shooter, 1975).

★

Patient colleague Zanele Mbatha of *Bona* magazine helped me with various translations. Any errors are entirely my own.

The 'Talking muthi' column in the magazine by Force Khashane, veteran journalist and practising sangoma, was a further source of valuable information. A kind, gentle man brutally murdered, he will be sorely missed.

Patricia McCracken lent a sympathetic ear during what turned out to be the worst eighteen months of my life, while Reg Vermeulen's occasional growls also helped.

★

Thanks must also go to Quercus, for their unstinting support and encouragement – to Nick Johnston, for making a very important phonecall, for Richard Arcus, for taking up the slack, and everyone else who helped get this one out there.

Then there are my editors Peter Lavery and Liz Hatherell, who knocked it into shape.

★

As with the first novel, the spirit of Goscinny and Uderzo hovered over the proceedings.

Then there are the 'stalwart companions' – Alan Cooper, Bobby Peek, Rob Askew and Andrew Gilder – who keep me sane.

As does Norma, who also continues to provide a welcome distraction.

Dr Paula, meanwhile, helped keep the black dog at bay (and was willing to discuss primitive brain surgery).

Speaking of medical matters, my apologies to Messrs Brook and Wheatley for appropriating a certain 'medicinal remedy' employed by the Induna.

Select Bibliography

Becker, Peter: *Path of Blood*, Panther, 1966; *Rule of Fear*, Panther, 1972; *Hill of Destiny*, Panther, 1972; *Tribe to Township*, Panther, 1974

Berglund, Axel-Ivar: *Zulu Thought-Patterns and Symbolism*, Indiana University Press, 1989

Binns, C. T.: *The Warrior People: Zulu Origins, Customs and Witchcraft*, Howard Timmins, 1974

Bryant, A. T.: *The Zulu People: As They Were Before the White Man Came*, Shuter & Shooter, 1967

Bulpin, T. V.: *Shaka's Country: A Book of Zululand*, Howard Timmins, 1975; *To the Shores of Natal*, Howard Timmins, date unknown; *Southern Africa: Land of Beauty and Splendour*, Reader's Digest, 1976

Fuze, Magema: *The Black People and Whence They Came: A Zulu View* (translated by H. C. Lugg; edited by A. T. Cope), University Of Natal Press & Killie Campbell Africana Library, 1979

Hamilton, Carolyn: *Terrific Majesty: The Powers of Shaka Zulu and the Limits of Historical Invention*, Harvard University Press, 1998

Kenney, R. U.: *Piet Retief: The Dubious Hero*, Human & Rousseau, 1976

Knight, Ian: *The Anatomy of the Zulu Army: From Shaka to Cetshwayo, 1818–1879*, Greenhill Books, 1995

Krige, Eileen: *The Social System of the Zulus*, Shuter & Shooter, 1965

Laband, John: *Rope of Sand*, Jonathan Ball, 1994

Lugg, H. C.: *A Natal Family Looks Back*, T. W. Griggs & Co, 1970; *Life Under a Zulu Shield*, Shuter & Shooter, 1975

Miller, Penny: *Myths and Legends of Southern Africa*, T. V. Bulpin Publications, 1979

592

Mutwa, Credo: *My People*, Penguin, 1971; *Indaba My Children*, Kahn & Averill, 1985

Omer-Cooper, J. D.: *The Zulu Aftermath: A Nineteenth-Century Revolution in Bantu Africa*, Longman, 1984

Ritter, E. A.: *Shaka Zulu: The Rise of the Zulu Empire*, BCA, 1971

Roberts, Brian: *The Zulu Kings*, Sphere Books, 1977

Samuelson, L. H.: *Zululand: Its Traditions, Legends, Customs and Folklore*, T. W. Griggs & Co, 1974

Stuart, J., & Malcolm, D. McK. (eds.): *The Diary of Henry Francis Fynn*, Shuter & Shooter, 1950

Taylor, Stephen: *Shaka's Children: A History of the Zulu People*, Harper Collins, 1995